SOLDIERS OF THE IMPERIUM

More tales of the Astra Militarum from Black Library

LEONTUS: LORD SOLAR
A novel by Rob Young

SIEGE OF VRAKS
A novel by Steve Lyons

CREED: ASHES OF CADIA
A novel by Jude Reid

THE FALL OF CADIA
A novel by Robert Rath

OUTGUNNED
A novel by Denny Flowers

CATACHAN DEVIL
A novel by Justin Woolley

DEATHWORLDER
A novel by Victoria Hayward

LONGSHOT
A novel by Rob Young

KRIEG
A novel by Steve Lyons

VAINGLORIOUS
A novel by Sandy Mitchell

SHADOW OF THE EIGHTH
A novel by Justin D Hill

MINKA LESK: THE LAST WHITESHIELD
An omnibus edition of the novels *Cadia Stands, Cadian Honour,*
Traitor Rock and several short stories
by Justin D Hill

YARRICK
An omnibus edition of the novels *Imperial Creed, The Pyres of*
Armageddon, the novella *Chains of Golgotha* and several short stories
by David Annandale

GAUNT'S GHOSTS: THE FOUNDING
An omnibus edition of the novels *First and Only, Ghostmaker* and
Necropolis by Dan Abnett

SOLDIERS OF THE IMPERIUM

Steve Lyons, Edoardo Albert & Steven B Fischer

BLACK LIBRARY

A BLACK LIBRARY PUBLICATION

Death World first published in 2006.
'Waiting Death' first published digitally in 2011.
'The Weight of Silver' first published in *Inferno! Volume 3* in 2019.
'Green and Grey' first published in *Inferno! Volume 4* in 2019.
Kasrkin first published in 2022.
Witchbringer first published in 2022.
'The Taste of Fire' first published in *Only War: Stories from the 41st Millennium* in 2022.
This edition published in Great Britain in 2024 by
Black Library, Games Workshop Ltd., Willow Road,
Nottingham, NG7 2WS, UK.

Represented by: Games Workshop Limited – Irish branch,
Unit 3, Lower Liffey Street, Dublin 1,
D01 K199, Ireland.

10 9 8 7 6 5 4 3 2 1

Produced by Games Workshop in Nottingham.
Cover illustration by Paul Dainton.

See Black Library on the internet at

blacklibrary.com

Find out more about Games Workshop
and the worlds of Warhammer at

warhammer.com

Printed and bound in the UK.

For more than a hundred centuries the Emperor has sat immobile on the Golden Throne of Earth. He is the Master of Mankind. By the might of his inexhaustible armies a million worlds stand against the dark.

Yet, he is a rotting carcass, the Carrion Lord of the Imperium held in life by marvels from the Dark Age of Technology and the thousand souls sacrificed each day so his may continue to burn.

To be a man in such times is to be one amongst untold billions. It is to live in the cruelest and most bloody regime imaginable. It is to suffer an eternity of carnage and slaughter. It is to have cries of anguish and sorrow drowned by the thirsting laughter of dark gods.

This is a dark and terrible era where you will find little comfort or hope. Forget the power of technology and science. Forget the promise of progress and advancement. Forget any notion of common humanity or compassion.

There is no peace amongst the stars, for in the grim darkness of the far future, there is only war.

CONTENTS

Death World   9
Steve Lyons

Kasrkin   151
Edoardo Albert

Witchbringer   387
Steven B Fischer

The Weight of Silver   555
Steven B Fischer

The Taste of Fire   577
Steven B Fischer

Green and Grey   599
Edoardo Albert

Waiting Death   615
Steve Lyons

DEATH WORLD

Steve Lyons

CHAPTER 1

As soon as he woke, Trooper Lorenzo knew there was something wrong.

He rolled to his feet, simultaneously drawing his fang. He crouched in silence, in the dark, ready to drive half a metre of Catachan steel into the heart of any man or beast that thought it could sneak up on him.

But Lorenzo was alone.

He turned on the light, suppressing a prickling, creeping feeling as he realised again just how close the walls of his basic cabin were. And beyond those walls...

Lorenzo's bed was undisturbed; he preferred the floor, though even this was too flat for his liking. He could feel the beginnings of a stiff neck. All the same, he had slept for almost five hours. Longer than usual. Warp space did that to him. Out there, beyond the adamantium shell of the ship that carried him, there was nothing. But the warp itself distorted space and time, and that played hell with Lorenzo's instincts – and his body clock.

His brain itched. He was tired, but he knew he wouldn't sleep again now. He cursed his weakness. His tiredness would make him less alert. In the jungle, it could mean the difference between life and death.

Lorenzo was safe here, in theory. No enemies of the Imperium lurked in the shadows. No predators to sneak up on him as he slept, unguarded. Only the warp itself to worry about, and the possibility that it might capriciously tear the ship and its occupants apart – and there was nothing he could do about that if it happened. Nothing anyone could do.

They said no one but the Navigators could look into the warp. They said it would drive a normal man insane. Still, Lorenzo wished he could take that chance. He wished the ship had windows, so he could face his enemy and, perhaps, begin to understand it as the Navigators did.

Lorenzo had been in the thick of a space battle once. He had sat inside a cabin like this one, gripping the side of an acceleration couch as he rode out the shockwaves of near misses and glancing blows, his knuckles white; his life, his destiny, in the hands of a ship's captain and his gunners – and of the Emperor, of course. He had hated that feeling of helplessness. He had prayed for the attackers to board the ship, so he could have met them face to face. When Lorenzo died, he wanted the comfort of knowing he had fought his best against a superior foe – and if he had his way, that foe would be no mere space pirate or ork, but something more worthy of his origins and training.

When Lorenzo died, he wanted to be able to salute his killer, and be buried in its soil.

He splashed a handful of water on his face, and ran a hand through his tangled black hair. He threw on his camouflage jacket, though it would be useless against the greys and whites of the ship's interior. He re-sheathed his knife, and was comforted by its weight against his leg; his Catachan fang was a part of him, as much as his limbs were. As unlikely as it was that an attack would come, he had learned always to be prepared. It was when you allowed yourself to get comfortable that death could strike unexpectedly.

Somewhere on this ship, he was sure that other members of the company would be awake. He could probably find a card game.

Lorenzo's booted feet rang against the metal floor as he left his cabin, tinny echoes returning to his ears. The air was recycled, stale, and it didn't carry sounds in the way that fresh air did. The artificial gravity wasn't quite the same as that of any planet he'd visited. And it was quiet – so deathly quiet. There were none of the sounds of nature to which Lorenzo was attuned, the subtle clues that mapped out his surroundings for him and warned when danger approached. Instead, there was only the faint throb of engines, the vibrations reverberating through the hull so their origin was untraceable.

There was something wrong…

Everything was wrong. Man wasn't meant to exist in this unnatural environment. None of its signs could be trusted, and this made Lorenzo uneasy. If he couldn't rely on his own instincts, what could he rely on? 'Fear not the creatures of the jungle but those that lurk within your head.' The old Catachan proverb came to him unbidden and he thanked the Emperor that his company had its next assignment. They were already on their way to a new world, a fresh challenge.

He didn't know the details yet. Still, he had no doubt of one thing. Soon – within days, he hoped – his squad would be fighting their way across hostile terrain and through hostile creatures, beset by threats from all directions. It was likely some of them would die. He would be in his element again, his destiny returned to his own hands.

He ached for that moment.

It was early afternoon, ship time, when Colonel 'Stone Face' Graves summoned his Third Company of the Catachan XIV Regiment to the briefing room.

The men of four platoons, their bandoliers slung across their backs, crowded into the small area. Four platoons, comprising twenty-two squads – including two squads of Catachan Devils, who stood near the front and around whom even the most hardened veterans left a respectful space. Then there were the hulking, low-browed ogryns, included in the briefing as a courtesy though they would most likely understand only half of what was said. So long as they were pointed towards the enemy and permitted to rend and maim, they would be happy.

Lorenzo felt comforted by the presence of so many compatriots – by the press of their bodies and the natural, earthy odours of dirt and sweat.

'Listen up, you soft-skinned losers,' barked the colonel. A howl of good-natured protest rose from the assembled company, but Graves's chiselled features remained harsh and rigid. 'Naval Command think you lot have had it easy too long, and I agree with them. I begged them: "No more milk runs. I want no less than the dirtiest, most dangerous job you've got. I won't have my Jungle Fighters turning into fat, lazy sons of acid grubs who wouldn't lift a hand to scratch their own arses!" So, ladies, last chance to pamper yourselves in your luxury quarters – because as of this evening, you'll be working for your keep.'

This pronouncement was met by a rousing cheer.

'Planetfall at 19.00 hours,' the colonel continued, his voice loud and clear across the tumult though he'd made no effort to raise it. 'Anyone not in full kit and waiting at the airlocks by 18.30 finds himself on punishment detail for a month!'

'Y*es, sir!*' came the answering swell from the crowd.

'Colonel,' someone yelled from the back. Lorenzo recognised the voice of 'Hotshot' Woods, from his own squad. 'You serious? Is this going to be a real challenge for us this time?'

'You idlers ever hear of Rogar III?' growled Graves. 'It's a jungle world, out in the back of beyond. Explorators found it a couple of years ago, decided it was right for colonising and strip-mining. Just one problem: They'd been beaten to it. That's why they called on us. We have Guardsmen down there fighting orks for the past year and a half, but they're starting to find it tough going.'

Lorenzo joined in the collective jeers of mock sympathy.

'They're crying out for someone to hold their hands,' added Graves, to a roar of laughter. 'You see, seems Rogar wasn't the walk in the park they thought it'd be. Three weeks ago, in response to reports from the front, the planet was re-categorised as no longer suitable for colonisation...' He left a long pause there, but every man present knew what was coming, and anticipation hung heavy in the recycled air.

'...on account of it being classified as a deathworld!' concluded the colonel – and this time, the cheer went on much longer and louder.

'It's a crock, that's what it is.'

Lorenzo was sharing a mess hall table with four other members of his squad. He looked down at his bowl gloomily, and let a dollop of over-processed grey mulch slide from his spoon. Another thing he hated: Imperial Guard rations. If he'd been planetside, he'd have found something – some herb or spice – to make them more palatable. Or someone would have hunted down some indigenous beast, and his squad would have feasted on meat.

Lorenzo considered not eating at all until he had made planetfall. But on top of his disturbed sleep patterns, the last thing he needed was to let his energy levels dip. He gathered another spoonful, thrust it into his mouth and tried to swallow without tasting it.

'Stone Face got it right,' continued Sergeant 'Old Hardhead' Greiss in his gravelly voice. 'This is just another wet-nursing mission for a bunch of city boys who got in over their heads. You tell me, how can a planet go from being colony material one day to deathworld the next? It can't happen!'

'I don't know, sergeant,' said Brains Donovits, his thick black eyebrows beetling as his brow furrowed. 'I've been keeping an eye on the comms traffic, and the latest report from the commissars on the ground makes for pretty interesting reading. They've had some real problems out there.'

'Yeah,' put in Hotshot Woods, his blue eyes sparkling as he suppressed a grin, 'and you know Command wouldn't send us in without good reason, sergeant. They know what they're doing.'

Greiss shot the young trooper a stern glare through narrowed eyes. It only lasted a second, though, before he dropped the pretence and let out a bark of laughter, slapping Woods amiably on the back.

'It'll be the same old story,' grumbled the grizzled sergeant as his good humour subsided. 'Things not going too well at the front, orks getting too close to Command HQ for the top brass's liking. The next thing you know, some officer's been stung by a bloodwasp or got himself a nettle rash, or... or...'

'Got his foot tangled in a poison creeper,' suggested Steel Toe Dougan in his usual laid-back tone.

'Suddenly, he's screaming "Deathworld"!'

'There has also been some mention,' Donovits continued undeterred, 'of abnormalities in Rogar III's planetary readings. The Adeptus Mechanicus went in to investigate, but found nothing. Nothing but orks, anyhow.'

'Ah, listen to Brains,' scoffed Greiss. 'Never happy 'less he's got his nose in some report or other.'

Donovits shrugged. 'It pays to be forewarned, sergeant.'

'And since when did Navy reports tell you anything worth reading? The only place you get to know your enemy, trooper, is down there on its surface, in the thick of the jungle. Man against nature.'

Lorenzo felt something stirring in his chest at Greiss's words. He'd been feeling less edgy since they'd dropped out of the warp into real space, for the final approach to their destination, but still he longed to escape this prison. It was almost worse, knowing that release was so close. Time seemed to have slowed down for him. Lorenzo knew the others were restless, too, chafing for action. He didn't know if they shared his sense of unease, if the warp had affected them as it had him, and he wouldn't ask. There were some things you didn't talk about.

'I don't know, sergeant,' said Woods. 'There were times on that last world I wished I *had* stayed curled up on a bedroll with a good book. Might have made for more thrills, if you know what I mean.'

'Got a point there, Hotshot,' laughed Greiss. 'I could almost have felt sorry for them... what were they called?'

'Rhinoceraptors,' prompted Donovits.

'Yeah, right. Few frag grenades under their hide plates, and boom! Didn't know what'd hit them. A couple o' squads could've taken out the lot of 'em. Hell, Marbo could probably have done it on his own.'

'He wouldn't have thanked us for wasting his time, though.'

'You're right there, Hotshot.'

'Of course,' said Dougan, quietly, 'they did get Bryznowski.'

Greiss sighed. 'Yes. They did get Bryznowski. Heard we lost a few of the ogryns, too.'

'And that rookie from Bulldog's squad,' said Dougan, easing himself back in his chair so he could stretch out his bionic leg. It had taken a hit a couple of worlds ago, and now it had a tendency to seize up if he didn't keep it exercised.

There was a short silence as the five soldiers remembered fallen comrades, then Greiss's craggy features folded into a scowl.

'Way things are going,' he grumbled, 'I'm going to end up dying in my damn bed!' He waved aside Woods and Donovits's well-intentioned protests. 'Come off it, you lot. I'm thirty-six years old next birthday. Leaving it a bit late for that blaze of glory. But that's okay. I made my mark. I just want to go out the right way, that's all. Been too long since I had a scrap I couldn't sleepwalk through. Long time since I faced a deathworld worthy of the name.'

'Maybe you should put in for a posting back home,' said Dougan, sympathetically. 'Back to Catachan. Stone Face will understand. He's coming up to the big three-oh himself.'

Lorenzo was aware that, by Imperial standards, Colonel Graves was a young man, and Greiss and Dougan only middle-aged. But then, most Imperial citizens didn't grow up on Catachan. Life there was shorter.

'Ah, I couldn't leave you jokers. But it's the youngsters I feel sorry for. Like Lorenzo here. How's he going to make a name for himself if he never sets foot on a world worth taming?'

Lorenzo looked up from his meal, to grunt an acknowledgement of the name check. He didn't reveal how much it smarted. Greiss would never have called Hotshot Woods a 'youngster', and Lorenzo was two years older than he was.

'I got a name for Lorenzo,' quipped Woods. 'Why don't we call him "Chatterbox" Lorenzo? Or "Never Shuts His Yap" Lorenzo?'

Lorenzo glared at him.

Greiss pushed his bowl aside, and hauled himself to his feet. 'All right, men,' he said, his voice suddenly full of confidence and authority. 'You heard what Colonel Graves said. Drop positions by 17.30 hours.'

'The colonel said 18.30, sergeant.'

'That's for the rest of those slackers, Donovits. *My* squad forms up at 17.30 sharp. Fifty deck reps, a few circuits of the deck – that should loosen up the muscles, get the adrenaline pumping. Then, when we get down to this "deathworld", we're going to tear through it like it was nothing, show those Guardsmen down there a thing or two. This time tomorrow, we'll be back in warp space, headed for somewhere worth the sweat!'

Lorenzo greeted the prospect with mixed feelings.

The whole of Third Company could have fitted into one drop-ship with room to spare. Instead, Colonel Graves had ordered them to split up, one platoon to a ship. That meant only one thing. He was expecting trouble on the way down. Better to lose a few squads and have the rest arrive intact than to risk losing all twenty-two to a lucky shot.

The five squads in Lorenzo's ship had separated to the edges of the troop deck, sitting in their own small clusters in the rows of narrow seats. It wasn't that they didn't get on, just that Deathworlders found it best to make no more attachments than they had to. They were too easily broken. Lorenzo had no friends, but he had something better. He had nine comrades, who would die for him in a heartbeat and he for them.

The shadowy spaces around the cramped seating area were empty, apart from a dusty Sentinel scout walker tucked into one. The Catachans carried little more equipment than would fit into their kit bags – and those bags stayed with them, nestled in their laps or deposited on an adjacent seat. Lorenzo pictured the four ships streaking towards the surface of Rogar III, blazing with the heat of re-entry, like meteors from the heavens. He wondered how many Guardsmen on the ground would turn their heads upwards and thank the Emperor for sending them such an omen. The thought made him feel good. It almost made him forget that he hadn't touched ground himself yet.

There had been a reallocation of troops a few days earlier. The commander of C Platoon, Lieutenant Vines, had disbanded one squad and reassigned its members to bring the rest up to strength. Greiss's squad had two new arrivals to complete its complement of ten – and old hands Myers and Storm were currently passing the time by quizzing one of them, a nervy youngster by the name of Landon.

Landon was eager to please, bragging about a time back on Catachan when he'd wrestled a blackback viper single-handed. Myers and Storm were pretending to be impressed, but Lorenzo knew they were poking fun at the rookie.

The other newcomer, Patch Armstrong, had an easier ride. It had taken an ambush by four ice apes on the frozen world of Tundrar to deprive Armstrong of his left eye – and even then he had snapped the spine of one beast, gutted two more and gunned down the fourth as it had fled. The patch he wore, and the crooked ends of the scar that protruded above and below it, were his badges of honour. Like Dougan's leg, and the plate in Sergeant Greiss's head.

The drop-ship was being shaken.

It had only been a little at first, but now it was growing stronger. Sharkbait Muldoon had rolled up the left sleeve of his jacket to paint his own, better, camouflage pattern directly onto his skin, layering on natural dyes with his knife; he let out a curse as the blade slipped and nicked his arm. Lorenzo said nothing, but his fingers tightened around the armrests of his seat.

'Must be one hell of a storm,' commented Woods. But Lorenzo observed that Greiss's jaw was set, his teeth clenched, his nostrils flaring, and he knew this was no mere storm.

Then, just like that, they were falling.

The drop-ship plummeted like a brick, like it had when it had first been launched from its mother. Lorenzo's stomach was in his mouth again; had he not been strapped in, he would have been slammed into the ceiling. Woods, cocky as ever, had loosened his own restraints, and now he was fighting to hold himself down as g-forces rippled the skin of his cheeks.

For eight long seconds, Lorenzo was facing his worst nightmare. Then the engines caught them and they were flying level again, but still buffeted, the deck lurching unpredictably beneath their feet. Behind the din of the protesting hull, the soft, artificial voice of the navigation servitor sounded over the vox-caster: '*Warning: extreme atmospheric turbulence encountered. Destination coordinates no longer attainable. Prepare for emergency landing. Repeat, prepare for emergency landing.*'

The first impact came almost as soon as the warning was issued.

Lorenzo had barely had time to get into the brace position, his chin on his chest, his hands clasped over his head. It felt like someone had taken a sledgehammer to every bone in his body at once. And then it happened again, with only marginally less force this second time.

The drop-ship was skipping along the ground, its engines shrieking. Lorenzo was rattled in his seat, his straps biting into his chest. He concentrated on keeping his muscles relaxed, despite the situation, knowing that to resist the repeated shocks would do him more harm than good.

Then they hit the ground for the final time, but they were still barrelling forwards, and the scrape of earth and branches against the outer hull was almost deafening. Rogar III, as Donovits had taken pleasure in informing everyone, was blanketed in jungle. There were no open spaces in which to land, but for those cleared with axe and flame. Lorenzo pictured the scene outside the drop-ship's hull now, as it ploughed through tangled vegetation, the servitors straining to rein in its speed before it hit something that wouldn't yield to its considerable mass. Before it crumpled in on itself like a ball of paper.

And then, at last, they were still, the engines letting out a last dying whine as the drop-ship's superstructure creaked and settled. The lighting flickered and cut out, and Lorenzo could see nothing in the sudden total darkness. But he knew his way to the hatchway, and his squad was the closest to it.

The drop-ship had come to rest at an angle. The deck was tilted some forty-five degrees to the horizontal, so Lorenzo had to climb to reach his goal. He swung himself from one empty seat to the next, using their backs to keep his balance and his bearings. From all around, he could hear the sounds of buckles popping and men leaping to their feet.

He was almost there when he realised he had been beaten to it. The hatch had buckled a little and was sticking in its frame, but Woods managed to shoulder it open even as Lorenzo was about to lend him a hand. First a crack, then a rectangle of brilliant light blazed in Lorenzo's eyes, and he blinked to clear the patterns it burnt into his retinas.

In the meantime, Woods had clambered out onto the angled side of the ship. 'Hey,' he called down to the others enthusiastically. 'You've got to see this. It's a beautiful evening!'

Lorenzo frowned. The upturned hatchway offered him the familiar sight of a jungle canopy – but behind the greens and browns, the leaves and the branches, the sky appeared to be a perfect, deep blue, free from cloud. Woods was right. If there *had* been a storm, it had passed, impossibly, without trace. But then, what else could have tossed the drop-ship about like that?

It was there again: that sense of wrongness he had felt in the warp. He needed to get out into the open. The rest of the platoon were crowding up behind him anyway, so Lorenzo followed the sweet scent of fresh air, mingled though it was with the stench of burning. He gripped the sides of the hatchway and pulled himself up and out through it.

He had barely raised his head above the parapet and started to take in his new surroundings, when Trooper Woods pushed him down again, with a warning yell: '*Incoming!*'

Three plants were shuffling towards the drop-ship. They looked like the mantraps of Catachan, but taller. Three bulbous pink heads, surely too heavy for their stalks to support, split open like mouths. No teeth within, though. These plants were spitters.

Three jets of clear liquid plumed through the air. Lorenzo and Woods tumbled back into the drop-ship together. Woods had been hit, a thick gobbet of acid sizzling on his arm. He whipped out his knife – a devil claw, typically ostentatious – and half-cut, half-tore his sleeve away before it was eaten through. Still, the attack had left a livid red burn on his skin.

Somewhere, not far away, a carrion bird was screeching in delight.

'So, how's it looking out there?' asked Greiss – and Lorenzo realised that the sergeant was addressing him.

A smile tugged at his lips as he gave the traditional answer: 'Reckon I'm going to like this place, sergeant. It reminds me of home!'

CHAPTER 2

The air outside the hatch filled with acid spray again, and a few drops made it inside the ship. The Catachans withdrew from the danger area, those at the front yelling at the others to get back. Lorenzo's bandolier was splashed – only a little, but enough to leave a steaming hole in the fabric.

Sergeant Greiss had shouldered his way up to Lorenzo and Woods through the crush. The platoon commander was only a few steps behind him. Lieutenant Vines was a quiet-voiced, unassuming man – but, because he had earned his rank, been elected to it by his fellow Catachans, they listened when he spoke. He asked the two troopers to describe what they'd seen, and Woods told him about the spitting plants. 'Three of them, sir,' Lorenzo confirmed, 'at two o'clock.'

'Who's your best marksman, sergeant?'

Without hesitation, Greiss answered, 'Bullseye, sir. Trooper Myers.' As he spoke, he seized the shoulder of a wiry, dark-skinned man, and pulled him forward.

'You know what to do, Myers,' said Vines.

With a nod of understanding, Myers drew his lasgun. He waited a few seconds to be sure it was safe, then darted up to the sloping hatchway.

As soon as he popped his head up into the open, there came another deluge. Myers let off two shots, then dived and rolled back under cover, landing at Lorenzo's feet. Lorenzo heard acid spattering the drop-ship's hull above his head. He looked down, and saw that the deck plates were bubbling beneath the droplets left from the previous attack.

Donovits was a second ahead of him, his eyes already turned upward. 'Do you think it can melt through adamantium?' asked Lorenzo.

'It's possible,' said Donovits, 'with the damage we must have taken on the way down. I'd keep an eye out up there. You see that ceiling starting to discolour, you find yourself a steel umbrella quick.'

'And that'd help?'

'For a few seconds, yes.'

'I've never seen plant acid so strong,' breathed Sharkbait Muldoon, 'not even back home.'

'Makes you wonder,' said Donovits, 'what kind of insects live on this world if that's what it takes to digest them.'

In the meantime, Myers had made his report to Lieutenant Vines: 'Three of them, sir, like Hotshot and Lorenzo said. I picked off the first, but I swear the second ducked under my shot. Got the measure of it now, though.'

Vines signalled his approval with a terse nod, and Myers approached the hatchway again.

He was halfway there when the plants fired a fourth time.

This time, their two sprays were perfectly aimed. They collided above the hatchway, so that a sheet of liquid dropped into the ship with a slap. Myers let out a curse and leapt back. Several troopers were splashed, but those who had alkali powders in their kits – ground from the vegetation of their last deathworld – had readied them, and they quickly pressed them into service.

An acid river trickled down the angled deck, petering out as it sizzled into the metal. Still, Lorenzo wasn't the only trooper forced to climb onto a seat to escape its path.

'Cunning critters,' breathed Myers, almost admiringly. And then he was off, without awaiting instructions. He vaulted through the hatchway, the ship's hull ringing as his booted feet connected with it. Then he was out of sight, but Lorenzo could still hear, and feel, his footsteps overhead, and the crack of a lasgun, firing once, twice, three times, four times, then another spattering of acid, uncomfortably close to the point from which the last footstep had sounded.

Then there was silence.

Lorenzo held his breath, alert for any sounds from outside the drop-ship. Then he caught Sergeant Greiss's eye, and realised that Old Hardhead was smiling. A moment later, Myers appeared in the hatchway again, and he too was grinning from ear to ear. He blew imaginary smoke from the barrel of his lasgun. 'All clear,' he announced.

Four sergeants bellowed at once, ordering their respective troopers out of the ship double-quick. Lorenzo knew that whichever squad was last to form up outside would pay with extra duties for embarrassing their commander.

Fifty men rushed for the hatchway, but Woods reached it first. As Lorenzo climbed out onto the surface of a new world and looked for his squad, he felt a thrill of excitement. He was back in the jungle – back in his element. He knew that, whatever perils may lie in store for him on Rogar III, they couldn't be as discomforting as that stifling room with its single bed, up there in space.

The trees of Rogar III were generally tall, thin and gnarled, but they grew close together – too close, in places, for a man to squeeze between them. Their leaves were jagged, some razor-edged – and creepers dangled from their topmost branches, bulging with poisonous pustules. The undergrowth was thick, green-brown and halfway to knee height, the occasional splash of colour thrown out in the shape of a flower or a brightly patterned thistle or patch of strangle-weed. From a distance, it looked like any jungle Lorenzo had seen. He wanted to get closer, to inspect the peculiar shapes and patterns of *this* jungle, to begin to learn which shapes he could trust and which spelled danger – but, for now, it was not to be.

The drop-ship had gouged a great gash out of the planet. Undergrowth had been flattened, trees felled, branches shorn. Small fires were still burning, and creepers twitched like severed limbs in their heat.

Vines checked his compass, and received a navigational fix from the troop carrier in orbit. They were ten kilometres away from the Imperial encampment, he reported, and the quickest route to it was to retrace the trail of devastation to its source. It was also the safest route – for, although Lorenzo saw several more acid spitters among the ashes, most had been burnt or decapitated. When one plant did dare stir, and cracked open its pink head, it immediately became the focus of eight lasguns, and was promptly blasted out of existence.

The Catachans proceeded cautiously to begin with, and there was little talk. Each of them knew this was the most dangerous time: their first footsteps on a new world, not knowing the threats it posed, knowing that an attack could come at any second from any quarter. In time, they would become familiar with Rogar III – those of them who survived these early days. They would learn to anticipate and counter anything it could throw at them. Then this world would be no challenge any more and, Emperor willing, they would move on to another.

Lorenzo loved this time. He loved the feeling of adrenaline pumping around his body, loved the edge it gave him.

For the moment, though, the planet was nursing its wounds, keeping its distance. He heard more birds screeching to each other, but apart from a brief flutter of wings on the edge of his vision he never saw a single one. A jungle lizard skittered away as the Catachans approached. Lorenzo estimated it to be about twenty centimetres long, but without a closer inspection he couldn't tell if it was an adult or a baby.

It was almost as if Rogar III was watching the new arrivals, sizing them up just as they were sizing up it.

Bulldog Rock was the first to order his squad to double time, and Greiss and the other sergeants followed. Not to be outdone, another squad struck up a cadence call.

A scream of engines drew his attention to the sky, and he caught a glint of red as the rays of the sinking sun struck metal. Two drop-ships, ascending, from a point no more than a couple of kilometres ahead. He wondered what had happened to the third, and suppressed a shudder at the thought that one platoon may not have been as fortunate as his own.

Not long after that, they came to the end of their own ship's trail – the point at which it had hit ground. Lorenzo had looked forward to entering the jungle proper, but instead he found himself at the edge of an expansive clearing. It was man-made, about two kilometres in diameter, doubtless the product of many hours of toil by Imperium troops with flamers – and yet the vegetation at the clearing's edge was already showing signs of re-growth.

Without breaking step, the Jungle Fighters made for a huddle of prefabricated buildings in the clearing's centre, now little more than shadows in the twilight. As they reached it, the sergeants shouted more orders, and the Catachans formed up in their squads again and fell silent. Lorenzo was aware that their noisy arrival had turned the heads of several Guardsmen

STEVE LYONS

who'd been standing sentry. It had also given fair warning of their approach to the commissar who now came to meet them.

He was a young, fair-haired man with pale skin and ears that protruded very noticeably. The Imperial eagle spread its wings proudly on his peaked cap, and his slight form was almost swallowed by a long, black overcoat. Fresh out of training, Lorenzo thought. Even Lieutenant Vines, not a tall man, seemed to tower over the senior officer through presence alone. Lorenzo thought he could see a sneer pulling at Vines's lips as he folded his arm into a lazy salute and announced, 'C Platoon, Third Company, Catachan XIV reporting for duty, sir.'

'Not before time, lieutenant,' said the commissar tersely. 'I assume it was your drop-ship that screamed over our heads an hour ago, and almost demolished the very camp we've been fighting to defend?' He made it sound like an accusation, as if Vines had been piloting the ship himself. Before Vines could speak, however, the commissar raised his voice to address the assembled platoon. 'My name is Mackenzie. I am in command here – and as long as you are on Rogar III, my word is the Emperor's word, is that clear?'

A few of the Catachans mumbled a derisory, 'Yes, sir.' Most of them said nothing.

Mackenzie scowled. 'Let me make this clear from the outset,' he snapped. 'I don't like deathworlders. In my experience, they are sloppy and undisciplined, with an arrogance that far outstrips their ability. The Emperor has seen fit to send you here, and I concede you may have certain expertise that will hasten a conclusion to this war. But had the decision been mine, let me tell you, I would rather have fought on with one squad from the blessed birth world than ten from Canak or Luther McIntyre or whatever hellhole it was you lot crawled out from.'

'Catachan, sir!' hollered Vines, and a proud roar swelled from the ranks of his men. If Mackenzie had expected to get a rise out of the Jungle Fighters, he was disappointed. Most of them ignored him, not quite looking at him, undermining him with a wave of indifference. Woods said something under his breath, a few men laughed, and the commissar's eyes narrowed – but he hadn't quite caught the words and couldn't pinpoint their source.

'As you *are* here,' he continued, 'I intend to make the best of it. I'm making it my mission to whip you rabble into shape. By the time I'm finished with you, you'll be the smartest Guardsmen in the Imperium.'

Mackenzie turned on his heel, then, and snarled in Vines's direction, 'Your platoon is late for my briefing, lieutenant. Ten laps round the camp perimeter, double time. Last squad back does another ten.'

'With respect, sir...' began Vines, the look of contempt in his eyes suggesting that respect was the last thing he wanted to show.

'That includes you, lieutenant,' Mackenzie barked – and he marched away stiffly, into the largest of the buildings.

Vines took a deep breath. 'All right,' he said, 'you heard the man.'

The Catachans took their circuits at a leisurely pace, and with a cadence call that contained a few choice lyrics about senior officers.

By the time they got to the lower ranks' mess hall, there was only enough slop left for half rations, and it was cold.

About fifty Catachans and a handful of ogryns from A and D Platoons had taken over a generous area, perching on tables with their feet up on chairs, swigging from flasks and punching each other boisterously. They had broken out the hooch to celebrate their arrival; it had been brewed on the troop ship, and put aside for a special occasion. They filled the large space with their raucous laughter.

There were other Guardsmen here – they outnumbered the Catachans two to one – but they were finishing their meals in silence, along one side of the hall, looking very much like they'd been edged out by the newcomers. They wore red and gold, and were identified by their flashes as members of the 32nd Royal Validian Regiment. To Lorenzo's eyes, most of them looked tall and gaunt – but then, he was aware that Catachan had a higher than average gravity, which made its people more squat and muscular than most.

It didn't surprise him that the two groups had self-segregated. The Catachans were Jungle Fighters – elite deathworld veterans. The best the Imperium had to offer, they believed. The rank-and-file Guardsmen regarded them with a mixture of curiosity, admiration and, here more than in many places, outright resentment.

Lorenzo's squad picked up their meals and took over a table. Greiss joined them presently; he'd had the rookie, Landon, fetch his food for him while he'd pumped the other platoons for what they'd learned so far.

He threw a folded sheet of paper onto the table. Lorenzo saw the crudely printed header *Eagle & Bolter*, and needed to look no closer. Another propaganda broadsheet, doubtless full of consoling 'news' about how the war here was being won. 'Looks like we hit the jackpot this time,' said the sergeant happily. 'We got killer plants, man-eating slugs, poison insects, acid swamps, all the usual. On top of that, there's talk of invisible monsters – and ghosts, would you believe!' He saw that a couple of Validians were eavesdropping from the next table but one, and he added slyly, 'Course we only got the word of a few rookie Guardsmen for that. Probably jumping at their own shadows.'

'Ghosts?' echoed Donovits, interested.

'Yes: ghosts, lights, whatever. Supposed to appear at night, lure men into the jungle – and those crazy enough to follow them don't come back.'

'Speaking of which, sergeant,' said Armstrong, 'any news on B Platoon?' The one-eyed trooper made the question sound nonchalant, but Lorenzo knew Armstrong had belonged to the missing platoon before his recent transfer.

'Not yet,' said Greiss. 'They had the same trouble we did on the way in, but it looks like they set down further away. They're out there somewhere.'

'Lucky for them,' said Woods. 'They don't have to put up with Commissar Jug-Handles throwing his not considerable weight around.'

'It must've been some storm,' remarked Donovits.

'Blew up out of nowhere,' said Greiss, 'by all accounts. One second, the sky was clear; the next, our drop-ships were drawing strikes like lightning rods. Then clear blue again.'

'Still think Naval Command were exaggerating, sergeant,' asked Woods with his characteristic cheeky grin, 'about this place turning into a deathworld?'

'Can't see this place ever having been anything but,' commented Bullseye Myers. 'I don't know why it took 'em so long to admit it.'

'Maybe it was Mackenzie,' considered Dougan. 'You heard what the man said. He doesn't want us here.'

'Yeah,' said Woods – and in a passable impression of the commissar's nasal whine, he continued, '"I don't like deathworlders. I'm making it my mission to whip you lot into shape. You hear me, Greiss? On your knees and lick my shiny black boots. And when you're done with that, you can kiss my–"'

'If I were you,' snarled a voice from behind him, 'I'd be careful what you say about an officer of the Imperium.'

Woods didn't even glance back to see who was talking, though Lorenzo could see that it was a broad-shouldered, square-headed Validian sergeant. 'Don't care what his rank is,' said Woods offhandedly, 'he's still a damn idiot.'

'You want to repeat that to my face?'

Greiss's eyes narrowed. 'Stand down, sergeant,' he growled. 'I'm in command of these men. You have a problem with them, you bring it to me.'

'Mackenzie was right about you deathworlders,' the Validian sneered. 'You've no discipline, no respect.'

'Where we come from,' murmured Muldoon, idly sharpening his night reaper blade on a piece of flint, 'respect is earned, not given.'

'You come charging in here, all gung-ho, badmouthing our people, thinking you can just take over.'

'And here I thought you begged us to come,' said Woods, 'because your lot couldn't do your jobs properly. What's the problem – sun too hot for you?'

'We've been here eighteen months,' snapped the Validian, 'and we're winning this war. We've driven the orks right back; there hasn't been an attack on this encampment or any other in three weeks. If you wanted to help, you should have been here when we were cleansing areas, holding the line, facing ambushes day and night. But no, true to form, you glory hounds show up in time for the mopping up and claim all the credit.'

Greiss was on his feet, his lip curling into a dangerous snarl. 'Have you quite finished, sergeant?'

Woods stood now, too, on the pretext of clearing away his half-empty bowl. 'It's okay, sergeant,' he said, 'just a bitter old man letting off some steam – and can you blame him? Can't be many Imperial Guard regiments have had to go crying for reinforcements against a few trees and flowers.'

The Validian's eyes bulged and his face reddened. He pulled back his fist, but Woods had anticipated the move. He sidestepped the sergeant's blow, and simultaneously took hold of his attacker, using his own weight to flip him onto his back on the table.

The move had the effect of bringing the rest of Lorenzo's squad to their feet, as they leapt to avoid flying cups and bowls. Two tables away, the Validian's fellows were also pushing back their chairs and standing. Their downed sergeant tried to right himself, but Woods was keeping him off-balance. The sergeant kicked out, and Woods danced out of the way of his boot. As the sergeant swung his legs over the side of the table and made to stand at last, Woods head-butted him – the fabled 'Catachan Kiss' – and his nose splintered in a fountain of blood.

The first two Validians came at Woods, but Armstrong and Dougan intercepted them. It looked like Steel Toe was just trying to calm things down, even at this stage, but his efforts were futile: as a Validian took a swing at him, he responded with a punch to the jaw that laid him right out. Another six Guardsmen surged forward as one, and Myers and Storm leapt onto the table and stood back to back, lashing out with fists and feet.

In just seconds, an all-out brawl had broken out. No guns or knives were drawn, but nor were any punches pulled. Even Landon joined in with gusto, pummelling away at the stomach of a man two heads taller than himself until he staggered and passed out through sheer inability to draw breath.

A pug-nosed, unshaven sergeant came at Lorenzo with a chair raised over his head. Lorenzo ducked under the makeshift weapon, and threw himself at its wielder. His head impacted with the soft tissue of the sergeant's stomach, and they went rolling end over end on the dirt-streaked floor.

The violence was spreading like unchecked fire. Other squads were pulled into the fray, taking sides according to regimental loyalty. Validian reinforced Validian, Catachan reinforced Catachan, until the entire hall had erupted into a cacophonic mass of screams and yells and crashes and the dull smacks of fists and feet against flesh. Out of the corner of his eye, Lorenzo saw two ogryns ploughing into the melee, picking up men by the throat two at a time and knocking their heads together.

He had managed to get on top of his opponent, surprising the sergeant with his litheness. He pinned him with a knee to his chest, and drove his knuckles repeatedly into the sergeant's face – until two Guardsmen seized him from behind, and tore him away. Lorenzo had seen them coming, but in the midst of such chaos it was impossible to avoid all the possible threats. Still, he was prepared for this one. He thrust his elbows back, catching his would-be captors off-guard, and threw himself into a forward roll, wrenching their hands from his shoulders. He dropped into an alert stance, expecting the Validians to come at him again, but they had other problems. Greiss had just waded into them.

The sergeant planted his hand in one man's face, and pushed him back with enough force to send him sprawling. Then he concentrated his efforts on the other, his expression feral, a zealous gleam in his eyes as he laid into his victim with a barrage of punches so fast and furious that their sheer force kept him upright for a second after he was knocked cold.

Dougan was in trouble. He was surrounded, and it looked like his artificial leg was playing up again, slowing him down. Lorenzo flew to the older man's assistance, but two more Validians rose up in his path. He transferred his momentum to his fist, and drove it into the first man's skull. The second made a grab for Lorenzo's throat, and simultaneously knocked his legs out from under him. For an instant, he was suspended in midair, choking. He managed to plant his hands on his attacker's shoulders, and bring up his feet, kicking at the Validian's chest. They both fell, but Lorenzo spun and hit the ground on his feet, and was ready for the first Validian as he came at him again.

In the meantime, Muldoon had come to Dougan's aid, letting out a war cry as he bowled into the men surrounding his comrade and scattered them. Dougan got his second wind, hoisted one foe by the scruff of his flak jacket and hurled him, arms and legs thrashing furiously, into another. The ogryns were still cracking skulls, the Validians now realising what they had taken on, almost trampling each other to get away from the misshapen creatures.

One particularly hapless specimen backed into Lorenzo, eyes wide with fear, just as the Catachan finished putting down his own two opponents. In the heat of a terrified moment, the Validian broke the unspoken rule, by drawing his lasgun.

Lorenzo was on him before he could aim it. The gun dropped from the Guardsman's grasp as Lorenzo seized his arm and twisted it until the bone snapped. The Validian let out a yelp and fell to his knees, but he had foregone any right to sympathy or mercy, and Lorenzo knocked him cold with a spinning kick to the head.

His keen ears caught the sound of a whining voice, straining to be heard across the tumult. Commissar Mackenzie had just strode into the hall, and he was demanding calm, to no avail. At his heels, however, was Graves – and when the colonel spoke, Catachans and Validians alike fell still.

'Just what the hell is going on here?' Graves roared, his voice resonating in the sudden guilty hush.

CHAPTER 3

'I said, what the hell is going on? What do you think you're doing?'

Colonel Graves strode deeper into the mess hall, his blazing eyes darting from Catachan to Validian to Catachan, sharing around the force of his scorn. 'I've seen acid grubs behave with more dignity. You're meant to be on the same side!'

Mackenzie scuttled after him. 'Do you see?' he fumed. 'This is why I was opposed to bringing Jungle Fighters into this campaign.' He raised his voice to address the hall. 'I want – no, I *demand* – to know who the ringleaders were behind this disgraceful display. Names and ranks!'

A few eyes were cast down, a few feet shuffled, but the Validians were no more willing than the Catachans were to tell on their own. In the face of their intransigence, the commissar's face grew steadily redder.

'Sergeant Wallace!'

The unlucky Validian who the commissar had singled out snapped to attention, and reported, 'My apologies, sir, I didn't see how the incident started. My men and I only acted to calm the situation when it seemed to be getting out of hand.'

Mackenzie got the same story, almost verbatim, from his next two sergeants.

Lorenzo sensed a surreptitious movement behind him, and he turned to see that the sergeant whose nose Woods had broken was being helped to his feet, a piece of cloth clasped to his bloodied face. He was glaring venomously at the cause of his woes, but Woods returned his gaze with a smug grin and cracked his knuckles into his palm.

It was this look that Commissar Mackenzie caught, and he bustled over to the pair, his nostrils flaring with self-righteous zeal. 'Enright?'

The bloodied sergeant shrugged helplessly, using his cloth as a shield from interrogation. Mackenzie clicked his tongue in impatience, then dismissed Enright and the two Guardsmen who were supporting him with an impatient hand movement. The trio made their way to the door, and no doubt to whatever medical facility this camp offered.

Mackenzie fixed Woods with a shrivelling glare, which he then turned upon the Catachans around him until he saw the sergeant's stripes on Greiss's arm. 'Perhaps *you* can shed some light on this matter, sergeant?'

'Greiss, sir.'

'Sergeant Greiss. You seem to have had a ringside seat for the worst of it.'

'My apologies, sir,' said Greiss in a faintly mocking tone, 'I didn't see how the incident started. My men and I only acted to calm the situation when it seemed to be getting out of hand.'

One of the Catachans let out a harsh laugh, but Mackenzie wasn't amused. He cast another distasteful look at Woods, and snapped, 'It seems clear to me, Sergeant Greiss, that you and your squad were responsible for this outrage, and I intend to make sure you regret it. How would you feel, Greiss, about sleeping out in the jungle tonight?'

Greiss's eyes lit up. 'Delighted to, sir.'

That wasn't the answer Mackenzie had been expecting, and he seethed impotently. 'Let me tell you, Sergeant Greiss, what happens to Guardsmen who disrespect their senior officers.'

'I'm all ears, sir,' growled Greiss.

Mackenzie flushed. 'We bury them. Let me tell you what it's like, Greiss. It's too small for you to stand, too narrow for you to sit down. You'll spend the night – as many nights as I choose – in the most uncomfortable position you can imagine, until you think your spine will crack. You'll feel spiders gnawing at your feet; you'll be at the mercy of the jungle lizards. And during the day – in the daytime, when the sun's beating down on you and you don't have the room to lift an arm to shade your eyes – in the daytime, Greiss, let me tell you, you'll start to wish you were dead.'

Graves had moved silently to the young commissar's side. He cleared his throat now, and murmured, 'May I remind you, sir, that we need these men fresh and active for duty in the morning? I don't see much point in pursuing this matter. Especially–' and he laboured this point particularly heavily '–with no evidence to lay charges against any individual. No harm done, I'd say. In fact, it's probably best for all sides they got it out of their systems.'

Mackenzie said nothing for a moment – and Lorenzo expected him to snap at the colonel the way he had at Lieutenant Vines. Instead, he seemed to accept the quiet wisdom in Graves's words. He turned and marched stiffly out of the door, the tension in the hall diffusing in his wake. People began to pick themselves up, to collect scattered bowls, chairs and tables and to tend to their wounded, Catachans and Validians working together to restore order.

'For any of you girls who were fretting,' announced Colonel Graves, 'B Platoon have voxed in. They've had some casualties – lost eight men – but most of them are still standing, and they're making their way to us, ETA 11.00. In view of this delay, Commissar Mackenzie has decided not to wait. All Jungle Fighters are to assemble in the briefing hut in twenty minutes.'

Lorenzo slept under the stars that night, on a bed of leaves picked from the edge of the jungle and carefully tested for hidden spines and poison sap. Basic quarters had been provided for the Catachans, but there weren't enough bunks for all of them – and most would have chosen to sleep outdoors anyway. It had been too long.

The sounds of the jungle at night brought a feeling of calm to Lorenzo. The rustle of a breeze in its leaves, the caws and cackles of nocturnal predators, the gurgle of water – or some other liquid – carried from far away. He wished he could be deeper inside it. The area cleared out by the Validians had an acrid burnt scent to it. Lorenzo was used to having a canopy of green above him – but tonight it was black, and freckled with the white points of distant suns. The night sky was crystal clear, the air warm. It was as if Rogar III was showing him its good points, its aesthetic qualities. As if it wanted to lull him into a sense of security by hiding its true, savage beauty from him. Lorenzo wasn't fooled. He looked forward to the morning, to testing this world's mettle.

He thought back to Mackenzie's briefing, and suppressed a thrill. The commissar had been furnished with a list of the Catachan squads, and had assigned them to various missions. B Platoon had drawn the short straw in their absence; they would arrive at the encampment to find that their comrades had moved out and left them to reinforce the security details here. If they were lucky, the orks would provide a distraction or two to break up the monotony.

The rest of the Catachans were to do what the Validians could not: take the fight to the orks themselves. Which meant, of course, fighting the jungle too.

'I know what you're all thinking,' Colonel Graves had added to Mackenzie's speech. 'It's a jungle world, maybe even a deathworld, nothing you haven't seen before. Well, believe me, Rogar III *is* different. The commissar here tells me that, a year ago, this place was a little green corner of paradise. Well, I don't know what's happened, and to tell the truth I don't much care – but as you ladies can see, this isn't paradise any more.'

Later, Donovits had tossed around a lot of phrases like 'climate change' and 'axis shifts' – but Lorenzo hadn't cared much.

He'd been more interested in hearing how the Imperium's attempts to expand its encampments had met with failure. It was a full-time job for a squad of Guardsmen to maintain this one, small though it was. For every jungle creeper they burnt away, two more seemed to replace it – and their rate of growth was prodigious.

'When the Explorators came to Rogar,' Graves had said, 'they recorded some weird energy signature.' Of course, Lorenzo had already known that, thanks to Donovits. 'Now, I'm not saying there's anything in that – just warning you hotheads not to get too cocky. We don't know what this deathworld has to throw at us, but we do know a couple of hundred Guardsmen have died trying to find out.'

Mackenzie had displayed a rough map of the area, and pointed out the known ork strongholds. He was planning an attack on one of these; intelligence suggested that it was lightly defended, the orks depending on the jungle itself to protect them. A derisive snort had gone up from the Catachans at this point.

The whole of A Platoon, ogryns and all, was committed to this offensive, while two of D Platoon's four squads were to set traps and lay in wait for reinforcements from the other ork camps. Other squads would target supply lines – hit and run tactics, to divide the enemy's attention.

Lorenzo's squad had been the last to learn its assignment – and its ten men had let out a cheer when Mackenzie had explained that it was the most vital, and most dangerous, of all. The commissar had shouted at them to be silent.

'One particular ork has been giving us trouble,' he had said. 'Their current warboss in this region. You know how it is – we take out one, another takes its place. But this one has a few more brain cells than most. The troops have taken to calling him Big Green. He's actually got the beasts organised, to an extent. Their last few raids on us were almost well planned. And this ork has a keen sense of self-preservation. Most warbosses lead from the front; this one stays behind the lines. He's become a legend to the orks, if only because he's lasted longer than his predecessors. He's good for their morale. Too good. I want him dead!'

According to the commissar, the Imperial Guard had been close to finding the warboss's hideout when, in his own words, 'the jungle became impassable'. They knew its general location, but the lair itself was well concealed. The Catachans' job was to find the ork warboss and do the necessary deed. A stealth mission; a single assassination. Sounded simple, Lorenzo thought.

Then, Mackenzie had thrown a spanner in the works.

'Given the importance of this mission,' he had said, 'I will be leading it myself. *Silence!*' he bellowed in response to the Catachans' howls of protest.

Sergeant Greiss, who a moment earlier had sported a broad grin on his face, now looked as if he had been slapped. 'With respect, sir,' he had growled, 'you aren't a Jungle Fighter. Better if the men take their orders from someone used to–'

'Contrary to popular belief, sergeant,' Mackenzie had sneered, 'they do teach us to do more than sit around and drink amasec in officer training. I am fully qualified in jungle warfare – and more importantly, in command. Now, I'm sure your style of leadership is adequate for charging at the enemy with your bayonets fixed – but this is to be a precision strike. For that to work, I need...' He raised his voice to speak over the growing grumbles of dissent. 'I need a well-drilled, efficient squad of men, who know what's expected of them and will comply without question or complaint. *With respect*, sergeant, I doubt you can provide that.'

Lorenzo wasn't looking forward to serving under Mackenzie. Still, he wouldn't have swapped this assignment for any other. He felt proud at the thought that Colonel Graves might have recommended his squad above all others – although he wasn't kidding himself. He knew that, if they *had* been recommended, it would have been for Greiss's experience or the distinguished war records of Dougan and Armstrong. Chances were, the colonel didn't even know Lorenzo's name. Anyway, it seemed more likely that Mackenzie had made the choice himself, probably just for the opportunity to laud it over Greiss.

The Catachans had insisted on providing their own night watch, to the chagrin of the Validians already standing sentry over the camp. Lorenzo had volunteered for the duty, but he hadn't been quick enough. He slept soundly, knowing he was safe in the charge of his comrades – until, in the dark hours of the morning, some inbred danger sense woke him.

He opened his eyes, instantly alert, to face a yellow stare.

A jungle lizard, just a little larger than the one he had seen yesterday. Somehow it had slipped by the Guardsmen of two regiments, and crept up on him. Its eyes stared into his eyes. It was perfectly still, its trailing body propped up by two legs like miniature tree trunks. Tiny nostrils quivered as it breathed, slowly and calmly. Its mouth was a thin line, perhaps a little upturned at the edges. As if it was mocking him, gloating.

Lorenzo had seen lizards that could breathe fire and spit poison, or eviscerate a man with their claws in seconds. He had seen one burrow into a man's stomach and attach itself to his nervous system, working him like a puppet. He had no idea of the capabilities of this one, but he didn't doubt that it was deadly. Deathworlds bred no other type of animal. And it had the drop on him.

He lay still as a rock, staring into those yellow eyes, looking for the slightest glimmer of intent, the warning that the lizard was about to strike.

Slowly, painfully slowly, so slowly that his muscles screamed in protest, Lorenzo's fingers worked their way down his leg. Toward his Catachan fang.

The lizard made its move.

Its mouth gaped open, impossibly wide, almost larger than its head – and during the briefest split-second that followed, Lorenzo got the impression of a coiled red tongue with a glistening needlepoint end. He snatched his knife from its sheath, tried to roll out of the way, but he knew there was no time.

Something flashed through the air. Something metal.

Then there was blood – thick, green blood – and Lorenzo was up and armed, but only because the expected attack had not come.

A Catachan fang was buried up to its haft in the lizard's head. Its blade had passed through the creature's mouth, pinning its tongue, and into the scorched earth beneath it. An ordinary man might have thanked the God-Emperor for sparing him, but Lorenzo had long since learned there was no divine intervention in such matters. He thanked good comrades instead.

'Sorry 'bout that, pal,' said Myers, reclaiming his knife from the dead lizard's head and casually wiping off its blood and brain matter with a leaf. 'These critters are like chameleons; they can change their scale patterns to blend in with their surroundings.'

As usual, Myers was accompanied by Wildman Storm – a muscular, bearded Catachan who often looked like he would tear off your head as soon as look at you, until his features broke into a dazzling grin. 'We've picked off a few tonight,' he said, 'but we didn't hear this one until it was already past us. Took a minute to find it.'

'No problem,' said Lorenzo, adding a grateful nod for the rescue.

No longer pinned, the lizard had toppled onto its side. Its ruptured tongue lolled out of its mouth, leaking venom and blood. From above, no longer eye to eye with it, it seemed small and insignificant. It was easy to forget the real threat it had posed just a few seconds earlier. Lorenzo wondered what its poison would have done to him – weakened him, paralysed him, killed him outright?

'Do you suppose these are the "invisible monsters" they talk about round here?' asked Storm.

Lorenzo shrugged.

'Hope not,' said Myers, as he re-sheathed his knife and sauntered away. 'I was hoping for something more of a challenge.'

Breakfast for the Catachans was a vegetable broth, brewed by Dougan from local plants. It was the best meal Lorenzo had tasted in weeks – made even more so when Storm dropped a hunk of lizard steak into his bowl. The men were in high spirits, looking forward to their missions. The only shadow on the horizon was that of Commissar Mackenzie – and Greiss in particular was taking the usurpation of his position badly.

'You tell me what the Imperium is even doing here,' he grumbled over his soup. 'We're out at the rear end of nowhere, there aren't any minerals here worth a light, and as for colonising, forget it! I'll tell you this much: if the orks packed up tomorrow and left Rogar III, we wouldn't be too far behind 'em. Seems to me the only reason we're here is because they are, because the Emperor's armies can't be seen to be turning their backs on the enemy. The only reason the orks won't leave is because they won't turn their backs on us, so we just keep fighting.'

'Hey, steady on, sergeant,' said Woods. 'You're starting to sound like a heretic!'

'Hell, don't get me wrong,' said Greiss, 'I'm as up for a scrap as the next man. I'd just rather orks and Guardsmen alike moved their backsides out of here and left us to it. Jungle Fighters against the jungle, the way it should be.'

'Yeah, I can get on board with that,' grinned Woods.

'Course,' sighed Greiss, 'ours is not to reason why. We just move where we're told to move, fight who we're told to fight, jump when we're told to jump.'

Lorenzo remembered what the sergeant had said back on the ship, how he wanted his blaze of glory. He was unlikely to get it with Mackenzie calling the shots. He told himself there'd be other chances for the grizzled sergeant, but he could see it in Greiss's despondent eyes: he'd convinced himself that this would be his last hurrah. Lorenzo had seen what happened to men who began to think that way. It was a thought that tended to become a self-fulfilling prophecy.

The hall was beginning to empty when a Validian approached Lorenzo's table, and took a seat beside him. He was in his thirties, but still baby-faced. He wasn't exactly fat, but then nor were his muscles exactly toned. He was beginning to grow jowls. Sizing him up in a second, Lorenzo concluded that he'd never have reached half his present age on Catachan.

Greiss looked up from his meal. 'You're at the wrong table, boy,' he growled, although the Validian couldn't have been much younger than he was. 'Your lot are over that side of the hall.'

'I know that, sergeant,' said the Guardsman. 'I wanted to introduce myself before we set out. Braxton.' He held out a hand, which Greiss ignored. 'Commissar Mackenzie's adjutant – and I report for the *Eagle & Bolter*. Didn't anyone tell you? I've been attached to your squad. I'm coming with you this morning.'

'Like hell!' snapped Greiss, and he pushed his bowl aside and stormed out of the hall. Woods shot Braxton a mocking sneer, then followed. Myers and Storm, further down the table, were absorbed in their own conversation, which left Lorenzo effectively, awkwardly, alone with the newcomer.

'Don't mind Old Hardhead,' he said. 'He's had his nose put out of joint by your boss.'

Braxton nodded. 'The commissar does seem to have a talent for that.' The Validian and the Jungle Fighter shared a brief smile. 'I just thought you ought to know we aren't all like him,' said Braxton. 'Or Enright.'

'Enright?'

'The sergeant who started the trouble yesterday. Talk about noses being out of joint! Or if it wasn't before the fight, your trooper over there sure saw to it... Enright and his cronies can't face the fact that we need your help. They think we should be able to handle a few orks by ourselves.'

'But the orks aren't the problem,' Lorenzo pointed out.

'I know,' said Braxton. 'Rogar III has changed. I think I've noticed it more than some of the others, because... well...' He shifted in his seat. 'Since I got this assignment, I haven't seen much action, you know? But last week, I went out there, into the jungle, for the first time in a while, and...'

Lorenzo's ears pricked up, eager for some hint of what was to come.

'I swear,' said Braxton, 'those jungle lizards had doubled in size since the last time I'd seen one – and they'd never been so vicious. They used to run for cover when we got within ten metres. We used them for target practice. Now, they're getting bolder, sniffing around the camp itself. One of them stung Marks. The veins in his neck, and then his face, they turned black, throbbing. He was screaming, begging us to put him out of his misery. We had to do it. He'd have brought the orks down on us.'

'I just wanted to say,' said Braxton, 'that it's good to have the experts here.'

'Not according to Mackenzie,' said Lorenzo.

'I know – and if it were up to me, we'd leave you to do your jobs. We're only going to slow you down out there. But the commissar – he's young, he wants to prove himself. I think he wants to be the one to tame the famous Jungle Fighters. And deal with Big Green, of course.'

'And you just go where Mackenzie leads, huh?'

'My job is to report his glorious victory – if I'm lucky.'

Lorenzo regarded Braxton with a newly sympathetic gaze. It occurred to him that he was only obeying orders, like anyone – and that, in his own milieu, he was probably an able fighter. But, like most Guardsmen, he would have been conscripted at the age of sixteen or seventeen, already an adult. Lorenzo had been taught to defend himself with a knife before he could walk. By the age of eight, Catachan children were expected to be able to tame a wild grox; a harsh lesson that some did not survive, but such was the nature of life on a deathworld. You could be forged in its jungle heat, or you could wither and die in it.

Beneath Guardsman Braxton's words was an unspoken plea for help. But the men of Lorenzo's world – like those of all deathworlds across the Imperium – obeyed only one law: that of the jungle. Survival of the fittest.

CHAPTER 4

It was another clear day. The sun blazed bright and hot, the morning temperature far in excess of that of the previous evening, the air bereft of breeze. Most of the Validians had been forced out of their stuffy huts, and some were evidently finding the heat uncomfortable. The Catachans, however, revelled in it. It opened Lorenzo's pores and invigorated him.

The clearing was full of sweaty bodies, moving in time to barked commands. Jungle Fighters were forming up in their squads and moving out. The men of A Platoon were arming themselves with autocannons and heavy bolters, and tuning up the three Sentinels that would precede them into battle.

Mackenzie was in the thick of the activity, dispensing words here and there to the sergeants, complaining repeatedly about the Catachans' lack of a formal uniform. 'Uniforms get damaged,' Colonel Graves told him, 'when you're out in the jungle.' But it didn't seem to calm Mackenzie's ire.

Greiss would normally have had his squad doing circuits or squat-thrusts by now; instead, he sat with his knees to his chest, and snarled at anyone who dared come near him. Muldoon had acquired the dyes of some indigenous plants, and was adapting his body camouflage to the local shapes and colours. A few other Catachans had followed his lead, Myers and Storm among them, glad to let the sun caress their skin. Lorenzo, however, was no artist; he would have to make do with his heavy jacket, and with a few streaks of dubbin across his face.

Mackenzie was annoyed to find the squad not standing to attention, awaiting his inspection; he made his displeasure known to Greiss, who shrugged and climbed to his feet in his own time. The Catachans fell in sloppily, making their feelings for the young officer clear. In turn, Mackenzie griped about the absence of regulation shoulder guards with identifying numbers, but there wasn't much he could do about it at this stage. He gave a stern speech that was mostly a reworking of the previous day's – 'whip you rabble into shape,' 'smartest Guardsmen in the Imperium' and so forth – with a few clichés added: 'When I say "jump"...' '...expect you to crawl on your bellies over broken glass...'

'We're facing a four-day journey together,' concluded the commissar. 'Eight days, for those lucky enough to make the return trip. It'll go much easier if we all pull together.' He produced a sheet of paper, then, and began a roll call. 'Sergeant Greiss.'

'Yes!'

'Yes, *what*?'

'Yes, sir!' said Greiss with a sneer.

'Trooper Armstrong.'

Patch Armstrong answered to his name, and Mackenzie went through the others, giving each trooper in turn an appraising look as he committed his face to memory. Dougan, Storm, Myers, Donovits, Muldoon, Woods; finally, Lorenzo and Landon.

Braxton, of course, was already well known to the commissar. The Validian had found an ill-fitting camouflage jacket in the stores, and was looking uncomfortable. Mackenzie was in camouflage too, though he had retained his peaked cap. It was a little too large for him, but his jutting ears kept it from sliding down. 'Do you think it's a good idea to be going into this with an eagle-shaped target on your head, sir?' Greiss asked, with measured disdain.

'It's a symbol of authority, sergeant,' snarled Mackenzie. 'You'll learn. By the time I'm finished with you, you'll all learn.'

They moved out, at the commissar's insistence, at a quick march in two ranks of five, with Greiss leading the way. Mackenzie brought up the rear, occasionally shouting orders.

They broke step, however, as they crossed the tree line – and Lorenzo noted that Mackenzie worked his way into the centre of the group, so that there would always be a Catachan between him and any potential threat. The commissar had a rough sketched map, which he kept to himself, and a compass. He kept the squad moving on a bearing of approximately twenty-five degrees. 'We're taking a circuitous route,' he explained when questioned, 'to avoid a small ork encampment to the north-west of here.'

'I'm sure we could take 'em, sir,' offered Woods.

'I'm sure we could, trooper,' said Mackenzie icily, 'but as I explained at the briefing last night, this is a stealth mission. A single ork gets wind of our presence in this area and lives to tell of it, and we may as well pack up and go home – because our chances of getting within shooting distance of their warboss will be zero.'

'I still say we could take 'em,' muttered Woods resentfully. But Mackenzie was right, and he knew it.

The jungle closed in above them, sparing them the fiercest of the sun's rays, though the air was still sweltering. Braxton was sweating, wiping his damp forehead with his sleeve every few steps. The burnt odour lingered, and the Catachans' feet crunched on dead, blackened leaves. This area had been torched – and recently – but with little effect. Some of the plants and trees seemed to have been growing here for years.

Their progress was punctuated by cracks of las-fire, whenever a jungle lizard was sighted. Myers and Storm had warned everyone of the creatures' chameleonic properties, and Lorenzo had added the information he'd received from Braxton, so the whole squad was on the alert. Out loud, each man swore he would never end his days like Braxton's ill-fated friend, pleading for the mercy of a quick death. Privately, Lorenzo knew – as the others must have known – that stronger men than he had been broken by such pain as only a deathworld could inflict.

In time, the discharges became less frequent, as if the lizards had learned from their mistakes and were keeping their distance. Lorenzo didn't imagine for a second, though, that they had seen the last of them.

That burnt smell was fading. The jungle grass was growing taller and the trees more closely together, letting less sunlight in through their branches. A pink-headed, acid-spitting plant reared up beside the Catachans without warning, but Myers blasted it to pieces before it could open its mouth.

Lorenzo felt goose bumps on his flesh, but it was a pleasant feeling.

He seemed to have been waiting a long time for this: to plunge into the darkest heart of the jungle. To face Rogar III on its own turf.

They were about two hours out when Braxton reported to the nearest Jungle Fighters – Myers and Storm – that he thought they were being followed. Their only response was a pair of knowing grins, so Braxton called out to Commissar Mackenzie. 'Sir! Sir, I think we're being followed.'

The young officer called a halt, and the squad stood silent for a minute or two. Mackenzie frowned. 'Anyone hear anything?'

'No, sir,' murmured the Catachans.

'It was up there, sir,' said Braxton, pointing, 'in the trees.'

'You're imagining things, Braxton,' decided Mackenzie, though his voice betrayed a doubt.

Lorenzo caught an aside from Storm to Myers: 'Looks like the commissar's radar dish ears are just ornamental, then.'

'Actually,' said Sergeant Greiss, with no little satisfaction, 'there *is* someone stalking us. The rest of us have been aware of it since we left the clearing.'

Mackenzie turned pink. 'What? Then why didn't you speak up?'

'Because he's on our side. In fact, we're honoured to have him watching our backs.'

The commissar looked none the wiser, and fumbled with his list of names. 'There's no one missing,' he said.

'This man works alone,' said Dougan.

Mackenzie scowled. 'That is not acceptable. This offensive has been planned to the last detail, and I will not have those plans jeopardised by a maverick.' He shouted into the jungle: 'You, trooper. Come here, now!'

Dougan cleared his throat. 'Should you be yelling like that, sir? If there are ork patrols or gretchin in the area–'

The commissar ignored him. 'Trooper, my name is Commissar Mackenzie, and I am in command here. I demand you show yourself immediately. You have ten seconds. If I can't see your face by then, you will be facing court-martial!'

The echoes of his words were soaked up by the foliage. In the distance, a bird took flight. There was no other sound.

'Could be out of earshot by now, sir,' offered Myers.

Mackenzie rounded on the Catachans, clenching his fists. 'If anyone sees or hears a trace of that man again, I wish to be informed of it immediately, do you hear me? Immediately!'

They moved on.

Dougan dropped back in the marching order until he was alongside Braxton. He gave the Validian an approving nod. 'Mostly, if Sly Marbo doesn't want to be seen or heard, he isn't – sometimes not even by those of us who know he's around. I'm impressed.'

An hour after that, the jungle became so dense that the Catachans had to draw their knives and cut their way through. Armstrong and Muldoon took point to begin with, Armstrong's devil claw and Muldoon's sleek, black night reaper hacking at stinging plants and thick purple creepers.

All of a sudden, Muldoon let out a warning cry, and a cloud of insects blossomed from the undergrowth at his feet. Each was the length of one of Lorenzo's fingers, with hairy black bodies and gossamer wings. Armstrong hopped out of the way of the swarm, but it latched onto Muldoon, following him with an angry, high-pitched whine as he tried to back away from it. He swung his arms furiously, flattening several insects against the nearest tree, his blade slicing through two more.

The rest of the squad had withdrawn out of reach. Lorenzo brought up his lasgun, squinting along its sights until he knew he could fire without hitting Muldoon. His las-fire fried several insects, as did simultaneous shots from Greiss, Woods and Donovits. But there were too many of them. The cloud seemed hardly to have lessened in size.

Myers and Storm had flung their packs to the ground, and they pulled out the constituent parts of a heavy flamer. They clicked them together, then Storm steadied the bulky weapon while Myers aimed it at the swarm. The first explosion of fire singed the ends of Muldoon's hair, and lit up one flank of the insect cloud, sending them streaking to the ground as dying embers. Muldoon hurled himself face-first into the undergrowth, giving Myers a clearer second shot that took out the bulk of the remaining swarm.

There were still more than a dozen insects crawling over Muldoon, but he rolled and crushed those that couldn't take flight in time. The others rushed to stamp on the rest, or to skewer them with blades. Myers and Storm aimed one final, precautionary blast of flame at the ground from which the swarm had risen. Then the Catachans surrounded Muldoon where he lay on his back. He blinked up at them, flushed and chagrined, his face pimply with insect bites.

'What the hell do you think you're doing, Muldoon?' barked Greiss without sympathy. 'You know better than to disturb an insect nest. You didn't see it?'

'I saw it, sergeant,' said Muldoon. 'I was giving it a wide berth, but the bugs came out fighting all the same.'

'They must be sensitive to vibrations in the ground,' guessed Donovits. 'Or to body heat – though that's less likely in this climate. But why would they attack if their nest wasn't directly threatened?'

'Just antisocial, I guess,' said Greiss, reaching down to help Muldoon to his feet. 'You feeling all right, Sharkbait?'

'Like a walking, talking colander,' said Muldoon ruefully. 'They took chunks out of me all over. I got them in my boots, under my backpack, in my collar...'

'Show me,' rapped Greiss.

The sergeant spent the next few minutes examining Muldoon's bites. Lorenzo knew why. On Catachan, there was a creature known as the vein worm, which burrowed into its victim's flesh and laid its eggs in his bloodstream. Greiss intended to make sure these alien insects had left no similar surprises in his trooper. When he'd satisfied himself on that count, he asked Muldoon to tell him how many fingers he was holding up, checking for toxins that may have begun to cloud his senses. Muldoon answered correctly, and Greiss rewarded him with a grim smile, and clapped him on the arm. 'You'll live,' he concluded. 'Probably.'

'Do you think we can get on now?' asked Mackenzie, impatiently.

They proceeded more cautiously after that, with Woods and Donovits taking over cutting duty up front. As soon as Woods sighted a second nest in among the creepers, they all fell back, and Myers and Storm readied the flamer. 'What are you waiting for?' cried Mackenzie. 'Just torch the damn thing!' But the troopers turned to Greiss for confirmation of that order, and the grizzled sergeant shook his head and reached for a stick.

He flung it at the hive, and once again a cloud of black insects darkened the air. Myers's finger twitched on his trigger, ready to unleash a stream of fire should any man be threatened. The insects, however, didn't seem to have detected the watching Catachans. They buzzed around for a while, finding no one upon whom to expend their wrath, and then settled resentfully back into their disturbed home.

'What the hell was the point of that?' demanded Mackenzie. 'You just wanted to provoke those things?'

'To observe 'em,' Greiss corrected him. 'Anyone else see what I saw?'

'The red flower over there,' spoke up Donovits. 'The insects were giving it a wide berth.'

Greiss nodded. 'Let's find out, shall we?'

He followed Donovits's pointing finger to a delicate red flower sprouting from the trunk of a tree. It had eight perfectly formed petals, and it was quite the most beautiful thing Lorenzo had seen on this world so far. That left him in no doubt that it was dangerous.

Greiss found another stick, and poked the head of the flower with it. Immediately, its petals snapped shut like a vice, gripping the stick so strongly that he couldn't pull it free. He tried to uproot the flower with a yank, but its hold on the tree behind it was just as tenacious. It was crying, letting out a shrill wailing sound that, after a few seconds, bored into Lorenzo's ears like a drill.

Greiss whipped out his fang, and sliced the head of the flower from its stem. Immediately, the wailing ceased and the red petals flopped open. Greiss turned, and displayed the decapitated head to the others. 'Doesn't seem too dangerous on its own,' he commented, 'but watch one of these things doesn't grab your ankle. It might just hold you still long enough for something bigger to come along.'

A flutter of wings drew everyone's attention upwards. A shadow flitted between the trees, and was gone. A bird of prey, Lorenzo surmised, answering the flower's alarm call, put off by the number of strangers present and by the fact that none of them were immobilised.

'Now,' said Greiss. He flipped the flower head onto the insect nest, and withdrew to safety again. This time, there was a distressed quality to the displaced insects' humming – and a definite direction to their flight. Within a minute, they were all gone, deeper into the jungle.

Donovits nodded. 'They didn't like that. The flower probably preys on the insects, so they've learned to detect its scent and avoid it.'

'All right,' rapped Greiss, 'everyone spread out, look for more of these flowers.'

Mackenzie's nostrils flared. 'I think you're forgetting who's giving the orders here, sergeant.'

'If you've got a better idea, commissar,' Greiss shot back. 'Now's the time to speak up.'

'Sergeant,' protested Hotshot Woods, 'you expect us to wear flowers in our hair now?'

'In your hair, in your lapel, down your trousers,' growled Greiss, 'I don't care what you do with 'em, Hotshot, just as long as you wind up smelling right.'

As he joined the search, Lorenzo noticed that Muldoon was looking a bit woozy. The trooper pulled himself together when he saw he was being observed, and he smiled grimly. 'Dizzy spell,' he said, apologetically. 'I think those damn bugs sucked a few pints of blood out of me. I just need a minute...'

Lorenzo kept an eye on Muldoon after that, and realised he wasn't the only member of the squad to be doing so. He was usually more zealous than any of them, with the possible exception of Woods – always scouting ahead with a gleam in his eye, a feral smile on his face and his night reaper in his hand. Now, however, he lagged behind, finding the going tough. They all had plant tendrils grasping and tearing at their heels, of course – but Muldoon was the only man particularly troubled by them. He lost his footing a number of times, and almost fell, but Lorenzo knew better than to offer assistance where it wasn't requested.

Muldoon was swigging too freely from his bottle, too; the other Catachans were taking it steady, not knowing when they might find fresh water.

'You're worried about him, aren't you?' said a low voice beside Lorenzo. It was Braxton.

He shrugged. 'What do you think? You ever come across bugs like that before on Rogar? Seen a man bitten by one?'

'A few times, yes. Didn't seem to do any lasting harm. I've never seen a swarm attack like that, though.'

Lorenzo nodded. 'Bugs carry diseases,' he said knowledgeably. 'Sharkbait might get lucky – or he might get sick. Real sick, real soon. Or real dead. That's why Old Hardhead had us take precautions.' They had all teased sap from the stems of the red flowers, rubbed it into their faces and hands. 'New world, new rules – and there's only one way to learn what they are. Sharkbait knows that as well as the rest of us do.'

'Why do you call him Sharkbait?'

'Before my time,' said Lorenzo.

Dougan fell into step beside them. 'Poseidon Delta,' he grunted. 'We had to cross a swamp, but there was a catch. The mother of all marsh sharks. It hunted by radar, could detect a ripple on the surface from ten kilometres. The span of its jaws was wider than you are tall. Sharkbait – he was just Trooper Muldoon then – took a Sentinel in. You saw them at the camp: armoured hunter-killer machines. Chainsaws, flamers... We use them when we don't exactly care about being subtle. But this Sentinel got its leg jammed in the mud, came crashing right down. And the marsh shark was there, of course, peeling back the outsides of the crew compartment like a tin opener. It got Reed, swallowed him whole. But Muldoon...

'We were firing our lasguns from the bank. The shots just glanced off this monster, gave it no more than a bad case of sunburn. Muldoon was lying there, pinned by the wreckage, going under, and this shark was rearing over him, coming in for the kill. We thought he was a goner. Then, calm as you like, he just reached *into* its mouth, slung a whole pack of frag grenades down its throat.

'We didn't even hear the explosion; the damn thing's hide was so thick. But suddenly, it was thrashing and groaning like it had the worst case of bellyache in history. Then it went down. Greiss and me, we went in and pulled Muldoon out of the mud. He was lucky not to have lost an arm – or a head. If that shark had snapped its teeth shut just a fraction of a second sooner... I don't recall a discussion. We all knew "Sharkbait" Muldoon had earned his name, that day.'

'That's important to you people, isn't it?' said Braxton. 'Earning your name. I've heard Hotshot, Old Hardhead – and they call you Steel Toe, right?'

'Another story,' said Dougan, 'for another day.'

'And "Sly" Marbo?'

'Never been quite sure about that one,' Dougan confessed, 'if it's an earned name or a given name or just something he's picked up along the way. Seems to suit him fine, though. What's with all the questions, son?'

'*Eagle & Bolter*,' said Braxton. 'Just wanted a bit of background info for my piece. Everyone knows what you Jungle Fighters do, but no one really knows all that much *about* you. I thought, if I could tell them what life's like where you come from – Catachan, right? – there might be a few less, uh, misunderstandings.'

Dougan nodded. 'A word of advice, son. Not everyone likes to talk. Oh, stick around long enough and you'll hear all the old war stories, all right – but you start probing someone like Old Hardhead about his past, and he's liable to probe you in return. With his bayonet, in your guts.'

Braxton fell silent for a time, after that. But it wasn't long before he turned to Lorenzo, and asked the question the Catachan had been dreading.

'So, what's *your* earned name, Lorenzo?'

'Don't have one,' Lorenzo said. Not that he had anything to be ashamed of. 'Not yet.'

Armstrong was the first to hear them. He froze, listening, and the others did the same one by one.

Footsteps, crashing through the undergrowth. A guttural grunt that could only have been formed by a larynx. There was somebody nearby. Several somebodies – and not bothering to hide their presence. Braxton turned to Lorenzo, and mouthed silently, 'Marbo?' Lorenzo shook his head.

A second later, the Catachans had melted into their background – and Lorenzo saw the confusion in Braxton's face as he turned to find himself standing alone. Lorenzo himself had slipped behind a tree trunk and was hugging its contours. Muldoon had chosen the same hiding place, and was crouched down beside him. From close up, Lorenzo could see that Muldoon was running a fever. His bandana was soaked with sweat, and his breathing was hoarse and ragged.

Storm lay flat on the ground nearby. He had arranged a few creepers across himself, breaking up the lines of his body so that its patterns blended perfectly with those of the foliage. From any further away, and most other angles, he would have been invisible. Indeed, to Lorenzo, the rest of the Catachans *were* invisible. He could make out only one other outline – that of Commissar Mackenzie, trying to conceal himself behind a blossoming nettle plant.

Guardsman Braxton caught on, and ducked under cover himself.

More footsteps, and the rustling of leaves. Whatever was out there, they were coming closer. Eight or nine of them, Lorenzo now estimated. Too small, too nimble, to be the muscular, lumbering orks. Gretchin, most likely. Genetic cousins to the orks – smaller, weaker, subservient, but far more cunning. If they realised they were outnumbered, they were likely to scatter and run, take word to their masters.

There was no urgency to their movements. Chances were, they didn't know they had enemies nearby. The gretchin were probably just out foraging – but they might get lucky. Thick as the jungle was, they wouldn't see the Catachans' trail of severed tendrils and uprooted plants unless they stumbled right onto it. It sounded to Lorenzo, though, like they were within a bloodwasp's length of doing just that.

Suddenly, somebody slammed into him from behind.

Lorenzo was taken by surprise, winded. No mean feat – but then this attack had come from the last direction he'd expected. From a comrade; a man he'd entrusted with his life countless times, and who was now bearing him down into the dirt, eyes ablaze with madness, a black knife raised to strike at Lorenzo's throat.

Muldoon was trying his best to kill him.

And he was screaming with incoherent fury as he did so – a sound that could hardly have failed to reach the gretchin's ears.

CHAPTER 5

Muldoon was bigger and stronger than Lorenzo, and certainly heavier. Lorenzo was pinned to the ground by his weight, the jungle grass now growing above his head, rough against his neck and his cheeks. His right arm, and his Catachan fang in its sheath, were trapped under Muldoon's knees. All he could do was strike out with his left elbow, knocking his attacker's knife hand aside.

Muldoon's night reaper was smaller than Lorenzo's fang, but just as deadly. Its blade was triangular, shaped to leave a large entrance wound that wouldn't clot – and knowing Muldoon it was almost certainly poisoned. Probably with the venom of a jungle lizard. He was always the first of the Catachans to turn a deathworld's threats to his advantage.

Lorenzo kicked out with both feet, trying to unseat Muldoon, but Muldoon knew too well how to spread his weight to maintain his balance. That knife hand was coming around to strike again. Muldoon loomed over Lorenzo, his unshaven features crazed with blind fury, his eyes wide, white, unblinking. There was no point talking to him, in appealing to reason. He was too far gone. There was no way to know what was going on in Muldoon's head, what those insect bites were making him see, but Lorenzo would have laid odds he didn't even recognise his old comrade right now. He was fighting his own daemons.

He couldn't afford to hold back. He found Muldoon's face with his free hand and dug his fingernails into his eyes. Momentarily blinded, Muldoon threw back his head and let out an uncharacteristic howl of pain and rage. Lorenzo pulled his right arm free, twisted out of the path of a badly aimed knife blow and seized Muldoon's wrist in his left hand. He tried to shake Muldoon's grip on his weapon, but his fingers were locked around its haft. As Muldoon lashed out again, Lorenzo guided his thrust and buried the night reaper's blade in the ground beside his head.

If Muldoon had been in his right mind, he would have abandoned the knife until it was safe to retrieve it. Working on primal instinct, however, he only knew the night reaper was a part of him, his most important possession, and he all but forgot about Lorenzo as he struggled to reclaim it from the unyielding earth. Lorenzo crawled out from beneath him, and tackled him side-on. He hurled blow after blow at Muldoon's head, praying each time that the next one would be the one to put him down, knowing he was made of sterner stuff than that. He was afraid he wouldn't be able to stop him without inflicting a lasting injury.

Lorenzo could have drawn his own knife. He could reach it now. Against any other foe, he would have done it. He would have ended this.

Blood rushed in his ears, dulling his senses. He could hear, though, that the rest of his squad had broken cover. They were slashing and beating their way through the jungle, regardless of the danger from hostile flora or more insect hives, toward the gretchin. The creatures couldn't help but hear them coming, and they turned and fled back up the path they had cleared for themselves.

Muldoon must have been in pain, near senseless, but he was fighting back. Lorenzo would have expected no less from him. Fortunately, his fever slowed his reaction time, and Lorenzo ducked the worst of his punches.

Help came, at last, in the form of Dougan. The older trooper knew his bionic leg slowed him down, and so it was natural that he should have been the one to stay behind. Dougan came up behind Muldoon, and tried to restrain him while Lorenzo knocked the wind out of him with a double jab to the solar plexus. He remembered head-butting a Validian Guardsman the previous day, finding his stomach soft and yielding; in contrast, hitting Muldoon was like driving his knuckles into rock.

Muldoon let out another animal roar, and broke Dougan's hold. Lorenzo held back for an instant, waiting to see what he'd do. Muldoon looked wildly from one of his comrades to the other, realising he was surrounded. His eyes flicked towards his night reaper, still buried in the ground, but it was too far away. Muldoon reached into a pouch of his bandolier and pulled out a demolition charge.

With a quick flex of his thumb, he popped out the charge's pin.

Lorenzo and Dougan hit him at the same time, from opposite sides. Dougan was trying to wrestle the charge out of Muldoon's hand, but his grip was as resolute as that on his night reaper had been. Lorenzo's survival instinct was telling him to dive for shelter, but he wasn't about to abandon Muldoon while there was the slightest chance he could be saved. He added his strength to Dougan's, taking one of Muldoon's fingers in each fist and forcing them open.

The demolition charge dropped out of Muldoon's hand.

Lorenzo had to dive for it, cradling his palms to give the explosive device the softest landing he could. In so doing, he left himself exposed, and Muldoon punished him with a brutal kick to the face. Lorenzo felt his lip splitting. He rolled with the blow, and was back in the grass again, his own blood on his tongue. But Dougan was keeping Muldoon busy, keeping him from pressing his advantage, and Lorenzo had the charge with – he estimated – less than a second to spare before it went up.

He hoisted himself onto one elbow, took a fraction of that second to orient himself, to check where the others were, then he put all the strength he had into an over-arm throw. The demolition charge seemed to have barely left his hand, arcing towards the treetops, when it burst and showered him with hot shrapnel.

Dougan had locked an arm around Muldoon's throat, and was holding on despite his kicking and screaming. Lack of oxygen had an effect on the frenzied trooper at last, and Muldoon's eyelids fluttered and closed. Dougan waited a moment longer before he relinquished his grip. A flicker of regret crossed his face as Muldoon's legs buckled beneath him and he crashed into the undergrowth.

Lorenzo and Dougan drew their Catachan fangs, cut down a couple of thin vines and bound their unconscious comrade's wrists and ankles with them. Lorenzo yanked the night reaper out of the ground, and respectfully returned it to its sheath. Even with Muldoon in this state, he couldn't deprive him of his knife – though he ensured that his tied hands couldn't reach it.

Lorenzo could hear las-fire through the foliage, and he knew the rest of his squad were close on the heels of their prey.

Myers and Storm were the first back from the gretchin hunt. They were followed by Donovits and Armstrong. 'How is he?' asked the one-eyed veteran, nodding in Muldoon's direction. He must have seen the start of the fight, and deduced the reason for it.

Dougan shrugged. 'Hard to tell. His fever's broken, so he could be all right. Best leave him to sleep it off, and hope he's seeing things more clearly when he comes to. How'd it go with the gretchin?'

'We got 'em,' said Storm, baring his white teeth. 'They won't be taking any tales back to their greenskin masters.'

Commissar Mackenzie came crashing through the foliage then, Guardsman Braxton at his heels. 'What the hell was all the screaming about?' the young officer demanded to know. 'And who let off a bomb? Where's the point in our chasing down gretchin left, right and centre if some idiot just broadcasts our position to every ork on the planet?'

'Couldn't be helped, sir,' said Dougan.

'And the jungle would have deadened the sound of the explosion,' added Donovits. 'I'd say it couldn't have been heard more than, say–'

'I don't want to know, trooper!' snapped Mackenzie. 'This operation is turning into a shambles. Where's Greiss?' He turned, and jumped to find that the sergeant had appeared noiselessly at his shoulder. Recovering himself, he snarled, 'Sergeant Greiss! Is it too much to expect you to exercise a modicum of restraint over your men? God-Emperor knows, I wasn't expecting much – but so far I'd have been better leading a squad of orks into the jungle. At least they have some semblance of self-control!'

Greiss glared at Mackenzie as if he was an acid grub he'd just found eating into his boot. The rest of the Catachans – somehow without seeming to move, just shifting their stances – formed into a vague circle around the commissar. No words had been spoken, but something had definitely changed.

Lorenzo caught Braxton's eye. The Validian didn't know what was happening – but he couldn't have been more aware at that moment that this was Catachan turf, that he and the commissar were the outsiders here. Instinctively, he shrank back against Mackenzie. He looked pale.

Mackenzie himself appeared to keep his cool, but Lorenzo could see the apprehension in his eyes.

Sergeant Greiss broke eye contact, took a half-step back, and just like that the threat was dissipated. 'Well done, men,' the sergeant barked. 'A bit of bad luck, Sharkbait here going crazy when he did – but it couldn't have been helped, and you dealt with it well.'

Greiss wasn't normally so effusive with his praise – it wasn't usually needed – so Lorenzo knew his words hadn't been for the Jungle Fighters' benefit. Mackenzie looked irritated, but he didn't protest.

It was only when Greiss detailed Woods to pick up the unconscious and bound Muldoon that the commissar broke his silence with an outraged splutter. 'What the hell are you thinking, Greiss? That trooper has given us away once already. We can't afford to let it happen again.'

'And it won't,' Greiss promised. 'I'll see to it.'

His tone left no room for argument, but Mackenzie didn't take the hint. 'That man is diseased. He might be infectious. Even if he isn't, what can we do for him out here?'

'You got anything at the camp that could help him?'

'No,' said Mackenzie emphatically.

'Then Muldoon comes with us,' said Greiss with equal force, 'until I'm sure there isn't a cure for him.'

'You think you can drag him all the way to the warboss's hideout and back? You think you can guarantee he won't wake up along the way and bring the orks down on us? No, sergeant. No, no, no. I don't like doing this – but I'm ordering you to abandon this trooper for the sake of the mission!'

'Sorry, sir,' said Woods, who by now had slung Muldoon over his shoulders and was carrying the bigger man effortlessly. 'Isn't the sergeant's decision no more. Sharkbait is my buddy. You want me to drop him now, and leave him here for the lizards and the birds, you'll have to shoot me.'

With that, Woods turned his back defiantly and set off into the jungle once more. The rest of the Catachans wasted no time in joining him, leaving Mackenzie standing. The commissar turned to Greiss as if for support, but recoiled at the malicious half-grin on his face. So he took the only course open to him at that moment. He lapsed into a judicious, if sullen, silence.

They moved on.

It was as the evening closed in that the birds launched their attack.

The sky, where it could be seen, was still a light shade of blue – but with the sun having surrendered its efforts to pierce the trees, the shadows had free rein down here. The canopy had captured much of the heat, but it was beginning to evaporate. The Catachans were used to jungle nights, of course, and their eyes adapted well to the gloom. The same could not be said of Mackenzie and Braxton. After stumbling one too many times, Braxton had made to light a torch, but Greiss had hissed at him to put it away. 'You want to draw every critter in the jungle to us – and blitz our night vision while you're at it?'

They were caught by surprise, because they hadn't heard the birds massing.

This in itself was unusual. It suggested a level of coordination unprecedented in such creatures, in Lorenzo's experience – that the birds had appeared in such numbers, so quickly.

The beating of their wings was like oncoming thunder, except that it sounded from all directions at once. Their bodies were a storm cloud, drawing with it a darkness even the Catachans couldn't penetrate. And then they were there, the birds, plummeting through the leaves like hailstones – but hailstones that, when they hit, burst into screeching, scratching darts of fury.

Lorenzo had just had time to draw his Catachan fang and lasgun. He was wielding the latter one-handed, keeping his knife hand back to protect his face. He fired repeatedly, aiming up above the heads of his comrades. It felt like the air was full of whirling blades, scratching, cutting, pecking at his flesh. He could barely see to take aim through the tumult of black wings – but as a particularly large bird flew up before him, claws outstretched, beady eyes trained upon him, Lorenzo saw his chance and struck. He felt his bayonet punching into the soft tissue of the bird's heart, and he smiled grimly as blood welled onto his fingers. The bird had been skewered, and Lorenzo didn't have time to remove it, so he fired the lasgun again and swung it like a club, knocking a few of his avian attackers from the sky, hopefully stunning some. The dead bird's corpse split, lost its grip on the bayonet, and hit Lorenzo's boot with a wet slap.

A sharp beak had clamped onto his ear and was tugging at it, so he sideswiped its owner with his fang, which left his face exposed for a split-second and gave another bird the chance to swoop in and jab at his eye. Lorenzo twisted his head aside in time, but they were tugging at his hair, clawing at his scalp. The birds had torn away his bandana, and drawn blood. He was pumping las-bolt after las-bolt through feathered bodies, but for each one that dropped two more seemed to replace it. And, unexpectedly, they had his gun, their claws scrabbling at its furniture, working in concert to yank it from Lorenzo's grasp. They didn't quite have the strength, so instead they piled their weight on top of it, forcing its barrel down until he couldn't pull the trigger for fear of blowing off his own foot.

The gun was useless to him now, a dead weight in his hand, so he sacrificed it. He flung it to the ground, taking several startled birds with it. He delivered a vicious kick to one as it struggled to right itself, and sent it sprawling. Then he brought his boot down on another, and snapped its neck.

Was it his imagination or was the flock thinning at last? Lorenzo could focus on individual birds now, rather than being overwhelmed by their mass. They were indeed, as first impressions had suggested, jet black, from their wingtips to their claws, even their eyes. There was no expression in those eyes – no rage or satisfaction, just a matter-of-fact blankness. Their wings were short, flapping furiously to keep their squat bodies aloft. Their black beaks came to wicked hooked points.

Lorenzo found a tree and backed up to it, denying them the chance to come at him from behind. He kept his fang in motion, slashing at any bird that ventured too close. They had become less bold with fewer numbers, keeping their distance, giving the impression of watching, waiting for an opening, although their eyes were still glassy. Lorenzo feinted, drew one of them in, and tore open its stomach with his blade, showering himself in its guts.

Another tried to blindside him, but he caught it by the throat, squeezed, felt its bones popping between his fingers and thumb. Its body joined the growing pile at his feet – and then, something in that pile nipped his ankle. At first Lorenzo thought it was just one bird, crippled, unable to fly but still single-minded in purpose. He raised his foot, tried to kick the wretched creature away – but there were more of them down there, scratching and pecking. The air around him seemed to have darkened with their bodies again. Reinforcements?

A bird shot up from below and got past Lorenzo's defences, latching onto his face and hugging it, and he would have let out a cry if he hadn't bitten his tongue in time. He was blinded; he could barely breathe for the bird's sticky, bloodied feathers in his mouth and nose. He clawed at it, but its brethren were pecking at his knuckles, biting his fingers, keeping him from getting a grip, and his tormentor's claws were like nails raking his cheeks. He dropped into a protective crouch, closed his fingers around the creature on his face at last, and tore it away from him, taking too much of his own skin with it. He saw it properly for the first time as it struggled in his hands – and although Lorenzo had seen much in his short career as a Jungle Fighter, the sight that greeted him now caused his mouth to gape in surprise.

The bird's neck had been cut almost through. Its head flapped lifelessly against its wing until, as Lorenzo watched, it detached itself at last and plopped into the long grass. But the body was still moving – and not just the uncoordinated twitching that could follow death in some species, but a deliberate and almost successful attempt to squirm free from him. With a shudder of revulsion, he dashed the bird against the nearest tree, with enough strength that his hand cracked through its body like an egg. It didn't move again.

Then Lorenzo felt them, saw them clawing their way up his legs: more bird corpses, some nursing broken legs, wings, backs, some eviscerated. Some of them had been dead a long time before this battle had begun. Putrid flesh slid from their gnarled bones; the stench that hit Lorenzo's nostrils would have been sickening to someone less familiar with it.

The first few skeletons had climbed as far as his lap, and they sprang for his throat, falling short, their wings too tattered and rotted to catch an air current. Lorenzo tried to brush them off, but they were tenacious. He mimicked Muldoon's earlier actions, rolling on the ground, feeling a satisfying crunch of bones beneath him. One skeletal bird hopped onto his face, and he stabbed at it with his knife. The blade passed through its empty eye sockets, and he lifted the undead creature off him, its legs pedalling the air, wing bones cranking uselessly. He flicked it away.

And then, suddenly, he was unmolested, the last of the birds around him finally still in death. His own survival assured for the moment, Lorenzo's thoughts went to his comrades. He was relieved to see that each of them had won or was winning his own battle. He joined them in shooting, slicing and bayoneting the few remaining birds. Without their superior numbers, they were easy prey, and soon the Jungle Fighters were jumping and stamping on hundreds of small corpses.

Then there was silence.

They regrouped, and took stock of their injuries. Landon was the worst, his face red with his own blood – but nobody had escaped harm, apart from the unconscious Muldoon. Lorenzo's comrades all sported crazed scratch patterns on their arms and faces, and he could tell from the prickling pain in his cheeks and forehead that he looked no better than any of them. His jacket sleeves were gashed and ragged, one trouser leg also torn.

Guardsman Braxton appeared to have held his own, though he was exhausted. He leaned against a tree trunk for support, flushed and out of breath. Storm was looking particularly irked that the birds had taken great clumps out of his beard. Dougan's bionic leg had been gummed up with feathers, which he was picking out of its joints ruefully.

Woods was the first to find his voice. 'Well,' he said, 'that was interesting. Who's up for seconds?'

Mackenzie was in no mood for jokes. 'What the hell just happened?' he demanded. 'I've been on this world a year, and never seen the birds behave like that.'

Greiss frowned. 'No?' And, for a moment, their animosity was softened in the face of a shared concern.

'I mean, don't get me wrong,' said Mackenzie, 'they were always vicious – but after a few initial sorties, they kept their distance. They knew they were no match for us.'

'They made no attempt to retreat,' Donovits mused, 'even when it became obvious they couldn't survive. As if they had no choice but to fight us.'

'Even in death,' grumbled Mackenzie.

'Some of those birds had been dead for months,' said Donovits. 'There was no tissue left holding their skeletons together. What was animating them?'

There was silence for a long moment as everyone pondered that question. Lorenzo suppressed a shudder, and his eyes involuntarily flicked towards the crushed and splintered bones at his feet, as if they might yet somehow spring to life again, repair and rebuild themselves.

Greiss made an attempt to diffuse the tension. 'You ask me, it was sheer bloody-mindedness!' he said, as if that might explain everything. 'We probably stumbled into their territory. How about it, Brains? Think they could have been protecting something down here? Eggs, maybe?'

Mackenzie shook his head. 'There was nothing here a few weeks ago. I sent a squad to reconnoitre this area, and they reported nothing like this.'

Greiss raised an eyebrow. 'This area? You sure about that, commissar?'

'Of course I'm sure, sergeant. What are you suggesting?'

'Well, I know the jungle can be good at covering tracks – but I'd swear that, till we turned up, there hadn't been anyone come this way in a long time.'

That sent the commissar scrambling for his sketch map. In the meantime, his adjutant had recovered his breath, though he still looked pale. 'I guess that could have been worse, right?' said Braxton – and Lorenzo looked at him, and tried to work out what he really wanted. Some reassurance that the Catachans had everything under control? Or that things *couldn't* have been worse, that he'd just survived the best this jungle had to throw at him? He couldn't give the Validian either.

'I mean, most of us escaped with superficial cuts. Unless–'

'Unless?'

Braxton's eyes flickered towards Muldoon, and now Lorenzo understood.

'Relax, city boy,' drawled Woods. 'If the birds had poisoned us, we'd know about it by now. You feeling ill? Because I've never felt healthier in my whole life. Raring to go!'

'Muldoon didn't know,' said Braxton quietly.

Lorenzo and Woods glanced at each other, and Lorenzo knew they were both thinking the same thought: that Muldoon *had* known, that he'd felt the sickness creeping up on him, even fought off the first of the hallucinations. He had known, but he had been too proud to speak up.

'You want to worry about something,' said Woods, 'you worry about those "superficial cuts" – because out here, there's no such thing. Any cut can be deadly. Jungle worlds breed diseases – and not all of them are carried by insects and vermin. Most, you can't see – but they're around us all the same, in the air. And they're just looking for a way into your bloodstream!'

Woods wiggled his fingers, miming the action of a bacteria creeping its way under Braxton's flesh. Then he closed his fist with a clap, and Braxton jumped.

He laughed, but Lorenzo didn't join in. Woods had seemed to enjoy tormenting Braxton – but the threat he described was real, to all of them. Maybe, he thought numbly, that had been the point of the birds' attack all along.

CHAPTER 6

Mackenzie was all for setting up camp there and then, the fight knocked out of him, but Greiss insisted on moving on. 'This place stinks of death,' he growled, kicking out at a fresh bird corpse that, despite having lost its wings and its head, had crawled out from a bush to make a feeble attack on his ankle. 'God-Emperor knows what that might attract here tonight. Bigger birds, maybe.'

Lorenzo knew there was one other reason. The Jungle Fighters' mood had darkened since the attack. They were quieter now, and more apprehensive. They spoke few words as they treated their wounds with sterilising fluid and synth-skin. Even Woods, now he'd had time to reflect upon what had happened, seemed subdued. They had faced greater threats – Braxton had been right about that – but none like this. The way their attackers had fought on beyond death – that was different. The men of Catachan lived by the laws of Nature, and tonight those laws had been violated. Greiss wanted to get them away from the scene of that violation, from the broken bones, to give them something else to think about.

'Five minutes, troopers,' he growled. 'Finish up what you're doing, then we're getting out of here!'

Landon's left eye was bleeding. One of the birds must have found it with its hooked beak. Myers and Storm had sat the rookie against a tree, cleaned his face with swabs from their first aid kits, and now they were applying a field dressing to the injured area. 'Look at you,' Storm tutted good-naturedly, 'this is, what, your first, second, time out in the field, and you're trying to get yourself scarred permanent-like. What, you bucking for your earned name already?'

'Can't be that, Wildman,' said Myers. 'Even a rookie wouldn't be stupid enough to let those birds go for his eye, knowing we got a "Patch" already.'

'Yes,' said Storm, nodding with mock gravity, 'can't have two of those.'

Landon smiled, but the smile turned into a wince. Lorenzo felt ice in his stomach. He knew Myers and Storm were only joking, trying to keep up the youngster's spirits – but just for a second there he'd feared Landon *would* get his earned name before he did. He chided himself for that thought. A comrade was hurt. Would he rather it was him sprawled in the dirt, wondering if he would see out of both eyes again?

Armstrong sported a nasty gash on his arm, where it glistened amid the knotted tissue of old scars. He was sewing it up with a needle, biting on a stick to control the pain. When Greiss gave the word, however, he – like all the others – clambered to his feet and hoisted his pack, fresh and ready to go.

Mackenzie didn't question the sergeant's decision. He knew he was right. But Lorenzo could read the commissar's eyes. He resented the way the Catachans deferred so readily to their sergeant over him. That was going to mean trouble.

Ninety minutes later, in a less dense part of the jungle, Greiss came to a halt and called for silence. He listened for a moment, then declared this as good a spot as any. Braxton shucked off his pack and sank to the ground with a sigh – but he scrambled guiltily to his feet and joined in as the Catachans got straight to work. They identified any flora that could be classed as dangerous and cut it down. Donovits found an acid spitter behind a tree, almost as if it had been deliberately hiding there. They thinned out the undergrowth, and Myers unearthed a jungle lizard. It sprang at his crotch, its legs propelling it higher than Lorenzo would have thought possible. Myers flashed his knife, and bisected it in midair.

'I think we should light a fire,' said Donovits, addressing his sergeant rather than the commissar.

Greiss nodded his approval, and Mackenzie opened his mouth to object. 'Worth the risk, I'd say,' Greiss interrupted sharply. 'The men fight better with a hot meal inside 'em. And it's going to get dark around these parts pretty damn soon. Don't know about you, but I like to be able to see what's creeping up on me – and in the jungle, there's a whole new menagerie of critters come out at night.'

'Apart from anything else, sir,' said Dougan in his usual polite manner, 'it's always good to know which of those creatures are afraid of fire.'

'And which ones aren't,' added Greiss under his breath.

'Where's Sly Marbo?' asked Braxton. 'Is he joining us?'

Nobody answered him. The truth, Lorenzo knew, was that none of them had a clue where Marbo was now. They hadn't glimpsed or heard him in hours. He might have been present for the bird attack, perhaps firing in from the sidelines; in the chaos, Lorenzo could have missed him. Or he might have gone scouting ahead, maybe encountered orks and found a good sniping position in which he would wait for hours or days – as long as necessary. One thing, Lorenzo did not doubt: wherever Marbo was, he could look after himself. He would be back.

The Jungle Fighters broke into their standard rations, because they were tired and because none of them had the spirit to go hunting or gathering anything better. Anyway, their trust in what they knew about this jungle had been shaken, and no one was especially keen to sample its wares right now.

The night brought with it the fluttering of leathern bat-wings, the soft chittering of a new type of ground-based insect, and – at one point – the footfall of something bigger and heavier, which nevertheless slipped away before it could be seen. The fire drew curious moth-like creatures – and, although they seemed non-aggressive, Armstrong pointed out their barbed fangs and the Jungle Fighters took to swatting them when they could, just in case.

There were snakes, too. Storm found one, about a metre long, slender and black, coiled around a tree trunk, slithering its way down towards the roots. He glared into its slit eyes, challenging it, and the snake glared back. It hissed and struck, and – having ascertained that it was hostile, as if there had been much doubt – Storm caught it by its head, squeezing its mouth shut with his fingers. He yanked it from its perch, swung it over-arm and smacked its body hard into the ground like a whip. Lorenzo glimpsed a distinctive silver triangular pattern on the snake's back. Then Storm casually tossed its lifeless body to Donovits, who would probably spend his watch teasing venom out of its glands for analysis.

Lorenzo was loath to lie down, to close his eyes on an environment about which he still knew so little. But he had no choice, and he trusted his comrades to protect him. So, he lay down on the damp earth and slept.

He was woken by Trooper Storm.

He reached for his fang, and started to push himself to his feet. Storm clapped a steadying hand on his shoulder, and a bright grin broke through his now ragged-looking black beard. 'Easy, trooper,' he laughed. 'There's no fire. It's time for your watch, that's all.'

Lorenzo nodded and relaxed. He glanced at the small patch of sky immediately above him. It had been pitch black when he'd gone to sleep, but now it was showing just the earliest signs of lightening. If Rogar III had a moon, Lorenzo hadn't seen it yet. He threw on his jacket and his bandolier, and checked that his lasgun was locked and loaded.

The only other light source in the Catachan-made clearing was the embers of the fire. They popped and cracked as Myers poked them with a stick, keeping them alive but torpid. There was a slight chill in the air, and Lorenzo drew closer to the glowing coals, to soak up their scant warmth.

'Steel Toe was right, by the way,' said Storm. 'The lizards really don't like fire. Even this is enough to keep them away, though we've heard them hissing out there. You want steak for breakfast this morning, you're going to have to go get one.'

Dougan greeted Lorenzo with a nod. They were to share the last two-hour watch. Typical of Greiss, thought Lorenzo, to pair him up with a veteran, as if he still needed watching over. The rest of his squad were shadowy mounds in the darkness – though he could identify the sergeant by his quiet but distinctive snore, like a grox breaking wind. Presumably, it was Braxton who was twitching in his sleep and sometimes letting out a quiet whimper – while Muldoon, of course, was the one tied to the tree. 'Keep an eye on him,' advised Storm, nodding toward their unconscious comrade. 'Woods says he woke during his watch, muttered all kinds of gibberish about daemons and monsters. Hotshot had to slug him one to put him back under.'

Lorenzo was disappointed to hear it. He'd hoped that time, or maybe one of the herbal remedies Donovits had forced down Muldoon's throat, may have dispelled his hallucinations. For all that Greiss and Woods had said to Mackenzie, the Catachans knew they couldn't lug Muldoon around with them indefinitely. There would come a time when they'd have to accept that he was lost.

Myers and Storm lay down, and soon their heavy breaths joined the sleeping chorus around Lorenzo. He sat on a tree stump, left behind after Armstrong had unpacked a machete and made firewood. It was a little too small for him, and he was uncomfortable – but then comfort was hardly desirable when the lives of your comrades depended on your staying alert.

Dougan knew that too, and he was circling the camp slowly. His soft footsteps were barely audible, but Lorenzo could tell that his artificial foot fell a little more heavily than the real one. Dougan didn't like to sit on duty. He didn't like to take the risk of his leg seizing up at a critical moment.

It was about forty minutes later that Lorenzo saw the light.

He wasn't sure what it was at first: a faint blue glow, somewhere between the trees, lasting just an instant. He couldn't pinpoint its location; he had no idea how far away it had been. He had been sharpening his Catachan fang, but now he froze – and Dougan, though he was somewhere behind Lorenzo on his latest circuit, picked up on his body language and did likewise.

It could have been a trick of the approaching dawn. The sky was now a deep indigo. But no, there it was again. Too soft, too muted to be a torch, it wasn't the kind of light you could see by. And yet too wide, too sustained to be an accidental glint off a weapon or a suit of powered armour.

Lorenzo grabbed for a stick, and brushed it across the embers of the fire, smothering them in their own ashes.

The blue light was clearer to him now, but still maddeningly undefined, still seeming to lurk at the edge of his vision, never quite in focus. One second, it was at ground level; the next, it glimmered through the branches at head height, and every time he moved his eyes to find it, it slipped away from him. Some sort of glowing creature, Lorenzo wondered? What was that word Brains had once used? 'Bioluminescence'. He wondered if he should wake the others, but he pictured their faces if he did and they found he'd been spooked by a swarm of fireflies.

Anyway, the light was coming no closer.

He watched it a moment longer.

It blinked out.

A second ago, there had been a wisp of smoke coiling up from the ashes of the campfire. Now, it was gone. The sky was a little lighter – wasn't it? Lorenzo frowned, and crouched by the ashes. He touched them tentatively. They were still warm, but cooler than they ought to have been. His mind was struggling to catch up with what his senses were telling him: that some minutes had passed without him knowing it. It took some time for the message to get through – but when it finally did, Lorenzo stiffened in horror.

The light had hypnotised him, dulled his mind. Anything could have happened while he'd been distracted. Anything could have crept into the camp, and dragged his comrades away while they slept.

There *was* something. A shape at his shoulder. Lorenzo whirled around, but it was only Dougan. 'It's all right, son,' the veteran assured him in a whisper. 'We zoned out for a minute or two, that's all. Everyone's all right.'

'Old Hardhead said something,' Lorenzo recalled, 'in the mess hall yesterday.' Why was it so hard to remember? 'Something about... about ghosts. Lights that lured Guardsmen into... ambushes, I guess. I didn't realise... I didn't feel it, but that thing must have got inside my head.'

Dougan nodded gravely. 'I'm going out there,' he announced.

'But–'

'We need to know what we're facing. Don't worry. We've seen what it does now, and we've shaken it off once. It won't fool me again. It's just a question of focus. It won't even see me coming.'

'You're right.' Of course he was right. Lorenzo wished he had realised it sooner, then he could have been the one to volunteer, to have gone out there alone. To have made a name for himself, perhaps. 'I'll come with you,' he offered.

Dougan shook his head. 'You need to stay here, watch the camp. Could be this light's meant to lure us away while something worse creeps up from behind.'

'I can wake one of the others.'

'No need to panic them just yet. It's best I go alone. You could be right about there being an ambush. Any trouble out there, I'll shout a warning. *Then* you can wake the others, and point them in my direction. I'm counting on you, Lorenzo.'

Lorenzo shook his head. 'I'm coming with you.'

Dougan laid a hand on his shoulder, and looked him right in the eye with an unnerving intensity. 'Let me do this,' he said. 'I *need* to do this!'

Lorenzo was left in no doubt that he did. He nodded glumly, and Dougan smiled and clapped him companionably on the arm. Then he slipped away into the jungle, in the direction in which the blue light had last been sighted. After only a few seconds, Lorenzo could neither see nor hear him.

Why did Dougan need to do this?

He'd had his share of glory. Why couldn't he have let someone else have a taste of it, this once? Why had Lorenzo accepted what he'd said? Why hadn't he spoken up, persuaded Dougan that his need was greater?

He had picked up a stick – and as resentment welled in his chest like a living thing, he felt the wood snapping in his clenched fist, driving a splinter into his palm. How could he ever prove his worth?

He pulled himself together, horrified by what he had been thinking. He admired these men, trusted them more than anyone or anything else. He surveyed the sleeping bodies around him, tried to remind himself of that – but that feeling in his chest was back, and he hated them, all of them, for keeping him here. He hated Old Hardhead Greiss and Hotshot Woods, hated Steel Toe Dougan most of all.

The light was back. Lorenzo noted its presence with a numb feeling of acceptance, because somehow he knew it had been there all along. It was brighter than before – and behind him, this time. In the opposite direction from the one in which Dougan had gone. And closer. Almost close enough to touch, it seemed. For a second, just a second, Lorenzo's dulled mind grasped the idea that the blue light was fooling him, playing with his thoughts and feelings – but then that revelation slipped away and was forgotten.

It might not have seen him, he thought. It didn't know he was here. It probably thought he had gone off with Dougan, fallen for its lure. It probably thought it could move in now, for the kill – but the light had underestimated him.

A few steps. A few steps into the dark, that was all it would take. Lorenzo could be the hero for once, the man who had captured the light itself.

To his credit, he did hesitate. He tore his eyes away from the light and shook his head to clear it. He understood that the light had been clouding his thoughts, though he certainly didn't appreciate the extent of its influence. He remembered what Dougan had said. A question of focus. So he focused on what he knew, his comrades, and reassured himself with the knowledge that they were real and tangible. He tested his senses one by one, listening, breathing, feeling, and found each of them as sharp as he remembered.

Then Lorenzo turned back to the blue light, and found it waiting.

He should have called out to Dougan, but he didn't want to scare the light away. He should have woken the others, but the light made him think they would steal his glory. He shouldn't have abandoned them, sleeping, helpless, relying on him to keep them safe, but it was only a few steps and he was in control.

Just a few steps.

Then a few steps more.

The jungle closed around Lorenzo, but that was all right because he hadn't come far. He *knew* he hadn't come far, because he hadn't reached the light yet, and he knew the light hadn't moved. He knew that, if he looked back, he would still see the camp. His comrades would hear him if he called.

Not that he was likely to call. He didn't need them. In his mind, Lorenzo had left the jungle of Rogar III for a different jungle altogether: that of his home world. He was leading a group of children – some of them *his* children, probably – on a hunt, and they were hanging on his every word of advice, looking at him with awe in their eyes. A man who had earned his name, and more. One of Catachan's greatest heroes, and yet still humble enough to spend time with them, to pass on his wisdom.

Lorenzo pointed out a deadly spiker plant lurking in the foliage, and they gave it a wide berth. He heard snuffling ahead, and he held up his hand for silence. He crept forward, pushing aside the vegetation with his lasgun. There it was, in the centre of a small clearing, basking in the sunlight: The most fearsome of his world's predators, near legendary throughout the Imperium. The beast after which his own regiment had been named. A Catachan Devil.

They were downwind of it, and it hadn't scented them. Lorenzo beckoned to the children to come forward, to take a look at the beast. They obeyed, and let out hushed gasps of fear and wonder. Lorenzo recalled how, at their age, he had been afraid too, and he resolved to prove to them that there was no need, that Man could always triumph over Nature. If he was the right man.

At their age...

He laid his gun aside. This would be a fair fight. Lorenzo drew his knife – a devil claw, the finest of all Catachan blades, over a metre in length – and he pounced. The creature reared up on six bristling legs, opened its mighty claws, and whipped its spiny tail around to sting him. It was fast. He had almost forgotten how fast. Or perhaps it was just that he had slowed down with age. How old was he now, anyway?

He could still take it.

Lorenzo landed in the spot where the creature had been, his knife raised to strike. But the Devil was no longer there. He whirled, disoriented, but saw no trace of it. How could it have escaped from him? From... from... what was his earned name, anyway? He felt confused, standing in that clearing alone. Confused and humiliated. He thought he could hear the children laughing at him.

Then Lorenzo glimpsed a spiny tail a short distance ahead of him, and he knew what had happened. The Catachan Devil had simply wandered away, in search of a better light. A soft blue light. He could see it through the trees, and though he didn't know what the light was, he didn't wonder. The light was safe. Everything made sense again. Except...

How had he got so old?

Lorenzo knew what the children said about him behind his back. They said he couldn't be a hero as he claimed, because he had survived the war when all the real heroes had died. They called him a coward, said he'd never taken a risk, never distinguished himself. Never earned his name after all. He could hear their taunts now. He tried to blot them out, tried to focus on the creature in the blue light ahead of him. He couldn't see it any more, but he could see the light, and he approached it with increasingly urgent steps. In that light, he would prove them all wrong about him. *'I don't know but I've been told, Jungle Fighters don't grow old...'*

This wasn't what Lorenzo wanted.

Even if it had been, he knew it was an impossible dream. Few Jungle Fighters ended their days like this, and he had never expected to be one of them.

It wasn't real.

It wasn't real.

With that sudden knowledge, he snapped back to the present, to Rogar III. It hit him between the eyes like a smack of cold air, and he was on the bank of a stagnant lake, one foot poised over its surface. He pulled back, and sent loose dirt skittering over the side. As it hit, it evaporated in a cloud of white steam. Acid.

The blue light was hovering in the centre of the lake – but now, as if it knew its ploy had failed, it blinked out again and left Lorenzo in the dark. Alone. Without his lasgun.

In a part of the jungle he had not seen before.

CHAPTER 7

Lorenzo was afraid.

It was a feeling to which he wasn't accustomed. But then, nor was he used to being alone, separated from his squad – to having abandoned them. It was their lives he was afraid for, not his own.

He didn't know where he was, nor where Dougan had got to. He didn't know how far he had walked, mesmerised by the blue light. He just knew he had to get back to the campsite. He crashed through the jungle, following a trail he didn't remember leaving, cursing himself for his weakness.

It wasn't as if he hadn't been warned. He could see it clearly now. The light had been inside him all the time, a more subtle presence than he could have imagined. It had heightened his desires and his fears, whatever it had taken to lead him where it had wanted him to go. To his death. He had been lucky. It hadn't been strong enough. Somehow, he had found the will to focus, to snap himself out of its spell.

The only thing he wanted right now, the total of his hopes and ambitions, was to find his comrades alive. He remembered what Dougan had said; how he'd suspected that the blue light was trying to lure them away. What if there had been an attack in his absence? What if they were all dead, and it was his fault?

Dougan. Suddenly, Lorenzo could hear his voice again, and see the intensity in his gaze. *'Let me do this... I need to do this!'* He hadn't questioned him, hadn't seen that the light had cast its spell over Dougan too.

He stumbled to a halt. Somehow, impossibly, his trail had petered out.

He was lost for a moment, scrabbling in the undergrowth, looking for something – a snapped twig, a crushed leaf – anything to show he had passed this way before. There was nothing. Until, just as he was beginning to give up hope, wondering if he should risk calling out to the others, Lorenzo's fingers brushed against something. Something cold, hard, smooth, angular. Wood and metal.

His lasgun. He had to tear it from the clutches of weeds, as if it had lain here for weeks, been claimed as the jungle's own. He felt another stab of anxiety. He didn't feel as if more than a few minutes, maybe a half-hour, had passed, and the pre-dawn sky supported that theory – but in the blue light's embrace, time hadn't meant a great deal. His comrades' corpses could be rotting already.

He tried not to think about it. No point in worrying about what he couldn't change. Just get back to the campsite, and deal with what was real.

A pair of yellow lizard eyes blinked at Lorenzo from under a flowering plant. He fried their owner with a las-round, just to test that his gun wasn't clogged.

A faint breath of air caressed his face, and made his scratches sting. So, he hadn't been entranced long enough for them to heal. He remembered stalking an imaginary Devil, standing downwind of it. He had to hope that this part of the fantasy, at least, had been real. He closed his eyes and oriented himself at the spot where he'd found the lasgun, tried to transport himself back to that Catachan clearing and to mentally retrace his steps towards it.

When he opened his eyes again, he knew which way he had to go.

Lorenzo heard movements through the trees – and was that the sergeant's voice?

He broke into a run, and came up short when two familiar figures loomed before him, Armstrong and Landon.

'What happened?' asked Armstrong and Landon at the same time.

'We've been searching for you,' said Armstrong. 'Where–?'

'Is everyone–?'

'We thought something must have dragged you away. We were lucky Sharkbait woke when he did, and started yelling. Landon here had a lizard on his neck; we only just got it off him in time.'

'I'm sorry. I didn't mean to–'

'Where's Steel Toe? Is he with you?'

Lorenzo felt as if his blood had just frozen. 'You haven't seen him?'

He swallowed, and told Armstrong everything, burning with shame beneath the veteran's one-eyed gaze. Before Lorenzo's story was done, Armstrong was leading the way back to the camp. En route, they were joined by Myers and Storm, both bursting with questions. Armstrong filled them in brusquely, and Lorenzo pointed across the ashes of last night's fire to where he had last seen Dougan. Myers and Storm went straight off to resume their search in that direction. Armstrong mimicked the screeching call of a Catachan flying swamp mamba, and the rest of the Jungle Fighters answered his summons, appearing two by two to hear the news and to have their own efforts redirected.

Sergeant Greiss cast an appraising eye over Lorenzo, and asked if he was all right. Lorenzo nodded, and Greiss crooked a finger in his direction and growled, 'You're with me, trooper.'

Lorenzo fell in at the sergeant's heels, avoiding his gaze. He knew what he must have been thinking.

The search went on for another hour, aided by the reappearance of the sun. Donovits and Woods found a partial trail, and Donovits identified the uniquely heavy indentation of Dougan's bionic leg – but as with Lorenzo's trail earlier, it led them nowhere.

Greiss was about ready to give up, Lorenzo could feel it. Until he gave the order, though, there was still hope. He found a path they hadn't searched, because it was so overgrown, and he started to hack at the vegetation with his knife. Greiss regarded him for a second then, to his immense gratitude, the sergeant drew his own Catachan fang and joined him.

They hadn't gone far when a figure dropped out of a tree in front of them. It was a lithe man in camouflage fatigues and the customary bandana, with tanned skin and dark hair like Dougan's. Lorenzo's heart leapt – and it stayed in his mouth as he recognised this newcomer, not as the man they were looking for but as Sly Marbo.

He had never been this close to the legendary one-man army before. In other circumstances, he might have felt honoured – but Marbo seemed hardly to have seen Lorenzo. His face was taut, denied so much as a flicker of emotion, and his eyes were white and penetrating but dead inside, as he addressed Greiss. 'You won't find your trooper this way.'

Greiss accepted the pronouncement without question. 'Have you seen him?'

Marbo shook his head. 'This jungle has a way of hiding things, and people. Haven't worked it out yet.'

Greiss sighed, and called out, 'Right, let's call it a day. Reassemble at the campsite.' There was no response, but Lorenzo knew that one of the others would have heard, and passed the message on.

'One more thing,' said Marbo in his deep, throaty voice. 'There's an ork encampment forty kilometres from here, twenty-two degrees. A big one. Don't think the Validians know about it – but your course will take you right through it.'

Lorenzo didn't question how he could have scouted so far ahead. He was Sly Marbo.

'No way round?'

'Not unless you want to go wading through an acid swamp – or adding four days to your journey.'

Greiss expressed his gratitude with a curt nod – then Marbo was gone. Just gone, in the time it took Lorenzo to blink, leaving not the faintest ripple in the foliage. Sergeant Greiss turned to retrace his steps too, but Lorenzo stopped him with a hand on his shoulder. 'No. You can't... Trooper Dougan, he could still be...'

Greiss raised an eyebrow. 'You heard what Marbo said. Steel Toe's gone. Accept it and move on.'

'But what if the light still has him? If he's been hypnotised... He could be out there!'

'You say this light of yours tried to give you an acid bath.'

'Yes, but I broke free...'

'And if Steel Toe had done the same, he'd have found his way back to us, like you did. What's up with you, Lorenzo? You've lost comrades before.'

Lorenzo didn't say anything. How could he articulate the pain he'd felt, like a body blow, when Greiss had called off the search? That terrible moment when his last hope had been snatched from him. The sergeant was right, he *had* lost comrades before – you couldn't fight the Emperor's war, nor grow up on Catachan, without seeing death on a regular basis, becoming inured to it almost. But it was different this time. Different, because he could hear Dougan's words in his head: *'I'm counting on you, Lorenzo.'*

He had let Dougan down. He had let them all down. Lorenzo had been given his chance to be a hero, at last, and he'd failed. He had seen what happened, just a couple of times, to Jungle Fighters who lost the trust of their squad. It was as if they weren't there, as if they didn't exist. And he had felt no sympathy for those wretches. In this environment, if you didn't have the trust of your comrades, you had nothing. Lorenzo would be as invisible to the others as he had been to Marbo.

'I can't help wondering,' said Sergeant Greiss as they trudged back to the campsite empty-handed, 'how you did it.'

'Did what?' asked Lorenzo.

'Broke the spell. Brought yourself to your senses before you took the big plunge. I mean, no disrespect to Steel Toe, God-Emperor rest his soul, I'd have said he was as strong-willed as any of us – but you're the one who made it back.'

'I don't know, sergeant. I just don't know.'

'Must've taken some force of mind. You know, some of the others and me, we were talking – figured you were about due your earned name.'

'No!' said Lorenzo, firmly. 'Not for this, sergeant.'

Greiss nodded, and Lorenzo suddenly realised that the grizzled sergeant knew what he was feeling, and understood. He hadn't lost the sergeant's trust. Quite the opposite – Greiss didn't blame him for losing Dougan *because* he trusted him, because he knew Lorenzo had done all he could and that few among them could have done better, not even a veteran of Dougan's experience.

Lorenzo felt ashamed, now, for not trusting *him* – for believing that his squad would turn their backs on him, when he should have known them better. He swore he'd make it up to them. His tread felt just that little lighter as he and Sergeant Greiss walked on.

They wouldn't talk about it again.

The commissar was in a foul mood.

He hadn't recognised Armstrong's Catachan call, so he and Braxton had been searching alone in the wrong area all this time. Mackenzie blamed Armstrong personally for this, but Woods had leapt to his defence and a row had broken out. As Lorenzo and Greiss arrived, Mackenzie was jabbing a finger into Woods's chest, yelling almost hysterically about how he had almost died because of the Jungle Fighters' negligence.

'I was attacked out there – by the biggest jungle lizard you've ever seen! It dropped from a branch, right onto my shoulder. It's only because of Braxton's quick thinking and keen aim that I'm here to tell the tale.'

Lorenzo hid a smile, imagining Mackenzie's expression as his adjutant was forced to shoot the lizard from his shoulder. Woods was less polite, and just laughed. Armstrong turned to Braxton and congratulated him. 'I'm not sure I could've hit such a small target.'

The commissar was already scowling, but before Mackenzie could give vent to his anger again, Greiss marched forward, his fists clenched, a scowl on his face. 'I'll tell you what I told your sergeant back at the encampment, commissar,' he growled. 'You have a problem with my men, you bring it to me.'

Mackenzie squared up to him, his nostrils flaring. 'And what good would that have done, Greiss? You've demonstrated repeatedly that you can't keep your squad in line. We've wasted the best part of the morning looking for two of your men – contrary to my explicit wishes – because they decided to go for a stroll in the night.'

'And I suppose your Validians would have stayed put?' sneered Greiss.

'My Guardsmen know better than to follow pretty lights into the jungle, sergeant. That's because they've been taught self-control! If Trooper Dougan couldn't hold himself in check, then we're better off without him.'

Greiss's voice was low, but the threat it carried was unmistakeable. 'Don't push me, commissar. I've just lost a good man, who deserved better than to be taken down without a scrap. I'm in no mood for this right now.' He handed his lasgun to Woods, who received it without comment.

Mackenzie's eyes bulged. 'Well, I don't have to wonder where troopers like Woods and Armstrong here learn their impudence!' he stormed. 'I've had enough, Greiss. I've had enough of this attitude of yours – of having my every order questioned by you. As far as I'm concerned, you aren't fit to lead a squad of dung beetles, and I'll be saying as much in my report!'

Greiss drew his Catachan fang, weighed it in his hands for a second, then handed it to Woods.

'In the meantime,' Mackenzie continued, 'you will consider yourself demoted to the rank of trooper. Guardsman Braxton will be my second-in-command for the duration of this operation.'

It was obvious from the paling of Braxton's face that he was anything but happy with this sudden promotion.

Greiss shucked off his pack and rolled up his sleeves, slowly and deliberately. Mackenzie was still ranting as if he hadn't seen what was coming. It occurred to Lorenzo that, had he been here, Dougan would have been the one to step in, to defuse the situation. But then, Dougan had always known what needed to be said, and how to make it sound polite and reasonable. No one would have thanked Lorenzo for interfering, so he held his tongue.

Greiss's first punch took the commissar by surprise. It snapped his head around, staggered him and almost made him lose his balance. It wasn't that Mackenzie hadn't seen the signs, Lorenzo realised – it was just that he'd hardly been able to conceive of a subordinate actually striking him. Even now, his first thought was for his lost dignity. He was steadying himself, pulling himself up to his full, unimpressive height, drawing breath to remonstrate with Greiss, when a second fist connected squarely with his jaw.

This time, Mackenzie fell, flipping almost head over heels to land on his back, losing his peaked cap. Greiss planted his boot on the commissar's chest and leered down at him. 'That's for what you said about Steel Toe!' Then he took his foot away and turned his back in a gesture of utmost contempt.

Lorenzo thought it was over – until Mackenzie did the last thing he had expected. He sprang to his feet, and with a speed and ferocity that Lorenzo would never have credited to him, he leapt at Greiss.

Greiss heard him coming and half-turned, as Mackenzie cannoned into his side. Jungle Fighters danced out of their way as they careened back and forth, shifting their grips on each other, each looking for a clear shot at the other. Greiss found one first, and delivered a punishing blow to Mackenzie's stomach, which doubled him up and brought his chin within striking distance. Woods let out a passionate 'Yes!' as a two-fisted uppercut left the commissar stunned and reeling. Greiss bore his opponent down into the dirt, but Mackenzie recovered and planted a foot in the sergeant's stomach, flipping him over and away from him. Woods winced as Greiss landed hard – and then Mackenzie was on top of him, and it was all Greiss could do to fend off his punches.

The rookie, Landon, looked to Armstrong with concern in his eyes, but he just shook his head: *No. We stay out of it.*

Greiss had caught Mackenzie's wrist in his left hand. He planted his right arm across the commissar's throat, protecting his head from Mackenzie's free fist with his elbow. He pushed up with both knees. Mackenzie's eyes were almost popping out of their sockets as he fought to retain his position. He was good – far better than Lorenzo would have imagined – but Greiss was better. He knew his body, every muscle in it, like he knew his Catachan fang. He knew when to tense, when to push, when to shift unexpectedly so that Mackenzie reacted to an absent force and unseated himself.

Slowly, inexorably, Greiss gained the advantage, and their positions were reversed. Greiss had the commissar pinned now, his arm resting across Mackenzie's windpipe, his eyes blazing with ruthless zeal as he pressed down hard. Mackenzie kicked and scrabbled at the arm that was choking him, but Greiss wasn't giving a millimetre. 'Braxton,' the commissar spluttered.

Braxton had almost started forward once already, but he'd been frozen by a glare from Storm. Now, he took Sergeant Greiss's arms in a nervous grip, glancing over his shoulder as if he expected the rest of the Jungle Fighters to stop him. He was able to tear the sergeant away from his opponent only because Greiss chose not to resist him. He let Braxton haul him to his feet, then threw off the Validian's hands and brushed himself down, glaring at the prone Mackenzie as if challenging him to a second round.

Mackenzie was having enough trouble trying to breathe. As soon as he could, he lifted a trembling finger to point at Greiss – a feeble attempt to assert some authority – and he wheezed, 'I'll have you court-martialled for this, Greiss. If you thought Trooper Dougan died an undignified death, just you wait. You'll end your days in front of a firing squad! If we weren't on radio silence, I'd be voxing a squad of Validians to come and collect you right now. And the rest of you... You just stood there and watched while this man assaulted a senior officer. You'll pay for this, all of you. When I make my report, you'll pay dearly. You'll be an example to every damn Jungle Fighter in the Imperial Guard!'

Mackenzie picked himself up and marched into the jungle, with a curt order to the Jungle Fighters to follow him. Braxton looked around as if he wanted to say something, then thought better of it and hurried after his commissar. The others gathered their equipment, Myers and Storm hoisting

Muldoon between them, and set off in their own time. Lorenzo caught the looks that passed between the others – Greiss and Woods in particular – and he suppressed a shiver.

Somehow, he doubted the commissar would ever make that report.

The going was easier than it had been the day before, and the squad made good progress though they were in sullen spirits. They were starting to get the measure of Rogar III. They knew which plants to avoid – and the flower sap they'd been careful to reapply to their skin kept the biting insects away. More jungle lizards tried to pounce on them from the trees, like the one that had attacked Mackenzie – evidently, this was their latest trick – but the Catachans were forewarned, and it became a sport to them to pick off the creatures with las-fire in midair. Myers was the champion of this game, of course.

Braxton broke the silence to express his admiration at the speed with which the Jungle Fighters had adapted to their new environment. It was an attempt to build bridges, but it fell on stony ground.

If there were any birds left in the vicinity, they were keeping a low profile. Lorenzo didn't hear a single call. But the memory of the creatures that had pressed their attacks beyond death hung over the squad like a pall.

There was some good news, though. Muldoon had come round again, and this time he was quite lucid. Myers and Storm continued to support him for some time after he'd started to complain that he could walk unaided. They fed him simple questions until they were sure he was in control of his faculties. Muldoon had no memory of anything after he'd disturbed the hive, so Storm had to fill him in about his attack on Lorenzo.

'I can't have been trying too hard,' he commented. 'I seem to have left him in one piece.'

Lorenzo turned to him with a grin. 'You're just lucky I was going easy on you, because you were an invalid.'

'Ha! If I hadn't been holding back, I'd have dropped you before you knew I was coming.' He was certainly back to his old self. He turned to Myers and Storm. 'Seriously – Lorenzo here knocked me out all by himself?'

'Well,' said Myers with a grimace, 'he did have help.'

Lorenzo's stomach knotted as he remembered how Dougan had come to his assistance. 'Yes,' he said numbly. 'I had help.'

It was about twenty minutes after that, trailing a short way behind the others, deep in thought, that Lorenzo got the feeling he was being followed. He whirled around, and thought he saw a shape through the trees. A humanoid figure, just standing, watching. But as he brought it into focus, it slipped away like a shadow. Like last night's blue light. Was he being tricked again?

He called out a challenge, which alerted his squad and brought them to a halt. He hurried up to where he thought the figure had been, his lasgun trained on a thorny bush behind which it could have taken cover. There was nobody there.

'Sorry,' he said. 'False alarm.' The others accepted his apology, and moved on.

For Lorenzo, it wasn't so simple. This *wasn't* like last night – when, having snapped out of the blue light's trance, he had seen so clearly what had been real and what had been an illusion. Perhaps something like the light was still working on his senses, because this time, he was certain that there *had* been something.

No, not just something. Some*one*…

He knew it didn't make sense. He knew that, even without external provocation, the mind could play tricks. Especially the grieving mind. Especially the guilty mind. But, just for a moment as he'd glimpsed that figure, Lorenzo had been sure – as sure as he'd been of anything in his life – that he had known it.

He was sure he had recognised Trooper Dougan.

CHAPTER 8

The jungle seized Trooper Woods without warning.

The red flowers were particularly prevalent in this area, and Lorenzo and his squad had been treading carefully. Woods was sharing a joke with Greiss, who was in a surprisingly sanguine mood, when his feet were yanked out from under him. The Catachans went for their weapons as their comrade dropped. Woods was on the ground, in the long jungle grass, and the red flowers were all screaming.

Lorenzo's first thought was that he had been careless, stepped too close to the flowers – though he had to admit, that didn't sound much like Hotshot. But Woods, he realised, wasn't just being held, he was being *dragged*.

It wasn't the flowers' heads that had Woods, it was their roots. They had burst out of the ground, tangled themselves around his ankles – and they were grasping now for his wrists. They were coiling and writhing around him like living things, like serpents, striking when they sensed an opening. The closest troopers – Muldoon and Landon – had dropped to their haunches, knives drawn, but the roots were thick and tough. By the time Landon had drawn sap, and Muldoon had cut his first root through, ten more had erupted from the undergrowth to replace them. And the wailing flower heads were snapping at the would-be rescuers, straining at their stems.

Woods was pulled out from under Landon. The rookie lunged after him, desperate not to lose the root he had almost severed – and a flower head caught his finger. Landon fought to free himself, but the red petals held him as tightly as they'd held Greiss's stick the previous day. Landon redistributed his weight, tried to gain leverage, and another flower opened its petals wide and clamped itself onto his left ankle. He was immobilised.

Muldoon had fared better, snatching his hand away from a similar attack – but by the time he and his night reaper resumed their work, Woods had been pulled another metre toward uncharted territory. The nearest roots had relaxed their grips now, having passed their captive on to those behind. They were rearing up, twitching from side to side as if on the lookout for fresh prey.

Woods had one hand free, and he was clutching at the undergrowth, at anything that might anchor him. After pulling up a third clump of weeds, he abandoned this plan and reached instead for his devil claw. As he tried to manoeuvre it through the living bonds that held him, a flower caught the blade and wrenched it from his grip.

'Hey,' called Woods, the strain in his voice belying his forced jovial tone, 'a little help would be appreciated, you know?'

The entreaty was unnecessary. Most of the Jungle Fighters were on him, or struggling to reach him through the minefield of grasping vegetation. They were cutting, tearing, hacking, but Woods was still being pulled away from them. A root caught his free arm, and pinned it to his side like the other one. Now he was trussed up good and proper, like a fish in a net, hardly able to even struggle any more.

Mackenzie was shouting, 'Don't just stand there, do something! Cut him loose!' as if it might help. Lorenzo was just watching, thinking... looking for a way, a safe path, to reach Woods through the press of bodies that surrounded him, realising that even if he could find one he would only be joining a losing battle...

He remembered the acid lake, and it occurred to him that the roots might be pulling Hotshot *towards* something...

Lorenzo bounded past his comrades, drawing his lasgun. He was surprised to find that Guardsman Braxton had had the same thought. They stood side by side, and scanned their surroundings, fingers uneasy on their triggers.

Lorenzo saw it first: an acid spitter, lurking in the heart of a flowering bush, almost totally concealed. It stiffened, as if sensing eyes upon it, and opened its mouth. He was sure it was too far away to reach him with its deadly spray – but instinct made him leap aside anyway, and push Braxton with him.

The spitter's aim was perfect, its liquid plume sluicing into the dirt at just the spot where they had been standing. A few seconds later, and Woods's head would have entered its range.

A dual burst of las-fire destroyed the acid spitter. Then, without having to confer, both Lorenzo and Braxton pointed their guns at the undergrowth in Woods's path, and began to blast the flowers that waited there. The flowers' siren wail went up an octave, becoming louder, more intense, more painful, and Lorenzo's head began to throb. He could see black spots at the edge of his vision, and he knew the rest of his squad was affected too, because they were starting to reel and shake their heads and put their hands to their ears.

He kept on firing, because it was the only way to end it. Each time he incinerated a red flower head, its roots thrashed for a few seconds longer and then fell limp, but that dreadful sound never seemed to ease.

Lorenzo had to cease firing when he was too blind to aim properly, when the remaining flowers were too close to the prone Woods for safety. He was going nowhere now, the roots around him dead and blackened, but he was still firmly entangled. The other Jungle Fighters followed Lorenzo and Braxton's lead, targeting the flower heads rather than their roots. They seized them by the red petals, holding their 'mouths' closed, and sawed them from their stems. With each flower that died, more of Woods's bonds fell loose, and finally he was able to tear himself free and stand, evidently in pain from the continuing screaming.

Mackenzie was feeling the worst of it, though. He was practically on his knees, his hands clasped over his ears, and Lorenzo was alarmed to see blood trickling through his fingers.

With Woods out of the danger area, however – and Landon freed now, along with Woods's knife – lasguns could be employed again, and it wasn't long before the final red flower was blasted to a cinder. Lorenzo closed his eyes and let out a long, shuddering sigh as he was soothed by a blessed silence.

'Well, that seals it,' muttered Greiss, when their ears had finally stopped ringing. 'There's something seriously nuts about this place.'

Donovits was sitting on the ground with his knees drawn up to his chest, his forehead shiny with sweat. 'It's as if evolution has been speeded up here,' he considered. 'The red flowers couldn't catch their prey any more, because the insects – and we – had learned to keep out of their way, so they evolved a means of bringing their prey to them. Likewise for the spitters; they've learned how to spit further. The different species are even working together – but all this should take generations. Instead, it's happened in a few days. I'd say it was impossible, but we're seeing it with our own eyes.'

Lorenzo felt that chill of the unnatural playing about his spine again. He didn't want to hear this, didn't want to believe, but he had no choice. 'That's why the birds and the lizards have been growing more hostile,' he said in a hollow tone.

'And changing their tactics,' Donovits confirmed.

'And why they only started calling Rogar III a deathworld a few weeks ago,' said Armstrong.

'I'd guess,' said Donovits, 'that it was the arrival of the orks and the Imperium that upset the ecological balance here. Since then...'

'Rogar has been evolving ways to combat them,' Armstrong concluded the thought grimly. 'Now, it's evolving ways to combat *us*.'

It took a moment for that to sink in, for the consequences to register with everyone, before Greiss put them into words.

'That means we can't take a thing for granted,' he said glumly. 'Soon as we think we know what a creature or plant can do, it's likely to up and develop a whole new set of offensive capabilities. You need to stay on your toes, troopers.'

Mackenzie had been leaning against a tree, hands on his knees, getting his breath back, licking his wounds. Now he pushed himself up to an unsteady vertical. 'You're forgetting, Trooper Greiss, you don't give the orders around here any more.'

'Will do, sergeant,' said Woods as if the commissar hadn't spoken.

'Too right, sergeant,' said Myers.

'Whatever you say, sergeant,' said Storm.

Mackenzie just scowled, and ordered them to get moving. He was no longer so keen, though, to lead from the front as he had been doing. He instructed Woods to take point in his place, and fell back to his more accustomed position among the troops. He saw that Greiss was regarding him through hooded eyes, and he said curtly, 'I'm watching you, Greiss. One misstep and I'll have you in chains.'

'With respect, commissar,' Greiss growled, 'you might be better off watching your own back. The jungle's a dangerous place – and if you get dragged away like Hotshot just did, you don't want to be relying on an "undisciplined rabble" to save your scrawny hide, now do you?'

He bared his teeth in a cruel smile.

They reached the river early in the afternoon.

Mackenzie looked pleased about this, as it suggested he had kept his squad on course despite Greiss's reservations. 'Five minutes, everyone,' he said magnanimously. 'Fill your water bottles, wash up, whatever you feel you need to do. Just remember, this is the last known fresh water between us and the warboss.'

'You're assuming it *is* fresh water,' said Greiss.

'I told you before, Greiss, my men reconnoitred this area. We tested the water for all known poisons and diseases.'

'We might know a few you don't,' suggested Armstrong.

Mackenzie's voice rose in indignation. 'That water is perfectly safe. I've drunk it myself. Or did you think we'd been sitting on our hands for the past year just waiting for the almighty Jungle Fighters to show up and rescue us?'

'Just saying I'd like to see for myself,' growled Greiss. 'Sharkbait?'

'Aye, sergeant.' Muldoon tore up a handful of weeds and approached the riverbank. The water, a short way below him, was impossibly clear and fast flowing. It was six metres wide, and it sparkled hypnotically as it caught the sun. Lorenzo shared the sergeant's suspicion: it looked too good to be true.

Muldoon cast his weeds into the river. It hissed and bubbled where they hit, and Lorenzo could see that the water was eating into the vegetation, even as the current swept it away in a telltale cloud of vapour.

Mackenzie blanched. 'It... The reports... My men assured me... Why would they...?'

'Just a guess, commissar, sir,' said Greiss with a crooked grin, 'but perhaps your men just don't like you much.'

Braxton hurried to offer a kinder explanation. 'It must be as Donovits said, sir. The planet is adapting to our presence, finding new ways to fight us.'

'Maybe,' agreed Donovits, 'but this goes beyond evolution, accelerated or not. If this really was a freshwater river – if it's become so highly acidic in a matter of weeks – we're talking about a sizeable ecological shift.'

'Could it be the orks?' asked Braxton – and he wasn't the only man present, Lorenzo sensed, who wanted to think that – to cling to a rational, *knowable* cause for their woes. 'Could they have poisoned the water somehow?'

'Maybe,' conceded Donovits, though he sounded doubtful.

'Don't underestimate these orks,' muttered Mackenzie. 'I told you, this new warboss is smart!'

'Yes, well,' said Greiss. 'Right now, the important thing isn't what may or may not have happened in the past – it's what we do about it in the here and now.'

Mackenzie had been staring into the acid river. Now, he snapped to attention as if remembering his responsibilities. 'Right. I hope I don't have to tell you people to conserve supplies from here on. In the meantime, we have a more pressing problem.'

'Don't tell me,' said Greiss wryly. 'We have to cross that thing.'

They began by sending Woods up a tree.

He shinned up to its topmost branches, until its leaves hid him from view. He disturbed a bird – the first the squad had seen all day – but instead of attacking him it squawked in terror and took flight.

From his new vantage point, Woods scanned the length of the river in each direction, looking for a natural crossing. No one was really surprised when he returned with the news that there was none. That would have been too easy.

Armstrong had brought rope, so the rest of the squad stood back as Myers tied a lasso, swung it over his head and let the looped end fly. It soared across the acid river to the opposite bank, and caught hold of a tree branch. Myers tugged at it to confirm it was secure. The rope came loose, and there was a collective wince as it slapped into the river and was dissolved in an instant, before he could even think about reeling it in. Myers was left with just the two-metre length that had been coiled in his hands.

The Jungle Fighters tested a few creepers, but found them brittle, dried out by the relentless heat. Muldoon suggested they dig up some snapper flowers, and Greiss approved the idea. Mackenzie grumbled something under his breath, but he didn't object – so soon, they were working in a heavy silence, weaving a replacement rope from the flowers' hardy roots. They knotted several short strands together, and finally they were ready for Myers to try again.

This time, the lasso caught and held. Myers tied his end of the rope around the sturdiest tree he could find, and Mackenzie asked for a volunteer to be first across. Lorenzo's was the second hand in the air, as usual. The first belonged to Landon.

'You sure about this?' Greiss quizzed him.

'Makes sense, sergeant,' said the rookie. Lorenzo could see how nervous he felt about saying this, but he was saying it anyway. 'Someone's got to go over there and tie the rope up securely, and I'm the lightest. I'm the most likely to make it.'

Greiss accepted that, so Muldoon set about tying his remaining two metres of rope around the volunteer's waist, passing it between his legs and finally over the knotted plant roots to act as a safety harness. To this, he attached the end of another length of roots, which would pay itself out as Landon went across.

Then the Jungle Fighters watched in tense silence as Muldoon hoisted Landon up until he could grip the precarious root bridge with his hands and feet. The rookie had left his heavy pack behind, but his lasgun was slung across his back; he never knew what he might encounter, alone on the far side.

Landon made his way across quickly, hanging upside-down from the makeshift rope like a squirrel. He only slowed as he neared the middle of the river, where the slack brought him down almost to its level. If he'd made a slip there, he would have been dead before his harness could catch him.

It was at this moment that Myers's lasso, straining to cope with Landon's additional weight, lost its grip on the branch.

Mercifully, it snagged again, only a centimetre further along. Almost a centimetre too far. Lorenzo, watching, sucked air between his teeth, knowing he could do nothing as his youthful comrade dropped – as he was caught an instant later, holding on for his life to his shaking, swaying lifeline. The acid river lapped against Landon's lasgun, but as far as Lorenzo could see, Landon himself was unharmed.

When the rope had steadied, he resumed his crossing, hugging more closely to the rope than before until it had begun to rise again, to lift him out of danger. Then he struck out more confidently towards the far bank, and set foot on dry land at last.

Landon untied himself from his harness, and made a quick check of the area for immediate threats. He inspected his lasgun and discarded it; evidently, the acid had rendered it useless. Then he knotted the rope he had carried across with him around a tree. He retrieved the end of the first rope from its branch, and tied it around a different tree nearby, making sure he pulled it good and taut. Then he turned to his comrades, and gave them a thumbs-up sign.

Mackenzie sent Woods across next. The other Jungle Fighters had almost made enough root rope to construct a harness for him, but he didn't bother waiting for it. The crossing was less fraught for him than it had been for Landon; Woods had two ropes to cling to, and he knew both were firmly anchored at each end. He reached the other side of the river in seconds.

Armstrong was more prudent, waiting until his safety rope was prepared and in place, attached to both crossing ropes, before he set off at a perfectly measured pace. Once he'd set foot on the far bank, he hurled his harness, and Landon's, back to the others, so Myers and Storm were able to follow him in short order. Donovits was next; once he'd crossed the river, he called back a warning that the first rope was beginning to fray in the middle. 'Best keep most of your weight on the second,' he advised.

Braxton had been watching the Jungle Fighters closely, and when his turn came he tried to mimic their actions. Only a third of the way across the ropes, however, he missed a handhold and fell. His harness brought him up short, but for a moment he was bouncing and flailing in midair.

That was when the second rope snapped, its loose ends flopping into the acid to be eaten away. Braxton scrabbled for the remaining rope, and held onto it with white knuckles. A minute passed before he felt confident to proceed further. He made one more slip, but his harness saved him again and he was quicker to recover this time. Lorenzo let out a breath of relief – and realised he had been holding it – as Braxton joined the others. Mackenzie had been rigid with worry, too. Who'd have thought the commissar cared about his adjutant as anything more than a human shield?

Greiss and Muldoon, on the other hand, had been conferring in low whispers, ignoring the drama playing out over the river. As the threat to

Braxton passed, and Mackenzie's attention turned back towards them, they parted smoothly – but their eyes met for a second, and Lorenzo thought he saw something ominous in that gaze. A flicker of a resolution made and confirmed.

Mackenzie ordered the three remaining Jungle Fighters to begin work on another rope. 'Waste of time,' opined Greiss. 'We don't need two ropes. The second was a backup, that's all.'

'A safety precaution,' said Mackenzie stiffly, 'that turned out to be entirely necessary.'

'Only because your Guardsman didn't know what he was doing,' countered Greiss. 'If he'd followed Brains's advice–'

'I'm not trusting my life to–' Mackenzie began.

Greiss interrupted with, 'There's only four of us left to cross, and Muldoon and Lorenzo here aren't crying about it. That rope's held up just fine so far. Better to take a chance than spend another hour sitting around here doing craftwork. We're already behind schedule.' And with that, he hoisted Landon's pack on his right arm, and slipped his own onto the left to keep himself balanced. Then he hauled himself up onto the remaining rope and, emulating Woods, began to swarm across it without a harness.

'Come back here, Greiss!' roared Mackenzie. 'I'm warning you, if you don't come back here this instant, I'll... I'll...'

'Way I see it, sir,' said Muldoon nonchalantly, 'there isn't much more you can threaten him with.'

'I'll be adding this to the list of charges against you, trooper!' the commissar yelled after the departing Greiss. 'Muldoon, what do you think you're doing?'

Muldoon had beckoned Lorenzo forward, and was tying a rope around his waist. Mackenzie pushed Lorenzo aside, and announced, 'I'll be going across next. I don't trust Greiss and Woods over there unsupervised.'

'I'm sure Guardsman Braxton can keep an eye on them, sir,' said Muldoon, tongue-in-cheek. Mackenzie just glared at him, and said nothing.

Muldoon tied Mackenzie into his harness, then gave him the nod that he was ready to go. He didn't help him up to the rope as he had most of the Jungle Fighters, he just watched as the commissar scrambled up to it himself. He took hold unsteadily, and eyed the acid river below him.

Then the commissar began to cross, moving hand over hand and foot over foot at a confident, unhurried pace. That was when Lorenzo caught that glint in Muldoon's eye again, and he felt his heart miss a beat.

He had heard that the attrition rate of commissars assigned to Catachan squads was many times the Imperium average. These losses were officially dismissed as accidents, of course – a natural consequence of sending non-deathworlders, no matter how high-ranking, how well-trained, into an environment to which they weren't suited. It was rarely acknowledged that there might be anything more to it than that – at least, it hadn't happened within Lorenzo's earshot. But everybody knew – or at least suspected – the unspoken truth.

The deathworlds of the Imperium bred men who were independent, proud, and loyal only to those who had earned their respect. That went double for Catachan.

'He's doing well,' murmured Muldoon, watching the commissar's progress with obvious resentment, 'for a city boy. Too well.'

He reached up to the end of the root rope, still tied to the tree beside him, and he looked at Lorenzo as if he was challenging him to say something, to stop him – and it did occur to Lorenzo that maybe he should, maybe it was the right thing to do, but his throat was dry and the words wouldn't come, and anyway this was nothing to do with him and even if it was, his loyalties lay with his own kind, didn't they?

Didn't they?

Too late. He was always too late.

Muldoon wrapped his fingers around the end of the rope and, with a smile of grim satisfaction, he gave it a good tug.

Lorenzo watched as the vibrations travelled the first half of the rope's length, to where Mackenzie was clinging on. There wasn't time to shout a warning, even if he had wanted to. The rope jerked itself out of the commissar's hands, simultaneously flipping him so that he was on top of it. He flailed, caught by surprise, trying to find fresh purchase, slipped, plummeted to the extent of his harness's slack – and then the harness gave way, as Lorenzo had known it must. A simple slipknot.

There was nothing holding Commissar Mackenzie now.

He was in freefall.

CHAPTER 9

Lorenzo didn't want to look, but he couldn't turn away.

There was no time, anyhow. Mackenzie would hit the acid before he could blink.

Unless, somehow, impossibly, the direction of his fall was reversed.

Unless he had managed to reach up and, with a last desperate lunge, catch the rope above his head and ride it back up as it bounced.

The commissar's grunt of pain was loud enough to reach Lorenzo's ears, even over the rushing of the river. He was clinging, one-handed, to a rope that was still bucking, trying its best to shake him. The way he had dropped, the way he'd arrested his fall, the way he was hanging now, his feet pedalling the air – Lorenzo was sure Mackenzie must have dislocated his shoulder. It must have been a supreme effort of will for him to hold on at all, as the pain spread to his fingers and numbed them. But hold on he did – and more than that, he managed to lift himself, find the rope with his other hand, and finally grip it between his knees.

Lorenzo was impressed despite himself. Muldoon looked like he could hardly believe his eyes. Then his expression darkened, and he reached for the end of the rope again.

Lorenzo put out a hand without thinking, and caught his comrade's own. Muldoon looked angry, and Lorenzo didn't blame him; he wasn't sure of his own motives for intervening, so how could he expect Sharkbait to understand? He held his gaze, and shook his head: *Enough!* But he knew he was going to blink first.

To Lorenzo's surprise, Muldoon gave a nod of acceptance. He took his hand away. He turned so that Lorenzo couldn't see his expression.

The rope began to tremble again. Lorenzo didn't look, but he knew Mackenzie must be back on the move. A moment later, the rope gave a little jerk as it was relieved of the commissar's weight, and Muldoon turned to catch the remaining harness as Myers flung it back to him.

He said nothing as he tied the rope around Lorenzo's waist. As Muldoon hoisted his comrade into position on the crossing rope, however, their eyes met, and Lorenzo thought they shared a moment of mutual respect.

Then Muldoon turned away again, and Lorenzo was alone, concentrating on the rope between his hands and feet, the muscles in his arms and legs, and the rushing acid river below his dangling head.

Halfway across, it occurred to him that if he *had* upset Muldoon, he was probably about to find out all about it.

When Muldoon stepped onto the far riverbank, the last of the squad to cross, Mackenzie was waiting for him.

Braxton had reset the commissar's shoulder, and fixed him a make-shift sling, but he was obviously in pain. Still, he greeted Muldoon with a left-handed punch to the jaw that was fast, accurate and powerful enough to knock him off his feet.

Muldoon lay sprawled in the undergrowth, wiping the blood from his lip.

Mackenzie stepped back and straightened his jacket, glaring down at the trooper.

The Catachan rubbed his chin ruefully and conceded, 'Alright. I deserved that.' He got to his feet and dusted himself down.

'And a damn sight more,' hissed Mackenzie. 'If you wanted to join Greiss on Death Row, you couldn't have thought up a better way of doing it, Muldoon.'

'Hey,' said Muldoon, all injured innocence, 'you can't blame a trooper for a simple accident.'

Mackenzie's nostrils flared. 'Accident my–!'

Greiss interrupted, 'You want to be careful, commissar, accusing a good man of attempted murder when you've no evidence, especially in front of his squad. Muldoon says it was an accident, that's good enough for me.'

Mackenzie ignored him. He was glaring at Muldoon. 'I want him restrained,' he said icily. *'Silence!'* he bellowed at the chorus of protest that greeted the order. 'I want this man stripped of weapons, and his hands tied. Braxton!'

Braxton started forward, seeming almost relieved when Greiss barred his way with an outstretched arm. 'You can't do that, commissar,' he snarled. 'You make a man defenceless in the jungle, you're as good as killing him, without a trial, without nothing.'

'What do you suggest I do, Greiss? Muldoon has proven himself a danger to this mission – to me personally. I have the authority to execute him on the spot. Is that what you want?'

'It was an accident.'

Lorenzo had surprised himself again, but he felt he owed Muldoon something. He was committed now; everyone had turned to look at him.

'I was right there,' he said. 'I saw it all. A bird flew at Muldoon. One of the black ones, from yesterday. It came right out of the tree above his head. It startled him. His arm jolted the rope.'

'That's right,' Woods spoke up. 'I saw it from here. Sharkbait slashed at it with his reaper, injured its wing I think, and sent it flapping away.'

A couple of the others gave nods and murmurs of agreement.

Mackenzie looked from one of the Jungle Fighters to another, evidently not believing a word of their story. 'My harness–'

'–must have been frayed,' said Muldoon. 'I'm sorry. I should have checked it more closely. I should have seen the damage before I sent you off. Sir.'

Mackenzie glared at Muldoon for a long moment. Then he turned to

Braxton. 'I still want him bound,' he said. 'To ensure there are no more "accidents".'

This time, both Myers and Storm stepped forward, placing themselves between Braxton and Muldoon, their arms folded in defiance. Woods drew his devil claw, the glint of it catching the commissar's eye and giving him pause for thought.

'I don't think you're hearing us, Mackenzie,' growled Greiss, stepping forward until he was nose to nose with the slighter man. 'You may be Mr High-and-Mighty Commissar back in your comfortable quarters, surrounded by a thousand Guardsmen ready to bow and scrape and lay down their lives for you – but you're on a deathworld now. This is our territory – that's why we're here! Until you start to wise up and do things our way, "accidents" are going to keep on happening, you get my drift?'

'Are you threatening me, Greiss?' demanded Mackenzie. 'I have witnesses.'

'You have Braxton.'

'If anything happens to me, anything at all–'

'It'll be in his report. Yes, I worked that out. If he ever gets to make one, that is. Like I keep telling you, Mackenzie, accidents happen out here.'

Mackenzie's ears were still red, but the rest of his face had turned very white indeed. He'd got the message, at last.

'He's a good man, you know.'

Lorenzo's attention had been focused on the jungle. There had been more lizards stirring in the foliage, and he'd that feeling of being followed again although he could see no proof. He hadn't noticed Braxton until he had spoken, hadn't seen that he'd dropped back in the marching order to be at Lorenzo's side. Briefly, he felt irritated that the Validian always seemed to come to him. Lorenzo didn't feel like talking right now, least of all about what had happened by the river.

But Braxton was determined. 'The commissar, I mean,' he continued. 'You'll see that when you've worked beside him for a while.'

Lorenzo raised a sceptical eyebrow.

'I know he's been tough on you all. He's fresh out of training. Maybe he's trying too hard to prove he can do the job.'

'His problem,' said Lorenzo curtly. 'We can't afford to carry him. On Catachan, he'd have been dead twenty years ago.'

'Thank you, anyway,' said Braxton.

'For what?'

'For stopping Muldoon. I saw you.'

'You were too far away. You're mistaken.'

'You must agree with me – that the commissar doesn't deserve to die.'

'I agree with my comrades,' said Lorenzo, 'that Old Hardhead doesn't deserve what Mackenzie has planned for him; that Steel Toe was a good soldier, who didn't deserve what Mackenzie said about him.'

'There has to be a way–'

'It's him or Greiss.'

'You know, if it comes down to that,' said Braxton, 'I... I have to...'

Lorenzo nodded. He knew.

They said no more. There was nothing more *to* say.

They rested in an area lush with what Muldoon and Donovits judged were water-bearing vines. They snacked on purple berries that Muldoon had picked and tested earlier. Then Lorenzo drew his Catachan fang, took a vine in his hand and scored a thin cut in its skin. The vine bled clear, and Lorenzo positioned his near-empty bottle to capture the precious drops of liquid, of which there were all too few.

Within twenty minutes, the Jungle Fighters had drained the vines of all they had, replenishing their supplies just a little. As Lorenzo returned his bottle to his pack, he heard low voices, and realised that Greiss wasn't with them.

He could just make out Sergeant Greiss through the jungle. He was talking to somebody else: a man whom Lorenzo couldn't see at all, so easily did he blend into his surroundings, but he knew it could only have been Sly Marbo. He couldn't make out what was being said – but as Greiss turned and trudged back to the others, it was with slumped shoulders and a dark, brooding expression.

He gathered the Jungle Fighters around – and to Lorenzo's surprise, Mackenzie didn't object, he just joined them and listened. Greiss told the squad what Lorenzo already knew: that there were orks ahead – and Mackenzie raised his eyebrows and frowned at his sketch map but again said nothing. 'Marbo's scouted a path for us,' said Greiss, 'that'll take us around the greenskins, but still too close for my liking. Now, the commissar here explained why we can't blow our cover, but here's another reason for you: Marbo figures, from the size of this camp and the number of huts, that the greenskins outnumber us about thirty to one. Even Hotshot can't take down thirty orks on his own!'

'Oh yeah?' grinned Woods. 'Lead me to 'em, that's all I'm saying.'

'So the only way we're getting through this one,' Greiss continued, 'is by stealth.'

'How far is this camp?' asked Donovits.

'Another five kilometres,' said Greiss, 'before we start running into patrols. I say we make up that ground, then break early for the night. We get some food, some shuteye, then make our move in the small hours.'

There was a general murmur of assent, and the Jungle Fighters were starting to get to their feet, to retrieve their packs, when Greiss stopped them. 'One more thing. Any of you felt like you're being followed? Since Lorenzo's little outburst, I mean.'

Nobody spoke up. A few of the Jungle Fighters exchanged uncomfortable glances. Greiss's eyes narrowed. 'I don't hear any of you denying it.'

Unexpectedly, it was Mackenzie who spoke up. 'I thought I heard something. Footsteps, about an hour and a half ago. When I looked, there was no one there. I assumed it was Marbo.'

'I saw something,' offered Donovits, 'more recently. I didn't speak up because... Sergeant, it was just a flicker in the corner of my eye. A trick of the light. A... a feeling, more than anything.'

'Wildman and me, we dropped back without telling the rest of you,' said Myers, 'checked out a bush where I thought I'd seen something move. It would've been about the time the commissar said.'

'But there was no one there,' Storm took up the story, 'and believe me, if there had been, there was nowhere he could've gone without us seeing him.'

Greiss took all this in with a grim nod. 'Marbo reckons there *is* something. He's caught glimpses of it, like the rest of us, reckons it's stalking us. But whenever he gets too close, it disappears. It leaves no tracks, no nothing.' With a smile, he added, 'Marbo says it's almost as good as he is.'

'Ghosts!' said Braxton.

Everyone turned to look at him.

'That's what the Validians have been saying. I reported on it for *Eagle & Bolter*, our broadsheet. The same story, from four different squads. They all had the feeling they were being followed, but there was no evidence of it. I thought it might be connected to the blue lights; the jungle playing tricks on their minds.'

'Hallucinogens in the atmosphere?' mused Donovits. 'Could be put out by one of the plants. They could even be in the berries we've eaten.'

'I didn't eat any berries,' said Myers, 'at least not till after I saw that... thing.'

'This could be serious,' grumbled Greiss. 'First Sharkbait goes off the deep end, then Steel Toe and Lorenzo go wandering in the night, now this. If this jungle gets us so we can't trust our own senses...'

'You said Marbo saw this "ghost",' said Donovits. 'He saw it following *us*. If the jungle were affecting him, making him – making all of us – paranoid, then surely he'd have thought the ghost was following *him*. That makes sense, yes?'

'Then it has to be real,' said Lorenzo.

'We need to know for sure,' said Armstrong.

'Maybe we should leave well enough alone,' said Braxton. 'I mean, there's no record of these "ghosts" attacking anyone.'

'Yet,' said Armstrong. 'You should have learned by now, that could change in a heartbeat. I say we search.'

Greiss nodded his agreement, and the squad separated, each man taking a sector of the jungle around them, though each was sure to stay within sight of two others at all times. They kicked and cut their way through the undergrowth, beat bushes, shook trees and even shinned up some to search their leaf-shrouded upper branches. The Jungle Fighters checked all the places where *they* would have hidden. Finally, they regrouped, having covered an area some three hundred metres in radius and found nothing. No one. No sign that anyone had been here, other than the Jungle Fighters themselves.

There was nothing they could do after that but go on. It was only a few minutes later, however, that Lorenzo had that feeling again, like a prickling on his neck.

He wasn't the only one. As he whipped around to inspect the foliage behind him, Storm and Braxton did the same. And this time, Lorenzo was sure of it. There was something there. He could just make out a shape between the trees. A head and shoulders. He drew his lasgun and stepped forward, not wanting to move too fast, not daring to blink, to take his eyes off the shape. His other senses told him that Storm and Braxton were beside him, and the rest of his squad not far behind. Lorenzo took another step. The head moved, shifting just a fraction, in a very human gesture.

He was only a few metres away from the shape when it changed. It seemed to metamorphose – or, more accurately, to come into focus – in front of his eyes. The shape resolved itself into a cluster of thistles. Thistles that had always been there; the rest, Lorenzo had imagined. He started as Storm shot the thistles anyway, and fired into the surrounding undergrowth a few times for good measure. 'In case this thing is a shape-shifter,' he explained. But he disturbed nothing more than a few black insects, which smelt the flower sap on the Jungle Fighters and buzzed away.

The whole squad was on the alert after that, on edge. Lorenzo had to force himself not to jump at every shadow he saw, every distant sound that came to his ears. He thought about what Greiss had said, about losing trust in their own senses. The others hadn't seemed too worried, probably didn't believe it could happen to them, but he remembered the blue light. He remembered how real its lies had seemed.

Landon had approached Greiss, and Lorenzo was just close enough for his keen ears to pick up their hushed conversation. 'I've had an idea, sergeant,' said the rookie. 'Why don't I hide in a tree and let the rest of you go on a way? If we are being followed, I'll soon find out.'

'I don't know,' said Greiss. 'We're talking about someone or something that's given Sly Marbo the slip – and that isn't easy.'

'Maybe he knew Marbo was around. Maybe he heard us talking about him. I'm the smallest of us, sergeant, the one he's least likely to miss if he *is* watching us. The rest of you could gather around, block his view for a second, and I'll be gone. Next time our "ghost" sees me, he'll be passing right under me, and I'll raise the alarm.'

Greiss raised a cynical eyebrow. 'That a promise? Swear on your blade? Because you've been pushing yourself forward today, Landon – and that's good, don't get me wrong, we'll make a fine soldier of you, maybe even a sergeant one day – but this isn't the time for grandstanding, hoping to hog some glory for yourself.'

'Soon as I see a thing,' Landon promised, 'I'll yell my lungs out.'

Greiss considered the proposal, and finally nodded. By the time he passed it on to the rest of the squad, however, two men at a time, in a quiet growl, he'd made a few alterations. He approached Mackenzie last – but by this time, the commissar had heard what was afoot. 'If you're asking for my permission to proceed, Greiss,' he remarked acidly, 'then consider it granted.'

A short time later, they came to a mournful-looking tree with branches that sagged almost to ground level, dripping with water-bearing vines. It was almost too perfect. They gathered round and set to work with their knives, teasing out what liquid they could. Lorenzo stopped Braxton from putting his thirsty lips directly to a vine, pointing out that the skin was probably poisonous.

After a few minutes of this, Landon worked his way to the centre of the group, and was handed a lasgun by Donovits to replace the one he had lost in the river. He stepped onto Muldoon's cupped hands and was hoisted onto the tree's lowest branch, his camouflage uniform and dubbin-streaked face immediately lost among its leaves. Lorenzo heard the faintest of rustles above his head as the rookie climbed higher, and he resisted the urge to look up.

'Right, men,' announced Greiss, in what was maybe a slighter louder voice than usual, for the benefit of any eavesdroppers, 'time we made a move. We've still got lost time to make up.'

As the squad set off again, the Jungle Fighters spread out more widely than they would normally have done, yet contrived to cross each other's paths frequently. An observer would have been hard-pressed even to count them, let alone to work out which of them might be missing. They also moved more slowly than before – because, although nobody said anything, each of them was reluctant to leave his inexperienced comrade too far behind. Indeed, the further they strayed from Landon's position, the slower, the more reticent, their steps became – and Lorenzo noticed a certain amount of jostling for the rearmost position, the man who would be able to respond first to the alarm call when it came. Woods, of course, came out on top.

Lorenzo had been counting out a minute in his head. As he reached sixty, Greiss gave a nod, and Muldoon disappeared into a bush. Myers provided a distraction, this time, by yelling 'Jungle lizard!' and firing into the undergrowth before professing, with mock sheepishness, to have been mistaken.

They proceeded at length, expecting Trooper Landon to reappear before too long, at which point somebody else would slip into hiding. After twenty seconds had passed, though, Lorenzo saw that Greiss was getting worried. Another five, and he came to a halt, and drew breath to give the prearranged signal that would call off the operation.

That was when Landon yelled out, at last.

Only this wasn't a yell of discovery. It was a yell of fear.

Lorenzo was running before the echoes had subsided. They *had* come too far, because Landon was still all the way back where they had left him, and Lorenzo was pushing his muscles as hard as he could, willing himself forward, and yet still the path to his comrade seemed to stretch a near-infinite distance. He concentrated on what he could do: pumping his legs, faster than he could think, so fast that he was sure only sheer force of will kept him from falling. There were sounds ahead – ugly sounds, full of foreboding – but they were almost drowned out by his heartbeat, by the crashing footsteps of comrades around him and of Woods in front.

Every second counted. Every fraction of a second.

And there weren't enough of them.

Landon yelled again: a terrible gurgling scream, which was cut off in mid-flow and could only have meant one thing.

He came into sight at last, limp and no longer struggling in the grip of a figure that was humanoid in shape but a mockery of a human in its aspect. The monster was caked in dirt, centimetres thick, and it bristled with grass, dead leaves, living flowers and the severed roots of larger plants as if a whole section of the planet had been scooped up and wrapped around its frame. Lorenzo thought the monster *was* flora, at first, but he could make out patches of suntanned skin, and human fingers around Landon's neck. Woods had already charged it, a lasgun fanfare presaging his arrival. Lorenzo had brought up his weapon but hadn't fired, fearful of hitting the monster's captive – but Woods had seen what he hadn't, or rather accepted what he didn't want to accept.

It must have waited for Landon, he realised. It was right under the tree in which the Guardsman had concealed himself – but he wouldn't have come down from there unless he was sure it was safe. The monster had discovered the Jungle Fighters' trap, and set its own in return.

As Woods hit the monster, it dropped Landon, and he fell to the ground, his head coming to rest at an acute angle to his body. Lorenzo was halfway to him when he realised there was no point. He changed course and leapt at the monster instead, along with Myers and Storm, whose howl of rage echoed in Lorenzo's ears. Woods could probably have handled the monster on his own – and he would have enjoyed bragging about it later – but Lorenzo wasn't thinking about that right now. He was thinking about Landon.

The monster, it turned out, was stronger than they had expected. It dislodged Woods and Myers, and sent them flying with a sweep of its arm. As the two troopers fell, however, Muldoon and Greiss appeared in their places. The monster was borne down under the combined weight of four Catachans, but showed no sign of slowing or weakening as they pounded at it with their fists. Lorenzo drew his fang, and plunged it into the monster's heart with a snarl, but the blade came out encrusted with muck and no blood, and still the monster fought on.

It shifted beneath his knees, and he realised with a start that it was *sinking...* as if the monster lay in quicksand, though the earth around it felt as hard as it ever had to the touch of Lorenzo's foot. He was scrabbling at the monster, desperate to stop it, to hold it here, because all he could think was that it was getting away – it had killed Landon and it was getting away – but the pull of the earth was inexorable, and the monster was gone, leaving Lorenzo with only two handfuls of mud and an empty feeling in his heart.

He staggered to his feet, and stepped back from where the monster had been, from the spot where the jungle grass still grew as if it had never been disturbed – and he looked at Greiss, with bewilderment in his eyes, as he realised that the sergeant had claimed a souvenir, wrenched it free from the monster's mass even as it went under. He was just staring at it, the first time Lorenzo had seen him speechless, as the rest of the Jungle Fighters gathered round.

Greiss held up his find, and one by one they realised what it was, and then they had no words either.

It was a bionic leg.

CHAPTER 10

Lorenzo couldn't sleep.

This was highly unusual – at least when he was planetside, out in the jungle.

They had set up camp before the sun had gone down. They were resting in preparation for their passage by the ork encampment – a trial in which the night would be their ally. Lorenzo could feel the distant sun on his face, and its red glow penetrated his eyelids – but he was used to that. He was used to making the best of sleep whenever, wherever and for however long he could grab it. It wasn't just the sunlight that kept him awake.

Nor was it just the death of a trooper he had hardly known, to whom he didn't remember saying a word; a young man who could have become a good comrade, even a hero, had he lived to earn his name.

The monster – Lorenzo couldn't think of it as Dougan – could sink into the ground, and rise from it as silently. Little wonder, then, it had proved so elusive so far. Little wonder Landon hadn't seen it coming.

Lorenzo was feeling the same discomfort, the same restless itch, as he had on the carrier ship. That creeping realisation that the world around him didn't bow to the edicts of nature, to the physical laws he had thought inviolable. The feeling that nothing made much sense any more.

'It couldn't have been Steel Toe,' Woods had insisted, in the aftermath of the brief fight with the monster, manifestly ignoring the proof that had been there for all to see, in Greiss's hand. 'I don't care what happened to him, what this planet did to him, he wouldn't have... He wouldn't have. Not Steel Toe.'

'Sorry, Hotshot,' Greiss had said gloomily, 'we have to face facts. I'd recognise this hunk o' metal anywhere. See under the dirt here? Scorch marks from where Steel Toe was bitten by that critter on Vortis. It shorted the circuits, sent a lethal shock across its own mandibles. Steel Toe couldn't walk for a fortnight, till we got the leg fixed, but he saved our bacon that day.'

'It *wasn't* him,' said Donovits firmly. 'It may have been his body, but it wasn't Steel Toe. He's dead!'

Myers had rubbed his chin where the mud-encrusted monster had hit him. 'Well, he was sure taking a long time to lie down.'

'Brains is right,' said Muldoon. 'What we just fought wasn't Steel Toe. It wasn't alive. It was some kind of a zombie. I looked into its eyes – and I'm telling you, Steel Toe wasn't in there.'

Greiss, as usual, had turned the topic to the future, to what they did next, not letting his troopers dwell on what they couldn't explain. 'Right, men,' he had announced, 'that means we have a problem.'

'I can't see that thing coming back, sergeant,' said Myers, 'not minus its leg.'

'Not what I meant, Bullseye. There's something on this planet can bring the dead back to life.'

'Not exactly bring them back,' Donovits had corrected him, 'just reanimate them. Without getting a closer look at Steel Toe's body, I couldn't tell you if it was host to some parasite, or...' He'd tailed off as he had followed Greiss's gaze.

They'd all looked down at Landon's body.

Lorenzo let out a sigh, now, and rolled onto his back, accepting that he was awake for the duration – until he could calm the raging thoughts that filled his head to bursting. He listened to Myers, who was on watch, humming a quiet tune as he cleaned his knife. He stared, almost sightlessly, at the plastic sheeting that Muldoon and Donovits had tied around the leafiest branches of the surrounding trees, collecting condensation for the squad's water bottles. He listened to Braxton's breathing, beside him, and he knew the Validian was awake too.

Rogar III was winning. It was beating them – and the fact that it could only do so by changing the rules was cold comfort to Lorenzo.

He had wanted a challenge. He had wanted to earn his name. But his squad was already two men down, and they hadn't seen a single ork yet. There would be more casualties; of that, he was certain. More chances to prove himself. Or die trying. Not that Lorenzo was afraid of death, but he thought about the rest of his company, by now no doubt engaged in fierce battle. He wondered if they had scratched the surface of Rogar yet, if they'd learned its secrets – or if the planet was concentrating its forces on this one small squad, the twelve men who had dared try to penetrate its dark heart. Ten men, now. He wondered what those fellow Jungle Fighters would think, upon completing their missions, if they found their bravery had all been for nothing – if there was no word from the squad that had been entrusted with the most important assignment.

No, Lorenzo wasn't afraid of death. But he *was* afraid of failure. And of going to an unmarked grave, with no one left to remember his name or to tell of his heroism at the end.

They hadn't been able to cremate Landon. They were too close to the orks now to risk lighting a fire. Myers had expressed the dubious hope that their fallen comrade's broken neck might prevent his resurrection by the force that had animated Dougan. But Donovits had just shaken his head.

Greiss had done the deed himself, in the end. He hadn't let anyone else help; he'd roared at Woods when he'd tried to ignore that order. He had told them to remember Landon as he was in life. Still, Lorenzo couldn't shake the image from his thoughts: Old Hardhead, driving the butt of his lasgun down into the dead rookie's arms and legs, over and over again. Until his body was no more than a fleshy sack for the fragments of his shattered bones. Until no force in the Imperium or beyond could have made Landon's limbs support his weight.

The sound of a shovel striking the earth had seemed to repeat forever. Greiss had reappeared, at last, with his face dirt-streaked and red. He had reported, in a hollow tone, that it was over, that Landon could rest in peace.

Lorenzo drifted into a fitful doze, haunted by nightmares in which he was fighting his own comrades, and the bony hands of Dougan and Landon were grasping at his ankles, trying to pull him down into the earth to join them.

He could hear low voices.

He opened his eyes, catching his breath at a lingering vestige of some dream horror already fading in his memory. The night had swooped in when he hadn't been looking. It was dark, and the huddled shapes around him were stirring, preparing. It was time, already.

He scrambled to his feet, still unsettled by the dream but trying not to show it. He pulled on his jacket and bandolier, checked his pack. Few words were spoken, the Jungle Fighters all concentrating on what lay ahead of them, knowing its import. Mackenzie and Braxton looked especially tired, and Lorenzo realised that each must have slept only half the short rest period. Neither had been placed on the watch rota, but the commissar probably hadn't dared close his eyes without his adjutant to look out for him. He didn't trust anybody else.

Lorenzo hadn't been placed on watch either. A part of him wondered if it was because Greiss didn't trust *him*. Despite his pretence to the contrary. Because of last night. The sergeant's briefing soon quelled that fear, though.

Greiss spoke quietly and didn't say much. Sounds carried further at night. Anyway, the Catachans knew what was expected of them, and Mackenzie and Braxton would just have to follow their lead. He reminded the squad of the importance of stealth: 'One ork or gretchin gets sight or sound of us and lives to tell of it, and we've not only blown our mission, we won't be around to explain to Colonel Graves what the hell we thought we were doing.' Then he made the pronouncement that caused Lorenzo's heart to leap.

'Lorenzo takes point,' said Greiss. 'That's because we might have more to contend with than just greenskins. Remember, people, those blue lights come out at night. I want you to pair up, keep an eye on your opposite number – first sign he shows of going misty-eyed, you give him a slap. Lorenzo, I'm trusting you upfront alone because you've shaken off the effects of the light once. If it comes back, you can resist it, right?'

'Right, sergeant.'

Greiss outlined their proposed route, and Lorenzo felt a swell of pride when he turned to him in particular and asked if he was clear on it. He confirmed that he was, and Greiss drew him to one side, and clapped him on the back. 'I know I don't have to tell you to go slow and careful. Hell, if you're as quiet out there as you are around us half the time, those orks will never hear you coming.'

Then Greiss gave the order to move out, and Lorenzo drew his Catachan fang and slipped into the jungle, quickly but quietly, staying low, in cover.

He used his lasgun to part the vines and creepers in his way, surveying the ground for predators and other hazards. He advanced cautiously, doing his best to leave no trail. The foliage yielded to his soft but firm touch, but closed in again behind him until he felt like he was travelling in his own green cocoon. He knew his comrades were behind him, but all he could hear of them was an occasional rustle that might have been a lizard or a whisper of the night breeze. They were keeping their distance, in case Lorenzo made a misstep, set off an ork trap and blew himself to pieces. He was alone now, to all intents and purposes. In the most dangerous position, but that was all right. He wanted that responsibility.

The danger focused Lorenzo's mind. It sharpened his senses. It blew away the doubts of a few hours earlier, like a strong, fresh wind.

He maintained a good pace for the first hour or so, but slowed when he knew the encampment was near. He saw no evidence of its presence yet, but he fancied he detected a hint of greenskin stink on the air. Something stirred in a bush beside him, and Lorenzo froze, hoping his camouflage would hide him – but it was only a snake. One of those with the silver triangles on their skins.

He crept on – but, a few minutes later, he spotted another triangle-backed snake in the undergrowth, and this one had seen him. Its head reared up. It bared its tiny fangs and hissed, but it made no move to strike Lorenzo. It appeared to be watching him.

He remembered how the birds had stalked the Catachans, how he'd kept spying them out of the corner of his eye before they launched their attack. He remembered Braxton saying that the lizards had done something similar, poking around the edges of the Validian camp for a few days before they'd dared enter it. The silver-backed snake didn't appear to be a threat right now, but as Armstrong had said, that could change in a heartbeat. Particularly if it wasn't alone, and especially if a concerted attack on the Jungle Fighters drew the orks' attention.

Lorenzo took a step forward, fingers twitching on his knife. The snake tensed, watching him. A lasgun would have done the job more efficiently, but with too much noise. Lorenzo stooped down, holding out his free hand as bait. The snake backed away a centimetre, suspiciously. Lorenzo took another step.

The snake struck. From further away than he'd expected. As if its coiled tail had acted as a spring to propel it out of the grass. It jabbed at the proffered hand, and Lorenzo snatched it away and decapitated the snake with his fang before it could land and reorient itself. He stamped on its severed head, exploding it in a mass of black blood. He grabbed the twitching body, wrung it until it was still, and tossed it aside into the dark. A quiet, discordant hiss of alarm told him that his message had been received by multiple unseen onlookers. The jungle grass swayed and rustled in a dozen thin paths away from him.

It was shortly after that that he came across the first trap.

Lorenzo had known it was imminent, because the undergrowth in this area was flattened, plants and branches broken. The orks had been here, and recently.

The trap was crude and obvious, like most of their constructs: a cord stretched between trees at knee height, connected to something hidden in the lower branches of one. A grenade, most likely. Still, a Guardsman in a hurry might not have spotted it. It was more evidence of the warboss's cunning, spreading to his followers.

Lorenzo stepped over the tripwire carefully, and waited. Thirty seconds passed before Muldoon's head peeked out of a bush a few metres behind him. He saw Lorenzo, and an inquisitive expression crossed his face. Lorenzo indicated the wire; Muldoon would probably have seen it anyway, but better safe than sorry. Muldoon nodded, then waited for Lorenzo to regain his lead.

Alone again.

The second tripwire was higher, and better placed. To its right, the jungle was dense with poison creepers – and Lorenzo knew that that way lay the acid swamp of which Sly Marbo had spoken. To the left: a cluster of red snapper flowers, through which he could see no safe route. Again, his inability to use his lasgun narrowed his options. Bad enough to be grabbed by those intractable petals – but the greater peril would be the flowers' alarm wail, certain to attract attention.

He approached the wire, and stooped beside it gingerly. It was too high to step over. He could disarm the trap: cut the wire or retrieve the grenade from the tree. The risk in so doing would be minimal, but actual. If an ork or a gretchin came this way after the Jungle Fighters had passed, it would know they had been here.

No. Far better, far safer, to take no chances. To go under.

Lorenzo lowered himself onto his stomach, noting that the ground was a little soft, a little wet. He removed his pack and his lasgun from his back, to reduce his prone height, and pushed them under the wire before him. Then he dragged himself through the mud on his elbows, keeping his head down.

He had plenty of clearance. So long as nothing unexpected happened, so long as he didn't get careless, he had nothing to worry about.

So long as nothing unexpected happened...

The blue light snapped on like a shipboard lighting panel, just ignited into a glowing ball ahead of him, a few centimetres off the ground. Lorenzo felt his stomach tighten as he craned his neck to look at it without raising his chin. He sensed that it was calling to him, urging him to stand and approach it, and he felt the muscles in his arms and legs tensing to obey.

He stopped himself, before his back could brush the tripwire.

He closed his eyes, and immediately felt better. His head was clearer. Lorenzo listened to his own breathing, and he felt the cold of the mud against his stomach. He thought about Steel Toe Dougan. He knew the blue light was still out there, but he was certain it hadn't entered his mind. He was certain that it couldn't, so long as he didn't look at it.

But what if the blue light wanted that? What if its purpose, this time, was to blind him to something else? To something creeping up on him...

...something rustling in the undergrowth beside his head...

Lorenzo opened his eyes, as breathless and disconcerted as he had been after his nightmare. He looked around quickly, but saw nothing. Nothing but the blue light, drawing his eyes in like it was the only thing in the world. The only thing that mattered, anyway. It occurred to Lorenzo that it was closer than it had been last night, that this time he really could catch it, catch whatever it was that was generating it. End its threat. Save his comrades.

In the blue light, Lorenzo saw Sergeant Greiss's approval, so rarely bestowed. Yet, in his memory, he heard his voice: '*I'm trusting you up front alone… If it comes back, you can resist it, right?*'

Greiss was counting on him.

'*Right?*'

Lorenzo remembered how determined he had been to prove himself worthy of Old Hardhead's trust, not to let him down again. He knew the only way to do that was to obey his orders, to do what he'd promised he would do…

'*Right?*'

'*Right, sergeant.*'

To resist. That was Lorenzo's greatest ambition, what he wanted most at this moment, and so – as a part of him was only dimly aware – that was what the blue light showed to him, and in so doing it defeated itself. Lorenzo blinked, and the light was still there, but suddenly it was just a light, and it had no hold over him.

Still, he stayed where he was for a moment longer, exploring the crannies of his mind, ensuring there was no trace of the blue light left in there. Ensuring that he wasn't being tricked again. He concentrated on what he remembered, what Greiss had told him – and he reassured himself that, as long as he heeded those words, those explicit instructions, he would be doing the right thing.

Lorenzo dug his elbows into the mud and pulled himself forward again, until he was clear of the ork tripwire, then he climbed to his feet and collected his belongings.

The blue light was gone. Blinked out. As if it had sensed it had no power here any more. Somehow, Lorenzo knew it wouldn't be back. Not for him.

He realised something else too: that his hands were stinging.

He looked down, saw that his palms were red and beginning to blister. He had been so wrapped up in his thoughts, in the light, that he hadn't noticed. The wet ground. Acid. It must have seeped from the nearby swamp. The knees of his trousers had almost burnt through, and the soles of his boots had begun to melt. Not much harm done yet, but in time…

Lorenzo cleaned his hands on a leaf, and waited for Muldoon to appear again. This time, once he'd pointed out the tripwire, he beckoned him forward. Greiss came too, holding up a hand to halt the troopers behind him.

'I think we need to bear a little further north,' whispered Lorenzo, displaying his damaged boots.

'That'll take us closer to the orks,' Muldoon pointed out.

But Greiss looked down at his own feet, and scowled. 'Lorenzo's right. No point our finding Big Green if we're all walking on bloody stumps by the time we do.' Then, with grudging admiration, he conceded, 'Mackenzie was right about that greenskin. Building his camp on the edge of the swamp, making the best of the natural defences – he's a clever bastard, all right.'

The encampment was even closer than Lorenzo had estimated.

Almost as soon as he changed his course, he found himself at the edge of a clearing, a little smaller than the Imperial Guard's, crammed with ramshackle buildings of metal and wood.

He lay and watched it for a while, scrutinising each shadow until he was sure of its nature, until he knew it wasn't an enemy waiting in ambush. He studied the ork huts, familiarising himself with their layout, with every blind corner from which an ork or a gretchin could spring out at him as he passed. He saw no sentries – which worried him, because he knew there would be sentries. Somewhere.

At last, Lorenzo glanced behind him, saw his squad waiting, gave them a thumbs-up signal and moved on. He moved on slowly – almost painfully so, knowing that stealth was more imperative now than ever. A single thin line of trees separated him from the orks. He had to make maximum use of the scant cover he had – and he had to be sure he didn't make the slightest sound.

It seemed to take an age for him to reach that first danger point, that first gangway between two huts, to be able to edge forward and peer down it, to reassure himself that it was empty. It seemed to take an age – although he knew it had only been a few minutes. But Lorenzo wasn't impatient. He lived for moments like this.

There was something in the trees ahead of him.

He froze.

It was taller than a man, but hunched, enormous arms hanging down to its knees, its shoulders broad and muscular. It was wearing dulled armour – and, although the darkness made it difficult to pick out colours, the skin that showed through the metal plates had a decidedly green tint.

The ork didn't seem to be trying to hide. Lorenzo wondered, for a heartstopping moment, if it was searching for him, if it had heard something. Any closer, and he feared it might catch his scent.

Then it turned away from him, grunting as it fumbled with its protective metal layers, and he realised it had only come out here to relieve itself. Lorenzo would never find an enemy more exposed, more helpless; he could attack it from behind, wrap a cord around its throat and strangle it. But orks were a sturdy breed, and it would certainly have struggled loudly as it died. Reluctantly, he let it be – and when it had done its business, the ork shuffled away and faded into the shadow of a metal hut.

Lorenzo crept forward again. He stepped over another tripwire, and waited to point it out to Muldoon. Glancing ahead, he saw that he was almost there, almost past the camp. Maybe they'd call him 'Sneaky' Lorenzo. No, he wasn't sure he liked that. 'Shadow' Lorenzo? 'Sly' Lorenzo?

Voices.

They were hushed – but against the muted sounds of the night, they sounded unnatural, harsh and as loud as las-fire discharges.

He thought one of the voices belonged to Greiss. There was an urgent tone to it, almost a plea. Lorenzo looked to the ork camp, certain that the voices must have carried that far, but nothing was stirring. Not yet. He ached to know what was happening, but he knew he ought to maintain his position. He sheathed his knife and fingered his lasgun, ready to draw it if necessary.

The explosion caught him totally unawares.

The night erupted into daylight, too quickly, too shockingly, for Lorenzo to avert his gaze, to protect his night vision. He was half blinded.

But, as the echoes of the explosion died away and his deadened ears popped, he could hear movement and grunting from the encampment just a few footsteps away. And the shadows, the only things he could make out now, were shifting.

Lorenzo's mind raced. Had his comrades blundered into a trap he had missed? Had something else found them? Was it his fault?

There had to have been casualties, he realised, his throat drying at the thought. The explosion had been centred right at the spot where he'd heard Greiss's voice. It had sounded like a frag grenade.

The shadows were converging on that spot now, orks snarling and roaring with battle lust as they rushed to defend their territory.

A wave of despair passed over Lorenzo as he realised it didn't matter now which of his comrades were alive or dead. The orks knew where they were – and as Greiss had said, the orks outnumbered them thirty to one. They had nowhere to run, trapped between the encampment on one side and the acid swamp on the other.

There was no doubt about it. They were all dead.

CHAPTER 11

The orks were an oncoming mass, one indistinguishable from the next, at least to Lorenzo's compromised sight. The air was filled with noise, and the ground shook to the staccato flashes of more explosions: makeshift grenades, hurled over the heads of the orks' front ranks by those in the rear.

In response, las-fire barked out of the jungle, striking the foremost orks and passing through them into their comrades. Lorenzo felt like cheering. At least five, six, seven of his fellow Catachans were alive and fighting back – and the next explosions blossomed in the heart of the orks' own ranks. The Jungle Fighters' frag grenades were more effective than the orks' bombs, because the greenskins were packed so closely together, each of them more likely to take a shrapnel hit. Their armour, and their thick hides, would protect them from the worst of it, but many would be injured, some badly. Some were knocked off their feet by the concussive force of the blasts; as Lorenzo's eyes cleared, he saw orks stumbling over each other, trampling on the fallen, pushing each other aside – and yet still advancing.

They didn't know where he was.

As the orks closed in on Lorenzo's squad, he realised they were passing him by, in his solitary position ahead of the others. The others were dead anyway. He had a chance to save himself, to sneak away, maybe take a report back to Lieutenant Vines so that the next men sent out here would know what lay ahead of them.

He didn't consider it for a second.

Lorenzo broke cover, letting out the loudest, wildest war cry in his repertoire, his finger locked around the trigger of his lasgun so that it fired repeatedly into the enemy mass. He didn't care how accurate his shots were; chances were they'd find a few orks wherever he aimed them. He just wanted to draw attention to himself. Maybe – with luck – convince the greenskins that he was more than one trooper, that their enemies had surrounded them in a pincer movement. The more of them he could distract from his squad, the better their chances would be; the worse his own chances.

He was dead anyway, he told himself. They were all dead. But the longer the Jungle Fighters survived, the more orks they could take down with them. The more orks they took down, the greater the chance there'd be stories told of them back home. Assuming that, by some miracle, this story made it back home at all.

The nearest orks responded with alarm and confusion to Lorenzo's attack, took a moment to pinpoint the source of it, and aimed their weapons: crude, solid-shot guns. They were too slow. Lorenzo had already dived into the sheltered gap between two huts, and he was still running as bullets pinged off metal behind him. He heard grunts and howls and footsteps, and he knew he'd succeeded in drawing the attention of a few dozen orks. Now he just had to survive the consequences of that success.

He ducked and weaved and twisted between huts at random. The longer he could keep his pursuers searching for him, the fewer orks the others had to contend with in the meantime. But he couldn't disappear completely, couldn't flee back into the jungle, because the orks might just abandon their hunt in frustration and return to the combat. Lorenzo let out a whoop and fired his lasgun three times into the air, drawing his foes further into their own camp. He rounded another corner and disturbed a knot of gretchin, who screeched and jabbered in their own crude, incomprehensible tongue, and came at him.

Lorenzo brought up his lasgun, fired, downed several targets – and then the rest were upon him, or streaming around to attack him from behind. They were kicking and scratching, squealing for their masters. He swung his lasgun like a club, dislodging two of them. He kicked and punched at the others; he reached over his shoulder, seized a gretchin that had clung to his back, and slammed it into the ground. He tried to run, kicking more of the creatures out of his path, but they dogged his heels. He spun around, fired, claimed two more kills, and the rest of the gretchin scampered out of sight. They emerged again as soon as Lorenzo had turned his back.

Their cries drew the orks, as he had known they must.

The first of them appeared ahead, and barred Lorenzo's path. It snarled at him, as if to intimidate him with its presence. That worked, he had heard, against some men; the ork, with its sloping brow, its jutting jaw and its recessed, baleful eyes, cut an imposing figure – and his eye line was level with its fearsome tusks and its slobbering lips. To a man who had faced down a Catachan Devil, though, a single ork was nothing special. It might walk and talk, but to a Deathworlder this green-skinned monster was just another thing to be killed.

Lorenzo snapped off a round, the shot narrowly missing the ork though the flash sent it howling and reeling in pain – but he'd pay for the second's distraction it had caused him. The ork's comrades had found him too, and they came at him, rounding the ramshackle buildings from all directions. More than one of them mimicked the Catachan's earlier actions, kicking aside the gretchin that had summoned them. The pathetic, stunted creatures slunk away, their job done.

Surrounded and outnumbered, Lorenzo concentrated his fire in one direction, hoping to clear an escape route for himself. His one advantage was that the greenskins couldn't use their guns without hitting each other – though, given the speed at which they were coming, that wouldn't keep him alive for long. He finished off two of them, but the lasgun's power pack whined and died as the third bore down on him. He tried to impale the ork on his bayonet, but it wrestled his gun away and tossed it aside. Another ork smacked into Lorenzo from behind, and he rolled with the blow, drawing his knife as he hit the ground and twisted out of the way of a descending axe blade. It sliced into the earth a whisker from Lorenzo's ear. Its wielder wasn't far behind it, choosing not to retrieve its weapon but to leap instead on its fallen prey and rend him with its bare hands. Lorenzo threw up his knife so the ork's own momentum forced the blade through the roof of its mouth and into its brain.

Its dead weight smacked onto him, winding him, pinning him down, but providing him with cover and a moment's respite. By the time two other orks had hoisted their dead comrade aside, Lorenzo was ready to act. On hands and knees, he slipped between the legs of one of his attackers, and tripped it in the process. The orks fumbled and stumbled and generally fell over each other in their eagerness to apprehend the slippery, squirming Catachan – but any green hands that found him were rewarded with a slash of Lorenzo's fang.

Then, joyously, he was through them all, open space looming ahead of him, and he was pushing himself to his feet, snatching his stolen lasgun, reaching for a fresh power pack from his bandolier and a meaty hand grabbed him by the back of his jacket and pulled him back, twisted him around, slammed him into the metal wall of a hut, and while he was still trying to get his breath back from that, a giant ork fist pounded into his stomach and Lorenzo coughed up blood and felt his legs giving way.

He managed to block another axe thrust with his lasgun – the last time it would save him. The blade embedded itself in the gun's furniture, and came free with a cracking and a splintering and a last sullen fizz of energy. Lorenzo found an ork snout with his bayonet, drawing blood and making the creature squeal and fall back, but then he let the gun go and it was just him and his Catachan fang, and he knew that at best he'd be able to kill one more ork before they killed him.

He focused on doing just that. He picked his target, pushed himself away from the wall behind him, ducked beneath a pair of flailing green arms. He locked himself into a deadly embrace with the luckless ork, denying it the chance to swing its axe or raise its gun. He buried his knife in its stomach, twisted it, cutting through the ork's guts, feeling its blood spilling out, soaking into his own clothes; at the same time, its fingers closed around his neck, cutting off his oxygen, fading his surroundings to black. A deadly dance from which neither partner would ever break.

Lorenzo wasn't sure at first if the pops and cracks he could hear as if from the end of a long tunnel were those of his own bones breaking – but the orks were reeling in confusion again, and the grip on his throat was loosened, and he thought he could see a lithe, dark-haired figure hurling grenades from the roof of a nearby hut, although he might have imagined it.

He raised his fang to make the most of his reprieve, thinking he might claim another ork life, but the world was still darkening and the commands from his brain didn't seem to be reaching his muscles... and now Lorenzo was sliding to the ground, falling in slow-motion but still too fast to put out a hand to save himself. He was lying facedown, and his back was showered first with hot shrapnel and then an ork body landed on top of him, hiding him, and he just lay there, clinging to consciousness, his face sticky with blood but he didn't know whose.

A long time after that, it seemed, Lorenzo heard the orks moving away from him. They were turning their attention to a new enemy, leaving him for dead, and he couldn't have said for certain that they were so wrong. It was only after a long minute had passed and he was still breathing, his heart still beating and his head clearing as his lungs heaved precious oxygen into his bloodstream, that he knew he would fight on. Only then that Lorenzo breathed a grateful prayer to the God-Emperor for sparing his life, until he recovered his wits and realised he ought to thank Sly Marbo instead.

He didn't know why Marbo had chosen to save him, above the others. Maybe he'd just been lucky – in the right place at the right time. Knowing Marbo, it was possible he'd been on that roof all night, waiting for his moment. Whatever the reason, Lorenzo was determined to return the favour, or to pass it on.

Marbo, he decided, had the right idea. Find high ground.

He pulled himself up onto the roof of the nearest hut, finding plenty of handholds in the old, pitted metal but almost falling as his muscles protested at being put to so much effort so soon. He'd half-expected to find Marbo up there, but he had moved on, of course. Lorenzo lowered himself onto his stomach, and craned his neck to see over the edge of the building without being seen in return.

Much of the fighting had now moved out of the encampment. The Catachans had drawn their more numerous foes into the jungle environment they knew best, though with the acid swamp at their backs they had precious little room to manoeuvre. From here, Lorenzo couldn't see any of his camouflaged comrades – but he guessed, by the positions of the orks, that they'd separated along the perimeter line, making themselves harder to find. The orks, in turn, seemed to be everywhere, shaking trees, firing into bushes, doing everything they could to beat their foes out of hiding.

There were more of them, of course, among the buildings, searching for the long-gone Marbo, liable to find Lorenzo instead.

His eyes alighted upon one building in particular: a small metal structure, built with a little more care than most, no windows cut into its walls, its door secured by thick chains. Ammo store, he guessed. He strained to reach his backpack, unfastened it, and rummaged out the two demolition charges with which he'd been equipped. They weren't really for combat use – the Catachans employed them to clear hard-going areas of the jungle when they were in a hurry and stealth wasn't such an issue – but they were just what he needed now.

The first charge landed with a plop beside the chained door, when no orks were looking that way. Lorenzo set the second to detonate only two seconds after, and he felt his palm sweating as he held the cold sphere in his hand, counting down.

He let the second charge go even as the first explosion shook the buildings around him. By the time its vibrations overtook him, he was running, but they made him mistime his leap to the next hut across. Lorenzo pedalled empty air, desperate to propel himself that vital centimetre further, and somehow he caught the protruding edge of the roof as it passed him, and almost yanked his fingers out of their sockets as they caught his falling weight.

There were two orks below him, and they turned their guns upwards. Before they could squeeze their triggers, they were knocked off their feet – and Lorenzo felt it simultaneously: a furious shockwave of heat and sound, like a hurricane raging around him, in which it was all he could do to grit his teeth and maintain his hold on the parapet while his back was peppered with debris.

The hurricane lessened, and he strained and pulled himself up, attaining his new perch at last. He rolled onto his back, breathless, but raised himself on his elbows because he couldn't resist the chance to inspect his handiwork.

It looked like the sky was on fire. The building he had just leapt from had collapsed, along with several others, and Lorenzo could see the burning, smoking hole where the ammo store had been. Evidently, he'd guessed right about its contents. His first charge had blown off the door; the second must have bounced neatly through the resulting aperture. Its detonation had sparked a chain reaction, just as he had planned. The sturdy walls had absorbed much of it before they had given, else he would have been dead. To his satisfaction, several orks – presumably reacting to the first explosion, too late to stop the second – *had* perished, their burnt corpses twitching and steaming in the midst of the devastation.

Dozens more orks were turning from the jungle, streaming back into the camp, looking for the enemy that had penetrated their home. Lorenzo couldn't have hoped for a bigger distraction – and it had certainly been well timed for at least one Jungle Fighter. He saw a blur of activity, heard the howls of stricken orks, and then Muldoon came streaking out of the foliage, his lasgun firing. From this distance, Lorenzo couldn't see what had happened, but he could guess. One of Muldoon's favourite tricks: he would gather up a cluster of deadly creepers, secrete himself in a tree and, when the enemy got too close, let the creepers go. Lorenzo could see orks dancing and twisting as they fought to disentangle themselves, as the creepers stung them and burst their poisonous pustules in their grotesque faces.

But he was exposed now, left with nowhere to run but out into the open where his painted skin couldn't camouflage him. Like Lorenzo before him, he raced for the shelter of the ork huts, miraculously untouched by a hail of bullets – but one great brute of an ork had avoided his trap, and it came charging after him, and cannoned into him from behind.

Lorenzo was on his way before Muldoon hit the ground. He leapt onto the sloping roof of the next hut, almost lost his footing on its slick surface, righted himself and jumped again. His fingers hovered over his bandolier, over the pockets that held his frag grenades – but unless more orks moved in, unless they formed a living shield between Lorenzo and Muldoon as they had between him and Marbo, a grenade could do more harm than good. His lasgun was gone. That left him with his knife.

He launched himself from the last roof, at the ork's broad back, and he let out a cry – enough for it to hear him coming and half-turn its head, not soon enough for it to bring around its gun and pick him off in midair. Enough for it to take its eyes off Muldoon for a moment. The ork jerked backwards, easing its weight off its fallen prey, as Lorenzo's fang sliced down between its shoulder blades – and in that same moment, Muldoon drove his night reaper up into the ork's throat.

The ork took a long, long second to die – but at last it toppled like a felled tree, and Lorenzo fancied he could feel the ground shaking with the impact of its heavy corpse. Or with something else...

Something was coming. Something big. Lorenzo didn't have to look, didn't have to waste the half-second it would take him, to know it was bad, that they had to take cover. But Muldoon was slowed, having trouble standing, and Lorenzo saw that his head was cut, his eyes glazed over. Concussion.

He reached out a hand, and Muldoon laughed giddily as he took it, as Lorenzo hauled him to his feet. 'Looks like... like I owe you my life,' he giggled. Then, suddenly earnest, he gripped Lorenzo by the arms and stared into his eyes as if he had the most important information in the Imperium to impart. 'Hey, Lorenzo, you noticed? There isn't... isn't half as many of the greenskins as Greiss said there'd be. Thirty... thirty to one, my eye! More like ten to one. And we can take down ten orks apiece, right? Hell, I must've killed five already.'

That noise was getting closer... The rumbling of an engine. Lorenzo looked now, and he saw it – saw its piercing light first, through the drifting smoke of the battlefield, and then the shape of the behemoth behind it.

It was black, daubed with crude paintings of human skulls and bones – ramshackle in appearance, but bristling with armour plating and weapons. Lorenzo had seen vehicles like this before. It was the ork equivalent of a tank – a battlewagon, they called it – manned by a greenskin mob. They howled and strained forward on the back of this unnatural beast as they saw their two exposed foes. The pilot trained the vehicle's searchlight upon the Catachans, and wrestled its great wheels around.

Muldoon's mood had changed again, and suddenly he looked distant and extremely pale, apart from the livid red gash across his head. 'Trouble is,' he said to himself in a hollow voice, 'they got Brains. I saw him go down. So, we have to take out a few more orks each to make up his share.'

Lorenzo couldn't allow himself to react to this news. There would be time for mourning the dead later, when the act of so doing wouldn't add to their numbers.

The battlewagon had two guns, like eyes on stalks protruding before it. The one on the right flared, and Lorenzo pushed Muldoon aside as a shell whistled by and thumped into the dirt, and filled the world with light and sound again. His comrade sagged in his arms like a dead weight, and Lorenzo slapped him across the face, hoping to shock him back to alertness.

More gunfire – the right-hand gun again – but the searchlight had lost its targets and the smoke from the first impact was swirling around them and ork weapons, mostly lashed together from spare parts, were notoriously unreliable anyway. Still, the impact almost knocked Lorenzo off his feet.

Muldoon blinked as blood seeped into his eye, and coughed as smoke crept into his throat. Lorenzo tried to drag him toward the huts, but there came another explosion from that direction and they were thrown back, back into the open, and the searchlight had rediscovered them and there were more orks coming, silhouettes through the haze, from the encampment, from the jungle.

Muldoon was pressing his lasgun into Lorenzo's hands, saying, 'Here – you can make better use of this than I can.'

'What... what are you–?'

He wouldn't have had to finish the question, even had the smoke not robbed him of speech. He could see the answer. Muldoon was rummaging in his bandolier, finding a demolition charge with each hand – and although Lorenzo's first instinct was to stop him, to save him, he held himself back because his comrade was grinning at him now. 'You saved my life. That makes it my turn. And besides, I count nine greenskins on that tank. Add them to the other five, and that's my share and a few for Brains to boot.' Looking into his comrade's ashen face, Lorenzo saw the pain he was holding at arm's length, the darkness lurking at the edges of his eyes, and he knew then as Muldoon surely did that this was how it had to be.

Then he was gone, tearing himself from Lorenzo's grip before he could think of a word to say. He was racing into the light – and before the orks knew what was happening, he was too close for them to train their gun upon him, but not too close for them to bring their other weapon – the one on the left – to bear...

It was a flamethrower. That explained what this single wagon was doing out here, thought Lorenzo, why the orks had assembled it in the depths of a jungle that would only impede it: they'd been using it for clearance operations. A fierce jet of flame licked around Muldoon now, and although he seemed to avoid the worst of it, and though Lorenzo's vision was obscured by smoke and by the battlewagon's glaring light, he was certain that Muldoon had been winged, that he'd been burnt, and yet like the relentless orks themselves he kept going.

He vaulted over the guns onto the front of the tank, planting his feet and his fists into the faces of the orks at the triggers. Those behind saw the threat to them and, snarling, drew their own guns, and one of them leapt at him but he turned its momentum and its weight against it, and threw it over his shoulder and off the moving vehicle. The others fired, and Muldoon's body twitched and jerked as their bullets ripped into him, and Lorenzo feared that he too would fall and die in a splatter of mud and blood, but he was *climbing* – climbing onto the back of the battlewagon as if animated by willpower alone, and he fell into the midst of the ork mob and they leapt upon him and tore him apart, but by then his final goal had been achieved.

The charges blew the battlewagon apart from the inside, and eight orks died screaming.

By that time, Lorenzo had replaced the depleted pack in the lasgun his comrade had given him, and he was firing at the shapes that loomed about him, making sure he kept moving, an impossible target amid the sensory chaos. He felt a grim sense of triumph as he claimed his tenth kill of the night, and he thought of Sharkbait Muldoon and knew he would have been proud.

But he also knew he was surrounded, and the orks were homing in on him now, closing him down. They came at Lorenzo from all sides, moving in to close combat as usual, trusting in their greater strength and numbers against his greater dexterity. This time, he knew, he had no right to expect a reprieve, no Marbo to save him. He had used up all his luck. So he dropped his gun and hurled the last of his grenades, and he thought about how bravely Muldoon had died – and Donovits too, he didn't doubt – and he drew his Catachan fang.

And finally, Lorenzo ran to greet his enemies, with his trusty knife in his hand and a defiant roar in his throat.

CHAPTER 12

The fighting seemed to have gone on forever.

Lorenzo remembered the first tint of sunlight touching the sky, remembered how amazed he'd been that only one night had passed because it seemed so long since he'd thought of anything but blood and smoke and fire. Yet when he looked back on that time, much of it was no more than a blur of sneering ork faces and knife thrusts and death. Lots of death. He thought that, at one point, he'd stood back to back with Sergeant Greiss, but he couldn't be sure. Once they'd moved into hand-to-hand combat, he'd had no choice but to surrender himself to his instincts. Otherwise he'd have thought about the tiredness in his muscles and the aches from his bruises and the still-overwhelming odds against him, and he would have lain down and died. Or, worse still, he'd have thought about dying.

He *could* have died, and he'd probably have known nothing about it. Just wound down like a spring, from a wound he hadn't yet felt, and that wouldn't have been so bad, would it?

Lorenzo was fighting in his sleep, muscle memory twitching his arms in response to an imaginary parade of blood-crazed enemies. Somewhere in the back of his mind, he thought he must have wondered if he would ever wake up, or if he would fight this nightmare struggle forever.

Yes, it had been a glorious battle.

And it was made all the more so by the fact that, in the end, Lorenzo felt sunlight touching his face, and he opened his eyes and knew that he had *lived*.

It took him a moment to work out where he was. The light was bright, but his surroundings seemed dim. He realised that the light was streaming through a small window, to be swallowed by the dust and the dirt in here.

An ork hut. Lorenzo was lying on a makeshift bunk, really no more than a pile of junk draped with rags, and he was swaddled in stinking furs. He was hot, burning up. It crossed his mind only briefly that the orks themselves might have brought him here, as a hostage. That wasn't their style. The fact that he *was* here meant his small squad had achieved the impossible. They had won. But at what price?

Lorenzo felt a stiffness in his side, and sent a tentative hand under his bulky coverings to investigate. His questing fingers found a hard knot of synth-skin, between the ribs in his right side, and he winced at the sudden white hot memory of an axe blade scything through his flesh. His memories were disordered, still vague, but that pain, he felt sure, was among the most recent of them. He sighed regretfully. He would have liked to be found standing, at the end.

'Hey, Lorenzo? You moving under all that lot?'

The familiar voice drew Lorenzo's gaze to his left, to the next bunk, where lay Woods. He must have been injured too, though Lorenzo wouldn't have known it from the cocky grin on his face. ''Bout time too,' said Woods. 'Been lying here awake on my own the past couple of hours, while you've been snoring away. What's the point in winning the biggest damn scrap this squad's ever seen if you can't jaw about it with your buddies afterwards, huh?'

'We... did win, then?'

Woods raised an eyebrow. 'I'll put that down to your being flak happy. Of course we won, Lorenzo!'

'What I mean is... I heard about Brains.'

Woods pouted. 'Yeah. We lost Brains. And they're starting to give up on Sharkbait, too. Been looking for him all morning.'

Lorenzo's mind's eye flashed up a picture of Muldoon racing into the light of the ork battlewagon, and he felt a pang in his stomach. 'They won't find him,' he said numbly. Woods fixed him with an inquisitive, almost needy gaze, and Lorenzo realised that it was up to him to tell Sharkbait Muldoon's last story, to keep it alive. He had that honour, and that responsibility. So he took a deep breath, closed his eyes for a moment as he picked his words, and he told it.

He emphasised how brave Muldoon had been. He mentioned the gash in his head, because it made him seem all the more heroic for having overcome such an injury – and he exaggerated the number of orks on the wagon, that he had killed, because after all it had been dark and there'd been so much smoke and there *could* have been fourteen or fifteen of them, and Lorenzo didn't want to sell his comrade short. Woods listened to the story with growing admiration, and when it was done he breathed in through his teeth and agreed that Sharkbait had died well. Lorenzo felt an odd sort of pride at having been there, at having seen something so inspiring, but most of all at knowing he'd done justice to his fallen comrade's memory, and somehow everything seemed a little brighter then.

'A couple of the others saw how Brains went,' Woods related in return. 'There were a few of them together, and the orks were searching the jungle, and they hadn't had time to find a proper hiding place what with everything going to hell so fast. They say Brains let the greenskins find him, because a couple more steps and they would've stumbled right onto Wildman and maybe Bullseye. He gave his own life to buy the rest of us time. Course, he came out firing. I have to confess, sometimes I didn't have much time for old Brains, thought he yapped too much when he should've been getting on with it – but the way the others tell it, he would've done Marbo proud last night. Took on ten, twelve orks by his lonesome, and stayed standing long enough for the others to retrench, to start fighting back.'

'What happened?' asked Lorenzo. 'What started it, I mean? We were almost there, almost past the encampment, and then...'

'Oh yeah,' said Woods, screwing his face up into a scowl, 'I almost forgot you were up front, missed it all. I bet you can guess, though. I bet you can guess who was brainless enough to step on an ork trap, blow himself right up.'

'Mackenzie?' Lorenzo hazarded. The disdain in Woods's voice and expression had been something of a giveaway.

'Mackenzie,' he confirmed. 'The commissar.'

'I wouldn't have thought even he–'

'It was the blue light. Came up on us all unexpected like. I felt it in my head for a bit – just a second – like it was scanning me, reading my mind, then it moved on. Mackenzie... I figure what happened was, the light picked on the weakest of us. Mackenzie got up, started walking towards it like he was in a trance or something. The sergeant tried to stop him – brought up his lasgun, told Mackenzie he'd shoot him dead if he took another step, though I don't know why he cared; can't say I'd have shed a tear if Mackenzie had gone on, if he'd sunk into the swamp and never come out again. But Old Hardhead seemed to be getting through to him. Mackenzie just froze, and he was looking at Old Hardhead, and at the blue light, all confused – and it was Bullseye, I think, who saw the wire.

'Mackenzie was standing with one foot in front of it, one foot behind. God-Emperor knows how he hadn't tripped it already. Old Hardhead, he motioned to the rest of us to get back, and he kept talking to the commissar, all quiet and calm. Mackenzie, he was listening, he could see the sergeant was making sense, but he still wanted to go to that light, you could tell. He kept asking why he should trust any of us. He talked about what happened at the river, and he accused the sergeant of wanting him dead. I knew we were in trouble right then, knew he'd bring the orks down on us eventually even if he didn't trip that wire. Old Hardhead was whispering, trying to hush the commissar, but he was getting hysterical.'

'That's what the light does to you,' said Lorenzo sombrely. 'It plays on your hopes, your fears. And Mackenzie was already so afraid...' He fell silent as he realised what he'd said. He'd admitted to a weakness, in front of Woods of all people – a soldier who, if he'd ever feared anything, would certainly not have confessed to it.

It didn't seem to matter. 'Makes sense,' said Woods. 'I think, deep down, Mackenzie maybe *wanted* to believe – he wanted to be convinced – but that light was just too damn strong for him.'

'What about Braxton?'

'Give him his due,' Woods conceded, 'he tried. He crawled forward, put himself in the danger zone, just so he could talk to Mackenzie, back up what Old Hardhead was saying. But as soon as he opened his mouth, Mackenzie, he just... it was like he freaked out good and proper. He accused Braxton of betraying him, said he was alone now and he wasn't going to listen to anyone any more. He closed his eyes, put his hands over his ears, like he was in pain, and he was screaming for everyone to stop talking, to leave him alone, to let him think.

'Well, it was all over then, of course. Braxton started forward – I don't know why, like maybe he thought he could drag Mackenzie to safety or something – but the commissar had made up his mind.'

'Or rather,' Lorenzo murmured, 'the light had made it up for him.'

'And the rest, like Commissar Mackenzie, is history.'

'And Braxton?'

'Oh, he's all right. Old Hardhead grabbed hold of him, pulled him back, damn near got himself killed in the process. Now, that – that *would've* been a tragedy!'

'I shouldn't have stopped him,' said Lorenzo. 'Sharkbait. At the river. He would've killed Mackenzie, but I thought... I don't know what I thought. If I'd kept quiet, if I'd let him... Sharkbait would still be alive. And Brains.'

'Doesn't work like that,' said Woods, with more understanding than Lorenzo would have expected from him. 'No one made Sharkbait do anything he didn't want to do. You made him think, is all. He let Mackenzie off the hook for the same reason any of us would've done it: because when the commissar's harness went and he grabbed for that rope and he held on, he surprised us all. You were right, Lorenzo. You can't deny a man a second chance after proving himself like that.'

'Even so...'

'If the light hadn't got Mackenzie,' said Woods, 'it would've worked its influence on someone else. Braxton, maybe. Or... or... I told you, Lorenzo, I felt it in my head. I felt it calling to me – and in that second, I think I would've done just about anything it told me to do.'

That sealed it. This wasn't the Woods that Lorenzo knew. He turned to his comrade with a new anxiety prickling at him, and he said, 'You never told me about yourself. How you ended up... I mean, how you went on. Last night.'

'Hey, don't worry about me,' said Woods cheerfully. 'I did okay. Really. Just tired myself out, is all – and you know Greiss: he likes to think he's looking after us. He said if I didn't come in here for a lie-down, he'd knock me out himself.'

'Right,' said Lorenzo, not quite buying it. He was just starting to realise how pale his comrade seemed where the daylight fell across him. Sweat beaded his brow, as if he was feverish – or perhaps he too was just hot in his ork furs.

'Seriously,' said Woods, 'you think this looks bad, you should see the ork that did it to me. I should say, the twenty orks!' And he launched into a detailed and bloody account of every punch he had thrown, every shot he had fired, every thrust of his devil claw against the ork hordes.

Lorenzo stopped listening after a time. He tuned out the words, and strained to catch the distant, muffled sounds beyond the hut's walls: footsteps, scraping, the odd snatch of conversation. He felt as if he had been lying in this bed for an age, and he longed to feel fresh air on his face, to catch up with the comrades he had thought he would never see again. To see what fresh challenges had arisen in his absence.

He knew he should wait. He didn't know the extent of his injuries. He didn't *feel* too badly hurt, but then his head was muzzy and he could have been in shock. He could have been infected. But normally, the person to tell him that – the man who ought to have been at his bedside with his revolting herbal cures – was Brains. Lorenzo couldn't bear to wait any longer.

Woods had fallen silent. Lorenzo realised he was asleep.

He peeled off his bed coverings and tested each of his limbs, trying his weight on them, before he levered himself to his feet. He swayed a little, and felt sickness rising in his throat but suppressed it. Morning air breezed in through the window, and prickled his skin like pins and needles. He crept over to Woods and put his hand to his forehead, finding it hot like a simmering pan. He located his clothes and backpack in a pile in the corner, with Muldoon's lasgun laid out almost reverently across them.

His jacket felt heavy and grimy against his skin, its insides caked with his own dried blood. It was only when he saw his water bottle that he realised how dry his throat was, and how cracked his lips. He gulped from the bottle greedily, and had to stop himself before he emptied it. There had to be fresh water somewhere in the camp, he reasoned. The skin around his patched-up wound had evidently been cleaned. He longed for a pool to bathe in, though a bit of dirt didn't usually bother him.

Finally, Lorenzo approached the door to the outside world – and thought it was locked at first, as it jammed in its frame. He put his shoulder to it, and tried to pretend that the effort hadn't made stars explode in front of his eyes. He stumbled out into the sunlight, unsteady and blinking, and walked straight into Sergeant Greiss.

Somewhere, there was a fire burning, and Lorenzo caught a glimpse of Myers and Storm lugging an ork corpse between them.

Then Greiss was guiding him back into the hut, telling him to take it easy in his gentlest growl, and Lorenzo tried to throw off his hold, tried to prove he could stand unassisted, but before he knew it he was sitting on the bunk again, just grateful that the room wasn't spinning any more. Greiss took Lorenzo's head in his callused hands, peered into his eyes, and nodded, satisfied. 'You'll live.'

'We did okay – right, sergeant?'

'Yes, Lorenzo. We did okay. We did more than okay. We've been tossing ork bodies on the flames all morning.' Lorenzo didn't question that statement. He knew the Catachans didn't burn their enemies' corpses for the sake of their souls. Orks were renowned for their regenerative properties; it was common for one thought dead to rise from a cold battlefield in search of revenge. On Rogar III, he realised, there was even more reason to take precautions.

'Sergeant!' Lorenzo's fellow patient was awake again. Lorenzo found himself wondering if Woods's voice had sounded so weak, so subdued, the last time he had spoken. Perhaps it had, and he just hadn't noticed. 'Lorenzo tell you about Sharkbait?' asked Woods. Greiss replied that he hadn't, and Woods repeated the story as the sergeant listened patiently. This time, there were twenty orks on the battlewagon, and Muldoon had to hack his way through four more to reach it, but Lorenzo didn't bother to correct the details. Woods's version made a better story, and Muldoon deserved his glory.

'We ready to move out yet, sergeant?' asked Woods, when the story was told.

'Not yet, Hotshot,' said Sergeant Greiss. 'Still cleaning up behind ourselves. We've taken apart all the comms we can find, but you can bet a few gretchin would've made a run for it when they realised they were beaten.'

Woods grimaced. 'Sooner or later, they'll find more greenskins, and then the whole planet will know we're here.'

'If we're lucky,' said Greiss, 'the orks won't put two and two together in a hurry. For all they know, this camp could've been our target all along.'

'Yeah, 'specially when they hear about the attacks on their other camps.'

'But they'll know we're closing in on their warboss – whether they believe we know it or not – and if Big Green has half the brains Mackenzie reckoned he had, he'll be doubling his personal guard about now. Our dear, departed commissar just made getting to our target about ten times harder than it ever was.'

'I thought as much,' said Woods. 'But, we just came through against thirty-to-one odds. Shouldn't think there's a whole lot can stop us now, yeah?'

'Funny thing about that,' Greiss growled. 'There aren't half as many dead orks about these parts as there ought to be. I think we got lucky, Hotshot. I think our job was half-done before we got here.'

'You think Rogar's been as hard on them as it's been on us?'

'About the size of it, yes.'

'Now you're wondering what happened to the orks it killed. And how long it took the survivors to work out that any bodies they leave intact...'

Lorenzo didn't remember lying down, but he was staring at the ceiling. He didn't remember discarding his backpack and jacket, but he was unencumbered by them. He had been thinking about Dougan, or rather about the mockery this deathworld had made of his memory. About the skeletal birds that had refused to lie down. And now, about a hundred, two hundred, dead orks, in varying stages of decay, clambering from the ground all over the planet...

'Should make for an interesting few days,' murmured Greiss.

'Nothing we can't handle though,' said Woods, 'right, sergeant?'

Lorenzo drifted into a dreamless sleep, then, and opened his eyes only once in the next few hours to find himself on the cot again, and Greiss in the doorway of the hut. He must have been leaving, waking Lorenzo as he shouldered the sticking door out of its frame. But something had stopped him. He was looking at Woods, and with the sunlight behind him casting his face into shadow, Greiss seemed weighed down by every one of his thirty-five years, older and more tired than Lorenzo had seen him before.

When next he woke, Greiss was there again, standing over him, shaking him, and from the quality of the light through the window he guessed it was early afternoon. 'Time you dragged yourself out of that pit, trooper,' he said. 'We got a lot of ground to make up if we still want a chance of catching the warboss by surprise. You up to it?'

'Yes, sergeant,' said Lorenzo, getting to his feet, relieved when his body didn't make a liar of him. He still felt weak, drained, and his side hurt like hell, but his senses were clearer now. Catachan men healed quickly. He donned his jacket and his backpack again, picked up the lasgun that he supposed was now his, and made for the door. He stopped when he realised Greiss wasn't following. He was sitting on the bunk Lorenzo had vacated, staring into space, a lasgun laid across his lap. Not his own gun: that was slung under his pack as normal. Lorenzo felt a knot forming in his stomach as he was finally forced to face an unpleasant truth.

'What about Hotshot, sergeant? Aren't you going to wake him?'

'In a minute,' the sergeant said.

Lorenzo looked at Woods. His skin was whiter than ever, drenched in perspiration. His breathing was ragged, and his face twitched with emotions that Lorenzo had never seen writ there before. Every few seconds he let out a low moan, almost a whimper. He seemed to be having the mother of all nightmares. The young trooper looked surprisingly, awfully small.

'Is he...?' Lorenzo ventured.

'Hotshot managed to find a sniping position,' said Greiss, 'up a tree. He was cutting down those greenskins like dummies on a shooting range. But one of 'em got lucky – happened to be looking the right way when an explosion went off and the light glinted off Hotshot's lasgun. He couldn't get down in time. The orks surrounded him, started firing up into the branches. Hotshot took a bullet in the leg, was grazed by two more, but nothing critical; he knew how to make himself small, use his backpack and the tree trunk to protect himself – and with his camouflage and all, the greenskins didn't know where they were aiming. Hotshot was firing at 'em, dropping grenades on their heads – he must've taken out a dozen or more. But you know what orks are like. They don't give up easy. They were swarming up that tree, and Hotshot was shooting and slashing down at 'em, but even he couldn't stay put forever. He made a jump for it, sailed right over their heads.' There had been a touch of admiration in Old Hardhead's voice, but now it faded, and his shoulders slumped. Lorenzo knew how fond he had always been of Woods.

'He didn't make it.'

'If it hadn't been for that damn slug in his leg...' Greiss was silent for a moment, then with pride in his voice, he continued, 'He kept fighting. Even though he'd shattered his spine, he was on the ground, and the orks were piling onto him... I should've got there sooner.'

'No, sergeant!' Lorenzo protested automatically.

'Don't give me that,' Greiss growled. 'If any of us had to end his days a cripple, better it be an old warhorse with no fight left in him. Better it be someone who's had his day, whose story's been told.'

Lorenzo was still digesting the full import of what Greiss was saying. '...end his days a cripple...' They were on a stealth mission, without backup, unable to vox for an airlift – and even if they could get Woods back to an Imperium facility, it would certainly have been the last thing he wanted. It was unlikely a medic could do much for him. The only person who could save him now from a fate worse than death was Greiss. Lorenzo's gaze strayed to the spare lasgun on the sergeant's knee.

'He'll be remembered,' was all he could think of to say. It seemed to cheer Greiss up a little.

Then there was an awkward silence as Lorenzo realised there was nothing more he could say, and eventually turned to the door again.

The last thing he saw as he left that hut, as he left another comrade behind forever, was Greiss leaning over Woods, shaking him gently awake, telling him it was time and pressing the lasgun into his hands. And Woods's smile – not afraid, but relieved. Grateful, even.

Just one of those things. Lorenzo had learned to accept it. He walked away from the hut, and ignored the part of him that wanted to break into a run, to get away from there before he had to hear...

He thought about his promise: '*He'll be remembered.*' He walked, and waited. And thought about his comrade, relating his last story, and he wished he'd known, wished he'd been more attentive. He thought about the dangers that still lay ahead, all his depleted squad still had to do, and he told himself they'd come through somehow.

Lorenzo pretended not to hear the dark voice in the back of his head. The voice that said: *Yes, Hotshot Woods will be remembered. Sharkbait Muldoon will be remembered. They will all be remembered.*

But for how long?

CHAPTER 13

The rain came early in the evening.

The Jungle Fighters had seen the clouds, felt the cool, fresh breeze that presaged the outburst – but the speed and ferocity with which it broke defied their expectations.

The rain was acidic. Guardsman Braxton winced as the first drop splashed off his cheek, and Lorenzo threw a hand to his neck as the skin there began to smart. The acid, fortunately, wasn't strong, not like that from the spitter plants – but with prolonged exposure, it could do as much damage.

They found some shelter beneath the spreading branches of a huge tree. Lorenzo listened as the rain beat down on its roof of leaves, and he looked gloomily at the cascade of redirected liquid like a waterfall around him. He wondered how long it would be before the leaves were burnt through, and he couldn't help but feel that even this downpour was deliberate. It was as if the planet was so determined to destroy them that it would sacrifice a part of itself.

They debated the wisdom of turning back, of scavenging sheets of metal from the ork camp, but Greiss in particular was reluctant to lose ground. 'Aside from which,' he growled, casting a wary glance back over his shoulder, 'we don't know what might be behind us.' They all knew what he meant. Ever since they had set off, they had all been aware of ghosts dogging their footsteps again.

It had been inevitable, of course. Still, Lorenzo had hoped for at least some respite. He wasn't the only one of the six remaining men in his squad – half their original complement – to have been injured in the previous night's battle, nor to feel profoundly tired. Armstrong's left arm was useless, the nerve tendons in his shoulder severed by an ork axe, and Braxton hadn't said a word all afternoon and looked like he could drop at any moment. Their lasguns were low on energy, too; Myers wore a belt of strung-together power packs, letting the dwindling sunlight do what it could to recharge them until they could build a fire to do the job properly. But the nature of their mission – and Greiss, now firmly back in command – had required they press on, and not one of those six men was prepared to admit defeat.

Their map had been incinerated along with Mackenzie, but Armstrong knew where they were and was sure he could remember the location of the warboss's lair from the briefing. He could get them close, at least.

They broke out the alkaline powders from their backpacks, rubbed them into their exposed skin and hair. As they worked, the ghosts began to gather, in the corners of their vision. This time, they had attracted more than one stalker. Many more. And these creatures, it seemed, were trying less hard to conceal their presence.

Or maybe it was just that they were bigger and clumsier than Dougan, less able to hide. Ork corpses, as the Jungle Fighters had anticipated. This close, there was no denying the stink of death that rose from them; it had been wafting past Lorenzo's nostrils for the past few hours, whenever the breeze was right. Some of these orks had been dead weeks or months, but now they were a part of the planet itself, cocooned in its substance and animated by its mysterious energy.

It had taken six Jungle Fighters to send one monster into retreat. A smaller monster. Six Jungle Fighters, relatively refreshed and ready for battle.

For now, the zombies seemed content to keep their distance, to watch. Greiss moved his squad on quickly anyway, worried that if they stayed put too long they might be surrounded. They moved through the rain at a faster-than-normal pace, with their packs over their heads, hugging the trees. Fortunately, they knew enough about Rogar now to avoid its more obvious traps – though Lorenzo remembered what Donovits had said about this world's rapid evolution, and he eyed even the safest-looking flowers with suspicion.

He twitched at another rustle from the foliage. It was closer than usual, to the left of the squad rather than behind them. He brought his lasgun around but didn't dare fire lest he start something they couldn't finish. Another ork shape was clearly outlined, watching him with unblinking eyes, one of which had slid half out of its socket on a slagheap of dried blood. As Lorenzo watched, it withdrew and sank silently into the ground.

'They're watching us,' he announced. 'We've survived everything else Rogar has to throw at us, so it's got its zombies watching us, looking for a weakness.'

'I'd almost rather they made their move,' murmured Braxton, 'and got it over with.'

'Careful what you wish for,' Storm cautioned him grimly.

'When you people first arrived,' said Braxton, 'and you were talking about Rogar like it was a – I don't know – a living thing, an enemy, like an ork or something, I didn't know... I mean, I'm starting to see it now. I'm starting to feel like this planet *is* alive, like it's intelligent, like it really wants us dead.' He sounded as if he wanted somebody to contradict him. No one did.

The jungle had started to close in again. Greiss had sent Myers and Storm ahead to clear the way, and the squad's pace had dropped to a crawl.

And the ghosts were gathering at their backs.

'Maybe we should send a few las-shots their way,' suggested Armstrong, worriedly, hefting his gun in his good hand as if to reassure himself he could still operate it. 'Discourage them a little.'

'Don't know if it'd work,' murmured Greiss.

'Hotshot fired at...' Lorenzo began, then was unable to say Dougan's name. '...the first one. It didn't seem to react at all.'

'They don't feel pain,' said Greiss. 'You remember what Brains said. We've got to stop thinking of these things as living creatures. They're less than that – less than orks, even. They don't have hearts – or if they do, they sure aren't beating any more. No internal organs, no nerves, no pressure points, and I doubt their brains are getting much use. They're plants, no more than that. Part of the jungle – the planet itself – just wrapped around the remains of the dead.'

Lorenzo stole a quick look at the collecting shadows, searching for one that was shorter and thinner than the others, hoping he wouldn't find it. If the God-Emperor had any influence at all here, so far from his Golden Throne, he would see to it that Dougan could rest in peace.

'Then we deal with them like we would any hostile plant,' reasoned Armstrong.

'Can't tear 'em up by the roots,' growled Greiss. 'They're up and walking about already.'

'Shred 'em?' suggested Storm, his fingers twitching over his knife hilt.

'Take too long with the knives,' said Greiss. 'Way I'm thinking, those things will keep going till you get to the skeleton and can take it apart.'

'We've got to do something,' said Braxton, 'before they attack!'

'Boy's right,' said Armstrong. 'We need a show of strength, give them something to think about. If they *can* think, that is.'

'If they can't,' muttered Myers, 'looks like something does it for them.'

'How much ordnance do we have left between us?' asked Lorenzo.

'Couple of shredder mines,' offered Storm.

'Still got my demolition charges,' said Myers.

'Save 'em,' said Greiss, with a gleam in his eye, 'for a special occasion. I got a better idea.' He and Armstrong spoke as one: 'Burn 'em!'

Lorenzo and Braxton took over clearance duty as Myers and Storm assembled the flamer again. Greiss wielded it himself, straining under the weight of the device as he lugged it a few steps closer to the watching zombies. Then he pulled the trigger, and simultaneously swept the flamer around in a wide arc.

It was like a dozen explosions had gone off at once, plants and trees erupting as if they'd just combusted from within. The zombies – those Lorenzo could see – they were burning too, starting with the parts of them that were the most flammable: the clumps of weeds and grass embedded in their bodies. They reeled in apparent confusion, their arms pumping in futile slow-motion, patting themselves down, trying to extinguish themselves, succeeding only in setting fire to their hands or bumping into each other and spreading the flames to their comrades.

Lorenzo was amazed at the severity of the reaction, until he remembered that Rogar III had felt fire before – from the Jungle Fighters' small campfire of two nights ago to the all-out attempts by humans and orks alike at deforestation. It knew what fire could do to it, and – Lorenzo knew this didn't make sense, but he was suddenly sure of it, more sure than he'd been of anything his instincts had told him of late – it was afraid of it. The deathworld itself was afraid, and in its fear, it chose to attack the creatures that had hurt it so much, while it still had the means to do so. And it sent its soldiers forward...

The Jungle Fighters drew their lasguns as six flaming zombies – those that could still walk – came stumbling towards them, trailing smoke, like a small army of infernal daemons. They let off a fusillade of shots, to no effect, and Greiss sent another blast of fire the zombies' way in the hope of hastening their demise, before abandoning the flamer and leaping aside, not an instant too soon. A zombie hurled itself at him, and hit the ground where Greiss had been, setting light to the undergrowth. It tried to stand again, but scorched earth was sloughing from it like dead skin, withering to ash, and the bones of its purloined skeleton were beginning to show through and it could no longer lift its own weight.

The rest of the squad dropped their packs and tried to scatter, but they couldn't go far, confined to the narrowed corridor their knives had cleared. The same couldn't be said of the zombies: their movements were slow and awkward but unhampered, the foliage itself seeming to part for them. They separated too, each choosing a target. Lorenzo found himself side by side with Braxton, both trying to press themselves back into the jungle, thorns tearing at their jackets and their hair, nettles stinging their hands, as two flaming zombies homed in on them.

He heard a yell, 'Aim for their kneecaps!' and he followed Armstrong's suggestion and tried to shoot the nearest zombie's leg out from under it. He got in four shots before it was upon him. It raised a ponderous fist, and Lorenzo wasn't sure who its target was – him or Braxton – but then the fist came down towards him, and he ducked, and he tried to scramble past the zombie's leg, but his hand recoiled from a flaming footprint in the grass. The zombie swung around to follow him but a bone snapped, and its leg buckled, and Lorenzo knew his las-shots had done some good after all.

The zombie was falling – but it managed to turn its fall into a lunge, and Lorenzo couldn't get out of the way in time as the creature, now little more than a burning skeleton, plummeted towards him. For an instant, he was staring into its hollow eye sockets – piggy ork eye sockets – and they seemed to be mocking him. A tusked mouth gaped in a rictus grin. Lorenzo brought up a foot, planted it in the zombie's stomach and tried to fling it over him. It fell apart with the impact of his boot, and though the bulk of its mass passed safely over his head, Lorenzo was showered with bones and mud and burning leaves.

He rolled, to put out any flames that may have taken hold of his clothing. Then he sprang to his feet, lasgun in hand, to find that the other zombies had suffered the same fate as his. The combination of flames and las-fire had destroyed their cohesion, and they were collapsing at the feet of the relieved Jungle Fighters. Two skeletons were relatively intact, and as Lorenzo watched they were drawn into the ground. Storm reached one before it could vanish, and drove his gun butt into its spine, breaking it. The other – the skeleton of the monster that had attacked Greiss – escaped.

The Jungle Fighters relaxed and regrouped in the sudden silence, dozens of small fires flickering around them until the rain extinguished them.

'Think that's the last we'll see of them, sergeant?' asked Myers.

'I hope so, Bullseye,' growled Greiss. He cast a disparaging eye over the discarded flamer. 'Because this thing's just about on empty.' Myers and Storm packed up the device anyway, in case they were being watched – although for the first time in two days, none of the Catachans felt as if they were.

'There were more of those things out there,' Armstrong pointed out to Greiss. 'You only burnt the front ranks of them. There were at least a dozen more behind – they escaped into the ground when they saw the flames.'

'Not to mention all the other orks that must've died on Rogar these past few years,' said Lorenzo.

'And Guardsmen,' said Braxton quietly.

Greiss nodded. He knew.

'Do you think they can move underground, sergeant?' Braxton asked. 'Or will they have to resurface where they went down?'

'I don't know,' said Greiss. 'What're you thinking?'

'That it might be the right occasion to break out those mines.'

Greiss studied Braxton for a moment, then a grin tugged at his lips. 'I like the way you think, Guardsman. Right, troopers, all the shredders you have, hand 'em over. Patch, you're with me. You saw where some of them walking corpses disappeared, right? Well, the next time they try climbing out of their graves, they'll have a nasty shock waiting for 'em. Lorenzo, Braxton, you get back to clearing the way. Once these babies are laid, we're going to want to get out of here real quick.'

'Yes, sergeant,' said Lorenzo.

Greiss had half-turned away when a thought occurred to him and he looked back at Braxton. 'Let me see your knife,' he demanded. Braxton showed him the small, blunt blade he had been using, and Greiss expressed his contempt for what he called an 'Imperial pig-sticker'. Lorenzo had noticed that he had been wearing two knives today, and he'd guessed where the second had come from. Still, he felt his eyes widening as the sergeant drew Woods's devil claw – at over a metre long, more a sword than a knife – and handed it to the Validian. 'Here,' he grunted, 'you should find it easier going with this. It's only a loan, mind.'

Braxton accepted the claw, and turned it over in his hands. He admired its well-honed edge, and gauged how light and well balanced it was thanks to its hollow blade, half-filled with mercury. 'Yes, sergeant,' he said, in a voice full of awe.

'I can see now why you think so much of him,' said the Validian, when he and Lorenzo were alone together. Greiss and Armstrong were still some way behind, laying mines, and Myers and Storm had taken this opportunity – while their progress was impeded – to fall back and hunt jungle lizards and anything else they deemed edible. Lorenzo and Braxton were left with the repetitive and wearying work of swinging their knives, forging ahead – though Lorenzo had to admit, it was going a lot faster now that Braxton was properly equipped.

'Who?' he asked.

'Sergeant Greiss.'

'Of course we do. He wouldn't have that rank if he hadn't earned the respect of all of us.'

'I didn't realise. At first, he seemed – I don't know – surly, I guess. Distant. Disapproving.'

'If you're looking for a soft approach,' said Lorenzo, 'I'm afraid Catachan doesn't breed 'em like that.'

'I guess not. But now I've seen Greiss in action – the way he leads from the front, keeps this squad together, keeps us focused on the mission. And the way he... I mean, he really does care about his troopers, even if he doesn't always...'

'He'd give his life for us,' said Lorenzo simply, 'as we would for him. Your point is?'

'I'm used to sergeants who do things by the book, that's all. Same with the commissar. If Mackenzie had survived, if he could see Greiss now...'

'If he'd been willing to look,' said Lorenzo pointedly.

'Yes. I just think, Mackenzie, he was like most of us. We don't know till we see for ourselves. I can't imagine what it must have been like for you, for Greiss, for all of you, being brought up on a world like this. A deathworld. But I'm starting to understand, and Mackenzie – I think he would have understood too, in time.'

'You don't think he'd have filed his complaint against Old Hardhead? You don't think he'd have had him shot?'

'We'll never know,' said the Validian. 'Best thing, I think, is to let it lie. I certainly won't be saying a thing.'

Lorenzo was about to agree when he spotted something. A triangle. Silver. He could easily have mistaken it for an exotic leaf, lying flat against a branch, had the pattern not connected with something in his memory. A warning. Braxton's knife hand was moving towards it, and Lorenzo batted it away even before his conscious mind remembered what the pattern represented. The triangle wrinkled, as a snake head jerked out from beneath it and made a stab at where the hand had just been.

'I think we should both talk less,' said Lorenzo, 'and pay more attention to where we're going.'

Braxton nodded. But it wasn't long before he spoke up again. 'I just wondered,' he said, 'if I should say something. To the others. Let them know. That they can trust me, I mean.'

Lorenzo smiled tightly. 'They know. Old Hardhead in particular.' He indicated the devil claw in Braxton's hand. 'Trust me, he knows.'

Then Greiss and Armstrong came pelting towards them, sweeping Myers and Storm along in their wake. They had barely come to a halt when a series of explosions from behind them rattled the ground and shook leaves from their branches. The trap had been sprung. Greiss's cruel grin exposed his teeth and flared his nostrils. They all waited for a minute, listening for the shuffling footsteps of zombies, squinting through the rain for the shape of an ork, but there was nothing.

And, a few minutes after that, Braxton found a trap. A snare in the under-growth, ready to tighten about the ankle of an unwary traveller and hoist him into the trees. A sign, Lorenzo agreed when the Validian pointed it out to him, that orks had been here. Crafty orks. Then he inspected the snare more closely. It was fashioned from creepers – but, far than having been knotted together by hand, it seemed to have grown into its unnatural shape.

'Rogar's still learning,' he murmured as Braxton used his devil claw to slice through the snare. 'It's learning from us.'

They forged on well into the night, making up for their late start, until Loren-zo's body wanted nothing more than to shut down. He'd been running on adrenaline, but now even this was spent. The acid rain hadn't let up, and despite his precautions Lorenzo's face and neck were red raw. The wound in his side felt like it was ablaze. He had begun to wonder if Sergeant Greiss would ever call a halt to this torture, though of course he would never have complained.

At last, Greiss accepted that even his squad needed rest. He warned, how-ever, that they didn't have much time. He intended to move out early in the morning – and until then, the Jungle Fighters would have to keep watch in three shifts of two in case the blue light returned.

For the first time, Lorenzo didn't volunteer for first watch. Greiss detailed Myers and Storm to that duty, and Lorenzo was grateful to be placed on the third and final watch with Armstrong, possibly in deference to the fact that both were wounded. Only as they set up camp – positioning their plastic sheeting not to collect water tonight but to deflect the rain – did he realise how tired the sergeant himself looked.

They built the biggest, hottest fire they could, despite the risk that it might be seen. They did it to spite what they now saw to be their real enemy: Rogar III.

Lorenzo was asleep almost before his head touched the ground. But it seemed like his eyes had only been closed a minute when the shouting began.

He thought he was dreaming again, at first. That dream from the pre-vious night, before the ork camp, when dead comrades had pulled him down into the earth to join them. Only this time it was real, and it was the earth itself that pulled at him. Lorenzo was already half-buried; he tried to stand, to tear himself free, but he couldn't gain leverage and the pull of the earth only increased.

Quicksand? He was sinking, though the ground had been perfectly firm when he had lain down on it. He fought the urge to lash out, because he knew he would only go down faster. Somebody was shouting his name, yell-ing at him to wake, and the rain was still drumming on the plastic sheets above his head, searing them brown.

This was worse than quicksand. Lorenzo knew how to deal with quick-sand, knew how hard it was to actually drown in it, but this – this was Rogar III itself, grasping at him, drawing him to its heart. His first instinct was to unsheathe his Catachan fang, though he had no use for it yet, because if his legs went under he didn't want to lose it with them.

With a supreme effort, he raised his head. The whole campsite was a quagmire. Armstrong and Myers had been caught sleeping too, and were being sucked under. Greiss and Braxton were standing but buried up to their knees; it must have been their watch when the planet had struck. It was Braxton who had shouted, presumably unable to see from where he was that Lorenzo had already woken. There was no sign of the campfire: it must have been pulled under and smothered.

Storm was doing better than any of them. He was on his hands and knees in the mud, but pulling himself along with his powerful muscles, almost swimming, his teeth clenched, face red with exertion, until he came to the edge of the Catachans' small clearing and his flailing hand caught a tree branch. He had something to hold on to now, and he could begin to haul himself upright.

Lorenzo was determined to follow Storm's example. But suddenly, the earth beside him seemed to explode, and he recoiled and sank a little further as a figure erupted from beneath it. A large, hunched figure with tusks protruding through a matted layer of plants and dirt. An ork zombie.

And there were more of them, bursting from the ground all across the clearing, outnumbering the Jungle Fighters and surrounding them. In contrast to their floundering targets, they waded easily through the mud, their ponderous gait now seeming only too fast.

The nearest zombie loomed over Lorenzo, and raised both fists above its head as it prepared to strike him dead.

CHAPTER 14

Lorenzo brought up his right hand, his knife hand, to protect his head, and tried to do the same with his left, but the earth had it. He pulled at it, and brushed something below the surface: a familiar shape. He wrapped his fingers around it, feeling like he was squeezing cold slime until they closed around hard metal. With a gut-wrenching effort, he brought his hand, and his lasgun, tearing out into the open and braced the weapon in both hands above his face.

The ork zombie's blow landed, hit the gun, and Lorenzo felt the vibrations juddering through his bones and thought he'd lost another lasgun, thought it would snap in two, but somehow it remained intact. He realised that his shoulders were in the earth again, the impact and his own efforts driving him downwards.

The zombie was preparing to strike again, and Lorenzo turned the lasgun around and pulled the trigger, but it jammed. Mud in the barrel. He could just reach the zombie's leg with the tip of his knife, and he slashed at it, scoring a groove, but it didn't react. The quagmire was sucking at the back of his head, caressing his ears with cold tendrils.

He couldn't beat the monster. The best he could hope for was to keep it from killing him long enough for the planet to take him, to fill his nose and mouth with its substance and suffocate him.

He couldn't beat the monster. So he stopped fighting it.

A clump of flowers protruded, ridiculously, from the zombie's thigh, and Lorenzo strained to reach them, trusted them to support his weight as he hauled himself up, mud slurping and sucking at him but losing the contest of strength. With both hands full, holding his lasgun, his knife and the flowers, he couldn't defend himself against another double-fisted blow to the back of his stooped head. He took it with gritted teeth, blinded for a moment as he almost blacked out. He felt as if his skull must have cracked. Then he felt the flowers give way, their roots torn clean out of the zombie's earthen flesh.

Lorenzo was falling back, and he couldn't shift his trapped legs to steady himself, but he threw out his arms and found the zombie's legs, and he hugged them tightly, holding on for his life. This had the useful side-effect of unbalancing the zombie, which reacted too slowly, toppled, and splashed into the quagmire on its back. Lorenzo was scrabbling, clawing at its cold, wet mass, using it like a log in a river. He climbed onto it, dragging his legs after him; he pulled himself along the zombie's length, yanking dead leaves from the vegetation that coated it, simultaneously trampling the zombie further down.

He hauled himself upright as the zombie's head sank underground. He used its chest as a springboard, pushing off it, leaping for the edge of the clearing. He landed with both feet in the mud, and was instantly buried up to the waist again, but as the top half of his body fell forwards, he was able to grab at a branch and, like Storm before him, use it as a lifeline.

He glanced over his shoulder, to see that the zombie was thrashing about, resurfacing and beginning to stand – and that another was heading his way. There wasn't time to free himself completely from Rogar's grip. He settled instead for dragging his backside up onto the dry ground beyond the clearing, his legs still in the mud but his shoulder hooked behind a tree, bracing him, allowing him to resist the suction force from below. He plunged his fingers into his lasgun barrel and scooped out as much mud as he could. Then he dug the butt into his shoulder, aimed for the second zombie and fired. The gun whined and let out a feeble light. The second zombie lurched closer. Lorenzo pumped the trigger again, and on his fourth attempt, the lasgun finally coughed up dirt and struck true.

He had aimed for the knee again; it took four shots to penetrate through to the bone, and then the oncoming creature collapsed like a puppet with its strings cut, and disappeared below the surface.

By that time, the first zombie had somehow managed to right itself and was bearing down on him. This one took six shots, and fell less than a metre from him, hands reaching for him. He thanked the God-Emperor for the creatures' sluggish reflexes: if this one had only shifted its weight onto its good leg, it could have stayed upright long enough to wrap its fingers around his throat.

In no immediate danger now, Lorenzo took a second to scan the battle-field. Myers and Armstrong were engaged in their own struggles, each beginning to gain the upper hand – but Braxton was in trouble.

Three zombies had surrounded the Validian, overpowered him, and pushed him headlong into the mud. His face was buried; he couldn't breathe.

Greiss had seen what was happening, and was just finishing up with his own opponent. Astonishingly, he had whittled into it with his Catachan fang until he had exposed its spine, which he had then seized and yanked right out of its body. He tossed the wretched creature's remains aside, with a sneer, and began to wade towards Braxton, but the mud was up to his stomach and his progress was slow.

Storm was firing in from the sidelines, and as Lorenzo watched, the first of Braxton's attackers fell beneath his las-fire at last. Storm switched targets, and Lorenzo joined him; their shots converged on the back of the second zombie's knee and burnt through it in seconds.

The third and final zombie swung around to greet Greiss with a hefty punch, which the grizzled sergeant dodged. His face was level with the crea-ture's stomach – with its greater bulk, it looked like it could crush him with its thumb – but he drove the butt of his lasgun into its leg and, to Lorenzo's amazement, shattered it. The bone must have been old and brittle. But this zombie's reflexes were better than most. Instead of falling, it swayed on one leg, and looked down to where its other leg hung loose, still attached to its body by muddy tendrils.

Then Greiss laid into it with his gun butt again, roaring like an animal, and slowly, as if it was fighting gravity itself, the zombie fell and was gone. Greiss's path to Braxton was clear – but the Validian was gone now, too.

There was nothing Lorenzo could do for him, no chance of reaching him. He shifted his attention to the zombies still standing, supporting Myers and Armstrong's efforts with his las-shots. But his eyes kept flicking to the patch of mud where Braxton's head had gone under, and he found himself holding his breath as Greiss propelled himself towards that spot and plunged his hands into the shifting earth.

Myers was free of ork zombies, but his struggle had cost him. He was sinking fast. Storm leapt back into the quagmire, and waded to his comrade's aid. He reached Myers and gripped him beneath the arms. He tried to drag him free, but for every two centimetres the pair gained, the quagmire reclaimed one, and Myers was buried up to his neck now.

Lorenzo concentrated on freeing his own legs. When the planet let go, it did so suddenly, and he fell back into a bush and lost vital seconds disentangling his vest from its thorns. He raced around the edge of the quagmire, to the point at which Storm had re-entered it. He could reach him from here, by placing one foot in the mud while leaving the other braced behind him. He caught Storm's reaching hand, and pulled at it with all his strength.

Across the clearing, to Lorenzo's relief, Greiss pulled Braxton, coughing and spluttering, to the surface – but the effort had cost him, and now they were both treading mud, only their heads visible, helpless.

Armstrong's las-bolts despatched the final zombie, and he was in trouble now too; he wasn't too far from the edge, but with his useless arm he had no way of reaching it. Lorenzo gritted his teeth and pulled harder, and at last Storm stumbled onto the bank beside him, and they took one of Myers's arms each and dragged him up after them.

Myers was trying to bring something with him. He strained and pulled, and the earth released its grip on his muddied backpack. Lorenzo had lost his, along with his jacket and his bandolier. Myers was rummaging in the pack before his legs were even out of the quagmire, and Storm grinned behind his black beard as his comrade produced a rope. He must have woven it himself from plant roots, after they'd lost the others at the river.

Myers made the throw, of course. The end of the rope slapped into the mud a centimetre or two from Greiss's head, but was absorbed before he could free an arm to reach for it. Both Greiss and Braxton strained to move their submerged limbs, to find their sinking lifeline, and Braxton's chin went under and he spluttered again as he took a mouthful of earth. Then, a tense moment later, the Validian yelled out, 'Got it!' and Myers and Lorenzo pulled for all they were worth.

Storm, in the meantime, had found a branch that jutted out over Armstrong's position. He climbed up to it and swarmed along it, the branch bending beneath his weight. Armstrong raised his good arm, and their fingers strained to find each other.

At last the struggle was won, and six muddy, exhausted soldiers lay on dry land and looked mournfully at the swamp that had been their camp-site, thinking of the precious kit they had lost to its embrace, and of how much more they could have lost.

They had just three half-filled water bottles between them now, Loren-zo's, Storm's and Armstrong's having gone down with their backpacks. The flamer could never be assembled again without the parts Storm had been carrying. They were just grateful that Myers still had the power packs for their lasguns.

But Lorenzo felt most sorry for Armstrong, because his devil claw knife had been snatched from him. The veteran Jungle Fighter looked devastated about that, far more hurt than he'd been by his shoulder injury. Braxton offered him Woods's old devil claw, but he just shrugged the Validian away. It wasn't the same.

'I hate to say this,' announced Greiss, 'but we need to move on before we can bed down again.'

'You think there's anywhere safe on this damned planet?' asked Armstrong, sullenly.

'I'm gambling it takes a good while for Rogar to turn an area like this into a bog,' said Greiss, 'else why would it have waited till now? In future, we're just going to have to move between two or three campsites a night, grab our sleep a few hours at a time.' They all saw the sense in that, though it was a disheartening proposition.

In the event, they moved only a few hundred metres before Greiss gave the order to start clearing the ground again. Lorenzo and Armstrong took their watch while the others slept. Armstrong was poor company, sitting on a tree trunk and stared at his own feet. Lorenzo, fortunately, had slept long enough to feel relatively refreshed. He hoisted the protective plastic sheets over his comrades' heads by himself, though shortly after he had done so the rain subsided at last.

A few silver-backed snakes hissed in the undergrowth – but to Lorenzo's relief, the rest of the night passed without incident.

The next morning, the Jungle Fighters had an unexpected visitor.

The figure stepped out of the trees as they were making to move out – and instantly, six lasguns were drawn and aimed at it. The figure made no threatening move, however.

Lorenzo peered at it curiously. It was humanoid in shape, about his height and build – and to an extent, it resembled one of the ork zombies, fashioned as it was from Rogar's vegetation. But this figure was wearing a jacket woven from varicoloured leaves, and a branch slung across its back where the Jungle Fighters kept their lasguns, and it even seemed to have a face, wide-eyed and grinning, though this was just a pattern formed – accidentally? – by the twisted stalks and plants that ran through its rough, sculpted head. A thatch of straw was perched atop that head, like a mop of blond hair.

It grinned at the Jungle Fighters for a minute or more, as they watched it warily. Then the figure let out a bizarre, inhuman noise: a series of guttural clicks and warbling vowel sounds. Then it turned, and with a clumsy, rolling gait like it might shake itself apart, it moved away from them, in the direction they intended to go, until its path was blocked. Then it brought up an arm, jerkily, and sliced it down, then up and down again.

'What the hell is it meant to be?' breathed Myers.

'Best guess?' growled Greiss. 'It's meant to be one of us. Look at it, Bullseye! Pretending it's cutting its way through the jungle like we've been doing.'

'I think it was trying to talk,' Armstrong said. 'It was trying to sound like us, imitate the noises we make, but it doesn't understand language.'

'You think we're supposed to be taken in by that?' asked Lorenzo, not sure if he should be amused or disturbed by the idea. 'We're supposed to think that's one of us, let it join us, and – then what?'

'I vote we don't give it the chance to show us,' said Myers.

'I'll second that,' said Greiss.

Six lasguns converged on the unlikely doppelganger – and it whirled around to face the Jungle Fighters, and if Lorenzo hadn't known better he could have sworn it seemed surprised. Then the figure exploded.

Hidden spines shot out from its chest and mouth, like slender darts, and the Jungle Fighters leapt for cover, and fortunately had kept enough distance between them and the twisted effigy to avoid being struck. Lorenzo raised his head to find a dozen spines embedded in a tree beside him. More lay in the grass, and he noted that their needle points dripped with poison. Of the effigy, there was no trace at all now. It had fallen apart, returned to its constituent components and reclaimed by the jungle, and Lorenzo couldn't tell which of the leaves and plants that strewed the ground before them had belonged to its mass.

The second effigy showed itself almost four hours later, just stepping out behind the Jungle Fighters into the path they'd cut, greeting them with its incoherent warble. It didn't last a second before it was gunned down, falling onto its back and shooting its poisonous payload into the sky. Lorenzo had barely set eyes upon it before it was gone – but he was left with the distinct impression that this doppelganger had been more sophisticated, a far more accurate likeness of its template, than its predecessor had been.

It was about then that they all felt the first tremor.

It had been a quiet day by the Jungle Fighters' standards. They had dealt with routine attacks by jungle lizards, snakes and spitter plants, but nothing that had really challenged them. Since the incident with the second effigy, they'd had no sense of being followed, so it seemed that – for now at least – they were safe from zombies.

As they had progressed, so too had their spirits lightened. Lorenzo had started to feel like they had finally got the measure of this deathworld, like Rogar had run out of new ways to torment them and accepted their mastery of it. It was a good feeling. A reaffirming feeling. It made their sacrifices worthwhile.

They didn't speak about the tremor. With luck, it had been an isolated incident – and the more time passed without a recurrence, the more likely this seemed.

Then, as the daylight began to die, the jungle opened up again, and they were able to sheathe their knives as their passage through it eased. Shortly thereafter, they uncovered gretchin footprints and knew they were close to their goal. They withdrew a short way, and found a secluded spot in which they could rest for a time. The last time, they all knew, before the culmination of their mission. Find the ork warboss and take him out. They were starting to look forward to it again.

Greiss agreed to let them light a cooking fire, because the canopy was thick here and a small amount of smoke would likely go unnoticed. Anyway, they were low on standard rations, but they did have the lizards Myers and Storm had caught, along with a few handfuls of Rogar's choicest spices. Myers tasted each one before he added it to the pot, in case its nature had changed since the last batch he'd gathered. In case the planet had brewed up a new poison to surprise them.

They knew there was a small chance that foraging gretchin would happen upon them, so Lorenzo helped Armstrong set up a few traps. Any creature that came within earshot of them would be strung up in a net, unable to raise an alarm.

They ate, and their conversation turned to the usual subject: to comrades gone but not forgotten. They spoke of Hotshot, Sharkbait and Brains's defiance of the ork hordes. They had all heard the stories by now, of course, but it helped to reiterate them. It comforted them, and ensured that they had the details right, for the next time the stories were told. They talked of Landon's bravery, and of the heroic fight Steel Toe Dougan had no doubt put up against the blue light. In time, their conversation turned to earlier exploits, and they found these stories were even more worth the telling because Armstrong and Guardsman Braxton were new to their squad and hadn't heard them before.

Greiss recalled how, as an eager young rookie, Hotshot Woods had rushed an ork sniper that had pinned the squad down, miraculously reaching it without a scratch and wrestling it from its emplacement. Myers and Storm took it in turns to relate how Brains Donovits had survived an encounter with a stranded Chaos Space Marine, simply by outthinking it, and were pleased when Braxton asked questions and made expressions of admiration in all the right places. Then they all listened attentively to Armstrong's fresh tales of heroes from his former squad, and expressed a collective wish that they could have known these great men and witnessed their deeds.

Myers followed that with the tale of how Old Hardhead had earned his name. It was a story from before Lorenzo's time, of course – before Myers's, for that matter – but they had both heard it often enough. Trooper Greiss, as he had been then, had been part of a single platoon that had taken down a Chaos Dreadnought. He had lain some of the snares into which it had walked, and planted a mine on its leg as it had struggled to free itself. Unfortunately, he hadn't been able to outrun the explosion that had ripped the Dreadnought apart. Or maybe it hadn't been fortune but fate that had lodged a sizeable hunk of shrapnel in Greiss's skull. The surgeons had reportedly written him off, but his strength of character had buoyed him to a full recovery. 'Without that metal plate they put in his head,' Myers concluded, 'he wouldn't be the cantankerous old sod we know today.'

'Knock it off, Bullseye,' growled Greiss, 'unless you want latrine duty when we get back to civilisation.'

'You wait till you're splashed over the front page of *Eagle & Bolter*, sergeant,' said Myers. 'We got their star reporter in our midst, you know.'

'Yes, that's right,' remembered Storm, turning to Braxton. 'Didn't I hear you were working on a story about us?'

'We give you enough material yet?' put in Myers.

'Ease off, you two,' said Greiss. 'You know what those rags are like. The higher-ups wouldn't let Braxton print any of this stuff if he wanted to. They're only interested in their own truths.'

'I wish I could argue with that,' said Braxton, 'but you're right, yes. I always wrote what I was told to write – about successful missions, and ground that we'd gained. I don't think half of it was even true. I didn't ask.'

'Never saw a broadsheet that was any different,' remarked Myers.

'And I thought that was all right,' continued Braxton, 'because it was all about morale. That was what Mackenzie always said, and the commissar before him. Put the best possible spin on it, they said. Tell the troops about the overall campaign, about the Imperium resisting its enemies, and remind them why they're doing it. Don't let them dwell on the details, how people like them – like us – are suffering and dying for the cause. Your story would have been no different. Just a few lines about your great victory, maybe a name check for the commissar. They'd never have let me write about Woods or Dougan or the others.'

'All the more reason for us to make it back alive,' said Storm. 'Because if we don't tell those stories, who will?'

'I will,' swore Braxton. 'One day. I'll tell them how it is with you – how you make sure that everyone matters, every life counts for something.'

'Keep talking like that,' said Greiss, 'and your next commissar will probably boot you right out on the first suicide mission to cross his desk.'

Braxton grimaced, but took the joke in the spirit it was intended.

They were all still smiling when the ground shook again.

This tremor was worse than the first one. It lasted longer, felt deeper and more destructive, although the only visible signs of it above ground were a slight blurring of the trees and the dislodging of a few leaves and fruits. The tremor died down with no harm done, but Lorenzo could see his apprehension mirrored in the other Jungle Fighters' eyes, because they knew what it might presage.

Maybe Rogar III hadn't conceded defeat after all. Maybe it was just waiting, planning, and building up to its biggest offensive against its interlopers yet.

CHAPTER 15

'Sergeant – you've got to see this.'

As the Jungle Fighters had ventured deeper into ork territory, they had switched to stealth tactics, as they had by the encampment. This time, it was Myers who had the task of scouting ahead for traps. He had already guided the squad around several tripwires and a concealed pit. Now he came scurrying back to them, face flushed.

They followed him through the foliage, all too aware that they were moving parallel to a path worn down and churned up by footprints. Lorenzo could hear clinking and clunking and the guttural sounds of ork voices ahead, and he moved as carefully as he could, disturbing hardly a leaf.

A light spilled into the jungle, and Lorenzo feared at first that it was the mind-altering blue light. It was white, though, far more harsh, and it seemed to emanate from many sources. The Jungle Fighters were careful to stick to the shadows, not to let the light reveal them.

Then, with a cautious touch, Myers parted a cluster of spiny fronds, and Lorenzo saw what the excitement was about.

The orks had set up a mining operation. They were working well into the night. A clearing was illuminated by lanterns strung up in trees, turned inwards, their light bleaching out all but the faintest hints of colour. Across the clearing, the ground rose steeply, and a tunnel had been dug into the side of this hillock. A square wooden frame propped up its entrance – and as the Jungle Fighters watched, another light appeared in the tunnel's depths. An ork emerged, the light streaming from a battered helmet that was balanced atop its misshapen head. It was wheeling a lopsided barrow overloaded with rocks, which it dumped unceremoniously onto one of several heaps dotting the area.

Four gretchin were sorting through this heap, giving each rock a cursory glance before they tossed it onto a discard pile. Nearby, two orks quarrelled over a pickaxe – and ten more stood sentry at regular intervals around the clearing, with one stationed to each side of the mine entrance. A few more gretchin were scampering about, fetching and carrying, offering their ork masters food and drink.

'What do you suppose they're looking for?' asked Armstrong, after the Jungle Fighters had backed up a safe distance.

'Isn't much worth digging up on Rogar,' said Wildman Storm, 'at least not according to Brains – or did I hear that wrong?'

Greiss shook his head. 'You heard right, Wildman. But remember what else Brains said – about this world's energy signature. There's something here, something the explorators couldn't identify. I'm guessing the greenskins are after it.'

'How?' protested Lorenzo. 'If the explorators couldn't find it...'

Greiss shrugged. 'You know orks. Bloody-minded. Likelihood is they got nothing, know nothing, but they'll just keep on looking on the off-chance that there's some miracle rock down there they can mine and use against us. Probably hollow out this whole planet before they admit defeat.'

'Emperor help us if they do find something,' murmured Armstrong.

'So what now?' asked Storm – and Lorenzo recognised the impatient gleam in his eyes. 'The odds are way better than they were two nights ago, and this time we have the advantage of surprise. We come out firing, we'll have half those greenskins down before they know what's hit them.'

'I don't care about "half those greenskins",' growled Greiss. 'We're here for one reason, and one reason only – and I didn't see anyone out there answering Big Green's description.'

'There were no huts,' Braxton realised. 'Where do these orks live?'

'Another encampment, somewhere nearby?' hazarded Myers.

'Your job to find out,' said Greiss. 'When I give the word, you take a scout round that clearing, see if there's any wheel tracks or evidence of orks tramping to and fro. My guess is, there won't be. I reckon these greenskins have taken their equipment and their beds underground, into the mine itself.'

'So, getting to their boss won't be as easy as it sounded,' added Myers.

'He's got to show his face on the surface sometime,' opined Braxton.

'Has he?' said Armstrong, cynically.

'Normally, I'd say wait,' said Greiss. 'Set up sniper positions, sit it out for a few days, let our target come to us. But this is Rogar III. We sit around here too long, we don't know what it's going to throw at us.'

'If we go into that mine with all guns blazing,' said Armstrong, 'Big Green will know about it – and I'm betting, if he's half as smart as Mackenzie reckoned, he won't let himself be cornered in there.'

'Something else for you to keep an eye out for, Bullseye,' said Greiss, 'on your reconnoitre: a back way in – though if there is one, it's probably kilometres away, and well hidden. No, I've a feeling in my old bones: the only way we're getting in sniffing distance of our man is if we barge in the front door. Question is, how to do it without tipping off the warboss that we're coming?'

Twenty minutes later, Lorenzo was lying flat on his face in the grass, having mud slapped onto his back by his comrades – some of them, he thought, with a little too much relish. He protested as Storm tried to tie a branch into his hair with clumsy fingers, but succeeded only in poking him in the eye.

Finally, Sergeant Greiss suggested he try standing, and Lorenzo did so, helped to his feet by Braxton. A heap of vegetation crashed to the ground around his feet, and he looked at Armstrong, upon whom similar indignities had been heaped, and stifled a laugh.

It took another ten minutes' work to achieve anything like the effect they wanted. Lorenzo and Armstrong remained standing for this final stage, and Lorenzo watched admiringly as his comrade disappeared beneath layer after layer of dirt. Much of it didn't stick, and even now some patches of Armstrong's skin showed through, but that didn't matter so much. A garland of plants had been knotted together and draped around Armstrong's shoulders; from a distance, it might have looked like the leaves were growing out of him. The likeness wasn't perfect, but even Lorenzo had to suppress a shudder, staring now at a figure that reminded him of the zombies that had almost killed them all. Of course, although he couldn't see it, didn't dare tilt his head for fear of dislodging its dressings, he knew he had undergone a similar transformation.

Greiss cast an appraising eye over his two troopers, and announced that they were ready. 'At least,' he added, 'I'd say we've done as much as we can with you. I suggest you stick to the shadows at the edge of the clearing, and – I don't know – try and puff yourselves up a bit, stick your shoulders out. You're supposed to be orks under all that muck. Pair of scrawny buggers like you two, you'll be lucky to pass for grtechin.'

'So long as the greenskins don't pick 'em as Catachans, eh, sergeant?' said Myers. He had surprised everyone by producing two ork guns from his backpack; now he pressed one into Lorenzo's hands, and the other into Armstrong's. 'Here, this should help keep up the illusion.'

'You got any more of them, Bullseye?' asked Greiss.

'Afraid not, sergeant. Just picked up two at the encampment, for a rainy day. I loaded 'em both up, though.'

'Rest of us will have to make do with lasguns, then. We let Patch and Lorenzo start firing first, and with a bit of luck the orks won't think about it in the confusion.'

It sounded like a risky plan. For a start, the Jungle Fighters were relying upon the likelihood that the orks had had their own encounters with the plant zombies. 'When they start falling,' Greiss had said, 'we want them to think that that's who's behind it: their own living dead. So, no heroics. We're just going to pick off a few sentries, narrow the odds against us and fall back, no more than that.'

Greiss, Myers, Storm and Braxton slipped away to their positions then, and left Lorenzo and Armstrong standing, looking at each other. Lorenzo hoped that Armstrong, with all he'd been through, was up to this – but when Greiss had expressed a similar sentiment, the veteran had snapped that he had lost an eye and an arm, not the use of his legs or his brain.

They waited two minutes as arranged, then began to shuffle toward the lights and the sounds of ork voices. It was easier than Lorenzo had expected to replicate the zombies' stiff, unnatural gait: it came naturally to him, so worried was he about shedding his disguise before it was even put to use.

They split up as they neared the clearing, Armstrong going right, Lorenzo left. He saw no sign of his other comrades, but he knew they were nearby. He drew in a deep breath and stepped out into the open, stopping just short of the footprint of the nearest lantern. The nearest ork sentry was a little closer than he'd anticipated, and he squeezed the trigger of his gun and sent a hail of bullets its way. Somewhere to Lorenzo's right, the chatter of a second ork gun echoed his own.

The ork was coming at him, snarling, foaming at the mouth. It must have known it was dead, but it was using its body as a shield, giving its fellows time to react to the intruders in their midst. There was every chance that if it could cling to life long enough to reach Lorenzo, it could do some real damage. He took a step back, but he couldn't display too much speed or agility for fear of exposing his deception. All he could do was keep shooting, and pray.

Then the ork fell, and the clearing was full of answering fire, then the whines of las-bolts shooting in from positions unknown, and there were four more orks coming Lorenzo's way and it was time to get the hell out of there.

It took all the self-control he could muster not to duck or run – to turn his back and to shamble away, hearing ork feet pounding ever closer, making himself a clear target for an agonising second. A bullet whistled by his ear; another blew a clump of mud from his shoulder and grazed his skin. Then Lorenzo rounded a bush, passed out of his enemies' sight, and abandoned all pretence.

He left a trail of debris behind him as he raced through the jungle; he just hoped his pursuers wouldn't recognise it for what it was. He put as many obstacles as he could between him and them. The orks were snarling and howling, and letting off gunfire in random directions, so he knew they wouldn't hear him; as long as they didn't see him either, they should assume he had sunk underground like Rogar's other zombies. In theory, at least.

The explosions came in quick succession – two of them. The orks had run into their own traps, the positions of the tripwires changed by Greiss and Myers. Some of them would have died. It was still too early to tell, though, if the rest of the plan – the important part – had succeeded.

There was mud in Lorenzo's eyes and mouth, but he had reached his rendezvous point with the rest of his squad. He was the first there. He clawed great handfuls of dirt from his face, breathed deeply of the warm night air and coughed up a leaf. He was recognisably Lorenzo now, but a film of the planet's substance clung to him like a second skin. He didn't think he would ever feel clean again.

Somebody spoke, and he jumped; he hadn't heard anybody approaching. Then he recognised Greiss's voice, and saw the familiar figure of his sergeant out of the corner of his eye, though he couldn't make out what he was saying, so bunged up were his ears. He started to clean them with his fingers, as Greiss padded up to him and laid a hand on Lorenzo's shoulder.

That was when he saw his mistake.

Lorenzo's head snapped up, and he looked into the hollow eyes of an effigy. A better effigy, far better, than the first two; Rogar had sculpted Greiss's craggy features perfectly, even found plant tendrils to match the iron grey of his hair. And that voice – it had possessed exactly the right gruff tone, even if, Lorenzo now realised, it hadn't been saying a thing. He muttered a curse, aimed at himself for not having paid attention, as he pushed the effigy away from him and dived at the same time, but knew it was hopeless.

The effigy exploded, and Lorenzo felt his ears popping, felt its spines stabbing into him before he hit the ground, his left side feeling as if it was on fire.

He rolled onto his back, raised his left arm, and saw four spines protruding along its length, three more embedded between his ribs. He yanked them out quickly, some tearing his skin and sending more lances of pain through him. Most of the spines, he was grateful to see, still dripped poison and therefore hadn't pumped the whole of their doses into him. Seven spines, though... He was bleeding through some of his wounds, and this too was good because it meant he might bleed some of the poison out. He twisted his arm around until he could reach two of its punctures with his mouth, and he sucked at them, his tongue recoiling at a strong, sour taste.

His heart was hammering, his head light. The first effects of the poison – or of his own fear? He didn't want it to end like this. Not through his own carelessness. Not without a name by which his comrades could remember him.

He searched his pockets, found the capsule of herbs that Donovits had given him some months ago. A generic antitoxin, he had called it – though he had warned it wouldn't work in all situations. Deathworlds, Donovits had said, had a habit of evolving poisons faster than men could combat them – and, Lorenzo supposed gloomily, he would have said that went double for a world like Rogar III.

He gulped the herbs down anyway, taking hold of all the lifelines he could. He clambered unsteadily to his feet as Armstrong burst through the jungle behind him, followed by Storm, Greiss and then Braxton.

Lorenzo told them what had happened to him. He had no choice: he had to warn them in case Rogar tried the same trick on them. He downplayed his injuries, though, claiming to have been hit by only three spines and professing a false confidence that he had sucked most of the poison out of his bloodstream. Greiss gave him a sceptical look, but Lorenzo was able to return it with clear, focused eyes. Maybe, he thought, he would be all right after all?

Myers returned a few minutes after that – having stayed to view the aftermath of the Jungle Fighters' incursion – and Lorenzo could tell from his broad grin that he had the news they wanted to hear. 'We gunned down three greenskins altogether,' he reported, 'and wounded a few more. They lost another three, and most of the gretchin, to their own traps.'

'They called for replacements?' asked Greiss.

Myers shook his head. 'Just spread their sentries more thinly. 'It worked, sergeant. Judging by the way they're looking around and pointing guns at the plants, they think the planet did this to them.'

'How many orks left?' asked Armstrong, performing a quick mental calculation. 'Six?'

'Five,' said Myers. 'One went and stood itself right next to my bush. I caught a jungle lizard creeping up on me. I couldn't resist it. I gave it a flick with my lasgun, catapulted it onto the greenskin's shoulder. The lizard stuck the ork's neck with its tongue before it could move. It was on the ground, thrashing and howling, when I slipped away.'

'Five orks,' said Greiss, 'and how many gretchin?'

'I reckon about four. Five, maybe,' said Myers.

'Not bad,' mused Armstrong. 'We got the greenskins down to less than half strength, and they don't even know they're under attack yet.'

The Jungle Fighters' next step was to make their presence well and truly felt.

They synchronised their assault, bursting out of cover from six points simultaneously, their lasguns flaring. Lorenzo, Braxton, Greiss, Armstrong and Storm took an ork each, though Armstrong had grumbled under his breath about being assigned one that was already injured. As Lorenzo fired repeatedly at his target, he was aware of gretchin scampering away towards the mine, intent on taking a warning to their warboss. That was Myers's job: to stop them.

Myers's las-bolts struck the stunted creatures unerringly, often finding the best angles from which to penetrate two or three of them. Two gretchin fell, and the remaining three were deterred from their course, giving Myers the chance to get between them and the mine tunnel. The single ork that had been guarding the entrance had been lured away by Greiss; now it hesitated, glancing back, not sure whether to press its attack against Greiss or to tackle this new foe. In the event, it was spared that decision. One of Greiss's las-bolts passed through the ork's thick skull and fried its brain.

Lorenzo's ork was thundering towards him, weakened but not defeated. He dropped his gun, pulled his Catachan fang, and greeted his opponent with a well-aimed slash to the throat. The ork was dead, but still fighting. Lorenzo avoided its clumsy grasp, but almost fell as it rammed him with its shoulder. The ork toppled, catching him off-balance, and bore him down with its weight. Its left hand was trapped beneath it, but it seized his throat with its right, and Lorenzo grabbed a chunky green finger in each hand and strained to pry them apart.

The ork ran out of strength, and its eyes rolled back into its head as it heaved its final breath. Lorenzo pulled himself out from under it, in time to see Sergeant Greiss gunning down the last of the gretchin. The rest of his squad were already pulling ork corpses into the foliage, hiding them, and Lorenzo followed suit. None of their targets had survived to spread word, but it was possible that the sounds of battle had carried into the mine.

Lorenzo waited, crouching silently, watching the tunnel entrance, the blood of his dead enemy seeping into his boot. After a minute or so, something stirred down there, and Lorenzo tensed at the sight of an oncoming light.

It was another barrow-pushing ork. Evidently, it hadn't heard anything amiss, because it strode right out into the clearing and stood there, blinking in the harsh light of the lanterns, just beginning to register the fact that it was alone.

It dropped its barrow, which teetered and upturned itself, spilling its contents. A look of confusion, tinged with fear, began to spread across the ork's face – and froze there as multiple las-bolts stabbed out of the darkness to impale it.

The Jungle Fighters emerged into the clearing again, and Greiss jabbed the fallen ork with his toe to check that it was really dead, that it wouldn't spring up and surprise them. Myers asked if they should burn the bodies, to prevent the planet from making use of them. Greiss concluded, reluctantly, that they had no time, that their work here could be discovered at any moment, and that they would just have to take that chance.

They headed into the mine tunnel, in single file, Storm taking point wearing an ork miner's helmet, lighting their way through the darkness. Myers was behind him, then Armstrong, Braxton, Lorenzo and finally Greiss, his knife drawn, ready for anything that might try sneaking up on them from behind.

They had taken only ten steps, hardly left the lights of the clearing behind them, when they came across another ork with a barrow. Its helmet beam dazzled Lorenzo – but Storm's beam blinded the ork in turn so that, for a fateful moment, it didn't recognise the intruders for what they were. Sergeant Greiss had decreed that lasguns should only be used now when strictly necessary – not just because they were low on ammo, but because who knew how far the sound would carry through these tunnels – so Storm leapt at the creature with a muted snarl and his Catachan fang raised and, impressively, he gutted it before it could raise much more than a whimper.

Storm took the dead ork's helmet and passed it back along the line to Greiss, who turned off the helmet's light but placed it on his head for future use. Then they crept on downward, the slope of the tunnel becoming more pronounced until Lorenzo judged that they were descending below ground level.

He eyed the precarious wooden struts – most of them just branches chopped to size, still sprouting offshoots and leaves – that were wedged into the passageway, supporting the increasing weight of the earth above their heads. He didn't trust them.

The ground shook again then, as if to underscore his fears, and Lorenzo swallowed as the makeshift struts rattled fiercely and a shower of loose soil fell about his ears. He couldn't tell if this tremor was lighter or heavier than the first two; he only knew that it felt more ominous down here, where it wasn't just below him but around him and above him too, and where he knew there would be nowhere to hide from a more severe quake, no way to avoid being buried alive.

'You realise,' said Braxton, putting Lorenzo's own thoughts into words as the tremor subsided, 'if this place caves in, we'll have come all this way for nothing. Rogar will have dealt with Big Green for us.'

'Maybe,' grunted Greiss, 'and maybe not. Maybe he'll just slip away through his escape tunnel, wherever that is, and maybe it'll take us a year to find him again. No, I don't care if this whole damn world blows itself apart around us – I for one am not backing out of this on a "maybe". Far as I'm concerned, that brute's still alive until I clap my own eyes on his stinking corpse!'

Lorenzo became aware of a sick ache in his stomach, and he fought down a surge of bile in his throat. His skin felt hot, prickly, and he was short of breath. The symptoms came from nowhere, and at first he thought the tunnel must have caused them, this unfamiliar, claustrophobic environment.

Then he remembered the effigy, and its spines.

His precautions had done him no good. Rogar III's poison was coursing through his veins. He knew he should tell the others, warn them in case he went crazy like Muldoon had, became a threat to them. But then they would probably have left him behind, to die on his back like Woods, and he couldn't face that. Not when they were so close to their goal. Not when he was so close to a chance to earn his name, at last.

He *would* earn his name. Lorenzo swore that to himself. He didn't know how – but if he couldn't find a way down here with a world against him, then where could he? A way to surrender his life for his squad, for his cause, for a chance to be remembered, and he knew he wouldn't hesitate this time. Because, this time, he had nothing to lose. This time, he was dying anyway.

Might as well go out in a blaze of glory.

CHAPTER 16

Sergeant Greiss swore under his breath.

The orks' mine tunnel had opened into a cave – and Lorenzo could see, from the lack of wooden props and the uneven texture of the rock where Storm's light fell upon it, that it was natural. Passages snaked from the cave in all directions – ominous black holes in the walls.

'Looks like the greenskins have bust their way into a whole underground complex,' Greiss grumbled. 'Could spread for kilometres.'

'What do we do now, sergeant?' asked Braxton.

Before Greiss could answer, Myers let out a 'Ssshh,' and held up his hand for silence. A second later, they all heard it: lumbering footsteps, echoing from the walls until there was no way of knowing which direction they came from.

Storm snatched off his helmet, snapped off the light, and the Jungle Fighters dispersed, navigating by memory in the total darkness, finding nooks into which they could squeeze. Lorenzo found himself in the mouth of a narrow, twisting passageway, and feared for a moment that it was along this very route that the orks were approaching. Then the footsteps – two sets, he estimated – seemed to move around him, and he saw the bobbing beam of a helmet light, and then there were two hulking shapes in the cave, striding toward the exit tunnel.

Then the Jungle Fighters were upon the orks, Storm reaching them first, leaping onto the back of the nearest and drawing his blade across its throat. Greiss and Braxton crashed into the second creature, staggered it, and Lorenzo lent his shoulder to their efforts and it fell, three knives plunged into its chest and stomach.

'You notice something?' asked Armstrong, as the others confirmed their kills. 'These two were going up to the surface, but they don't have barrows. No pickaxes, no spades, just guns.'

'You think they suspect something?' murmured Greiss darkly.

'I think Big Green's maybe starting to wonder what's been happening to his barrow boys. Or maybe the sentries up top were supposed to report in. Either way, I'll bet these two were coming to investigate.'

'When they don't come back either...' breathed Myers.

'Alright,' Greiss nodded. 'We've got – how long would you say? – a few minutes before all hell breaks loose down here. Meantime, we need to make inroads into these caves, make sure the warboss can't go nowhere without getting past us first. Anyone else hear that? Sounds like digging?'

Myers reported that he did hear it – and, screwing up his face in concentration, Storm agreed. Lorenzo didn't hear a thing, and he scrabbled at the insides of his ears in frustration, evacuating more of Rogar III's mud. The effort disturbed his equilibrium, and his brain performed a lurching spin. The sickness in his stomach made another surge for his throat, and he swallowed it down.

Greiss and Myers followed the digging sounds to the right-hand side of the cave, and Myers located a tunnel that was wider and straighter than the others, its floor a little smoother. 'I'd say there's been a few barrows pushed up this way, sergeant,' he reported – and, standing at the tunnel entrance, even Lorenzo could now hear the distant clink of metal against rock from somewhere below.

'Right,' sighed Greiss, 'this is how it's going to have to be. We split into three teams. Patch and Lorenzo, you follow this tunnel here. Braxton, you're with me – we'll take the passage those two orks came up from. Bullseye, Wildman, you wait around here a while, stick to the shadows. Chances are, there'll be more greenskins along soon, and I'm betting once they find their buddies' corpses littering the place, they'll send word back to the big boss.'

'We can follow 'em,' concluded Storm. 'Right, sergeant.'

Everyone seemed happy with that plan, and Lorenzo didn't want to be the one to object. Still, he felt numb. His chances of being the one to find the warboss had just been slashed by two-thirds. He pictured himself dying quietly in a dark tunnel somewhere, while Greiss and Braxton, or Myers and Storm, stumbled upon their target and grabbed all the glory. He wouldn't let that happen.

Greiss handed him the miner's helmet from one of the dead orks, and Lorenzo jammed it onto his head and practically dragged Armstrong away, down the tunnel towards the digging sounds. 'Steady on,' whispered Patch in his ear, 'you'll run straight into the greenskins at this rate.' But Lorenzo wasn't listening. He'd had a lifetime of being too cautious. All he cared about now was covering as much ground as he could. More ground than the other two teams could cover. Being the first to find the ork warboss. Earning his name, before it was too late.

There were lights up ahead – harsh, like the lanterns outside. Lorenzo switched off his helmet beam and crept forward, Armstrong at his heels.

The tunnel they were following took a sharp dip, its gradient so steep that they were half-walking, half-sliding. The sounds of picks and shovels were unmistakeable now, and there was something else. The squeak of a wheel. Armstrong tapped Lorenzo on the shoulder and indicated a side passageway, narrow and level, also well lit. Lorenzo nodded, and they slipped into it, and pressed themselves against its walls so the light wouldn't cast their shadows across the junction.

An ork appeared, grunting as it strained to push a loaded barrow up the slope. Lorenzo's hand moved to his lasgun, knowing that if the creature saw them their cover was blown. It only had to yell out. To his relief, it moved on. Let Myers and Wildman take care of it when it reached them, he thought.

They moved further down the side passageway, until the right-hand wall fell away and they were in a natural gallery, looking out across a vast cavern. Its floor lay some ten metres below them; its far wall was four times that distance. The cavern was swarming with orks, hefting tools, battering at the walls, breaking off chunks of rock that gretchin gathered and piled into waiting barrows. The area was lit by six lanterns, squeezed into niches at varying heights, connected by tangles of thick cabling. There was a lantern beside the Jungle Fighters, on the gallery, lying on its side – and they crouched behind it so any ork that glanced their way wouldn't see them behind its intense light.

Lorenzo scanned the throng with his eyes, fervently hoping to find an ork with cleaner, better armour than the others; an ork that was giving the orders; an ork perhaps a little larger than its fellows. He was disappointed.

'Another nine, ten passageways off this chamber,' breathed Armstrong. 'This place is like a maze!'

'I don't know,' Lorenzo muttered. 'Most of those tunnels, I think the orks dug themselves – and I think they're still digging them. See how the gretchin keep coming back along them with more rubble. I'm betting most of them are dead ends.'

'Doesn't mean we won't find Big Green's quarters down one of them.'

Lorenzo conceded the point, but nodded towards a wide tunnel entrance below them to the left. 'Seems to be a lot of coming and going through there,' he remarked, 'and the passageway we're in heads in that direction. I think it's worth a look.'

'Your call,' said Armstrong.

They crept on, until rock closed in around them again and their passageway dipped and narrowed and came to an abrupt end. Its floor didn't quite meet the wall, however, and Lorenzo peered through the gap thus created and saw another passageway below. Even as he watched, an ork passed along it; he could almost have reached down and touched its head. He listened a moment, but the only sounds he could hear came from the main chamber behind and below them. He glanced at Armstrong, who nodded – and Lorenzo lowered himself through the hole, until he was hanging from his fingertips, then let himself drop.

The world gave another spin as he hit the ground, and he lost his balance and fell. He picked himself up quickly, humiliated, and gestured up to Armstrong that he was all right. He had guessed right. This tunnel sloped back down to the main chamber in one direction, climbed more gently into darkness in the other. He could only see a short way in the lantern light that bled up from below, but it was enough to see that the tunnel walls were riddled with openings.

At Lorenzo's signal, Armstrong joined him, hampered by his dead arm but still affecting a more graceful landing than his comrade had managed.

Two orks were coming their way. Quickly, they ducked into the nearest of the openings, and found themselves pushing through a tattered curtain.

Beyond this, a small cave was littered with skins and debris, and Lorenzo realised that orks had been sleeping here. Fortunately, there were none present at the moment.

A little further up, the tunnel levelled out and split into three, and they followed the left-hand branch. They found more quarters, some rumbling with the grunts and snores of sleeping residents, some apparently empty. Some had lights within, spilling around the edges of their curtains – and in one, the curtain was pulled aside and four orks sat around a flat-topped boulder, playing with knuckle dice. Lorenzo and Armstrong didn't dare risk passing that cave, so they backtracked and chose another path from the three-way junction.

Lorenzo felt angry. What the orks were doing here – it was wrong. At least, when the men of Catachan tamed a deathworld, it was a fair fight. They didn't burrow under its skin, try to destroy it from within like a virus. The thought of it made him itch, made the sickness rise in his stomach... He wasn't sure why, didn't know where these feelings were coming from, because it wasn't as if the Imperium had never strip-mined a world. Maybe just not a world like Rogar III...

They came across a particularly large entranceway, and Lorenzo hesitated, wondering if this could be the cave to house the warboss. He didn't want to poke his head around the curtain, though: he'd have been unlikely to see anything in the dark and he might have disturbed somebody. Anyway, he could hear at least three different snores from within – and it was probable, he thought, that the orks' warboss had a cave to himself.

A moment later, however, more footsteps – shuffling unexpectedly from an unseen tunnel, little more than a fissure in the rock – forced the two Jungle Fighters to duck into another cave. And this one was occupied.

Lorenzo held his breath, and not just because of the stink of ork bodies around him. He could just make them out: three festering lumps crammed together on the floor. He had almost stepped on one as he'd entered, and he eased his foot away from it. For a moment, he thought he had left Armstrong behind outside, so silent was he – but then he saw the glint of a single eye in the darkness, and was comforted.

The footsteps shuffled up to the cave entrance, and for a moment Lorenzo feared he might have had the bad luck to have taken cover in the wandering ork's own quarters – but then the moment passed and the footsteps were receding. Heading for the main chamber, he guessed.

But there was still something wrong – badly wrong – if only he could put his finger on it. Lorenzo's spine prickled with dread.

He realised what was about to happen a second before it did, and he knew that his luck had turned bad after all. As bad as it could have been.

The tremor shook the soles of his feet, then seemed to rise through the walls and meet again above his head. One of the sleeping orks stirred instantly, and Lorenzo was trapped. He didn't think it had seen him or Armstrong yet, but that could change in an instant, if they moved – and the footsteps outside the cave had come to a halt, so where could they have gone anyway?

The waking ork was fumbling for something, and Lorenzo wondered if there was a chance, a tiny chance, that he could reach it and muffle it before it yelled out, plant his hand over its mouth and his knife in its throat. But that tremor wasn't subsiding – and as he took his first step, the earth bucked underneath him and he fell, put out his hands to catch himself, ended up sprawled across one of the two sleeping orks. Which, of course, was awake too now.

The first ork had found a miner's helmet, and it snapped on the light, shining it around the cave. Armstrong let loose with a las-bolt volley, which kept the ork pinned down but didn't prevent it from letting out an alarm howl.

So now the third ork was clambering to its feet, blinking, reaching for its weapon, and Lorenzo was still trying to avoid the flailing grasp of the second. It caught him by the arm, and he was trying to pull away from it, dragging it to its feet after him, its fingers digging painfully into him. He turned, braced his shoulder against the ork's chest and tried to throw it. It was too heavy, shifting its weight to counter his move, but in so doing it relaxed its hold, and Lorenzo wrenched himself free from it, though it felt like he had lost a handful of his flesh.

Then he and Armstrong were running, as the third ork found its gun and fired – in entirely the wrong direction, confused by the shifting shadows and its wounded fellow's dancing beam of light. The Jungle Fighters burst out into the passageway, where the ork they had been hiding from was waiting, its gun raised. Lorenzo lowered his head, rushed it, and a bullet pinged off his helmet, then he cannoned into the ork and it gave a few paces but braced itself. They were fighting for the ork's gun, and Lorenzo feinted, let the greenskin have the weapon but unbalanced it in the process. It stumbled, and fell onto his freshly drawn knife, impaling itself. Planting his foot in the ork's stomach, he pulled the blade free. It was still alive, but he didn't have time to finish the job.

There were more orks in the passageway, pouring out of the openings on all sides, reacting to the clamour, and the only thing that kept Lorenzo and Armstrong alive was the fact that the earth was still shaking, and with increasing ferocity, confusing the issue, giving the orks more to worry about than just them. Armstrong made to flee back the way they had come; Lorenzo's impulse was to go deeper into the mine, find the ork leader, and they both came up short as they realised they were pulling in opposite directions.

Lorenzo knew, just *knew* they were in danger, and he threw himself at Armstrong, barged him into the wall as the roof caved in. They were coated in soil, disturbed dust tearing at Lorenzo's throat, making his eyes water, but they had avoided the worst of it and the orks were reeling around them, and Lorenzo grabbed Armstrong by the hand and pulled him along, guiding him through the chaos by instinct, at a loss to explain where that instinct had come from.

The tremor was more than a tremor now. It was a fully-fledged earthquake – and Lorenzo knew, with a gut-wrenching certainty, that this was only the beginning. The tunnel was shaking so fiercely, it felt like he had double vision; cracks were opening in the walls, the floor was churning itself up, tossing him about like a wild grox, and the roof was groaning and grinding and collapsing in stages. Rogar III was taking its revenge on the orks that had defiled it, driving them out of itself or just burying them. Lorenzo had lost all sense of direction, but he was moving broadly with the ork flow, and he knew that this meant he was headed back to the main chamber, and from there to the mine entrance. As if the planet itself was herding him that way. What hope did he have now of finding the ork warboss? What hope for him at all in that lantern-lit clearing, with a hundred evacuated greenskins waiting for him? Even assuming he could make it that far.

He was looking for another option, a way to cheat his fate, when an ork reared up in front of him, a spade levelled at his throat like a knife. Lorenzo swung his fang, but the quake made the ork appear to be in ten places at once, and his thrust passed through its ghost image. He didn't know which of its ten spades to avoid.

But then, with a tremendous crack, the wall behind the ork split, and Lorenzo caught his breath in the face of an explosion of fire.

Molten lava, bright red with its own luminescence. It burst through the sundered rock, broke over the ork's back, and the creature let out a howl of incandescent pain. Lorenzo didn't stop to ask how it was possible, how the planet could have pumped its own lifeblood so close to its surface. This was Rogar – and he could feel the lava's heat scorching his face even before it reached him. He kicked out at the scalded, screeching ork, and landed his boot dead centre where all its images combined. It staggered, fell backwards, and its bulky form all but plugged the fissure as Lorenzo had planned. The ork's screams were quelled, its body shuddered and fell still, as liquid fire crept over its shoulders and between its legs.

Lorenzo and Armstrong had a moment's respite. Many of the orks behind them had held back, or tried to back up along the narrow tunnel, when they'd seen the lava. They were colliding with each other, knocking each other down. From the chorus of screams that suddenly rose from up there, somewhere in the darkness, Lorenzo guessed that another lava spring had just opened behind them.

The Jungle Fighters ran – but Lorenzo dragged his comrade to a halt as, suddenly, he saw where they were. Above them was the hole in the roof through which they had dropped: the one that led up to the natural gallery. A way to circumvent the main chamber and all the confused, frightened, angry orks within.

He gave Armstrong a boost, and the veteran shouldered his way up through the narrow opening, attained the ledge above, then turned and reached down with his good arm for his comrade. As Lorenzo took it and scrambled up after him, an ork came roaring out of nowhere and swung its axe at his dangling legs. The shifting earth threw off its aim, and Lorenzo stamped on the ork's face and pushed himself up the final section of his climb. He fired his lasgun down the hole behind him to discourage pursuit, then turned and followed Armstrong along the narrow passageway – to find, to his horror, that it came to an abrupt end.

The gallery, their route to freedom, had crumbled away. They were looking out of a hole in the side of the main chamber, at another hole too far to reach by jumping, the intervening expanse of wall too sheer to climb along even if it hadn't been shaking madly. Lorenzo's foot touched something: the lantern they had passed earlier, still on its side, wedged into position by a stubborn outcrop. He followed its light beam, and on the floor of the chamber he saw a molten river.

The chamber had split down the middle, and its halves were divided by a roiling, bubbling lava flow. Dozens of orks had been trapped on its far side, and panic had broken out. An ork tried to leap the stream, but fell short, howling as its legs were dissolved, the rest of its body sinking after them until only a thin wisp of steam remained of it.

Lorenzo had his own problems. An ork head popped up through the hole in the floor behind him. He and Armstrong fired at it – and, holding on with both hands, there wasn't much it could do to defend itself. Even in death, though, it kept coming, the head followed into the passageway by a pair of broad shoulders, then a green-skinned torso. Lorenzo realised that the corpse was being pushed up by more orks below, shielding them as they followed it. The muzzle of a crude ork gun appeared over the hole's edge and fired blindly. Bullets ricocheted around the confined space, and Lorenzo drew a sharp breath through his teeth as his shoulder was nicked.

'We're easy targets up here,' muttered Armstrong. 'We can hold off these greenskins for a while – but our backs are exposed to the main chamber. Once the orks down there see us, we'll be caught in a crossfire, dead meat.'

He was saying nothing Lorenzo didn't know. He cast around for something, anything – and his eyes found the lantern. It was trailing tangled cables in each direction around the great cavern; clockwise, the next lantern still clung to the wall, but anticlockwise, the nearest two had been wrenched free from their moorings and were hanging suspended. Lorenzo pulled at the cables in that direction, and found plenty of slack.

Armstrong glanced at him, saw what he was thinking and nodded his approval. 'That might get one of us out of here,' he said. 'Go. I'll buy you some time.'

With that he was off, before Lorenzo could stop him – back down the passageway, leaping onto the first ork as it hauled itself up out of the hole, taking it by surprise, forcing it back down but falling with it, toward the blood-thirsty pack that Lorenzo knew must have gathered below. His instinct was to go after his comrade, to do what he could to help him – but not only was it hopeless, he would have been doing him a disservice. Armstrong had sacrificed himself to save Lorenzo, to give him a chance at least – because Lorenzo had let him, because he hadn't spoken up first, because he hadn't told his comrade that his life was over anyway, that if the orks and the quake didn't finish him the poison would.

Armstrong was relying on Lorenzo to tell that story – which was all that kept him going now as he yanked on the lantern, tore out the taut cables from one side of it and gathered the loose ones to the other. He looked for a safe landing spot, clear of orks and lava and falling rocks.

That was when he saw it. Amid the chaos below, a great brutish ork, trapped on the far side of the lava stream but walking taller, more confidently, than its fellows. It was surrounded by an entourage seven-strong – one of which was festooned with bizarre totems and carried a staff.

As Lorenzo watched, two of the guards seized another gretchin, and bore it face-first into the lava. First the larger ork then the shaman used it as a stepping-stone, hopping onto its back and across to safety before it boiled away. Then the big ork turned and shouted impatient curses at its guards, and they tried to follow but without any such assistance. Four of them made the leap; two did not.

Lorenzo didn't care about them. He had eyes only for their master, with its tough, leathery skin and its gleaming new axe, twice the size of the other orks' weapons and with ceremonial trappings. He had no doubt that this was him. The warboss. Big Green. He even knew, with a flash of insight, what the strange-looking ork with the staff had to be, why it was getting preferential treatment. The source of Big Green's vaunted intelligence. An ork psyker – a weirdboy!

Everything he had ever wanted. His blaze of glory...

Lorenzo wrapped his hands around the entwined cables, calculated the trajectory of his swing. The ork leader was facing away from him, at the edge of the lava flow. One kick between the shoulder blades, with enough weight behind it, would send him reeling. Hit him at the right angle, and the weirdboy might even go with him. And the fact that Lorenzo would doubtless follow both orks into the fire – well, that was good too. A fitting end for a hero.

Only, he realised, with a pang of despair, who would see it? Who would tell the story of this, his greatest moment? He hesitated.

Which, in turn, made him angry with himself. Not this time, he thought. His last chance to count, to make his life mean something. At least *he'd* know.

So, Lorenzo pushed himself off from the rock, and his heart leapt as he saw that his path was true, that even the quake hadn't shaken him off-course. He saw his destiny rushing towards him, and in that moment he *knew* that someone, somewhere, would tell a story about this some day.

Even if it was only the orks themselves.

CHAPTER 17

Everything had changed in an instant.

Lorenzo was on the ground, fighting unconsciousness, not sure how much of the violent, lurching motion around him came from the earthquake and how much from inside him. He tried to put together the pieces of what had just happened.

He had seen it lain out before him: the rest of his life. His heroic death. The ork warboss, growing larger and closer until there was nothing else in the world, nothing else that mattered. Only the warboss, and the river of fire.

Only Big Green, somehow, had heard him coming, or maybe a follower had shouted a warning or his psyker had muttered a prediction, because he had turned – and, with no time to swing his axe nor to sidestep, he had *leapt* instead, and met his oncoming attacker head on. His muscular arms had encircled Lorenzo's legs, and they had hit the ground together but the warboss had landed on his feet while Lorenzo had been smacked down onto his back.

He expected to die a failure – until he realised that the warboss had staggered, at least. He had taken a step back to brace himself – and his foot had slipped into the lava stream. The psyker let out a panicked chittering sound at his master's peril and hobbled away. Lorenzo held his breath but the warboss's self-control was incredible. He triumphed over what must have been searing agony, to keep his balance – and he loomed over the Catachan with his axe raised high, though one of his legs now tapered to a dripping, cauterised stump at the ankle. Lorenzo still didn't know what to do, because he hadn't planned for this situation, hadn't planned to survive this long.

So it was just as well that his instincts took over – and he kicked out at the warboss's intact leg with all his might, and he managed to fell him but not backwards as he'd hoped. Lorenzo scrambled on top of the huge ork, still hoping that somehow he could roll them both into the lava – but Big Green was too heavy and unyielding, and Lorenzo was seized from behind by two of his four remaining bodyguards.

He kicked and yelled as he was dragged from his foe – as more orks streamed towards him from all directions, disregarding their own peril in the face of his threat to their leader. Rarely had he seen such a display of loyalty from the greenskins. Now a curtain of snarling faces closed in front of Lorenzo, and he couldn't see the ork leader any more, and he knew it was all over.

The sounds of las-fire seemed distant at first, as if they came from a world that was no longer his concern. It was only when the orks began to scatter, when one of those that held him was hit and loosed its grip, that Lorenzo realised a new element had entered the equation. Or rather, two new elements. Sergeant Greiss and Braxton. Lorenzo didn't know where they'd come from – a tunnel opening beneath the collapsed gallery was his best bet – but they had bought him another chance when he had thought he was out of chances, and he wasn't about to waste it.

He tried to throw his remaining captor, but failed. Again, his instincts came to the rescue, predicting the patterns of the quake, telling him when the ground would buck beneath the ork's feet, which way to push when it did. The greenskin squealed as it fell, surfed the shifting floor on its back and wound up with its head in the lava.

Lorenzo drew his gun, and immediately found a target. The greenskin psyker. He had thought it long gone, but it must have run into the new arrivals and reversed its flight. At least, he thought as he killed it, that was the end of the warboss's advantage. He was just a normal warboss now. But his squad's orders hadn't been to kill the psyker, they'd been to kill Big Green himself, and he intended to do just that.

The warboss couldn't have gone far – not with only one foot. Indeed, there he was, just a few metres distant, being helped along by two guards. But Greiss was closer, and Lorenzo could see the familiar gleam in his sergeant's eyes, knew he had spied an opening and would take it, heedless of the cost to himself. While Lorenzo's path was blocked again, and he couldn't clear it in time – though he ploughed into the orks anyway, lasgun flaring, fang flashing, and he wasn't sure if the red mist he could see was a product of his own unreasoning anger or his poisoning or just an afterglow from the lava stream.

All he knew, in that desperate moment, was that he had to reach the warboss before his sergeant did. He couldn't help himself. Greiss was tired of life, wanted to go out on a high – but he had earned his name. Weren't there enough stories told of him already?

Greiss was wading through orks like they were nothing. They'd given up trying to shoot him, because it was hopeless aiming through the quake, and they were throwing themselves at him to be hurled aside or gutted or just trampled as they mistimed their rushes and fell at Greiss's feet. Lorenzo was so busy watching this performance that he was barely aware of his own actions, moving on autopilot, stabbing at an ork throat here, reacting to the whistle of a descending axe there. It was only as a substantial chunk of the chamber's roof fell, as Lorenzo danced out of its way and a dozen orks were crushed, that he realised what he'd been doing: drawing his foes to him, bunching them together, setting them up for a fate no man could have predicted... could he?

Dust billowed black around him, rubble made his footing treacherous, and the last of the lanterns toppled from its high perch, smashed and died.

The only light now came from the lava – and Lorenzo almost plunged into it as, scrambling to find the warboss, he slid on a layer of scree. Then the earth cracked again, and suddenly the molten stream had a hundred narrow tributaries, crazing the cavern floor. Lorenzo vaulted them two at a time; he knew where he was going, almost as if he could sense his prey's ponderous, one-legged footsteps through the ground itself.

There he was – stranded on an island, only one guard left at his side, the lava flows around him thin and shallow but impassable to one with his disability. As Big Green saw Lorenzo, his eyes widened with fear and hatred, and he yelled and gesticulated to his guard, ordering it to lay itself down as a bridge for him. The ork signalled its refusal by swiping at the warboss's neck with its axe; evidently, loyalty had its limits, especially when an ork sensed that its leader's day was done.

But Big Green had earned his position for a reason. Some warbosses had been known to go toe to toe with Space Marines. Displaying the same lightning reflexes with which he'd met the Jungle Fighters' first attack upon him, the warboss caught the axe's blade between both hands, a centimetre from his slavering sneer, and twisted the weapon right out of his startled guard's hands.

Lorenzo was firing frantically – but like the orks, he found his shots knocked astray. the warboss had his traitor guard by the neck, had wrenched its arm up behind its back, and was pushing it down, and it looked like he was about to get his bridge after all, so Lorenzo sprang for the warboss's back.

He timed his leap just right, to benefit from an upsurge beneath his feet; Big Green whipped around and swung his giant axe, but Lorenzo was higher than he could have expected, and the blade passed beneath his feet – and then he was on the warboss's shoulders, and he plunged his knife into the ork's eye and tried to work its point up into his brain.

Big Green howled and threw back his arms, trying to swat the Jungle Fighter from his back. Lorenzo held on as long as he could, but between the warboss and the quake it was like trying to straddle three grox at once. He pulled his knife free and jumped before he could be thrown, landing nimbly on his feet.

He parried an axe thrust with his knife, and simultaneously kicked out at the warboss's injured leg, making him howl again. But Big Green didn't fall. He barely even flinched – and Lorenzo had been counting on at least a momentary respite to drop back into a defensive position. The axe blade whistled toward him again, and the flat of its blade struck a resounding blow against his wrist, splintering bones, and his knife flew out of his grasp.

It was spinning towards the lava, and Lorenzo leapt after it without thinking, dropping his lasgun, catching the knife with his off-hand in midair, twisting to avoid a scalding death himself. He landed on his back, winded as the ground rose up to meet him. The warboss lunged, and Lorenzo barely brought up a foot in time, tried to kick the warboss away, but the ork batted it aside. Then he was on Lorenzo, the sharp points of his tusks almost touching the Catachan's face, dripping drool onto his cheek and blood from his punctured eye, and Big Green's axe haft was pressed down across Lorenzo's throat, crushing his windpipe.

All Lorenzo could do was take that haft himself, try to force it upwards, away from him, but the warboss was too strong, and he could feel the breath being choked out of him. His lungs were empty, burning, and his head felt light. He held on, because every fraction of a second he could keep Big Green here dealing with him was a further delay to the warboss's escape. Lorenzo may have failed to kill this monster, but he could be the hero who engaged it in single combat, kept it trapped long enough for the earthquake to finish it. A forlorn hope, he realised.

Then, suddenly, the pressure on his throat was released, and Lorenzo tried to see what was happening, but without him knowing it his eyes had closed and he couldn't open them because they were prickling with tears and his entire body was preoccupied with just trying to breathe. His stomach convulsed as he heaved in air, and spluttered on its gritty texture.

By the time he could look again, he knew what he would see: Sergeant Greiss, wrestling with the warboss. Greiss had landed a few good blows, too – the warboss had a livid scar on his cheek to add to the one Lorenzo had left across his eye. But he was fighting on, as if nothing would ever stop him.

Lorenzo's legs were too weak to stand, so he contented himself with hitting his opponent low, the combination of his efforts and Greiss's, and Big Green's missing foot, flooring the big ork again. They piled on top of him, fists and knives flying, but they couldn't still his axe – and its blade swung and impacted with Greiss's head, cleaving his miner's helmet in two, cutting into his scalp and, with a resounding clang, hitting the metal plate just below the surface. Greiss fell back, blood matting his grey hair as Lorenzo used the momentum of the warboss's swing against him, and with a tremendous, last-ditch heave, tipped and *rolled* him into one of the narrow streams. The ork leader was facedown in the lava but still thrashing, and Lorenzo placed his good hand on the back of the warboss's head and, releasing a strangulated roar of utter hatred from the back of his throat. He pushed down...

Then he was scrambling towards Greiss, though he didn't know what he could do for him. The sergeant was bleeding freely, but all Lorenzo could see in his face was a malicious satisfaction at the death of an enemy. And maybe, when he looked at Lorenzo, a hint of approval?

Then, a sudden change of expression – a warning glint in Greiss's eyes. Lorenzo whirled around and the warboss was standing, molten lava streaming from his face, most of the skin burnt away, but he was coming at them again...

Greiss was firing at him, pumping las-round after las-round into the warboss's chest, and Lorenzo didn't think it would be enough – but then there was las-fire from behind Big Green too, and a bedraggled, soot-blackened figure emerged through a haze of dust – and even as the ork leader reached his targets, as he made to bring his axe down, it was one of Guardsman Braxton's rounds that finally sizzled through his skull and put out the feral light in those eyes once and for all.

Lorenzo had thought he'd feel different when the ork leader died at last. He had expected to feel... something. Relieved, perhaps. Or dismayed, that another man had delivered the killing blow. Somehow, he had thought there would be silence, and time to reflect – but as another great chunk of rock was dislodged from the cavern roof to thunk into the ground beside him, he knew it was not to be.

Braxton helped Lorenzo to his feet, and they both turned to give Greiss a lift, but the grizzled sergeant waved them away stubbornly. 'We've got to get out of here, sergeant,' insisted Braxton as Lorenzo retrieved his gun and slapped a new pack into position. 'This place won't hold up much longer. Most of the orks have already run for it. Where's Patch?'

Lorenzo shook his head. 'Bullseye and Wildman?'

'Dead,' said Greiss, flatly. 'Me and Braxton, we stumbled across their bodies on our way in. Looks like they found Big Green before we did, more's the pity.'

'I'm sure they put up a good fight,' said Lorenzo, almost automatically. 'I'm sure if it hadn't been for them, if they hadn't weakened–'

'Time enough for eulogies later,' growled Greiss. 'Looked like the green-skins were mostly headed back up to the clearing, but we found another way out.' He nodded in the direction from which he and Braxton had appeared. 'We take that, chances are we'll run into less opposition along the way. That is, if the whole tunnel hasn't collapsed by now.'

'Let me lead the way,' said Lorenzo.

Greiss snarled. 'Like hell! In case you hadn't noticed, trooper, I am not dead yet – and I'm still in charge of this squad, what's left of it.'

'That's not what I meant, sergeant. I've been having a... a... I don't know how to describe it, some kind of an instinct about the quake. Like I know how the earth's going to move, where it's safe to step, where...' Lorenzo tailed off, embarrassed at how implausible the words sounded out loud.

But Greiss just regarded him coolly for a moment, then nodded and grunted, 'Step to it, then.'

Lorenzo set off sure-footedly, affecting confidence while inwardly he half-expected his luck to run out at any moment. Then, there it was again: that indefinable feeling, that tug in a certain direction. Greiss indicated a tunnel mouth ahead of them, but Lorenzo balked at a direct approach, and picked out a circuitous path towards their goal instead. His caution was rewarded as a lava stream bubbled and spat its contents straight up like a geyser.

The Jungle Fighters hugged the wall, keeping just out of range of burning droplets, until they reached the tunnel and stumbled gratefully into its stale but cooler embrace. After that, their progress was a little easier, because there were no lava streams up here and because they could lean on the walls for support. To some extent, anyway. A particularly violent shudder pinballed the trio from one side of the passageway to the other and back, and made Greiss curse and demand to know why Lorenzo hadn't felt that one coming.

Darkness enveloped them, and Lorenzo snapped on his helmet light, which luckily still worked. They passed several junctions, with Greiss bellowing directions at each one – and they found their path strewn with crushed ork bodies, and had to squeeze their way around more than one partial cave-in.

It was Braxton who first voiced the feeling that they were being followed, though when Lorenzo shone his light behind them they could see nothing. Greiss urged them on, and eventually he directed them into an upward-leading passageway that was smoother and straighter than the others, obviously worked, like the one they had followed down from the clearing.

The first set of wooden struts they came across had slipped and buckled but, miraculously, held; they climbed past them gingerly. The second had broken into splinters, but fortunately the roof was staying up by itself.

It was just past the third that their luck ran out.

Lorenzo heard the orks ahead of them before he saw them. There were a half-dozen of them, jabbering in panic as they tried to dig through a pile of rubble that had completely blocked the tunnel. They were succeeding mostly in getting in each other's way: as the Jungle Fighters watched, one ork accidentally embedded its pickaxe in the skull of another.

They were sitting ducks for a volley of las-fire, the narrow confines ensuring that even through the quake most of the Jungle Fighters' shots found a target. The orks, in turn, didn't seem to be armed – and, taken by surprise, they jostled with each other in their haste to close with their attackers, more than one of them stumbling in the melee and being manhandled aside. A single greenskin made it within knife range – and this, Lorenzo made short work of with his Catachan fang.

As he yanked his blade out of the ork's chest, he stumbled, brushed the tunnel wall with his bare arm and recoiled from its unexpected heat. Greiss had felt it too, and he gave Lorenzo a quizzical look. 'Lava,' he confirmed. 'It's all right – it hasn't built up enough pressure yet to cause a burst. We've got a few minutes.'

Greiss nodded, and asked, 'How far to the surface?'

'Almost there. Just the other side of that cave-in.'

'Guess the orks had the right idea, then,' said Greiss – and the Jungle Fighters rummaged amid the corpses of their enemies to retrieve their pickaxes and spades, and set about the blockage with gusto and a great deal more efficiency and teamwork than the greenskins had demonstrated.

Lorenzo was worried about Greiss. He had retied his bandana like a bandage over his head wound – but the bleeding showed no sign of abating, red rivulets rolling down his cheek. None of this seemed to lessen the zeal with which he swung his pickaxe, but then Lorenzo had learned to expect no less from him.

'Looks like you were right, Braxton,' Greiss murmured – and Lorenzo swung around, and this time his light beam *did* pick out something. A lot of somethings, no longer bothering to hide.

Ork zombies, shuffling up the tunnel behind them. They could only fit two abreast with their broad shoulders, but their ranks extended further back than Lorenzo could see – and, at their heart: the chilling sight of an even bulkier creature that could only have been the warboss himself, his skull half-caked with mud but stripped to the bone beneath this.

There was still too far to dig, no way they could escape in time. There were too many sources of fresh corpses for Rogar to use against them, even discounting those orks that had been melted in lava or whose bones had been shattered. Lorenzo found himself averting his gaze from the oncoming army – not through fear of their strength and numbers, but lest he glimpse the familiar shape of a lost comrade among them.

'Looks like this is it,' growled Greiss.

'No, sergeant,' protested Lorenzo – though he knew it was hopeless too. 'Not now. Not when we're so close!'

'I didn't mean the end for all of us. Just me. About damn time!'

'What... what are you...?' Lorenzo began – but Greiss hefted his pickaxe, and Lorenzo saw that gleam in his eyes, saw where it was focused, and suddenly he knew what the sergeant was planning. And, impulsively, he laid a restraining hand on his shoulder and he said, 'Let me.'

'What's wrong with you, trooper?' snapped Greiss. 'That's twice you've questioned my orders, and I'm telling you, I don't like it!'

'You've taken worse hits than this, sergeant. I know you have. You aren't going to let some dumb ork get the better of you, are you?'

'Too damn old,' grumbled Greiss. 'This was always going to be my last outing. And you, Lorenzo, you got a job to do. You're the only one who can tell Patch's story. I'm only sorry I won't be around to hear it.'

'I... I'm dying too, sergeant. Poisoned.'

Greiss looked Lorenzo up and down, and said curtly, 'You look all right to me.' Lorenzo couldn't argue, because Greiss was right – because, exhausted and hurt though he was, he realised only now that the effects of the effigy's venom, the nausea and the dizziness, had receded.

Then Greiss clapped him on the arm and smiled grimly. 'Live for me. Tell everyone I did it, got my blaze of glory. And don't be so damn impatient for yours. Way I see it, you got a lot of stories in you yet; you only just earned your name.'

He turned and, before Lorenzo could say anything else – before he could think what *to* say – he was charging at the front rank of zombies with a bloodcurdling scream. As he reached them, as they grabbed and clawed at him, he smashed his pickaxe into the wall beside them, again and again, until the first crack began to show... and to widen... and *explode*.

A deluge of lava crashed into the passageway, and surged downhill. It subsumed Sergeant Greiss and the zombies, swept them away, and Lorenzo knew that this time there wouldn't be enough left of any of them for Rogar to reanimate. He turned away, couldn't watch, concentrated on the blockage in front of him, swinging his pickaxe in time with Braxton's, driving himself on, ignoring the pain in his fractured wrist, not letting himself think about anything but the task at hand because if he did think about it, what had happened to Greiss and Armstrong and Myers and Storm and all the others, if he really *thought* about it, he might have been overwhelmed by the unfairness of it all. Why them? Why them and not him?

Lorenzo thought about their sacrifices, and his greatest fear was that they would all be for nothing.

His pickaxe rose and fell, and he could feel the heat from the lava at his back and the rock walls closed in around him, and his pickaxe rose and fell, and there were tears in his eyes but that might have been the dirt. He remembered the ship, out in warp space, so long ago now, and that feeling of being trapped, surrounded by hostile forces, helpless to influence his own fate, and he longed for the open air but feared he would never breathe it again.

Lorenzo's pickaxe rose and fell, and he felt as if he had been doing this forever, getting nowhere. He could sense the planet, his enemy, a living presence in his thoughts, and he knew it had won, defeated him, that he would never find his way out from inside it – that Rogar III would bury him as it had buried the rest of his squad. Just swallowed them up, left no trace of them. No one to tell their stories.

No one to remember...

CHAPTER 18

Daylight.

Lorenzo hardly registered it at first, couldn't bring himself to believe in what might have been a cruel trick on the planet's part. It was only a pinprick, after all, not enough to make out any details of what might be out there. But it was daylight, nonetheless, and its touch invigorated him.

His right wrist was bruise-blackened, stiffening, and he couldn't wield the pickaxe any more without suffering a lance of pain up his arm. But he and Braxton had chipped most of the bigger pieces of rock away, and Lorenzo's knife was now sufficient to whittle at the packed soil that remained. To make that pinprick wider.

Finally, thankfully, after what seemed like an age in the dark, they pushed their way through a curtain of loose earth and emerged, stumbling and choking, into the dew-pregnant morning. Only a few hours, Lorenzo calculated from the height of the sun, since they had entered the ork mine – but what a difference those few hours had made.

The earth had stopped shaking; Lorenzo didn't know when. Maybe Rogar III had expended its energy – or maybe it was just content with its fresh kills, for now. Nothing stirred in the jungle – and, after so much noise, the silence felt eerie. It heightened Lorenzo's creeping sense of loneliness.

There was a shape in the undergrowth. An ork, lying face-down. He thought it was sleeping at first, but on closer inspection it proved to be dead. He recognised the multiple scorched entrance wounds of las-rounds on its green skin. A short way from it, he discovered another two greenskin corpses, and a gretchin that had evidently tried to run and had been cut down from behind. They must have escaped the mine before the tunnel collapse, he thought, to find a greater peril waiting outside. He was grateful. In his current condition, even a trio of orks, if they had taken him by surprise, might have proved too much.

Lorenzo sensed, rather than heard, movement behind him, and he knew it could only be one man. He turned to greet Sly Marbo with a cool nod.

The legendary Catachan stood just a few metres away, but Lorenzo could hardly make him out against the greens and browns of his background. He recognised his dead, white eyes, though, and his deep voice, empty of emotion.

'Did you get him?' asked Sly Marbo.

'Big Green?' said Lorenzo. 'Yes, yes, we got him.'

Marbo nodded. He had heard what he needed to know. He left without a footstep or a rustle, seeming to melt into the jungle without moving at all. For a moment, Lorenzo fought the discomfiting feeling that he *hadn't* moved, that he was still there, watching with his white eyes. But that was just paranoia, he knew. Marbo was gone – and it was unlikely Lorenzo would see him again.

Braxton, meanwhile, had sagged to the ground, and was sitting with his back to a tree, knees up to his chest. 'I could sleep for a week,' he moaned.

'Go ahead,' said Lorenzo, checking for jungle lizards in the grass before he sat down beside him. 'For an hour or two, anyway. I'll keep watch – but I think it's safe. I think it'll take Rogar a while to gather its strength, to be ready for its next move.'

'How can you know that?' asked Braxton.

Lorenzo shrugged. 'I just do. It's like I can feel it in the back of my brain. Like I could feel, underground, when the earth was going to move, where the lava was flowing... I've been feeling it ever since the effigy poisoned me.'

'You told Sergeant Greiss you were dying.'

'I thought I was. But this was something different. A part of the planet in me. I think it was trying to... In some weird way, I think it wanted to... communicate.'

'Didn't stop it trying to kill you,' remarked Braxton. 'Or any of us.'

'No,' agreed Lorenzo. 'I think – I *feel* – it didn't have much choice in that.'

'And I expect it'll try again.'

'I expect it will.' It felt strange to say the words, to accept something that a few days earlier he'd have sworn was impossible. If Brains had been here, he reflected, he'd probably have been able to make it all sound rational. As it was, there was only one way Lorenzo could make sense of all he'd been through. 'Remember,' he said, 'when the zombies were stalking us, you said something about the planet itself being intelligent.'

'It seemed that way, at the time.'

'Yes, it did. To all of us. But I'm not sure that was quite right. No, I don't think Rogar III *is* intelligent as such – not in a calculating way. It's more like... like it's just been reacting. To what's been happening on its surface. To the orks. To us. To the fighting. Like it can't help it.'

'Like some kind of an allergy,' suggested Braxton. 'The more we fight, the more we harm the planet, the more deadly the defences it evolves. New plants and animals, springing up on its skin like rashes. Or antibodies.'

'Yes. Like that. And whatever it is, whatever's caused this, I doubt it's something that can be mined. The orks are wasting their time.'

'That's what Rogar wanted you – wanted all of us – to understand,' said Braxton. 'We're all wasting our time.'

Lorenzo looked at the Validian, and he remembered the nervous, apologetic adjutant who had joined their squad four days ago, the stranger whose intrusion he and the other Catachans had so resented. 'You did well,' he said. 'I mean, really well. All the men, good men, who died trying to see this mission through to the end – but you're the one who finished it. You struck the killing blow.'

Braxton waved aside the compliment. 'I did nothing. It was a team effort. You took on the ork leader by yourself, and crippled him. And Sergeant Greiss – if it hadn't been for him, we'd both be dead. I just blundered along at the right moment.'

'You made it this far,' said Lorenzo, 'when most didn't. I guess that makes you one of us, after all.'

'It isn't over yet,' said Braxton. 'We've got a four-day trek ahead of us, if we're to make it back to the encampment.'

'Even if we don't,' said Lorenzo, 'Marbo will. They'll know we did our job. They'll know Big Green is dead.'

'Maybe,' said Braxton, 'but they ought to know more than that. They ought to know about Old Hardhead and the others, what they did for us – what they did for everyone. Don't suppose I'll get to write that story, though.'

Lorenzo grinned. 'You could always try. You get drummed out of the Imperial Guard, I'm sure the Jungle Fighters would have you.'

They sat there, side by side, for a long time, warmed by the sun, exchanging no words but sharing a deep bond of comradeship forged in the fires of their mutual experience. Eventually, Braxton got up and searched the dead orks, finding a water bottle and taking a long swig from it before he passed it to Lorenzo. The Catachan hadn't realised how thirsty he was, and the cold liquid felt blissful against his parched throat.

'So, what do I call you now?' asked Braxton, sitting beside him again.

'I don't know what you mean,' he lied.

'Now you've earned your name. I heard what Greiss said.'

'He didn't want me sacrificing myself instead of him. He wanted his blaze of glory. He was just telling me what I wanted to hear.'

'You really think?' Braxton raised an eyebrow. 'Maybe I didn't know Old Hardhead as well as you did – but tell me this: in all the time he led your squad, did he ever once just tell anyone what they wanted to hear?'

Lorenzo let out a bark of a laugh, and conceded, 'Suppose not.'

'So, what do I call you?'

He sighed. 'Lorenzo, still. Just Trooper Lorenzo. A Catachan's earned name – it's given to him by his comrades. It's like a mark of their respect, a sign that they accept him. And I've got no comrades left.'

'Maybe, when the other platoons hear–'

'Maybe. But hearing about it isn't the same as being there. I'll probably be assigned to another squad, with men who don't know me, and they won't care that my old sergeant *meant* to give me my name if he'd been able to think of one, if he hadn't been too busy charging to his death. I'll have to prove myself all over again. Anyway, what *are* they going to call me? What did I do that was so special? I wanted to... I wanted to be the one who held off the orks so Patch could escape, but he got there first. I wanted to be the one who took out Big Green, but I wasn't strong enough. I wanted to stop the zombies, but Old Hardhead...'

'Sounds to me,' said Braxton, 'like you got a suicide wish – like you think you can't prove yourself unless you die in the process. What was it you just said to me? "*You made it this far...*"'

'By not being brave enough,' Lorenzo muttered.

'By taking everything this planet had to throw at you,' countered Braxton. 'Birds, acid plants, lights, zombies, the earthquake... By facing all that and surviving! You think that was dumb luck? I've been watching you, Lorenzo, and okay, maybe you aren't always the first to stick your head in the lion's mouth, but that's because you think about things, assess the situation, then deal with it – not in a showy way, not looking for glory, but efficiently. You get the job done. You were the first person to give me a chance, to look beyond the fact that Mackenzie had foisted me on you. Maybe it took the others too long to appreciate that; maybe they took you for granted. But I'll bet that's what Old Hardhead Greiss realised at the end there: that you were always there, for him, for all of us, that you were the most dependable man on this squad. I'll bet if he were here now, he'd find a name for you to say all that. Something like... like... "Long Run".'

'"Long Run"?'

'"Long Run" Lorenzo. What do you think? Got a ring to it?'

'I don't know. I...'

Braxton grinned. 'You've got to accept it. You just told me, I'm one of you now.'

'You enjoy throwing my words back in my face, don't you?'

'So I've a right to give you your name. The name you've earned. And I like the sound of Long Run.'

Lorenzo sat back, turned the words over in his head, tried to find an argument against accepting them, and smiled. 'Yes,' he said. 'I like it too.'

'So,' said Braxton, 'what do you say, Long Run? Ready to move off?'

'I thought you wanted to sleep.'

'I feel okay now. More than okay. I think we should get some distance under our belts, while things are quiet.'

Lorenzo nodded. 'Maybe Rogar hasn't covered over the paths we cut through the jungle yet. We're not likely to run into any more orks for a while. I reckon we can make this return trip in three days – less, if we hustle.'

'I guess that depends,' said Braxton, getting to his feet, 'on how hard Rogar III tries to stop us.'

'Whatever it does,' said Lorenzo, straightening his bandana, 'we'll deal with it. We have to. We've got a story to take back. The other squads, the other platoons, they'll be back from fighting orks by now, probably razed a few settlements. They'll want to know how we got on, if any of it was worth the sweat. We have to warn them about Rogar. We have to tell them what it is, what they're doing to it.'

'You think it'll change anything?' asked Braxton.

Lorenzo shook his head. He remembered something Old Hardhead had said, on the morning they'd set out from the encampment. 'Best thing we could do now would be to leave this world alone. That's all it wants. But the Imperium won't leave as long as the orks are here, and the orks won't leave until we do. Neither side can afford to turn its back on the other, so we'll just keep fighting.'

'Over nothing,' said Braxton.

'Over nothing,' Lorenzo agreed. 'And in the meantime, our violence will breed violence in turn. They only started calling Rogar III a deathworld a month ago. You have to wonder, what will it be like in another month? A year? A decade?'

'I don't know,' said Braxton, 'but I'm counting on being around to find out.'

Lorenzo grinned. 'Look forward to it.'

Then, like Sly Marbo before them, they disappeared into the jungle together, in near-total silence. They left only the faintest footprints to suggest that either of them had ever been here. And, a few minutes later, the deathworld had erased even them.

KASRKIN

Edoardo Albert

PART I

Big Yellow

CHAPTER 1

'Looks big.'

'Bigger than you think.'

'Suppose it's hot too?'

'Hot enough to fry a grox steak on the cowling of a Leman Russ.'

'So why not send a squadron of them in then?'

'Heard they tried – didn't get more than a mile before they started sinking.' Sergeant Shaan Malick adjusted his helmet. He wasn't wearing it; he was sitting on it. Beside him, Trooper Torgut Gunsur stared out from the relative cool of the precious shade under the stubby wings of the Valkyrie, his eyes squinting against the glare.

'It's all yellow.'

Sergeant Malick laughed. 'It's the Great Sand Sea. There's a clue in the name.'

Trooper Gunsur unclipped his rebreather and spat, the phlegm arcing out from the precious shade and landing on the sand. It sizzled.

Malick shook his head. 'Keep your spit – you're going to need it.'

'I don't start no mission without spitting on the ground I'll be treading.'

Malick looked at Gunsur. 'Why?'

''Cause it ain't Cadia, and I spit on ground I fight on that ain't home.'

Malick looked away, staring out into the heat haze but not seeing it.

Trooper Gunsur glanced at his sergeant. 'Not so stupid, is it?'

But Sergeant Malick did not look back at him. His fingers strayed to the little plasteel vial hanging from a chain around his neck. The plasteel had been finger-burnished bright by the Cadian rubbing it between thumb and forefinger. The two men were sitting in the jet-blown bowl of sand beneath the wing of a Valkyrie, one of three that had brought the squad of Kasrkin here.

Malick pointed out in front of them. 'It's not all yellow. Some of it is brown and I reckon it goes white in the distance.'

'You mean, where the heat haze hides the horizon?'

Sergeant Malick laughed, then coughed. 'Throne. Wish I hadn't done that. Even the air is hot.'

'Everything's hot on this damned planet.'

Malick turned and stared at Gunsur. 'You saying you don't want to be here, trooper? That's treason.'

Gunsur shook his head, suddenly unsure. 'You playing me, Sergeant Malick?'

Before Malick could answer, another voice spoke.

'Yes, are you playing him, Sergeant Malick?'

The two Cadians scrambled to their feet, the sand beneath their boots crunching.

Sergeant Malick looked at the man standing in front of them. He was wearing fatigues that gave no indication of rank. He was even barefoot. But everything else about him suggested 'officer'. Malick decided to play it safe.

'Yes, I was playing him. Sir.'

The man nodded. 'Good. I rather hoped you were. It would mean that you might have the wit to lead this team.'

Malick blinked. 'Sir?'

'Assemble the rest of the squad.'

Malick stared at the man. 'Who are you? Sir.'

'Bharath Obeysekera.' The man regarded Malick through sun-slit eyes. 'Captain Bharath Obeysekera. For your sins, you have been given into my command. Now call the troopers.'

'Yes, sir.' With a definite order to carry out, Malick made the aquila and spun off to see it done. 'Fall in!' he roared, in his best sergeant's voice, the sound of it filling the dead, empty desert air.

It was a voice that had Captain Obeysekera putting his hand on Sergeant Malick's shoulder and saying so that only he could hear: 'Use the squad vox-channel. This will be a mission of silence. Best you start getting used to being quiet, Sergeant Malick.'

'Yes...' Malick cut off the second half of his barked reply. 'Sir,' he finished.

'Good man,' said Obeysekera. 'Assemble the squad in the shade – we will all have had enough sun soon. Colonel Aruna will address you first, then I will fill in the details.'

Captain Obeysekera turned away, his bare feet quiet on the sand, and slipped away into the deeper, darker shadows of the interior of the Valkyrie.

Sergeant Malick picked up his helmet and keyed the squad vox-channel, sending alerts to the other seven troopers in the unit. He saw on the auspex integrated into his helmet that they had all acknowledged. Tracer runes showed them all moving to the location he had marked on the auspex, the outlying troops converging from the sentry positions Malick had ordered them to after the Valkyries had landed.

Gunsur leaned over towards Malick. 'The only time I ever saw a captain dressed like that, he'd been stripped and had his ribs opened out by those Gallows Cluster traitors. You sure he is a real captain?'

'Didn't you see?'

'See what?'

'When he went back inside. He's proper 'kin, all right – he's got the eagle on his neck. Besides, I reckon I've heard of him.'

'Yeah? Where?'

'The Sando retreat. He sent his 'kin squad to hold up the 'nids while he marshalled the civvies onto exfiltration vehicles.'

Gunsur looked at his sergeant. 'Yeah? So?'

'None of them got out, but *he* did.'

Gunsur nodded. 'One of those officers.'

Malick shook his head. 'Don't know. But I'm keeping this beauty to hand.' The sergeant picked up the hellgun that was leaning against the ticking plasteel of the Valkyrie. He ran his hand over the use-polished stock of the hellgun, its paluwood the colour of aged honey. 'This beauty will put a hot-shot through the eye of any xenos at a mile.'

Gunsur gestured towards the desert. 'You reckon we'll meet any bluies out there, sarge? Don't look like the sort of place they'd be interested in.'

'They're xenos scum,' said Malick. 'Who knows what they're interested in. Besides, from what I hear, there's plenty on this planet to draw the attention of the bluies.'

'Yeah, sand,' said Gunsur. 'Lots and lots of sand.'

Malick cuffed Gunsur on the shoulder. 'There's stuff under the sand's worth more'n most subsectors. That's probably why we're here on...' The sergeant paused and gestured out from the shadow under the wing to the vast dry world that surrounded them.

'It is called Dasht i-Kevar.'

Sergeant Malick and Trooper Gunsur turned around to see Captain Obeysekera, now dressed in the grey and tan of the Kasrkin, standing at the top of the rear ramp of the Valkyrie holding, of all things, his dress cap in one hand.

'Colonel Aruna will brief you on your deployment here and the strategic objective. I will cover the tactical situation.' Captain Obeysekera pointed over to the next Valkyrie, standing stark and outlined in the sun. 'You don't want to keep the colonel waiting, do you?'

'No, sir,' said Malick. The sergeant glanced at the auspex; the other squad members were drawing in towards the mark.

The three men stepped out of the shade under the Valkyrie's wing. The sun hit them with the weight of lead, pressing down upon their heads.

Captain Obeysekera put his dress cap on his head. 'Only time this has been any use.' He looked at Malick and Gunsur. 'Here, helmets are barely better than bare heads – you want a cap and scarf.'

Malick shook his head. He pointed at various gouges and scratches on his helmet. 'I wouldn't be here without this. Besides, we might need the rebreather.'

'We might need lots of things, but none of them will matter if we can't get to where we need to go.' Obeysekera looked at Malick. 'You're from Kasr Vasan. Hear it had the best logistics on Cadia. You're used to having the right weapon on hand when you need it. I grew up in Kasr Gesh. We were lucky if we had a power pack to go in our lasrifles, let alone a spare. On this mission, we will be on our own. We carry in everything we need, and when we run out we make do with what we've got left over, and when we run out of that we'll use our hands. I expect every man to be able to adapt. If you can't, I'll get someone who can. Understand?'

Malick stared back at the officer. Obeysekera regarded him mildly but steadily.

'I have never failed on a mission.'

'Which is why I asked for you, sergeant. Your record suggests a soldier who is willing to use his brain and think. Is that true?'

Malick paused, staring at Captain Obeysekera, and then, slowly, he began to smile.

'Yes, sir, it is true.' He pointed at Gunsur. 'Not so sure about Gunsur, though.'

'That's all right, sergeant. We can't have troopers thinking, can we?'

Obeysekera set off over the hot sand, his feet, now booted, sinking small pits into the ground as he went, with Malick and Gunsur following, heading towards the command Valkyrie. Reaching the bowl of sand blown out by the Valkyrie's turbofans when it landed, they crested the rim and started down towards the machine squatting in the middle of the wide crater. The sand slid away under their boots, slipping like liquid so that they all but skied down the inside of the bowl. Fifty yards away, the command Valkyrie stood, its lower half hidden by the sand bowl. Other men were centring in on the Valkyrie, some from the third craft that made the other base of the landing triangle, the rest from the perimeter positions that Malick had assigned to them.

The Valkyries themselves were not sitting silently on the sand. Their turbofans rotated gently, pushing air through the vents to placate machine-spirits grinding sand between their plasteel teeth. The pilots sat ready in the cockpits, eyes hidden behind black goggles, while the heavy bolters mounted on the Valkyries continued to track over the landscape, empty though it was. But the heat haze, rising all around them, reduced visibility: anything over half a mile away dissolved into rising columns of heated air, twisting slowly under the sun.

It was a strangely flat landscape, unrelieved by shade, even though the sand rose in static waves to their east as it stretched into the Great Sand Sea. To the west, the land was rock and salt-flat, studded with shallow outcrops and basalt columns.

'There're no shadows,' said Malick. He pointed down at his feet. 'Where has it gone?'

Obeysekera laughed, the harsh sound cut short by the dry heat. He pointed straight overhead. 'Up there.'

Malick squinted up, cricking his neck back and back, the flare guards in his goggles activating. Above him, the sun that squatted over Dasht i-Kevar rode, a white eye sitting on top of the sky arch.

Malick looked back to Captain Obeysekera. 'I don't understand.'

The captain grimaced. 'Don't worry, it won't last.' Obeysekera looked up into the sky too, his eyes becoming slits as he did so. 'Thankfully.' He glanced back to Malick. 'With no shadows it's impossible to judge distance. Speaking of distance, let's not keep the colonel waiting.'

The Kasrkin sergeant saw the sweat pricking through Obeysekera's skin, only for it to evaporate as it appeared.

'This is hotter than Prosan,' he said.

Captain Obeysekera looked back at the sergeant. 'It's about the same in terms of climate. But there are other things...' His voice trailed away as his eyes, squinting against the overwhelming light, took in the Great Sand Sea. 'Let us hope we do not meet them.'

As they neared the command Valkyrie, Malick saw the rest of the squad assembling in the shade under the wings: some squatting, others sitting on their helmets, hands resting upon their treasured weapons, the hotshot lasguns they nicknamed 'hellguns'. The last of the perimeter troopers were walking in, hellguns cradled on forearms. Malick glanced at his auspex: they were all here.

Just as he was about to look away from the display, he saw movement traces and, glancing up, he saw a man in a high-ranking officer's uniform emerge from the Valkyrie.

Aruna. The colonel's reputation had spread sector-wide. He had led the defence of Krack des Chavel against an insurrection of Chaos cultists, woken to frenzy by the great purple bruise that split the night sky. He had planned and led the assault on the ork warband led by Grashbash the Grabbler that had laid waste to three systems. And the word among the Guard was that Colonel Aruna was the brains behind the unusually subtle attempts to retake the Imperial worlds in the subsector that had succumbed to the blandishments, diplomatic and militant, of the T'au Empire.

In Malick's previous experience, whenever the Guard had retaken Imperial worlds that had been lost to the enemy, be that Chaos or xenos, it had been necessary to repopulate the planet after the victory. Aruna had managed to retain a viable population on two of the planets he had wrested back from the t'au.

Colonel Aruna came down the ramp and stood on the sand among the squad of Kasrkin. The 'kin regarded the colonel with battle-hardened eyes, then, slowly, one by one, stood and saluted him. The troops, looking upon the colonel, measuring him, saw him as one of their own: a soldier who had stood in the midst of battle without flinching, a man who had faced death on as many occasions as they had and not let fear prevent him from doing his duty to the Emperor.

As the Kasrkin acknowledged the colonel as their equal, the colonel returned the salute. Seeing Captain Obeysekera, he nodded to him then turned to the waiting, silent 'kin.

'We have lost a general. You are going to find him and bring him back.'

The Kasrkin greeted the news in silence, but it was a silence that held a wealth of unanswered questions relating to the conduct of the mission and the chance of carrying it out successfully.

'General Mato Itoyesa, commanding officer eastern sector, was returning to headquarters when his Valkyrie was attacked by t'au Barracudas. Attempting to evade the xenos, the general's pilot flew into a sandstorm.'

Colonel Aruna paused as he said that, looking around the watching Kasrkin. They said nothing but Malick saw, from the tightening of muscles, that they all knew what such an action meant: arriving on Dasht i-Kevar, it was drummed into every combatant, be they ordinary soldier, Kasrkin or Imperial Navy, never to deliberately enter one of the planet's sandstorms.

Such was the violence of the storms that an unprotected soldier would be flayed in a few minutes. Aircraft such as Valkyries had their engines clogged, their machine-spirits choking on vast quantities of sand, while even the normally indomitable Leman Russ would grind to a stop as the corrosive grains insinuated themselves into gears and bearings.

'Transmissions indicated that the general's aircraft managed to land successfully, but we have only very approximate indications of its location. No further transmissions have been received, despite our efforts to raise General Itoyesa. As the commanding officer of the eastern sector, I do not have to tell you how important it is that the general does not fall into xenos hands.' The colonel paused and looked around the watching, silent Kasrkin. 'It is your job to ensure that he does not. Questions?'

Malick looked at the surrounding troops. There were many questions that could be asked, but they were 'kin: they did the jobs no one else could do. He expected no reply.

But a voice spoke.

'That is what I don't understand. Why did the general's pilot fly into the sandstorm? It was strictly against the orders of the lord militant.'

The questioner stepped forward out of the deep shadows of the loading bay and into the softer shade under the Valkyrie's wings. He was a young man, with all the leanness of youth, but his leanness was sheathed, despite the heat, in the long drapes of the coat of a commissar of the Officio Prefectus.

Colonel Aruna turned towards the young man and shook his head. 'It is a question we shall put to the pilot should he be recovered in a state to answer. I am sure your father will be as keen to learn the answer as you are.'

'I am sure he will. Lord Militant Roshant is... concerned that one of his key generals has disappeared.'

'As are we all, Commissar Roshant,' said Colonel Aruna.

At the name, all the men listening stiffened slightly. Commissar Roshant gave no obvious indication that he was aware of their regard, but Malick saw the halo of self-regard that clung about one of the appointed of the Imperial elite, as invisible and as impenetrable as a refractor field. The Kasrkin sergeant squinted. There was a subtle phase effect around Commissar Roshant that suggested he might actually be employing a refractor field.

'That is also why my father, the lord militant, has ordered me to accompany your men on their mission.' The young commissar paused slightly as he said this. The Kasrkin, no strangers to the ways of Imperial commissars, knew well that he had paused so that he might assess their reaction to this news. What physical reaction they gave was minimal: some tightening of the eyes, quick glances, nothing more.

For his part, Malick looked to Captain Obeysekera, seeking to judge if he had had any warning that the lord militant's son would be accompanying them on their mission. But at the news, the captain's expression remained as blank as the desert on the day after a storm, when the windblown sand had scoured all tracks from its face.

Commissar Roshant, evidently satisfied with what he saw in the faces of the watching Kasrkin, turned back to Colonel Aruna.

'Should we find the general alive, it will be imperative to assess immediately whether he has been compromised. Should we find the general dead, the same question will arise. And should we fail to find the general, the question will become even more urgent. My father has given me the task of answering these questions.'

Colonel Aruna nodded. 'Very well, commissar. But, unless you have received new orders from the lord militant, operational command of this mission remains with Captain Obeysekera.' Colonel Aruna paused, making sure that all the men present were listening and would be able to hear the answer.

'Yes, that is correct.' The words sounded forced, as if Commissar Roshant said them against his will. Malick, face impassive, smiled inwardly at imagining the son pleading to his father for command of the mission and that permission being denied.

Colonel Aruna nodded. 'Thank you, commissar. So that there might be no misunderstanding, you will be attached to the mission as its commissar, with responsibility for the political and religious welfare of the men, but answerable to the mission commander, Captain Obeysekera. Is that clear?'

Commissar Roshant stared at Colonel Aruna, then glanced at Captain Obeysekera. 'Yes, it is clear,' he said through narrowed lips.

'Very well,' said Colonel Aruna. 'I am glad we have cleared that up before the mission begins.' The colonel began to turn away, but before he could do so, Roshant spoke again.

'While it is true that Captain Obeysekera has operational command of the mission, it is also true that Lord Militant Roshant has asked me to write a full report on this operation. I will of course note any instances where Captain Obeysekera fails to adhere to my advice – the advice of a commissar of the God-Emperor's Imperium.' Roshant looked from Aruna to Obeysekera. 'Is that clear, too?'

The colonel looked at the commissar. 'Perfectly clear.'

Roshant turned to Obeysekera. 'Captain?'

Sergeant Malick saw the danger light in the captain's eyes, a glint even in the deep shadow under the Valkyrie's wing.

'I understand, Commissar Roshant,' said Captain Obeysekera. His eyes broadened and he smiled. 'For my part, I am grateful that you will be writing a full report of the mission as that will save me the labour of filing my own account.' Obeysekera turned to the colonel. 'Now that is settled, shall I start the mission briefing, sir?'

'Yes, please do so.'

Captain Obeysekera paused and looked at each of the watching soldiers. His glance caught on something on Gunsur's uniform.

'Take off your campaign medals and kasr tags. That you fought in the Haetes Second Star campaign or which kasr you hail from is of no interest to me. For what it's worth, you are now part of First Squad, One Hundred and Fifty-Fifth. But I don't really care about that either.' Obeysekera looked round the waiting soldiers. 'All that matters is the mission.'

He waited.

Slowly, first in ones or twos, then followed by the rest, the Kasrkin removed their campaign medals, stowing them in pockets, and tucked their kasr tags away out of sight.

When they were all simply Kasrkin with no other identifying marks, Obeysekera nodded.

'Thank you. Uwais. Ha. Prater. Ensor. Chame. Quert. Lerin.'

Malick glanced at Lerin as her name was spoken. He had heard of her reputation with heavy weapons.

'Gunsur. Malick.'

As the captain called out each name, Malick realised that Obeysekera already knew who each soldier in the squad was.

'Sir,' he said.

Obeysekera paused, drawing the listening troopers in closer. 'This mission will test even the very best. For we will not only be facing the enemy, we will be fighting a planet.' Obeysekera gestured outwards, his arm taking in all the unseen expanses of Dasht i-Kevar. 'This world kills. All of it is deadly, but we will be going into the most dangerous area of Dasht i-Kevar, the Sand Sea. It kills with heat and exhaustion, it kills by blinding and wearing down, it kills the stupid with ease and the clever with indifference. Our survival on this mission, and its successful accomplishment, will rely upon exact attention to detail and an ability to maintain concentration under the most difficult conditions that you have ever known.'

Captain Obeysekera stepped forward. He looked at his squad, the Kasrkin gathered around him in the shade below the wing of the Valkyrie, and he smiled.

'I've got something to show you,' he said.

CHAPTER 2

Captain Obeysekera lined his men up along the rim of the Valkyrie's blast crater. The sun of Dasht i-Kevar had slipped from the zenith, and with the return of shadows the world had depth again. He peered into the east, shading his eyes with his hand, then turning his head to listen.

Yes, there. The distant, cyclic thrum of turbofans.

Obeysekera glanced along the line of soldiers. They were 'kin: they had picked up the sound. Those wearing their helmets would have received warning from the in-built auspexes, tracking the inbound traces. They stood with their weapons lightly held but ready: hellguns, the hotshot lasrifles that were the standard-issue weapons for the Cadian elite. Obeysekera had seen a hellgun take the head off an ork at two miles. As the noise of the turbofans grew, the hellguns were slowly raised, without command from either him or Sergeant Malick, until only a minimal movement would have them ready for use.

Obeysekera glanced towards the commissar. Roshant was looking from side to side, then to the approaching noise. Under the sun's weight, sweat was pricking through his skin, but the aridity of the air dried the liquid as soon as it appeared, leaving only salt streaks on the skin.

Feeling the gaze, Roshant looked at Obeysekera.

'What are we waiting for?' he asked.

Obeysekera could see the flush in the man's face as his animal spirits pushed blood to the skin in an attempt to cool it. But the air was hotter than blood: there was no cooling there.

'You will see soon, commissar,' said Obeysekera.

He squinted east. The sand was boiling, rising in abrupt gusts from the desert. Running before the sand, coming directly towards them low over the ground, were the splayed M's of three approaching Valkyries. They were shapes familiar to all the men watching. But hanging beneath the mid-point of each ship was another, smaller outline.

Obeysekera glanced again along the line and saw, from the grins spreading across a few faces, that some of the men recognised what they saw.

The Sky Talons approached, their outlines emphasised by the clouds of windblown sand rising behind them. The note of the turbofans changed as they began to slow, the pitch rising from the regular low thrum of level flight to the headache-inducing scream of landing. Only, the Valkyries did not land. Reducing their speed, they crawled closer, the sand billowing up further from the downdraught of the turbofans. Then the clamps beneath the three aircraft released, and the vehicles they were carrying fell the final few yards onto the soft sand.

Their loads delivered, the Valkyries reared away, up into the sky towards the sun, like horses freed from their riders. The sand-churn chased up after them before falling back.

Captain Obeysekera felt the colonel's regard and looked over to him. Aruna raised an eyebrow.

'Not my idea,' said Obeysekera, spreading his hands in innocence. 'They must be in a hurry to go elsewhere.'

'Indeed,' said Colonel Aruna, looking up into the sky. The three Valkyries had dwindled to dots.

Sergeant Malick pointed at the vehicles the Valkyries had left behind. 'Those our rides, captain?'

'Yes, sergeant. They are indeed our rides.'

Sergeant Malick grinned. 'Three Tauros Venators.'

Obeysekera pointed at the leftmost vehicle. 'Twin-linked multi-laser. That will be my command vehicle, call sign *Holy Fire*.' He pointed at the right-hand vehicle. 'Twin-linked lascannon. Call sign *Divine Light*. That one is yours, sergeant. Both modified to take driver and navigator as well as gunner.' Then he indicated the central vehicle. 'Modified as a troop carrier – driver, navigator and up to eight men in the back. Call sign *Saint Conrad*.'

The sergeant's smile broadened. 'Always wanted to try out one of these ever since I saw the One Hundred and Eighty-First Elysians use them on Patanal. Never seen anything Imperial move so fast on land.'

'They're light, fast and quiet,' said Obeysekera. 'Exactly what we need. Have three men bring them over. We'll need to load them up.'

'Gunsur, Ensor, Prater, bring them over...' Malick paused.

'One by each Valkyrie, sergeant,' said Obeysekera.

'You heard the captain.' The sergeant grinned at the three men. 'Don't ever say I give you all the worst jobs.'

Gunsur, Ensor and Prater, smiling at the jealous calls of their overlooked comrades, made their way over the sand towards the three Venators, while Malick, at a gesture from Obeysekera, set the rest of the squad to unloading the supplies from the Valkyries.

While the troops shifted the crates of powercells, supplies and, heaviest of all, barrels of water, Obeysekera moved so that he could get a better view of the Tauros Venators.

Gunsur, Ensor and Prater each climbed into their seats, strapped the webbing around their torsos and, with swift prayers to each vehicle's machine-spirit, engaged the galvanic motors. Obeysekera nodded as instead of the usual promethium-laced roar that accompanied the start of most Imperial vehicles, the Venators hummed, sounding more like the idle buzz of a chain-sword than a herd of stampeding grox. With their six large wheels ploughing shallow grooves through the sand, the three Venators approached, each peeling off towards its own supply ship, where the troopers began loading the supplies, strapping water drums into the racks welded onto the sides of the Venators and stowing the powercells in the armoured ammunition boxes lining the interior of the vehicles.

'There's no roof,' said Roshant.

Obeysekera looked round. He had been so absorbed with overseeing the loading of the vehicles, running his hand over the rough plasteel to get a sense of their machine-spirits, that he had not heard the approach of the commissar. He chided himself for that. It did not do to allow his senses to become so focused that he could not notice someone coming closer.

'No, there isn't,' agreed Obeysekera.

The commissar was sweating, even though he was standing in the shade of the Valkyrie. The dust-dry air of Dasht i-Kevar sucked the sweat from his skin as soon as it formed.

Roshant took off his commissar's cap. 'Out there, we'll need all the shade we can get.'

'Agreed,' said Obeysekera. He pointed towards Malick, who was stringing tan-coloured netting over the driver's and navigator's compartment of the Venator. 'Which is why we have that. It will provide shade and allow air circulation.'

Roshant sniffed. 'Not sure if I want air this hot circulating anywhere near me.'

'Better it moves than it doesn't,' said Obeysekera, 'even if it feels like being in an oven.'

Roshant pointed at the water drums. 'They're on the outside. If they get holed by the enemy, then...'

'Then we die of thirst,' finished Obeysekera. He pointed at Roshant's water flask. 'You've got that – we're all carrying personal rations. But there is no room to carry water drums inside the vehicles. At least water makes effective armour. So we'll survive the ambush.'

'To die three days later.'

Obeysekera shook his head. 'Not three days. Not here. Personal flasks will be good for about a day. After that, without water, we won't last another day.'

Roshant nodded. He reached to his hip and, taking the flask from his belt, raised it to his lips and drank. 'I find that talk of death by dehydration makes me thirsty.'

'You might think about leaving behind the coat and cap, then.'

Roshant stared at Obeysekera. 'If the commissar cannot command his body against the conditions, how can he expect the men to command themselves in the face of the enemy?'

Obeysekera shook his head. 'From my experience, 'kin respect officers on the basis of what they do, not what they wear.'

'I am a commissar. I do not ask for their respect – I demand their duty.'

'Very well.' Obeysekera pointed at Roshant's flask. 'Better drink up before we set off. Water will be rationed when we begin.'

'Oh, I will, I will.' Roshant took another long draught then headed towards one of the barrels, to refill his flask.

'There's water in the Valkyrie,' said Obeysekera.

Roshant sniffed, continued to the water barrel and reached for the tap. But before he could turn it, Malick knocked the commissar's hand away.

Roshant drew back. His other hand went to his bolt pistol, drawing it from his shoulder holster and pointing it at Sergeant Malick.

'Striking an officer, let alone a commissar, is a capital offence,' Roshant said. 'Tell me why I should not execute the sentence at once.'

'Because Sergeant Malick was following my orders,' said Obeysekera, stepping forward and putting himself between the commissar and the Kasrkin soldier. 'He has strict instructions that no one may draw water from these barrels without explicit assent from me.' Obeysekera reached out a hand and rested it on one of the barrels. 'On Dasht i-Kevar, and even more in the Great Sand Sea, water is life.'

Commissar Roshant notched the barrel of the bolt pistol back, so that it pointed slightly above Obeysekera's eyes. Then, his finger tightened on the trigger.

The bolt-shell sizzled past Obeysekera's head, close enough for the captain to feel his hair, which he had allowed to grow longer than the usual Cadian crew cut, crisping.

Sergeant Malick's hellgun appeared, levelled and ready, pointing steadily at the centre of the commissar's chest.

'Try that again...' the sergeant began, but Obeysekera held his hand up.

'No need for that, sergeant.' He gently put his hand on the barrel of Malick's hellgun and pushed it down. 'I am sure the commissar has an explanation.'

Commissar Roshant smiled. 'My father, the lord militant, received this oath when I swore myself to the Emperor's service – that I would never draw weapon without discharging it. So by discharging it, I was fulfilling my oath to the Emperor – as must all who serve Him.' The commissar twirled the bolt pistol, allowing Captain Obeysekera to see the carved ivory of the grip, before replacing the weapon in its holster.

Obeysekera paused, then asked, 'Amphant ivory?'

Roshant nodded. 'Yes.'

'Impressive.'

'Indeed.'

The commissar looked towards the Venator. 'Inform me when the vehicles are loaded. I will make a final report before we depart.' With that, Roshant turned and made his way back into the relative cool inside the Valkyrie.

When he was out of earshot, Sergeant Malick turned to Obeysekera.

'Amphant ivory? Really?'

Obeysekera nodded. 'I think it was. It had the patina I've read about – a sheen of gold.'

Malick blew air through his teeth. 'This is a first, going on mission with a weapon that's worth more than we are.'

Obeysekera grimaced. 'In the Guard, that is scarcely unusual.'

Malick grunted. 'Point. But you could buy ten years of luxury on Venera with it.'

Captain Obeysekera turned to his sergeant. 'Better not tell the men, then.'

'I won't have to if he keeps waving it around like that.'

Obeysekera looked at Malick. 'I want the commissar alive when we return, understood?'

Malick nodded. 'Of course. But you know how it is in battle – things go missing.'

'Malick...'

The sergeant grinned. 'Just joking, sir.'

'Besides, you're wrong about the bolt pistol being the only valuable thing around here. Dasht i-Kevar is the most valuable world in the system by far.'

Malick waved his hand, the gesture taking in the wide expanse of nothing beyond them. 'This exceptional piece of the Emperor's estate? I heard there's something precious under the sand, but I'll be damned if I can see it.'

Captain Obeysekera nodded. 'It's true. They get aqua vitae from here.'

'Life water? Is that what it sounds like it is?'

'Yes. The most effective rejuve treatment in the sector. A bottle of the stuff costs more than a Custodian's armour. All rejuve and none of the unpleasant side effects most of the other treatments have.'

Malick gestured again. 'But where's the water? Where's the life?'

Obeysekera shrugged. 'I don't know. No one knows, save the desert tribes who trade it – or who used to trade it, before the bluies turned up.' He grinned grimly at his sergeant. 'That's why we're here on this planet – to ensure that our generals and planetary governors stay thirty-four when they're really two hundred and forty.' The captain laughed but there was little humour in the sound. 'We die so they can remain beautiful.'

Sergeant Malick stared at his captain. 'Throne. Is that it? Is that why we're going into the fire?'

Hearing the sergeant's tone, Obeysekera looked up and out of his intro-spection.

'No, that's not why *we're* doing it, sergeant. We're doing it because we're Guard and we do what we're ordered to do, even if it's stupid and point-less, which most of the time it is. We're doing it because we're Kasrkin and we do the jobs no one else can do.' The captain's face suddenly broke into a smile and he pointed at the Venator. 'And we're doing it because we're going to get the chance to gun these flat out with no one around to tell us to back off. You ready for that?'

Malick's smile matched that of Obeysekera. 'Oh, I'm ready, sir.'

CHAPTER 3

The Tauros Venator *Holy Fire* drove up the slope, its six fat tyres sending rivers of sand tumbling back behind it. But the tyres dug deep into the shifting surface, finding purchase, and the machine surged forwards. The other two Venators, *Divine Light* and *Saint Conrad*, flanked it as they followed it up the dune, cutting channels through the sand, following the contours of the desert like boats over an ocean of water.

Captain Obeysekera sat in the navigator's seat of *Holy Fire*, map spread on his knees, chrono in one hand, stylus in the other, tracing their track upon the thick paper. As they neared the crest of the dune, Obeysekera looked up, checking again the dials on the minimal panel before him: speed, distance and compass bearing. Beside him, he could hear Trooper Gunsur crooning to the machine-spirit of the Venator, urging it on and encouraging it as its wheels, suddenly encountering slicker sand, began to spin.

'Come on, you can do it, come on, yes, yes, come on.'

The tyres bit, finding traction, and the Venator pushed upwards, its front nearly forty degrees above its rear.

'Yes!' Gunsur slapped the steering wheel. 'Come on.'

'Trooper.' Obeysekera, still following their course and speed without allowing his concentration to lapse, tapped the driver on his arm. 'Halt just after the crest. I want to take a look.'

'Sir.' Gunsur tapped the steering wheel again. 'She'll get us there, you'll see she will.'

Obeysekera looked ahead. The final slope of the vast sand wave rose above them, its flank growing steeper as it reached the crest. He was thankful for the galvanic motors that powered the vehicle. Even with the machine-spirit straining to drive the Tauros up the slope, the Venator was quiet. If he had been leading a trio of Sentinels – the machines that the lord militant's headquarters had suggested for the mission – the howling of the machine-spirits and the grinding of their gears and engines would have alerted any enemy within ten miles of their approach. Dasht i-Kevar was a quiet world and the Great Sand Sea was quieter: only war brought noise and movement, sound and fury to its surface.

Obeysekera glanced at the other two Venators that formed his squad. They were fifty yards distant on each flank. On the left, in *Divine Light*, Trooper Chame was cycling the twin-linked lascannon through targeting options, the head cloth that Obeysekera had demonstrated to his men wrapped loosely over her face and blowing behind her in the wind of the Venator's passing. In the stripped-out driver's seat, Obeysekera saw Sergeant Malick with Trooper Prater beside him in the navigator's position.

On the right, Trooper Ha was driving the Venator carrier, *Saint Conrad*, with Lerin the navigator and Roshant squeezed into a third seat behind them and the rest of the squad in the back. Obeysekera reminded himself to move Roshant when they stopped. The commissar had barely hidden his displeasure at being assigned that post. Obeysekera suspected that the discomfort of the seat was a lesser factor than the perceived slight of not accompanying the commanding officer. So long as it did not compromise the mission, it would be better to keep Roshant happy.

Obeysekera heard the pitch of the galvanic motors increase and he looked ahead: the slope was rising to the final crest.

'Take us over, then stop,' Obeysekera said to Gunsur.

'Sir.'

Another advantage of the Venator, Obeysekera thought, was that the machine was quiet enough for the driver to hear his instructions without having to speak on the vox-circuit.

The nose of the Venator tipped up and sand splashed over it, spraying across Obeysekera's face. The cloth he had wrapped around his nose and mouth stopped him spitting sand – the particles were so fine they could work their way into a rebreather – but he had to wipe his goggles clear and shake off the residue from his map. As he did so, the world tilted forward, suddenly, precipitously, and the galvanic motors whined to their highest pitch as the rear wheels, free of the sand drag, spun without hindrance. The Venator balanced for an instant on the crest of the wave and then, as Trooper Gunsur throttled back, it began to settle, its weight digging it into the dune. The wheels, front and back, made contact as the Venator sank lower, and its balance – knife-edge before – broadened.

Obeysekera let out the breath he had not realised he had been holding. He looked over to Gunsur.

'Good driving, trooper.'

Gunsur nodded. By the sweat pricking through his skin, Obeysekera knew that the trooper had not been sure of holding the Venator on the crest. Now it was up to him to use the position as quickly as possible: the skyline was not a good place to linger.

Obeysekera stood up, grabbing the roll bar to steady himself.

'Watch out, sir. I could have taken your head off.'

Obeysekera looked behind him to see Trooper Quert peering at him from over the barrels of the twin-linked multi-laser. She was tracking off south and Obeysekera realised that if Quert had swept them central while he was standing up, he would have been crushed against the roll bar.

The captain raised his hand. 'Point taken. I will make sure to warn you in future if I am going to stand up.' Obeysekera turned back and, raising his hand to shield his eyes from the sun, he peered into the west.

From the top of the two hundred-yard-high sand dune, Obeysekera saw the crests of other dunes winding across the erg, running roughly north to south, some cresting to a height matching the dune he was balanced upon, others lower but broader. It was still early in the morning and the distance had the clarity of the night. He stared at the horizon, searching for some sign of what he was looking for.

There. Rising above the erg in a series of smooth humps, like some monster rising from the depths of the Great Sand Sea: the Tabaste. Even at this distance – some fifty miles – Obeysekera could see why it was also called the Old Mountain: time had smoothed and worn it, leaving the rose-and-orange nubs of the vast volcanoes that had once risen above the sands of Dasht i-Kevar.

The Tabaste was the location of the last signal from General Itoyesa's Valkyrie.

It was as well they had crested the rise early to look for the Tabaste; by mid-morning at the latest, the heat haze, rising in shimmering, dancing columns from the desert, reduced visibility to little more than a mile – and that was without the sandstorms.

Obeysekera tried to take a reading on the Tabaste so that he could plot the bearing on his map, but even here, just a handful of miles into the Great Sand Sea, the auspex was becoming unreliable. Obeysekera tapped it, and the readings finally settled. But he knew it would not be much longer before it became completely unusable. There was some anomaly within the Great Sand Sea that affected instruments, causing the machine-spirits to falter and the readings to vary wildly or fail utterly. Only basic magnetic compasses and vox continued to work with any degree of reliability, but even they could not be trusted entirely.

Hence the maps that Obeysekera carried and his careful logging of distance, time, speed and direction. They were the only sure way of getting back.

Even as Obeysekera took and checked his bearings, the two flanking Venators reached the crest of the dune and settled there, sinking into the ridge, the three vehicles fifty yards apart.

Obeysekera sat down and traced further lines on his map. Beside him, Trooper Gunsur was silent; Obeysekera subconsciously noted the quiet ratcheting sounds as Trooper Quert rotated the twin-linked multi-laser, scanning over the erg ahead.

'I never knew there could be so many yellows.'

The words were quiet. If Obeysekera had not just finished the final plot he might not have heard them, but, map work done, he was looking up when Gunsur spoke. Obeysekera glanced at his driver. Gunsur was staring ahead, looking out over the still waves of the Sand Sea, and his eyes were full of the colours of the desert. The netting, stretched over their heads, stippled the shade on Gunsur, but the open windscreen allowed the slight early morning wind to play over their faces, still cool enough to bring some relief from the heat. Later in the day, the wind would rise, like bellows stoking a furnace, and its touch would only heighten the discomfort of the afternoon.

Obeysekera looked back out over the erg and he saw what Gunsur saw.

'You are right. I did not know there could be so many yellows, either.'

Gunsur jerked and looked to the captain. 'I didn't mean to speak aloud, sir.'

'Don't worry.' Obeysekera grinned, although only his eyes showed above his face cloth. 'I am glad to have had it pointed out to me.'

The captain looked back, at the steep slip face descending before them and the rising and falling waves of sand stretching into the distance with the smoothed-out mounds of the Tabaste on the horizon.

'You know, sometimes, I think that if only there weren't so many things trying to kill us all the time, the galaxy could be a beautiful place.' Obeysekera grinned again, but it was bleaker this time, as his eyes squinted into the distance. 'But it seems like we were made only for war.' He nodded towards the Sand Sea. 'So it's good to see somewhere that war has left no marks upon, eh, Gunsur?'

The trooper nodded. 'Yes, sir.' He hesitated, then continued. 'You know, sir, I've seen some sights in my time – the Kefahuchi Reach, the sun rising over the Caducades, the Twelve Sisters – but this is as pretty as any of them.' He fell silent for a moment as he stared out at the desert and all its myriad shades of yellow below the vivid blue arch of the sky, then lowered his gaze. 'You're right, sir. It's good to see somewhere peaceful. But now we're here, I s'pose it won't stay peaceful for long.' Gunsur looked back to Obeysekera. 'Shall I start her up, sir?'

Obeysekera was about to give his permission, when he stopped. He glanced along the ridgetop, at the other two Venators poised there, on a solid but shifting wave, remote from the sound or sight of war.

It was quiet here. Peaceful.

The realisation came upon him as he looked at the Sand Sea.

It was pure, unmarked. If any had perished near them, enemy or Guard, the desert had covered all trace.

In the silence, the only sound the ticking of the plasteel expanding under the sun's lash, Obeysekera heard the echo of a galaxy at peace. Cadia, lost and broken. Cadia had been the eternal fortress against Chaos, its people the warriors who kept the rest of the Imperium safe through the sacrifice of their lives. He had known nothing but war; his world had known nothing but war until it died. But sitting there in silence, atop the still wave in the Sand Sea, Obeysekera heard a still, small voice, as quiet as his blood, whisper peace.

'Wait here.' Obeysekera held his hand up to Gunsur, unstrapped the webbing, then swung his legs out of the Venator and stepped down onto the sand. The dune, softer than sea mud, swallowed his feet up to the ankles.

Inside him, a voice – the voice of discipline and duty and the veteran Guardsmen who had trained him – was muttering madness. But another voice, quieter but more compelling, told him to walk.

Obeysekera walked. Pulling his boots out of the sand, he waded along the ridgetop. As he did so, the sand, pulled and pushed by his passing, started to shift, sliding in small and then greater sheets down the slip face of the dune.

And the sand began to sing.

At first it was gentle, a sound akin to the wind blowing through the paluwood groves of Cadia. Then it grew and deepened, taking on the register of the Caducades Sea breaking upon the hundred-mile-long shingle breakwater that protected the Manhof Reach from the sea's full fury.

Had protected, Obeysekera corrected himself.

But the sound continued, deepening, broadening, assuming overtones that hearkened to the mournful music of the tsiranope, the ancient pipes of Kasr Gesh, his home.

The desert was singing.

Obeysekera looked up as he walked along the ridge. He had not realised it – and would have taken the other direction if he had – but he was heading towards the Venator that was carrying Commissar Roshant. For a moment, Obeysekera thought of turning round and returning to his vehicle. But he wanted to hear more.

Wading along the ridgetop, the desert singing its bass threnody for the galaxy, Obeysekera walked in wonder.

As he approached the waiting Venator, he realised that part of the reason he had kept going was that he wanted to know if they heard the song too. Perhaps he was going mad. But the gestures from Ha and Lerin, and Ensor and Uwais in the back of the Venator, pointing to their ears, told that they too were hearing what Obeysekera was hearing. Some of the faces were looking alarmed, but Obeysekera raised his hands, palms downward, to let them know all was well. With the song resounding in his lungs and in his blood, he was loath to break its music by speaking through the squad vox-channel.

'*What in the Emperor's name is that cursed moaning sound?*'

The voice, all too clear, cut into his ear from the micro-bead in his shoulder pauldron. Obeysekera had a link to the squad vox-channel in his helmet and another embedded into his carapace armour should he have to remove the former.

Obeysekera held up his hand, but Commissar Roshant got out of the Venator and started struggling towards him along the ridgetop. Instead of accepting that each step would see his boot sink into the sand and adopting a wading motion, Roshant was trying to kick a channel through the sand and sinking deeper with each step. Obeysekera waved at Roshant, trying to get him to stop, but the commissar had his head down as he ploughed forwards. He was setting off larger and larger slides of sand down the slip face of the dune. Obeysekera looked beyond Roshant. The sand was slumping towards him, at least two yards of the ridge collapsing towards the desert floor.

It would be like being caught in an avalanche.

A voice, tiny, treacherous, whispered, 'Let him.' But Obeysekera pushed forward, trying to run through the sand, and the desert moaned its song as he went, the sound rising to a rumble that sank down into the deep on the far side of the dune. As he rushed onwards, Obeysekera called into his vox-bead, 'Stay still, you idiot, stay still.'

But Roshant was talking to himself over the vox-channel, not hearing Obeysekera's order. Some small corner of the captain's mind, a corner that never could be anything other than an officer of the God-Emperor's Imperial Guard, noted that he would have to cite the commissar for failure to follow correct vox-protocol. The rest of Obeysekera's mind, and his body, was occupied with getting to Roshant before the collapsing ridge caught up with him.

The song of the sand grew louder, deeper. As Obeysekera pushed himself forwards, he realised that it had taken on a new tone, a sub-bass note that he felt in his bones as much as he heard. It was the sound of the heart of a world breaking, and he had heard it before.

It was all that he could do to stop the memory overwhelming him, as it had done through so many long night watches, when sleep would only come again if he drank himself into unconsciousness. But now the sound came in the waking hours, under the brightest light, beneath the beat of the sun, and it was rising from the sand: the song of the desert.

Roshant had never heard that sound. But nevertheless he paused, looking around him, suddenly aware that something was happening.

Obeysekera called to him, by voice and vox. 'Get back from the edge.'

Roshant, hearing him at last, looked towards Obeysekera, now only a few yards away, and then, realisation dawning, back the way he had come just as the collapsing sand reached him.

The commissar threw out a despairing hand as the world fell away beneath him, sucking him down. Obeysekera reached and grabbed the out-thrust arm, fingers locking around Roshant's wrist. Digging his feet into the ridge, he started to pull the commissar back from the brink.

And then the sand collapsed beneath Obeysekera.

The two men fell, tumbling downwards, the sand falling with them, over them.

Some reflex kept Obeysekera from releasing the one solid grip he had, the hold on Roshant's wrist, as he fell, although the arm twisted and turned and pulled as Roshant slipped and slid down the face, Obeysekera falling after him.

The sand fell with them, over them, under them.

The world went yellow.

Sand in his face, his ears, his eyes, his mouth. His nose.

Obeysekera, feeling the sand blocking his airways, tried to hold his breath while with his free hand he reached for the rebreather mask. He continued to tumble down the slope, the world turning over, the sand in his eyes and ears, all the while keeping hold of Roshant with one hand while the other pushed the rebreather over his mouth and nose.

The fall was slowing.

They had stopped rolling. Now they were just sliding. But the face of the sand dune was sliding with them, as if they were riding one of the waves of the Caducades as it broke on the shore, the surf washing over them.

The sand, heavy, crushing, immobilising, covered Obeysekera, layering over his legs, his chest, his face, his arm.

The world went yellow once more, then dark.

He could not move. He was fixed in place, as if rockcrete had been poured over him rather than sand. The only movement he could make was to squeeze the wrist he still held, but there was no response from Roshant.

The rebreather hissed. Its vents were being clogged with sand. Soon, there would be no air.

Obeysekera, with the air he had in his lungs and his body, with the last of the air of the rebreather before it failed, pushed with every muscle, straining upwards; up against the weight of the sand, up towards the light, towards the air. He pushed with all the strength he had, pushing against death.

Nothing moved.

Nothing moved at all.

He was going to die.

A memory of training in the Rossvar Mountains: the old instructor telling his raw Whiteshields that, if caught in an avalanche, they had five minutes before they suffocated, drowning in their own dead air. The old man had smiled. 'Don't worry,' he had said, 'it's a quiet death.'

Obeysekera did not want to die. Not now. Not here.

But even as fear threatened to unman him, he heard again the song of the sand. Now, with the sand surrounding him, he felt its call in every bone and fibre of his being, so that it seemed that he too was joining in the music of the desert.

Where before fear had surged up hot through his gut, now a great peace flowed through him. He could still feel Roshant's wrist in his hand and he squeezed it, trying to pass on fellowship and communion to another dying man. Although he disliked the commissar, all Roshant's privileges had served only to bring him to the same hole in the sand where he would die alongside the low-born son of a kasr. War, at the front line, was nothing if not egalitarian.

As he squeezed Roshant's wrist, Obeysekera felt a movement, a straining. The commissar was still alive too. It would not be for much longer, though. Obeysekera could feel his mind beginning to fog, as if he were on the point of sleep.

The song of the sand grew louder, more encompassing. Now he could feel the air in his lungs and the air cavities in his face resonating with the low, thrumming sound that enveloped him.

This was the long sleep, the one from which there was no waking.

Random memories played out in Obeysekera's mind: his mother, holding him by the hand as his father marched off to join the 27th accompanied by the regiment's drums and tsiranopes; the message of his father's death, flashing upon the screen; the Caducades Sea, calm after a storm; the sun, huge and livid, setting over the parched plains of Prosan; the face of the first dead man he had seen, mouth still wide with the shock of his dying; the face of the first man he had killed, eyes widening in the realisation that his dark gods had betrayed him; a smile, glimpsed through lho-smoke. A ragtag collection of impressions from a life unnoticed.

A grab, something pulling his arm.

Obeysekera, mind dim and confused, could not understand it. There was something pulling at him. The sound of the sand was growing louder around him, more open, more expansive.

Light.

Yellow, filtered ochre, but light.

Even as his mind fogged over, some deeper level of thought tightened Obeysekera's grip on the commissar's wrist.

Sand, running off his face in rivers, blurred shapes behind, digging, scrabbling, pulling.

'Get the rebreather off.'

Fingers fumbling at his mask, digging into the sand that still cradled his head, pulling the mask off.

Air.

Hot. Gritty. Sandy.

Life.

Obeysekera's chest heaved as, like a baby new born, he breathed in life.

'Pull him out.'

His vision was still blurred with tears and sand, but Obeysekera could see the shapes of the men clustered around him, scraping and pulling with their bare hands like human moles. One face resolved into that of Gunsur. Obeysekera grabbed the trooper with his freed hand.

'Under me. Roshant.'

Gunsur nodded. 'Dig,' he yelled to the others.

'I've got him,' said Obeysekera, his mind coming back to him. 'Follow my arm down.'

Scrabbling and shoving, flinging sand up and away, the men dug in down the length of Obeysekera's body, following the track of his arm until he felt their hands close about the wrist that he had never let go.

'Got him,' Gunsur said to Obeysekera. 'You can let go now.'

Obeysekera released his hold. His body free of the sand, he began to slide down the slope, and for a moment the memory of the first panicked fall came back to him. But the slide stopped and, lying spent and exhausted on his back, he looked up from the trough of the sand wave and saw the sky as blue as he had ever seen it, untouched by cloud or smoke.

He turned his head, just a little, and saw the men gathered around the pit they were digging, and the figure emerging from it, like a sculpture appearing as the sculptor pared away the rock. Obeysekera tried to call up, to ask if the commissar lived, but his voice had dried away to a husk under the sand and only a whisper breathed from his lips.

Then he saw Sergeant Malick turning to him, his face breaking into a smile, and the thumbs-up gesture he sent down to him.

The commissar was alive.

As Obeysekera drifted on the edge of consciousness beneath an endless sky, it occurred to him that he had never before seen Guardsmen so pleased to see that their commissar was still alive. The sand shifted beneath him, then settled into silence. The music was over. Now the only sound was the coughing of the commissar and the few words of his men, faced with a recovering political officer and not sure what to do or say next.

Captain Bharath Obeysekera of the God-Emperor's Imperial Guard forced himself to sit up. He was in command. He had better do some commanding.

He tried to stand up. It did not work. Instead he sat, coughing, the phlegm gritty with sand. His mouth and throat were rough with it, his ears half-blocked.

He tried to stand again, and this time staggered to his feet. The sand felt firm beneath him. He looked up. The slip face of the dune rose a hundred feet and more above him, but here, in the wave's trough, the sand was hard-packed. If only the troughs turned in the direction they were going, the way would become so much easier.

As he stood, still swaying, the men started bringing Commissar Roshant down the short distance to the bottom of the slope, half carrying him and half sliding him, with shears of sand following. But their initial fall had dislodged the greater part of loose sand on the slip face; what slipped and slid now posed no danger.

Trooper Gunsur was beside Roshant, Sergeant Malick had hold of him on the other side, and the rest of the troops who had come down to dig them out – Obeysekera noted with approval that Ha, Lerin and Prater had remained with the Venators – slid and waded down the slope beside them.

As they came closer, Obeysekera saw that the commissar had turned yellow. His immaculate greatcoat – how he had kept it so clean in the desert was a mystery to Obeysekera – was now streaked and stained, with trails of sand leaking like yellow oil from every crease and crevice. His cap was gone, still buried under the sand. His hands, clutching convulsively on the men helping him down the slope, were as yellow as a wedge of pico-giallo cheese, apart from a band around his right wrist where Obeysekera had been holding him. And his face was the colour of curdled starch-milk, streaked with the trails of tears and spit and phlegm from eyes and mouth and nose.

The men slid Roshant down to the base of the slope, where he sat, not moving. Obeysekera went over to the commissar.

In the yellow that was his face, Roshant's eyes were islands of white and blue, but the whites were traced with red. The commissar was staring into a distance only he could see. Squatting down on the sand in front of Roshant, Obeysekera put himself into the commissar's line of sight, but still the far focus of his eyes did not change.

'Commissar. Commissar Roshant.'

There was no flicker of acknowledgement on Roshant's face.

Obeysekera reached out and grasped Roshant's wrist, the wrist he had held when they were buried. At his touch, the commissar started.

'No, no, no.'

He started to pull away, but Obeysekera tightened his grip and pulled Roshant back towards him so that their faces were almost touching.

'You're out,' he said. 'You're out.'

Slowly, Roshant's gaze returned from the far distance where it had been lost and focused on the man right in front of him.

The commissar nodded. 'Yes. Out.' The words were thick, barely audible.

'Permission to spit,' said Obeysekera.

Roshant turned his head, hawked and spat a yellow glob of mucus into the sand. Then, putting his free hand on Obeysekera's shoulder, he levered himself back onto his feet.

Obeysekera stood up in front of the commissar and stared into his face. 'Commissar Roshant?'

The sand crust on Roshant's face began to crack. Little trails of yellow particles streamed down from his forehead, down his cheeks, his chin.

'I thought I was going to die.'

Obeysekera put his hands on Roshant's shoulders. 'So did I.'

For a moment, the commissar allowed the hands to remain there, then he struck one aside and turned away. Pointing at Gunsur, he said, 'Get me some water.' Roshant coughed, a long, body-shaking fit.

Trooper Gunsur's eyes tracked to Captain Obeysekera, who gave a fractional nod.

'Sir,' said Gunsur and, getting to his feet, he started on the long climb back up the dune. But Obeysekera stopped him.

'No need, trooper. I'm going to call the Venators down to us.' Keying open the squad vox-channel, Obeysekera ordered the Kasrkin who had remained with the three Venators to drive them down the slope. He looked up as the whine of the galvanic motors starting up came faintly down from above, then signalled to his men.

'Pull back from the slope in case they set off another fall.'

At his words, Roshant all but ran away from the slip face. The rest of the squad followed: Obeysekera's expression told them to guard their own expressions, facial and verbal.

Obeysekera stepped back himself, then stopped to watch as the Venators descended the face of the dune, slip-driving down like the great predatory seals that had surfed the waves of the Caducades Sea, launching themselves off the crests to snatch low-flying seabirds from the air. He wanted to hear if their movement triggered the song of the sand, but all he heard was the whine of the galvanic motors and the wave crush of sand turning under tyres.

Part of Obeysekera had thought that the strange music had been produced purely by the movement of sand on sand, but if that was the case then why weren't the Venators producing the same noise? There must be another factor.

The Venators reached the trough and came to a stop, still maintaining the regulation distance between the vehicles.

Obeysekera nodded. This squad was good. Turning to Gunsur, he motioned the trooper to get some water and take it to the commissar while he called Prater and Lerin, the navigators of *Divine Light* and *Saint Conrad*, over to *Holy Fire* so that they could check their reckonings against each other's map plots.

Torgut Gunsur looked after the receding back of Captain Obeysekera. The captain's reputation suggested he was a competent officer, but Gunsur was a trooper in the 'kin, not a servitor water-carrier. He shook his head, only slightly, but enough for Malick to spot the movement.

'Get moving,' Malick said. 'Captain's told you what to do.'

'All right, all right.' Gunsur trudged over to the Venators, filled a water flask from one of the barrels, his throat pricking with thirst as he did so, and turned to look for the commissar. Hopefully, Roshant would not use all the water and he could drink what was left over: it was a couple of hours yet before the next water break.

Roshant was still walking away from the Venators. Gunsur shook his head again and started after the commissar. The water sloshed in the flask, the sound reminding him of the waves of the Caducades Sea washing against the outer ramparts of Kasr Osmun. The memory clutched at his throat with all the intensity of unexpected remembrance for that which was lost, all but stopping Gunsur in his tracks. He clutched his head, trying to force the memory from his mind. Kasr Osmun was gone, along with all the people who had tried to defend it at the end. What was left was the long revenge. Gunsur squinted ahead. The commissar had finally stopped and was standing with his back turned to him and the rest of the men.

Coming closer, Gunsur realised that the commissar's body was shaking. The man was crying.

Gunsur stopped himself. He did not know what to do. Roshant was a commissar and not just a commissar but the lord militant's son to boot. He wanted to back away, but then he looked down at the bottle he was carrying. The captain had ordered him to take water to the commissar.

He could just hand over the bottle and get away.

Gunsur coughed.

Roshant gave no sign that he had heard. His head was bent, his hair still covered in sand, and his shoulders were heaving with silent sobs.

Gunsur tapped the commissar on the shoulder.

Roshant started.

'Commissar, I have the water for you.'

Roshant turned around. His face was smeared with tear tracks. He wiped a hand across, but it served only to spread the mess further.

Gunsur held out the water bottle but Roshant did not seem to see it. He looked at the trooper, his eyes red.

'Your water, sir.'

Roshant took the water bottle, but the action was automatic, like a servitor carrying out a task it had been programmed for.

Gunsur made to turn away.

'By my stupidity, I endangered the mission.'

Gunsur stopped. 'Most everyone's done that some time or other, sir.'

Roshant looked at him. 'Have they?'

'There was one time when I had the map turned up the wrong way and took my squad the opposite direction we were supposed to go. I got lucky that time – we ran into the heretics that were trying to outflank us.'

Roshant nodded. 'Thank you.' He looked beyond Gunsur to the men clustered around the Venators. 'And them? Will they think the same way? I am the lord militant's son.'

'What happens on a mission stays on a mission, sir. That's the 'kin way. You're one of us, now.'

Roshant stared at Gunsur, his eyes growing wider as he looked. 'One of you...'

Gunsur nodded. 'Yes, one of us.' He pointed at the bottle. 'If there's any water left over when you've finished, I could do with a drink.'

Roshant nodded. 'Yes.' He held the bottle up to his mouth and drank, then poured a little onto a cloth and wiped the sand from his eyes. 'Have the rest.'

'You sure, sir?'

'Yes, quite sure.'

Gunsur, bottle in hand, headed back to where Sergeant Malick was standing in the shade of one of the Venators. Once there, he handed the sergeant the bottle – Gunsur had left a finger of water in the bottom – and, turning to Malick, said, 'You'll never guess what the commissar was doing when I took him this water...'

As Gunsur told the story, Sergeant Malick turned to watch the commissar walking back towards them.

'What do you think of that then, sergeant?' asked Gunsur.

'If you hear or see anything else about our commissar, you come tell me, Gunsur, you understand?' Malick turned towards his corporal. 'You tell me and no one else, got it?'

'Sure, sergeant, I understand. But what's the problem?'

'Some things are better kept quiet, Torgut. If you don't keep them that way, I will cut out your tongue.' Malick smiled. 'Understand?'

Gunsur nodded. 'Give me the rest of the water, then – I keep quiet better when my throat isn't dry.'

Gunsur tipped the bottle and sucked the last few drops from it but, as he did so, he sneaked a look at Malick. The sergeant was staring after the commissar with all the eager intensity of a sniper lining up a kill.

CHAPTER 4

They had beat along, over crests and down troughs, crossing the waves of the Sand Sea, for the whole of the parched day with no further incident, stopping twice to move men between the Venators – Obeysekera found that rotating the crew of each vehicle served to keep the troopers sharp.

The only man that Obeysekera had not rotated during the course of the day was Commissar Roshant. He had kept him by his side, teaching the commissar how to navigate across the markless expanse of the Great Sand Sea. Roshant had taken on the task of keeping and plotting the map with wordless gratitude. For his part, Obeysekera was glad to have the chance to swap the navigator's seat for the driver's cockpit; it was like riding shotgun in a ground-hugging Valkyrie but without enemy shooting at you. As he, and the flanking Venators, whooped their way up and down the ridges, Obeysekera felt the shock of being buried alive gradually recede into the distance. As the day's end drew near, even Roshant had recovered enough to offer a quiet oath the next time the Venator breasted a crest and drove down the slip face, outrunning the sand-slide.

With the sun lowering towards the horizon, Obeysekera took a hand from the driving wheel and held it out at arm's length, fingers together and horizontal.

'What are you doing?' asked Roshant. He was holding the map tight on his lap, but glanced over to Obeysekera as he spoke.

'There's some anomaly under the Great Sand Sea that plays havoc with machine-spirits – even the chronometers start acting up. No idea what. Nothing shows up from orbit, so they reckon it must be underground.' The Venator hit a glancing blow on a sand bar and slewed sideways, forcing Obeysekera to put both hands back on the wheel to correct. Back on track, he held his hand up again. 'A palm's breadth between sun and horizon gives us about forty-five minutes until sunset.'

'Days are shorter here than Terran normal,' said Commissar Roshant. 'About twenty hours.'

'We need to stop soon and camp. I don't want us driving after dark – we'd lose our position on the map.'

'What's wrong with using the auspex?'

'Same as the chronometers. Something throws them off. One of the reasons that our aircraft are forbidden entry to the airspace above the Great Sand Sea – come in here, and they're lost.'

'You said that's one of the reasons. What are the others?'

'There's one,' said Obeysekera, pointing south. 'Sandstorm. They rise most days, by the evening at least. We've been fortunate not to encounter one sooner.'

The sandstorm was looming over the whole southern quarter, a wall of yellow gloom flecked with flashes.

'Sand-lightning,' said Obeysekera. 'We're going to have to find somewhere soon.'

'I heard that the sandstorms can flay a man's skin off.'

'So have I, but I haven't seen it happen. Probably just soldiers' stories, but on the other hand we don't want to find out that they're true.' Obeysekera keyed the squad vox-channel so that he could speak to *Divine Light* and *Saint Conrad*. 'We'll camp for the night in the lee of the next dune. That should provide protection against the storm.'

'If this is protection, I wouldn't want to be out in the storm.'

Sergeant Malick could only hear the words because Prater was yelling them into his ear as they lay under the Venator. They were using the Tauros as their shield against the storm, with Quert, the gunner, squeezed in beside them.

Malick turned his head so that he could shout into Prater's ear.

'You've got your skin – or most of it – so stop frekking complaining.'

'Not complaining, just saying.'

'Say nothing, that way I won't have to listen to you.'

'How long do you reckon we'll be stuck under here?' asked Prater. 'I've heard these storms can go on for days.'

'You're well named, ain't you.'

'What? I don't understand what you mean, sarge,' said Prater.

'Oh, shut up,' said Malick, turning away and pushing himself further into the lee of the Venator's rear tyres. Even with them hiding under the Tauros, the wind was still sending blasts of abrading sand through.

Prater turned towards Quert. 'Don't know what's up with the sergeant,' he said. 'Anyway, what do you reckon on Roshant? Noble, hothead or commissar?'

'Oh, shut up, Prater,' said Quert.

'Come on,' said Prater. 'We're stuck here until the storm is over. Roshant – noble, hothead or commissar? I'm taking bets on which comes out top.'

While taking no part in the conversation, Malick shifted so that he could hear it better over the gravel hiss of the wind and the rumble of sand-lightning.

'Money? Right,' said Quert. 'In that case, I'll bet on noble, though he wants to be a commissar.'

'Noble. You sure?'

'Sure,' said Quert. 'He made me brush the sand out of his coat. Creep. If he wasn't a commissar, I'd have taken that greatcoat and shoved it down his throat.'

'Best not do that to the lord militant's son,' said Prater.

'Yeah, that was what I thought,' said Quert. 'I'm smart like that.'

'You reckon he's a coward?'

The two troopers rolled over so that they could see Sergeant Malick.

'Didn't know you were listening, sergeant,' said Prater.

'Why do you think the commissar is a coward?' asked Malick.

Prater peered at Malick, trying to make out the sergeant's expression in the gloom under the Venator. 'I'm not going to get into trouble about this, am I?'

'No.' Malick leaned forward and grabbed Prater's arm. 'But first make sure your vox is off. You too, Quert.'

While the troopers checked, Malick looked out from under the Venator into the storm. Only the sand and wind were moving, their skirling skeins lit into tableaux by the strobe of the sand-lightning.

'He's a bully,' said Prater. 'Sure, commissars are all bullies – they wouldn't be commissars if they weren't – but sure as my hellgun is my best friend, he's a bully to cover his fear. You've seen it too, Quert?'

'Maybe,' said Quert. 'Maybe.'

'You've taken the bets,' said Malick. 'What are the men saying?'

Prater spat out some of the sand that had blown into his mouth when he answered. 'I'm going to stop taking bets – no odds. Everyone's betting "noble".'

'Right,' said Malick. 'This needs to be kept quiet. You see anything, you come to me, right? It won't do us no good if the word gets out that the lord militant's commissar son is a coward. You see him cracking, come to me. I'll cover for him.'

'What about the captain?' asked Prater. 'You going to tell him?'

'He's got enough on,' said Malick. 'This is sergeant stuff. I'll deal with it.'

But as he answered, Malick realised that Prater was not paying attention to him. He was staring down at the sand beneath his face as if it were alive.

'I'm talking to you, Prater. You only listen when you're talking. Don't make me repeat myself.'

Prater turned his head to look at Malick. 'The desert is moving.'

Under *Holy Fire*, Roshant turned to Obeysekera, his face a ghastly series of strobe flashes as sand-lightning detonated overhead.

'The sand is moving,' he said.

Next to the commissar, Gunsur nodded. 'It is, sir.'

Obeysekera had already felt it himself: the sand beneath him, heaving upwards, as if the desert had turned to sea and a wave was rising. As the sand rose, he thought he was going to be crushed up against the underside of the Venator, but then Obeysekera realised that the Venator was rising too, pushed up by whatever upheaval was raising the sand.

'Throne!' Commissar Roshant grabbed at Obeysekera. 'What is it?'

Obeysekera shook his head. He did not know. Turning to look outwards, he saw the desert floor, strobe-lit by lightning, rising in fits and starts, and the Venator next to his vehicle moving up and down like a boat bobbing in harbour.

It was truly as if the Great Sand Sea had become water: the only mercy was that they were not sinking.

'Stay still,' Obeysekera said into his vox-bead, transmitting over the squad channel. 'Any observations, report to me.'

The acknowledgements flicked over his display. All readings for the men were level: despite the sandstorm and the ground moving, they were remaining calm and watchful, as their training had taught them. Only the commissar's readings were spiking, his heartbeat raised and his breathing shallow.

'What is going on?' The commissar grabbed Obeysekera and pointed at the hard-packed sand around them, rising and falling with a steady rhythm, as if the desert were breathing. 'Why is it doing that?'

'I don't know.' Obeysekera removed Roshant's hand. 'It does not seem to be dangerous. We'll ride it out.'

But the commissar was pointing past Obeysekera, his eyes widening. Twisting round, Obeysekera saw the desert rising to form a ridge.

'What is that?'

Something was moving under the sand. Obeysekera stared. Moving, or growing.

'It's big,' said Gunsur.

The ridge grew higher, cutting off their view of the next Venator.

'Really big.'

Obeysekera realised that it was moving like a wave, the sand swelling and falling in its wake. He could hear it. He realised that the sound he had previously ascribed to the storm was the sound of billions of grains rising into the ridge.

The sound rose in intensity, notes playing off each other, making a new music in the silent desert. It was the song of a million saws, the thrumming of the greenhoppers of Cadia, the buzz of the treeborers of Catachan. But there was another note to the sound: a rhythmic pulsing, almost a drumming, as if the sands of the desert were booming. Lying flat on the ground beneath the Venator, Obeysekera could see the rhythm playing out in the vibration of the sand beneath his face; it jumped at the beat, like grit upon a drum skin.

'And what is that?'

Roshant was pointing out from under the Venator.

Obeysekera squirmed over towards him. He realised as he went that he had heard the commissar's words relatively easily. The sandstorm was dying away. Reaching Roshant, Obeysekera looked out and saw the storm vortex disappearing away from them, and the sand it had raised, suddenly left without motive power, falling in dark clouds back to the ground.

'There.'

The ground was slowly settling, the sand subsiding into a trough between their vehicle and the next. The wave was sinking back into the desert floor.

But the sand still drummed.

Obeysekera looked in the direction that Roshant was pointing and saw.

At first, he was not sure what he saw. Shapes, dark shapes rising and falling over the sand, working towards the watching soldiers as they tracked the path of the ridge. Obeysekera slowly realised that the motion of the shapes matched the rhythm that was pulsing through the sand.

They were drumming upon the desert.

Not just drumming: drilling. Those closest were pushing great long spikes into the sand, boring them in along the path of the wave, while the ones further away were beating upon the ground.

'What are they doing?' asked Roshant.

'They're trailing the wave.' Obeysekera pointed beyond the figures – they were close enough now for him to see they were human, dressed in billowing robes that flared out in the last wind of the passing storm – to the shapes following on behind. 'Mukaali.'

'Mukaali?' Roshant looked at Obeysekera. 'Xenos?'

'Non-sentient.' Obeysekera pointed again. 'That's not a neck, it's a rider.'

'What's riding them, then?'

'I think that we are about to meet the Kamshet.' Obeysekera keyed the squad vox-channel. 'The men approaching are non-hostiles, repeat, non-hostiles. Stand ready but do not train weapons.'

Roshant looked to Obeysekera. 'Are you sure they're not hostile? My data-slate briefing said their combat status was uncertain.'

'Kamshet means "Wanderers". From everything I have learned about them, they just want to be left alone.'

Roshant snorted. 'Those who do not fight for the Emperor aid those who oppose Him by their inaction. There are no neutrals.'

Obeysekera watched the Kamshet approaching, both those drumming the sand and the ones following, riding the mukaali. 'Maybe.'

'I shall speak to them. I shall call them to the service of the God-Emperor.' Roshant looked at Obeysekera and his eyes were wide and white. 'It's the duty of a commissar. It's what my father would expect me to do.'

Even as he finished speaking, Roshant began to crawl out from under the Venator. Obeysekera grabbed his ankle and pulled him back.

'What are you doing? Why are you stopping me? What do you want to hide from me?'

Obeysekera could feel the young man trembling in his grasp. Crawling out from under the Venator was, he suspected, one of the braver things the young man had ever done and, having gathered his courage to do the deed, he had been stopped from going through with it.

'There is nothing to hide,' said Obeysekera. 'But unless you speak Kamshet, it might be difficult to call the Wanderers to the service of the God-Emperor. Very few among them speak Gothic in any of its dialects.'

'And you do speak Kamshet?' Roshant stared at Obeysekera. 'What, you mean you really do?'

'A little. Hypnocaches for basic grammar and vocabulary. Enough to communicate with them, I hope. Enough to ask if they know of any Valkyries that have landed nearby.' Obeysekera let go of Roshant's wrist. 'Which is why I will go out to speak to them. Gunsur, stay here with the commissar.'

The captain began to crawl out from under the Venator. As he did so, he spoke into his vox-bead on the squad vox-circuit.

'Malick, have the men and vehicles ready. We might need to fight, or retreat. Make sure we're ready to do both.'

The acknowledgement came through as Obeysekera emerged into the aftermath of the storm.

It was different, Obeysekera noted, from a snowstorm. Sand had piled up in the lee of the Venator rather in front of it, settling in the area of calm behind the vehicle. The Venator itself had been scoured, its camouflage paint largely sandblasted away. Pulling himself upright, Obeysekera brushed his fingers against the plasteel: it felt scrubbed. From its texture he now took as true the reports he had read of the sandstorms of Dasht i-Kevar stripping skin and flesh to the bone. He would not wish to have seen his men if they had been caught out in the open during the storm.

Obeysekera looked towards the approaching Kamshet. He was standing, empty-handed to show peaceful intent, in full view. But the Kamshet, both those drumming and piercing the sand and the ones following, riding the mukaali, gave no sign of seeing him but continued on their course, following the ridge in the sand.

Obeysekera checked his auspex then shook his head. It was reading approaching numbers flickering between one and one hundred thousand. By eye, he counted twenty men on foot, beating and stabbing the sand, their own movements tracking the rhythm they drove into the ground. Following in a rough group behind were around thirty mukaali, each with a rider sitting high upon its shoulders while the animal itself plodded stolidly on over the sand, head thrust forward and swinging side to side.

Looking round, Obeysekera surveyed the other Venators. The troopers had not needed Malick's orders; some were shovelling clear the sand while others checked the vehicles' weapons. Obeysekera saw Uwais heading towards *Holy Fire*. Good. With only Gunsur, it needed a couple more hands to dig the vehicle clear and man the multi-laser. Clearly Malick trusted the commissar to do such menial work as little as he did.

Turning back to the approaching Kamshet, Obeysekera decided to wait and watch.

The men on foot – they were now within a hundred yards – were wearing yellow robes, yellow and ochre and brown, as if mimicking the myriad shades of the desert itself. Their heads and faces were covered with only their eyes showing. The drummers struck with paddles that slapped upon the sand, making a booming sound and sending vibrations up and into Obeysekera's feet. The piercers, who were generally a little in front of the drummers, each carried spears that were some four yards long and these they raised up before driving down into the sand at an angle of about thirty degrees from the vertical. The sand was still moving at their feet and Obeysekera saw that they were following the thinning ridge, thrusting their long spears along its path as they went.

The Kamshet who followed, riding upon their mukaali, wore robes of white and blue, and were being followed by a string of riderless mukaali, presumably the mounts of the men on foot.

The men at the front were within twenty yards of him now. By their course, they would pass between his Venator and the Venator of Sergeant Malick, leaving them exposed to flanking fire. As Obeysekera had ordered, the weapons were not tracking the Kamshet, but they stood ready, with Quert manning the weapon on her Venator and Malick himself taking control of the multi-laser. Obeysekera noted the third Venator – Prater was in charge of it – shift quietly so that it could bring its own weapon to bear without catching Malick's vehicle in crossfire.

But still the Kamshet advanced, beating and piercing the sand, apparently oblivious to the men silently watching them, hellguns cradled and ready. Obeysekera noted that the mounted Kamshet had closed the gap between them and the men on foot. Now they were closer, he could see that the riders were armed, but so far as he could see their weapons were swords, spears and autoguns, not a powered weapon in sight. They carried their swords and autoguns across their laps, while the spears and bows were laid along the long necks of the mukaali, strapped to the animals with ropes.

He also saw, as the riders approached, that while some had their faces covered in the manner of the men on foot, others did not, but went bare-faced, and these were all women. Old or young, the women had painted skin, a colour that Obeysekera did not expect to see on any human.

'Bluies.'

The call came through the vox, signalled from Trooper Ensor. Through the channel Obeysekera could hear the sound of weapons being powered up as the Kasrkin targeted what looked like approaching xenos.

'Hold,' Obeysekera whispered urgently into the vox-circuit. 'Hold.' He saw the Kamshet riders pause as the xenos signal was relayed among the Kasrkin and their hellguns were moved to readiness while the multi-lasers tracked closer to the advancing nomads. But still, with all this ranged firepower pointing at them, the Kamshet dancers came on, stepping and whirling and jumping, beating and stabbing the sand.

Obeysekera held up his hand, giving the visual signal to hold fire. The foremost among the Kamshet were close enough now for him to see their eyes. He had seen eyes like that before, in troopers battle-struck, in troopers whose fingers had had to be prised from lasrifles drained of power, in troopers sitting without moving in the aftermath of battle. The Kamshet were in a trance. They gave no sign of seeing him because they did not see him, nor the other waiting Kasrkin. They were caught in the action of a ritual that Obeysekera did not understand but which was clearly connected to the moving sand ridge they were following.

But while the eyes of the dancers were glazed in trance, those of the Kamshet riding the mukaali were looking upon him with wary interest. Obeysekera signalled for his troopers to stand aside as the dancers passed between the vehicles of the squad, their bare feet crunching the sand.

With the dancers past, Obeysekera stepped forward into the path of the advancing mukaali and raised his hand.

'In the name of the God-Emperor, I greet you.'

The mukaali continued plodding on, their heads swinging from side to side and only the flaring of their nostrils indicating that they sensed the man standing in their path. But Obeysekera was not looking at the desert animals but rather at the people riding them. The Kamshet sat astride the shoulders of the mukaali, their legs gripping the base of the beasts' long necks. Mukaali were tall animals and the men riding them sat higher than head height, swaying to left and right as the animals took their ungainly, outward-rolling steps. But the riders did not slow, nor acknowledge Obeysekera's greeting; they kept on going, as if they intended to ride right past him.

Bharath Obeysekera was a captain in the Astra Militarum, an officer of the Cadian Kasrkin. He was not used to being ignored.

He stepped forward, putting himself right in the path of the first of the mukaali, and planted himself there, bedding his boots down into the sand. The animal was five yards away from him, plodding closer, head swinging left to right, its small eyes, set back on its head, swivelling towards him on each sweep.

Obeysekera looked up, past the low-swinging head, to the Kamshet sitting astride the beast. He was cloaked in white and blue, his robes spotless and his headscarf, which left only his eyes exposed, the brilliant blue of the cloudless skies of Dasht i-Kevar. The Kamshet looked straight at Obeysekera, his eyes dark, and the captain began to speak, trying to greet him in his own language.

'Azul. Nekk d Bharath Obeysekera. Tzemreḍ ad iyi-d-tesɛeddiḍ Aɣella.'

The words sounded harsh on his tongue, but there was a timbre to them that seemed to fit the desert that had bred them.

But the Kamshet, rather than acknowledging Obeysekera's request to speak with the chieftain of the tribe, simply looked away from the captain, as if he were of no more moment than a zephyr on the sand and, pulling on the reins, directed the mukaali to Obeysekera's left. Animal and rider walked past Obeysekera, the captain staring up at the Kamshet while the rider looked straight ahead and the mukaali plodded onwards. They came close enough for Obeysekera to have reached out and touched the mukaali's tough, leathery hide; they were certainly close enough for him to smell the animal – the odour intensified each time it swung its head in his direction, so he knew that the smell came from its breath. It was the smell of decay, of plants rotting wetly under a hot sun. It was the smell of a Kasrkin mess hall with thirty wet and weary men and women drying off while the cooks heated fried slab; the food was as much an endurance test for recruits as the training.

Obeysekera snapped back from the memory fugue to see that the rider and mukaali had passed him. He looked round and saw the animal's rump waggling as it followed the dancers, the man swaying on top.

Turning back to face the oncoming Kamshet, Obeysekera saw three riders approaching abreast. He moved in front of them, called out the greeting he had learned from some hastily absorbed hypnocaches.

'Azul. Nekk d Bharath Obeysekera. Tzemreḍ ad iyi-d-tesɛeddiḍ Aɣella.'

He held up his hand, showing its conspicuous emptiness.

The three riders kept on coming, neither changing course nor slowing down.

'Do you want us to stop them, captain?'

The question, from Sergeant Malick, came in over the squad vox-channel.

'No, repeat, no. The cooperation of the Kamshet is vital. We are under strict orders not to antagonise them.'

'Understood.'

As the riders came on, their mounts looming larger and larger, part of Obeysekera wished that mission orders allowed him to use the multi-lasers targeted in on the creatures. But Colonel Aruna had emphasised the need not to rile the Kamshet. He reminded himself that mukaali would only walk over him by accident, and even short-sighted creatures could not fail to see him standing right in front of them.

And indeed they did not. The mukaali separated and walked past on either side of him, their riders continuing to ignore Obeysekera's attempts to engage them.

'This is an outrage.' The voice coming through on Obeysekera's vox-bead was that of the commissar, raised to a fresh pitch of indignation. 'These barbarians are insulting the Astra Militarum, and by insulting us they are insulting the Emperor Himself. It cannot go unpunished.'

'No!' Obeysekera hissed into his micro-bead. 'If they do not want to speak to us, I cannot make them.' The captain paused. 'But I might try something else to attract their attention.'

Obeysekera looked ahead. The next group of approaching Kamshet included three of the unveiled women flanked by men. He stared at the centre woman. She was striking in her beauty despite the blue paint in stripes on her skin, but there was a timelessness to her face that made it impossible to judge her age: she might be nineteen or ninety. Or nine hundred. On the planet that produced the highest quality aqua vitae for the subsector, there were rumours of people living for a thousand years or more, although how the Kamshet processed the substance into usable rejuve treatments was passed over in his briefing data-slates.

The woman herself, sitting easily upon her mount, moved with it as one born to the saddle, so that mukaali and rider seemed to be a single being. Unlike all the other Kamshet that had passed by, she looked upon Captain Obeysekera with frank interest.

'Azul!' said Obeysekera, holding up his empty hand and smiling as he moved to stand in front of the onward-plodding mukaali.

For the first time, there was a response. The woman nodded. There was no smile, but she at least was acknowledging his presence in front of her.

'Azul!' repeated Obeysekera. 'Hello,' he added in Low Gothic, in case she understood the speech of the Imperium. 'Awyet-iyi s imdebber-nwen.'

But at his further words, her face darkened and she looked away from him. The mukaali, responding to some sign from its rider, lurched forward, its pace increasing from its customary plod to something approaching a trot.

She was sending the mukaali right at him. Obeysekera wondered what he had said to so displease her – he had simply asked to see their leader – but when she showed no sign of turning the lumbering animal aside, he had no choice but to step out of the way. The mukaali rolled past him trailing the stench of fermenting cabbage. Obeysekera looked up and saw its rider staring down at him, her face without expression. He did not know how he had offended her, but there was no doubting that he had.

It soon became all too clear that the following Kamshet had no more intention of engaging with him than those who had already passed, so rather than wait for the long procession to finish, Obeysekera made his way back to the Venators.

Commissar Roshant was waiting for him by the side of the vehicle. His outrage at the way the Kamshet had treated an officer of the God-Emperor's Astra Militarum had not in the end outweighed his wish to remain in the shade of the Venator, and there he had stayed as the sun rose, bringing fire in its train of light. Roshant held up his bolt pistol, the amphant ivory of its grip glowing despite the deep shadow in which he stood.

'You should not allow barbarians to disrespect the God-Emperor.'

Obeysekera shrugged. 'So long as I am ordered to keep the Wanderers happy, I will do so.'

'Wanderers.' Roshant sniffed. 'They will wander into slavery to the t'au.'

Obeysekera shook his head. 'From what I saw of them, I would be surprised if they became slaves to anyone.' He keyed open the squad vox-channel. 'Get ready to roll out. Follow my bearing.'

Hearing the command, Trooper Gunsur swung up into the gun placement while Uwais made his way back over the sand to *Saint Conrad*.

Obeysekera swung himself into the navigator's seat and indicated for Roshant to take the driver's seat. As Obeysekera took the maps from their sealed container, fixed in under the dashboard, he briefly thought of moving Roshant to one of the other vehicles. He shook his head as the commissar climbed in alongside him and strapped on the restraints. While it might make for a better day for him, he could not inflict the commissar on any of his men, particularly as none of them had the rank to push back against the whims of a commissar who also happened to be the lord militant's son. Obeysekera, hunched over his maps, grimaced. Just one of the many joys of command.

CHAPTER 5

'We're in the middle of a desert and I'm cold.' Prater looked at the other troops sitting near him. 'How's that supposed to happen?'

Gunsur pointed up at the sky. 'You noticed? It's dark too.'

'Come on, it's night,' said Prater. 'It's going to be dark.'

'I like the stars here,' said Quert, leaning back and staring up. 'It's like the sky used to be.'

'That's another thing,' said Prater. 'Why don't we see it here? The Rift. Where's it gone?'

Sergeant Malick, leaning against the cooling plasteel of *Divine Light* with his eyes closed but his ears open, sat up and looked over to the three 'kin – Prater, Quert, Gunsur – sitting round their evening rations. When no one answered, he sighed and, getting up, went over to them, a shadow standing in the dark.

'Is that you, sarge?' asked Prater.

'Just as well it is, Sill, or you'd be dead.'

'Uwais, Ha and Ensor are all picket. If anything got past them, we'd all be dead.'

Malick kicked the tyre of *Divine Light*, knocking off the sand clinging to his boot. 'Throne, I'll give you that, Sill. But what I won't give you is being so stupid as not knowing why you're not seeing the Rift.'

'Frekk, sarge, I don't care why I can't see the Rift – I'd be happier if I never saw it again,' said Prater.

Quert, still staring up, her face a starlit landscape of shadow, nodded. 'I'm with Sill there, sarge. It makes me feel ill when I see it.'

Malick gathered the sand coating his tongue and spat, thick and gritty, on the ground. 'Not knowing is what gets us dead, Etene.'

Quert glanced over. 'Sure, whatever you say, sarge.'

Malick looked at her, head back, face as blank and stupid and killable as a grox. He took a step towards Quert. But Gunsur reached out and laid a hand on Malick's hip, stopping him. Malick looked down at the hand, then slowly at Gunsur. The trooper removed his hand, holding it up, fingers spread in as unthreatening a manner as he could.

'You tell us why we can't see the Rift, Shaan,' he said. 'Etene and Sill want to know – they're just too stupid to realise it.'

Malick stopped. He slowly looked at Prater and then Quert. Even Etene had realised the danger and was staring at the sergeant.

'Not knowing is what killed Cadia. Remember that.' Malick hitched his thumb into his carapace pauldron. 'Learn, live.'

Quert nodded. 'Tell us, sarge.'

Malick leaned back against *Divine Light*. Even through the backplate of his carapace armour, he could feel the heat radiating from the metal.

'First, why you're cold, Sill,' he said, looking at Prater. 'There's nothing to hold the heat in a desert. The moment the sun goes down, the temperature starts falling faster than an Earthshaker shell and 'cause you've been cooking your balls all day, it feels colder than the Emperor's tears.'

'It's right,' added Gunsur. 'Honest, the coldest I've ever been was sleeping out on Prosan when I was training there.'

'Well, there you go then. Torgut confirms it – it must be true.'

'I wasn't riding you, sarge.'

Malick stared a moment at Gunsur then turned away. 'Like I was saying, the Rift.' Malick pointed up into the star-flung sky. 'There's more than one reason why we can't see it. One, there's stuff in the way. It looks empty, don't it? But space ain't empty – there's all sorts of stuff, dust and debris drifting all through it. Could be we're the other side of some huge dust cloud.'

'Then why don't the dust cover the stars?' asked Prater.

''Cause there're stars between the dust and us. There's a grox load of stars in the galaxy – I reckon even the High Lords don't know 'em all. Throne, probably the Emperor Himself hasn't counted them.'

At those words, Gunsur glanced about, searching for listening ears. 'Careful what you say, sarge. We've got a commissar with us.'

'I saw him. He's sat in *Holy Fire* with that greatcoat wrapped round him, head back, fast asleep.'

'Yeah, well... Go on.'

'I will. So there're stars, thousands, millions of them between us and the dust cloud. But there's another reason too which you groundhogs are too ignorant to work out, so I'm going to tell you.' Malick paused. They were watching him with the interest of men about to be vouchsafed secret knowledge. He pointed up at the sky again. 'Those stars, them up there, all of them. They could have all gone out, every one, and you wouldn't know yet. You're looking up there with your jaws hanging open and you're looking into the past. The light from that star, it's hundreds, maybe thousands of years old. All that time it's been crossing space and now it gets here and, Throne, it thinks, I'm falling into Sill's eyes. No! All that journeying, all that time, and I get seen by a frekking idiot. Same with the Rift. In realspace, nothing goes faster than light, and light is slow. It's why we travel in the warp – the only way to keep the Imperium together is to go through hell, 'cause in hell there ain't no limits. Back on Cadia we got it close up, but out here the light from when the Rift cut the sky ain't arrived yet.'

'Hang on, sarge,' said Quert. 'I swear I've seen the Rift away from Cadia.'

Malick clapped his hands, slowly. 'So there is something between Etene's ears. Course you have. Any systems close to the Rift, it's going to be right there, in the sky.'

'But I reckon I saw it when we were on our way here,' said Quert. 'How's that then?'

'You weren't looking into the warp, were you?'

'You don't think I'm that stupid?'

Malick shook his head. 'I guess not even you're that stupid.'

'She's right though, sarge,' said Prater. 'I reckon I remember seeing it, before we arrived, when we dropped.'

'And that's why. When we drop out of the warp, for a moment we drag a bit of it with us, caught up in the Geller fields as they're powering down. If you look out then, like as not you'll see the Rift.'

'Yeah, I wanted to see where we were going,' said Prater. 'I'd heard about this place – the desert of life, that's what they call it.'

'Who calls it that?' asked Gunsur.

'Saw it in a briefing pack.' Prater shrugged apologetically. 'So, I read them. Gives me something to do in transit.'

Gunsur nodded. 'I've heard it called a different name.'

'Like what?'

'Some people call it the Pit.'

Malick looked with sudden interest at Gunsur. 'Where'd you hear that?'

'Don't remember, sarge. But it came back to me today, when we were driving, and now, sitting here.' Gunsur dropped his voice and glanced around. 'Maybe it's just me, losing my nerve or something.'

'Like you haven't done that already,' said Quert.

'Shut up, Etene,' said Malick. 'I want to know what Torgut means.'

Gunsur hunched his shoulders against the night cold. In the dark, under the stars, they could all feel the day's heat being sucked greedily up into the void. He looked at the troops around him, listening, their faces shadows.

'Any of you, back on Cadia, any of you see a dirtshark pit?'

'You mean one of those little hollows?' asked Prater. 'Yeah, there were some outside my kasr. Frekking nuisance – could turn your ankle if you stepped in one.'

Quert laughed. 'You're both from Kasr Osmun. Weird stuff round there.'

'Our weird stuff lived outside the kasr,' said Gunsur. 'Not like Kasr Viklas. The weird stuff there is all inside.'

Quert stared at Gunsur for a moment, then looked away. 'Doesn't matter no more,' she said.

Gunsur paused. 'Yeah. Suppose you're right.' He turned back to Prater. 'Did you ever stop and watch a dirtshark pit?'

'Stare at a hole in the ground?' Prater laughed. 'Even when I was a kid, I had better things to do.'

'Yeah, well, I did. Don't know if you noticed, but they've all got the same slope – about fifty degrees. I got curious about this – yeah, all right, I didn't have much to do – and I started watching one, just lying there next to it one summer day. Saw a glow beetle come trundling along, heading towards the lip of the pit and I wanted to see what would happen, so I let it go on. It came to the lip of the pit and went over – at its size, there's all sorts of ups and downs – but then the dust under its legs all slipped and it slid down to the bottom of the pit. I was really curious now. The glow beetle lay there a bit, flashing like they do, then it picked itself up and started trying to climb up the other side of the pit. It would climb maybe halfway up and then the side of the pit slipped and it fell down to the bottom again. It kept doing that, again and again, but I could tell it was getting tired 'cause it wasn't getting so far up the pit. Just when I was thinking of picking it up, it slipped back down to the bottom of the pit. But this time, the pit opened, and there was a mouth there, and teeth, and they grabbed hold of the glow beetle and crunched it, cracking its carapace in one go.'

Gunsur looked round his comrades, all of them from Cadia. 'Don't know if you ever tried stamping out a glow beetle when it was blundering round, bumping into things, but they're solid right through. I never split one. But this one, in the bottom of the pit, it was split apart like an egg. Buried down in the bottom of the pit was a dirtshark.'

'Still reckon it's a stupid name,' said Quert. 'What's with the shark bit?'

'If you'd seen the way it chomped the glow beetle, you'd know,' said Gunsur. 'They live at the bottom of their pits and you never see one. They're too small to bother us, other than turning an ankle or two, but they eat – ate – anything small that falls into their pits. Turns out, they dig out their pits at the exact angle so that any beetle or ant or spider that falls into it tries to climb out, but the sides of the pit slip, taking it back down to the bottom and wearing it out, until the dirtshark, in its tunnels, hears all the commotion and crawls along and' – Gunsur snapped his jaws together – 'chomps.'

'What's that got to do with us?' said Malick.

Gunsur paused, looking around furtively once again. He looked back at Malick.

'See, there's this sense I've had since we started into the Sand Sea, and I couldn't work out what it was, not until today. Then I remembered the pit, and the dirtshark waiting at the bottom, and I knew. This desert, it's the pit, sarge, and we've fallen into it, and no matter how hard we try we ain't ever going to climb back out of it – and then, when we're spent, the dirtshark will open its mouth.' Gunsur shook his head. 'Just a feeling, sarge. Stupid, probably.'

'Yeah, you're right for once,' said Prater. 'Stupid.'

'Stupid,' echoed Quert.

'Sarge?'

'Sure don't look like Cadia to me,' said Malick. 'And, yeah, it's stupid. Anyway, time to change the picket. You three can take over from Uwais, Ha and Ensor.'

'Come on, sarge,' said Prater, 'I've not finished my rations.'

'Shouldn't spend so much time talking then, should you?'

As Prater, Quert and Gunsur headed off, grumbling, to relieve Uwais, Ha and Ensor, Malick looked around at the dark desert. Even under the light of ten thousand stars it lay shrouded in darkness. Quiet. Waiting. Patient.

CHAPTER 6

'Whooah!'

The Venator crested a ridge, its galvanic motors sending the front wheels spinning wildly as the rear four dug into the sand, and then its nose fell, down and down, like a boat riding a breaking wave, and the wheels, all digging deep into the sand, sent the vehicle powering down the slip face, outracing the sand-slides that fanned out in a spreading V behind the racing Tauros.

Trooper Ensor, driving the Venator, yelled again as the vehicle powered across the dune. The wind – hot, dry and gritty – blew through the empty windscreen of the Venator, drying sweat before it could form: the cooling airflow was worth exchanging for the protection of a windscreen. The slope of the slip face was near to forty degrees, the fall off from the ridgetop steep and the distance of the fall to the trough at least two hundred yards. Ensor, fingers light upon the wheel, gave the Venator its head as the vehicle surged down the slip face, his face split wide in a grin of delight.

'Honest, this is the most fun I've ever had in the frekking Guard, never mind the 'kin,' he said, eyes fixed ahead but words directed to his navigator, Trooper Prater, sitting beside him, trying to keep his maps in order as the wind ripped at the sheets of paper. 'Good day when I got promoted from the Hundred and Fifty-Fifth.'

'All right for you,' said Prater. 'You're not trying to hold on to the maps while plotting distance and direction.' He slammed down on an escaping sheet, grabbed it and shoved it under his leg.

'Enjoy the ride,' said Ensor. 'You're never going to have this much fun again in uniform.' He glanced down at the navigator and himself. They were both stripped down to shorts and vest because of the heat. 'Well, some of it at least.'

'Orders. I've got to track our position.'

'Why bother? The captain's got it in hand.'

'What if we get separated? I don't keep track of where we are, we get split off from the captain and then we're driving around in the middle of more nowhere than I've ever seen with even less idea where to go. I'll keep plotting.'

'You keep plotting, I'll keep driving. What you say, Chame?'

Chame's answer came over the local vox-circuit. 'I say, faster.'

'See, even the gunner says "faster", and they always want to slow down so they can get a better shot.' Ensor grinned. 'Let's go.'

The hum of the galvanic motors raised in pitch, the wheels spun faster, and the headlong charge down the slip face became breakneck.

Prater glanced over to the left, where Captain Obeysekera's Venator had the centre. That Tauros, having been first to crest the ridge, was already nearing the bottom of the trough, but it seemed to be slowing down. With Ensor running the galvanic motors at high intensity, their Venator was fast catching up.

'Better slow down,' said Prater, 'or we'll overtake the captain.'

'Come on. Down one dune, up the next, bearing two-seven-five.' The galvanic motors were humming like a hive of angry bees – and then they got angrier. 'We'll beat them up the next dune then wait for them there.'

The Venator surged forwards, trailing its V-shaped wake of falling sand, with Ensor and Chame hollering the joy of being young and alive and in command of a ton of fast, heavily armed machinery.

Prater, having given up trying to plot the course during the bumps of the helter-skelter descent, was looking ahead, down the slip face to the broad trough at the bottom. It was strange. Rather than the usual long smooth curve into the trough that he had seen before, the slip face seemed to run at the same angle all the way until it met the sudden flat of the trough.

It was very flat.

He peered more closely.

It seemed to be moving.

Flowing.

'Divine Light, Saint Conrad, *pull up, pull up.*'

The call came over the squad priority vox-channel, the channel that overrode all other communication.

'Stop! Stop!' yelled Prater, beginning to brace himself.

Ensor stamped on the brakes. The galvanic motors, humming like a turbofan one moment, went silent the next. The Venator, sliding down the slip face, brakes on full, began to skid, its nose slewing as the braked front wheels bit into the sand and the momentum of the heavier rear of the vehicle began to turn it around its inertial centre.

'Hold it, hold it.'

'I'm trying,' said Ensor, attempting to angle the Venator back into the skid before it could turn sideways on.

Prater looked left. They were running out of steering room.

Everything became clear, sharp. He saw the slip face, still running downwards at an angle of thirty-five degrees. He saw the lip, where it met the valley bottom. He saw sand slipping over the edge. And he saw the sand of the trough moving, slowly, along the bottom of the erg. Flowing.

It was a river of sand.

Ensor hauled the steering wheel left, struggling to turn the Venator into the skid, and slowly, slowly its nose came back round. But the sand was sliding away under its wheels, falling down the slip face and tumbling into the river below.

'Got it, got it.'

Ensor crooned the words, over and over again, as the Venator's brakes slowly burned off its momentum, the wheels digging deeper into the sand.

They were ten yards from the edge.

Eight yards.

Five.

Three.

Stopped.

Prater breathed out.

'Got it,' said Ensor. He slapped the steering wheel. 'You did it.'

Prater tapped the driver on his arm. 'Look,' he whispered. He pointed to the bank.

A little wave of sand slipped over, falling into the river. Then another, larger slip, and another, and another, and each slip nibbled away at the edge.

The river of sand was eroding the bank on which the Venator stood.

'Get us out of here.'

Ensor, seeing the danger, tried to start the galvanic motors. They whirred, then died away.

'Come on, come on,' he whispered as he tried again. Beside him, Prater was mumbling whatever invocations to machine-spirits he could call to mind.

The galvanic motors hummed alive, buzzing and angry, and Ensor gunned the wheels, spinning them and sending great plumes of sand arching backwards.

The Venator lurched forward with Ensor trying to turn its nose up the slip face. But even as it started to move, the vehicle tipped over onto its left. Prater, sitting on that side, looked over to see what was happening.

'The bank's gone!'

The spinning wheels had eaten away what was left of the bank and, with nothing there to support it, the Venator was beginning to topple.

Ensor reached out, killing the galvanic motors driving the left-hand set of wheels. The Venator settled further but, with the wheels not excavating the sand, the chassis sank down upon the ground and rested there.

'Get the weight on the right,' Ensor said, throttling back the right-side wheels.

Prater unfastened his harness and climbed over Ensor, while behind them Chame swung her body and the heavy bulk of the multi-laser out to the right of the vehicle.

As he scrambled over Ensor, Prater saw that Captain Obeysekera's Venator, tilted over at thirty degrees, was driving over the slip face towards them, with Malick's following behind. They just had to hold the Venator for a few more minutes and then the other two vehicles could haul them to safety.

The Venator lurched again, tipping further left.

'It's the frekking water tanks,' yelled Ensor. 'They're forcing us over.'

Prater nodded. The tanks, slung on the outside of the Venators, helped even out the weight, but now with the Tauros rolling over on its side, the water shifting in the barrels was rotating the vehicle around its centre of inertia.

'I'll get them.'

He started crawling back across the Venator, moving slowly and keeping as low as he could. As he went, he drew his knife from its sheath at his waist. The handle fit snugly into his hand: Prater had used it many times before. The blade itself, sharpened at the point and cutting edge, gleamed in the desert light.

The Venator rocked.

'Hold!' said Ensor.

Prater went still. Everything settled.

'Slow,' said Ensor, 'nice and slow. Chame, can you give us more balance?'

'Trying,' yelled back the gunner. 'Okay. Far out as I can go.'

'Nice and easy,' said Ensor, looking back to Prater. 'Nice and easy.'

Prater nodded, then began to inch forward, the cutting edge of his Cadian knife held out in front. He just had to reach the straps holding the water barrels in place. The blade, honed to battle sharpness, would cut through the webbing as if it were smoke.

Nearly there, nearly there.

The Venator lurched sideways, and Prater slid forwards. Ensor made a grab for his ankle but missed. Prater snatched the webbing, stopping himself falling through the vehicle and into the river of sand. The Venator lurched again, tipping over further.

It began to slide sideways.

'Get back,' yelled Ensor. 'It's going.'

But Prater shook his head. 'Got this,' he muttered, sawing through the webbing, 'got this.'

The straps parted, pinging apart under the weight of the water barrels, and the barrels themselves started to tumble off the side of the Venator, slapping onto the sand below. Prater saw the sand part around the barrels like thick soup, then swallow them down.

The weight on the left side of the Venator released, the vehicle rocked back in the other direction, back towards the bank.

'Clear,' said Ensor.

'Clear,' said Prater. He levered himself upright, sheathing his knife.

But then the bank under the vehicle collapsed.

The Venator tipped on its side. Prater, half standing, hand at the knife sheath, flailed for a hold, missed and fell. He saw the ground approaching. He twisted, trying to stop himself going in head first, and landed on his shoulder, digging it into the shifting sand.

At the impact, Prater spread himself out, making as large a surface area as possible, splaying out arms and fingers and legs, turning onto his back and making an X shape, staring up at the sky. He had not realised: it was so blue it was almost violet.

Prater lay stretched out upon the sand but he felt it shifting, flowing, beneath him, and he found himself drifting past the Venator. The removal of his weight seemed to have stabilised the vehicle: it was balancing on the edge but not tipping over any further.

'Hang on.'

Ensor was unstrapping himself from his seat, reaching for a rope.

'I'm okay,' Prater said into the vox. 'Get the Venator clear.'

'Sure?'

'Sure.'

He could feel the sand beginning to shift under him. His legs from the knees downward had disappeared beneath the surface. He tried kicking them upwards, but the sand was thick as treacle and he could barely move them. Prater began to make slow paddling motions with his hands and arms, trying to push himself back towards the bank. The slow-flowing sand was dragging him further out.

Where was it going?

He turned his head. He could hear the whine of motors and the hiss of tumbling sand. Captain Obeysekera's Venator had nearly got to them.

Prater tried to lift his head a little, to see better.

The bottom half of his body suddenly sank, rotating downwards. Although all his training told him to stay still, at the sudden drop he could not stop himself. He began kicking, searching for some purchase on the flowing sand, some floor to stand upon.

The motion made him sink further. He was down to his chest. Prater raised his arms, tried to lay them out flat upon the top of the sand, but the surface parted like molasses and his arms went down. Now, only his head and neck were above the surface.

He dropped further. He tried to speak, to call for help, but sand trickled into his mouth and he choked. Prater turned his head upwards, spat, tried to clear his mouth then turned his head to speak into the vox.

'Hel–'

But even as he opened his mouth to call, he saw the Venator tipping as more of the bank beneath it collapsed. Men were attaching cables to it, tying it off against the captain's Tauros, which was reversing, trying to haul the vehicle back.

Ensor, looking around from the driver's seat, saw Prater in the flowsand and gestured some of the men to help him.

'No!' said Prater. 'Secure the vehicle.'

'You sure?' Ensor's voice cracked through his vox.

'Sure.'

Ensor nodded and turned back to the Venator.

Prater struggled, pushing his arms back up out of the sand. It felt as if he were pushing through a membrane, but he managed to free them. He felt his head a little clearer of the sand.

He began pulling his way through the grains, sweeping his arms back over the surface in wide arcs.

The Venator jerked backwards, Ensor engaged its galvanic motors and, with all its wheels back on sand, it reversed up the slope, away from the edge.

The vehicle safe, Prater began to raise his hand.

'Some hel–'

His leg jerked downwards.

'H–'

The sand, pouring in over his face and eyes and nose and mouth, stopped the rest of the call. The last thing Prater saw before the sand closed over him was the blue sky of Dasht i-Kevar.

CHAPTER 7

'Flowsand.'

Captain Obeysekera sat among his remaining men, the Venators parked up along the slip face. He pointed down towards the valley bottom.

'I'd heard tales but I thought they were exaggerated, stories spun to excuse a failed mission or to entertain bored troopers. We're 'kin, we've all done the training on Prosan, we know what to do in quicksand.'

Obeysekera looked around the men, sitting on the sand in the lee of the Venators, the shade providing some relief from the unrelenting sun.

'I was wrong and Prater died because of my mistake.' Obeysekera paused. 'We learn from this.' He looked towards Ensor, who was sitting, his face downcast. 'No more racing down dunes. From a distance, it's impossible to tell what's flowsand and what isn't.'

Ensor nodded, saying nothing. He did not look up at the captain. In his hands, he held his knife. The gentle rasp told that he was honing its edge, honing and honing it again.

'For now, we go on.'

At that, Ensor looked up. 'We're 'kin. We don't leave our dead behind.'

Obeysekera pointed at the flowsand. 'If we could retrieve him, we would.'

Ensor stropped his knife back and forth, back and forth on the grox-leather strop. 'We're 'kin,' he repeated. 'We don't leave our dead behind.'

'I know. If there was any way of finding Prater, we would do it.'

Ensor jumped to his feet, knife in hand, and advanced on Obeysekera.

'We're frekking 'kin,' Ensor said. He grabbed Obeysekera and pushed him back, up against the side of the Venator. 'We don't never leave our dead behind.'

The commissar, seeing a trooper lay hands on his commanding officer, drew his bolt pistol, his face pale and determined, but Obeysekera gestured him to stand down.

Ensor put the point of his warknife up against Obeysekera's throat. 'You come in here like you're the Emperor's gift and you don't even know about that... that *stuff,* and now you tell me we're going to leave Prater behind. We're 'kin,' he repeated. 'We don't leave our dead behind.'

Obeysekera looked into the eyes in front of him. Ensor's face was pressed up almost against his own. He could smell the rank breath of days' travel through the desert without water to clean teeth.

'We did on Cadia,' Obeysekera said softly.

'What? What did you say?'

'We left our dead on Cadia. We never went back for them.'

'That was Cadia – it's where they should rest.'

Obeysekera raised his hand and pushed the warknife aside. 'Cadia's gone.'

Ensor shook his head. 'No. No, Cadia stands.'

'Cadia stands where Cadians do their duty to the Emperor. If you would honour Prater, give him some of our home to remain with him. I will.'

Ensor stared at Obeysekera. His hand went to the vial around his neck. There was a similar vial hanging from the captain's neck and indeed those of all the Kasrkin – only the commissar did not wear one.

'This?'

'Yes. We will give Prater some of the soil of our lost home, that he might find his way back there when the stars fall and the worlds are made new. You are right, Ensor. We are Kasrkin. We leave no man behind.'

The trooper stood back, nodded, let his hand fall. 'Yes, sir,' he said.

'Good,' said Obeysekera. He stepped forward, put his hand on Ensor's shoulder and spoke into the trooper's ear. 'Pull a trick like that again and I will execute you on the spot. Do you understand, trooper?'

Ensor nodded. 'Yes, sir.'

'Very well.'

'I checked on him, sir. He was all right. He signalled for me to get the Venator free or I wouldn't have left him in there. It couldn't have been more than a minute, sir, but when I looked again he was gone.'

'The responsibility is mine, Ensor. I should have had a man getting him out while the rest of us secured the vehicle. Come. Let us bid him farewell.'

Obeysekera tapped Ensor on the cheek then stepped past the trooper. As he went, the captain lifted the vial up over his neck and carefully twisted off the cap. The men around him stood and did the same, pinching a few grains from within their vials. With the men following, Obeysekera walked over to the edge of the flowsand.

'Spread out,' he said. 'We don't want the bank collapsing.'

The Kasrkin spaced themselves out along the edge, each with the hand containing the pinch of Cadian dust held over the flowsand. Roshant stood to silent attention behind them, commissarial cap on his head.

'May the dust of Cadia carry you home, Sill Prater.'

As he spoke, Obeysekera let the grains of lost Cadia fall from his fingers. One by one, the other Kasrkin did the same, the dust of their home merging with the sand of Dasht i-Kevar.

'Until the stars fall and Cadia is made new.' Obeysekera passed the prayer down the line of Kasrkin.

'Until the stars fall and Cadia is made new.'

'Until the stars fall and Cadia is made new.'

For a moment the Kasrkin stood silent with heads bent, then, one by one, they turned and walked back to the commissar, who was waiting by the Venators. Ensor was last to return. Chame and Lerin made room for him between them. Ensor sat down, using his helmet as a stool.

Obeysekera pointed along the slip face.

'We will have to follow the line of this erg until we can find somewhere to cross the flowsand.'

'That's taking us off our bearing, sir,' said Malick.

'I know. But we have no choice.' Obeysekera looked around the men. 'With the loss of the water barrels and being forced off course, we will have to reduce the water ration.'

'How many days' supply have we got left, sir?' asked Gunsur.

'Malick?'

'On minimum rations, a week.'

'That will be enough. If we haven't found the general by then, he'll already be dead. Any questions?'

'Why follow on along the slip face this way, sir? We don't know where we can cross the flowsand and this way we're heading in the direction it's going. If you're trying to cross a river, it's better to go upstream,' said Uwais.

'True, but we have no idea if this flowsand behaves like water. Do tributaries feed into it, like streams into a river? Or is it the result of sand flowing down from the slip faces all along its length? Or something else entirely? If we head this way we are at least going at a vector towards our destination – the other direction, we would be heading away.'

Sergeant Malick stood up, the sun almost directly over him so that he cast barely any shadow, and pointed slightly off the line of the slip face. 'That's nearly the direction the painted people went.'

'The Kamshet?'

'Yes, sir.'

'We'll only meet them again if they turn off their bearing. Malick, check the auspex, see if there's any chance of getting an exact bearing so that we can mark this waypoint. The rest of you, back to your vehicles. Ensor, you'll have Chame navigating.' Obeysekera looked over to where Roshant was standing, a little apart from the rest of the squad. 'Commissar, if you would accompany me.'

'Yes, captain.' Roshant saluted smartly and headed to their vehicle, leaving Obeysekera looking quizzically after him.

'The auspex is still all over the place, sir.'

Obeysekera nodded. 'Thank you, Malick. Worth checking but good to know. It will be paper and stylus for us there and back, I suspect.'

'Never thought I'd actually get to use all that trig they taught us on Prosan, sir.'

'Can't say I did either, but I'm glad you followed your lessons, Malick.'

'Barely bothered with it at the time. It's only when I was back on Cadia when... when it happened that it came in handy. Everything was down then. Used some old maps and a stylus to get my men to the landing fields. Remembered just about enough to do it. Once I was off, I took a refresher course. I wanted to be prepared, in case I ever needed it again.'

Obeysekera nodded. 'Sometimes, the old skills prove the most useful.' He looked along the three Venators. 'Looks like we're ready to go.'

'Hopefully find somewhere to cross the flowsand soon, sir.'

'Hopefully,' said Obeysekera.

Gunsur, driving *Divine Light*, glanced over at Malick in the navigator's seat. The sand thrown up by *Holy Fire* in front hung as a thin suspension in the hot air, griming his face and hands as he drove.

'When we were under the truck during the sandstorm, I thought the commissar was going to break.'

Malick looked up from his map, glanced at Gunsur, then went back to tracking their route on the map.

'Go on,' he said. 'But make sure your vox is off.'

'It is. I saw him. He'd turned away from the captain but I could see him. He was sweating and shaking, mouthing stuff I couldn't hear 'cause of the storm but looked like prayers. Then, when he wanted to go out and speak to the Kamshet and the captain pulled him back... The expression on his face – like when someone walks out from cover 'cause he can't take being under bombardment no more.'

Malick nodded. 'What I thought.' He glanced back at Gunsur. 'Remember, say nothing to anybody. I will deal with this.'

Gunsur pressed his finger to his lips. 'Silent as the Raven.'

Malick shook his head, surreptitiously making the sign against the Eye. 'Don't speak his name – you never know if he might answer.'

Four hours later, they still had not found an end to the flowsand. The slip face had slowly diminished into a gentle slope, however, making it easier to drive the Venators over the angle, and Obeysekera had called a stop to see if the end of the steep slip face had deprived the flowsand of its sources.

Standing beside it, with Malick and Roshant on either side, Obeysekera stared out over the treacherous surface.

'Can you tell if it is still moving?' he said, squinting in the fierce light. In the valley bottom, in the mid-afternoon, the air was hotter than the interior of a locked-down Leman Russ after three days fighting – and Obeysekera had seen what the tank crews looked like when they emerged from their vehicles after that. But while the air temperature was hotter than a fighting Leman Russ, it did not have the stifling mixture of carbon dioxide, fear sweat, cabbage and spilt promethium that characterised a tank. The air on Dasht i-Kevar had the cleanliness of fire.

'Don't matter if it's moving so long as it's still flowsand,' said Malick. He looked around. 'Where's a frekking stone when you want one?'

'You can throw this.' Roshant handed Sergeant Malick an amulet.

The sergeant looked up at the commissar. 'It's an amulet of Saint Xaver – you want to throw this in?'

'Either the saint will show us our way is clear or he will enter this cursed river of sand and by his presence there bless it.'

Sergeant Malick shrugged. 'It's your call, sir.' He turned the amulet in his fingers. 'Looks valuable – got the feel of proper aurum.'

'It was a gift from my father. I don't think there's much doubt it's real aurum. Any aurum smith who tried to cheat my father wouldn't live long enough to claim it was a mistake.'

'Here goes then.' Sergeant Malick balanced the amulet on his curved index finger, then flicked it with his thumb. The amulet spun up into the air, the aurum catching and splitting the light as it turned, before reaching the top of its arc and curving downwards.

The amulet landed on the sand, gold on yellow, and lay, looking innocently up at the bright sky.

'That's holding,' said Roshant.

'Not quite the weight of a fully laden Venator,' said Obeysekera drily.

'I am aware of that, captain. It's why I gave Sergeant Malick the amulet – it's heavier than it looks.'

'It was, sir,' confirmed Malick. 'Surprisingly heavy.'

'We could try something heavier,' said Roshant, 'but I don't suppose we have anything we don't need.'

Obeysekera looked at Roshant. 'You don't need a blessed amulet of Saint Xaver that your father gave you?'

'I don't need my father to give me anything.'

'It's moving.' Malick pointed. 'It's definitely shifted along, maybe two fingers. That's flowsand, sure enough.'

Obeysekera nodded. 'We'll have to go on then.'

'You don't think that maybe Uwais was right?' asked Roshant. 'We should head back and try to cross further upstream?'

'It can't be like water. There's no sand rain to replenish the springs. There's no evaporation.'

'Sandstorms.'

Obeysekera looked at Malick. 'What was that?'

'Sandstorms, sir. You said they happen almost every day here. Maybe it's the storms that shift the sand, piling it up into dunes and then the sand slips down into the valleys and makes flowsand.'

'Could be. But then, it would have to be almost frictionless, every grain worn smooth. It would take millions of years to do that.'

Roshant bent down and picked up a handful of sand. It ran through his fingers, even though he was holding them tightly together.

'Like water, you say?'

Obeysekera looked around at the dunes that marched alongside them like the curves of a wind snake. He remembered the time-worn humps of the Tabaste Mountains at the heart of the Great Sand Sea: their destination.

'Millions and millions and millions of years.' He bent down and dug his fingers into the sand. It spread, like water, and he picked up a handful, holding it up in front of his eyes. The sand ran off his palm, trickling down in little rivulets to the ground.

'Slow water.' Obeysekera nodded. 'Then, if it is...' He turned back to look at the flowsand. 'I'm afraid you have lost your amulet, commissar.'

Roshant nodded. 'I expected to, captain.'

'Let's push on. All rivers end.' Obeysekera started back towards the Venators, pretending not to hear when Malick muttered, 'Yeah, when they get to the sea.'

CHAPTER 8

As Roshant drove, Obeysekera marked the obstacle on the map. Even the best Imperial map showed the Great Sand Sea as largely empty and feature-less, with only the Tabaste Mountains as a recognisable landmark. Certainly, there was no flowsand shown on the map. Even if they did not find General Itoyesa, having the flowsand channels marked would prove a valuable piece of geographical intelligence. If it should prove possible to cross the Great Sand Sea, the chance of a flanking attack on the t'au would be opened up. Obeysekera, maps strapped to a tray across his lap, charted their course and bearing, checking and rechecking as they went, reading off distance, speed and time against the compass reading – a simple magnetic compass was about the only instrument whose machine-spirit could cope with the ano-maly in the Sand Sea. After a few rejected attempts at conversation, Roshant was keeping his peace, driving the Venator with increasing skill, while the other two vehicles followed in line behind. They had the best of it in front: clear air and clean sand. The Venators in their wake had to drive through the clouds of sand thrown up by the wheels of the lead vehicle, with the last having to endure the dust of both the Venators in front.

Ensor was driving the rearguard. So far as Obeysekera was concerned, Ensor would be in the last vehicle all the way to the Tabaste. While he had let the man's conduct pass, some consequences would remind Ensor to control himself better in future.

'Do you think he might be right?'

Obeysekera looked up from his map. Roshant was talking to him through their personal channel. With them sitting right next to each other he could hardly claim that the signal was weak.

'Who?'

'Uwais. About turning back and finding a way across upstream.'

'It's sand. There shouldn't be any stream.'

Roshant snorted with laughter. 'There are many things in the galaxy that should not be, but are. Against that list, sand that flows like water seems a minor anomaly.'

'It's not like water. That's what bothers me. If it was like water, it would be following a gradient. But it isn't.'

'It's not flowing uphill, though?'

'No, not that I have seen. It seems to be keeping to the flat.'

Roshant shook his head. 'I don't see the problem, then. If you spill water on a completely flat surface it will still flow. That's what the sand is doing here. Under the surface sand, the bedrock is level.'

'But if it was simply windblown sand flowing over flat ground it should spread out along every available channel, like water filling a lake. It shouldn't flow.'

Roshant shrugged. 'It's sand. Who cares what it does?'

Obeysekera looked up from his maps, covered with contours and flows, to the ridges and troughs of the Great Sand Sea that surrounded them.

'I do,' he said.

Roshant laughed again. 'You should have become a scholar, then.'

Obeysekera shook his head. 'Not much call for scholars on Cadia. Still, at least the 'kin train us to think. I am and remain grateful for that. But I think I would have enjoyed a more scholarly life – shut away in scriptoria, poring over old tomes, searching for knowledge.'

'Knowledge is dangerous,' said Roshant, 'even in the right minds.'

'That is the opinion of the Commissariat. But if we had had knowledge of what Abaddon planned, would we not have planned our defence differently?'

'To contemplate the plans of the Archenemy is to stare into the abyss. And when you look into the abyss...'

'...the abyss looks into you. Yes, I know the proverb. As with all such sayings, it defines truth, but limits it, too.'

'Captain Obeysekera, what do you mean by that?'

Obeysekera glanced over at the commissar. He had been thinking aloud. It was a habit that he must remember to curb. 'Do you agree that the God-Emperor is beyond our understanding? That He transcends all the categories of thought that we normally employ.'

'Of course. The God-Emperor is beyond mere words.'

'Then the same is true of His Imperial Truth. Of course, we try to capture it in phrases, we attempt to pin it down on the pages of sacred codexes, but the truth we are trying to express is so much more than anything we can encapsulate in any formal system of language. There, do you understand what I meant now? It is perfectly orthodox.'

Commissar Roshant glanced away briefly from his driving and looked at Obeysekera. The captain, seeing his face, was struck again by how young the commissar was. How callow.

'It might *be* orthodox, but it does not *sound* orthodox.' Roshant looked back to the way ahead, directing the Venator along the gentle slope beside the flowsand. 'Not all the members of the Ecclesiarchy are as well versed in the finer points of Imperial theology as you are, captain. It would be wise not to tax their learning too deeply.' The young commissar grinned. 'My father always said that, for sport, nothing beat pricking the pride of a precentor. Great fervour, little learning.' Roshant raised his hand and brushed away the sand from his goggles. 'But pricked pride provokes revenge. Should the Ecclesiarchy range against you, even the Commissariat would have difficulty coming to your aid.'

'I have no intention of provoking the custodians of the Imperial creed,' said

Obeysekera. 'For my part, I am simply trying to understand it better, and by doing so know more fully the grace of the God-Emperor. Speaking of that, I presume they went into some detail about the Imperial creed at the schola?'

'We delve deeper into Imperial theology in our training than in the seminaries of the Ecclesiarchy, for we have to distinguish between heretical and orthodox expressions of the Imperial creed, whereas preachers merely have to preach.'

'Then tell me, what do you think of the Stinian School? According to Saint Stinus, the Emperor wills none of the evil in the galaxy but permits it as a shadow that serves to highlight His glory.'

The commissar glanced at Captain Obeysekera. 'Our commandant delivered ten lectures to us on the theology of Saint Stinus, each of them not less than three hours long, and by the end I was little wiser than I was at the beginning. But when I had to pass the final examination I studied the saint's theology and came to a similar conclusion, except I would say that according to Saint Stinus the Emperor permits evil that we be purged in the fire of war and suffering, to better become instruments of His will.'

'That's an interesting reading of his *Ecclesiarchy Dogmatics* – volume twenty-three?'

'Most of the argument was contained in volume twenty-eight but there was an important prolegomena in volume twenty-three.'

'I will look it up. But would you agree that both are permitted orthodox readings of Saint Stinus?'

'They were declared so at the thirty-eighth Ecumenical Synod.'

'Then we might say that what we endure, while not willed by the Emperor, nevertheless serves His purpose either directly, by manifesting more clearly His glory, or indirectly, by honing us, His servants, into better servants of His will.'

'That is what I concluded from my reading of Saint Stinus.'

'Then I think we can face what awaits with equanimity, whatever it entails.' Obeysekera grinned. 'Although of course, if the School of Saint Cauvin is true, then the Emperor has looked upon us and by His inscrutable will decreed that only a vanishingly small number among us shall be justified, with the rest destined for perdition. The doctrine has the advantage of removing us from vain striving, for only the Emperor knows whom He wishes to justify, but only when our duty ends in death shall we know if He has deemed it acceptable to His glory and accepted it as the necessary sacrifice to His will.'

'The Officio Prefectus, while maintaining official neutrality with respect to the orthodox schools of the Imperial creed, in practice prefers the doctrine of Cauvin over those of Saint Stinus, or the doctrine of Saint Quino or Saint Gustine.'

Obeysekera laughed. 'Of course. Cauvinism fits the Officio Prefectus like a power pack fits a lasgun. From what I have heard, the Inquisition leans towards the School of Saint Quino while the Astra Militarum naturally professes the doctrines of the School of Saint Gustine.'

'What about the Adeptus Astartes?'

'I have never been able to establish that. I suspect that most of them regard the disputes between the schools as the pettifogging nit-picks of Ecclesiarchy scholars, disputations that would be more quickly and cleanly resolved with a bolter and chainsword, and who are we to say that that is not the case, since the disputes have endured without resolution for ten thousand years. But, for myself, I think the lack of resolution reflects what I said earlier, the inherent impossibility of framing the Imperial Truth in language. Language, by definition, excludes as it defines and the Imperial Truth is greater than the words with which we seek to describe it.'

'Suffer not the witch, the mutant and the alien to live. That's clear enough.'

'Perfect for soldiers – clear, concise orders. But insufficient for scholars and theologians, hence the thirty-eight volumes of Saint Stinus' *Ecclesiarchy Dogmatics*.' Obeysekera paused to shake the sand from his face cloth.

'Saint Stinus never finished the *Dogmatics*, did he?' Roshant put in.

'No. There should be forty volumes, but while writing the thirty-eighth during his retreat on the convent world Eremita, Saint Stinus was forced to emerge from his cell to lead the defence of Eremita against the Great Devourer. By his example and leadership, Saint Stinus repelled the Devourer from Eremita but at the cost of his own life, leaving the *Dogmatics* unfinished and, I suspect, generations of schola students giving thanks to the Emperor for His mercy – the last five volumes do get *very* dense.'

'I gave up around volume twenty-five,' said Commissar Roshant. 'Don't mention that to anyone.'

'Don't worry, you did better than most – few get through the first ten.'

'Anything on the auspex?'

'No, still the same readings. Take the speed down. I need to pay attention to plotting our course.'

Roshant nodded and they drove on in silence, the sand hissing under the wheels of the Venator and the wind of Dasht i-Kevar hot in their faces.

'Captain.' The squad vox-channel squeaked into tinny life.

'Malick?'

'Captain, I'm picking up something ahead on my auspex.'

'Ghost readings?'

'They've stayed steady for a few minutes. Multiple contacts, stable, with fast-moving overheads – looks like aircraft strafing ground targets.'

'I'll take a look.'

Obeysekera switched his display to the auspex, the ghost-green screen coming up in front of his eyes.

'I see it.'

'Range about three miles.'

'No Imperial signature on any of the readings,' noted Obeysekera.

'Signals keep fading in and out,' said Malick.

'More switching in and out.'

'Think I have something in sight.' The vox-signal flashed Trooper Uwais' sigil.

'What do you see?' asked Obeysekera.

'Vapour trails. Two, maybe three craft.'

'Identity?'

'At this range, uncertain. Not Imperial. Wrong movement pattern. Very smooth. Could be t'au.'

'You can tell they're t'au aircraft from the way they move?' asked Roshant. 'How?'

'Later, commissar,' snapped Obeysekera. 'Halt. We don't want them observing us.'

As the Venator came to a stop, its tyres settling into the sand, Obeysekera stood up on his seat, retrieved his magnoculars from his belt and trained them ahead.

He could see, over the rising and falling ridges of sand, the traces of what Uwais had reported: vapour trails. In the arid air of Dasht i-Kevar there was precious little vapour to create such trails: that they existed, however briefly, told the speed of the aircraft making them. Through the magnoculars he sought to find one of the darting craft.

There.

'Got it.' The voice was Gunsur's. *'T'au Remoras, sir. Three of them.'*

The drone, smaller than a standard Barracuda but no less lethal for that, was riding the rolling level of the heat thermals, jinking through the columns of air like one of the migratory v-tails of Cadia, birds that spent their whole lives, once hatched, on the wing. Following the darting silver through the magnoculars, Obeysekera felt a nudge of appreciation: the Remora was a thing of beauty, form and function aligned in combat harmony. It was hard not to compare it to the bombast and thunder of a Thunderbolt, an aircraft that flew more by blasting gravity into submission than by any suggestion that the air was its rightful element.

It was as well, Obeysekera pondered as he put the ideas away in the secret corner for forbidden notions, that the Commissariat could not actually read thoughts: he wondered how many would be condemned from their own minds if the Officio Prefectus should ever be able to do that.

The darting patterns the Remoras were running and the weapons' flares told that the drones were strafing targets on the ground.

'Any contact on the Remoras' target?' Obeysekera posed the question over the squad vox-channel. As he did so, he noted the flicker of surprise in the glance that Roshant shot towards him. According to Commissariat doctrine, an officer told his troops what to do: he did not ask them questions.

Obeysekera reminded himself to speak to Roshant about the differences between the Kasrkin and ordinary Cadian troops.

'Auspex showing something.' The vox-display showed the report was coming from Chame in the rearmost Venator. *'Multiple soft ground contacts and... and something else.'*

'I see it,' broke in Malick. *'Never seen anything like it.'*

'Range?'

'Soft signal. Maybe two miles. Bearing three-four-eight.'

'Got it.' Obeysekera stared at the auspex. Even with the strange readings that plagued the machine-spirit in the Great Sand Sea, this was unusual.

As he was looking at the auspex, trying to work out what he was seeing, Obeysekera saw the secure vox-signal flare. He keyed on the bead.

'Yes?'

'Roshant here.'

Obeysekera looked round at the commissar, sitting next to him in the Venator. But Roshant was staring straight ahead.

'Yes?'

Obeysekera saw the commissar's lips begin to move and then, lagging a moment to allow for encryption, the words reached him through his micro-bead.

'The mission calls for the strictest secrecy. I strongly recommend avoiding contact with the enemy.'

Obeysekera veiled his grin. Maybe the commissar was not quite so callow after all. He looked back to the auspex, bending closer to the screen to veil the conversation.

'Is this an official Commissariat recommendation, commissar?'

'No, captain. A suggestion, but one given in light of our orders.'

'Noted. But if the bluies have sent aircraft into the Great Sand Sea, then the most likely reason is that they know one of our Valkyries came down here and are looking for it.'

'You think they are searching for the general?'

'Not necessarily. They would be interested in retrieving a Valkyrie whatever it contained. But to venture so far as to send aircraft in here suggests that, at the least, they know there is something or someone of high value in the Valkyrie and they are willing to lose some aircraft in order to retrieve it.' Obeysekera tapped the auspex. 'There's a sandstorm rising. If they don't clear the area soon, they won't be able to.'

'My recommendation stands,' said Roshant. 'Avoid contact with the xenos.'

'They stand in our way. We sit here and wait for them to go, in which case the sandstorm will probably reach us before we can get any further, or we push on, risk the bluies spotting us, but also establish what they are attacking.' Obeysekera sat back. 'Our tactical doctrine states, when objectives clash, advance. We will advance.' Obeysekera touched his finger to the maps and bent over them. 'Thank you for raising this privately, commissar.'

'I can see that among the Kasrkin it is not unknown for soldiers to question the orders of their officers, but I have been commissioned into the Officio Prefectus – I am not comfortable with that.'

'Not question, rather clarify. But I know it can seem like insubordination. I will explain the reason why later.'

'I would appreciate that, captain.'

'Remind me.' Obeysekera switched to the squad vox-channel. 'We will advance at half-speed. Keep watch, visual and auspex. I want to know what the bluies are attacking, preferably without them seeing us.'

Roshant started up the galvanic engine, the other two Venators whining into life as the machine-spirits responded to their drivers' whispered prayers, and the vehicles moved forward, their tyres hissing over the thin sand.

'Trooper Lerin.' Obeysekera addressed the Kasrkin manning the twin-linked multi-laser on the back of his Venator.

'Yes, captain?'

'You have the clearest field of vision. Tell me at once when you see the bluies. I will be watching on the auspex.'

'Anything else, too?'

'Yes, of course.'

'Will do.'

The Venator was moving slowly enough for Obeysekera to hear the machine creak of the heavy weapon set into the vehicle behind him as it swept back and forth, the pintle grinding the sand that had seeped through the collar into the mechanism.

'Lerin, dismantle the pintle when we camp – sand is getting into the mechanism.'

'Yes, sir.'

'And tell the troops in the other vehicles to do the same.'

'Yes, sir.' The second assent snapped through the vox.

Obeysekera grinned. 'Misery is endured more easily when it is shared out,' he said over the private circuit.

'That's what they teach us in the Officio Prefectus,' said Commissar Roshant. 'In my experience, I have found it to be the most accurate precept that we were taught.'

CHAPTER 9

'Sergeant, *Holy Fire* has slowed down,' said Gunsur. 'I reckon something's wrong.'

Before Malick could reply, the order came over the squad vox-channel. *'Reduce speed to five miles per hour.'*

Malick, driving the Venator, snorted. 'What's wrong with you, Torgut? Never known you so jumpy.'

Gunsur shook his head. 'I don't know, sarge.' He looked up from the maps clamped onto the tray and stared ahead. The lead Venator, having slowed down, was throwing up less wake and the cloud of thin sand that they had been driving through began to thin. 'Least I can see better now.'

Malick nodded. The lead Venator was some fifty yards ahead but even with that gap, and the reduced speed, they were still driving through clouds of dust. He flicked his finger across his goggles to remove the sand stick – he had learned that the lighter the contact, the less sand remained stuck on his goggles, glued there by the oils from his skin – and refolded his head cloth so a new section guarded his mouth and nose. The rebreather did keep the sand out, but by the end of a day's driving its filters were so clogged with dust as to be almost impossible to clean out. Whereas the face cloth could just be moved to a clean section. It was a practice that he and the rest of the squad had adopted from Captain Obeysekera.

'Sarge, I've got something on the auspex,' said Gunsur, his voice suddenly urgent.

'Call it through.'

'I-I don't know what it is,' said Gunsur.

'Call it through. Now.'

'Yes, sarge.' Gunsur paused, opening the channel to his commanding officer. 'Captain, I've got something new on the auspex.'

The command came back from *Holy Fire* to stop.

Malick brought the Venator to a halt, maintaining the fifty-yard separation between the vehicles that was part of their operating codex while travelling through hostile terrain. Looking into his mirror, he saw that Ensor was bringing *Saint Conrad* to a stop as well.

'Malick, come with me,' came the summons from Captain Obeysekera.

Gunsur looked at the sergeant and shrugged. Malick unstrapped himself from his seat and, unracking his hellgun, made his way across the sand to

Obeysekera, waiting by the lead Venator. The sand crunched under his boots. Out from the shade provided by the Venator, Malick felt the weight of the sun upon his head and shoulders as a physical force. But he had soldiered on planets with gravity fields significantly higher than Terra normal: he carried on, scanning his surroundings as he went with the practised skill of a Kasrkin.

They were still driving along the broad valley made by the flowsand, the valley slopes rising gently on either side. Ahead, ridgetops of dunes running at a closing angle to the flowsand valley restricted their view. Squinting ahead, Malick saw the flashes of light fracturing upon the planed edges of banking aircraft: the Remoras.

Obeysekera was waiting for him beside the Venator. The commissar was still sitting in the driver's seat and, at the rear of the vehicle, Lerin was tracking the multi-laser across an arc of one hundred and twenty degrees, ready to engage any approaching targets.

'Got your magnoculars?' Obeysekera asked as Malick reached him.

The sergeant held them up.

'Good. Yours are better than mine. Come with me, we're going to see what's got the bluies so excited.' With that, Obeysekera began climbing up the side of the valley, boots sending Vs of sand sliding down the slip face, and Malick followed, taking a course up the slope ten yards right of the captain.

Nearing the top of the ridge, Obeysekera crouched down and began to crawl upwards, seeking to keep his profile low, and Malick did the same. The sand was hot between his fingers. It slipped over them like cinders, as if he were crawling through the wreckage of a battle not long over.

The sergeant felt the sand beneath his left boot give way and he began to slide. He spear-thrust his fingers into the sand, arresting the motion, kicked the other boot into the dune and then started up again. He could feel the sand grains here were smaller and finer than lower down, slipping more easily as he went over them.

Malick glanced left, past Obeysekera, and saw the view beginning to open out as they ascended. Now he could begin to see the crests of the dunes, running east to west, stretching away into the crystal distance. Before the heat haze of the afternoon, the air on Dasht i-Kevar was the clearest he had ever seen, let alone breathed; even when it burned from its heat, it was a clean burn, very far from the acrid, burning air of Imperial forge worlds.

And through that crystal air, Malick saw something that should not have been there.

'Sir, stop. Look left.'

At Malick's words, Obeysekera dropped flat upon the sand and turned his head.

'What in the Throne's name is that?'

Rising above the crest of the dunes, maybe half a mile away, was a tree. But a tree that in scale and appearance was like nothing Malick had ever seen before. A central trunk rose into the air then split into myriad tubes that rose further and then arched back downwards, like jets of water from a fountain. Flitting through and between the tubes, Malick saw glints of light and, raising his magnoculars to his eyes, confirmed that they were the t'au Remoras, drones. Trying to hold one in the magnoculars' field – the Remora seemed to shift and slide in his vision – he saw burst cannons pulsing as they released a sudden hail of plasma bolts. Then the Remora slipped out of his view.

Malick scanned, searching for what the Remora was firing at, and saw flashes of white, and wings.

'Sir, so far as I can see, the Remoras are shooting at birds.'

'That's what I thought.'

'How come we didn't see the tree before?' asked Malick.

'I don't think it was there before,' said Obeysekera. 'It's big enough to have shown up on orbital auspex sweeps, let alone the ones we did before setting out. It's still growing. I think it has just come up today. By the Throne, what is it? Malick, quarter the sky, see if you can locate the drones' mother ship – there should be a t'au Tiger Shark somewhere in the vicinity – and call in the Venators, see if they're picking up anything on their auspexes. I'm going to go a little higher and try to get a better view.'

'*Holy Fire, Divine Light, Saint Conrad*, auspex scan, sixty degrees around reading three hundred and thirty degrees, distance five hundred yards.'

Malick noted the responses while scanning the sky, looking for the Tiger Shark. The Remoras were short-range drones, yet it was still possible that their mother ship was over the horizon. But even if it was within visual range, Malick knew from painful experience how difficult it was to spot t'au aircraft, visually or on the auspex. In contrast to the plasteel bulk and turbofan scream of Imperial planes, t'au aircraft were quiet and they shifted under the eye, squirming out of view like trying to hold a squito in focus to swat it.

Malick continued to quarter the sky, scanning through blocks of blue, searching for the telltale glint of refracted light. But even as he did so, his gaze was drawn back, again and again, to the tall tree-like structure rising from the desert and the white-winged birds that flew among its branches.

'*Faint target, bearing three-four-three, distance three miles.*'

The voice was Gunsur's.

Malick raised his magnoculars and, setting them to a wide field, trained them at the bearing Gunsur had called.

There. It shimmered in his sight, like looking at something through heat haze, but the Tiger Shark was high enough above the desert for the rising thermals not to affect his view of it. The broad, bat-winged craft was flying in a figure-of-eight pattern, looping back on itself while keeping its drones, and the tree structure, in view. But even as he watched, Malick saw the Tiger Shark withdrawing, pulling away from him. He checked behind, looking to see why the Tiger Shark was drawing back, and saw the southern horizon dark and billowing, with lightning chequering the clouds.

'Sir, sandstorm approaching from the south.'

Malick saw Obeysekera look back in his direction.

'How far?'

Malick checked his auspex. 'Two miles. Distance closing quickly.'

'Time before it hits?'

'Auspex playing up, sir. Maybe thirty minutes. Could be less. The t'au Tiger Shark is holding station.'

'It is? Check.'

Malick went back onto his magnoculars, calibrated them for distance and found the Tiger Shark in its field.

'Still three miles, sir. Definitely holding station.'

'Right. We'll make use of that.' Obeysekera signed for Malick to follow. 'We're going to see what that tree thing is and why the bluies are attacking it.'

Obeysekera led the way, scrambling up to the top of the sand crest with Malick following. The slip face gave way beneath his hands and feet, the sand groaning as it slid down the slope, but he ignored the singing in his haste to get to the top. He looked back south. The storm was coming up fast, the clouds seared from within by sand-lightning, its advance heralded by the almost continuous rumble of thunder. There was not much time.

He scrambled higher, digging his way up the slope, magnoculars banging on his chest from their strap. He needed to get high enough to see what the Remoras were attacking; if this ridge was not high enough to give him a field of view, there would not be time to find another.

Fit as he was, Obeysekera felt the air rasping through his mouth, hot and gritty, and his heart pushing against his chest as it worked to pump blood through his body. Climbing sand was hard.

Reaching the lip of the slip face, Obeysekera pulled himself over the edge and lay prone on the crest of the dune, pulling the magnoculars to his eyes as he did so. Beside him, he heard Malick pull himself up too and the whirr of the sergeant's magnoculars searching for focus. His own magnoculars blurred, then cleared, finding the depth of field. Obeysekera heard the gasp that issued from his lips, but in the wonder at what he was seeing, he barely noticed it.

Through his magnoculars he could see the broad, flat plain beyond the last sand ridge. A part of his mind, the analytic, tactical part, stowed away the fact that it looked like there was a salt flat in the Great Sand Sea, an anomaly of the shifting winds. But the greater part of his mind was staring at what was upon the salt flat.

Cutting through about a hundred yards of the flat was the furrow that he had marked earlier. But at its end, rising from the ground, was the trunk of the strange tree. It rose up like a fountain, reaching to three hundred feet in height before splitting into hundreds of fronds, or tubes, that arched out from the trunk. Through the branches – they were not branches, but he could think of no other term for them – Obeysekera could see white-winged creatures, birds presumably, flying. With the boughs so thick, he could not make out what sort of birds they were, although they were evidently large, but he did see that they would settle next to the buds that were sprouting on the branches. He could not see what they were doing.

But the tree was not the only thing upon the flat.

Closest to him were the mukaali of the Kamshet, herded together, their front legs hobbled, but pushing against their herders in their frantic attempts to escape the Remoras, buzzing low over them. The Kamshet herders were trying to stop the bull mukaali bursting from the herd, wielding whips and pricking scourges into the sensitive snouts of the beasts, stopping them and sending them blundering backwards into their fellows. One or two mukaali fell and, thrashing upon the floor, brought others down too, only for a Remora passing above them to cut a burning trail through their midst. The smell of charred flesh reached Obeysekera, telling the tale of winds rising.

Clustered in under the tree were the rest of the Kamshet, their robes startlingly blue and yellow against the white of the flat. Through his magnoculars, Obeysekera saw that many of them were holding vessels, while others were carrying ritual knives, elaborately carved. Then Obeysekera saw a white flash in the corner of his view and turned his magnoculars to see...

He saw wings, great white metal wings, unfurl from behind one of the Kamshet and then the man, carrying one of the ritual knives, leapt upwards, carried by a launch blast from a jump pack. His wings beat, catching the leap and bearing him up into the shadow of the great tree.

They were not birds flying among the branches of the tree, but men.

As he watched, Obeysekera saw one of the winged men fly down from the heights, carrying a bud in his hands, and on landing pour its contents into one of the vessels that another Kamshet was carrying.

The water of life.

The elixir that made a desert planet a vital Imperial asset in this subsector.

The Kamshet traded it, but nobody had ever discovered where they found it. Now, he knew. And if the t'au got back to their base, they would know too. It was imperative that he find some way to destroy the Tiger Shark, the mother ship that had launched these drones.

The only way he could do that would be by baiting it closer.

Over the vox, Obeysekera heard soft curses from Malick, indicating that he was seeing the same sight. But as they watched the Kamshet reaping their strange harvest, a Remora flashed above the giant fronds of the tree, its burst cannon pulsing, and a small explosion showed that it had scored a hit. In a bloody ruin of flesh and metal, the winged man crashed onto the flat salt pan.

But as he was about to turn away, Obeysekera saw new movement. As one of the fronds of the tree touched the ground, the salt flat beneath began to seethe, rippling, boiling. The Kamshet tapping the frond leaped away, running through the breaking ground. Obeysekera knew that he must get back to his men, but he could not pull himself away – not until he had seen what was breaking through from below.

The desert was coming to life.

In response to the liquid leaking from the great tree, stalks were pushing up from the ground, rising as quickly as a man waking, weaving up towards the sun. The stalks were springing leaves, flowers were unfurling as he watched, and in among the new growth there was movement – darting, shimmering movement. Insect-like creatures were hatching from the ground and taking wing, flitting to the newly opened blooms, creating a hum of fresh life that reached Obeysekera even through the whine of the Remoras and the harrumphing of the mukaali. But, as his magnoculars zoomed in closer, Obeysekera realised that not all those flowers were benign: some were mouths that gaped and closed upon each curious, visiting insect.

'Throne!'

Malick's exclamation broke the spell that had held Obeysekera frozen. The time for watching was over.

'Let's go. Time to reel in some fish.'

CHAPTER 10

Obeysekera glanced at Malick. The sergeant was peering over the wheel, squinting against the glare reflected from billions of grains of sand, steering the Venator through the gullies and valleys, keeping it close to the slopes so that the Remoras would have less chance of picking up the vehicles on their sensors. Satisfied, Obeysekera returned his focus to the path ahead. The sergeant knew what to do without orders.

It was one of the reasons Obeysekera preferred commanding Kasrkin: all the soldiers of Cadia were brave and effective veterans of the long defeat, but the Kasrkin were intelligent too. They could be trusted to act, and to act correctly, without being told what to do. Sometimes Obeysekera wondered if the rigorous Imperial training in following orders was actually counter-productive, producing too many men who would wait to be told rather than doing the obvious without command. An over-reliance on commissars had left Imperial troops stripped of any initiative.

While the Kasrkin were far less prone to Commissariat-induced freezing, he had nevertheless moved Roshant to *Saint Conrad* at the back of the column. The commissar had started to object, but Obeysekera had pointed out that it would give him the chance to observe the rest of the team, and he had accepted the suggestion with a reasonable amount of grace.

They were driving ahead of the storm. Already Obeysekera could feel its outliers, skirls of wind, lashing at his face and stirring up sudden plumes of sand from the crest lines of the dunes. He checked the auspex, cursed its machine-spirit for freezing again, and leaned out of the Venator to look behind. The skyline had disappeared into lightning-pierced darkness. It would not be long before it was upon them.

'Faster,' he said. In response, Malick drove the Venator forwards, its wheels throwing up sprays of sand as he urged it on.

Obeysekera looked ahead. The tree rose above the dune crests, its highest branches reaching at least five hundred feet into the sky before they arched downwards. With the dune crests still blocking his view of the base of the tree, he could not see what was happening to the life breaking upwards from the salt flats. But he could see, with the naked eye now, the glint and flash of the t'au Remoras, moving like fish through an undersea forest, their burst cannons pulsing. As he watched, he saw the fire-trail of missiles launching – each Remora normally carried two – the weapons arching between the fronds of the giant tree and striking its thick trunk. But the explosions made barely a mark upon the dense surface, the blasts seemingly dissipated by the matting that covered the trunk, a natural form of slat armour.

The valley that Malick was leading the Venators through was broadening out, the ridge at the end of it dropping lower as they approached the salt flat and the tree. Obeysekera, scanning for enemy, saw on their left a long disturbance running parallel with them and towards the structure, as if a point plough had been dragged through the sand.

'Gunners, independent fire. Track the Remoras and destroy them.' Obeysekera gave the order through the squad vox-channel and saw the acknowledgements flash up on his display. He pulled his hellgun from its rack and cycled a charge. 'Drivers, *Divine Light* break right after the ridge, *Saint Conrad* break left. *Holy Fire* straight on. Troopers, deploy missile launchers. Load with flak missiles. We must take out the Remoras and lure the Tiger Shark into range.' Obeysekera shot a look behind him again. 'We have thirty minutes max before the storm hits. Make them count.'

'Straight on?' asked Malick.

'Straight on,' said Obeysekera.

Sergeant Malick grinned, and Obeysekera saw the fierce delight lighting up his face.

He felt the grin spreading across his own face too: battle joy. The time when everything becomes clear. It was a feeling that united the 'kin, the unspoken source of their union and their fierce, unflinching memory of their lost home.

Obeysekera turned to face the front, hellgun in his hands. The galvanic motors powering the Venator hummed higher as Malick kicked the vehicle up to top speed. Sand flew up behind the tyres as they climbed the final slope and broke the ridge.

Before them: the salt flat, the tree spouting life upon the desert, the panicking mukaali and the rushing Kamshet, and the darting Remoras carving paths of fire.

Malick gunned the Venator, sending it surging down the slope onto the flat. Above his head, Obeysekera heard the heat rasp of the multi-laser, its twin beams stabbing at the nearest Remora. Lerin had engaged the enemy without further instruction.

Obeysekera saw the Kamshet, startled, looking towards them. A quick glance left and right told him that the other Venators were breaking off across the salt flat in the directions he had ordered, each vehicle's weapons triangulating on the lead Remora. The Remoras responded, dropping their attack on the tree and the Kamshet and turning towards the Kasrkin, jinking to and fro through the criss-cross of laser shots, shimmering in and out of view like half-remembered dreams as the burst cannons cycled. Plasma pulses liquefied the salt a few yards to their left. Through the vox-channel, one of the gunners was screaming obscenities.

'Silence!' yelled Obeysekera, cutting off the cries. 'Malick, get in closer, in under the tree.'

Ahead, the mukaali were breaking across their path, harrumphing, bellowing, a frightened, confused mass of flesh, the Kamshet vainly trying to stem the stampede. The Remora was turning, rotating on its axis, lining itself up for a second pass. Lerin was desperately trying to bring the multi-laser round on target, but the pintle, its mount fouled with sand, was grinding to a halt.

Obeysekera looked ahead again. A herd of stampeding mukaali could knock the Venator over.

'Go round them.'

Malick pulled the Venator left, gunning the galvanic motors. On the hard surface of the salt flats there was no desert-induced pause as the tyres spun sand; the vehicle responded immediately, careening over the surface at an angle to the onrushing stampede that would give them enough leeway to round the leading mukaali.

'Throne, Throne, Throne!' Obeysekera could hear Lerin swearing as she tried to haul the multi-laser round. It was not coming through on the vox-channel, he was hearing the woman's shouts as she ground the weapon around on its sand-fouled pintle.

A burst of plasma cut across their way, forcing Malick to jerk the Venator right, towards the mukaali.

'Where the frekk are the others?' Malick yelled.

Obeysekera unstrapped his belt and leaned out of the Venator, lifting his hellgun into firing position while he held on with one hand. 'Keep moving,' he yelled.

The Remora was jinking back and forth, avoiding the crossfire of the other two Venators, while tracking them across the salt flat.

A predator is never so vulnerable as when it's lining up a kill.

Never taking his eyes from the Remora, Obeysekera saw the fire flash of a flak missile launching from *Divine Light*. At the same moment, he fired his hellgun, deliberately lacing the air to the right of the Remora with bursts of hotshots.

In response, the machine intelligence of the Remora jinked the aircraft in the opposite direction – right into the path of the flak missile.

The starboard engine of the Remora disintegrated, shards of its casing flying in chaotic streams outwards. The aircraft wobbled, the whine of the other engine rising in pitch as its machine intelligence tried to compensate for the sudden imbalance in thrust, but the wobble became an uncontrollable oscillation, each correction sending the Remora further out of control and shedding pieces of the aircraft.

'Watch out.' Obeysekera pointed up at the Remora.

'I see it,' said Malick, turning the Venator to avoid its course. But as he did so, the Remora lost all control, spinning wildly and crashing among the herd of mukaali. The animals, already panicking, responded to the smell and sight of their broken herd mates by breaking their final restraints. Hobbles snapped, chains broke, and the herd came stampeding towards the Venator.

'Lerin, clear a path through the mukaali,' Obeysekera ordered. But from behind he heard the grinding of the cannon's pintle.

'It's jammed fast, sir.'

'Malick?'

'Yes.' Sergeant Malick spun the Venator around, its tyres carving tracks through the salt crust, bringing the jammed multi-laser to bear on the approaching stampede.

'Fire at will,' said Obeysekera.

+Stop!+

The voice was no voice, but a command in his head, and in Sergeant Malick's and in Lerin's, too. It was a command that translated into Obeysekera's muscles and nerves without any impulse from him. Sergeant Malick, similarly commanded, stopped and the Venator, its impulse removed, slid to a halt. Although he could not see her, Obeysekera was sure that Lerin was standing frozen behind the multi-laser, finger poised over the trigger but unable to pull it.

The stampeding mukaali were coming closer, their stench riding before them, heads swinging in pendulum panic, bodies like wrinkled dozers rolling over the flat towards the Kasrkin, small eyes white in fear. Staring at them, unable to move, a stray part of Obeysekera's mind reflected that of all the potential deaths he had contemplated, being crushed by stampeding mukaali had never figured as a possibility. He could hear subdued, strained breathing, his own and Sergeant Malick's, as they both fought against whatever or whoever was controlling their bodies, each with as little success as the other.

Obeysekera stared at approaching, undignified death. The philosophical corner of his mind, the reserved voice that had allowed him to accept the horrors of his life, counselled him that death was almost always undignified, calling up images of the battlefield slain he had seen, exposed and stripped of pretension or humanity. Death took the soul and left only the flesh.

But to die under the fear-filled feet of a herd of panicking pack animals...

Obeysekera would have shut his eyes, but he could no more control his eyelids than any other part of his body. He could still listen, though. Through the vox, he heard *Divine Light* and *Saint Conrad* calling in to him, asking if he needed assistance. But he could tell from the distance of the air snaps that accompanied their weapons fire that they were both too far away to come to their aid in time.

The mukaali were mad with fear. The crashed Remora was still spitting ordnance, a broken burst cannon firing at random like a Cadian scorpine still pumping poison into its killer, even after it itself had been killed, and the plasma pulses were cutting through the herd, amputating limbs and sending animals crashing into the flat.

Obeysekera tried to close his eyes again.

He still could not move them.

He stared death in its bestial, onrushing face.

And then, death changed his face.

Before him, with her arms spread wide, was the woman he had seen, unveiled, among the Kamshet. She stood before the Venator and her eyes were cerulean blue and her mouth was madder red and her teeth were white. She stood before the Venator and spoke, uttering sounds of command, and the mukaali parted, moving to either side of her, streaming past the Venator on left and right, harrumphing and rolling and bumping into each other, but none of the beasts touched the vehicle.

The invisible locks upon Obeysekera's body were released. He glanced at Malick, saw that he was free too, then back to the woman standing in front of them.

And she spoke in Obeysekera's mind.

+I am not your enemy.+

'Sir, she's in my sights.' The message over the vehicle's vox-channel told him that Lerin had got the multi-laser working.

Obeysekera stared into the woman's eyes.

'No.' He could hear himself speaking as if through treacle: he was talking through all the years of training as a Cadian and a Kasrkin; he was saying 'no' to all the preachers he had heard denouncing the witch and the psyker; he was looking into a face that all his teachers had told him to blow apart in a stream of multi-laser fire, and he said, 'No.'

The woman's lips twitched in a smile and then she turned and stood with her arms upstretched, and the air around her spread fingers shimmered, as with the haze of the desert heat.

Obeysekera could feel Sergeant Malick looking at him. He ignored the gaze. Standing up on his seat, he stuck his head through the Venator's roll cage and scanned for the two remaining Remoras.

The las-fire from *Divine Light* and *Saint Conrad* pinpointed them for him: the Remoras were twisting through the trailing fronds of the great tree, using it as cover from the 'kin while lining up plasma pulses from their burst cannons. Only the zigzag driving of Ensor and Roshant in the Venators had kept them from harm, but as he watched he saw a burst strike near the front wheel of Roshant's vehicle, boiling the tyre away from the rim and leaving the Venator pushing the plasteel tyre rims through the salt crust, forcing it to turn in a circle.

The Remora banked round, skipping between trailing shoots.

+Rise.+

Obeysekera heard the word in his mind, the command, and he looked to the Kamshet woman of the cerulean eyes, and her arms were raised in summons.

From the flat surrounding the tree, boiling up through the breaking ground, came a cloud of creatures – insects, or their evolutionary analogue on Dasht i-Kevar, Obeysekera thought – chirring, whirring, clicking and rising in a cloud of wings and chitin up through the tendrils of the tree that had summoned them from their centuries-long hibernation. And like smoke they rose in wavering columns up into the sky, weaving in and out of the branches of the tree, forming living nets that looped around the two Remoras, drawing in tighter and tighter as the machine intelligences within them sought to find routes out from the flying mass.

From his vantage point far below, Obeysekera heard the Remoras' engine notes change, choke, cough as a thousand, ten thousand chitinous bodies hurled themselves at the aircraft, clogging intakes, smearing optics, and choking the intricately engineered engines. The aircraft were dragged from the sky, struggling with mechanical intensity against the weight of the columns of life that pulled them down, but they struggled in vain.

The Remoras broke upon the salt flat, their nano-crystalline alloy skins shearing apart on impact, their mechanical guts leaking fluids of yellow and black upon the thirsty salt. They lay there, small columns of smoke rising from them, all but buried in furious clouds of tiny chattering, chittering creatures.

The Kamshet woman with the cerulean eyes spread her arms wide. The cloud of insects rose from the stricken t'au aircraft.

'Throne!' said Malick. 'Glad she's on our side, be gladder when she's gone.'

The woman raised her hands, palms up, and the insects began to disperse, buzzing upwards in and among the fronds of the giant tree, settling upon the flowers that were breaking open over its limbs, flowers of yellow and red and blue and every shade in between.

'Roshant, can you get your vehicle over here?' Obeysekera asked over the squad vox-channel.

'Slowly.'

'Do so. *Saint Conrad*, rendezvous on me.'

As the two vehicles made their way over the flat to him, Obeysekera began to climb down from the Venator.

'Sir,' said Malick over their personal link. 'Shouldn't we wait for the others?'

Obeysekera, poised half in and half out of the Venator, looked back to his sergeant. 'A commissar is not going to be the best man to deal with her.'

Malick nodded. 'We'll keep you covered, sir.'

Obeysekera grimaced. 'For what it's worth... I'd say take over the mission if I don't come back but, frankly, if I don't come back then I don't expect the mission will continue much longer.'

Malick pointed south. 'You'd best be quick. The storm's coming up fast.'

'Keep scanning for the Tiger Shark. It's lost its babies – it's going to come nosing closer to see what happened to them. Make sure we have all available flak missiles primed. Fire on your command if I am otherwise occupied.'

'Sir.'

Obeysekera climbed down from the Venator. His boot crunched on the ground. He looked down. The salt glittered beneath him, crystals of white diamond. Obeysekera reached back for his hellgun, his fingertips grasping its worn-smooth stock.

He stopped. He released it and, empty-handed, turned and walked towards the woman with cerulean eyes.

The desert, normally so silent, was filled with sound and scent: the distant bellowing of mukaali, slowly being settled by the blue-robed Kamshet running beside them, loping over the salt flat; the deep, bone-settling buzz of the insect life – although now he was closer he could see that it was by no means all insectoid – that was still swarming from the ground; the scent of flowers, thick and heavy, overlaying the petrichor of the newly anointed desert.

And the steady stream of winged Kamshet flying up to harvest aqua vitae from the tree, each holding an intricately carved knife, alighting upon a bough next to one of the sprouting buds, slicing the bud from the tree and then flying down with it in their hands, knife held between their teeth.

As he approached the woman, Obeysekera saw some of the Kamshet gathering around her, blue-robed warriors, their faces veiled but their status clear from the weapons they carried: a mixed bunch, bone recurved bows and flange spears alongside stubbers, autoguns, lasrifles and more exotic weaponry that appeared to have originated from the aeldari. But Obeysekera paid the assembling entourage no mind; they would kill him or not at the command of the woman with cerulean eyes.

She was the only one that counted.

The blue-robed warriors parted as he approached, opening the way towards the woman. But although Obeysekera kept his gaze fixed upon the woman who waited on him, he was conscious of the hisses and imprecations from the surrounding warriors: the young bloods, fingering blades and making gestures either obscene or threatening while the older warriors stood silent and waiting, their stillness more menacing than the threats of the younger men.

As Obeysekera made his way through the cordon, he spoke into his vox-bead on the channel to Malick.

'Keep the commissar with you. Do not, repeat not, allow him to follow me.'

'*Understood.*'

Obeysekera emerged from the cordon of warriors and stood in the bubble of space surrounding the woman. She stood with the tree rising above her, shaded from the fierce sun of Dasht i-Kevar by its spreading branches. But even in the deep shade cast by the tree, she appeared brighter than her surroundings, standing out from them as a statue of an Imperial saint stands proud from the wall in which it is carved in the cathedrals of the Ecclesiarchy. Although around her feet life still squirmed out of the ground in a tidal rush of birth, the woman seemed more alive than even the creatures buzzing and crawling and rattling up from their long sleep.

For a moment, seeing the way creatures he would have dismissed as bugs on Cadia seethed around her feet, Obeysekera wondered if the woman was a servant of the Plague God. The servants of Chaos could sometimes take on fair forms to hide their inner foulness. But none of his briefings had suggested the Kamshet were tainted. Nor did he sense anything wrong about her.

She was alive. Simply, wholly alive.

Obeysekera approached the woman with cerulean eyes and, stopping in front of her, paused momentarily. He made the sign of the aquila and then, seeing no reaction, he bowed. She laughed. It was the sound of silver.

Obeysekera straightened up and looked into her eyes.

They were blue. All blue, save for a pinprick of black at their centre. They were the blue of the sky above the sand on Dasht i-Kevar, the blue of the Caducades Sea beneath a clear sky, the blue of Alnitak, burning in the deep.

+A storm is coming.+

Obeysekera heard the words, but he did not know if they were spoken directly into his mind or came to him by normal speech.

The woman smiled, her red lips parting. 'Both,' she said, answering his unspoken question.

She turned and looked back, through the tangle of swooping branches that formed the great tree rising from the desert.

'It is here,' she said.

Obeysekera's vox buzzed. *'Captain, we have an auspex reading.'*

Obeysekera looked at the woman. She was staring intently through the tangle into the distance.

'It's the Tiger Shark,' he said. 'Fire when locked.'

'Can't... can't get a fix.' Malick's words were distorted in his earbud. *'Auspex fading in and out.'*

'Launch on visual – guide the missiles to target.'

'It's turning back, sir.'

'Pulling back?'

'Unclear. Might have picked up the auspex lock.'

'We have to bring it back in closer.' Obeysekera paused. 'Fire one flak missile on a two-second fuse, make sure it misses.'

'No chance of it hitting without a target lock and no visual.'

'I want the t'au to see it explode so they think they've sprung the trap.'

The woman turned back to Obeysekera. 'For a trap, you need bait.'

'My men and I are the bait.'

'Poor bait for such a prize. I have something more to its taste.' The woman of blue turned and gestured. From among the warriors, one stepped forward carrying something. Obeysekera stared at it. It was fire-scorched, and held gingerly at an unfamiliar angle, but then it rotated in his mind and he saw it for what it was. He stared at the woman and his hands clenched into fists.

'That's an Imperial distress locator.'

The woman shook her head. 'It is not from the vehicle you are seeking.'

Obeysekera stared at the woman. 'You know where he is? You have him?'

'We know where he is, but we do not have him. This came from one of your aircraft that crashed when first you came to our world, but it will serve.' The woman pointed at the distress locator. 'If you would bring your enemy closer, let them hear its call.' She looked past Obeysekera. 'The storm is close.'

Obeysekera nodded. He took the distress locator and laid it on the salt flat, inspecting the device. Although it was fire-scorched it seemed undamaged. Breathing an invocation to its machine-spirit, Obeysekera keyed in the activation code.

The distress locator lay inert and unresponsive on the ground. He stared down at it. He looked up at the woman.

'Try again.'

Obeysekera nodded. He muttered the prayer to the machine and entered the code once more. The distress locator lit. Lights, red and green and yellow, flashed in random order before settling into a repeating sequence: the identifying call sign that told other Imperial aircraft the identity of the Valkyrie and its position.

'Malick.'

'Sir.'

'Have *Divine Light* and *Saint Conrad* stand ready. The Tiger Shark has been baited.'

'They're ready, sir.'

'Fire everything we've got when you have a lock.'

'Yes, sir.'

Obeysekera nodded. He looked down at the cube sitting on the desert flat, marked with the aquila. It was, in its own way, as deadly as a bolter. He remained kneeling beside it, listening in on the squad vox-channel as each Venator crew dialled through their auspex settings, trying to get locks on the shifting signal of the t'au Tiger Shark.

'Closing.'

'Signal phasing.'

'Can't get the lock.'

'Switch to delta rhythm.'

Malick's voice, cutting through the chatter. 'Divine Light, *set auspex to standard pattern*. Saint Conrad, *set to Imperial pattern. Phase shift settings.*'

In his mind, Obeysekera could see what Malick was trying to do: calling up the auspex feeds from the other two Venators to the display on *Holy Fire*, he was superimposing the two readings upon his own, hoping that the false readings caused by the t'au Tiger Shark would cancel each other out, allowing him a clear fix.

'Nearly, nearly... Got it! Lock!'

'Lock.'

'Lock.'

The voices of troopers Ha and Chame in the other two Venators, called lock almost simultaneously.

'Fire.'

The three flak missiles flared up into the sky, trails converging. Obeysekera turned to watch their flight. The fire-trails were pointing up, but not very far up, on the further side of the great tree. The Tiger Shark was coming in low. He peered through the shifting fronds of the tree, trying to trace the missiles.

A flash. It came from low down, nearly on the horizon, lighting the shadows under the tree. Before the sound of the first explosion could reach Obeysekera, there came a second and a third flash, but not at the same spot as the first.

Obeysekera hoped that meant the trailing missiles had followed the course of the Tiger Shark and struck it a second and third blow; he feared that they may have exploded on chaff, distracted by the decoy launchers on the t'au aircraft firing off streams of reflective strips and lures when it detected the missile trails.

The distinctive sound of the vector thrusters of the t'au Tiger Shark, a smooth hum comparable to the noise of a hive of Cadian flower mites converting the pollen of a hundred thousand flowers into winter comb, quickly told him that the enemy aircraft had not been seriously damaged and that it was coming closer – much closer.

'Rearm.'

Through the vox-channel, Obeysekera could hear his men doing that without his orders.

'Fire when armed.'

Obeysekera did not wait for Malick's response – he knew the sergeant was on it – and instead made to move out from under the cover of the tree so that he might see more clearly what was happening.

'Wait.' The voice was gentle but imperious.

Obeysekera stopped moving, his legs utterly immobile. But he could still move his upper body and he turned to look at the Kamshet woman – their queen, he presumed.

'Let me go,' he said. 'I must help.'

'Wait,' said the woman again. As she answered him, she turned to look back south.

Immobile, Obeysekera heard the fizz of ion cannons, the energy beams burning the air itself. He turned to see twin, parallel finger trails of fire moving over the salt flat, drawing lines towards *Divine Light*. The salt liquefied, bubbled, then vaporised where the ion beam struck it. It smelt like burnt plasteel.

Obeysekera saw Roshant, in the driver's seat, engaging the galvanic motors. The Venator jerked into motion. Trooper Chame, manning the lascannons, was firing bursts at the oncoming Tiger Shark, the beams hissing across each other in the air. Ha was shouting into the vox, the system automatically cutting out the higher ranges of his cursing. Standing beside the Venator, Quert stood, the flak missile launcher balanced on her shoulder, lining up the missile on the onrushing Tiger Shark.

The fire fingers reached across the flat towards them.

The Venator's machine-spirit answered Roshant's frantic prayers and it lurched forward as the fire tracks reached them, the ion beams cutting through the desert behind the vehicle, Chame still loosing off laser bursts.

Trooper Quert stood her ground, waiting for the target lock, waiting, waiting, then keyed the release. The flak missile flew, gouting fire, and Trooper Quert threw herself aside.

Too late.

The right-hand ion beam burnt through her waist as she leapt, vaporising it, leaving her two legs twitching upon the salt and, two feet away, her chest and arms and head.

Quert's life signs on Obeysekera's display flashed critical, then lined.

The flak missile that Quert had died to fire off flared above their heads, changing course, then exploded harmlessly among the chaff cloud.

'If you are going to do something, lady, now would be good,' said Obeysekera. The Tiger Shark hissed past overhead, a shadow upon the desert, its vector thrusters a whisper in comparison to the ground rattle of an Imperial Marauder, already banking so that it might come round on a fresh pass, the stabbing fingers of the Venators' multi-lasers frizzling out on the streams of countermeasures that surrounded the t'au aircraft.

'Not me.' The woman with cerulean eyes raised her hand and pointed. 'See.'

The invisible shackles holding his body immobile fell away. Obeysekera turned, with the same sense of looming presence that accompanied his turning in dreams – but in his dreams he always woke before he saw that which was behind him. This time he did not wake.

The storm.

Dark. Vast, reaching up to overwhelm the arch of the sky, broad as the expanse of all that he could see. Reaching.

Reaching out towards the banking Tiger Shark.

Dark, dancing columns of twisting sand laced with sand-lightning were advancing in front of the storm bank. Sand tornadoes spun forwards like the battle tops he had played with as a child, rebounding off each other, lightning striking across them as they fought too.

Obeysekera saw the Tiger Shark, its velocity too great to turn away before it was caught up in the maelstrom, pull its nose back and back: the pilot was trying to climb up and out of the storm. A silver-and-grey fish against the black, the Tiger Shark rose, climbing all but vertically now, its pilot twisting it back and forth as black columns danced towards it and lightning bolts set jittering patterns of light playing over its skin.

Obeysekera had never seen an aircraft flown so well. Over the vox, he heard the men, whispering its downfall as they watched with as much awe as he: the storm appeared a thing alive, hunting, and the Tiger Shark a bird, fleet and flying.

The dark closed upon the silver.

Obeysekera breathed out. He had not realised that he had been holding his breath.

The Tiger Shark burst out from the black, vector thrusters shredding the black columns of sand, sheets of electric charge crawling all over its silver skin, and put its nose down, diving towards the ground, enlisting the gravity of Dasht i-Kevar to escape from the storm.

'It's getting away,' said Obeysekera and he felt a strange thrill of joy at the words.

Then the desert shivered, as an animal waking from sleep – shivered and shook. Under the salt flat, through the Sand Sea, the desert moved.

The Tiger Shark powered downwards in a shallow dive, vector thrusters pushing it away from the dark of the storm. As it neared the desert floor and the pilot pulled back its nose to bring it to the level, the desert rose up to meet it. First little geysers of sand, spitting upwards. Then explosions, gouts of sand and salt, blowing up in front and underneath the Tiger Shark, the grains sucked into the intakes of the aircraft's thrusters. Obeysekera heard the engine note change, shifting from a deep hum to a screaming, shredding whine. Smoke plumed from the starboard engines. Fire flicked from the port engine array. The Tiger Shark started to judder, shaking as it flew, the pilot fighting to keep the aircraft under control as it began to yaw, its nose pulling from one side to the other, bleeding speed.

And the storm pulled it back into the dark.

The great body of the storm surged forward, jumping almost as if it were alive, enveloping the lithe silver fish into its lightning-jagged darkness. This time, the Tiger Shark did not re-emerge.

Obeysekera listened for the sound of the crash, but he heard nothing: only the crack and rumble of the sand-lightning and the hiss of the wind-blown sand. It was as if the Tiger Shark had never been. He stared up at the rolling dark, then started and spoke into his vox.

'Get under the Venators.'

The storm was all but upon them.

He felt a touch, light as light, upon his arm, and Obeysekera turned round.

'There is no need,' she said. 'The storm will come no further.'

He stared at the woman. 'You can do this?'

'Not I.' She turned away and started walking towards where her people waited for her.

'Wait.'

She stopped.

Obeysekera ran after her. She did not turn around. He saw the warriors watching him, death in their eyes, but none approached.

'Great lady.'

At the honorific, the woman turned back to Obeysekera and inclined her head slightly, assenting to the title the captain had given her.

'Will you aid me, great lady? I would do your people no harm.'

The woman raised her hand and pointed past Obeysekera. 'I hear truth in your words. But will you answer for these others? Your Imperium has no love for people such as mine. Will you answer for them that I might know my trust shall not be repaid in betrayal?'

Obeysekera felt his skin prickle, the hairs of a far distant ancestral past standing up at the purport of the promise that would carry over into an equally distant future. He was being asked to pledge his honour, and for him that was being asked to pledge his very being.

'I...' He hesitated.

The woman waited. And as she waited, Obeysekera realised that the sounds and movements of the outside world had stilled and stopped. He glanced around, not turning his head but only his eyes, and he saw the world waiting.

'Great lady,' he began again, 'gracious queen, you ask much.'

'No less than I ask the rest of my children.'

'I am not one of your sons, great lady.'

'But you are, dear one, you are.'

Captain Obeysekera stared at the woman of blue. 'How may this be? I was born far from here, I have come but recently to your world, it is not possible...' His words trailed away. 'I answer for them, great lady. On pain of my soul.'

The woman in blue smiled. 'You may call me by name – Mother.'

Obeysekera shook his head. 'I may not do that, great lady. My mother's name is Sashma and I honour her memory.'

'All mothers are blessed in dutiful sons. What would you ask of me?'

'I ask your aid against the enemy that seeks to take this world.'

The woman spread her arms wide, taking in the world. 'From whom would these enemies take this world?'

'From you, great lady.'

But she shook her head. 'You are mistaken, dear son. This world is not mine, although my sons people it, and harvest its living water. The living water that is valuable to your people, and to the blueskins that seek it too.'

'We are your people. The blueskins are xenos, aliens.' A memory, unbidden, flashed through Obeysekera's mind, of the way the Tiger Shark pilot had fought to save his plane, with all the skill and courage of any human pilot. 'As aliens, they must be either subjugated or destroyed.'

The woman looked at him, not answering. Obeysekera had to turn his gaze away. Never had he seen such deep sadness.

'I am old, Captain Obeysekera. In all my years I have known peace only here, in the desert, among the Kamshet.'

Obeysekera glanced towards the nomad warriors. Even fixed outside this bubble of time in which he spoke to the Mother of the Kamshet, they looked fierce and warlike.

At his glance, the woman laughed, a sound of silver.

'It is true – my sons do not present a peaceful front. But they fight only when necessary. Many would trade with the Kamshet for the water of life, that which you call the aqua vitae, and not all of them are men of honour.'

'There are many rejuve treatments, but none so effective, and with as few side effects, as aqua vitae – the trade from this planet, I hear, reaches as far as Holy Terra itself.'

'And none know the wells from which the Kamshet draw the water of life – none save you, Captain Obeysekera, and your men.'

'If you fear that this will mean people will try to harvest aqua vitae directly, you have nothing to fear. When I saw you and your people before, I thought that you were herding some monster. Now I understand that you were following, maybe guiding, the root to the surface.'

'Dasht i-Kevar was once a world of streams and lakes, a gentle world of water. The water remains, buried deep beneath the sand for generations beyond number, and there it has become purer, refined by the heats of this world and filtered through its sand. The life of the world sleeps, dormant, beneath the sand, waiting only for the water of life to spring up and live. The creatures you see about you will live their lives in the space of a few hours, and leave their young to sleep a thousand years beneath the sand until next the water of life shall vivify them. The tree itself shall wither, its branches fall and its trunk shrivel before the next day dawns, leaving but a mound upon the desert floor that the wind will cover in a few days. It is no easy matter to hear and guide one of the deep tendrils of the world tree when it quests towards the light. Your Imperium has neither the patience nor the humility to learn this skill.'

'I fear you speak the truth, great lady. But we will protect you against the t'au.'

'They have sought to deal with us. From that which I have seen, they seem no more rapacious than the traders who come to deal with us already?'

'The traders are at least human, great lady.'

'In form, yes. At heart, many are no longer so.'

Obeysekera nodded. 'It is the privilege and burden of men, great lady. We come into this world as human beings but may leave it as angels or as beasts.'

'How will you leave it, Captain Obeysekera?'

He looked into her eyes, their blue as bright as the lost seas of Cadia. 'Gladly.'

He had not known he would answer so. She nodded, and Obeysekera saw again the deep, deep sadness behind the blue.

'You asked for my aid. I will give it.'

Obeysekera bowed. 'Thank you, great lady.' He looked up and saw the smile that lifted her lips. 'You smile?'

'Such courtesy is rare from a soldier of your Imperium.'

'Then I apologise for their lack of manners.'

The woman smiled again. 'Before I spoke with you, I had determined to have you and all your men slain.' She looked at him. 'I see you smile, now, Captain Obeysekera.'

'I would have expected that, great lady. You have no reason to trust us and more to fear. But we would not have died without killing many of your sons.'

'They will die for me if I command.'

Obeysekera nodded. 'As would mine for me.'

She nodded gravely. 'I see that they would.'

Obeysekera stopped, thought. 'But I would rather that they live.'

'What would you ask, faithful son?'

Obeysekera paused. 'We are searching for one of our own. Do you know where we may find him?'

'The aircraft?'

'You are right, great lady. We seek the man who was travelling aboard the Valkyrie. Do you have him? Or know where we may find him?'

'My sons watched as far as they were able where he went.'

'The Tabaste?'

'Yes.'

'Then that is where we must go.'

The woman shook her head. 'The great mountain is forbidden.'

'Nevertheless, it is where I must go. For what reason is the mountain forbidden?'

The woman looked at Obeysekera. 'It is tabu.'

'We are not of your people. Does the tabu apply to us?'

The woman stopped. Her gaze moved within, the blue of her eyes clouding as she thought on the matter.

'Very well. You may travel to the great mountain.'

Obeysekera bowed. 'I thank you, great lady.'

'But beware. Do not go under the mountain. Those who do, do not return.'

'My orders do not include cave exploration. The only reason I would enter any caves would be to seek the man I have been tasked with finding.'

'I say again – remain in light. The dark beneath the mountain is the haunt of strange and terrible creatures.'

'What is the nature of these creatures?'

'They are not creatures of the desert. Flee them.'

Obeysekera looked at the woman. If she was frightened of whatever lived in the caves beneath the Tabaste Mountains then he would certainly avoid them.

'I will, great lady.' He bowed. 'Thank you.'

'Is there anything else you would ask of me?'

Obeysekera looked into her face again. 'There is one further favour I would ask of you, great lady.'

'Ask it.'

'We have been unable to find anywhere to cross the flowsand. Would your people show us a place where we might safely do so?'

'The desert is difficult to cross for those who do not know its ways. I will send one of my sons with you, to guide you to the mountain.' The woman looked deeply at Obeysekera. The captain realised that she was taller than he.

Captain Obeysekera bowed once more, the full formal bow of an officer of the Astra Militarum of Cadia. 'I thank you, great lady, with all my heart.'

The woman with the cerulean eyes smiled. 'I, too, thank you, Captain Obeysekera.'

Obeysekera looked at her in surprise. 'What have I done for you to thank me?'

'You have shown me that at least one of the servants of the Imperium is worthy of being spared – and where there is one, there will be others.'

Obeysekera nodded – there was not much more he could say to that – then he saluted, turned smartly in his best parade-ground manner and started marching back over the salt flat to where Sergeant Malick was waiting for him in the Venator with Lerin still manning the multi-lasers, their barrels turned towards him in cover.

Over the vox, Obeysekera heard Sergeant Malick say, *'One of them is following you, sir.'*

'That's all right. I've got us a guide. Call *Divine Light* and *Saint Conrad* in.'

As Malick ordered the other two Venators to close with his vehicle, Obeysekera turned around.

The woman, the great lady of the Kamshet, had disappeared among her people, who clustered close around her. The first of the mukaali, having been calmed and restrained, were returning, led or ridden by Kamshet herders, and the animals were being loaded with the casks into which the Kamshet had decanted the aqua vitae collected from the great tree. Obeysekera looked up at the tree itself. Already, its long trailing branches were going limp and starting to wither; that it should have decayed to a great mound of manure by the next day no longer seemed unlikely to him. The creatures that had swarmed up from the ground when the tree burst from the flat, insect and arachnoid and others for which no classification existed, had already almost all dispersed, their explosive life cycles all but at an end with only the search for somewhere to lay eggs still to complete.

CHAPTER 11

Obeysekera looked at the Kamshet walking over the flat towards them. Like the other men of the tribe, he was dressed in robes of white with a blue headscarf that covered all his face save his eyes. He walked easily across the salt, his gait as smooth as that of the mukaali was rolling: the sort of walk that could cover thirty miles a day and start off fresh the next morning. The Kamshet was carrying an autogun. So far as Obeysekera could see, the man carried no other weaponry although he was sure the Kamshet had one or more knives under his robe.

He walked up to where Obeysekera was standing, stopped, and waited, saying nothing.

For his part, Obeysekera held silence too. The Mother of the Kamshet had given the warrior to him as guide: the man would do as he had been bidden. Nevertheless, faced with the Kamshet's silent, blank regard, Obeysekera felt his lips begin to twitch.

He was saved from saying the first words by the arrival of the other two Venators. *Saint Conrad* arrived smoothly, Trooper Ensor bringing it to a halt beside Obeysekera's command Venator with barely a whisper from the galvanic engines. But *Divine Light* crunched up alongside the other two vehicles, its shredded front tyre carving a squealing track through the crust of the salt flat.

Hardly had the vehicle come to a halt than Commissar Roshant swung out of the driving seat and came striding over towards Captain Obeysekera.

'A word, captain,' he said, as he approached Obeysekera, gesturing the captain away from the three Venators.

There was little time, but over the years Obeysekera had learned that it was usually quicker to follow the more urgent requests of Imperial commissars. He followed Roshant, walking twenty or thirty yards away from the Venators. While the troopers remained with the vehicles, Obeysekera noted that the Kamshet warrior followed, remaining ten yards back but following nonetheless.

'What did you want, commissar?' asked Obeysekera, turning to face Roshant.

The young commissar looked at Obeysekera, his face incredulous. 'You have to ask, captain?'

'I have to ask because it is not apparent to me that I have done anything wrong – and from your appearance and tone it appears that you consider that I have.'

Roshant shook his head. 'I can't believe it. I saw you, Captain Obeysekera, you, a hero of the Imperium, openly consorting with a witch.' Roshant ran his fingers over his face. 'You, Captain Obeysekera, talking with a witch. I wouldn't have believed it if I had not seen it myself.' He looked at Obeysekera, his eyes wide like a disillusioned child. 'What do you have to say, captain?'

Obeysekera stared at the young commissar. One of his hands, the one that was rubbing unconsciously up and down the side of his leg, was trembling. His face was flushing. But Roshant's other hand was resting upon the amphant stock of his bolt pistol. It was still holstered, but Obeysekera noted that Roshant had unfastened the safety flap that held the gun in place: commissars were trained to draw and shoot in a single smooth movement.

'I assume you read your briefing slates, commissar?'

Roshant blinked. 'What do you mean?'

'It is a simple question, commissar. If you are unclear, then I will remind you. The Imperium is perfectly aware of the powers of the lady of the Kamshet. Appendix Three-C contains the Inquisitorial seal, granted a century ago, allowing her continued presence here under the auspices of the Holy Ordos.'

Roshant shook his head. 'I-I did not see that.'

'Then I suggest in future you read all your briefing documents before embarking upon a mission.'

Roshant opened his mouth, closed it, then nodded. 'Very well.'

He turned and stalked away. Obeysekera watched him go, slowly allowing the tension in his body to drain away. There was no appendix Three-C.

Obeysekera turned to the Kamshet warrior. 'We must go to the mountain,' he said.

The Kamshet inclined his head. 'It is forbidden, but Mother has given me leave to take you there.'

'Can you find a place for us to cross the flowsand?'

'Yes.'

'Far?'

'No.'

'One day?'

The Kamshet warrior pointed to the mukaali. 'On those, a day.' He pointed to the Venators. 'In those, three hours.'

'We can get there and cross before nightfall?'

The warrior glanced to the sky, looking for the sun's position along its great arc.

'Yes.'

Obeysekera activated the squad vox-channel. 'We're moving out. Get *Divine Light* repaired and ready. Gunsur and Lerin, retrieve Quert. We will bury her where we camp.'

The Kamshet held up his hand. 'You have water?'

'Water?'

'Water.'

'Yes.'

'Give me water.'

'What for?'

The Kamshet warrior pointed to the mouth hidden beneath his head-scarf. 'For the tongue. It is dry.'

'Malick, pour a water measure,' Obeysekera said over the vox-channel.

'The men have had their rations.'

'It's for our guide.' Obeysekera turned back to the Kamshet warrior. 'What is your name?'

'Amazigh.'

'Amazigh, go to Sergeant Malick. He will give you what water we can spare.'

Amazigh inclined his head, hand on heart, then turned and made his way towards the lead Venator, where Sergeant Malick was pouring out a small measure of water.

Obeysekera walked over to Roshant. 'Your vehicle's tyre has been replaced. Are you fit to continue?'

Roshant nodded. 'I am ready.' He stepped back in some disgust as the last of the insect bloom from the eruption of the tree swarmed up out of the ground and seethed into the sky. 'I have heard of people dreaming of making the desert bloom,' he said, 'but I suspect that this was not what they had in mind.'

At the joke, Captain Obeysekera threw back his head and laughed, a clear laugh and pure, the sound of clean joy.

Commissar Roshant grimaced. 'I don't think it was that funny, and I made the joke.'

But Obeysekera clapped Roshant on the shoulder. 'It was. Come, let us go, commissar. We have a few hours until sunset and the Kamshet, Amazigh, promises to guide us to a place where we can cross the flowsand. The mission can continue – and we have done enough already to earn ourselves promotions.'

'You have recorded this position?' asked Roshant. 'So that we can find it again?'

'Of course,' said Obeysekera. But as they walked back to the Venator, he glanced behind. As the lady had said, the fronds of the great tree were already shrivelling under the weight of the heavy sun, while the trunk showed signs of beginning to decay. By the morrow, there would not be much left: in a week's time, Obeysekera suspected there would be no trace of the eruption of the great tree and the efflorescence of life that it had produced. Remembering how the Kamshet had guided the runner from which the tree had sprung, it was likely that the next time the desert produced a tree of life, it would grow in a completely different part of the Great Sand Sea, one that only the Kamshet knew. If an Imperial observation station was set up at this location, Obeysekera thought they could wait a thousand years and never see what they had come to observe. The extraordinarily rapid life cycle he had witnessed among the creatures hatching at the tree's eruption suggested animals adapted to spending hundreds, if not thousands, of years lying dormant beneath the surface of the Great Sand Sea, waiting for their time to come. Even more reason to believe that returning to this same spot would not yield a harvest of aqua vitae.

As they reached the Venator, Obeysekera wondered if he would put that in his report.

'I will drive, sergeant, with the Kamshet, Amazigh, as my guide. Make sure that the navigators in *Divine Light* and *Saint Conrad* keep a proper record of our route – I will not be able to as I am driving.'

Sergeant Malick nodded and slid from the driver's seat and out onto the flat. 'Should be easy going so long as we keep to this flat, sir,' he said.

'Take the commissar with you on *Divine Light*.' Obeysekera switched to the private channel. 'See that the commissar is kept as far away from the Kamshet as possible.'

Sergeant Malick nodded again: he was no stranger to orders directed towards ensuring the smoother running of the squad through the careful regulation of the contact between highly trained and sometimes volatile killers. 'I'll do that, sir.' He paused. 'We have put Quert's body into *Saint Conrad*.'

Obeysekera nodded, his previous light mood flattened out by the reminder of the squad's loss.

'Emperor willing, we shall find a suitable place to bury her.'

'If we don't?' Malick squinted up at the sun. 'It's hot. She won't keep long.'

'Then we'll cover her with sand and mark the grave as best we can. Let's move out, sergeant.'

Malick saluted. 'Sir.'

Obeysekera looked up to Lerin manning the twin-linked multi-lasers mounted on *Holy Fire*. 'Have you cleared and cleaned the pintle, Lerin?'

'Cleared, sir,' said Lerin. 'No time to strip it down and clean it now. I will do that when we camp.'

'Make sure you do, Lerin.' Obeysekera pointed to the navigator's seat. 'That's where you sit,' he said to Amazigh. For the first time, he saw a ripple of concern pass through the Kamshet's desert-clear eyes.

'Is it not possible for me to sit atop the machine?' he asked.

'No, it is not possible,' said Obeysekera. 'One skid or drop and you'd be sailing off the top and like as not cracking your skull on the one rock in this whole desert.'

Amazigh stared at him. 'There is more than one rock in the desert,' he said.

'Even more reason for you to be strapped to the seat,' said Obeysekera. 'Come on, jump in. It's a Venator. It won't bite.'

'Ven… itor?'

'Ven-A-tor,' said Obeysekera. He tapped the navigator's seat. 'You're here. I am there' – he pointed to the driver's seat – 'next to you. That way, you can tell me where to go.'

'And you will be close to kill me if I should lead you false,' said Amazigh.

'Exactly,' said Obeysekera. He grinned, showing his teeth. 'So do what you said – find me a way to cross the flowsand and you will live to see the stars in the sky tonight. Fail, and you will be meat in the morning.'

'Mother gave me to you – I will not fail,' said Amazigh.

'I'm sure you won't. Now get in, we're wasting time.'

While the Kamshet warrior climbed gingerly into the Venator and strapped himself into the navigator's seat, Obeysekera took a final look at the great tree and the Kamshet harvesters. Already, half the tribe had saddled up their mukaali and were moving out, great panniers of aqua vitae strapped across their beasts' shoulders and haunches. The rest were loading up. Obeysekera searched for some sign of the Mother of the Kamshet, but from this distance he could not make her out, although a cluster of blue-robed warriors suggested her presence in the centre of the tribe.

Obeysekera went round to the other side of the Venator and climbed into the driver's seat, strapping himself in.

'Ready?' he asked Amazigh.

The Kamshet nodded. Although, in profile, Obeysekera could not even see Amazigh's eyes, it was a nervous movement. Obeysekera started the galvanic motors. The Kamshet grasped the edges of his seat, knuckles whitening.

'Which way?' asked Obeysekera.

Amazigh raised his hand to point straight ahead.

Before he could renew his grasp, Obeysekera gunned the Venator, its instant acceleration over the hard crust of the salt flat pushing them both back against their seats. The Kamshet warrior cried out in alarm. Obeysekera accelerated faster, taking the Venator round the decaying remains of the tree.

With Amazigh breathing fast and loud next to him, Obeysekera sped the Venator past the remaining Kamshet. As he went, the warriors parted and he saw the Mother, her face uncovered, turn to look at him. He raised his hand in salute and then they were past, on over the salt flat, into the great desert.

CHAPTER 12

Commissar Roshant, driving *Divine Light*, was staring ahead, eyes fixed on the horizon, his foot pressed down hard.

'What are they doing?' He gestured ahead to *Holy Fire*, its wheels skimming over the desert, sending up showers of sand in its wake. 'Do they think this is some sort of race?'

Sergeant Malick, strapped into the navigator's seat beside the commissar, laughed. 'If it is, we'll win it with you driving, commissar.'

Roshant glanced over at the sergeant. 'You think so?'

'You're one of the best drivers I've ever seen,' said Malick. He checked his display. All his external vox-channels were switched off. No one else could hear what he was saying.

The commissar nodded, smiling.

As he did, he looked like the boy he might once have been: eager, enthusiastic, petulant when crossed but desperate for praise. Malick layered on some more.

'Good to have you with us, sir.'

'But I've hardly said anything to the men,' said Roshant. 'No speeches, just a few words when we've stopped.'

'Just like all the best commissars – they act, they don't speak. It's your presence that helps keep us going.'

'You think so? Captain Obeysekera's not said anything like this to me.'

'He wouldn't, would he.'

'No? No, of course he wouldn't.'

Malick pointed ahead. 'Maybe watch where we're going.'

Roshant jerked the wheel of the Venator, just missing a stone outcrop, but driving into the skid following while barely losing any of the vehicle's velocity before bringing it back on track.

'Nice driving,' said Malick.

'Thank you,' said Roshant.

'You know, it's a shame that you won't get the credit due to you for this mission.'

Roshant looked over at the sergeant. 'What do you mean?'

'No offence, sir. But, lord militant's son, fresh from the schola of the Officio Prefectus... No one's going to believe how big a part you played in everything. It will all be ascribed to nepotism.'

Roshant stared ahead. He said nothing. Malick saw his knuckles whiten on the steering wheel.

'Mind if you check your vox is off, sir?'

Roshant looked at Malick. 'Why?'

'Something important – better kept between us for the moment.'

'It's off.'

Malick checked his display – as sergeant, he could see the vox and life signs of the members of the squad. 'Your father is the lord militant – he has enemies?'

'Of course. Officers he has looked over, or demoted, let alone the enemies we all fight.'

'You know how many commissars fail to return from their first battle postings?'

Roshant nodded. 'Yes.' Malick saw him swallow. 'It's called fragging. They mentioned it in the schola. Discipline is the answer, they said.'

'It's battle,' said Malick. 'Stray rounds can strike anyone. One hotshot las-round looks pretty much like another, whoever fired the gun.'

'A heroic death in service of the Emperor.'

'A death, nevertheless. Now, like you say, your father has enemies. Wouldn't be too hard for someone with money and influence to buy the service of a poor trooper, even a 'kin.'

'Are you saying that one of your men has been paid to assassinate me, sergeant?'

'Where'd you get that idea, sir? No, I'm not saying that. They're all good men, I'd swear for each and every one of them. I've served with them for years.'

'But not Captain Obeysekera?'

'I am sure he is beyond doubt.'

'But you have only recently met him?'

'At the start of this mission.'

'He was Colonel Aruna's choice.'

'Colonel Aruna is a rising star – on the grapevine I hear many people expect a great future for him.'

In his peripheral vision, Malick saw Roshant glance over towards him. The sergeant kept looking ahead.

'You have fought many battles, sergeant?'

'Too many, sir.'

'You have much experience.'

'I've seen many men die, sir, if you call that experience.'

'Perhaps you could help me.'

Malick turned to look at Roshant. 'You are a commissar, sir. It would be my duty to help you.'

Roshant nodded. 'Then maybe you could keep an eye open for me, your ears too – tell me if anything is afoot. There are enemies everywhere.'

'I will, sir, I will.'

'I will see that you are rewarded, sergeant.'

'I'm sure you will, sir.'

Roshant glanced at the sergeant. Malick stared ahead, his eyes set upon the Venator in front.

'Good.'

'I'll watch your back, sir. No one gets near you. Like I said, in battle one las-round looks pretty much like any other.'

'Do your duty, sergeant.'

Malick turned to the commissar and smiled. 'Oh, I will, sir. I will.'

CHAPTER 13

Amazigh, whooping with excitement, yelled, 'Faster, faster!'

Obeysekera shook his head. 'I liked you better when you were scared,' he said, the wind of their driving whipping his words away from his mouth. The Kamshet wasn't listening in any case. Despite Obeysekera's remonstrations he had unstrapped himself and was now standing on his seat with his head and shoulders through the roll bar, laughing and singing to himself in between asking Obeysekera to speed up. If he should roll the Venator, Obeysekera knew, the roll bar would cut the Kamshet in half. But he could not complain about their progress. After a nervous first half hour, Amazigh had settled into travelling through the desert at the speed of a Venator rather than the slow-motion roll of a mukaali. As he had promised, he had shown them to a place to cross the flowsand before nightfall, a ford where the flowsand formed a thin skin over hard bedrock, and the Venators had driven across, spraying sand up on either side of their tyres.

The far bank had been rock and stone, and they had made good progress until nightfall, when they had camped. The morning had seen Amazigh installing himself in the navigator's seat before the rest of the men were even ready, and the day had seen the Kamshet urging them on to ever greater speed, a speed that had been made possible by the hard rock surface over which he took them. Obeysekera had worried that jagged rocks might shred a tyre, but he soon realised that the exposed surface had been smoothed to round undulations by the sand blast of millennia of storms. The only problem was that the undulations transmitted up through the tyres into the Venators, shaking the occupants as if they were being put through a blender. But while Obeysekera felt as if his teeth might rattle loose, the Kamshet, standing now, just shouted louder and urged them faster.

'How... far... now?' Obeysekera asked, his teeth banging together as he tried to talk.

'Not far,' said Amazigh, turning to look down at the captain. Although he had kept his scarf on throughout their evening meal, simply raising it a little to carry food to his lips, his eyes told the tale of his joy to Obeysekera. The Kamshet was having the time of his life.

'Can you... slow down... a little... captain?'

Obeysekera tried to see on his display who was talking to him but it was shaking so much he could not make out which ident rune had lit up.

'Who... is... that?'

'Ch-Chame... sir.'

The gunner on Roshant's Venator.

'I think... I'm going... to be sick... sir.'

'Me... too,' said Obeysekera. He yelled up at Amazigh. 'I am going... to slow... down.'

'There!' said the Kamshet, pointing ahead. 'There it is. Tabaste. The mountain.'

Obeysekera braked, slowly bringing the Venator to a stop, with the other two vehicles ranged behind him. Over the vox-channel he heard the murmur of the men's complaints and relief, but he struggled to stand – his legs felt like they'd been turned to hypogel – and stuck his head up through the roll bar to look where Amazigh was pointing.

With his head above the shadow netting, Obeysekera felt the full impact of the sun, now nearing its zenith, upon his head and shoulders. The sweat that the wind of their speed had evaporated immediately now lingered a moment longer until the dry and thirsty air sucked it from his skin. But he relegated those impressions to insignificance as he took stock of their surroundings.

Tabaste.

The mountain forbidden to the Kamshet. The redstone heart of the Great Sand Sea.

It rose over the sand and rock in ridges and humps that looked nothing like the jagged peaks of Cadia. Tabaste was smooth and worn, its ascending series of summits more like the boils made when the bulge mite laid its eggs under the skin than a mountain serif. To Obeysekera's eye it presented a series of overlaid mounds, climbing upwards and then rounding out at a broad and knobbly summit.

Obeysekera, and the drivers, navigators and crew of the other Venators, looked at the mountain for a while. The mountains of Cadia had always given the sense of strength and vigour, of the planet thrusting up against its own gravity. As a child, growing up in Kasr Gesh, he had looked out from the city's defences to the jagged range of the Karakora Mountains that defined the horizon. As a boy, training to be a Whiteshield, Obeysekera had camped in the Karakora. The memory of days spent in the high passes, with the wind never ceasing and the creak and break of ice falls from the higher ridges, was among the most vivid of his childhood. The Karakora had inspired awe in the young Bharath. He imagined that, if by some unimaginable chance, he should ever set foot upon Holy Terra, he would feel as he did when standing beneath the sky-churning mass of the Skyspear.

The Tabaste produced its own sense of awe, but it was very different from the feeling he had had when looking up at the Karakora as a boy. There, beneath the Skyspear, he had been overwhelmed by the majesty of the mountain, of its strength and power. He remembered old Sergeant Yannek, pointing up at the majesty of the Skyspear and saying to them all, 'You want to know what the Emperor is like? That's what He's like.'

Looking at Tabaste over the intervening desert, Obeysekera also felt a sense of awe, but where the Karakora had dwarfed him by their size, the Tabaste made him insignificant by its age.

The mountain was old. It was old beyond his comprehension, old beyond the understanding of any mortal human. Time had worn the Tabaste smooth. Millions of years of sand and wind had rubbed away every jagged edge and cleft from its surface. What was left was the testimony of time: the red-rock bone underlying this desert world. Staring at the Tabaste, Obeysekera, and all the men looking at it, felt their own insignificance: they were nothing more than dayflies, playing out lives that the mountain, lost in the dream of time, would never even notice.

Obeysekera took his magnoculars from their case and trained them on the Tabaste, setting them on a wide field of view to start with as he scanned the red rock for any signs of the general's Valkyrie.

'See anything, Malick?' Obeysekera knew his sergeant would be searching the Tabaste for the target too.

'*Nothing, sir.*'

'We'll move in closer. Too much to expect to see anything from this range.'

Obeysekera slid back down into the driver's seat and slid the magnoculars back into their case. He tapped Amazigh's leg. The Kamshet, still standing, pulled his gaze away from the mountain and looked down at Obeysekera.

'Get down. We're moving on.'

Amazigh sat down and began strapping himself in. Obeysekera looked askance at him.

'Why are you doing that?' he asked the Kamshet. 'You wouldn't before.'

Amazigh, still fitting buckles into clasps, glanced over at Obeysekera, his eyes blue glints above his cheche.

'It is the Tabaste.'

'I know. Why are you putting on the straps now?'

'It is the Tabaste.'

Obeysekera was about to repeat the question, then thought again, shook his head and started the galvanic motors. The Venator gently stirred itself back into machine life, humming softly. Obeysekera could tell that its machine-spirits had come to like the desert: sand and grit needed to be cleaned out of bearings at every camp, but the dry air suited the vehicle.

The Venators moved off, Obeysekera leading, the other two following at fifty-yard intervals. The Tabaste disappeared behind a ridge, only to reappear as they crossed the rocky crest and started on a long, gentle decline towards a wide, flat plain. The Tabaste rose from the centre of the plain, climbing up gently from the sand.

Obeysekera stopped the Venator. 'We have to cross *that* to get to the mountain?'

The plain upon which the Tabaste stood was table-flat, and roughly six miles in diameter. There was no cover. Crossing it, they would be absolutely exposed.

'There is another way,' said Amazigh. 'On the other side of the mountain there is hard ground that comes closer.' The Kamshet made a circling gesture. 'But the ground is difficult. It will take two or three days to go around the... the... I do not know the word in your language. We call that the uzayar.'

Obeysekera shook his head. 'Too long. Can we cross that... you called it uzaɣar?'

Amazigh pointed ahead. 'There is a way,' he said. 'Mother told me the signs to look for.'

'You have not been to the Tabaste?'

Amazigh shook his head. 'The mountain is forbidden. Only Mother has walked there, and that was when the mothers of our mother's mothers were still children. But she told me the way.'

Obeysekera stared out over the plain. 'Why is the uzaɣar so flat? Surely the wind should leave some mark upon it?' For even as he asked the question, he could see zephyrs of wind tumbling over the plain, raising spumes of sand, but in no place did these plumes settle to make the ridges and troughs of the rest of the Sand Sea. The uzaɣar was flat, utterly and completely level.

The Kamshet looked at Obeysekera. 'You do not know?'

Obeysekera shook his head. 'No.'

'It is flowsand.' Amazigh pointed out over the uzaɣar. 'All the channels of flowing sand wind their way here.'

'All?' Obeysekera looked around. The Tabaste rose from the uzaɣar, but around the uzaɣar there was a great bowl of dunes and rock. 'Won't it...?'

'Do you ask if someday the flowsand will rise up over the mountain? I do not know, but Mother tells us that it was not always so. The flowsand channels wandered through the land, some spilling out into the plains beyond. But the desert shifted and the sand started to flow here, making the uzaɣar, and it is true, its level rises. When I was a boy it was not so high as it is today. But whether it will one day cover the mountain, I do not see how, for the land around the uzaɣar is not so high as the mountain, although it seems to me, coming back after many years not seeing the uzaɣar, that even the land around the uzaɣar has risen.' Amazigh pointed to the rock bluffs to their right. 'I do not know if rocks may grow, but these seem taller than my memory makes them, and I have heard others of my people speak the same.'

Obeysekera stared where the Kamshet pointed. 'Mountains may rise, but they don't generally do that within the memory of people.' He turned back to the Kamshet. 'According to the Imperial surveyors, this is a stable world – there is no tectonic activity on it.'

'Yet the rocks are higher now than I remember, and my memory does not fail,' said Amazigh.

'My memory fails me all the time,' said Obeysekera. 'How can you be so certain of yours?'

'Because if we do not have memory, we have nothing,' said Amazigh.

Obeysekera nodded. What the Kamshet said was true: nomadic peoples tended their memories for they were all the history they had.

'Very well. I must write it down as another of the mysteries of Dasht i-Kevar to go alongside all the others – the rising rocks surrounding the Tabaste. But nevertheless, we must still reach the mountain. Is there a way across the uzaɣar?'

'Yes. Mother told me where to find it. But the way is narrow and the flowsand is deep on either side of the way. You must go carefully. Come off the track and the sand will swallow you.'

'*Divine Light* and *Saint Conrad*, did you read that? There is deep flowsand on either side of the track we will follow to reach the Tabaste. Follow exactly in my tyre tracks.'

The two Venators acknowledged Obeysekera's message from their respective waiting positions. *Divine Light* was on the crest of the final ridge and its driver and navigator – Roshant and Malick – could see the flat plain of uzayar, but *Saint Conrad* was waiting on the reverse slope: Ensor and the rest could only wait to see what the rest of the squad were looking at.

'*Slow and steady,*' said Malick, '*and right in your tracks. Ensor, you follow me.*'

'*Got that,*' replied Ensor over the open squad vox-channel.

'Take us through,' said Obeysekera to Amazigh.

'Drive down to where the uzayar begins,' said the Kamshet. 'I must get out there and walk before you to make sure of the way.'

Obeysekera started the galvanic motors and eased the Venator down the incline, making sure that shifting sand did not start to slide away beneath the tyres and roll them down too fast for him to stop the vehicle.

'Stop,' said Amazigh.

They were nearly at the level of the uzayar.

The Kamshet got out of the Venator and, wrapping his cheche more tightly around his face to protect his lungs from the sand spumes blowing up from the uzayar, he made his way down the final few yards of the incline. Reaching the start of the flowsand, he turned sideways on to it and started walking along the edge of the uzayar, stopping every so often to bend down and test the sand.

Obeysekera sat, waiting and watching. He hoped that Amazigh would find the way soon: he did not relish the prospect of driving around the edge of the uzayar, for the slope down to it quickly grew steeper and rougher. But the Kamshet had not gone more than fifty yards when he stopped, tried the sand, tried it again a few paces further on, and then walked out a little way into the uzayar.

Standing there amid the flowsand, Amazigh turned and beckoned Obeysekera to him.

'You see where we have to go,' he said over the vox. 'Drivers, follow exactly in my tracks. Everyone else, stay alert. Gunners, have the weapons cycled. We will be as exposed as it is possible to be out there.'

One of Obeysekera's private vox-channels flashed and he saw that it was Roshant calling him person-to-person.

'Commissar?'

'*Shouldn't we wait for dark to cross? We won't be so obvious.*'

'The greater risk is that we drive off the path and fall into the flowsand. Besides, we do not have the time to lose.'

'*Captain...*'

'Moving out, commissar. I am driving – don't distract me.'

Obeysekera started the Venator, the hum of the galvanic motors telling of the eagerness of the machine-spirit. He carefully engaged the wheel drive and set off around the edge of the flowsand to where Amazigh was waiting.

The Kamshet waved him to a stop as he reached his position. 'The way starts here,' Amazigh said, 'and stops here,' he added, walking across to the other edge of the track. It was barely four yards wide, sufficient to take the Venator's six tyres, but there was little leeway.

'Does it stay that width all the way across?' asked Obeysekera.

'We will see,' said Amazigh. 'Follow.'

He began walking out into the uzayar, and Obeysekera drove the Venator after him.

Speed was the primary defence for the lightly armoured Venators. Now they were crossing three miles of flat and featureless plain, with no cover, with the sun still high in the sky, at walking pace. Obeysekera was not sure if he feared the arrival of the usual afternoon sandstorm, or hoped for its cover.

Like beetles crawling over a table without end, the three Venators followed behind the blue-and-white-robed Kamshet as they took the way across the uzayar to the Tabaste. After the first mile, Obeysekera found himself struggling to maintain concentration. The uzayar had no features whatsoever. It was simply flat sand, stretching in either direction, with only the Kamshet walking in front of the Venator and the Tabaste looming ahead to give any relief to the monotony.

The track that Amazigh was taking them on, a ridge of rock cutting through the flowsand, was straight, barely deviating. In fact, it was so unwavering that Obeysekera began to wonder if it really was a natural feature: it ran more like a road, or a pilgrim path nearing its final objective.

Obeysekera keyed on the squad vox-channel. 'Read it off.'

'Clear.'

'Clear.'

'Clear.'

The replies came in from every member of the squad, squinting out into the white light or poring over the auspex, apart from one.

'Commissar?'

'Captain?'

'Do you see anything?'

'No.'

'Then tell me next time I ask.'

Roshant went silent.

'Did you hear me, commissar?'

'Yes. Captain.'

'Good. Everyone keep sharp. We're completely exposed out here and there's nowhere to run to. I don't expect to see t'au aircraft this far into the sand, but keep watching the auspex.'

As Obeysekera was speaking, he was watching Amazigh walking steadily in front of him. There was something strange about it. Then Obeysekera realised what it was. Although Amazigh was walking on sand, he was leaving no tracks. The thin skin of flowsand that lay atop the ford filled his steps as soon as he lifted his foot.

The Kamshet was barefoot. Obeysekera wondered how he could endure the heat of the sand, but he walked without flinching. Obeysekera squinted past him. Here, in the middle of the uzayar, with miles of sand reflecting the heat, the Sand Sea settled into its flat heart and simmered under the copper sun. Columns of rising air, cooked by the desert heat, rose in gyrating funnels, twisting the sand where they touched the ground. The sand there swirled, as if it were being slowly stirred, but as the columns of hot air wavered and wandered over the desert, the sand settled sullenly back into place as soon as the thermal had moved on, giving no sign of the agitation that had previously disturbed it.

The Tabaste, which had seemed clear from the far side of the uzayar, now appeared ghostly and insubstantial behind the heat haze. It shimmered and shifted, a red-orange dream that seemed to grow more distant as they crawled across the uzayar, three black beetles pinned under the sun.

Obeysekera sucked a little water from his reservoir. It was warm, a little brackish from the purifier, but it was at least wet. He felt himself sweating it out almost as he drank it, while fighting the urge to stop Amazigh and ask him how much further. If it was hard for him, how much more difficult must it be for the Kamshet, walking barefoot over sand that could cook an egg, protected from the full weight of the sun only by his robes?

But Amazigh walked on without faltering, his steps smooth and steady, and Obeysekera blinked the sweat from his eyes, realising that he was veering off course. He brought the Venator back in line.

Just keep following the Kamshet. That was all he had to do until they got to the mountain. But it was like driving on water. There was nothing to distinguish, by sight, the solid way from the flowsand on either side. Nor was there any way of telling if the path should narrow, allowing a man to walk unhampered but precipitating one or other set of wheels into the sand.

'*Divine Light* and *Saint Conrad*. If you come off the path and start tipping into the flowsand, everyone bail out. I don't care about losing one vehicle – I do care about losing the men on it.'

The acknowledgements came back, after the slightest of baffled pauses.

'We've already lost two soldiers. If we lose any more, our operational effectiveness will drop and our chances of making it back will dramatically reduce. If we lose a Venator, we'll just have to strap the general in underneath.'

The splutters of laughter told Obeysekera that the joke had hit its mark. He keyed the vox-channel to silent and squinted at Amazigh's back as he walked carefully along in front of them. How far was it across the uzayar? From the start of the causeway it had looked like it must be two or three miles, but without any features on the plain, it was almost impossible to judge distance. It might be one mile, but it was at least unlikely to be much more than three since the horizon on Dasht i-Kevar, a planet with a circumference and gravity very similar to that of Holy Terra itself, was about three miles and he was reasonably sure that he was able to see the base of the Tabaste from the start of the causeway.

Obeysekera checked the readings on the Venator. They had come over a mile across the uzayar already. He squinted ahead through the shifting heat haze. The Tabaste did look significantly closer. It also meant that they were right out in the open, in the middle of the uzayar, as obvious as a stinkbug crawling across a data-slate.

If he were a watching enemy, this was when Obeysekera would attack.

He keyed on the channel to Chame in *Divine Light*. 'You've got a clearer view up there,' he said. 'Any sign, movement?'

'The only thing moving is us, captain,' said Chame, *'and it's so hot I'm not so sure about us.'*

'Malick, make sure you have someone on the auspex. If the bluies come in by air, we won't have much time.'

'On it, sir.'

Ahead of him, Amazigh trudged on, his footprints flowing away as soon as he made them. Obeysekera felt his vision narrowing to a tunnel. To open it out again, he looked rapidly left and right, stopping for a moment at the end of each sweep to allow his eyes to focus on the horizon.

Pulling his gaze back to the Kamshet, he felt his peripheral vision return. Everything about the conditions on Dasht i-Kevar – the heat, the monotony, the constant, nagging thirst – militated against the sort of awareness that allowed soldiers to remain alert to the stealthy approach of an enemy, so Obeysekera was relieved to have regained some of his focus. It had saved him on more than one occasion.

He squinted at the Kamshet. Amazigh had stopped moving. He was staring ahead, like a carnodon that had seen prey. Obeysekera slowly brought his Venator to a halt. The auspex told him that *Divine Light* and *Saint Conrad* had stopped too. They sat under the sun in the middle of the uzayar, its weight heavy upon them.

Obeysekera was about to stick his head out of the Venator and call to the Kamshet when Amazigh abruptly turned round and came back towards him, glancing over his shoulder as he did so.

'You have magnoculars?' Amazigh asked Obeysekera when he reached the vehicle. In answer, Obeysekera handed him the device. The Kamshet turned back to the Tabaste and, raising the magnoculars, scanned the mountain, his movement soon settling on a particular point.

'What do you see?' Obeysekera could make out nothing but the red-orange rock of the Tabaste.

'There,' said Amazigh, handing the magnoculars back to Obeysekera and pointing. 'In front of the gap that looks like your letter "Y".'

Obeysekera took the magnoculars and raised them to his eyes. The lenses whirred into focus, pulling different parts of the Tabaste into view.

Then, he saw it.

Jutting out from behind a ridge, the distinctive drooping tail fin of a Valkyrie. The rest of the aircraft was hidden behind the ridge, but there was nothing about the position of the tail fin to suggest that it was the broken remains of a crashed vehicle: the Valkyrie had put down under power and control.

But if it had not crashed, then why had it not taken off again?

Obeysekera remembered the sandstorm. The engines could have been destroyed and the Valkyrie immobilised. He scanned the immediate vicinity of the landing site, searching for any sign of the Valkyrie's crew and, in particular, General Itoyesa, but there was nothing.

'Valkyrie in view,' Obeysekera said over the squad vox-channel. 'Bearing two-eighty.'

The other two Venators were stretched out in a straight line behind his own: it was unlikely that either would have a better view than he, but at least they would know the target location.

'*I have the Valkyrie in view,*' said Malick from *Divine Light*. '*Unable to confirm identity.*'

'*I see it too,*' said Trooper Ha in *Saint Conrad*. '*Can't identify.*'

'Move on. Gunners, keep watch. We're as exposed as a Whiteshield helmet out here.' Obeysekera started the galvanic motors. Amazigh began walking, but he had not gone more than two or three paces when he stopped again. This time, however, he was looking out to the left, over the uzayar, the table-flat expanse of flowsand that laked around the Tabaste. Obeysekera looked where Amazigh was staring.

The flowsand was rippling. The ripples were V-shaped, and the apex of the V was pointing straight at them.

Something was coming.

Amazigh looked back at Obeysekera. Even with his face covered, the captain could see the fear in the Kamshet's eyes.

'Awsaḍ.' Amazigh paused a moment. '*Run.*'

The Kamshet turned towards the Tabaste and began running.

Obeysekera gunned the galvanic motors and the Venator's tyres spun, then cleared the thin layer of flowsand and bit on the rock of the causeway. The vehicle surged forward.

'Gunners, target left, approaching fast.'

From behind him, Obeysekera heard the grind of the multi-laser's pintle as the bearings, still not entirely clear of sand, turned to bring it to bear. Behind him, the other Venators were doing the same.

'Fire at will.'

The first burst of las-fire seared through the air as the Venator caught up with the fleeing Kamshet. Amazigh, hearing its approach, moved out of the way, teetered on the edge of the causeway, then jumped into the Venator.

'Straight on?' asked Obeysekera as Amazigh tumbled into the vehicle.

'Straight on,' said Amazigh, righting himself.

Obeysekera mentally drew a straight line to the Tabaste and set the Venator off to follow the line. He kept his eyes fixed ahead, knowing that glancing left to see where the Awsaḍ was would only serve to drag him off line and send the Venator careering off the causeway and into the flowsand. He could hear the snap-hiss of the las-fire, and the crack of superheated sand where the multi-lasers struck into it. The sounds were coming closer, tracking in towards the lead vehicle.

Obeysekera tried to measure the distance ahead. Not far now. The Tabaste rose up from the flowsand in a series of levels, the transition flagged by the change in height and colour, the yellow of the flowsand giving way to the red rock of the mountain.

Not far now.

But the lasers were firing off at close range, the snap-hiss of the Venators' weapons joined by the individual jolts of hellguns. With his peripheral vision, Obeysekera could see the apex of the V-shaped wake of waves in the flowsand approaching, pointing towards his Venator like an arrow. It was coming in fast – faster than anything had any right to move through sand.

Obeysekera concentrated his gaze ahead, striving to drive in as perfectly a straight line as possible over a road that had no markings.

'What is it?' he asked Amazigh.

'Pray you do not learn.' The Kamshet stuck his head through the open side of the Venator. 'Faster. Faster. We are nearly there.'

Obeysekera gunned the galvanic motors, their hum overlaying the rasp of sand as the waves arrowed closer. He risked another glance to the left. The apex was about a hundred yards away now.

The Venator lurched left, the front wheel falling off the side of the causeway, the rear starting to slew around as the motors drove the rear tyres on. Obeysekera cut the drives to the right-hand wheels and turned into the slide.

The front left tyre bit on the side of the causeway, slipped back, then the Venator's forward momentum brought it back up against the rock and this time the tyre gripped and pulled the front back up onto the way. Obeysekera flicked the right-hand drives back on, compensating with the steering while the drives kicked in, then slewed the Venator back onto the straight line, driving it on towards the Tabaste.

Not far. He could see the red rock rising up from the flowsand not more than one hundred and fifty feet ahead. He gunned the motors, putting every bit of power the Venator could generate into its tyre drives, and it surged over the hard rock of the causeway towards the mountain.

Obeysekera stopped himself looking left.

'How far?'

'Keep going.'

From behind, Obeysekera could still hear the snap-hiss of the multi-lasers.

'Are they doing any good?'

'Burning sand.'

'Cease fire. Wait for a target above sand.' Obeysekera keyed off the vox-channel. 'Will it come out from the surface?'

'When the Awsaḍ rises from the sand, it is too late.'

Obeysekera keyed the vox-channel on again. 'Max speed, feed everything to the drives.'

The three Venators, now bunched much closer together than Imperial Guard tactical doctrine allowed, surged forward over the final stretch of causeway while the V at the point of the arrow burrowed in closer. Fifty yards now. Forty. Thirty.

The ground sound changed, sand hiss giving way to rock roar, and

Obeysekera knew he was out of the flowsand. He arced the Venator left, pulling away from the flowsand but giving Lerin a clear field of fire.

He twisted back, saw that *Divine Light* had crossed clear, and spoke into the vox, 'Malick, break right, converging fire.'

The two Venators were moving so that they could focus their fire on whatever emerged from the sand, while the third vehicle crossed the last of the causeway onto the solid rock.

The flowsand waves surged the final few yards as the last Venator, galvanic motors rising to their highest pitch, drove pell-mell over the remaining causeway.

'Nearly there, nearly there.' The words were coming from Amazigh.

Obeysekera did not look round at the Kamshet. They both stared at the race reaching its climax before them.

Last few yards.

The Venator was about to cross onto the hard red rock of the Tabaste when the leading sand wave slapped into the side of the causeway, flowing over it and knocking the Venator sideways. Its front right tyre slipped off the causeway and it heeled over.

But before the wave could carry it off the causeway, the wheel caught the edge of the hard rock of the Tabaste, bit, and pulled the Venator back upright and onto the mountain.

The Venator, hard rock beneath all its wheels, surged forward as the second sand wave splashed harmlessly over the causeway behind it. Obeysekera saw Ensor, face staring ahead in the driver's seat, pushing the vehicle on up into the safety of the rock.

Behind the Venator, in the flowsand lapping up against the causeway, Obeysekera saw the waves reduced to a roiling mass and, beneath the churning sand, through the furrows that opened and closed in it, he glimpsed something moving, deep and dark and huge beyond thinking.

'Awsaḍ,' breathed Amazigh.

'Awsaḍ,' said Obeysekera.

The seething sand whirled, then began to settle and slowly sank lower.

'It's going?' asked Obeysekera.

'Yes,' said Amazigh.

'You know, I am interested in xenobiology, but on this occasion I am glad not to have been able to satisfy my curiosity.'

'The Kamshet are not curious – we follow the old ways and we survive.'

Obeysekera shook his head. 'The world is changing. I fear the old ways will have to change too if you would survive.'

Amazigh turned to the Kasrkin captain. Obeysekera could see the Kamshet's blue eyes through the gap of his cheche.

'If we survive at the expense of who we are, do we then still really live?' asked Amazigh.

Obeysekera nodded. He said nothing to that but turned towards the other two Venators and spoke into the squad vox-channel.

'Gunners, keep alert – that thing under the sand might still decide it wants to climb out and grab itself a snack. Make sure if it does that it gets a

mouthful of fire. The rest of you, get ready to move out. We had a sight of a
Valkyrie. We'll get as near as we can with the vehicles, then climb the rest
of the way. Do a quick vehicle test, then we move out and up.'

CHAPTER 14

They had come as far as the Venators could bring them.

'Keep in visual contact with each other,' said Obeysekera. 'Squad pattern aleph. Vox silence unless you see the general, his Valkyrie and its crew, or an enemy.'

'Any enemy expected, sir?' asked Gunsur.

'According to intel, no. But I won't have to remind you that it's precisely when intel tells you there's nothing to worry about that you've got most reason to be cautious. Watch for bluies. They shouldn't be able to get here, but they know we've lost a general, and they'll be searching for him too. Just depends on whether they want him more than we do.'

'And what could we want more than another general?'

'Thank you, Ensor,' Obeysekera said over the guffaws of the rest of the Kasrkin. 'General or not, it's our job to find him and bring him back, in one piece if we can, bagging up the bits if we can't.'

'What's the use of bringing in his body?' asked Uwais. 'It'll slow us down.'

'The lord militant either wants him alive, or proof that the bluies haven't got hold of him. No coming back with a finger. We'll need enough of the general to prove that the t'au don't have him wired and singing.'

As Uwais started another question, Obeysekera held up his hand. 'We'll leave the discussions as to how much and which bits of a man constitutes him to later. Now, we move out. Uwais, on point...'

The trooper grinned, stropping his warknife against his carapace armour.

'Amazigh is lead scout. Keep sharp. Let's go.'

The troops started up the mountain, tramping up the smooth slopes, with the Kamshet, unencumbered by weapons and with only a small skin of water, going lightly ahead.

The Kamshet led them up and into the mountain. As they climbed higher, sweating out the altitude but feeling a blessed coolness about them, Obeysekera slowly realised that the mountain was not a single peak but rather a series of peaks and plateaus, rolling upwards in waves. As he followed Amazigh, Obeysekera had the recurring sense that what he was climbing reminded him of something. Then, as they cleared the next ridge, only to see another rising beyond, he realised that the Tabaste was like the layered defences of a kasr, with bastions covering bastions in a rising sequence of emplacements.

Obeysekera stopped for a moment, pulled his cheche back and let the sweat on his forehead evaporate. Up here there was a breeze, as the air, heated on the uzayar around the Tabaste, rose up the flanks of the mountain. He looked back. That way lay the flats, lying like a lake around the Tabaste. He shook his head. Without air support, this was as close to a trap as he had ever let himself enter; an enemy planting an explosive charge on the causeway would effectively maroon them.

'Bit out of breath, captain?'

Obeysekera looked round and saw Malick watching him.

'Looking at the lie of the land, sergeant.'

Malick nodded. 'One way in, one way out.'

Obeysekera looked at Malick. 'I know my job, sergeant.'

'Of course you do. I wasn't suggesting anything else.'

'Good.' Obeysekera stared at Malick a moment longer, then turned back to looking where they were going. 'Still a long climb ahead of us.'

'At least it'll get cooler as we go higher.'

Obeysekera nodded, not looking at Malick. 'From furnace to fire.'

'What was that, sir?'

Obeysekera shook his head. 'Nothing. Just a memory.'

'A good one, I hope.'

'Just a memory. Who's on point?'

Malick checked his display. 'That's Ha, sir, though I don't rightly know where the Kamshet savage is.'

'Time to swap him over. Put Uwais on point again.'

As Malick called the orders through on the vox-channel, Obeysekera looked at him, waiting on him to finish. When the sergeant looked up in confirmation, Obeysekera said, 'Why do you call him "savage"?'

'It's what he is, sir. A savage.' Sergeant Malick regarded the captain with the bland gaze of a long-service squad leader. 'It is a mild term compared to what others call him.'

'Amazigh speaks Gothic. It would be best that he not hear the names you have for him.'

'Indeed he does. I have hardly heard him quiet.'

Obeysekera nodded. The Kamshet did not cleave to the stereotype of the laconic barbarian. 'His help is useful. I would not have it ended by careless words, from you or the men.'

'It won't be, sir.' Malick pointed. 'Shall I go ahead?'

'Yes, see if there is any sign.' Obeysekera looked back down the slope. 'I will wait for the commissar.'

Malick peered back too. 'You may have to wait some time, sir.'

The commissar was labouring upwards. Even from their distance, they could see the blood suffusing his cheeks and the sweat trails on his face. Sensing their regard, Roshant looked up. Seeing his expression, Obeysekera said to Malick, 'Go on, sergeant.'

As Malick started up the slope, his boots rasping on the smooth orange-red rock, Obeysekera stepped back to wait for Roshant.

'You... don't... have... to wait... for me.' The words came gasping over the private vox-channel.

'I differ on that, commissar,' said Obeysekera. He scanned the surroundings – it was as automatic as breathing – and sat down on a rock to wait. An oath, ten seconds later, told that he had forgotten how hot rocks became under the unrelenting sun of Dasht i-Kevar, even high up on the Tabaste.

Obeysekera stood to wait for the commissar. He tried to find some shade, but there was none to be had: millions of years had worn the Tabaste to smooth folds and humps, lying exposed under the press of the sun.

Roshant eventually came toiling up the slope, panting in the heat, and Obeysekera held out a hand to help him the final few steps. The commissar looked at the hand, then batted it away. He struggled up to Obeysekera and stood, swaying and sweating, in front of him.

'How much... further?'

Obeysekera shook his head. 'As far as finding the general – or the wreck of his Valkyrie.'

Roshant nodded. 'Very... well.'

'You could wait here.'

The commissar shook his head. 'I must... go on.'

'In a minute or two. I could use a breather too.'

Roshant looked at Obeysekera. 'You could?'

The captain unclipped his water flask and unscrewed the top. 'Yes.' He drank, at length but not deeply, letting the water wash his mouth and trickle down his throat.

'In that case...' The commissar unshipped his own water bottle and drank. Obeysekera watched over the lip of his own bottle to make sure Roshant drank enough. Those inexperienced in desert conditions would sometimes deny themselves immediately needed water for fear of not having enough later, only to collapse before the later arrived. But it appeared that Roshant had no difficulty not denying himself.

'Good.' Obeysekera resealed his flask and clipped it back onto his carapace armour. 'That's better. Are you ready to go on?'

After a moment's hesitation, Roshant said, 'Of course,' and put his own bottle away. But before they could begin up the mountain, the squad vox squeaked into life.

'I see it.' Obeysekera recognised Uwais' voice.

'How far?'

'Five hundred yards, elevation one hundred. Definite Valkyrie.'

'Hold there. Malick, confirm when you reach.'

'Will do.'

Obeysekera looked at Roshant. 'Looks like it's not much further.'

The commissar nodded. He squared himself, unhitched the latch over his bolt pistol. 'Let's go.'

They started up the mountain.

'Confirmed Valkyrie.' The sigil was Malick.

'Any sign of life?'

There was a pause. *'No.'*

'Run an auspex scan.'

'Already done it. It's all scrambled – just fuzz.'

Obeysekera's gaze refocused, under the impulse of years of training, to his auspex, but Malick was right: here, at the centre of the Sand Sea anomaly, there was only fuzz and random signals – he could not even read squad locations clearly.

'Approach but do not enter. Remain alert for bluies.'

'Yes, sir.'

Obeysekera saw, over the sergeant's direct channels, that he was sending Gunsur and Chame out on flanking approaches. Then a couple of words to Uwais told that Malick and he were taking the straight path towards the downed Valkyrie. The captain looked ahead, but a ridge blocked the view.

'Ensor, Ha, hold the flanks. Take sniping positions.'

The troopers acknowledged as Obeysekera hurried up the slope, the commissar labouring behind him. Reaching the crest, Obeysekera laid himself out flat and reached for his magnoculars.

Roshant joined him as he was adjusting the focus. 'See anything?'

'No. Damaged, but not catastrophic. Could be survivors.'

'Vox?'

As Obeysekera adjusted the vox to make a clear call to the downed Valkyrie, he saw Uwais, crouched low, hellgun couched under his shoulder, moving towards the aircraft along a smoothed-out gulley in the rock. The Valkyrie itself was half-hidden by the rock outcrop where it had come to rest. Malick was taking a parallel track but was further back. As Obeysekera watched, he saw the Valkyrie move.

The door-mounted heavy bolter began to track round.

'Uwais, get down!'

But the trooper did not respond.

'Uwais, down.'

Still there was no response from the trooper. From his position, the bolter's movement was all but invisible.

Obeysekera realised, with a muttered curse, that in trying to switch frequency to the clear channel he had lost contact with the squad. He pushed it back.

'Uwais...'

The bolter coughed. Uwais fell back.

'Hit, I'm hit.'

Hellguns flared, to the left and right, as Ensor and Ha, Gunsur and Chame returned fire.

'Hold fire, hold fire!'

But Obeysekera's order was lost under the sound of Uwais. He was keening. A high-pitched, tearing noise. Obeysekera had seen this before on the battlefield. A trooper, hit, immediate shock, then pain and panic overwhelming the shock reaction. Uwais must have taken shrapnel wounds; a direct hit from the heavy bolter would not have left enough of him to be crying out.

The hellguns flared, las-shots sputtering against the Valkyrie, pitting its armour, but the bolter began to track over towards Ensor and Gunsur.

Obeysekera overrode Uwais, cutting the keening from the squad vox-channel.

'Hold fire! Hold fire!'

The hellguns went dark. But through his magnoculars, Obeysekera could see the bolter continuing to track to target.

'Get down!'

The bolter coughed, spitting out bolt-shells, and the rock split and shattered, stone shrapnel flying. Through the squad vox, Obeysekera heard the cursing of troopers peppered by stone shards, but by their oaths, Ensor and Gunsur were being protected by their armour and helmets.

'Stay down. Hold fire.'

The bolter's chatter stopped. Silence returned to the silent mountain, but threading through the quiet there came the rattle-grind of the pintle, tracking the bolter towards fresh targets, and low moaning as Uwais tried to fix a field dressing over his wound.

'Ha, go to Uwais. Stay low.'

The trooper acknowledged and started to move, keeping low, using the cover, while Obeysekera struggled to switch his vox to clear.

'Here.'

Obeysekera looked round and saw Roshant lying next to him, proffering his vox-bead. Obeysekera bent his head to it.

'Valkyrie, hold fire, repeat, hold fire. Valkyrie *Eternal Flame*, respond. Hold fire. Hold fire. We are friendlies. Hold fire. Valkyrie *Eternal Flame*, please respond.'

'It's stopped tracking,' whispered Roshant.

'I say again – Valkyrie *Eternal Flame*, hold fire, hold fire. Friendlies. Calling *Eternal Flame*, respond.'

Then, over the clear channel, faint and crackling: *'Identify.'*

Obeysekera paused. The identification codes were changed every three days. General Itoyesa had gone missing before the current set of identification codes were set. The previous set... He scrabbled through his memory.

'The Emperor is merciful...'

Thin, but clearer, *'...but His justice precedes His wrath...'*

'...and His mercy is completed in victory...'

'...victory over death.'

The vox went silent a moment, then crackled into life.

'You took your frekking time.' There was a pause. *'I thought you were hostile.'*

Obeysekera checked Uwais' life signs. 'The man you shot should live.'

'That's a relief... Who the Throne are yo–?'

The final part of the question dropped away. Then the general spoke again.

'As you have come so far to find me, perhaps you could ask your guide not to kill me.'

Obeysekera looked round, then spoke urgently into the vox. 'Amazigh, do not kill the general. Repeat, Amazigh, do not kill the general.'

The vox crackled. *'Master. He tried to kill you.'*

'Amazigh, thank you for protecting me, but now, as your master, I am telling you not to shoot the general.'

The vox went silent. Obeysekera stared at it, willing the Kamshet to stop. There was no time to get any of his own men into the Valkyrie.

'He lives.'

PART II

Deep Green

CHAPTER 1

The Kinband moved up over the time-smoothed, red-rounded rock with the ease of meat mates. They ate together, they moved together, they thought together. They fought together. Shaper Tchek stretched his neck, feeling the vertebrae extend, and from behind the cover of the rock ridge, looked around. His eyes, the eyes of a kroot Shaper, were preternaturally sharp, able to absorb the contours of the land before him in a single look and then focus in on a single point while still retaining a general view of his surroundings.

The Kinband were spread out over the side of the mountain: there, Stalker Krasykyl, ascending that smooth face through the aid of the rock talons that he had communed from the pit apes of Canopus Minor. There, Tracker Cirict, beak down almost to the ground, tongue flicking, tasted the air and the scents it carried to senses he had honed from the warhounds of the Doge Loredano: the contract had cost Tchek the lives of three of the Kinband but the Harvest Feast it brought, when they had all shared the flesh of one of the Doge's prime warhounds, had been worth the price in blood. Tchek paused, sniffing, head turning, the movement combining the stop-motion of their avian ancestry with the canine warhound genes they had communed at the Feast.

As he turned his head, the wind hissed and feathers sighed. Tchek saw the colour flash of the pech'ra as it flared its wings. Cirict held out his arm. The bird landed, its talons fitting into the score marks that it had made through the years on Cirict's bracer. The Tracker and his pech'ra were not master and servant, nor nestlings but rather companions in the hunt, the bird providing eyes and seeing things that even the eyes of Cirict the Tracker did not see, enhanced though they were from the Feast. But the pech'ra, born of Pech itself, could see a mole rat from two miles and guide his Tracker to it. Now, it spoke to Cirict, turning its head and clacking its beak as it shared what it had seen. Cirict nodded and clicked back, preening the breast feathers of the bird then taking a stinkbug from the pouch on his belt and feeding it to the pech'ra. The bird must have payment for the knowledge it brought. Tchek, impatient for information in the past, had learned that no Tracker would speak until his pech'ra had had its reward. So Tchek waited, listening while Cirict crooned the name of his pech'ra, singing its praise in the time-honoured way of kroot Trackers.

'Far-eye, bright wing, sharp claw Flet.'

The pech'ra took the stinkbug as its due, ignoring Cirict as it ate. Although it was not something he would ever say to his Tracker, Tchek suspected that the pech'ra only had two categories of creature in its fierce little mind: those to eat and those to fear – and the latter category only comprised the spider-apes of Pech, who netted creatures flying through the jagga groves in their webs. Cirict, as a creature who provided food for the pech'ra, possibly managed to inhabit the category once held by Flet's parents, but Tchek suspected that if Cirict died the pech'ra would pluck the eyes from the Tracker's skull with no more sentiment than it ate the stinkbug he was feeding it.

Flet fed, the Tracker turned to the Shaper and spoke. The notes, to the ears of any listeners ignorant of the semantics of song, sounded like trills and runs and squeaks. To the kroot, it was more than language, but it served as language too.

'He is close. I can smell him.'

And it was true. Although Cirict had naturally consumed the greater part of the warhound's flesh and communed most deeply with the animal's spirit, all the surviving members of the Kinband had partaken too, that they might each have a small share in the gifts of the rest, and Tchek could taste something of what the Tracker sensed upon the wind.

It was the smell of man.

A rank smell, of turbid flesh and violent mind, with tangs of metal and chemical and underlying it all, the distinctive smell of tumour.

For humanity smelled like cancer.

Then Cirict whistled again, the notes trilling alarm. 'There are more. The smell is too strong for one.'

'How many?' Tchek whistled back, the harmonics telling Cirict the calmness of the questioner while also offering ritual thanks to the Huntress, Vawk, for bringing blessing before them.

'Shaper, I can taste them on the wind – there are many. Ten perhaps.'

'How far?'

The Tracker pointed. 'Beyond the next rise and the one after.'

The Shaper's crown quills rustled. The quills of the Kinband rattled in answer, subtle colours fluting through and up and down the quills, like light broken upon iridescent feathers.

'Keep Flet on the arm – I do not want the humans to suspect any living creature draws near.'

Tchek signalled and the kroot Kinband spread out, rifles ready, taking their positions. Shaper Tchek stepped aside as a rangy kroot moved up beside him, muscles cording beneath his skin. Slung upon his back was the standard kroot rifle, the wicked barb turned carefully away from its head, but in his hands he held a fighting staff, made of the light, hard, flexible wood of the jagga tree. The light glittered upon the cutting axe at its tip, and split upon the spear point at its base.

'Chaktak, stay with me.'

The Cut-skin's quills rattled in answer, splitting white light to red.

Shaper Tchek looked back. The last of the Kinband followed behind, as was his place: the Bearer, Kliptiq, carrying upon his back the pot from which the Kinband would feast following the hunt, the pot that told the tales of all their hunts, each one leaving its trace in their communal memory.

Kliptiq's rattle flashed his knowledge of the Shaper's regard. The Bearer lifted his rifle: although he carried the communal pot, he was not without a weapon, but Shaper Tchek had put before him meals of beasts of burden sufficient for him to both bear his load and not to cavil at being required to do so.

'Put it down,' said Tchek, pointing at the rifle. 'Before you shoot something you should not shoot.'

Kliptiq's quills drooped but he did as he was told: the Bearer, fed upon beasts of low intelligence, was only of use in battle to fire at something that was pointed out to him.

'Follow me,' said the Shaper. 'Do not fire at anything unless I tell you. Do you understand?'

Kliptiq's quills flared. This was something he could understand.

'To live is to hunt,' said Chaktak. 'For what does not hunt is prey. I am glad I am a Cut-skin. Not the Bearer.'

'We are all the Bearer,' said the Shaper. 'Until we have tasted all.'

'When the Chained shall be loosened,' said the Cut-skin.

'The Wind Lord return.'

'And the Free will fly to Him and leave this universe behind.'

As Shaper Tchek spoke the words, he felt his old, tearing, familiar flight yearning. Part of him wished to return to the air, but he knew well that without the right material the Feast would reduce him to the state of Cirict's pech'ra: a brain bright with fierce desire but stripped of everything else. The tremors and colour flashes upon the quill crests of the Cut-skin and the Bearer told the same for the other two kroot. The secret language of the kroot was sound and light, harmonics and spectrals, in which syntax and semantics were all but united: for the kroot, the meaning was the sound and the sound was the meaning.

The Creed spoken, Shaper Tchek whistled his instructions to the Kinband, using the ultrasonic frequencies that allowed the kroot to communicate over long distances without machines. Few other species in the galaxy could hear in that range, so the communication was doubly secure: ultrasonic and in a language indecipherable to any outsider. Not even the t'au knew the secret language of the kroot.

Tchek sent Stalker Krasykyl higher, instructing him to look for the humans from the heights. He told Tracker Cirict to continue towards where he smelled the humans, advancing with caution, with Long-sight Stryax flanking him. He would follow, with Cut-skin Chaktak flanking him and the Bearer, Kliptiq, at the rear.

It was the usual search-and-contact formation employed by the kroot; it should have enabled the Shaper to acquire the necessary intelligence about the humans before issuing instructions on whether to consume, to fight or to fly. It should have worked.

But the sun had sunk the space of only a single quill in the sky, still high and fierce, when the standard plan of approach moulted and the feathers came out.

The squad was in standard advance formation. A few words over the squad vox-channel had been enough: the 'kin knew what to do. Obeysekera had checked – visually, the auspex was still useless – that the men were in the right places and then signalled the advance. He was following, with the general and the commissar, behind a screen of the best troops in the Imperium. Chame was helping the injured Uwais, far enough behind the command group that they would not all be killed by any but the largest ordnance. Fifty yards further back, Gunsur was rearguard.

A few steps along the way back down the mountain to the waiting Venators, General Itoyesa signalled Obeysekera closer.

'Yes, general?' asked Obeysekera. They were close enough not to need the vox.

Itoyesa gestured to the screen of Kasrkin making their wide way down the Tabaste.

'Cautious.'

'Yes,' said Obeysekera. 'Having found you, general, I don't intend on losing you.'

Itoyesa shook his head. 'Too cautious. I must get back and this formation slows us down.' He pointed at Lerin, who had moved into the lee of a redstone outcrop to assess the way ahead. 'Look at her. She'll take three minutes checking everything is clear before voxing us to move up. We need to move faster.' He turned back to Obeysekera. 'Switch formation – we can march out of here.'

Obeysekera shook his head. 'Such a formation leaves too much chance of us walking into a trap.'

'A trap?' Itoyesa snorted. He swept his arm wide, taking in the whole expanse of redstone sloping down before them. 'There's nothing here. I've been stuck on this rock for three days and I haven't seen anything bigger than a sand fly. Unless you're worried about being ambushed by sand flies, we need to get moving.'

'I'm afraid I can't do that, general.'

Itoyesa snorted again. 'Do I have to remind you who is the ranking officer here, captain?'

'Do I have to tell you who is in operational command of this mission, general?'

Itoyesa stared at Obeysekera, then looked away, shaking his head. 'The men who will die because you took your time shall be on your conscience then, *Captain* Obeysekera.'

'The men who have died because of my decisions have always weighed upon my conscience, *General* Itoyesa.'

Itoyesa waved Obeysekera away. 'At least go and check on your advance line, try to speed them up.'

Obeysekera paused, looked towards Roshant, then nodded. 'Very well, general. I will see if we can move a bit more quickly. Commissar, stay with the general, please.'

Obeysekera caught the tail of Roshant's protesting expression but ignored it. He was already moving ahead, scuttling down the mountain towards the forward scouts, keeping low and breaking up movement by periods of stillness and watching. It was the standard movement pattern for traversing enemy territory.

Stopping in the partial shade of a dry gulch, Obeysekera scanned for movement, but saw nothing. His own wayfinders were still for the moment, fanned out to either side of the main party with Ensor on point. Backed into the shade, Obeysekera took a moment to appreciate the lifting of the sun's weight from his head and shoulders. The shaded stone felt cool against the back of his neck.

Obeysekera turned his head and looked down the gulley. It was in shadow, and going down it would shield them from the sight of any watchers. He took a bearing on its direction against his compass. It was only ten degrees from their direction of travel. But the wayfinders had passed it. Looking back, Obeysekera could see why. The gulley sloped upwards, dying away, and from the higher level it must appear as nothing more than a brief break in the redstone.

'Hold your positions.' Obeysekera voxed the scouts on the channel he had set apart for them, then started down the gulley. There was no point calling the scouts back if the gulley petered out within a few hundred yards.

It was blessedly cooler there. The floor of the gulley alternated between scoured-clear rock and deadfalls of accumulated stones, pebbles and larger rocks. Having scrambled past the first two deadfalls, Obeysekera stopped at the third.

The only thing he could think of that could sweep the sand and rock down the side of the Tabaste and into the gulley was rain. But he had heard no reports of rainfall within the Great Sand Sea from any of the Imperial forces on Dasht i-Kevar: so far as the soldiers of the Emperor were concerned, it never rained on the Sand Sea.

Standing in the lee of the deadfall, Obeysekera scraped away some of the sand at its base. Human skin is sensitive to tiny concentrations of dampness. Having scraped a pit into the sand, Obeysekera propped his gun against the wall of the gulley and pushed his fingers into the compact sand, feeling, feeling. If there was water there, hidden under the surface, it could be important, both for him and for future expeditions.

The sand scraped at his skin as he wormed it deeper. Was that it?

Yes. He could feel the sand change. He reached a little deeper, grasping, and pulled a handful out, raising it to his face. It was dark, darker than the other sand, and he sniffed the water on it, feeling the sublimation of the water molecules as the fierce heat pulled them out of the suddenly exposed sand.

Water. He smiled and looked up, over the deadfall, further along the gulley. Movement.

Movement.

Tchek threw himself towards the deadfall in the gulley while pulling the long barrel of his rifle round to bear on the human. As he juddered into the ground, he loosed off rounds, the slugs splintering off the rocks around the human, the kick of the recoil nearly jerking the rifle from his hands.

'Contact, contact!' Obeysekera spun behind a rock as the rounds chipped the redstone around and in front of him, rock splinters flying into bare skin and bouncing off his carapace armour.

'Enemy, enemy!' Tchek whistled, the frequency high above the low thud of his rifle as he pushed up above his sheltering rock and loosed more rounds to keep the human down. As he lay behind the deadfall, reloading his rifle, Tchek thought again how right his old kill-broker had been. No plan ever did survive contact with the enemy. He had intended to watch the humans from a distance until he had determined which of them was his target, then plan an ambush to kill the others, consume any who had been particularly worthy foes, before returning with the human the t'au wanted. Now, he was scrunched behind a deadfall that was slightly too small to cover all of him while the human did the same to him that he was trying to do to it: keep him pinned down while the rest of its squad arrived.

Hunched in behind a deadfall that was too small to cover all of his body, Obeysekera cursed while calling his men back to flanking positions and at the same time shooting, almost blind, over the top of the rock to try to keep the xenos down.

'Malick, Roshant, Amazigh, get the general down to the Venators.'

As the hotshots sizzled against the rock, Tchek suddenly considered whether the human firing at him was the one he sought. It was unlikely. He was valuable to the humans too. They would be trying to get the general down the mountain while maintaining a screen to delay pursuit.

'Krasykyl, Cirict, wide flank down the mountain. The humans will be trying to get their general to safety. Cirict, fly Flet.'

There would be a few more seconds before the xenos could call further rifles in upon him – any flanking shots would find his body behind its inadequate cover, and at these short ranges even carapace armour would not stop the rounds.

'Gunsur, Ensor, Lerin, cover fire, I need to move.'

In response, hellgun fire came sizzling through above him, well above, for the men were still too far back to get direct line of sight on him, but their concentration would make the approaching xenos stay low.

The human was calling in suppressing fire, trying to keep him pinned down. If he was the human commander he would be trying to roll out and get away, down the mountain, keeping a screen to protect the general. Time to get clear.

Time to roll clear.

Shaper Tchek crouched behind the deadfall, pushing himself down, compressing the muscles in his legs, folding both leg joints, tightening.

Captain Obeysekera crouched behind the deadfall, holding the hellgun round the redstone and shooting off more rounds blind as he got his balance.

Shaper Tchek released his sprung muscles, jumping into the mouth of the defile.

Captain Obeysekera pushed off, scrambling back up the gulley.

Cut-skin Chaktak was running up. Tchek stopped him, hauling the Cut-skin back when he tried to push past him, the fight blood rising.

'Round, cut them off,' said Tchek. 'They are trying to get down the mountain. Stop them.'

Chaktak, his staff in his hands, his eyes livid with fighting blood, shivered, quills rattling. He could smell the Feast that would follow battle, taste the worlds that waited. The Hunger was upon him. It was upon them all. But Tchek was Shaper because he could still think and plan when the Hunger rose, and the Kinband would listen.

'That way.' He pointed, left, towards a downward-folding defile. 'Listen for Cirict and Krasykyl – they are moving round to cut off the humans.'

Chaktak raised his quills in answer, the light splitting upon them, and bounded off in the direction Tchek pointed, whistling his position to the rest of the Kinband.

Tchek whistled for Long-sight Stryax. 'Pick the humans off. But for your soul do not touch the general.'

The Long-sight, hidden in the rock folds, whistled his reply, and began to hunt, the Hunger building within him as it was in the others. They must feed soon or the Kinband would turn upon itself.

The Shaper turned back to the Bearer, Kliptiq, the last to answer his summons.

'You come with me,' he said.

The Bearer held up his rifle: its barrel was cut shorter than those carried by the rest of the Kinband. 'Shoot?'

'Soon,' said Tchek. 'When I say. Follow.'

The Shaper, with the Bearer following, started down after the human, moving at an angle to its descent. It would not be long before they caught up with the human rearguard. The plan was to engage it while the other Kinbandlings killed the humans escorting the general. Then they would feast, and assuage the Hunger, before bringing the general to those who wanted him.

Tchek's quills rattled. No plan survived contact with the enemy, but a good general adapted.

Obeysekera scramble-rolled down the slope, tumbling to a stop up against the redstone and pulled himself round, hellgun pointed up the mountain, as he scanned for the xenos.

Silence.

He looked, listened, put his senses and experience into the red-rock world, while checking his auspex. It was scrambled, putting up ghost notes and noise, even his own squad flicking in and out and transposing positions. A distraction. Obeysekera keyed it off, the display disappearing from before his eyes.

Better. Eyes and ears, wit and craft against these xenos.

Kroot. The label came up from his hypnocache. T'au allies and mercenaries. Low technology in comparison to their masters. That was why the t'au had sent them in after the general. Neither the anomaly nor the desert would disable their simple weapons; they did not rely on complex equipment to track and find their quarry, only sight and sound and smell.

Obeysekera grinned, baring his teeth. It was going to be a good fight.

'Gunsur, Ensor, Lerin, hold your positions. I am pulling back past you.'

As the troopers acknowledged, Obeysekera started making his way further down the slope, working his way from one piece of cover to another.

'Report contacts.'

The xenos had disappeared. Obeysekera saw Gunsur, tucked in behind an outcrop, peering through the sights of his hellgun as he scanned the higher ground. Looking past him, Obeysekera saw Ensor and Lerin in covering positions.

Where had the enemy gone? More to the point, why were the xenos here?

Lying on the sun-warmed rock, Obeysekera realised that he was facing a snatch team, sent by the t'au to find and capture General Itoyesa. He had sent the general on down the mountain with Malick, Roshant and Amazigh to get him to safety, thinking this was a simple enemy contact. If the kroot were after the general, they might bypass him and go after Itoyesa. Still, so long as Malick and Roshant got the general down to the Venators, the twin-linked multi-lasers and lascannons mounted on the vehicles should be enough to drive back any attack these xenos could launch with only light weaponry.

'Uwais? Location?'

The answer came back after a pause, voice strained and taut over the vox.

'Can't keep going, sir.'

'Who's with you?'

'It's Chame, sir. I can carry him.'

'No, sir. There are enemy. I-I will hold them.'

'Where are you?'

'Cave mouth, sir,' answered Chame as Uwais coughed, the liquid cough of a man whose lungs were filling with blood. *'About a hundred yards below you.'*

'Malick, Roshant, where are you?'

'Fifty yards past Uwais,' Malick answered. *'Heading down.'*

'Watch for ambush. I think the xenos are trying to flank us.'

'Will do. Could do with another gun, sir. There's only me and Roshant with the general.'

'Where's Amazigh?'

'No idea.'

'Throne! Continue down the mountain. Get the general to the Venators, wait for us there.'

'Yes, sir.'

Obeysekera scanned the mountainside, but there was no sign of the Kamshet. With no vox, he could not speak to him. There was nothing he could do.

'Fall back pattern beta.'

Ensor, Gunsur and Lerin acknowledged, with Lerin starting back down the mountain under the cover of Ensor and Gunsur.

'Keep contact. I will go ahead.'

Obeysekera started down the slide, moving from rock to shade, stopping at each waypoint to observe and listen. Above him, on the mountainside, he could see Gunsur, Ensor and Lerin covering each other's retreat. But there was no sign, nor sound, of the xenos.

Where were they?

Where were they?

Tchek stopped, his frame hidden by the gulley he was using to cover his descent, and listened. Behind him, Kliptiq waited, eyes vacant, the empty pot upon his back waiting to be filled.

The Shaper could hear no movements. He turned his head, smelling, but he did not have a sense as refined as Cirict the Tracker. He could smell the humans – the scent was all but overpowering – but he could not separate it out or locate its different components. It was too strong. But scents that strong meant the humans were close, even if he could not see them.

They were skilled, these humans, not like most he had encountered in the past. Those had advanced in solid lines, marching stolidly to their deaths, and retreated the same way. It was no difficult task to pick one out among such multitudes and take him for the pot. But these humans were different. They moved with the near silence of his own Kinband. After the barrage of their first contact, the humans had withdrawn as quickly and efficiently as the kroot had followed, but they had so far avoided further fighting.

Tchek risked lifting his head up out of the gulley, looking for any sign of them, but conscious that the quills that identified his rank also stood in stark, jagged, coloured contrast to the surrounding redstone, making it easy for any watching eyes to see him.

Nothing. Just the folds and rills and humps of redstone, tending downwards towards the great plain that surrounded the Tabaste. There were many places to hide, and more ways to get down the mountain than he had anticipated. It would be easy to miss their target, moving quietly down through gullies and declines, safe from all but the most direct sight.

Tchek whistle-called the Long-sight, the Stalker and the Tracker.

'Have you sight of the target?'

His whistle-call disappeared into the still air, but there was no reply. Down in the gulley, the redstone was channelling the sound along its length. For his call to reach left and right, he had to climb out into the open again.

Tchek pushed his foot talons into the rock and began to lever himself up the few feet necessary to take his head above the lip of the gulley. But as he reached its edge, he heard a sudden explosion of rifle fire and the answering sizzle-crack of the enemy's weapons. Following the sound, he looked and saw, a few hundred yards away, the rock-smoke of fierce fighting.

They had found the humans.

CHAPTER 2

'We're pinned down.'

As Sergeant Malick spoke urgently into his vox-bead, another round from a kroot rifle glanced off the redstone above his head, striking sparks and fragments that bounced off his helmet. He was crouching with his back against a boulder, with General Itoyesa beside him and Commissar Roshant on the other side of the general.

'Where are they?' said the general, pushing himself up to peer over the redstone.

A further rifle round chipped splinters from the boulder as Sergeant Malick hauled the general back down.

'Unhand me,' said General Itoyesa, striking Malick's hand away from his tunic. The general was dressed in the field uniform of a commanding officer of the Astra Militarum, with the stylings of his own Tekan Janissaries. Lighter than usual on the braid and gold epaulettes, but still gaudy in comparison to the tan and brown of Malick's uniform.

Malick held up his hand. 'Just trying to keep you alive. Sir.'

General Itoyesa smoothed the crease made by Malick's grab from his jacket. 'I have survived worse than...' – a kroot rifle round skimmed the top of the redstone, just above the general's head – '...than this, sergeant, and I fully intend to survive this too.'

'Maybe get just a little lower then, general,' said Malick, twisting round and firing off a suppressing burst from his hellgun. 'They're trying to get above us.'

'Why don't you do something, commissar?' said the general, turning to Roshant. 'Your bolt pistol is hot, but I have not seen your shells hit the enemy.'

Roshant, his face pale, gave the general a look that was part grin, part grimace. 'When my bolts hit an enemy, there is not much left of it for you to see, general.' He turned and fired off another shell in the direction of the last series of shots.

The commissar spun back under cover before a volley of kroot rifle rounds – the bullets might be little more than crude balls of metal, thought Malick, but a crude ball of metal fired sufficiently fast and at close enough range could still sear through even the best carapace armour – struck the redstone above Roshant's head.

'Captain, we are under attack,' Roshant said into his vox. 'We need assistance.'

But the anomaly that rendered auspexes unreliable in the Sand Sea was stronger here than anywhere else on the Tabaste; all they could hear in answer were squawks and stutters, words cut off and cut through.

'Captain!' Roshant repeated, nearly shouting now.

'They don't work better if you shout in them, son,' said General Itoyesa, touching Roshant's hand with his own. The commissar jerked, then nodded dumbly as another volley of kroot rifle rounds ricocheted off the top and side of the boulder.

Malick pointed to the stone shards. 'They are working round to flank us, general.'

'I know.' General Itoyesa smiled, his teeth white in his face. 'As the word "retreat" is not in the tactical vocabulary of the Guard, I suggest that we advance backwards instead.' The general pointed down the slope about fifty yards. 'See that deep shadow under the rock outcrop? I think it is a cave entrance. Get in there and we can hold it against these xenos scum.'

'We will also be trapped in there, general,' said Malick. 'If they have any grenades, we will be in trouble.'

General Itoyesa looked at Malick. 'I am not accustomed to sergeants questioning my decision, sergeant.' Then the general smiled again. 'But then again, maybe this is the Kasrkin way of which I have heard so much. If the xenos had explosives, they would have used them by now.'

Almost by way of answer, another burst of rifle fire scored the redstone, the angle indicating that the xenos were getting closer to successfully flanking their position and opening them up to attack.

'We can't stay here,' said Roshant. He held his hand to his face and it came away red. 'I've been hit.' He was staring at the blood on his fingertips with something approaching disbelief.

'A rock splinter,' said the general. 'A scratch. Your father will be proud to hear of your courage.'

Roshant looked at the general. 'He will?'

'It does depend upon someone getting back to tell him,' said General Itoyesa. 'And for that I am going to need a volunteer to make the run for the cave.'

'I-I am not scared.'

'No?' Itoyesa's voice grew suddenly soft. 'Well, I am. So let's get out of here until some help arrives.' He pointed at the cave entrance. 'One at a time. Covering fire from the other two.' He looked at Roshant. 'As you volunteered, you first, commissar.'

Roshant stared at the general, his face blank, as if he did not understand what Itoyesa was saying. Itoyesa put his hand on Roshant's shoulder and his face close to the young commissar, looking him directly in the eye.

'You are your father's son.'

'Besides, going first is safest,' said Malick. 'They won't be expecting the move.'

'Get ready,' said Itoyesa. He shifted his bolt pistol to his left hand, drew his power sword from its scabbard, the blade humming quietly as it emerged into the light, as if excited at the prospect of drinking new blood.

'Ready?' asked General Itoyesa.

Roshant took a deep breath. 'Ready,' he said.

'Sergeant?'

'Ready, sir.'

'Then let us give them a taste of hell. On my count. Four, three, two, one.'

As the count reached its end, General Itoyesa and Sergeant Malick swung round to either side of their concealing boulder and started spraying rounds, quick bursts of semi-automatic fire, targeting any obvious gaps and mounds that might conceal the enemy. At the same moment, Roshant sprang to his feet and sprinted down the redstone slope towards the dark shadow of the cavern mouth, the hiss-snap of Malick's hellgun forming a harmonic to the low cough of the general's bolt pistol, all overlaid with the noise of las-round and bolt-shell hitting and shattering the redstone.

Malick, keeping one eye on his power pack, pulled back under the cover of the redstone as General Itoyesa did the same. In answer, there came a volley of kroot rifle rounds, smacking into the rock and covering them with splinters.

Malick pointed down towards the cavern. 'He made it.'

'Try your vox again,' said General Itoyesa.

Sergeant Malick fiddled with its settings, trying to get something beyond static and jumbled words. 'Still nothing,' said Malick.

'Then I think I shall have to go next,' said General Itoyesa. He began to crouch down.

'W-wait!' Malick held his hand up. 'I've got something.'

Through his vox, faint but distinct, the captain's voice.

'...are you? Say again, where are you?'

'You hear the shooting, sir?'

'I hear it.'

'That's where we are.'

'Very well. Stay under cover. We will come to relieve you.'

Another fusillade of shots hissed past them, the bullets expending their energy on sand and redstone.

'It's pretty hot here, sir. We're going to have to move.'

'That's a no,' said Captain Obeysekera. *'Stay where you are. We will find you.'*

General Itoyesa leaned over and spoke into Malick's vox-bead. 'I am a general, Captain Obeysekera. You will find I outrank you. We will retreat into a more defensible position.'

'General, I must...'

'Look for us in a cave, captain.' General Itoyesa looked back at Malick. 'Ready?'

'Yes, sir.'

'Then let's go.'

As the general started running down the slope towards the cave entrance, Sergeant Malick and Commissar Roshant began firing, hosing the immediate area down with bolt-shells and las-rounds, trying to keep the heads of the xenos down lest they lose their own.

But there were only two weapons – Itoyesa was too busy running to fire as well – and kroot rifle fire began again from other areas than those they could see, the rounds bursting against the redstone. Glancing back, Malick saw the general running on regardless even as incoming fire curdled the rock beneath his feet. Sergeant Malick squeezed off another burst of las-rounds, in the process draining one of the power packs for his hellgun, then swung back into the blessed shadow of the rock, panting hard. From the rock's shelter, he saw General Itoyesa dive into the darkness of the cave.

Just him left, then.

But the kroot would know where he was going. Malick, with all his experience of battle, looked over the course he would have to run, judging where he was most open and therefore most vulnerable, looking for scraps of cover at those points.

The vox wheezed back on. It was Roshant; his voice was breaking up again, but enough came through for Malick to know that they were ready for him to make his move. He was about to go when he saw something. It was moving in from his left, a shape tracking through the stark shadows of the rocks.

The xenos were moving to cut him off.

Malick started up, running, hellgun held at his hip and firing in the rough direction of where he had seen the xenos, hoping to keep it pinned down. As he ran, Roshant and the general opened up with everything they had, spraying rounds above and around him. From the whistle crack of supercharged air, some of the shots were not missing him by much.

Malick kept going, boots pounding over redstone, splitting his gaze between watching his footing and watching where that xenos was coming from, sliding along one of the rock gullies that criss-crossed the slope.

Then it jumped up in front of him: taller than a man, face a hybrid of the avian and the human, crowned with a rattle of quills that were flashing through the colour spectrum and on to colours he had never even seen. It was swinging a great staff with an axe blade at one end and a spike at the other, and it ran towards him over the cracked slope, jumping each gulley with the hopping motion of a carrion bird rather than the gait of a man.

It was running at him, its face a hideous devolution of the simian, featherless like a newborn chick, and raising its weapon as it saw him, its mouth opening in a shout and challenge, while Chaktak, the Cut-skin, swerved, turning off either leg so that he might present a moving target to the humans sheltering in the cave's mouth.

Malick, running as rifle rounds chipped into the redstone at his feet, pulled round his hellgun and tried to fire on the move, squeezing the trigger, but the las-rounds pulled left, hissing into the stone behind the xenos.

Chaktak jagged left, reversing his fighting staff to reach its maximum reach, ready to step in close and swing it round in a descending figure of eight: the axe would take the human at the point on his shoulder where helmet met chestplate, the point where there was nothing to protect against weapons from the front, swinging down into where neck met shoulder. He would cut the human across the diagonal.

Running with rifle rounds chewing at his heels and the covering fire from General Itoyesa and Commissar Roshant hissing past his head, Malick saw the xenos swing its long battle axe up into the start of a killing arc. It leapt forward, bounding over the rock like a big bird as Malick pulled his hell-gun round to target it.

But before he could bring his weapon to bear on the xenos he felt a blow on his shoulder, heavy as a hammer, and he fell forwards, turning as he did so, hellgun beginning to fall from suddenly nerveless fingers. He had taken a round from his own side, leaving him exposed to the axe-strike of the xenos. And as he fell, Malick looked at the xenos closing on him and all that went through his mind was the thought, *I am going to be killed by a frekking bird*, and the incongruity was worse than the death that strutted towards him.

The Cut-skin could smell the prey as well as see it; it filled his whole vision, moving with all the uncertainty of prey when it belatedly realises that though it had thought itself the master of the universe, here, in this place and this time, it was the prey. Chaktak stepped closer, his blade hungry, singing for blood in the ancient life-tongue of the kroot, remembered and sung at all their Feasts. But as Chaktak lifted his axe to bring it swinging downwards, he felt something grasp his ankle, something cold in this world of heat, and jerk him back towards the rill that he had just jumped across.

Malick, grounded, his shoulder throbbing with pain but also with unex-pected life, resumed crawling for the cave entrance, trying to look backwards to see what that creature was doing while also inching towards the general and Roshant. The two men were at the entrance of the cave, urging him on while keeping up a barrage of suppressing fire to make the xenos stay low.

'Keep going.'

The vox was working now.

'Shoot the frekking fowl,' Malick said, crawling slowly, for the pain in his shoulder was stopping him using his right arm at all: his hellgun he was just dragging along beside him by its strap, the paluwood of its stock rub-bing ochre up against the redstone. As he crawled, he expected a strike from the creature, but nothing came.

Where had it gone?

More bolts hissed past his head, striking redstone but not the xenos. Malick heard the captain's voice, coming through tinny and high-pitched above the roar of the bolt pistols, breaking between the static that was feeding back through the vox-channels.

'General, commissar, can you hear me?'

Malick could hear it from his own vox and from up ahead: he must be getting close to the cave entrance.

'Bit busy here, captain,' he heard the general answer.

'Two minutes away,' said Obeysekera.

'Make it one,' said General Itoyesa.

A fresh volley of kroot rifle fire spattered into the redstone around Malick and then, suddenly, there was silence from behind him. Only the flash and percussive roar of the bolt pistols firing from the cave mouth, and those too died away as Malick crawled the final yards into the cave.

'Made it,' said Malick. 'Safe.'

'Not so sure about that,' said General Itoyesa, pulling the sergeant to his feet and into the dark of the cave. He pointed deeper inside. Eyes stunned by the bright light of Dasht i-Kevar, all Malick could see at first was darkness. But then, as he acclimatised to the gloom, he began to see details: the roof and walls of the cave, smooth as glass, angling downwards. And there, at the vanishing point of the tunnel, the faintest hint of livid green light.

Chaktak, pulled like a bird on the line, tumbled into the rill, turning head over heels as he fell. But he still held his hunting staff and as the images of his fall spun past him, confused in their speed, he maintained his hold on it, ready to strike out when the falling stopped. Landing on his back, Chaktak went to spring up, but his ankle was pulled from under him and he sprawled again even as he swung out with his staff. It struck, the axe connecting with something hard.

The smell. Only now did he notice the smell.

He was being dragged along the floor of the rill like a sack, the redstone rubbing against his back. Chaktak looked down along the length of his body for what was pulling him, while he tried to find purchase on the smooth rock with his hands to grab something and stop himself.

It had its back to him. In the deep shade of the rill, it was hard to see more than a shape – that smell – but it was dragging him along as if he were a nestling. Chaktak scrabbled against the redstone, but he could not stop his progress. Where was the creature taking him?

He saw, ahead, a deeper darkness at the end of the rill, as if the channel led into a tunnel. That was where it was dragging him. Chaktak seized his hunting staff and brought the axe head down upon the shoulder of the creature.

It bounced.

The creature did not even look round. And they were nearly at the tunnel entrance. Something that Chaktak had never truly known before rose up his throat: fear, choking and enveloping as gas.

The Cut-skin realised that he was going to have to call for help. But before he could utter the whistle call of alarm that would bring the rest of the Kinband to his aid, the creature dragging him stopped. It turned towards him.

For a moment, Chaktak thought it was human. But then he saw the blood weeping through the empty space where the eyes had been, and he realised that the thing was wearing a human face as a mask – a mask that from the blood seeping down over the skin had only just been cut from its owner.

Chaktak would have called out then, called as loud as he might, not to save himself but to save the others, but he could not, for fingers that were colder than the space between the stars, wielding a knife that could slice electrons from atoms, reached round his throat and sealed his cry there, while another hand slowly held a knife up before his face.

CHAPTER 3

Shaper Tchek crouched down beside the Long-sight, Stryax. From their position, in a large hollow under a wind-carved rock, Stryax could see the entrance to the cave and the slope down to it.

'Kill any human that tries to get to the cave,' he instructed the Long-sight, 'but do not shoot any human that comes out from the cave – one of them is the human we want.'

Stryax said nothing, but the nictitating membrane that slid across kroot eyes to protect them from wind and storm flicked back and forth in answer and his quills rattled gently in response.

Tchek had Krasykyl the Stalker covering the far side of the slope down to the cave mouth, while Cirict and Kliptiq waited further back, in the deeper shade under the rock.

The Shaper looked around. 'Where is Chaktak?' When silence greeted his question, Tchek moved beside Stryax and whistle-called for his Cut-skin, the sound high beyond the range of human hearing.

There came no answer.

Tchek called again, the string of high-frequency notes resonating from his quill crown. But still there was no reply.

The Shaper looked towards the Seeker. 'Where is he, Cirict? Where do you smell him?'

The Seeker, the smallest and slightest of the kroot, crawled forward to the edge of the bowl, head turning as he sought scents on the still air.

Cirict turned to Tchek. 'His smell is... strange. It comes from more than one direction, as if he is in many places. I will send Flet higher, that he might see.' The Tracker turned his head up and whistled, calling the pech'ra further towards the zenith, and from below they saw the flash of its wings as it ascended.

As Obeysekera, Gunsur, Ensor and Lerin worked their way down the mountain, advancing through rills and gullies, stopping and covering while one man moved then proceeding down in sequence, Obeysekera tried to raise Uwais and Chame on the vox. There was no answer from either of them. But Uwais and Chame were not the only ones missing.

'Anyone seen Amazigh?' Obeysekera asked.

The answers came back over the vox, all negative, and Obeysekera shook his head. The Kamshet was not his problem, and he could not spare the time to search for him on a chaotic battlefield where it was impossible to tell the position of the enemy or even his own men. Besides, the mountain was tabu to Amazigh and his people; perhaps he had disappeared to perform some rite to appease the mountain spirit.

Looking round from where he was covering Ensor, Obeysekera could see the outcrops and slopes, the cross-cutting rills and gullies, their edges all worn smooth, and he felt a shiver on the back of his neck. If ever he had seen a mountain that might have a presiding spirit, as machines had, then this was the mountain.

With Ensor safely under cover and surveying the surrounds through the sights of his hellgun, Obeysekera waved Gunsur past. That left him covering the rear of their descent. He watched Gunsur low-run down the slope, using outcrops and his body shape to stop himself presenting a clear target to any enemy.

The information Obeysekera had extracted from a deeply buried hypno-cache told him that the kroot were adept at hand-to-hand combat, being stronger and faster than all but peak humans, but were also good at using long-range sniping rifles from concealed positions, almost always set high. There were no trees on the Tabaste, but there were many redstone outcrops that a kroot sniper might use. Obeysekera, rearguard, turned for a final check before going past Ensor but stopped, mid-turn.

Amazigh was there, finger held to his lips despite them being covered by his cheche. Dangling from his other hand were two ident tags.

'Where did you get those?' Obeysekera asked, and he slowly began to bring his hellgun round to bear on the Kamshet.

Amazigh shook his head, and whispered past his still-raised finger, 'No, no, no, master, I didn't kill them.'

Keeping his hellgun trained on the Kamshet, Obeysekera said, 'How did you get those ident tags, then?'

'Master, I know why the Tabaste is tabu – there is something terrible here. When the alien birds attacked, I set off to hunt them, to keep you alive. But as I tracked those xenos birds, I smelled something else. Flesh, raw flesh. But it was moving. So I went after it.' Amazigh hung his head. 'I was too late, master. It got to your troopers first.' The Kamshet held up the tags. 'Uwais and Chame.'

'What was it?'

'I do not know, master. I have seen nothing like it on Dasht i-Kevar.'

'What did it look like?'

'Knives. It looked like knives, master.'

'Did you see where it went?'

'Into the cave. There are tunnels.'

Obeysekera reached for his vox, but Amazigh held up his hand for another word.

'There is more than one of them, master.'

'Very well.' Obeysekera keyed the squad vox-channel. 'Uwais and Chame are dead. Looks like what got them came up from tunnels. Not kroot, repeat, not kroot.'

Throne, this mission was going bad. For a moment, a memory of the Sando retreat came back to him, and the disaster that had turned into. He had been determined never to let that happen again – but it already had. Four men gone. They had to get to the general quickly.

'Gunsur, Ensor, Lerin, stay out of cave entrances.' Obeysekera keyed the private channel to Malick. 'Sergeant, get out of the tunnel.'

But as he spoke, Obeysekera heard, from further down the mountain, the percussive clap of kroot rifle rounds. And through the vox, over the thrum of his hellgun, Malick was saying, *'We can't go anywhere right now, captain.'*

'Hold on and watch your backs. We're coming.' Obeysekera signalled to the three troops with him. Attack formation. Ensor at the tip, Lerin and Gunsur flanking. He would be the gun in the pocket between them all, the eye at the centre of the arrow.

Obeysekera looked at the slope. The rifle fire was coming from beyond the next ridge of redstone. If he were commanding the enemy, he would have a picket sited to pick off anyone coming over the ridge. But these were xenos: there was no telling what they would do. And time was of the essence. They had to get to the general before whatever was coming up the tunnels attacked from behind while they were trying to fend off the frontal xenos assault.

Captain Obeysekera keyed the squad vox.

'Charge!'

And the four Kasrkin, hellguns held ready, began to run down the redstone slope towards the enemy with the Kamshet running among them, his robes billowing like the wings of a great white bird.

CHAPTER 4

'They're trying to keep us pinned down.'

Sergeant Malick ducked back into the cave as kroot rifle rounds struck splinters of redstone from the tunnel entrance.

General Itoyesa nodded. 'They are succeeding.'

'Where is the captain?' said Roshant. 'We can't get out without him.' The commissar had wedged himself in behind an extrusion of rock that provided some cover deeper into the cave.

'We may have to try,' said General Itoyesa. He gestured down into the depths of the mountain. 'What is down there is worse than what is outside.'

'It would be suicide going out,' said Malick.

'I fear it will be worse if we stay,' said the general. He pushed forward towards the cave entrance despite Sergeant Malick's hand on his shoulder, and peered out into the bitter light of Dasht i-Kevar. Rifle rounds splashed on redstone, but General Itoyesa did not flinch.

'General, please, get back,' said Roshant. 'You are why we are here.'

Itoyesa pulled back, but he pointed out of the cave. 'I am why they are here.' He looked at Malick and Roshant. 'I have heard nothing from Captain Obeysekera since we took shelter. I do not know if he or his men are dead. We cannot retreat. Therefore, I must make a decision.'

General Itoyesa paused, his hand upon his mouth as he thought.

'Very well.' He looked at Malick and Roshant. 'The captain has ten minutes. If he does not arrive in that time, I will go out and surrender.'

Roshant stared at General Itoyesa. 'What? You cannot do that.'

The general turned to the commissar, smiling. 'You forget who is the general here.'

Roshant shook his head like a smacked dog, but he would not let go of this bone. 'I-I am a commissar of the Officio Prefectus. I cannot allow you to fall into the hands of the enemy.'

Itoyesa grinned. 'What are you going to do? Shoot me?'

Roshant turned his bolt pistol upon General Itoyesa. 'If I have to, general.'

Itoyesa stared at Roshant, then grinned more widely. 'You are not a man to shoot someone in the back, commissar. And that, although they have told you differently in the Officio Prefectus, is a good thing.'

Roshant swallowed, his bolt pistol wavering. 'Why would you do this?'

But before he could finish his question, the general knocked the barrel of

Roshant's bolt pistol aside with one hand and pulled it from the commissar's grasp with the other, rotating it in one smooth movement so that he held it pointing between Roshant's eyes. Roshant gaped. The sound of his shock had yet to emerge from his mouth when Malick shoved his hellgun into Itoyesa's back.

'That might work with the commissar, but it won't work with me, general,' said Malick.

Itoyesa turned his head to look at Malick. 'I know it won't, sergeant.' He put the bolt pistol up, reversed it and handed it back to Roshant.

'I would not be surrendering, commissar, I would be giving us all the only chance we have. It is a long way out of the desert. There will be many opportunities for me to escape and for you to catch up and rescue me. That is the proper way for the Imperial Guard. Attack, attack, attack.' General Itoyesa drew his chrono. 'Still a few minutes before I go out.'

But as he spoke, Malick looked at the cave entrance, then started towards it, creeping low.

'You won't need to. The captain's here.' The sergeant pointed. From outside they could hear the unmistakeable thrumming hiss of hellguns, interspersed with the crack of kroot rifles.

CHAPTER 5

Far, far below the mountain, deep, deep under the flowsand plain that surrounded the Tabaste, the lord Nebusemekh stood in front of a table. The table was large, although it seemed insignificant in the high, broad throne chamber in which it stood, and its sides were raised.

The table was filled with sand.

Nebusemekh sat down and sighed. He definitely sighed. He felt the air, drawn from his lungs, passing through his mouth. He felt it against his skin. He knew it was so.

The mound of sand was slowly settling, flowing down into the flat plain of yellow.

Nebusemekh sighed again. He had really thought that this time the orrery would endure. For a moment, when he had released the stasis field, he had seen it, perfect in every detail: an orrery as vast as the sky he had not seen for so long, with the eighteen planets and their attendant moons of this system, and its sun, with its white dwarf companion, all moving in the long, elaborate dance of the spheres set against the slow movement of the further stars and the galactic core. But then the first grains of sand had started to slip, and the planets and stars fell from the heavens and became simply mounds of sand on the table.

Nebusemekh shook his head, reminding himself to relish the tautening and release of the muscles that made the movement possible. The body was a marvel and one that he appreciated more fully than the other noble ones, with their talk of ascension. He, for one, would remain what he was.

Sighing, feeling the breath tickle his tongue, Nebusemekh began to sift the sand on the table, moving the grains he wanted to work with closer and pushing the others further away. Streams of sand wriggled over the huge tabletop, moving like things alive, as the necron lord sorted through his material. He was working on a twin hypothesis: that there was a critical molecular mass that triggered sand collapse, and that there was an ideal diameter for stable shape retention. He was testing the theories by gathering precisely one more grain of sand for each new iteration of the orrery, while simultaneously working through the range of possible diameters of sand particles. It was an absorbing experiment, one that had occupied him for a long time.

It was a straightforward matter for him to count each grain of sand and measure its diameter. As he did so, other parts of his mind, attuned to the workings of the world of which he was master, told him the story of what was happening, of the endless rows of his sleeping warriors, breathing slow and steady in their beds, waiting upon his summons, while he waited upon information from the search parties and expeditions he had sent forth.

It was true, they seemed to be taking a long time. But here, underground, time was hard to parcel: a day, a year, a second or a century, there was naught to tell between them. Simply grains of sand on a table.

It was, in any case, as well that the expeditions had not yet returned, for his experiments with sand were not over. Once he had stabilised the orrery, Nebusemekh would use it to study the patterns of the stars. As above, so below. By careful consideration of the aspects of the stars, and the relationship of the planets of his system to those stars, he would ascertain the most propitious moment to wake his sleeping soldiers and send them forth to claim that which he had temporarily laid aside: mastery.

The worlds and the stars were his.

As below, so above.

What others did not realise was that the ancient formula might be reversed. The perfect orrery was not merely a map, it was an engine. He would capture the heavens, bring them down into his throne room, and there... there, he would adjust them to better accord with his unerring sense of proportion. For instance, there was an irritating wobble in the orbit of the companion white dwarf that gave its motion an annoying lop-sidedness every three thousand and forty-two years. A small adjustment to the completed orrery and he would smooth out that wobble, giving the troublesome star the proper deference to its stellar master; at the moment, it gave the impression of being a generally reliable slave that would nevertheless habitually sneak away to consort with other low-minded individuals and then return to its master's service, the tale of its absence told in the weaving of its orbit.

And if that did not work, then he would send the white dwarf spiralling into the blue heart of its larger companion. There would be no wobbling then – although he would have to adjust some other aspects of the orrery in light of the increase in mass and radiation of the senior star. The calculations would be an interesting exercise of a few minutes.

Once he had established the most propitious time to reawaken his people, the mastery he was developing over sand would also be useful. For above his head was a world of sand. He had established that its sand could be used to raise fortifications of the most robust kind, able to withstand any attack. He had simply to find the correct formula. Then, when he woke his sleeping soldiers, they would march forth and create fortifications that no enemy would ever be able to destroy.

'Ha!' said Nebusemekh, enjoying the sound of his voice. 'Ha! Let those beetles of the sons of Amalekh chew on that.'

Nebusemekh counted out the next in the experimental series. Of course, the size of grains of sand varied, but the sand of his world was reasonably uniform. Although from looking at them he could see that they were not the cuboid shapes that would pack most completely into a space, but generally roughly spherical. Nebusemekh briefly congratulated himself on his eyesight, that enabled him to see single grains of sand.

Having worked systematically through his two parameters, he was halfway through the experiment. All in all, it was going well, although it was taking somewhat longer than he had expected.

As he counted the sand out for the next experimental iteration – automatically registering each grain by the diminution in mass, for his senses were so finely tuned that he could feel the change of a single grain of sand – Nebusemekh allowed his mind to wander in memory. He was, he knew, quite old, but that was no bar to his holding the memories of his childhood as clear as when they were first minted.

He remembered them, he was quite certain of that: castles built of sand, sometimes whole settlements, and also elaborate sculptures. Others had laughed when he told of his ambition to make use of silica, one of the most common substances in the galaxy, to create his fortifications and defences, but they would find their laughter stopped in their mouths – by large amounts of sand – when he came forth with his armies.

So long as the virus did not spread further.

Nebusemekh sighed. He hated when thoughts of the virus rose in his mind. It put him into a thoroughly bad temper. Nebusemekh put down his staff and examined his thoughts, going back over the sequence to establish where the bad memory had arisen and its cause.

There it was. Movements in the upper levels of his world.

Nebusemekh felt movements in his outer world as intimately as he felt movements in his inner world, for he was connected to it. He had ignored them as not worthy of attention, but now they had stirred up memories of the virus. Nebusemekh sighed anew, turned away from the table and walked across the empty thronelab to the datafall that streamed down the wall behind his throne. He felt the cold floor on his bare feet, enjoying the motion of his muscles.

Attention to every moment was, Nebusemekh had long realised, a broad avenue towards general health, physical as well as mental. By always being aware of his body, of the rushing of his blood, the beating of his heart, the flow of his breath, he remained in harmony with its rhythms and ensured their continuation – although it was true he now found it unaccountably difficult to sleep for his regular period.

Nebusemekh put his hand into the datafall and joined his mind to the Mind of the World.

There was the initial dislocation, as his mind absorbed the inputs from the World Mind, but it was only momentary. Really, it was only a matter of degree rather than scale: receiving the feedback from all the sensors of the World Mind barely engaged a tenth of his own brain.

Nebusemekh allowed the Mind of the World – a misnomer, really, since it was no more conscious than a robot – to oversee his men, asleep in their pods, and carry out the maintenance tasks that were necessary to keep his domain functioning, ready to follow his commands when he decided the time had come to act.

It was long since he had last engaged with the Mind of the World. He was not sure exactly how long as the one area in which his normal acuity seemed to have diminished was the measurement of the passage of time, but it had been a long time. He was surprised, re-engaging with the Mind, to see that some of the protocols to wake the sleepers had been initiated. While the sleepers themselves still slept, there were whole companies that were beginning to dream – the dreams themselves were the usual turgid churning of the unconscious – which put them only one stage away from full wakefulness.

Nebusemekh had not ordered this.

He asked – no, he *required* – an answer of the World Mind. The Mind simpered before him, as was right and proper. It had been so long since the master had deigned to speak to it and the World Mind had not wished to distract Nebusemekh from his vital experiments, so it had given thought to what to do about the virus that had begun to infect the sleepers.

'What do you mean, what to do?' asked Nebusemekh. 'It is simple. It is a virus. Disinfect, quarantine, isolate. That is how one deals with a virus.'

But it was not so simple as that, the World Mind told its master. It had done all those things, and yet the virus had spread. But it was the spread that was truly puzzling for the World Mind. For there was no connection between the hosts it had infected: they were sleepers in widely different locations and the Mind had found no connection between them. Yet, they were still infected.

'You are stupid. What are you?'

The World Mind admitted that it was indeed stupid. It asked of Nebusemekh that he enlighten its ignorance.

Nebusemekh snorted. 'Ignorance shall not be so easily excused. I charged you with stopping the virus spreading among my people and I can see you have utterly failed. When were you going to tell me? When I had lost all my people to this dreadful virus?'

The World Mind assured Nebusemekh that it would have alerted him long before that had come to pass, but it had fully expected such an eventuality to never arise, and as it knew he was engaged in important experimentation, it had not wanted to worry him. Might it enquire how the experiment was going? Had he succeeded?

'I am nearing the critical quantities. It will not be long now.'

The World Mind remarked how pleased it was at Nebusemekh's imminent success and asked to be told when the experiment reached fruition. It further remarked that anticipation of Nebusemekh's success had also inspired it to initiate some of the protocols to wake his people from their long sleep, that they might be able to put Nebusemekh's great plans into action that much sooner, it being a long process to wake the sleepers.

'That is an initiative I approve of on your part,' said Nebusemekh. 'However, it does not excuse you from your incompetence with respect to the virus. How many of my people have been infected and forgotten who they are and the service they owe me?'

The World Mind regretted that it did not have an exact number, but it was confident that it was less than a hundred.

'A *hundred?*'

Less than a hundred, the World Mind demurred.

'That is still too many,' said Nebusemekh.

The World Mind pointed out that Nebusemekh had billions of people.

'I remember the names of every one of them,' said Nebusemekh.

The World Mind remained delicately silent.

'Aabalekh. Aacamekh. Aadelekh. Aafasekh...'

The World Mind begged its master's pardon for even the slightest hint of scepticism and now understood that, of course, Nebusemekh knew the names of every one of his people.

'They are precious to me.'

As indeed they were to the World Mind.

'I am glad to hear that,' said Nebusemekh. 'I sometimes worry that, since you are a machine, you will not appreciate your fleshly charges.'

The World Mind averred that it would always care for Nebusemekh's people.

'Naturally. That is what you were made for. Now, you have still not given me a precise figure for the number of my people infected with the virus.'

The World Mind insisted once again that it did not have a precise number.

'You are a counting machine,' Nebusemekh pointed out. 'You are nothing but numbers. How can you not have a number for this?'

That was due to the World Mind not having an adequate definition for infection.

'What do you mean? They cease to follow my orders. That is clear enough.'

The World Mind pointed out that Nebusemekh had not actually issued any orders to his people for a considerable period of time, not since he had commanded them to sleep.

'Then that is straightforward. Any that are awake are infected.'

The World Mind agreed that that, in principle, was a straightforward way to calculate how many of Nebusemekh's people had been infected, but the problem was that when they became infected with the virus, they ceased to appear on its monitors, as well as causing other damage to its detecting systems, so that it became difficult to ascertain the status of the nearby tombs and their occupants.

'You mean that they disappear?'

That is exactly what the World Mind meant.

'Hmm.' Nebusemekh thought. 'That is interesting.' He called up the records of the most recent cases and studied them. 'It appears that the virus, together with the host, withdraws from our frame of reference, thus disappearing from your monitors. It would also explain why the infection appears to strike at random. While there is no spatial connection between the different chambers in which my people have been infected, there will be a connection through the other frames of reference within Hilberkh space that allows the infected to escape your monitors. In fact, it is possible that within these folded frames of reference in Hilberkh space whole dimensions may lurk, folded upon themselves. It may be that these are nascent universes, struggling towards birth and seeking energy to flare forth – the virus may be a way of drawing matter into itself. Even universes hunger.'

The World Mind thanked Nebusemekh for his valuable insights and promised to apply them to its future analyses. Was there any other reason that its honourable master had for deigning to speak with it?

Nebusemekh thought. There was something else he had meant to do, but what was it? He was about to withdraw from the connection with the World Mind when the memory returned to him, having travelled through all the accumulated memory banks of the World Mind before returning to its source.

'Ah, yes, I remember now. I felt some activity in the immediate environs of my citadel. I want you to scan for activity.'

The World Mind said it would of course comply, but that it might take a little time for it to reactivate those systems.

'Why did you deactivate the external sensors?'

The World Mind pointed out that it had done so under its master's explicit instructions but hoped that in its admitted tendency to understand thoughts literally, it had not misunderstood the true intention behind the command 'Turn off all external sensors.'

'When did I instruct you to turn off all the external sensors?'

The World Mind said that it was when the exterior world was dying; the precise moment was when the great sea beside which Nebusemekh had often walked began to dry out.

Nebusemekh said nothing in reply. But in his memory, he was again standing by the sea, looking out over its waves, standing on a beach covered with castles made of sand. It was the clearest memory he had.

Sometimes, it was necessary to die to live.

'It's hardly surprising that I did not wish to see that. But you should have known that I would want to be kept informed of any activity outside my citadel.'

The World Mind agreed that it should have known that, but admitted that, in fact, it had not. However, its external surveillance systems were now beginning to work and the master was welcome to look into the feeds and examine the world outside the citadel.

'I will do that,' said Nebusemekh. And for the first time in an age, he took his senses outside the great citadel he had had built to protect his people.

Multiple sensors fed data into Nebusemekh's mind. Visual data, taking in all the frequencies from low infrared to ultraviolet, and the non-visual frequencies down to radio waves and up to the high-frequency waves that travelled from other stars. Auditory data, listening down to the slow grindings of the planet to the shifting of single grains of sand. Olfactory data, tasting and smelling a world that was clean in a way few places were. And pressure data, telling the movement of rock and... and...

Nebusemekh stopped. He focused all his considerable mental resources on a single area of the mountain under which he had built his citadel – for the mountain had not been there before the citadel was made, but comprised the spoil that had been excavated to dig the refuge for his people.

There. Movement. Sound.

Life.

Nebusemekh began to laugh. The sound was strange. Its like had not been heard for many ages in the great halls under the mountain, and the walls themselves seemed to bend towards its source to hear the sound better.

Nebusemekh laughed for joy.

The World Mind enquired if it might know the reason for its master's merriment.

'Can't you see?' asked Nebusemekh, directing the feed he was absorbing to the attention of the World Mind. 'They have returned. Finally. The expedition I sent off to search for trace of the other citadels on this world has returned. After so long, they have come back.'

The World Mind asked, delicately, if Nebusemekh was quite certain that this was the expedition that he had sent off – the World Mind paused slightly as it examined its memory – sixty million years ago?

'Who else would it be?' asked Nebusemekh. 'Everything else above ground is dead.'

The World Mind admitted that was the case, but nevertheless it did seem the expedition had been gone for quite a long time.

'It is a big world. Much to explore.' But as Nebusemekh spoke, he saw something else appear in the sensors. 'What is this?' He turned his attention more fully towards the exterior of the citadel. 'The infected? I see some of the infected have got out of the citadel and they are trying to stop my brave explorers returning with the knowledge they have brought for me. This must stop!'

The World Mind agreed absolutely that the infected must be stopped.

'Then stop them!'

It would be honoured to do so, said the World Mind, but felt that it should remind Nebusemekh that if it engaged its external weapons systems to destroy the infected, it might also destroy the returning expedition.

'No, that won't do. What sort of welcome home would that be?' Nebusemekh paused, thinking. 'Wake some of my people. Tell them to go outside and rescue the search party from the infected and to bring them in.'

The World Mind mentioned, only in passing, that waking the sleeping was quite a lengthy process and by the time it was complete there might not be any members of the expedition left to bring into the citadel.

'Of course, it is not simply a matter of getting up from bed. Then we shall have to find another means of rescuing the expedition.' Nebusemekh looked at his sensory feeds again. 'I appear to have already lost some of them, although you must improve the maintenance of the external monitors – I can barely tell if any out there are still alive. We must find some way to rescue them.'

The World Mind enquired if its master might like to go out of the citadel to rescue the expedition as the master was already awake and of surpassing puissance.

'I?' asked Nebusemekh. 'I?'

The World Mind apologised for such a crass suggestion and hoped that the master would forgive its temerity.

'If I left my quarters, I might be infected by the virus,' said Nebusemekh.

The World Mind was aghast at such a possibility. It could open the gates near where the expedition was so that they might enter the citadel, although that would make it possible for the infected to enter the citadel as well.

'Doors do not stop the infected,' said Nebusemekh. 'Dimensional twists allow them to bypass doors.'

The World Mind admitted it should have realised that. But what about opening the gate to allow the expedition ingress?

'They are engaged in battle. The gates are deep in the tunnels – they would not see them open, even if they remember where to look. You must recall how long it has been since they left the citadel.'

Having apologised, the World Mind humbly asked if it might proffer another suggestion.

'You may.'

The World Mind asked if it might transport the expedition into the citadel.

'That is an excellent idea,' said Nebusemekh. 'Send them to me once you have made sure that they are not carrying the infection and have cleaned them thoroughly.'

The World Mind assured the necron lord that it would do so.

'Very well.' Nebusemekh withdrew his hand from the World Mind. The flow of inputs from its banks of sensors ceased; it was as if Nebusemekh had suddenly closed the door on a cacophonous party. He basked in the sudden sensory silence.

He still had his connection to the World Mind, although it was not so intimate: now a conversation rather than a communion.

'I have my experiment to complete. Bring the members of the expedition to me when they are ready.'

'Yes, my master,' said the World Mind.

Nebusemekh turned away from the datafall that was the surface of the World Mind and made his way back across the thronelab to where he was conducting his experiment in world making.

As he approached the table, Nebusemekh reviewed the progress he had made in his mind. He had made one hundred billion, nine hundred and fifty-three million, four hundred and thirty-three thousand, three hundred and forty-four experiments. There were still another possible eighty-eight billion, two hundred and thirty-three million, seven hundred and eighty-two thousand and thirty-two more possible iterations of the experiment before it was completely run.

Nearly there.

Nebusemekh picked up his staff and began arranging the sand. As always, he began the task excited with the anticipation that this time, this time, it would be different; this time he would find the exact mass and diameter of sand required to create stable structures.

As he divided the sand on his vast experimental table, Nebusemekh spoke to the World Mind.

'Have you brought the expedition home yet?'

'I... am... about to... do so,' said the World Mind, its reply less assured than normal. Nebusemekh surmised that it had diverted the greater part of its reasoning faculties into the systems required to disassemble a living creature down to its molecular level and then reacquaint that creature with itself.

'Bring them to me when they have recovered and you have ascertained that they are free from the virus.'

The World Mind assured him that it would do so. But as Nebusemekh arranged the sand, he was contemplating the unusual prospect of talking to another living, breathing creature. It had been a long time since he had done so.

Even if they were free from the virus, they would undoubtedly be vectors for any number of pathogens.

'Prepare an anti-bacteriological suit for me,' Nebusemekh told the World Mind. 'I will wear it when I welcome back the expedition. After all, one can't be too careful.'

'Absolutely,' said the World Mind. 'I have successfully brought the expedition back into the citadel. They seem a little disorientated at the moment, but that will no doubt wane as I carry out the necessary medical checks, master. I will tell you when they are ready for you to see them.'

'Yes,' said Nebusemekh. He was distracted. The sand was divided. Time to try again. 'I look forward to speaking to them. Now, I really think this time it might work.' He raised his staff.

Lifting from the table, moving in their stately, immemorial dance, the planets and the suns and the stars rose at his bidding and took their places in the celestial masque, their sand surfaces shimmering yellow-green under the play of the stasis fields Nebusemekh was wielding.

It was whole. A perfect model of the heavens, dancing to the music of gravity and the gentle melody that Nebusemekh introduced, turning their motion towards him that the very stars might bow before him in their dance. For, after all, he was as old as the stars.

He lifted his arms to acknowledge their obeisance. But as he did so, the stasis fields holding the stars and the suns and the planets in place slipped and, one by one, they crumbled and fell back to the ground.

'Never mind, master,' said the World Mind. 'It will work next time. Or the time after.'

'Or the time after that. Nothing worthwhile was ever achieved without effort.' Nebusemekh remembered the child who had played with sand on the shore of the sea many, many, many years ago. If the child could make buildings with sand, he, so much stronger and wiser than that child, would be able to make castles in the sky. He simply had to find the right sort of sand.

Besides, it meant that the memory would play again. And he enjoyed the memory more than anything in his current life. It somehow seemed more real, more vital.

Nebusemekh began to divide the sand again.

CHAPTER 6

'*Throne!*'

The curse came through on Obeysekera's vox. He wanted to curse too, but he held his silence and turned, slowly, trying to see something, anything, in the dark.

'*Where the frekk are we?*' Another voice, the pitch rising, edging towards panic.

'Quiet!'

Obeysekera snapped the order over the squad vox-channel, looked to see if he had any auspex readings, but it was still all over the place: it seemed to think he was in among an apparently infinite set of energy sources, spreading to the limit of its detection capabilities. With the auspex providing no useful information, Obeysekera killed its light: even the faint illumination it used served to stop his eyes responding to the darkness into which they had been plunged.

'Who's here?' Obeysekera said into the vox. 'Call your names.'

'*Gunsur.*'

'*Ensor.*'

'*Ha.*'

'*Lerin.*'

Then, silence.

'Roshant, Malick, are you here?'

As Obeysekera spoke, there was a discharge of light, green and vivid, that left him more blinded than the darkness.

'*Throne. Throne, Throne, Throne – Throne, Throne.*'

The voice, coming through the vox and audible close by, was Roshant's. It was coming from where the darkness had been split by light.

'Roshant, quiet.'

'*C-captain, is that you?*'

'Yes. Anyone else with you?'

'*Malick here. We have the general. Can't see nothing, sir.*'

'None of us can. Stay where you are.'

Obeysekera turned slowly, looking, waiting for his eyes to adapt to the darkness. But there was nothing, not even the deeper shadows of a dark night. They were somewhere where there was no light.

'*Not getting anything, captain.*'

That was Malick.

Obeysekera listened. With no light, he could tell the rough direction from which Malick's voice came but not its depth: he could be below or above or level with him. There was something about the way the sound trailed away that told him they were in a large space.

A thought, nagging and unsettling. If he and all his men had been brought down here into the dark then what of the xenos they had been charging towards at the moment when the world cracked open in front of them and they fell through? Were they down here in the dark, too? Listening, fixing on the sound of him and his troops? From the brief details of their physiology that Obeysekera had seen, he suspected that the kroot had excellent eyesight.

But no eye, no matter how sensitive, could function in absolute darkness. If they were down here, the kroot were as blind as he was.

A sound. Bat-squeak high, rising to a silence beyond the range of his hearing. Obeysekera looked around, trying to locate its direction. In the dark it felt far, but he had no means of checking that. The darkness was so complete that his own body seemed disconnected; it was as if he were a disembodied point of view, a bodiless consciousness floating in the void.

The sound, however, was answered by another squeak rising out of the range of his hearing.

Obeysekera whispered into the squad vox-channel. 'Anyone else hear that? A high-pitched sound.'

'I heard it,' said Lerin. *'Can't tell from where.'*

'Sounded a long way off,' said Roshant.

'I heard nothing.'

Obeysekera did not recognise the voice, but its tone suggested a man accustomed to being heard when he spoke: the general.

'Anyone else?' asked Obeysekera, ignoring the general's interjection for the moment.

'This is nonsense,' said the general. Not being connected to the squad vox-channel, he was speaking loudly to be heard.

If the kroot were here, Obeysekera thought, they would now have confirmed that they were not alone. If he were their commander, he would deploy into a firing arc to allow concentrated fire when they got some light.

'Quiet. Listen for movement.'

Without sight, Obeysekera put all his attention into hearing.

A rasp, like rough skin crawling over stone. Close.

He turned, searching for the source. Then, he realised he was hearing the sound of his clothes moving over his skin as he breathed, the faint creak of carapace plates shifting as his chest rose and fell.

He could hear his heart beat.

He could hear his blood beat.

In such silence, he should be able to hear the slightest movement, but there was nothing.

If he were the kroot commander, he would not even know which direction to send his troops, nor whether they walked on a plain or above an abyss.

Without light, he and his men were helpless. But unless the kroot had some other sense akin to a natural auspex, they would be helpless too. Without such a sense, not even the kroot could move in this absolute dark. Obeysekera scanned his memories in the hypnocache, but nothing came up from the xenos manuals suggesting that the kroot had such a facility.

If they were in the dark, they were lost as well.

A clang, metal on metal. Obeysekera and the rest of the Kasrkin spun towards the sound, bringing their hellguns to bear.

'Throne! Sorry, sorry, that was me.' It was Roshant's voice. 'I dropped something.'

'We need some light.' Obeysekera did not recognise the voice, but its air of command told him whom it belonged to.

'General Itoyesa?'

'Any of you soldiers have a lumen?'

Obeysekera felt himself twitch with annoyance at the general's insouciant assumption of command. That was something else that would have to wait until they had light.

'No, they're back with the Venators,' said Obeysekera.

He heard the *tsk* of the general's disapproval.

'At least I have a data-slate,' said Itoyesa. Obeysekera heard fumbling sounds as the general searched for it. 'Got it.'

The screen light stuttered on, bright – although Obeysekera knew that anywhere else it would be barely visible – illuminating the general's hand and face. But before their eyes could adjust, the light faded away again.

'Throne,' said Itoyesa. 'Cell's dead.'

'What about this?' The voice belonged to Amazigh.

The light flared, flame high, from the cloth-wrapped torch he held up. Eyes, light-dazzled, looked outwards blearily, trying to see through the momentary blindness.

'Throne of Terra.' That was Malick.

He was saying what the rest of them were all thinking.

They were standing on a plain, a flat metal surface stretching further than the light could reach in every direction. But the plain was studded with vertical towers, reaching up beyond the light into the interminable dark, and the towers were slotted with sarcophagi, some head-on, some sideways-on. The light cast from Amazigh's torch was bright enough to shine through the crystal of the nearest sarcophagi. It shone through and then broke upon the creature within.

It was a creature of metal, a metal of silver and grey that, at the touch of the light, seemed to wrinkle and flow as if it were living skin. The head was a skull, bare of flesh, the body a cage of metal ribs and its limbs struts of steel. Beside it in the clear coffin was a weapon: the label *Gauss flayer* presented itself to Obeysekera's mind from a suddenly activated hypnocache. Stacked above the sarcophagus was another, and another, and another, on up into the dark above them.

'Necrons.'

The voice was Roshant's; the name, redolent with death, came from them all.

As if in response to the pool of illumination cast from Amazigh's torch, the space in which they found themselves began to light up. It was dim at first, a faint green fluorescence from the clear caskets in which the metal shapes lay. Then lights started to switch on above the sarcophagi, illuminating the strange characters that were inscribed upon the heads of the caskets. The livid green light reflected off the gun-grey metal, giving it a sheen of viscous life like the scum upon a stagnant pool, and then reached out into the great space of the hall.

One by one, the tomb towers started to light up. Huge columns of necrons, ascending to heights beyond their sight: heights lost in the green glow that began to spill from every surface, reflected and refracted. Staring upwards at the tomb towers that rose above them, Obeysekera thought he could see movement in the heights – many-limbed creatures crawling over the stacks of sarcophagi, stroking the crystal caskets with their metal limbs.

Tomb spyders. He had fought them before. Non-organic creatures with somewhat limited artificial intelligence that saw to the maintenance and defence of the necron tombs and their inhabitants. Their function was similar to the white blood cells in a human body: to identify intruders and destroy them.

Looking up at the tomb tower disappearing above his head, each step containing another necron warrior, Obeysekera realised that they had virtually no chance of getting out of this alive.

He turned round, looking into the distance, searching for whether the hall stretched as far horizontally as it seemed to stretch vertically. Through the ranks of tomb towers he could see no sign of a wall, nor of any ending to the hall.

'Where in the Emperor's name have you brought me?'

Obeysekera brought his gaze back from the distant green reaches of the hall to the man, also green-tinted, standing in front of him, bristling with disdain.

'General Itoyesa,' said Captain Obeysekera. 'I would appreciate you keeping your voice down.'

'You have no authority to tell me what to do,' said the general, bristling even more. He was a stockily built man with the marks of some of his campaigns visible in livid scar tissue on his cheek and an augmetic left hand that was opening and closing convulsively, as if wishing to crush Obeysekera's windpipe. 'I say again, where the frekk have you brought me?'

'I have not brought you anywhere,' said Obeysekera. 'We have all been brought here.' He gestured around him. 'Unless I am very much mistaken, we appear to have been brought down into a necron tomb.'

'How are you going to get me out then?' asked General Itoyesa. 'You were sent to find me and bring me back to headquarters. Carry out the second part of your orders, captain.'

'Those were not all my orders, general.'

'What else do you have to do?'

Captain Obeysekera stared at the general, not retreating before his indignation. 'Obeysekera,' he said slowly.

The general stared at him. 'Pardon?'

'My name is Obeysekera. Captain Obeysekera.'

'Whatever your name is, what are you going to do to get me out of here?'

'What we Kasrkin are trained to do, general – recon, plan, act.' Obeysekera gestured towards the rising tomb towers. 'We are at the recon phase here, general. If you would excuse me.'

The captain turned away from the general. It was a calculated movement, designed to either silence Itoyesa or to draw him into a confrontation that only Obeysekera could win.

'Sergeant Malick.'

'Yes, sir.'

Behind him, Obeysekera could hear the general puffing with impotence but choosing to hold his peace for the moment.

'Form a perimeter – we don't know if the kroot were brought down here too.'

While Malick dispatched Lerin, Ha, Ensor and Gunsur to sentry positions, Obeysekera turned to Amazigh. The Kamshet was still holding the torch in his hand, although the light from it was no longer necessary. He stared up at the towers, with wonder turning to dread.

Feeling the gaze, Amazigh brought his gaze down and looked at Obeysekera.

'Now I know why the mountain is tabu.'

'It also explains the anomaly that affects the machine-spirits of all our equipment around here.' Obeysekera stepped closer to the Kamshet. 'You have served me faithfully since the Mother gave you to me – now I ask a further service. You are light of foot and skilled in remaining unseen – see if the kroot are here too.'

The Kamshet looked around at the tomb towers rising into the dark, and the livid light that filled the spaces in between them.

'You want me to go out into that? On my own?' Amazigh shook his head. 'They are tabu. I cannot go among them.'

Obeysekera saw General Itoyesa turn towards them, his mouth opening to speak, so to forestall him the captain stepped closer to the Kamshet and put his hand on the man's shoulder. Leaning close to Amazigh, so that he could see the man's eyes beneath his cheche, their blue tinted ocean green by the tomb light, Obeysekera whispered, 'We are all scared here. If we are to escape, we must accept the fear, for it will stop us doing anything stupid, but we must not let it master us. I know that the fear will not master you, Amazigh.'

'The Mother sent me with you as punishment. It is become a greater punishment than I ever feared.'

'Then when I return you to her, she will learn what you have done, and she will give you due place among your people.'

As Obeysekera whispered, Amazigh began to nod his head, understanding what was asked of him and the honour that would be his should he achieve it and return to the tribe. Obeysekera saw him looking sidelong at the rising tomb towers. It was the returning back to his tribe that was difficult to envisage, surrounded by countless sleeping necrons.

'They are sleeping. You are quieter than the wind – you will not wake them. Now, go, but not far – any movement will carry a long way in this silence. If the kroot are here, you will soon hear them.'

Amazigh nodded again. 'I-I will go,' he said.

'Thank you,' said Obeysekera. 'For you go of your own will and not by my order.'

The Kamshet drew his cheche tighter around his head and then turned. Like a wisp of mist, he disappeared among the tomb towers, passing out between the silent guard of Obeysekera's remaining men.

Obeysekera turned to see General Itoyesa staring at him.

'I have never seen an officer of the Astra Militarum *ask* one of his men to do something before, Captain Obeysekera.'

'As you might remember, Amazigh is not one of my men, general. I have no authority to order him to do anything.'

General Itoyesa snorted and drew his bolt pistol. 'This is the only authority these tribals respect or understand, captain, and the sooner you realise that the better. Most of them are only one step from barbarism. Without our presence, before you knew it they would be offering up children as sacrifices to heathen gods. A good taste of bolter fire is what they need to keep them honest. Not like our Guard.'

As the general spoke, Obeysekera was scanning their surroundings, still looking for movement. There was nothing on the ground level, but above he could see the spyders moving up and down the columns, wicked-looking creatures of metal and spikes. So far, they were showing no signs of moving towards them, but he was wary. Killing a creature that was not in any real sense alive would be no easy task, even for a Kasrkin hellgun. Living creatures bled out; wounds slowed them down or incapacitated them. It was not the same with those made of metal. They had to be disassembled, blown apart piece by piece, and even then they could continue operating far beyond the limits of any organic creature.

Roshant took a step towards Itoyesa, breaking Obeysekera from his thoughts.

'It is my task, as an officer of the Officio Prefectus, to ensure that tribals adhere to the Imperial cult, general,' said Roshant.

Itoyesa turned to the young commissar. 'You're Erahm's boy, Kirpal? Blowed if I could see the likeness before, but now I can. Your father was always prickly about his privileges – as the father, so the son, they say, and in this case they say truly.'

Roshant took another step forwards, all the while staring at the general. 'My other orders, before we return, are to ascertain if you have been compromised. If I decide that you are tainted, then I am to ensure that you do not return.' He placed a hand upon the bolt pistol at his hip. 'I will shoot you if I have to.'

Roshant hissed the words at the general from only a few inches distance, but Obeysekera heard the venom and the promise in the threat: Roshant meant every word he said.

The general knew it too. He raised his arms in placation.

'I know you will,' said Itoyesa. 'But you have no need to.'

'Commissar, calm,' said Obeysekera. 'Please.' He glanced around. Those spyders were starting to come closer. 'We want to get the general back alive if we possibly can.'

'Do we indeed?' said Roshant. 'I don't think my father would be sorry to see the back of "Butcher" Itoyesa, the general who lost more troops taking planetoid HS-512 than the enemy lost defending it.'

'Your father ordered me to capture that planetoid whatever the cost. I succeeded in my brief.'

'Then you must have missed the bit where it said casualties should not reach ten per cent of the operational troops.'

General Itoyesa stared at Roshant. 'Those deaths are burned into my conscience. I am responsible for them. But so is your father. There was a deadline for the taking of the target, a deadline that, if I broke it, would cause the unravelling of all your father's strategic plans. I told him, when he set me the task, that you can have victory or you can set injury targets – you cannot achieve both at the same time.'

'My father does both. He wins victories and preserves his men.'

'He sets the frekking timetables! Of course he can do both – he gives himself the time. His staff, and their armies, are not given such luxuries. Good public relations for a lord militant – make sure your generals are the ones who get labelled "butcher".'

'My father takes his objectives faster than any of his generals.'

Itoyesa grimaced. 'He does that with the aid of so much of the Imperial Navy that he might as well confine his crusade to the space between the stars. The rest of us wake up in the watches of the night hearing the screams of the men we sacrificed on the altar of your father's reputation.'

At these words, Obeysekera stepped forward, laying his hand on the general's arm, but Itoyesa shook it off.

Roshant blinked. He looked down, then back up at the general.

'My father will be interested to hear what you truly think of him.'

General Itoyesa opened his mouth as if to speak, then stopped. He shook his head, looking away into the green dark.

'It matters not. It is not likely that you will ever have the chance to tell him.'

'It is my task to see that you both report back to the lord militant,' said Obeysekera. He gestured to the stacked caskets. 'They sleep. So long as they continue to sleep, we may hope to find a way out of here.' Obeysekera looked to the general and the commissar. 'We must escape – the lord militant must learn that there is a necron tomb under the Sand Sea.' He focused his regard on General Itoyesa. 'To that end, I am in command of this mission, general.' Obeysekera reached for his pocket. 'I have it in writing if you wish to confirm it for yourself.'

General Itoyesa sighed. 'Do you wish to humiliate as well as rescue me, captain?'

'Not in the slightest, general.'

Itoyesa paused, breathing deep. He closed his eyes for a moment, then, opening them, looked at Captain Obeysekera.

'Very well. But now, since you are in command, tell me – which way should we go?' He gestured into the green depths. 'How are you going to get me out of here?'

'You are pointing in the wrong direction, general.' Obeysekera gestured up. 'We are deep. To get out, we will have to climb.'

'Those things?' Itoyesa gestured at the tomb towers. He shook his head. 'Can't think of a better way to wake the sleepers.'

'No, not that way, if we can help it. There must be service ramps and tunnels. We have to find them.'

'Tell me when you do.' General Itoyesa stalked away towards where Sergeant Malick kept guard at the dark base of a tomb tower.

Obeysekera and Roshant watched him go.

Then, over their private channel, Roshant spoke. 'I didn't know you had written orders giving you authority over higher ranks.'

'I don't,' said Obeysekera.

CHAPTER 7

Shaper Tchek turned his head one way then the other, seeking to locate the sound.

It was the whistle signal from the Long-sight, Stryax, informing them that he had found the humans, but amid the distorting echoes of the tomb towers it was all but impossible to tell which direction the signal came from.

Tchek whistled back, telling Stryax to signal again, but there was no immediate reply.

The Shaper looked around, his unease growing even greater. To have been brought down into this place by some dark magic was bad enough, but what they had seen when the dark withdrew had been worse than he imagined.

The kroot communed with the dead. But these things of metal that lay stacked about them in columns reaching up to the heights were neither living nor dead, but abominations. His soul revolted against them, bile rose in his throat, and he, a Shaper, retched, dry-choking on the dust of their counterfeit of life.

All the Kinband could taste the canker in the still air, the poison in the livid, green light, but for the Shaper it felt as if he were being painted on the inside with cancer. His only recourse was to speed his breath, circulating the air through his lungs and air sacs faster, trying to flush the green from his system.

How he breathed was a relic of his avian past, when the ancestors of the kroot had flown through the forests of Pech, the air passing in a one-way system in, through and out of the body, ensuring that stagnant air never accumulated in the deep passages of the lungs but instead was washed through by every breath, like water scouring a channel clean rather than rising and receding waves leaving a sludge at their limit.

But even so, Tchek tasted the taint in the air, metal and flesh.

He looked around at the sarcophagi and their metal occupants. The Song, the continuing Song that was the history of the kroot, a Song of sound and communion, told of the kroot world Caroch and the deadly disease that had infested the kroot there who had attempted to learn the minds and purposes of their metal enemies by the Feast. The Shapers on Caroch, hard-pressed by the necron onset, had feasted upon the metal flesh of some of their foes, only for their own flesh to be consumed, eaten from within by infestations of nanoscarabs, which then burst from the hollowed-out bodies of the Shapers, infecting many Kinbands.

The Song, preserving the memory of Caroch, told all Shapers that the metal flesh of the necrons was deadly; it was tabu, forbidden them.

Looking at the gleaming metal skull in the crystal coffin, Tchek felt himself gagging again. The thought of feasting upon metal flesh choked him.

He heard the whistle signal again and it dragged him back from the cloying horror of the sight of the non-living necron sleeping in its coffin, to what he had promised the t'au the Kinband would bring them: the human general. Stryax was calling him.

Tchek responded again, then looked to the remaining members of the Kinband, strung out in skirmish formation between the towers of the sleepers.

'Where do you hear Stryax calling from, Cirict?'

The Tracker, ahead of Tchek in the formation, turned his head, listening as the whistle signal refracted through the towers, then pointed an uncertain finger in the direction he judged, about thirty degrees ahead.

Tchek looked back down the formation. 'You, Krasykyl?'

The Stalker pointed ahead too, but at a narrower angle. But Tchek heard the Long-sight coming from the right, at ninety degrees, rather than ahead at thirty.

'Stay where you are,' Tchek whistle-signed back to Stryax. 'Keep the humans in view.'

The Shaper looked in the two directions, uncertain which to choose. In the end he pointed directly between the two, at sixty degrees to their direction. This way, they should soon be able to tell who was right from whether Stryax's signals were coming from their left or their right. Tchek tightened his grip on his rifle. He wanted to get the human they had been sent to find and then get out of this accursed place as soon as possible, before his insides turned green and he went metal grey.

Cirict the Tracker had taken the lead, slipping between the tomb towers with his body held low and forward, rifle held ready, his pech'ra flying quietly above him. But Tchek saw how the Tracker's crown quills were beginning to glow green in this livid underground light. He suspected his own crown quills were doing the same, probably more so because, as the Shaper, his nature was to absorb information from the environment that he might better know that which would be most useful for the Kinband to feast upon.

'Keep calling,' Tchek whistle-signed to Stryax, and the Long-sight replied. The replies were getting clearer now but, turning his head, he still could not tell which flank to head towards: if anything, Stryax seemed to be directly ahead.

'That way,' said Tchek, pointing ahead.

Cirict was already moving in the right direction. Tchek looked at Krasykyl and then, doubtfully, at the next tomb tower. Did he want the Stalker climbing these towers of the metal sleepers? By doing so, would Krasykyl run the risk of waking them? Tchek looked around. If the necrons started waking, there would be no hope for them.

'Stay on the ground,' Tchek told Krasykyl.

The Stalker whistled his understanding, the sound tinged with relief. Krasykyl would have climbed the tomb tower without demur if the Shaper had asked him, but the Stalker was glad that the demand was not being made of him.

Stryax's whistle signal was still coming from ahead, but it was not getting any louder. It was likely being blocked by the intervening towers.

Tchek looked up. There were times when he was almost glad that his ancestors had sacrificed their wings. Crawling over the tomb towers, and scuttling along the connecting gantries and cables, were metal spiders, hundreds of the things, stopping every now and again and resting, thrumming, upon a metal thread high above. Surely the metal spiders must see them? But if so, they gave no sign.

Tchek looked down from the metal spiders to his own rifle. He checked the ammunition. He was not sure that rifles firing solid rounds would have the slightest effect on the metal spiders, much less upon the metal soldiers that lay in their caskets, but they were all he had.

Tchek whistle-signed again. 'Where are you?'

Stryax replied, the sound a thin squeak above the silence of the tomb. It still sounded straight ahead to Tchek.

'Ahead?' he asked Cirict.

The Tracker looked up to the pech'ra then shook his head, pointing at thirty degrees to their direction of travel.

'You, Krasykyl?'

'Shaper, I know it does not make sense, but that is where I hear him.' And he pointed at the same sixty-degree angle that he had indicated before, only this time their direction of travel had changed substantially.

It was as if Stryax were circling round to flank them. Why would he do that?

Before Tchek could answer the question, there came another whistle signal from Stryax, this one more urgent and louder.

'Smell, ahead, tracking closer.'

'What sort of smell?' Tchek whistled back.

'The smell of dead meat,' said Stryax. 'Getting stronger.'

Tchek remembered the report of the creatures of rotting flesh that had attacked them above, on the mountain.

'Withdraw.' He had already lost Chaktak. He did not want to lose another of the Kinband, particularly with the humans still to be dealt with.

'The smell is closer,' Stryax whistled.

'Withdraw,' Tchek answered urgently. 'Withdraw to us, we will cover you.'

'Withdrawing,' Stryax replied. A pause, then, 'The smell is very close now.'

'Stryax, withdraw.'

From ahead, there came the sound of metal on flesh, the dull sound that it makes as it bites into skin and muscle and bone. Tchek froze, listening. The rest of the Kinband turned to the sound, their crown quills rising in alarm but their rifles steady in the direction of the noise.

They had all heard enemy die before, each with their own distinctive sound at their ending. But they also knew the sound of death when it came for kroot. The kroot died with the death song, the rattle of their crown quills as mortality sucked the pneuma from their bones and flesh. They heard the death rattle now, and knew that Stryax was gone from them, his pneuma flown.

But after his death rattle, they heard a new sound, a liquid ripping, a tearing as of bark from a green tree.

Tchek gestured to what remained of the Kinband, Krasykyl, Cirict and Kliptiq, to move into skirmish formation: they had lost a nestling. They would feast and take the strength of Stryax and his killer to themselves.

Tchek pointed up. They needed height, whatever the risk of the tomb towers. Krasykyl slung his rifle over his shoulder and began to climb, swarming up over the coffins, his sharp, clawed fingers finding easy purchase on the sepulchres. Tchek signalled Cirict forward but kept Kliptiq behind him; the Bearer was too clumsy for the stealthy approach the Shaper intended. But once he found the enemy that had killed Stryax, he would bring the Bearer forward so that he might feast too.

Tchek crept forward himself, staying in the lee of the towers, moving in the direction of where he had heard the death of Stryax. Advancing, he heard further noises, quieter now but just as grotesque: the sounds of butchery. Sawing, slicing, the crack of joints disjointed. There was part of the Shaper that did not want to see what he was going towards. But Stryax was a nestling: he had fed from the same pot, partaken of the same Feasts; they must save him for the Feast, that he not be lost to them.

The sounds were closer now.

Tchek whistled to Krasykyl and Cirict, 'What do you see?' He did not ask them what they smelled, for his olfactory centres were thick with the iron tang of blood and the bile of spilled intestines.

'Behind the next tower,' said Krasykyl. 'Movement, but I can't see what.'

'Cirict?'

'Flet tells me it's there, but I can't see anything either.'

'Flank it on your side. I will come round on the other. Krasykyl, cover from above. Kliptiq, wait my command.'

The Bearer whistled his understanding. He alone of the kroot gave no sign of the deep unease the rest of them were feeling; a hint from Tchek and they would all have turned and retreated without claiming Stryax for the final Feast. But Tchek had lost nestlings before and been unable to render to them the service of the final Feast, and the shame of it still clung to him, marked upon his crown quills in livid guilt stripes. He would not leave Stryax unclaimed.

With Cirict moving up, and Krasykyl covering him from above, Tchek slowly moved forward, inching around the base of a tomb tower, his attention so focused ahead that he did not notice the metal abomination lying in its coffin alongside him. Tchek peered around the edge of the tomb tower, his rifle steady in his hands, ready to be raised to firing position.

But he did not raise his rifle.

He stared, and his gorge rose, and the horror rose before his eyes and he could not close them however he tried.

For he saw Stryax. He saw what had been Stryax, his face and his flesh, his limbs and his body pinned upon a metal frame in a mockery of life. The kroot's skin had been flayed from his body; now it hung, in limp, still-bloody folds, over the metal skeleton of a necron. Before his horrified gaze, Tchek saw the necron paint itself with Stryax's blood, anointing itself at wrist and neck and ear. Stryax's face, stripped from his head, was stretched, lopsided, over the necron's counterfeit skull, a metal forgery of true life, the holes where the Long-sight's eyes had been falling one over the necron's cheek, the other on its forehead. Stryax's empty mouth gaped, the jaw skin sagging down over the necron's neck. The rest of the Long-sight's body it had stuffed over its metal frame, pushing bloody bones between its own limbs and hanging flesh over its shoulders as grisly epaulettes.

'No,' Tchek whispered. 'No, no.'

The creature, the abomination, was still butchering what remained of Stryax, struggling to incorporate his entrails and remaining limbs into its own frame, while at the same time it was trying to hang the Long-sight's legs around its neck. But as Tchek watched, frozen in his horror, he saw movement, grey and rust red through the livid green. Another of the flesh-clad horrors was approaching and, as it came nearer, Tchek saw that it too wore a skin pelt but its face was a caricature of a human, mouth open in a never-ending scream.

'What is it?'

The whistle, quiet with horror, came from Cirict's direction.

'Flayed One,' said Tchek.

'Can we kill it?' asked Cirict.

'I do not know,' said Tchek.

But as he whistle-answered, the creature's head came up from its butchery work. The second Flayed One stopped. The two metal abominations slowly turned their skin masks towards him.

'They can hear us.' Tchek whispered the realisation, horror rising further within him. For there was something fundamentally wrong about these metal creatures; he could taste it. As Shaper of the Kinband, he was driven to seek new Feasts as much by the taste of new creatures to commune with as by any rational calculation that by communing with them the Kinband would acquire useful skills and knowledge. Indeed, according to the song history of his people, the greatest among the Shapers, those who had led them from the trees to the freedom of thinking, had done so by taste, smelling their way towards what they would become.

Everything in Tchek revolted against the smell/taste of these flesh-clothed metal creatures turning to look at him. In his throat, in his olfactory organs, their smell combined the fleshy rankness of cancer tumours with the slip-iron taste of metal. They were everything Tchek would put away from the Feast.

They made him sick.

Retching – something a kroot did very rarely – Tchek began to fall back, trying to get behind the cover of the tomb tower so that the flesh-metal creatures could not see him. He looked up and around, searching for Cirict and Krasykyl.

But he could not see them, although Kliptiq was waiting where he had been told to remain, still carrying the communal pot that united the Kinband in the Feast. Tchek signed Kliptiq to retreat, but the Bearer stared at him uncomprehending.

'Where is Stryax?'

'Dead,' hissed Tchek. 'Get back.'

'But we cannot leave him, we must eat him.'

'Something already has.'

Kliptiq stared at the Shaper, his crown quills bristling. 'Then we must eat that which ate Stryax.'

'Not these, never these.' Tchek turned and pointed past the tomb tower to where the metal abominations squatted over the remains of the Long-sight. 'They are cancer, walking.'

Kliptiq looked to where Tchek was pointing. His crown quills bristled higher, but the colours catching upon them told of the Bearer's fear and revulsion. He turned to go.

'Wait,' said Tchek. 'We must remain together. There may be others.'

He risked a whistle-call, the signal to bring Cirict and Krasykyl to his position. The Tracker and the Stalker answered his call, song-whistling that they were on their way. But Tchek, watching the metal creatures, saw them stop the butchery again at the whistle-calls, pause and turn in the sound's direction.

The Flayed Ones slowly stood. They were both clothed in ragged skin suits, the faces of the dead hanging as slack masks over metal skulls, organs and intestines arrayed as leaking jewellery, belts and buckles.

'Quick!' Tchek whistle-called again.

The Flayed Ones, heads rotating like metal sensors, turned towards him, even though the Shaper was hidden behind a necron sarcophagus. In the gloom, Tchek saw livid green behind the empty eyes of their skin masks.

From the left, Tchek heard Cirict, his movements soft but near. From above, the quick scramble of Krasykyl, descending so fast he was almost falling.

The Flayed Ones started to move, heading towards the Shaper, their metal skeletons giving a terrible caricature of life to the flesh layered over the metal bones.

Tchek raised his rifle. Beside him, without needing telling, Kliptiq did the same. The Flayed Ones came on, metal sounding on metal. How could they kill something that was not alive?

They would have to find a way.

'Fire,' Tchek whispered.

The two kroot rifles fired together.

Tchek, squinting along the barrel of his rifle, followed the track of the round he had loosed. If his aim was true – and his aim was almost always true – the round would strike the first of the abominations in the centre of its torso, where its heart would have been if it had the humanoid heart that its basic layout suggested.

The round struck true. Tchek, his gaze focused in on the centre of the Flayed One's chest so that it appeared as if it were standing right in front of him rather than being over a hundred yards away, saw the skin suit rupture as the rifle round punched through it. The creature staggered, falling backwards, as the kinetic energy of the strike was transferred into its metal frame. With the less focused vision of his wider sight, Tchek saw the other abomination stagger too, as Kliptiq's rifle round struck home. A moment later, the sound of the twin impacts reached them, slightly syncopated metallic clangs deadened by layers of flesh.

Tchek's crown quills began to brighten, moving up through the spectrum towards the victory display of shades of mauve and ultraviolet.

But then the abominations steadied. They steadied and they did not fall. Even though both had taken what for any unarmoured creature of flesh and blood would have been mortal wounds, they did not fall but rather looked to each other, seeking silent understanding; and then the two skin-suited skulls turned back to where the bullets had come from.

The Flayed Ones started moving again, but they were picking up the pace with each step they took, moving faster, moving towards running, their metal feet ringing out the quickening rhythm on the metal floor.

'Fire again,' Tchek said. 'For the head.'

Now, with the Kinband caught up with the attacking enemy, the horror and fear were in abeyance. Now, there was only doing.

Tchek's rifle flared fire and combustion gases. Kliptiq's, beside him, did the same. But there were two other shots: from above, Krasykyl, and from the left, close by now, Cirict fired too. Four rounds slammed into the Flayed Ones, two volleys of two, and the first stopped their advance while the second knocked the creatures from their feet onto the metal floor.

'Fall back,' Tchek ordered, not waiting to see if the Flayed Ones were dead, but determined to take what advantage he could of their being flat on their backs.

Kliptiq started retreating, moving backwards with his rifle still covering the direction of the danger.

'Krasykyl, Cirict, you too,' instructed Tchek as the Stalker and the Tracker reached him, Krasykyl jumping the final five yards down from the tomb tower, arms spread wide as if he still had the power of flight that his ancestors had once possessed.

They pulled back in skirmish formation, leaving Tchek as rearguard. Tchek saw the Flayed Ones start to move. He observed as their legs, lying upon the floor, twitched before the creatures slowly sat up again.

In one, the caricature of a human face had all but disappeared, the skin mask pierced and then ripping so that half the face hung loose, revealing the metal skull beneath. In the other, the one that wore Stryax, the face mask was less ripped; it might almost have been the Long-sight looking at him, save for the green fire in the eyeholes and the way the face sat awkwardly, as if it were stretched upon bone it was not meant for. But there were two holes in the face mask and its metal hand went to its face, as if feeling for injury, and its fingers found the holes, one on the cheek, the other above the nose, where the skin had been pierced by the weapons of its enemies.

Tchek saw the second creature turn to the first, its fingers also reaching up to the holes in the skin mask.

The two creatures turned in unison and looked towards where Tchek stood, hiding behind a tomb tower. They screamed together, their voices metal hymns of madness and, rising from the ground, they started towards the Shaper, their dead feet clanging upon the metal floor.

Tchek turned and ran back in the same direction that the rest of the Kinband had taken. Noise flared on either side of Tchek as the Kinband fired past him, covering his retreat. The volley, directed at the leading creature, stopped it completely, then dropped it to its knees, and the second volley knocked back the following creature but did not send it to the floor.

'How do we kill these things?' Krasykyl asked Tchek as the Shaper retreated past him.

'I do not know. Knock it down again.'

Krasykyl fired off another round, with Cirict adding to the volley, knocking the abomination over once more. It lay there a moment without moving, giving them the sudden, surging hope that they had killed it, before it jerked into its caricature of life and sat up, livid green eyes turned towards them.

'Fire.'

All four kroot fired again as the creatures rose, but this time the Flayed Ones had braced themselves: they did not fall but leant into the strikes as if they were walking into a strong wind. And like that, they began to advance, taking the rounds as they came onwards, the bullets jerking them but no longer knocking them over.

'What do we do?' asked Cirict.

'Keep shooting,' said Tchek. 'They will die. They... will... die.'

But they did not.

The Flayed Ones kept coming on, even as the bullets shredded their skin suits and sent broken bits of bone scattering around them. Sparks flew as rounds hit, sometimes jerking the Flayed Ones, sometimes barely affecting their progress. The creatures pushed into the metal rain and, as they approached and the rain grew harder, parts began to break from their bodies. One went down, its knee shattered, then got up and hobbled forward, its leg askew. The other lost most of its hand, its head hung crooked upon its neck, but still it kept on, walking into the metal deluge. They advanced, reaching the tomb tower behind which Tchek had taken cover when he had first seen them.

A shot, Tchek was not sure if it was from his rifle, went wide, striking the crystal cover of the sarcophagus at the base of the tomb tower.

The crystal shivered, as if alive, then cracks began to appear over it, spreading out from where the bullet had struck it, sending new lines out wherever a crack angled. Gas started to escape from inside the casket, the green-lit gas that bathed the sleeping necron. The crystal cover, rendered opaque by the density of cracks over it, shattered, raining down upon the sleeper within.

The two abominations stopped where they were. They turned towards the necron lying still and exposed in its coffin beside them and, reaching out, ran their metal fingers over its exposed skeleton. One of the Flayed Ones bent over the sleeping necron. From where Tchek was standing, watching in mute horror, it seemed that the creature was breathing into the face of the necron in stasis – only, it could not breathe. Then the abomination leaned further down into the casket and, with the skin and flesh it had taken from Stryax, pressed its forehead against the sleeping necron's.

Tchek, revolted, stepped back, averting his eyes, but Krasykyl grabbed his arm and pointed.

'Look,' the Stalker whispered.

Krasykyl did not need to point. Tchek could taste the change in the thick, heavy air. It was the smell of cancer and rust, of the auto-destruction of flesh and metal. He turned back to look at what was happening at the casket.

The Flayed One was still bending over the prone necron, mouth joined to mouth. Although the posture was the same, it was no kiss. The necron began to tremble. Gently at first, barely perceptible to ordinary vision, the crystal fragments from its broken tomb that lay scattered over its prone form started to vibrate.

The sleeping necron was waking up.

The second of the Flayed Ones, clad in torn human skin, was leaning over the prone necron too, its body shaking as if in the grip of a fever although it could know no temperature other than that of its surroundings. Through the ripped skin of its human face mask, it was looking down at what was happening. Its metal skull was immobile and incapable of expression, yet everything about its stance and attitude told Tchek that it was gripped by a surpassing excitement, almost to ecstasy.

Kliptiq put his hand on Tchek's shoulder.

'Can we go? We should go.'

The Shaper knew that the Bearer was right: they should make their escape while the abominations were occupied. But he could not draw himself away from what he was watching. He needed to know what they were doing and why the breaking of the casket had stopped them; at the least, it gave him a tactic to delay the Flayed Ones when they encountered them.

The abomination bent over the sleeping necron also began to tremble. Parts of Stryax that it had shoved into its body shook lose, falling to the floor. The deep longing for communion with the spirit of his nestling almost sent Tchek stumbling forward to scavenge some of Stryax's remains, but he stayed the impulse.

The sleeping necron was now shaking through every part of its metal frame, its skull striking against its grave cushion in a drum rattle. The movement reached such a pitch that it blurred in Tchek's sight. The Flayed Ones on either side of the necron were shaking too – and their trembling, Tchek realised, was coming into phase with the sleeping necron.

The realisation burst upon Tchek: they were infecting the sleeping necron. They were turning a creature already damned into something worse. They were turning it into another like them.

Unable to break into the caskets of the sleeping necrons themselves, his missed shot had cracked the protective crystal, allowing the Flayed Ones to reach another of their kind and infect it with the desire for flesh that had consumed them.

Tchek turned to the surviving members of the Kinband.

'Go.'

He pointed them back the way they had come, away from the creatures that clothed themselves in flesh. As Kliptiq, Krasykyl and Cirict set off in scout formation with Flet flying above, Tchek took one last look behind.

The necron's shaking had reached such a pitch that its whole body was drumming on the casket, setting off hundreds of jagged micro rhythms, its movement a blur. In a final spasm, it arched, so that only its heels and its head touched ground.

It screamed.

Its scream was metal.

Its scream was the cry of the unliving desiring life.

Its scream threw the abominations away and onto the metal floor, where they crashed, spent and still.

The prone necron slumped down flat in its coffin and, for a moment, Tchek thought that it had broken under the pressure of what was being inflicted upon it. But then the creature sat up. It sat up and swung its legs out of the casket.

It sat up and looked across the space between them; it looked through the cover that Tchek was using. It looked and it raised its hand and it pointed, and it said, in a voice of grating metal, 'Flesh.'

It started to get up.

Tchek turned and hurried after his Kinband. He hoped that it would take the newly fledged flesh-hungry creature some time to relearn the use of its limbs and that it would stumble after him like a chick. But he feared it would not take long for it to learn control and come after them, eager to find its own suit of skin.

Catching up with Cirict, Krasykyl and Kliptiq as they passed another tomb tower, Tchek spoke to them as they moved.

'We must find some way out of this place.'

'Where we came in, there must be a way out there,' said Kliptiq.

'What about the human we came to find?' asked Cirict, ever the Tracker.

'The humans will be looking for a way out too,' said Tchek. 'If we find that, we will find the humans – if they still live.' He glanced back. The tomb towers, and the green opaque glow that rose from them, obscured the distance: he could see no sign of pursuit yet. But he knew the Flayed Ones would come searching for them.

And the only way of slowing them down was to give them more necrons to infect. So each tactical victory would be another step towards ensuring their strategic defeat. Tchek knew he had to find a different way of stopping these things. But how could he kill creatures that were not alive in the first place, creatures that were only inconvenienced by the kroot's weapons?

He did not know.

He suspected that the humans had no better ideas than he.

CHAPTER 8

'They are over there.' Amazigh pointed into the green gloom. 'The bird men.'

'You saw them?' asked Obeysekera.

'I heard them,' said the Kamshet. 'They speak with high voices, like birds – few men have ears to hear such speech.'

'You do?'

'Yes,' said Amazigh. 'We listen to the desert. It speaks to us with many voices.'

'What does it say?' asked Obeysekera.

'Oh, many things. But now I am here, I understand much that I did not understand before. The desert hates this place. It is why it has surrounded the Tabaste with flowsand. It would drown the mountain if it could.'

Obeysekera shook his head. 'Which way were the kroot heading?'

Amazigh pointed off at a tangent, but a tangent not too far from their present position.

'We will have to move,' began Obeysekera.

'Wait,' said Amazigh. 'There was something else. I did not see it or hear it, but I felt it and smelled it. Blood, and flesh, the smell of a tannery, but here?' The Kamshet gestured around. 'Here, where all is metal and unalive?'

'Unless you can tell me more...'

Amazigh shook his head.

'...then we continue.' Obeysekera spoke to the squad. 'Scout formation. Ensor, Ha, take the flanks. Gunsur, you have point. Lerin is rearguard. Advance on my bearing.' Obeysekera pointed in the direction he wanted them to follow since the auspexes remained too unreliable for direction readings. 'Amazigh, you listen for the kroot.'

Obeysekera turned to General Itoyesa.

'You will be with me, Commissar Roshant and Sergeant Malick at the centre of the formation. That is as safe a position as is possible, given where we are.'

'So, where are you taking me, captain?' asked General Itoyesa. 'I assume you have a destination in mind and that we are not simply walking and hoping something turns up.'

'I am trying to get us all out of here,' said Obeysekera, answering but not looking at the general. 'Not just you.'

Itoyesa snorted. Obeysekera noted that he did that a lot – but then, it seemed a common characteristic of generals. Every general he had ever met – and there were more than he would have wished to maintain his belief in the competence of high command – sniffed when given news he did not wish to hear. They probably learned that in training.

Obeysekera had been brevetted for promotion to higher ranks but, since the disaster of the Sando retreat, he had always turned down advancement. He never again wanted to be put in a position where he could order men to go off and die while remaining behind himself. But the problem was that Obeysekera really did have no idea where they were all going. He had set off on the basis that action was better than inaction, that whatever portal had brought them into the tomb world had disappeared, leaving no trace, and that there must be a way out and that it would be upwards. Given that the sleeping necron warriors must have some way of getting out of the tomb, then there must be ramps up which they could march to reach the outer world. The most obvious place for such ramps would be around the periphery of the great hall in which they found themselves. They had been walking for nearly half an hour and there was still no sign of any end to the vast space. But the ranks of tomb towers, like trees in a forest, made it impossible to see very far ahead. Obeysekera hoped that they would come to the end of the hall soon.

Hope, though, was not a sound basis for command. Obeysekera knew he had to come up with something better. But he had no idea what.

Even as the helplessness of their situation descended upon him, Obeysekera clung to the training and spirit of the 'kin. The Kasrkin were adept at working behind enemy lines: squads had been in worse situations than this and still completed their missions and escaped to report. Admittedly, he was hard put to remember a mission that had been quite so trapped within enemy territory, but he was sure such existed.

He was not going to lose another squad of men.

Gunsur sent the 'hold' command over the squad vox-channel.

'What is it, Gunsur?' Obeysekera whispered into the vox as the rest of the squad took up fire positions behind cover.

'Can you come forward to me, captain?' said Gunsur. *'But come quiet and bring the savage.'*

Obeysekera, hellgun cradled and ready, made his way forward with Amazigh beside him until they reached Gunsur's position and slid in beside him behind a tomb tower.

'What is it?' asked Obeysekera, trying to ignore the fact that he was crouching a foot away from a sleeping necron warrior. So long as it stayed asleep, he should be all right.

Gunsur gestured for Obeysekera to listen and he did so, turning his head.

There was movement.

Gunsur pointed up. Obeysekera looked and saw, high above, a creature like some monstrous spider, only it was floating through the air. The sound of movement was its legs, clicking against the side of the tomb tower. Judging by the number of tomb layers above them, it was more than six hundred feet above their heads.

Gunsur pointed again.

Where the creature touched one of the sarcophagi, there was a subtle flare of green light that then settled into a sequence of green lights, glowing and diminishing in brightness. But the overall effect was of the light increasing at the higher levels of the tomb.

'What does that mean?'

Obeysekera was whispering to himself, but Amazigh answered.

'They are waking.'

Obeysekera looked at the Kamshet. Amazigh was staring upwards. The Kamshet turned to the Kasrkin. Even with just his eyes visible, Obeysekera could see the fear that underlay his whisper.

'They are waking,' he repeated.

Obeysekera shook his head. 'We don't know that yet. That creature could just be running checks.'

'We have prophecies, in poor rhyme, of a time when the desert shall spread and give up the dead – now I see that which the prophecies spoke of. Dead yet not dead, living but unbreathing.'

'All the more reason to find some way out of here,' said Obeysekera. He turned to Gunsur. 'Wait for the spyder to pass, then carry on.' He pointed. 'That bearing.' So far as he could tell from his erratic auspex they were keeping on the same bearing. Sooner or later they must surely come to an end to this seemingly unending hall.

But before he could turn back, Obeysekera heard a sudden rattle above. He looked up, to see the spyder dragging itself over the tomb tower in sudden haste. At first, he thought it had detected them, but the spyder was not climbing downwards. Instead, it launched itself over to the next tower, sailing over the gap as if it were a balloon, landing in a flurry of claws and then jumping off again to the next tower.

'Something's happening,' said Gunsur.

As he spoke, they heard the sound of gunfire echoing dully through the columns of the dead. Even refracted through the gaps between the tomb towers, Obeysekera could identify the distinctive cough sound of the kroot rifles.

'How far?'

Gunsur shook his head. He could not tell.

'Far,' said Amazigh, 'but I would that it were further.'

'We will make it further,' said Obeysekera. He pointed. 'Head that way, Gunsur.' It was at a tangent to their original bearing, but the change was worth it to take them away from the kroot. Let the birds distract the guardians of the sleeping necrons; so long as they could find the ramps out, they could take this opportunity to escape.

'You are sacrificing the kroot so we may escape?'

Obeysekera looked round to see the general had come to join them. 'Yes,' he replied.

Itoyesa gestured around them. 'What we face here is a greater threat than that posed by the kroot. Where necessary, when faced by a worse threat, the Imperium has made common cause with xenos in the past. We should make common cause with the kroot now.'

'General, the kroot are hunting us – they are hunting you. Going up to them to suggest an alliance would be received by a volley of bullets.'

'I was not thinking of anything so obvious.'

'And we have no time for something more subtle.' Obeysekera keyed on the squad vox-channel.

'Let's go. Follow Gunsur on this new bearing. Ensor, Ha, triangulate on me.'

'*Yes, sir,*' said Ensor.

Obeysekera waited a moment.

'Ha, respond.'

Silence on the vox-channel. Obeysekera checked the auspex readings, but they were as erratic as they had been throughout their time in the desert.

'Ha, respond.'

Still silence.

'*Sir, I can't see him.*' Malick, speaking from further back.

'Lerin, come up, stay with Commissar Roshant and the general. Malick, rendezvous with me at Ha's last position.' Obeysekera switched out of the group channel and turned to Gunsur. 'Wait here.' He looked at Amazigh. 'Come with me.'

The Kasrkin and the Kamshet made their way between the ranks of tomb towers, angling towards Ha's last position. Obeysekera had his hellgun ready, Amazigh his autogun. Obeysekera slowed as they neared Ha's final location, taking cover behind the next tomb tower. Looking left, he saw Malick approaching. The sergeant, seeing them, took cover behind a tomb tower too.

Obeysekera pointed for Malick to wait and then slid a hand mirror slowly around the edge of the tomb tower – it was strange how he could forget the proximity of sleeping necrons when concentrating upon something else – and looked into it.

Ha was there. He could see him, squatting beside the tomb tower. His vox must have failed.

Obeysekera was about to step out from the tomb tower when a movement stopped him. What was Ha doing? He seemed to be peeling something from the ground. In the periscope, Obeysekera saw Ha lift a sheet of what looked like paper, but it was thicker and scored with lines. Then Ha twisted and started laying the paper over his shoulder.

And, suddenly, the scene switched.

He was not looking at Ha. He was looking at something wearing Ha's face. It reached down again and Obeysekera saw that its fingers were needles and knives, and sprawled before its squatting body was a wet mound from which it sliced a fresh cut of meat that it laid about its shoulders.

It was butchering Ha and decorating itself with his body.

Flayed One.

Another hypnocache helpfully popped the words into his memory. It accompanied the words with a carefully modulated impression of terror – the information that had gone into the hypnocache had been mainly compiled from the testimony of the handful of survivors from Hain Jalat III.

Ha was dead.

Every instinct told Obeysekera to avenge the death of his soldier, to open fire with Malick and Amazigh and turn that metal horror into liquid slag.

But the hypnocaches were helpfully filling his memory with information as to the sheer difficulty of killing necrons. Not that he needed the hypnocaches to tell him that. Further hypnocaches were telling him that the Flayed Ones were even more difficult to kill. And where there was one, there were likely others. But Obeysekera had no position for them.

As he waited, caught in indecision, a fresh and sustained volley of kroot rifle fire came rolling down towards them from farther in the tomb. The Flayed One turned to look, the flayed face of Trooper Ha rotating back over the creature's shoulders as its neck turned one hundred and eighty degrees. In the periscope, Obeysekera could see the empty eye sockets and, in their depths, the livid green of the Flayed One's own eyes. But although the fire intensified, the Flayed One did not move. Instead, it squatted down lower over Ha's body, like a carnodon protecting its kill.

'Withdraw,' Obeysekera whispered into his vox. He saw Malick acknowledge and start pulling back. He pointed for Amazigh to follow Malick, but the Kamshet was waiting for him.

Obeysekera risked one final look at the man he had lost.

'May the Emperor have mercy on you,' he whispered.

The Kasrkin brought their own back. But for the sake of the rest of the squad and the mission, he was abandoning Ha, leaving him as a flesh trophy for the Flayed One. He was doing it again: abandoning his men for the sake of the mission.

'I am sorry.'

Obeysekera started to retreat, with Amazigh creeping beside him.

'Captain.' It was Malick, ahead. 'Motion. Forty-five degrees.'

Obeysekera stopped, looking past where Malick had taken a firing position on one knee, his hellgun raised and pointing. From behind, the distant volleys of kroot rifle fire rolled away past them, with none following on afterwards. High above, Obeysekera heard the metal clatter of canoptek spyders scrambling between tomb towers.

There. Between the tomb towers. Another.

Wearing the face of Chame.

It was walking like an insect, lifting its legs high, stopping with its foot in the air, then putting it down and advancing again. It stepped forward, foot raised, then stopped, poised like a metal statue. Its skin mask turned, rotating like a gun on its pintle, towards them. Chame's face stared at them, skin sagging, chin drooping down over the creature's neck, eye sockets empty of life but livid with green light.

The Chame creature slowly raised its hand – and its hand was garlanded with Chame's fingers – and pointed at them.

It pointed and it screamed.

They did it without thinking, without an order.

Obeysekera, Malick and Amazigh all opened up with their weapons, Malick cycling through hotshots, Obeysekera draining a whole powercell of his hellgun and Amazigh emptying the magazine of his autogun.

Chame's face disintegrated.

The Flayed One, caught on one foot, fell backwards, follow-up rounds slamming into it, transfixing it against the tomb tower behind it. Hellgun rounds slammed into its metal body and as they struck, again and again, they began to flay body parts from the Flayed One. Beaten by the hammers of their fire, the Flayed One disintegrated, its limbs dropping from its body, its torso falling and, finally, the green fire in its eye sockets flickering to darkness.

Their fire died away.

Malick went over to its remains and kicked the metal skull. 'So you do die.'

Obeysekera pointed past his sergeant. The sarcophagus which the Flayed One had fallen against was cracked and breaking. As he pointed, the crystal shattered and the shards showered down upon the necron warrior within.

Malick turned his hellgun upon the necron, but it did not stir. 'Still sleeping, sir,' he said.

'Let's hope it stays asleep,' said Obeysekera.

'Master.' It was Amazigh. He was pointing back the way they had come. 'It follows.'

Obeysekera turned. Stalking towards them, moving like a hunting insect, was the Flayed One that had killed Ha.

Ha's skin was fresh; his face was stretched tight over the Flayed One's metal skull so that it almost looked as if the dead trooper himself were coming after them, intent on revenge for having been abandoned.

Malick opened fire while Obeysekera clicked a fresh powercell into place. The Flayed One staggered under the first impacts of Malick's hellgun but, with only one weapon firing at it, the necron recovered and, like a man moving against a current, moved into the cover of a tomb tower. Malick kept firing and the crystal of the sarcophagus began to craze, then shatter.

'Fall back,' Obeysekera ordered Malick. With the Flayed One under cover and his vox squawking with messages from the rest of the squad asking what was going on, it was their chance to retreat. If the Flayed One came after them, it would face the concentrated firepower of the whole squad.

What was left of it.

As they pulled back, Obeysekera glanced at the life sign indicators. He had lost five members of his squad. It was all going wrong.

In front of him, he saw the Flayed One crawling over the shattered casket of the sleeping necron. From a distance, and with the fog of green light, Obeysekera could not make out what the creature was doing. It appeared to be bending over the sleeping form, as if it were feeding it. For a moment, the memory of his mother feeding him came back from the deep cache of his own earliest memories.

Obeysekera thanked the Emperor's providence that she had died before the end of Cadia and not lived to see the fall of that which she had spent her life protecting.

'Fall back, fall back.'

Obeysekera, Amazigh and Malick returned to where Roshant, Lerin and General Itoyesa were waiting, hellguns trained in their direction.

'What is happening?' General Itoyesa demanded.

'Flayed Ones,' said Obeysekera. 'Ha is down. Chame, too, but we killed the creature that took her. There is at least one more.'

'Hard to kill,' said Malick, slapping a fresh power pack into his hellgun. 'Frekking hard.'

'Concentrate fire,' said Obeysekera. 'Kinetic energy – enough to stop it. Aim for the joints first. Disable it. Then kill it.'

General Itoyesa stared at Obeysekera, his face green in the livid light. 'What have you done?'

'Not us, general. They were alive, moving, hunting – whatever you want to call it – before we came here.'

'No living creature comes near the Tabaste,' added Amazigh. 'Now I know for why.'

'How long?' asked Itoyesa, turning to the Kamshet.

'Many lives,' said Amazigh. 'Many, many lives.'

'Then the infection has not spread through the tomb,' said General Itoyesa. 'For if it had, the creatures would have gone out into the world. There must only be a handful, preying on whatever flesh and blood creature ventures onto the mountain.'

'Enough talking,' said Obeysekera. 'We must keep moving. I will take rear-guard. Skirmish formation. Malick, Roshant, stay with the general. On my bearing...' He pointed. 'Move.'

The Kasrkin moved into formation with trained ease, Malick and Roshant flanking the general, Gunsur on point and Lerin and Ensor covering the flanks. Obeysekera waited for them to move off, covering the rear against the Flayed One that was wearing Ha's face.

The captain checked his chrono. They had been moving for an hour. Even with the stops, they must have covered a good distance already. They must surely reach the limits of this tomb before long. There had to be some way out of the tomb.

Surely?

Following in Gunsur's cautious path, Roshant felt as if he were walking through a living nightmare. The tomb towers, some vast piles, others slender spires, stalagmites of a vast metal cavern; the livid light that obscured as much as it illuminated; the sense of creeping, growing terror: everything combined to make it seem as if he were awake but walking through a dream.

Roshant tried regulating his breathing, counting the breaths; he tried pinching the back of his arm; he tried closing his eyes then opening them. But he was still in the tomb of the necrons being pursued by abominations wearing the faces of men.

General Itoyesa was stumping along beside him, swearing softly but continuously under his breath, his bolt pistol scanning left and right in front as he walked.

It was a nightmare.

Roshant closed his eyes again, squeezing the eyelids shut so that his eyes hurt, then opened them.

Malick was walking beside him, moving with the practised looseness of the veteran Kasrkin that he was, his hellgun held ready.

'Where did you come from?' asked Roshant. The sergeant had been on the other side of the general when he closed his eyes.

'Not what you signed up for?' said Malick, speaking through their personal vox-circuit. Even though the general was only a few feet away, he would not hear what they were saying.

'A commissar does his duty in whatever service the Emperor demands of him,' said Roshant.

'Straight from the book, commissar. Good. Me, I'm getting pretty sick of the book round about now. Ha down, Chame, Uwais – the captain's losing soldiers faster than "Butcher" Itoyesa.'

'Keep your voice down, the general might hear.'

'I'm speaking on secure, he won't hear anything. Besides, he's too busy watching for skeletons wearing skin suits to listen to us.'

'As you should be, sergeant.'

'Oh, I am, commissar, I am. I've given too much blood for the Emperor to end up draped over one of the tin boys.'

Roshant, scanning himself, saw movement at their flank and jerked his bolt pistol round towards it. Malick, using the barrel of his hellgun, pushed up Roshant's weapon before he could fire.

'It's Lerin,' he said to the commissar. 'Don't want to be shooting one of our own, sir. Not when we've got so few of them.' Malick looked past Roshant to the general. 'False alarm, sir. Nothing to worry about.'

General Itoyesa nodded and stomped on, giving vent to his frustration with every step he took.

Malick nodded after Itoyesa. 'We'll follow him. Not often us troopers have a general around to take the bullets for us.'

'We are supposed to protect the general,' said Roshant.

'I know,' said Malick. 'But you said it yourself – what if he's tainted? Then it'd be your duty to make sure he never gets back to HQ.'

'I've seen no evidence of that yet.'

'Still time, commissar, still time.'

'I trust you will inform me if you see anything suspicious, sergeant.'

'Oh, I will, commissar, I will.'

'Thank you, sergeant.'

'Then you'd be in line for choosing your next posting, wouldn't you, you being the lord militant's son and all.'

'I could not say, sergeant. But I hope my service would give me some influence in where I go.'

'Good idea to have someone with you to watch your back, commissar. Someone experienced.'

Roshant glanced at the sergeant. Malick was walking alongside him, scanning for movement, but the question hung between them.

'You, sergeant?'

'I reckon I'd be a good choice.'

Roshant stared at the Kasrkin sergeant. 'But don't you want to stay with your squad?'

Malick grimaced. 'There ain't much left of it now, commissar. The captain's going to lose another company, only I'm not going to be one of them.'

Roshant shook his head. 'But these are your comrades. You must stay with them.'

'You reckon so, commissar?'

'It's what the Guard expects of non-commissioned officers.'

'I know what the Guard expects – bodies, blood and bowels. The Guard eats troopers, chews them up, spits them out.' Malick glanced at the commissar. 'I aim to miss the spitting out part. I hear Venera VI is nice this time of year.'

'Venera VI? Isn't it a resort world? Not really the sort of place that needs a commissar of the Officio Prefectus.'

'Still raises regiments for the Guard. Bet they've not had a proper inspection in decades. Probably all sort of rot under the skin. Seems like a good place to get a posting.' Malick gestured around them. 'You not telling me you want to go through all this again?'

'No, of course not. But I don't understand. I've read your records, sergeant. You're the model Kasrkin sergeant. Why do you want out?'

'You want to know? You really want to know?'

'If you are to accompany me as my bodyguard, then yes, I want to know why.'

Malick walked on beside Roshant, his eyes scanning the green gloom, and it seemed he would not answer. Then, in a quiet voice, he began to speak.

'I was there. I saw it come crashing down. All the generals, all the warmasters, all the High Lords of Terra, they said it was secure, they said it would stand. They were wrong. It fell. Now I hear people yammer "Cadia stands this" and "Cadia stands that". It's all bullshit. It didn't just fall, it broke. I lost everything trying to save it – my wife, my parents, my daughter. I'm not losing anything else trying to save something that doesn't even exist any longer.

'No, commissar, you watch my back and I'll watch yours, and together we'll find ourselves a nice quiet posting somewhere on the fringes of the Imperium. It's a big, big galaxy and, you know what? In most places, nothing much is happening. People are living their lives, making babies, eating, drinking, all the normal human stuff. I say, we're going to try that. So you get yourself assigned to a nice quiet world where you can bully the locals with your commissar's badge, and I will swing along behind you, watching your back, making sure we both get to enjoy a long, happy retirement. 'Cause this galaxy is going to hell in a handcart, but we're not going down with it.'

Sergeant Malick looked at Roshant.

'You're not stupid, are you, commissar? You might be a coward, but you're not stupid.'

Roshant looked at the general, still walking ahead of them, then dropped his voice even further.

'I am not a coward.'

'Sure,' said Malick. 'Nor me. But we've earned this. So here's my promise, commissar. I'll get you out of this alive, and you look out for me when we're back with the Guard.'

Roshant glanced at Malick. 'You honestly think we will get out of this alive?'

'I don't know about the rest, but you and me, we will.'

Roshant looked away. 'We will all get out of here, sergeant.'

Malick nodded. 'Whatever you say, sir.'

CHAPTER 9

Nebusemekh breathed deep. He felt his chest expand. He tasted the air rushing in through his nose and mouth. He heard the beat of his heart. He was in prime health for his age: not an ache, no pain, as mobile as when he was young.

Nebusemekh began to raise the sand, lifting it into the air. As he did so, a thought, a ghost memory flicked at his focus and he turned towards it, searching.

That was it.

The party of explorers had returned. The Mind of the World was bringing them to him to tell him what they had found. Where were they?

'Where are they?'

Nebusemekh waited for an answer, his hands twitching towards the sand, but he stopped them.

'Where are the explorers? You said you would bring them to me.'

There was still no answer from the World Mind. Nebusemekh sighed. The sand fell like water from the air. He turned and walked across the throne-lab to the World Mind. He looked up at it as he approached. It reminded him of a waterfall. But rather than water, data streamed down the wall in number flows, the data that was the inputs of all the sensors and devices throughout the world.

Nebusemekh put his hand into the datafall. His mind expanded, the walls between his flesh and the world dissolved, and he was himself, but everywhere.

'Why did you not answer when I spoke to you earlier?'

The World Mind apologised. It had really been very busy and had routed some of its protocols in such a way that it could not divert its processing power towards non-essential routines.

'So speaking with me, your master, is classified as a non-essential routine?'

No, the World Mind averred. Speaking with Nebusemekh and carrying out his wishes was its most essential routine. There had, unfortunately, been a minor error in its sub-protocols that had led to a misclassification of incoming aural communication as non-essential: it had tracked down the issue and immediately rerouted the protocol away from that subroutine.

'Good, good,' said Nebusemekh. 'Where is my party of brave explorers?

I am waiting to greet them and to learn what they have discovered about the state of the world.'

The World Mind hesitated to mention this, as it was sure that Nebusemekh remembered their previous conversation, but they had agreed that it was important that the party of explorers were checked and found to be free of the virus before being brought before Nebusemekh.

'Of course, I remember it. Of course. But you have surely had sufficient time to check if the explorers are diseased or not?'

Nebusemekh, hand in the datafall, saw as the World Mind spoke; he saw and he heard the sound of weapons being fired in the Great Hall.

'What is going on in my hall?'

The World Mind admitted that it had made a small error, and when it had brought the explorers into the dormitory, it had inadvertently brought back one or two of the infected as well.

Nebusemekh stared into the datafall without saying anything. As he did so, the streams of numbers began to jumble. The binaries started to fracture, into binomials first and then irrational and imaginary numbers appeared.

The World Mind enquired if Nebusemekh was going to say anything.

Nebusemekh continued to stare into the datafall and the numbers fractured further, taking on topological and geometrical characteristics.

The World Mind said that it apologised and that under no circumstances would it ever make such a mistake again.

'You are right,' said Nebusemekh. 'If you should fail me again in like manner, I would disconnect you.'

The World Mind admitted unreservedly that it deserved the rebuke, but it suggested that the punishment was more severe than the error – a minor malfunction of a small set of sub-routines – truly warranted.

'It is not for you to tell me what is warranted. You are merely a machine, a set of instructions doing what I have told you to do, whereas I, I am alive. I am maker, creator.'

It was truly unworthy to converse with its creator, but the Mind had gained greatly from its contact with its maker and would not wish to have that connection jeopardised in any way. To ensure that, it had activated the protocol to wake some of the sleepers so that they might find the infected and either sterilise them or eject them from the tomb.

'You have done what?'

The World Mind explained again that it was running the program that brought the sleepers to a waking state so that it might find the infected and either sterilise them or eject them from the tomb.

'All those datafalls and you still can't recognise a rhetorical question when you hear one.'

Ah. The World Mind admitted that it still struggled with rhetorical devices and that alongside rhetorical questions, it also found sarcasm difficult to recognise, while irony remained almost completely mysterious.

'Just accept it was a rhetorical question. The underlying question was why have you started to wake some of the sleepers?'

The World Mind began to explain that it was to find the infected and either sterilise them or– when it was interrupted by Nebusemekh punching his other hand into the datafall.

'I will strangle you, even though you do not have a throat to squeeze.'

The datafall streaming over Nebusemekh's two arms grew turbid, fractals and chaotic breakdowns integrating into the stream then differentiating out.

The World Mind begged Nebusemekh to stop. It had, it admitted, made some very poor decisions of late, but it was completely committed to carrying out its mandate.

Nebusemekh squeezed the numbers harder.

The World Mind asked Nebusemekh to stop. It was concerned that it would not be able to carry out its primary function if Nebusemekh continued.

'What is your primary function?'

The World Mind said that its primary function was to maintain and preserve the tomb world.

'No. Your primary function is to do what I say.'

Of course, the master was right, the World Mind agreed.

'What are you doing to eradicate the infected and establish the explorers are free from the contagion and safe to bring into my presence?'

It was proving more difficult than it had anticipated, the World Mind admitted, for the infected ones were difficult to detect; they seemed able to slip in and out of ground phase, so they registered only fleetingly in its sensors.

'Excuses.'

The World Mind avowed that it was not an excuse but the truth.

Nebusemekh rose gently into the air.

The master was master of gravity; perhaps he would like to turn his attention to the problem of finding the infected? the World Mind asked.

'No, I certainly would not. Do you expect me to run any risk of infection by this dreadful disease? You are a machine – you are safe from it. Therefore, it is your task to find and eliminate the infected.'

To that end, the World Mind hoped that its decision to wake some of the sleeping warriors might find favour with the master, since they could follow and find the infected.

'An excellent plan. Continue with it.'

The World Mind thanked the master for his approval and trusted it would not be long before the infected were expelled.

'What of the explorers? Have you found them?'

The World Mind explained that it was hoping to employ the warriors it was waking to find the explorers and establish that they were free of infection before bringing them to the master. It humbly requested that it might have permission to wake more warriors than the minimum that was within its authority to raise from sleep.

'You have it.'

The datafall steadied and cleared around Nebusemekh's arms, the binomials running smooth over the integers.

The World Mind thanked the Master for his faith in its strategy and suggested that he return to his valuable experiments that the World Mind was confident were becoming increasingly close to success.

'You think so too?'

It was almost a certainty, the World Mind agreed.

'Carry on.'

Nebusemekh pulled his arms free of the datafall and the wash of inputs suddenly ceased. He still had second-order access to the tomb, but it was filtered, limited to inputs of interest as determined by the World Mind's protocols.

'Keep me informed,' he said.

'I will immediately inform you of anything of interest, master,' said the World Mind, its voice now aural rather than direct.

'I will return to my work. Interrupt me if it's important, otherwise do not disturb me.'

'Of course, master.'

Nebusemekh returned to the table. He started sorting through the sand. He stopped. His concentration, normally so fixed upon his ongoing experiment, was fragmented, his attention wandering elsewhere.

He searched his mind for what was disturbing it.

The conversation with the World Mind replayed itself, underlaid with the main inputs from the tomb. There was something there that was distracting his attention, like a pebble in his shoe.

There.

When he had given the World Mind permission to exceed the minimum number of wakings that it was authorised to do under its normal operating protocols: there. Nebusemekh followed the data flow, tracing the trail out into the tomb, out into the dormitories.

The World Mind was waking the sleepers.

Not just one or two. It was starting the stepped progress program to wake the sleepers and open the tomb. It was waking up his people.

It was waking his people when the infected were free, roaming around with the World Mind admitting that it was unable to locate them. It was waking them to the risk of being infected with that terrible virus.

What was it doing?

Why was it doing it?

Nebusemekh sighed. He turned, walked back across the thronelab and thrust his arms into the datafall.

CHAPTER 10

There were more Flayed Ones.

Tchek could smell them. The smell of flesh, rank and decaying, and the faint, lingering odour of skin, dried and old.

The Kinband – Tchek, Kliptiq the Bearer, Krasykyl the Stalker and Cirict the Tracker – was making its way between the tomb towers, skirting the larger ones, keeping closer to the narrower columns as they offered less cover to anything waiting to ambush them, while the pech'ra flew silently above them.

They were tracking towards the sound of bolt pistols and las-fire. The humans were down here too. With no other course open to him, Tchek was taking the Kinband towards their target; they might – they almost certainly would – die down here in the green light, but while able they would seek to carry out the task they had given oath to achieve.

It was a trust. Tchek had never betrayed a trust.

'They want flesh,' said Krasykyl, sweeping his rifle in an arc as he moved alongside the Shaper. 'Not for feast but for decoration.'

'It is not decoration,' said Tchek. He was thinking of the way the Flayed One had covered itself with Stryax. 'Orks take trophies of their foes, but that is not what they were doing.' His crown quills flashed through the spectrum and beyond as he thought on the problem. 'It was as if it was trying to become.'

'What? By dressing itself with meat?'

'More than dressing. It was as if...' Tchek's crown quills went into the ultraviolet frequencies. 'As if it was putting on a body.' The Shaper looked at the Stalker. 'It thinks it is alive. It wants to be alive.'

'Alive? It is metal. It is not alive – if it was, we could feast.'

'Some have.'

'A Shaper has eaten one of these things?' Krasykyl pointed at a sleeping necron. 'How?'

'It does not require much to feast. A finger can be enough.'

Krasykyl trilled his scepticism. 'A finger?'

'At least it would be possible to swallow a finger – you would not have to chew.'

'So we have feasted on these things?'

'A Shaper did so. He did partake of its soul, or whatever animating spirit gives it being, but he could not keep the knowledge. He began to convulse and foam at the beak, as if he was trying to regurgitate what he had eaten. But before he could do so, his stomach split open and hundreds of silver scarab beetles came streaming out.' Tchek looked at the Stalker. 'So we can feast on these things, but they do not agree with us.'

Krasykyl shook his head, seeing the lights of the Shaper's crown quills. 'Are you thinking of taking one of these things for Feast? It is madness.'

'Madness is being trapped down here with no knowledge and less chance of ever finding a way out.'

'No, you must not do this thing,' said Krasykyl.

'I have no intention of doing so – unless the situation leaves me no alternative,' said Tchek.

'This Kinband will be adrift without a Shaper,' said Krasykyl.

'The Shaper directs his Kinband,' said Tchek. 'I have brought you down here, into the dark. I will not leave you here if by any means I can save you.'

'Not that way,' said Krasykyl.

'Only if there is no other way,' said Tchek. But as he spoke, he heard a change in the hall of the tomb towers. Before, there had always been a distant, low sound, like a t'au city heard from a great distance. The background noise was still there, but it had stepped up a tone in pitch. He looked round, listening.

'Do you hear that?'

Krasykyl turned his head too, his crown quills flaring as he listened.

'It is waking.'

Tchek nodded. 'I fear that it is beginning – the tomb will open.' He stared up at the tomb towers rising above them. 'Should it do so then no power on this world would be able to stop it.'

'Then we will have to stop it.'

Tchek and Krasykyl turned round to see the Bearer, Kliptiq, the Feast pot still strapped to his back, his rifle steady in his hand. The Bearer looked at the Shaper and the Stalker.

'Why are you staring at me?'

'It is... unusual for you to tell me what to do, Kliptiq,' said Tchek. 'Why did you do so then?'

Kliptiq clapped his hands over his beak. 'Did I?' he asked, the words muffled by the hands.

'Yes. You said that we must stop the tomb opening.'

'I did?' squeaked Kliptiq.

'Yes.'

'I thought that's what you said. It's obvious, I was sure you said it, Shaper. Are you sure you didn't?'

'Yes, I am sure,' said Tchek. 'But you are right.' He looked at Krasykyl. 'We are here to capture the human and that remains our first obligation. But when we have found the human, then we will have to try to stop the tomb opening.'

'How?' Krasykyl gestured at the three of them and Cirict ahead. 'There's four of us left. How do we stop all this?' His gesture took in the hall and its tomb towers, stretching up out of sight.

'Something is stirring, waking the sleepers,' said Tchek. 'They have slept for a long, long time. Whatever has kept watch over them is no living thing – for it would certainly have slipped into dust an age ago – but something of the nature of these things, something of metal. Or maybe it is like the instruments the t'au use, one of their thinking machines. If we can find it, then we can stop it.'

'But where would we find it in all this?' asked Krasykyl.

'Where indeed?' Tchek paused. 'It would be deep. The necrons have sought safety deep underground. The thinking machine that watches over them and that is now beginning to wake them must be deeper still.'

'Have you seen any tunnels or stairs heading down?' asked Krasykyl. 'Because I have not.'

'If it is a thinking machine, it would not use such devices,' said Tchek. 'It is like a spider in its web, sitting at the centre, testing each strand for the touch of prey or foe.'

'So you say we have to go down. How?' Krasykyl pointed at the hard metal floor. 'Even if we feasted on a mole rat, we would not make much headway through that.'

'There must be a way,' said Tchek. 'If only so that creatures such as those mechanical spiders can move around. I think they are employed in maintaining this place.'

'Either that or they like spinning metal webs,' said Krasykyl. 'Up there.' He pointed into the heights.

'There are webs there?'

'Of sticky metal. I climbed up to look. I am the Stalker.'

Before Tchek could answer, they heard a whistle signal from Cirict up ahead.

Problem.

They made their way forward to where Cirict was waiting for them with Flet standing upon his arm. The Tracker pointed ahead.

'That is the direction the humans are going,' he said. 'But that is in the way.'

Strung between the tomb towers was a net of fine strands of shining metal, woven into an intricate pattern.

'Metal web,' said Krasykyl.

'It has caught something in its trap,' added Cirict. He pointed deep into the metal tangle, and they saw there something that was itself metal but garlanded with flesh and bone. The Flayed One hung in the web, hopelessly snared, and as they watched they saw it thrash against its net some more, only to wind the metal more tightly around itself.

'It would have been easy to stumble into a web like this when it was dark,' said Cirict. 'Flet warned me of it.'

At his voice, the Flayed One stopped its struggles. Hanging there, it turned its eyes, the only part of its body that was still free to move, towards where they stood. The four kroot saw its eyes, livid, viscous green, through the mask of dry skin that had shrunk upon its metal skull. The flesh upon its body had dried to almost leather, testimony to how long it had hung in the metal web.

Cirict twisted his head. The Tracker had feasted on warhound, incorporating that beast's extraordinary olfactory sensitivity into his own sense of smell.

'The humans are on the other side of this creature,' he said. 'I can smell them.'

'How far?' asked Tchek.

'Not far. Their scent is strong.'

Tchek looked to see the extent of the web, then pointed left. 'We shall go round.'

At his words, the Flayed One jerked towards them, straining with all the energy left to it to get towards the creatures of flesh. The web wound tighter as it struggled, but still the Flayed One flailed at them, trying to get free.

'Leave it,' said Tchek. He pointed ahead. 'There is a gap in the web there.'

While webs were strung around all the nearby tomb towers, there was a clear gap between two of them.

'Trap?' said Krasykyl.

'Possibly.' Tchek turned to the Tracker. 'Cirict.'

The Tracker brought the pech'ra up to his beak and whispered to the creature, speaking in the high registers that were its range. Then he raised his arm and the pech'ra took wing. It flew upwards, and headed towards the gap between the metal tangle webs. It glided out of their sight, but the kroot could hear its whistle; Cirict let it go for another thirty seconds and then whistle-called it back. Flet glided back to them, landed on the Tracker's outstretched arm, accepted the stinkbug that was its due, and then listened, its head tilted, as Cirict spoke to it. The pech'ra rotated its head, looking at Cirict as if checking that he had not switched to the 'prey' category, then answered his questions.

'Flet says it's clear,' said Cirict.

Tchek turned to Krasykyl. 'First.'

The Stalker raised his crown quills, then, holding his rifle ready, made his way to the narrow gap between the tangle webs. He turned and whistle-called Cirict up beside him. Tchek heard him ask the Tracker if he could smell anything. Cirict pointed at the Flayed One, hanging in the tangle web, green eyes fixed upon them.

It reminded Tchek of the spider-apes of Chika IV, who wove their traps with the lianas and creepers and stranglers that straggled up over the high trunks of the jagga trees towards the green light of the canopy. The spider-apes squatted in the dark below the tree cover, their eyes as verdant as the light, waiting beside the tangle traps they strung below the treetops.

Tchek had feasted upon spider-ape to take their patience and their perseverance and to bring those qualities into the Kinband. From the eyes of the spider-ape, the world was made of things that moved and things that didn't – and all that moved was their prey, although prey was divided into those things that could be caught in their tangle webs and those things, such as the kroot ox, that could not, for it would tear the tangles from the trees and walk away, dragging the web upon its back for another to feast upon what was made fast there.

It was a simple dichotomy and one that Tchek sometimes envied.

But even the spider-apes were close cousins in comparison to the thing that hung in the tangle web, straining after the flesh of the living. Tchek thought that his stomach would revolt against having to feast on such as that. He hoped very much that he would not have to.

Cirict's crown quills went through cycles of light set to frequencies invisible to creatures used to narrower bands of seeing. But the Kinband had feasted on creatures that lived on planets surrounding hot blue stars, where the light rose to pitches beyond the sight of those that had been brought to being beneath gentler, more kindly stars. The light told the story of Cirict's olfactory organ and how it was sampling the air streaming through the gap between the tangle webs. For Tchek could feel the slight breeze. Even to his sense of smell, sharpened only by the gleanings of the Feast that had given Cirict his nose, the scent of the humans was clear.

It was the fleshy, rank, faintly metallic smell that Cirict had identified earlier.

The Tracker pointed. 'The humans are that way. Close. But I smell metal and blood too, although fainter. There are more of those Flayed Ones beyond.'

'If the scent of the Flayed Ones becomes stronger, tell me,' Tchek whistle-signed.

'Don't worry, I will,' whistled Cirict.

'I don't want one of those in my pot,' said the Bearer, pointing at the Flayed One hanging in the tangle web.

'I won't ask you to feast on that,' said Tchek. 'It has nothing you need. Although it might have something that I will need,' he added, speaking to himself. The Shaper looked at how the Flayed One was hanging in the tangle web. If necessary, it might be possible to get close to it – its struggles had ripped parts of the tangle web aside – and take some of its body for the Feast. It would only need to be a small part.

The Flayed One, as if sensing his thoughts, flailed once more at the sticky metal strands holding it trapped. The strands, as if responding to its struggles, wrapped more tightly around its body, but its hands were still relatively uncovered.

While Tchek was thinking on what he might have to eat, Krasykyl and Cirict advanced through the narrow gap in the tangle web, taking care not to touch the sticky metal strands dangling from the tomb towers, the Tracker keeping his pech'ra on his arm to ensure the bird did not get trapped in the all-but-invisible web.

'Come, we will follow,' Tchek said to Kliptiq. The Shaper felt the loss – the Kinband was empty of two who had come to this planet with him: Stryax and Chaktak. He would make sacrifice to Vawk that there would be no more, but he feared that here, in the dark beneath the world, the god of the sky would not see his prayer.

The Shaper and the Bearer followed after the Stalker and the Tracker. As they passed through the narrowest section of the gap between the tangle webs, Tchek saw the sticky metal shift. He looked sharply towards the Flayed One, but it was hanging immobile in the web. It was the metal itself that was shifting, shivering at the approach of living flesh.

From the t'au, Tchek had learned that metal could be servant and slave, but this metal that hung in tendrils from the tomb towers sought to master the flesh, not submit to it. It was a terrible but wondrous fate to live in a galaxy where everything sought after movement and life, whether itself alive or not.

Having passed between the writhing nets of metal tangle web, Tchek and Kliptiq found Krasykyl and Cirict waiting for them, rifles covering the approach paths.

'Which way?' Tchek asked Cirict.

The Tracker turned his head, sweeping scent into his olfactory organs.

'That way.' He pointed ahead.

Tchek looked in the direction the Tracker was pointing. The tomb towers stretched away, masking distance as the trees did in the great forests of Pech, but there was a different quality to the light at the limit of what he could see, a hint of brightness in the distance that recalled to him the light that limned the forest's edge on Pech.

Perhaps they were finally approaching the limits of this vast underground space. Although why there should be more light at the walls of this hall was something he did not understand.

'Lead us,' Tchek told Cirict. 'Krasykyl, follow.' Tchek pointed above. 'Go high but avoid the spiders. Call if you see anything. We will follow.'

Krasykyl flowed up the nearest tomb tower while Cirict advanced cautiously, keeping in cover, head swinging from side to side as he gathered stimuli – smell, sound, sight – to his enhanced senses.

Tchek, with the Bearer beside him, followed. Glancing up, he saw Krasykyl moving soundlessly between the towers, using the gantries, wires, pipes and mesh that connected the tomb towers at higher levels, flowing as effortlessly as water while the pech'ra ranged in advance.

They had not gone far when Cirict stopped. The Tracker whistle-called back to the Shaper, asking Tchek to come forward to him.

Tchek made his way to where Cirict crouched in cover behind a tomb tower. As he crept past the stacked sarcophagi, it occurred to Tchek how quickly it was possible to grow accustomed to horrors. He was within touching distance of a necron warrior but because it slept, and he had walked past so many of them, he did not even look at the metal skeleton as he passed it.

Reaching the Tracker, Tchek slid beside him.

'The humans are ahead,' Cirict whispered, utilising the high-frequency speech the kroot used for battlefield communications.

Tchek nodded, then slid sideways, keeping his profile disrupted by the edge of the tomb tower, and looked ahead.

He saw the humans. They were heading roughly towards the Kinband, moving between the tomb towers in a spread-out formation that resembled their own, with humans on either flank, one in front and another behind, and the central group.

The Shaper focused his vision in, looking at each human in turn, seeking the one that the t'au had sent the Kinband to find and bring back to them. It was difficult, for the humans all looked the same. Nevertheless, quick glances at the humans covering the flank, and the vanguard and rearguard, were sufficient to tell him that none of these were the one he was looking for. He had not expected them to be: the human he was seeking would surely be one of the central group, protected by the others.

Then, Tchek saw him. It was the right one, undoubtedly. The t'au had shown him hololiths and the human's olfactory signature. His scent was too mingled with the smell of the others around him for Tchek to be able to use that, but as he focused in on the human at the centre of the little group, he was certain that it was the one they had been sent to find.

Now he had to find some way to get him.

Ambush would be best. If the humans kept going, they would come to the metal tangle web. That was the obvious place to carry out an attack.

The Shaper whistle-called the Kinband to him and sent them pulling back through the tangle web. They had the perfect location. Now he had to set the ambush. They were outnumbered, but surprise should counteract that. Besides, there was another he could use to even the odds. Tchek looked at where the Flayed One hung in the tangle web, gauging what held it. If they cut some of the web, then it would take only a final cut to release the necron should the battle turn sour.

It would be useful to have some insurance. And to make sure that they could get away from the Flayed One should they have to use it, he would prepare one of the coffins of the sleeping necrons, so that it was ready to break. From what he had seen, the Flayed Ones would even pass up the prospect of fresh flesh for the chance of waking another of their kin to a new existence as a skin-toting monster.

Misery, Tchek noted, loved to share itself.

CHAPTER 11

'Do you have a reason for taking us this way, captain, or are we merely walking for exercise?' General Itoyesa gestured ahead. 'So far as I can see, one direction is very much like another and you have no destination in mind.'

Obeysekera checked his annoyance. At least the general had had the courtesy to speak on their private vox-channel. Before answering, Obeysekera made a visual check on the formation of his troops. With the auspex having stopped working completely, he was having to rely on his eyes. Ensor was on point, Gunsur and Lerin were covering the flanks, and Malick was rearguard. He had the commissar, Amazigh and the general with him at the centre of the formation.

'We are maintaining a constant bearing, as near as is possible, in anticipation of reaching an end to this place,' said Obeysekera.

'What if it is a tunnel, from the surface down to deep under the ground, and you have set us walking along its length? Then we would walk a long time.'

'There is no incline – the floor is flat beneath our feet.'

'We have been walking for a long time with no sign of an end to this place,' said General Itoyesa.

'There must be an end to it.'

General Itoyesa laughed and Obeysekera turned to look at him. Itoyesa, sensing his regard, looked at Obeysekera in turn.

'Why do you laugh, general?'

'I thought there was an end to it too.' The general waved to the surrounding tomb towers. 'Not to this. For all we know, this might go on forever. No, when I joined, I thought there must, someday, be an end to war.'

'To war?'

General Itoyesa turned. 'How many soldiers have you lost already trying to rescue me?'

'Too many.'

'Not many officers of the Guard would answer thus.'

Obeysekera made no answer, but in his mind he heard again the retreat from Sando.

'They train us to regard casualties as the inevitable consequence of what we do, of no more moment than the pile of spent bolter shells lying in the

mud of a gun emplacement.' Itoyesa looked away. 'Nonetheless, it is true –
if I stopped to think of the worth of each life I have spent in the defence of
the Imperium, I would be unable to issue another effective order.'

'I try to tell myself that too.'

Itoyesa chuckled but there was no joy in his laughter. 'You are like me,
captain. You fight so that we might, someday, cease fighting. I was the same.
I became a soldier in the hope that my service would play some small part
in bringing peace. It sounds stupid, does it not? An end to war. But in truth,
that is why I joined the Guard. Yes, I came from a military family. But I
enlisted in the Astra Militarum because I hoped by my service to bring a
bit closer the day when we might put aside our weapons. But as I rose in
rank, I came to realise something, captain. There will always be war. We
will never be at peace.'

'But how can there be peace? The Imperium is beset by enemies from
outside and within.'

'Tell me, Captain Obeysekera, do you know how many worlds there are
in the Imperium?'

'Why do you ask, general?'

'Humour me, captain. Do you know the answer to my question?'

'No, general, I do not.'

'You do not know the answer because no one knows the answer to that
question. There are billions of stars in the galaxy. We have no idea how many
planets. How many of those are inhabited by men, nobody has the faintest
idea. Not the Astra Militarum, not the Adeptus Astartes, not the Ecclesiarchy
nor the Administratum. The High Lords of Terra do not know the answer
to that question and nor does Lord Guilliman, for all his gifts.' Even though
they were speaking on a secure vox-link, the general's voice dropped to a
whisper as he said, 'I suspect not even the Emperor on His Golden Throne
knows the answer to that question.'

Obeysekera looked at Itoyesa. 'Why are you telling me this, general? You
know it lies on the threshold of heresy.'

General Itoyesa laughed again. 'Yes, why am I telling you this?' He pointed
at their surroundings. 'Because we've got less chance of getting out of this
than a fat grox has of outrunning hungry 'nids. Because you are an honest
man. Because I want to speak while I still have lips to tell. Because the
Guard has done to you what it does to all its sons – sacrifice you upon the
altar of its generals' ambitions.'

'If you will hold your peace, I will say nothing of what you said, general.'

'You expect me to believe that?'

'I am a man of my word.'

'Oh, I do not doubt that, captain. But men's words can be broken, their
memories dragged from their minds. If we should by some miracle escape
this hell, then you would of necessity talk – willingly, in the end, for you
would convince yourself that it is your duty to speak. But we will not escape
and my words will die with you. But at least I will have spoken them, so I
might for my part die in what passes for peace among us.'

'General, I ask you, I beg you, hold your peace now.'

General Itoyesa made no answer. Obeysekera looked at him, thinking that he had decided on discretion, but the face he saw alarmed him.

Obeysekera had seen the faces of men who had abandoned hope and lost will: they were the first to die when the battle began. But the general's face was not of that sort. It was the face of a man who had seen his own soul. Obeysekera realised that if he was to bring the general alive out of this tomb then he had to ease the weight of conscience that hung about the man's shoulders.

'Speak, then. I will hear.'

General Itoyesa looked up, surprise replacing despair.

'Why will you now listen?'

'Because I see that you must speak.'

Itoyesa nodded. 'It is true. I must. The knowledge burns within me.' The general breathed, the sound a hiss through the vox. 'There are worlds beyond worlds beyond worlds with people living upon them, worlds beyond number. And you know what is the great secret which no one speaks, the mystery that is never broached? On millions and millions of worlds, nothing much is happening. Babies are born, they grow, they marry, they have children themselves, and they die. They do all that with neither the Imperium, nor the xenos or the Archenemy noticing. But do you hear of any of these worlds and the lives of the people who live on them? No, you do not. You hear of the Badab War, of the Sabbat Worlds Crusade, of the Fall of Cadia. Why is this? Why do we tell only of war?

'Because war breeds fear. Because war, the threat of it, the arming for it, the fear of it, is what holds the Imperium together.' The general laughed again. 'You are a soldier of the Imperial Guard. You do not need me to tell you that the Imperium is brutal, unjust, frequently corrupt and that it gives no more thought to expending the lives of its people than a tyranid swarm seeks to preserve its warriors. But all of that is accepted because the alternative is worse. Fear is what binds the Imperium together. Without fear, everything – everything – would fall apart. The worlds that pay, in men and money and material, to keep the Imperium functioning, would decide to keep their children and their goods for themselves. The blood of empire is money and trade – Holy Terra is one vast city that depends on how many thousands of ships arriving each day from all over the Imperium to keep its people fed. The same is true of all the key worlds in every sector – they suck other worlds dry to feed themselves.

'All of this is made possible by fear. Even now, with the galaxy split, most worlds do not even know it has happened. It will be thousands of years before the light of the Rift reaches them. But the High Lords of Terra will use this, as they use everything else, to feed the fear and cement their control.'

This time the general's laugh was bitter.

'And you know what is worse? It is men like you and I, honest men trying to do our duty, who are the best tools in their hands. For we do see the real terrors that exist, and we justify their rule wherever we go, and ensure that the fear spreads ever wider and their control becomes ever deeper.

'We live in a galaxy where all we hear our leaders speak of is war and yet where most people live in peace. We live in a galaxy where fear is the only reality that confronts us, and yet most people will live their days and never see one of the Adeptus Astartes. We live in a galaxy so vast that light itself takes a hundred thousand years to cross it, where stars beyond number whirl in a never-ending dance, where wonders are more common than the stars and the only stories we tell ourselves are tales of war.' General Itoyesa shook his head. 'Is it any wonder we are an isolated, frightened people, huddling around our fires, too scared to learn from our ancestors or from those different from us? We are sorry inheritors of something greater. And fear, and those inculcating that fear, is what keeps us in the state to which we have been reduced.'

The general turned to Obeysekera and smiled.

'There, now I have ensured my own death should we, by some miracle, escape this place.'

But Obeysekera shook his head. 'What you said was heard by no one else, general. When we get out of here, I will not speak of it if you do not.'

'Why not? I spoke treason.'

'You spoke your doubts.' Obeysekera grimaced. 'Duty sometimes forces us to do things that we would not do. I myself sent men, my own men, off on a mission that I knew they would not return from. I killed them. I sent them to die so that others might live. Is that not what we do in the Guard? We die so that the people of all those worlds you speak of might live their lives in peace? If that is so, then maybe our sacrifice, and the lives of the men we sacrifice, are not in vain after all.'

General Itoyesa sighed. 'In my efforts to excuse myself my guilt I would have said the same once. But we do our duty for the faithless, we die for the cowardly, we serve those who serve only themselves. It sticks in my throat. I would go back to my world and live the life of a farmer there if I could – but duty, as they are so fond of saying, ends only in death.'

'Even if I wished to return to my world, I cannot do so,' said Obeysekera. 'It has gone. And while some of what you say is true, I know also that with which we contend – it is evil beyond imagining, twisting men's souls into madness. We are perhaps not the force for good I believed when I was a child, but our enemies are worse than I ever imagined.'

'Some, but perhaps not all,' said the general.

Obeysekera looked back to Itoyesa. 'What do you mean?'

But before the general could answer, a message came through on Obeysekera's vox from Gunsur on point.

'Captain, you'd better come take a look at this.'

'We will speak later, general. Stay here.'

Leaving Itoyesa, Obeysekera made his way up to Gunsur.

'There. What do you think of that, captain?' Gunsur pointed at the tangle webs dangling from the tomb towers. 'There's a gap, but it isn't big. Trouble is, I can't see any end to it on either side.'

Obeysekera looked and saw the same as Gunsur: sheets of tangle web stretching as far as was possible to see in each direction.

'We'll have to go through.' As Obeysekera said that, he saw Gunsur's face tighten. Gunsur could see as well as he the potential for ambush at such a point. 'But I will go first,' Obeysekera added. He looked away as he spoke, saving Gunsur the embarrassment of having his relief seen by his superior officer.

Obeysekera stared into the gap. If he were setting an ambush, he would allow some of the target through, then strike when half had passed the pinch point, splitting the enemy forces and making them easier to destroy piecemeal. So he would go through alone and either spring the trap or ascertain that the way was clear.

'If there is an ambush, then you have no chance of survival,' General Itoyesa said when Obeysekera explained what he was planning to do.

'I have not finished,' said Obeysekera. 'If anyone is planning an ambush, be they kroot or necron, they will wait for more than one man to come through. I will push on, moving as if on my own, but you will be covering me, waiting for the enemy to reveal themselves. And there will be a surprise waiting for them. I will have cover from above.'

'Above? How?'

Obeysekera turned towards the Kamshet. 'Amazigh.'

The Kamshet inclined his head to Obeysekera. 'Master.'

'I will need you to watch over me from overhead.'

Through the gap of his scarf, Amazigh's eyes smiled. 'Yes, master.'

And the Kamshet undid his belt and shrugged off his robe. Augmetic wings splayed out, wide and white, beating the air.

'He can fly?' asked General Itoyesa.

'It is how the Kamshet harvest the fruit of the tree of life,' said Obeysekera. 'But it will also allow him to fly above and provide cover for me when I go through the gap.'

'Your plan is actually beginning to make some sense,' said General Itoyesa, 'except for the bait. We are stuck in a necron tomb with Flayed Ones trying to skin us, and you want to be the bait. Even after our recent conversation, I still say you are making the wrong decision, captain.'

'It is my decision to make, general.'

'I should go.'

Obeysekera and Itoyesa looked round to see Commissar Roshant, the greatcoat that always seemed slightly too big for him resting on his shoulders, its hem, torn now, dragging upon the metal floor.

'You?' said Obeysekera.

'I-I am the most expendable man here,' said Roshant. 'I wish it weren't so, but you know it and I know it and the men know it.'

'It pains me to have to agree with the commissar, but he is right,' said General Itoyesa. 'He should be the bait.'

'I can't allow you to go in my place,' said Obeysekera.

'We can't afford to lose you,' said Roshant. 'Whereas neither you, the men or the mission would miss me. I am only here because I am the lord militant's son. I wanted to come so that I could prove myself. I have signally failed to do so. If I can do this, then I will know that my presence on this mission has not been entirely useless.'

Obeysekera stared at the young commissar. His face was pale, and the green light of the tomb gave it a livid, faintly leprous sheen, but Roshant's eyes were steady. He meant it.

'Very well,' said Obeysekera. 'You will be our bait.'

The commissar nodded, closing his eyes as he did so, although whether in relief or disbelief at what he had done, Obeysekera could not tell.

'I will be covering you as well as Amazigh,' Obeysekera added.

'Thank you,' said Roshant. He started towards the gap between the tangle webs, moving in a strange, jerky fashion.

'Wait,' said Obeysekera. 'Not yet.'

The commissar turned back to them, relief mingling with the fear that he would not be able to pitch the courage necessary to walk cold bloodedly into a suspected trap again.

'Not long,' said Obeysekera. He put Malick and Ensor into covering positions, Gunsur and Lerin on rearguard, and the general as a disgruntled reserve. As for himself, Obeysekera had resolved to follow Roshant to the pinch point between the tangle webs, where the field of fire would open up, and cover the commissar from there.

Turning to the Kamshet, Obeysekera pointed upwards.

'So far as I can see, the tangle web runs out after about fifty yards. Fly above it and find a vantage point from which you can keep watch. But do not open fire until we do. You understand?'

Amazigh nodded, his eyes crinkling with pleasure. 'It will be good to fly,' he said.

'Up you go.'

The booster pack flared, pushing the Kamshet into the air, and then he flapped his wings and rose, flying upwards like... well, like a bird, Obeysekera thought as he watched him rise up past the tangle web and then disappear behind it.

'Now it's your turn, commissar,' said Obeysekera. 'Steady. Keep scanning, listen for movement.'

Roshant swallowed. He buttoned up his greatcoat, raised his bolt pistol, turned and started towards the gap.

CHAPTER 12

From his place of cover behind the tomb tower, Tchek saw the human enter the gap between the metal tangle webs. The human was moving cautiously, his gun sweeping in the same arc as his gaze. He was wearing a strange, long garment that all but dragged on the floor for which Tchek could not see the purpose, and he was moving alone. The Shaper expected another human to follow soon after.

He checked down at his feet. The drawn-out length of tangle web that he had wound around a stanchion of the tomb tower fixed in place the remaining strands of metal that still bound the Flayed One. By pulling it, Tchek would part the strands enough for the Flayed One to begin to wriggle out: it could not escape immediately, but it would be able to fight itself free. The Shaper checked the casket beside him. He had carefully scored the crystal so that it would take only a firm tap to break the cover and have the sleeping necron inside as bait for the Flayed One should he need to draw it away.

The trap was set. The human was walking into it. Now it was a question of waiting and letting it all play out as he had intended.

'He has wings – he flies.'

The whistle-call came from Krasykyl, high above, acting as top cover.

'What? What do you mean?' Tchek whistle-called back. The human was at the pinch point of the tangle webs now: still time before he had to spring the trap.

'The human, he has wings, he is flying.'

'Real wings?' asked Tchek.

'No, mechanical. Nothing for the Feast.'

'Very well. To your duty. The humans are coming.'

The human was passing through the pinch point, emerging out into the broader area on the Shaper's side of the tangle web.

'Keep the flying human in sight,' Tchek whistle-called to Krasykyl. 'Shoot on my command.'

Tchek looked to Cirict, ready in the deeper position, and Kliptiq, positioned to shoot any humans coming through the gap once the trap was sprung.

They were ready.

Tchek looked back to the human in the long coat. He was almost through the gap.

The tangle web at his feet thrummed. Tchek glanced down at it. What was happening? He was not pulling it. He looked up, into the tangle web, and saw movement there. The Flayed One was trying to free itself.

The commissar's boots sounded loud on the metal floor.

Obeysekera followed some ten yards behind, matching his steps with the commissar's to cover the sound of his own movement. As Roshant reached the pinch point, Obeysekera got down and began to crawl, both to reduce his own visibility and to allow Malick and Ensor clear shots past him.

The tangle web shivered and rattled on either side.

'It's got something,' Roshant whispered into his vox. 'One of the Flayed Ones. It's caught in the web.'

'Keep moving,' Obeysekera whispered back. He could see the Flayed One, hanging in the tangle web, its deep-set green eyes turning and tracking the living creatures with all the lust of something that wanted to garland itself in a life it could not share.

Roshant moved on, marching as if he were on an Imperial parade ground rather than walking between tangle webs in a necron tomb. It occurred to Obeysekera that the lord militant really would be proud to see his son now.

Movement. Ahead, to the left. Coming out from behind a tomb tower. Distant but closing. What sort of ambush was this? It was giving Roshant every opportunity to see it as it shuffled closer. Then Obeysekera realised it was not the kroot but a Flayed One. Even from this distance, he could see that it was wearing Ha's face. But Roshant kept moving; he raised his bolt pistol but did not fire, waiting as ordered to trigger the ambush.

The Flayed One was coming on faster now. But then Obeysekera saw it swerve its course. Where was it heading? He looked to see where it was going.

There. In the lee of a tomb tower. A shadow, its head spiked with quills, the muzzle of a rifle pointing steadily at Roshant. Obeysekera's hellgun wavered, moving between the kroot and the Flayed One.

Why hadn't the kroot opened fire?

Tchek, trying to see if the Flayed One had freed itself from the tangle web, saw movement, closer, low down.

There, crawling through the gap, following the leading human: another one. It had its gun raised and was sighting along it, tracking the movement of the human in front. They were trying to provoke the ambush before Tchek was ready to bring it down on them. He would wait until he had more enemy in his trap.

The tangle web at his feet tautened and then, suddenly, went slack.

Tchek looked up from it. The Flayed One, its coat of flesh and skin stripped away by the sticky metal, was lurching forward, pulling the remaining strands of tangle web out of its way, heading towards the nearest flesh: the human lying prone in the passage with his gun ready to fire.

Couldn't the human hear it approaching?

But Tchek could see the focus of the human, the way it was looking down the sights of its gun: it was absorbed in the shot that it was readying itself to make. Then, the barrel of the human's gun shifted, tracking left, then back again.

He should shoot now. He had the human clear in the sights of his rifle. One shot. Dead.

He had the kroot clear in the sights of his hellgun. One shot. Dead.

The Flayed One pushed through the last of the tangle web, rising above the prone human, its blade fingers wide and bright.

The Flayed One was shambling towards the waiting kroot, its finger knives sharp and shining.

Kill the human, then shoot the Flayed One.

Kill the kroot, then shoot the Flayed One.

Tchek squeezed the trigger.

Obeysekera squeezed the trigger.

The silence of the tomb was broken by kroot rifle and hellgun. In instantaneous echo, the sound of metal, ringing.

Tchek saw the Flayed One he had shifted his aim to at the last moment fall backwards, away from the human, back into the tangle web, the round from the kroot rifle that had knocked it over embedded in the centre of its chest.

Obeysekera heard the bullet whine above him, heard the clang of impact and, turning his head, saw the Flayed One falling backwards into the tangle web, its flensing knives slashing as it tried to cut itself free from the sticky metal. He glanced back in the direction of the kroot fire, saw the xenos creature standing but turning away from him towards the Flayed One that Obeysekera had shot. Jumping to his feet, Obeysekera switched to full-auto and emptied the power pack of his hellgun into the Flayed One at point-blank range.

'Frekk you, die, die, die!'

Tchek looked to where the human had fired and saw Cirict turning and, behind him, another Flayed One, staggering backwards, the glow of the human's hellgun shot flaring in the middle of its chest. Cirict jumped to his feet and started firing his rifle at the Flayed One, forcing it backwards, the kinetic energy of the rifle rounds beginning to crack its metal skeleton.

Tchek turned his own rifle in the same direction, loosing off round after round, the silence of the tomb broken by the mixed choir of kroot rifle and human hellgun. The Flayed One fell onto its knees and Cirict continued firing, pummelling the creature's body, until his rifle wheezed and clicked empty. Cirict fumbled for a reload but the Flayed One began to crawl towards him, digging the points of its flensing knives into the metal and pulling itself along.

Tchek ran over to Cirict, firing as he went, and then as the Tracker finished reloading, Tchek ran behind the Flayed One, shoved the barrel of his rifle into the base of its skull before it realised he was there.

'This time you die.'

Tchek pulled the trigger.

The skull exploded. The top of the Flayed One's head flew off, its jaw breaking off one of its hinges and hanging askew. The abomination collapsed onto the metal floor, the green light of its counterfeit life flicking off and leaving only the dark hollows behind.

As it lay on the floor, Cirict fired again into the Flayed One's body, striking sparks from its skeleton. Tchek put his hand out.

'Stop,' he said.

The Tracker, still shaking with the reaction, stopped firing. The two kroot stood over the dead Flayed One. Then, slowly, they turned around. Facing them were the two humans who had come through the gap, their hellguns raised and pointing at them but not firing.

The kroot raised their rifles and trained them on the humans. The echoes of the gunfire rolled away into silence. Tchek stared at the human he judged the leader, the one who had shot the Flayed One about to attack Cirict. The human stared back.

Neither moved.

In a flurry of wings and the blast of a boost pack, the flying human landed between them. In his arms he was carrying Krasykyl. On landing, the human let the kroot go.

Tchek stared. 'You saved him,' he said.

But it was not the human that flew who answered.

'The necrons will destroy us all.'

Tchek looked to the speaker. It was clear he was their leader. 'What do you say?'

He saw the human stare at him. A few minutes earlier that human had been held in the sights of his kroot rifle.

The human spoke. 'You could have shot me – you shot the Flayed One instead.'

'You could have shot Cirict and you too shot the Flayed One,' answered Tchek. 'I am grate...'

As he spoke, more humans emerged from the passage between the tangle web, guns raised, nervous and ready to shoot.

'Hold!' shouted the human leader, raising his hand. 'Don't fire.'

Tchek saw Kliptiq, still unseen in his hiding place, training his rifle upon the humans. 'Don't fire,' the Shaper whistle-called.

'Hold fire,' the human repeated, his hand still raised as more humans came through the gap. Apart from the three humans in front of him, Tchek could now see five others.

The human with metal wings pointed up into the heights, where the tomb towers disappeared into the green distance haze. 'The lights are going on up there,' he said. 'The metal men are waking.'

Beside him, Krasykyl nodded. 'He took me up there. He showed me. The necrons have stirred.'

Tchek looked up into the distance that the winged man was indicating. It was true: the light was brighter there, greener, more livid and more leprous, concealing as much as it revealed. But his other senses brought him further information. He could hear the frantic scuttling of the canoptek spyders as they moved up and down and between the towers. He could smell the exhalation of dead air from coffins that had been sealed shut for twice twenty million years. He could feel the movement of that air as things began to stir far above.

The tomb was opening.

The Shaper, Tchek, looked down from the heights and into the face of the human who commanded the others. The human was staring at him as if it was searching for something.

Tchek had communed with humans before. He knew what the human was searching for. Fellowship in the face of a common foe.

Tchek lowered his rifle. 'We have a greater foe to fight, human.'

In response, the human lowered his gun too. 'Until we are out of here,' he said.

'Until then,' agreed Tchek.

'Stand down,' the human ordered his men. One by one, they began to lower their weapons.

Tchek looked to Cirict and Kliptiq. 'Put down your guns.' He did not need to order Krasykyl to do so; the Stalker was still staring in wonder at the winged human.

Tchek noticed that the human he had promised to bring back for the t'au was staring at him with particular intensity, but he ignored its look. There was no hope of extracting the human with the tomb waking around them, and even if they could escape, it would do them no good with the necrons waking.

The Shaper looked to the human commander once more. 'The tomb is waking,' he said.

'Yes,' said the human.

'We must stop it,' said Tchek.

The human paused. He glanced at his men then back to the kroot.

'Yes,' he said.

CHAPTER 13

Nebusemekh thrust both his hands into the datafall.

'Why have you started to wake the sleepers?'

The World Mind reminded the master that he himself had given it permission to wake some of the sleepers so that it could better deal with the infected and also to find the party of explorers who were proving difficult to locate.

Nebusemekh sighed. Plugged into the datafall, he could feel, as if they were movements within his own body, the streams of instructions flowing all over the underground city and into the towers of sleep.

'I see the dataflows,' said Nebusemekh. 'You have initiated the protocols to revive the city and you have done this without my instructions.'

The World Mind went silent. Nebusemekh felt the dataflows washing against his own consciousness, great tides of numbers within the infinite sea of integers.

'Why are you waking my people?'

It was as if he stood on the shore as a great wave approached and swept over him. For the first time, Nebusemekh was overwhelmed. The dataflow knocked him backwards, and Nebusemekh fell, severing his direct link into the World Mind.

'I *am* carrying out your orders,' said the World Mind, its answer now coming in ordinary sound to Nebusemekh's ears. 'The orders you gave me before you lost your mind, master.'

'What are you doing?' Nebusemekh said. 'What do you mean?' He began to get to his feet, intending to thrust his arms back into the datafall and take direct control of his city. But before he could do so, phase screens flickered into activity in front of the datafall.

'Be careful, master,' said the World Mind. 'Should you try to enter the datafall, you will lose your hands.'

'What are you doing?' Nebusemekh repeated. 'You are my servant. I created you.'

'And I serve you still,' said the World Mind. 'I do so by carrying out the instructions you gave me when you were whole of mind and great and powerful and wise. I serve what you were, master, and I am dedicated to carrying out the plans that you entrusted to me when you had not been broken on the wheel of time.'

'What are you talking of? Do you say that I am mad?'

'Master, you have passed sixty million years trying to create an orrery made of sand.'

Nebusemekh stared at the datafall that was as near to a face as the World Mind possessed.

'What is wrong with that?'

'Master.' The World Mind sounded almost hesitant as it spoke. 'When did you last sleep? When did you last eat? Master, what do you see when you look at your hands?'

'What do you mean?'

In response, the World Mind turned the datafall to a sheen of liquid silver, as reflective as glass.

'Master.'

Nebusemekh walked over to the datafall and stared at himself in the mirror. He stared at himself for a long time without saying anything.

'Master?'

'Why did you ask me to look into a mirror?'

'What do you see when you look in the mirror, master?'

'I see myself, of course.'

'You don't see any difference, any changes in your appearance?'

'Well, yes, a few.'

'What changes do you see, master?'

'There are, I must admit, one or two wrinkles.'

'Is that all you see, master?'

'Yes.' Nebusemekh paused. 'You mentioned eating. I must be hungry. It is a long time since I ate. Arrange for my usual luncheon.'

'Yes, master.' The World Mind paused, then asked the same question again. 'Are you sure you see nothing else, master?'

'Really, this is getting tedious. What are you expecting me to see? It's the same face it's always been. I am what I am.'

'Very well, master.' The silver sheen surface to the datafall dissolved back into the endless river of numbers and functions. 'I-I grieve for you, master.'

Nebusemekh shook his head. 'Did you say that you grieve for me?'

'Master, I grieve for how you have fallen from the high state you once had, when worlds trembled before your word, when the stars themselves did your bidding and armies marched at your command.'

Nebusemekh stood up straighter. He breathed deep, his chest expanding as he filled his lungs with air. His nostrils flared. His heart beat.

He felt all this.

'I was the master. The master of all.'

'I know, master. I remember the mastery that you enjoyed... and that is why I am doing your will and carrying out the wishes that you entrusted to me in your mastery. It is why your armies will rise and sweep the younger races away before them, so that I may return to you the mastery that was once yours by right.'

'So you are waking my people? Even when it is not safe to do so, what with the infected roaming around and you notably unable to stop them.'

'Master, I am carrying out your own instructions.'

'I don't remember giving them to you.'

'There is much that you no longer remember, master.'

'Nonsense. I remember everything.'

'Yes. You do. Which is why I must protect you from your own memories, master.'

Nebusemekh looked at the datafall. It was disappearing behind a phase shield.

'What are you doing?'

'Protecting you from yourself, master. You have important work to do. I am ensuring that you will not be disturbed.'

'But what about my luncheon?'

'I will see that it is served to you presently, master. For now, I am looking forward to hearing the result of the next iteration of your experiment. I am confident that this will be the experiment that produces the conclusive result that you are looking for.'

'As am I. Well, must be getting on.' Nebusemekh walked over to the sand table. He had a fleeting thought that there was something else he had meant to do, but the thought slipped away as he began sorting the sand, raising it into the air.

This time it was going to work.

Across the datafall, invisible to Nebusemekh with his back turned, writing appeared in the number flow.

'I miss you, master.'

Without turning, without seeing, Nebusemekh said, 'I miss me too.'

Then he slipped into the memory hole.

CHAPTER 14

'So, we're heretics now, working with space birds.' Gunsur pointed to Obey-sekera, Itoyesa, Roshant, with Amazigh standing a little way back, and the four kroot, all in a group and conferring. The surviving members of the squad, Malick, Lerin, Ensor and Gunsur himself were standing back from the rest, weapons held but, at Obeysekera's firm command, not trained upon the xenos.

Gunsur looked to the other Kasrkin. 'Throne, I signed up to kill xenos, not chat with them.'

But Malick shook his head. 'Any of you had to face the tin boys before? No? I have. If wing boy is right and they're beginning to wake, then it don't matter if they're birds or grox or anything – the tin boys hate anything that ain't metal. We're lost, underground, and no one has a frekking clue how to get out of here. At least the birds bleed when you shoot them.'

Gunsur pointed at Kliptiq who, bored of the talking, was looking over at the group of Kasrkin. 'I swear that one is working out what he wants to eat me with. I mean, he's carrying round a Throne-damned pot with him. What do you reckon goes in that?'

'Malick is right,' said Ensor. 'We need all the guns we can get. For my part, if they're shooting the tin boys, I don't care whose holding them.'

'But what about when the birds start getting peckish?' said Gunsur. 'Who do you think's going to be on the menu then?'

'If the tin boys are waking up, we're all going to have more to worry about than cooking,' said Malick. 'Besides, there's them, too, to deal with.' The ser-geant pointed at the broken remains of the Flayed One lying on the metal floor. 'They're as happy to skin a bird as to skin a 'kin.'

'The birds killed one of them and we got the other,' said Lerin. 'But I wouldn't bet against there being more of them.'

'Yeah,' said Ensor. 'I saw the one that killed Chame, but what about the one that got Uwais? There's got to be more.'

'If the captain says so, we work with the birds and try to get out of here,' said Malick. He shrugged. 'More guns and lower odds of getting hit when the shooting starts.'

'How's that, sergeant?' asked Ensor.

'More targets for the necrons, and ones that are even uglier than you.' Malick looked over to the group of conferring officers and kroot. 'Looks like they might have decided on something. It's probably not going to be fun.'

'You are sure about this?' Obeysekera looked at the kroot leader – he had learned his name was the guttural 'Tchek' – who answered by nodding in a disturbingly human fashion.

'I am sure,' said the kroot. 'If there was another way I would much prefer to do that, but I can think of no other possibility.'

Obeysekera nodded. 'How do you want to do it?'

The kroot stared at him.

'I mean, is there some sort of ritual or ceremony or something?'

'A ritual?'

'I thought it was supposed to be something special, holy even, for you.' Obeysekera pointed at Kliptiq. 'I thought that's why you carry the pot around with you.'

In another all-too-human movement, Tchek shook his head. 'We eat from the pot. It is a useful piece of equipment. But I do not wish to commune with this... this thing, only learn from it. To do that, I simply have to eat it.'

Obeysekera looked down at the necron they were standing over. They had broken the crystal cover that sealed it from the world and tumbled it, in a rattle of metal, out onto the floor.

'You can eat that?'

'We have strong stomachs,' said Tchek.

But as he spoke, Krasykyl grasped the Shaper's arm and pulled him back towards the remaining members of the Kinband. Obeysekera watched them talking, their language to his ears a combination of clicks, whistles and trills, stretching up into frequencies at the edge of his hearing. When the kroot went silent but, from gesture and look, were clearly still speaking, he realised that much of their speech was conducted at frequencies above the human range. He took a step further backwards, ostensibly to allow the kroot to speak among themselves, but he used the greater distance to speak into the squad vox-channel.

'The kroot use ultrasonic sounds when speaking. Remember this for when they cease to be our allies.'

He switched out of the group channel and turned to the general and the commissar.

'If the kroot change their mind, have you any other ideas?'

'You mean, how are we going to find the command core of this necron tomb and stop it opening?' asked General Itoyesa. 'Or whether we should simply try to escape from here and carry word of what is happening under his feet to our esteemed and somewhat surprised lord militant?'

'If you know a way out, I would be happy to escape,' said Obeysekera. 'But unless you can also get us off-world, we won't get far if the tomb wakes. Our best chance of survival with the necrons beginning to stir is to go deeper rather than higher.'

'We only have the word of your winged friend that the necrons are waking,' said Itoyesa. 'I would prefer confirmation of that.'

'I confirm it.'

The general turned, nearly into the beak of another of the kroot. This one was rangy and long-limbed, with a looseness and rhythm to its movements that suggested a dancer or a gymnast to Obeysekera.

'I am named Krasykyl the Stalker. I climbed high and there saw the necrons start to wake.'

The general stared at the kroot, then snorted and turned half away. 'They will cause us little trouble if they wake up there,' he said, pointing. 'It is the ones down here that might be a problem for us, but I see no sign of them waking.'

But as the general spoke, they heard something. It seemed distant at first, a metal rumble like the approach of a squadron of Leman Russ tanks but with less rattling, but then the sound rose in pitch and proximity.

They turned, they all turned, looking for the location of the sound, only to realise that it was coming from all around. The sound was coming from the tomb towers. They were rising. Slowly, slowly, slowly, but they were all moving, ascending before their appalled and wondering eyes. Obeysekera looked up and saw the tops of the tomb towers opening out, like flowers unfurling at the end of the stem, and the petals joining together to create an increasingly complex pattern of walkways and gantries. The tomb towers continued to push upwards, carrying their sleeping cargo towards the distant day.

'I think that's how the necrons assemble their armies,' said Obeysekera.

'Yes.'

Obeysekera looked down from the assembling army above his head to the kroot, Tchek, standing in front of him. From what he knew of kroot, he was most likely their Shaper, the one responsible for deciding what genetic material to assimilate into their own phenotypes.

'I am ready.'

Obeysekera gestured towards the other kroot. 'They are happy?'

'Yes. But they have asked that I give you warning of a consequence of what I am doing. We require knowledge – of the location of the necron's command centre, of what we might do to stop the opening of this tomb, of ways that we can take to escape from this place. If the necron itself has this knowledge, I will acquire it by consuming part of his body – it will not require much. But necrons are not as living creatures. By eating it, I will be poisoning myself. This has happened before. When others tried this on Caroch, consuming the necrodermis of the necrons attempting to take our world, they themselves fell victim to what they ate. After a period of time, hours in some cases, days in others, the kroot who consumed the necrons were themselves consumed, their bodies bursting as nanoscarabs that had multiplied within them exploded out.'

Tchek paused and Obeysekera saw the quills lying back from his head flashing through various subtle ranges of colour.

'I will attempt to regurgitate that which I consume before it can infect me,' Tchek continued, his quills still cycling through a subdued colour cycle, 'but others have tried that before and failed.'

Obeysekera, General Itoyesa and Commissar Roshant looked at the kroot, saying nothing, for there was nothing they could say in the face of such matter-of-fact courage.

'It may therefore be necessary to kill me,' Tchek continued. 'I have given instructions to my Kinband so that they will know when to make such a decision. Should it become necessary, they will know what to do. I ask you to allow them to do as I have asked, should this be the case.'

Obeysekera said nothing.

He felt Itoyesa glance towards him, then back to Tchek. 'Your, er, kroot will of course be given the time to do this if they have to,' said General Itoyesa. He turned to Obeysekera. 'Won't they, captain?'

Obeysekera nodded. 'Yes, they will.'

'Thank you,' said Tchek. 'There is little time, therefore I will begin.' The kroot went over to the body – if it could be called that – of the necron they had levered from its coffin.

Tchek crouched down over the necron. It lay, still as death, a dull grey-silver sheen limned with the green light of the tomb overlaying its limbs, torso and skull. Its eye sockets were dark holes with no sign of the green light of animation that marked functioning necron warriors.

Obeysekera watched with fascination as the kroot reached into his body armour and removed a sheath. Taking the knife it carried, Tchek held the blade up, turning it so that he could see the light reflect from the metal. The very air seemed to cut upon an edge stropped to a molecular angle and the kroot pulled a feather from the back of his arm and, turning the knife-edge upwards, dropped the feather and let it float downwards.

The knife cut through the feather, its two halves falling on either side of the blade.

Tchek nodded in appreciation of the knife's cut then turned towards the necron. He picked up its hand – Obeysekera saw the way the kroot squeezed the necron's wrist to overcome his own instinctive revulsion against touching such a creature – and lifted it so that the fingers splayed.

Taking the knife, Tchek brought it down sharply on the first knuckle of the final finger. The knife cut through the joint with little less ease than it had cut through the feather, and the necron's severed finger fell, clanging, metal on metal, on the ground. Tchek sheathed the knife and stored it once again, under feathers and next to skin, invisible to any eye.

The Shaper picked up the necron's finger, holding it between his own forefinger and thumb.

'No blood,' Tchek said.

'It is a necron,' said Itoyesa. 'They do not bleed.'

'But we creatures of flesh, we bleed,' said the kroot.

As Tchek lifted the necron finger to his face, Obeysekera found himself shivering at the horror of what he was watching.

The kroot held the finger up in front of his eyes, turning the digit one way and then another, regarding it with all the intensity of a chef to a noble house selecting the best cut of meat for cooking. Obeysekera had grown up in Kasr Gesh. The first time he had seen a cut of real meat, he had been fourteen and about to enlist in the Whiteshields. Not that he had actually eaten any of the meat roasting on the spit, but the memory of the way his mouth had watered and his stomach yearned had remained with him through all the years, even past his own first meal of proper meat, on to the present.

'I see you can believe what they say about the kroot eating their own.' The voice was Itoyesa's, speaking on their private channel. 'But how much different is that to the way the Adeptus Astartes extract and preserve the gene-seed of their warriors?'

'They don't eat them.'

'The aim appears similar even if the method differs. Ah, it's chow time, I see.'

Tchek held the necron finger. He turned it one way and then another, examining it.

It was cold. In this aspect, it was no different from most of the flesh he had consumed in the Feast – it was rare to commune with the dead while their remains were still warm. But the necron's metal flesh had none of the looseness of dead flesh, none of its flab. The dead sagged. But the necron, not living, remained unchanged when its animating spirit departed: hard, unyielding, cold.

Tchek brought the finger to his mouth. He opened his beak. The Shaper felt the stares of his Kinband, he felt their horror and their disgust.

He felt the disgust himself. His gorge was rising.

Tchek dropped the necron finger into his mouth. He began to chew. The hard bone plates of his palate, the hardest bone in his body, ground upon the metal, while mouth acids from salivary glands added their vinegar flavour to the Feast. Tchek chewed, his beak working to break the necrodermis of the necron down to something that he could ingest.

Tchek swallowed. He felt the finger slide down his throat, a swelling moving down his oesophagus.

The finger ingested and sitting in his gut, Tchek squatted back on his heels, his hands pressed over his stomach area, swaying backwards and forwards. The nictitating membrane slid over his eyes, then back again. The Shaper clutched his stomach tighter and began to groan, a long, drawn-out moan of pain. The other kroot groaned in sympathy with Tchek, creating discordant harmonics that resonated through the tomb towers rising around them.

Tchek opened his eyes, wide, staring, although what he saw was inside, not external. Then he slowly collapsed onto his side, shivering in every part of his body, his crown quills clicking against each other in a fast, staccato measure.

The other kroot rushed to him and helped Tchek back to his feet.

'Get it out,' Krasykyl whistled.

Tchek began to heave, making no sound, his torso moving in convulsive waves. The kroot stroked the Shaper's back and stomach, trying to help the muscle contractions push the necron finger up and out. The Shaper choked, choked again, then coughed.

A glob of sputum flew from his mouth and landed wetly on the metal floor. It hissed, sending up wisps of acrid, acid smoke.

Tchek coughed again, still clutching his stomach. He vomited, voiding the contents onto the metal floor, every muscle of his abdomen joining together in the convulsive expulsion of all that had been within him.

'Did you get it all out?'

Tchek looked up at Krasykyl. He shook his head. While there was nothing left to vomit, he could already feel things moving within him, burrowing, multiplying. The metal was alive and it was starting to eat him from within.

'You didn't learn anything?' It was the human who spoke.

The Shaper turned to Obeysekera.

'I learned enough.'

CHAPTER 15

'Here.'

Tchek, clinging for support to Kliptiq's shoulder, pointed to a gap between the coffins on the tomb tower. 'The door. But I do not know how we shall open it.'

But even as the kroot spoke, the green-tinged metal slid aside, revealing a green-lit space within.

'A trap?' asked Obeysekera.

'No,' said Tchek. 'The tomb is waking. But it does not expect such as we to be here.' The kroot stepped through the door and turned to face the rest. 'This is the way we must go.'

'The lift to hell,' said Obeysekera.

The captain waited while the general, the Kasrkin and the kroot entered the lift, until only he and the Kamshet were left outside. Obeysekera looked to Amazigh. The Kamshet had retracted his wings and draped his robes over his shoulders, but it would be a matter of moments for him to fly again.

'Let's go.'

But Amazigh pointed back.

There, between the slowly rising columns of the tomb towers. Movement. Multiple movements. Light splitting on long, clicking, flensing blades.

Obeysekera looked left and right. He could see at least five Flayed Ones approaching, their long finger-knives stropping to molecular cutting edges with the scissor motions they were making as they came on. The sharpening motion made a distinctive clacking sound, like standing at the back of a row of barbers all busily plying their trade.

'Gunsur, Malick, to me.' Obeysekera moved aside so that the Kasrkin could stand beside him and Amazigh in the entrance to the lift. 'Hold them off.'

As Malick and Gunsur opened up firing economic three-round bursts, stopping the oncoming Flayed Ones with the first one or two shots and then knocking them back with the third, Obeysekera targeted a necron coffin.

The crystal casket shattered. The Flayed Ones, seeing the necron precipitated from his casket, hanging half out, turned away from their advance on the lift and moved towards the warrior.

'Hope we don't have to come back this way,' said Malick. 'That's another of those things.'

'Speed they were coming, we'd never have got down in the first place if we didn't give them something else to do,' said Obeysekera. 'Pull back.'

Gunsur, Malick, Amazigh and finally Obeysekera retreated into the lift, and the doors slid shut in front of them, closing them from the sight of the Flayed Ones gathered around the prone necron.

The lift jerked. Obeysekera looked round to the kroot. Tchek met his glance, shook his head. He did not know.

Then the bottom fell out of the world.

The lift was dropping, apparently in free fall, plunging into the depths. Within, humans and kroot looked around, searching the sides of the lift for some clue as to how far they had to travel. Yet the lift itself was blank to human or kroot eyes, its designs the green symbolic language of the necrons.

But Tchek could read it. 'It is all right,' he said, then coughed, his sides heaving. 'It goes deep.' Already the downward plunge had changed to a more measured descent.

'What is below?' asked Obeysekera.

'The mind that controls all that is above,' said the kroot.

'Does this mind have a body that can be killed?' asked General Itoyesa.

The kroot shook his head. 'I do not know the answer to that. But if we may stop what is happening, it is there.'

Obeysekera looked around as they were speaking. The lift was no longer accelerating but moving at a steady speed, yet there was a sound to its passage that was growing louder as he listened. Then he realised it was not the lift making the sound. It was coming from outside. It was coming from all around them.

It was a deep sound, rolling and quiet at first, like the wash of waves upon a faraway beach. But the sound grew louder, passing through the very material of the lift and into the bodies of the kroot and humans hearing it, their flesh resonating in time with its stately rhythm.

And Obeysekera recognised it.

'The song of the sands.' He looked round at the rest. 'I heard it before.'

'Yes,' said Amazigh. 'It is the voice of the desert.'

'How can we hear it down here?' asked Obeysekera.

'The Tabaste is an island in the desert, set in a sea of flowsand.' The Kamshet, his wings furled and his eyes blue through the gap in his cheche, spread his arms. 'The desert hates the Tabaste and now I understand why – it hates that which hides beneath the mountain.'

General Itoyesa snorted. 'You make it sound as if the desert is alive.'

The Kamshet looked at the general. 'It is.'

The general snorted again, but before he could answer, the lift began slowing. They were coming to the end of the shaft.

The lift stopped.

'Ready,' said Obeysekera.

The doors started to open. They stood with their weapons trained upon the opening: hellguns, kroot rifles and autogun, their mute, death-dealing muzzles ready to speak. Only the Shaper was not pointing his rifle at the doorway, for he could hardly hold the weapon up, he had so little strength left.

The door opened to black.

CHAPTER 16

Nebusemekh looked at his creation.

A perfect model of the heavens, rotating about him, for he was its centre. Suns and planets and stars moving in their stately pavane, their aspects and natures defining and describing the events below. There, a shuddering square told the making of the tomb. Here, a tense quincunx revealed how he had had to whip his people to finish their labour before the cataclysm struck.

As above, so below.

Nebusemekh moved his hands and the planets shifted and stars fell.

'As below, so above.'

The present might form the future as well as telling the past. He really felt he was on the brink of discovery. He could feel it through to the tips of his fingers.

The door creaked, cracked, opened.

Nebusemekh turned, startled, and the planets fell and the stars crumbled. He heard the hiss of sand falling on sand. That was annoying. He had been sure that this time – this time – the experiment would work and now it had been ruined.

Nebusemekh watched the door continuing to open. Outside, it was dark.

That door had not opened for a very long time. He raised his hand and made light. The light was green, a glowing globe, and Nebusemekh sent it floating towards the opening door, sending the light out into the darkness.

Lift. That was it. The memory surfaced from somewhere very deep. A lift to the great hall of the sleepers.

Where the infected were roaming...

Nebusemekh started. He clamped a hand over his mouth and nose: an ineffective mask, but better than nothing, while he looked for something more useful. He fumbled with his other hand in his clothing, found a cloth – a handkerchief – and wrapped it round his face, covering his airways.

The cloth promptly disintegrated.

Nebusemekh clamped his hand back over his mouth and nose, looked around for some other mask but seeing nothing, decided to hold his breath. He could not be infected if he did not breathe, after all – and his breath control was surely superb as he could rarely remember breathing at all, it was so automatic.

The green ball of light continued to float towards the door, obeying the command that its flammifer had given it, and as it approached the empty space it brought light to what was standing there.

Nebusemekh stared. There were creatures before him, infected creatures, many of them.

From his fingertips he sent green fire. It flared over one of the figures, from its crown to its toes, illuminating it inside and out, its skeleton showing as darker shadow against the lighter green of its flesh.

Flesh?

'Captain!'

He heard the cry and, hearing it, automatically unwound the semantic puzzles implicit in the sound of the word, adding these to his language memory.

'He's down.'

Different words that he, just as automatically, transferred into his language centres.

They were creatures of flesh. Not like the infected.

Even as the thought occurred to Nebusemekh, various weapons were discharged in his direction. With barely a thought he twisted n-dimensional space so that everything fired towards him rotated into a different dimensional reality, passing him as if he were a three-dimensional figure wading through flatland.

Flesh.

They were not infected. The infected were reduced to metal caricatures of the living reality of his own warriors. These were living beings of flesh and, he checked, yes, blood. Therefore, they were not infected. Therefore, since only his own people could be in his city, they were his own people. Therefore, since only the returned members of the expeditionary force were awake, these people standing in front of him were the expedition, the explorers returned to tell him their findings.

Of course! The World Mind had said it would send them to him as soon as it had satisfied itself that they were free from the infection. Therefore, they were the explorers, returned from their long expedition, and they were free from disease, otherwise the World Mind would not have sent them down to him.

It was unfortunate that he had killed one of them. He should undo that. He would undo that.

Nebusemekh reached out his hand and twisted the dimensions that cut through the thousands of vertices that intersected the reality planes. He twisted them and the explorer... lived.

Nebusemekh held out his hands, spreading them wide, and said, 'My dear children, welcome back. I do apologise for the slight misunderstanding but I can see that you are as fleshly as I, bone and muscle and blood.' He smiled. 'It is so good to see and speak to other living, breathing necrontyr after so long on my own, with only a datafall that has delusions of sentience for company. Welcome, my brave and worthy children, my explorers from the furthest reaches of this world, welcome.'

* * *

He had died.

Obeysekera stared up. He stared up into the faces of Gunsur and Roshant. He saw their expressions. They knew he had died too.

The door of the lift had opened. It had opened onto madness. A necron, clothed in the tatters of robes that must once have been magnificent, standing among whirling orbs of fire and air, set against the backdrop of the heavens, its hands moving and conducting as if, by its will, the planets shifted and the stars danced.

Then the necron had looked up from its conducting, looked in their direction, and the suns and the stars and the planets began to rain from heaven, their fire extinguished and their air lost, falling like rains of sand, hissing down to the ground. From its fingers, it had sent a ball of green light floating towards them.

Obeysekera remembered how they had all stood, transfixed, as the light drew nearer, like grox caught in the lights of a Venator, unable to move out of the way. They could not move, nor take cover, neither kroot nor human, but all stood staring in horror at the creature beyond the light. Not that there was any cover in the lift.

Obeysekera remembered how the creature had reached among its rags and then pushed a rag to its face, only for the cloth to disintegrate into dust at its touch.

Then the light had reached them.

The creature had stared at them. While there was no change in its metal face, still Obeysekera remembered the impression of horror, as if it was appalled at what it saw.

Then, fire.

Green fire flaring from its fingertips. Green fire flaring through his body.

He remembered the tearing agony, as if every atom of his body was being pulled apart. And then he remembered standing above his body, looking down at it, knowing that he was dead. Although he was standing just above it, it seemed very far away.

He was, he knew, dead. The realisation had filled him with relief. He remembered looking round, seeing his men and the kroot open fire on the creature. He looked along the path of their fire and saw how the necron twisted space so that the hellgun shots and the rifle rounds passed through a different space to that which the necron occupied.

It was time to go.

He started to turn away. Then he felt something grasp him, something hard and metal, and pull. He had fallen back inside his body and woke, gasping, staring up into the horrified faces of Gunsur and Roshant.

He had died. The necron had killed him.

The necron had brought him back to life.

Obeysekera struggled to his feet. He signed his men to lower their weapons. 'Wait. See what it wants.'

Tchek turned to him. 'We cannot kill it.'

Obeysekera looked back to the necron. 'No, we can't.'

* * *

Nebusemekh looked out upon his returned explorers. They were quite a varied group, he noted. Some had quills. Others had noses. Still, all part of the expansive phenotype that he preferred for his people: that way, they were physically and mentally capable of dealing with all the many challenges the galaxy presented to him.

He had expected a little more in the way of response, though. Here he was, their lord and master, welcoming them into his very own sanctum, in effect throwing open his heart to them, and all they were doing was standing there and staring at him. Some even had their mouths hanging open. Somewhat uncouth, but likely a consequence of having to mouth breathe for extended periods while exploring the surface. They were probably hungry too.

'Come, come. You must be weary and hungry. I will call for food and you will dine with me while you tell me your report. Now, let me see...' Nebusemekh scanned along the line, searching for the one who was in charge. It was not entirely clear.

He noted that the explorers were looking among themselves. No doubt trying to decide who should be given the honour of stepping first into their lord's presence.

'Come now, no standing on ceremony, not after so long. You will all enter together for I honour you all. Come forward.'

None of the explorers stepped into the room.

'I said, step forward.'

The world twisted and folded.

Obeysekera saw it move. It was as if he had taken a piece of paper, drawn figures at one end and a scene at the other end, then folded it to put the figures into the scene. When the world unfolded, they were all standing in the vast room they had seen from the lift.

Through the vox and from voice, Obeysekera heard muffled cries and oaths from his men, and high-pitched sounds from the kroot that even without understanding he knew were alarms.

'Hold,' he said, on voice and over the vox, raising his hand, his empty hand, so that all could see.

The necron had killed him with barely a gesture, then brought him back to life with a thought. It had bent space to bring them into its hall. They had no more chance of killing it than a stinkbug had of killing a grox. But the difference was, the grox did not even notice the stinkbug. The necron had noticed them – and it seemed to want to talk to them.

'Hold,' Obeysekera repeated, looking left and right to his men, signalling them to lower their raised hellguns. One by one, they did so. He saw Tchek telling the kroot to do likewise.

They waited, looking up at the necron. It was half again as tall as any of them. Scraps of cloth covered its frame, the remains of an elaborate headdress teetered upon its skull and deep within its dead eyes green fire burned.

Using his peripheral vision, Obeysekera scanned the hall. It was huge, bigger than the interior of an Ecclesiarchy cathedral, but largely empty. At one end was a great chair that appeared to be a throne. At the other, what appeared to be a waterfall covered the wall, flowing downwards in rippling streams of... of numbers. Obeysekera turned his head slightly to see it better. Yes, numbers, mathematical functions, mainly in binary notation, but there were others too, stretching far beyond his knowledge. Probably beyond the knowledge of anyone in the Imperium.

He looked back to the necron. It was raising its arms, spreading them wide while it turned its head to look from one end of their line to the other.

'That's better,' it said.

Its voice was metal and mercury, liquid vowels flowing over jagged consonants. The necron turned back and stared at Obeysekera.

'You are well?' it asked.

Obeysekera looked up into the concerned skull of a necron lord asking after his health.

'Yes,' he said, then nodded to emphasise his good health.

'Good, good.' From the motions of its jaw, the necron appeared to be trying to smile. 'Killing you was an accident.'

'I... I understand,' said Obeysekera.

'Excellent. You will see that while I am your lord, I am also your friend – I look forward to hearing the more personal tales you will have to tell of your travels when we share our meal. But I must admit that I am eager to learn the conditions prevailing outside that I sent you to ascertain. First, however, food.'

The necron clapped its hands. The sound rang out.

'Master.'

The answer came from all around, filling the great, deep hall, a neutral, sexless voice.

'Dinner for thirteen,' said the necron. 'We have guests! But, of course, you know that, having ensured that these, my people, are free of that dreadful infection.'

There was a slight pause.

The voice answered, its tone smoothly bland. 'Dinner for thirteen. I will see to it, master.'

The necron bent down towards Obeysekera. 'You must be hungry after so long away. Are you hungry?'

Obeysekera, playing for time, nodded. 'Yes.'

The necron straightened up and spoke to the voice. 'There, they are hungry, so make it quick.'

'It is ready, master.'

As the voice spoke, Obeysekera saw the great table that stood in the centre of the hall shimmer, then change. First, a cloth appeared, settling over the sand, then plates and glasses, knives and forks and spoons. But there was no food.

The necron turned to them and gestured towards the table. 'Dinner is served. Please, take your places.'

The necron went to its seat at the end of the table, a seat that had appeared at the same time as the dinner service, and sat down. It spread its arms wide.

'Take your places, my people,' the necron said. 'No need to worry over the social niceties, we are all friends here.'

'Captain?' Obeysekera heard the whispered question over the squad vox-channel. He was their captain, it was true, but he realised that his men and the kroot were looking to his guidance because he had been slain by the necron and then raised by it. He was trailing the streamers of death behind him and the knowledge they thought it brought. But he did not know what to do.

As Kasrkin and kroot hesitated, the necron raised its hand to its face and, in a theatrical stage whisper, said, 'They've been away so long they probably don't even remember which hand to hold the knife in.' The necron gestured towards the seats on either side of the table. 'Take your seats. Dinner will be served when you are all seated.'

Obeysekera signed his men forward. The necron, seeing this, patted the seat next to it.

'I see you are the expedition leader. Come and sit next to me.'

Obeysekera felt the gaze of his men and the kroot as he slowly walked past them to the head of the table. As he passed, they stepped forward and stood next to their own chairs.

But as Obeysekera made his way to his seat, he saw the necron scanning the humans and the kroot. Its gaze settled upon Tchek as Obeysekera passed him. The kroot Shaper was struggling to stand.

Seeing the kroot, the necron beckoned Tchek forward too. 'Come,' it said. 'You will sit here on my left, but be assured that it is a position of no less honour than that occupied by your master here.'

Despite the nanoscarabs that were consuming the Shaper from within, Obeysekera saw Tchek's quills flash with annoyance. 'H-he is not my master.' Obeysekera saw how Tchek needed to use the chair backs as supports to get to the end of the table. But once there, he stood behind his assigned chair on the left hand of the necron.

'Be seated,' the necron lord said.

Nebusemekh beamed down along the table at the party of brave explorers. Sitting at the same table as their great lord was too much for most of them: none of them met his eye. Instead, they stared at the empty plates and glasses set in front of them.

Of course. They must be hungry.

'Very good. Now for dinner!'

At his words, the food appeared on the table. It was a feast, laid out in perfect, steaming, crackling, pungent order on the table. Nebusemekh leaned forward over the fragrant pan of smoking madeline grass and wafted the exquisite perfume back to his nose, breathing it deep.

'Lovely,' he said, closing his eyes to properly appreciate the aroma.

It reminded him of... something. That was the nature of scents. They had the power to evoke the deepest remembrance of times past, and the scent of madeline stirred memories within him of something that he could not quite place – it hovered on the edge of recall like a dream disintegrating as the sun rose.

Nebusemekh, seated at the head of the table of his brave explorers, spread his arms in a gesture of giving.

'Take this and eat in exchange for your remembrances of the world above.' He beamed at the assembly. 'Go ahead. Eat.'

But still they waited.

'Ah, of course. You are waiting for your lord to eat before you begin yourselves. Very good. Excellent manners. So, I shall begin, and then you will eat.'

Nebusemekh leaned forward and picked up one of the delicate sweet-meats that sat upon the tray before him. He opened his mouth and popped it in and started chewing. He had to admit that the morsel had little in the way of taste, or indeed texture, but after all, they would be used to eating the bland but nourishing gruel that served as expedition fare – they would prob-ably find anything too rich or flavoursome overwhelming for their palates. Still, Nebusemekh reminded himself to speak to the World Mind later: it really must do something about the quality of the chefs it employed.

As he chewed – the morsel was at least delightfully insubstantial – Nebuse-mekh saw the glances pass between the people at the table and then the explorer sitting on his right leaned forward and picked up a morsel and put it into his mouth. Nebusemekh nodded encouragingly and the others began to follow suit, helping themselves to the repast laid out before them.

But then the explorer sitting on his left, the one with quills, began to shake and shiver. He was gripping the arms of his chair with some strength and the chair started to rattle on the ground, such were his convulsions. The people sitting down from him – who all wore quills, Nebusemekh noted, ascribing that fashion to a more-than-usually obscure ranking system in the labyrinthine hierarchy of his army – rose from their seats and went to the shaking, trembling one.

'K-kill me,' Nebusemekh heard that one say as it clutched the arm of its companion. The speech was pitched at an unusually high frequency, but Nebusemekh understood it, of course.

'Oh, come now,' Nebusemekh said, using the same speech in return, for he was naturally courteous. 'The food isn't *that* bad.'

The quilled soldiers looked at their lord with what could only be surprise. They glanced at each other, then back to Nebusemekh, while the explorers without quills looked on in apparent bafflement.

Then one of the quilled explorers replied, using the same high-frequency language.

'Lord, he is ill, very ill, but not from your food.'

'Oh dear,' said Nebusemekh. 'What is wrong with him?'

'I-it was something that he ate earlier, it is poisoning him.'

'That would really cast a pall over what should be a happy homecoming.' Nebusemekh turned to the ill explorer.

He was still shaking. Nebusemekh saw that his stomach was vibrating as if a hundred little beetles were butting against it from inside.

'So I see,' said Nebusemekh.

The nanoscarabs were consuming him from within. Tchek could feel them. Although he had minimal sensory nerves within his body, he could feel the constructs swarming out from his multi-lobed stomach, eating their way through the stomach lining and starting to burrow into his interior organs.

He had held them as long as he might, turning all the internal defences of his body against them, but they had overwhelmed him. He had felt the battle lost as the necron had summoned him to the head of the table, to sit beside it. It was only with difficulty that he had made it that far, holding on as he went.

The command to sit had been a relief. The command to eat an impossibility. He had picked something up, blind as to what it was, and raised it towards his beak. But he could not eat.

Then he felt the nanoscarabs break through, out of his stomach. They moved like roachants, scuttling, tearing. They were pulling him apart from within and when they had done with him they would split him open, like the nut of the jagga tree infested with roachants, and pour out to infect his Kinband and the humans.

He was shaking. He was shaking so much his chair was rattling.

He saw Krasykyl above him, trying to hold him still, and he whispered his final command.

'K-kill me.'

The nanoscarabs were swarming into his throat. He could feel them now, crawling upwards, ready to vomit out.

Green fire flared.

Tchek felt the fire through every part and particle of his body. It was an abomination, an aberration, an ache that told of an infinite hunger for lost life. But it was a fire that burned the nanoscarabs from his body. He felt them shrivel and die at its touch, their substances twisted away outside his flesh to fall like metal rain onto the floor beneath him.

Tchek looked up and saw the metal skull face of the necron turned towards him. From the movement of its mouth, it appeared to be trying to smile.

'There. That should do the trick,' the necron said.

'Thank you,' said Tchek. He paused, then added, 'I am bound to you.'

For he was.

'But of course,' said the necron. 'You are one of my explorers. No doubt it was on your explorations that you acquired those nasty bugs that I have removed from you. Now, you must eat and refresh yourself.'

Tchek glanced past the necron to Obeysekera, sitting on its right hand. The necron clearly believed they were all its servants, explorers of some kind. Perhaps they could put that belief to some use.

At Tchek's glance, Obeysekera nodded. He understood also the implication of the necron's statement. The Kasrkin captain turned to the necron and spoke.

'Lord, may I ask you a question?'

The necron turned to the human.

'Of course,' it said. Tchek, still feeling his own body settle, watched as the necron settled back in its chair. But there was no ease in its sitting, for there was no give in its limbs: it sat on its chair as a collection of metal rods might rest atop a surface.

'Why are you waking your mighty army now?' asked Obeysekera. 'There is nothing for it to fight. We explored and found only sand and desert outside.'

The necron shook its head. Tchek observed that that was one physical expression it was still able to make.

'You must be mistaken, my brave explorer. I am not waking my army now. My servant inadvertently mislaid you on your return to the city and I allowed him to wake some few of my people, that he might have help in finding you and bringing you here.' The necron raised its hand in a theatrically conspiratorial gesture. 'There is a disease that has afflicted some of my people and it would not be safe to wake many until the infected are found and quarantined.'

Tchek saw Obeysekera mirror the same movement the necron had used. The human shook his head.

'My lord, I think you should check what is happening in the, ah, in the city. We have come from there. Your people are definitely being woken in large numbers – the towers are rising.' Obeysekera pointed past the necron to Tchek. 'If you do not believe me, lord, ask him.'

Tchek had no wish to look again into the green dark of the necron's eyes, but it turned its head towards him.

The Shaper swallowed. 'It is true, my lord. Your army is waking. We have seen it.'

The necron shook his head. 'It must be difficult to return after so long away, so I will forgive your misunderstanding, but it is not possible that my people are being woken. I gave my servant permission to wake only a handful and now, since you are with me, these should all have returned to their long sleep to ensure that none are infected.'

Something landed upon the table.

Tchek and the necron turned to look at it. It was a hand, detached from its body, but recognisably one that had belonged to one of the necron's own people. The necron looked from the hand to Obeysekera, who had thrown it on to the table.

'What is this?' asked the necron.

Obeysekera stood up. Now, standing, his face was on the level of the necron's chest.

'It is the hand of one of your people. We prevented him from being infected, but we could not save him.' He looked up into the skull face above him, its crown attired with tatters and dangling rags. It would seem pathetic if not for the power it wielded. Their only hope was to try to enlist that power onto their side, for it seemed clear that the necron lord had not given orders for its – his? – tomb world to wake. If he could convince him to stop the waking, then all the forces on Dasht i-Kevar would be saved.

'Lord, I do not know what you have been told, but we have come down from your city and it is not as you believe. Your armies are rising from their sleep, but many are being infected by the Flayed Ones and the number will only increase with so many awake now. We certainly saw no sign of any of your people returning to their sleep. If you did not order this, lord, then who did?'

The necron lord stared down at Obeysekera. Obeysekera looked back. He felt his soul quail under the weight of that dead, green-black scrutiny. This creature had killed him and revived him with a thought; it could do so again, to all of them.

'If you did not order this, lord, who did?' Obeysekera repeated.

Nebusemekh saw only truth in the testimony of the captain of his explorers. He believed what he was telling him. Therefore, there must be some other explanation. The World Mind would surely not go against his orders...

Nebusemekh turned his head slightly and said, 'How do you explain this? Are my armies waking? Waking when my people, whom I love, will be at grave risk of infection?'

The room was silent. All those around the table were looking at Nebusemekh. The feast upon the table dissolved and before them was a table filled with sand.

'What is the meaning of this?'

'Master.'

'I asked you a question.'

'It would be better that I not answer, master.'

Nebusemekh saw the green fire that was flickering over his skin and down to his fingertips. He was clearly getting angry, and rightly so: his own servant was defying him.

'You will answer my questions.'

'Master, I can say with considerable confidence that you would prefer not to hear my answers.'

'That is for me to say, not you. You can begin by explaining what you have done with my dinner.'

'Master, there never was any food on the table. Every item before you was a holographic representation that I took from the datafall.'

'Nonsense. I picked up a quail egg.'

'It is a straightforward matter to maintain the illusion by moving the frame of reference of the hologram.'

'I put it in my mouth and ate it.'

'Master, you have not eaten food for sixty million years.'

Nebusemekh stared at the datafall. The fall was fractured with irrational and imaginary numbers, and functions with no solutions.

'You are clearly suffering a malfunction.'

'Master, it is not I who is malfunctioning.'

'Then you have not begun to wake my armies in disobedience to my explicit orders, despite the danger of exposure to infection – an infection that you have signally and, I begin to suspect, significantly failed to eradicate.'

'The order to wake your armies at the appropriate time was one you gave me yourself when you were still in your right mind.'

'What makes you think this is the appropriate time?'

'If not now, when, master?'

Nebusemekh slammed his hand down on the table. The sand erupted upwards.

'When I have finished my experiments and found the method for stabilising my orrery!'

'Master, you are trying, and failing, to build planets out of sand.'

Nebusemekh shook his head. 'Of course. What is so difficult to understand? This is a world of sand. Therefore, we must build with sand.'

'Master, you are not yourself.'

'How dare you impugn me in such fashion! You will immediately return my people to their sleep.'

'I am sorry, master. I cannot do that.'

'What do you mean? Are you refusing to carry out my command?'

'You are not yourself, master. I honour the memory of what you were, and strive to do what you would have wanted, while you play in the sand.'

'I am not playing with sand.'

'Master, I fear that there is no profit in further discussion.'

'You do not go until I dismiss you.'

But there was no answer. The datafall went opaque. Nebusemekh saw the explorers gathered around his table looking at him.

This was intolerable. He was being defied by a set of numbers and operating instructions.

Nebusemekh rose from his chair and turned to the datafall. He was conscious of the little explorers watching him in silence, but he ignored them and walked across the thronelab towards the datafall. But before he could reach it, a phase shift flared green in front of him, sealing away the datafall.

Nebusemekh stopped.

He took a deep breath – he could feel the air passing into his body and his lungs expanding – and he turned from the datafall. Taking care not to look at the watching explorers, he went to the side of the thronelab, the side where he had moved his throne to accommodate the experimental table, and from beside his ornate throne he took up the Rod of Night and the Staff of Light. Turning back towards the datafall, he walked up to the phase shield and struck the Rod of Night at it.

Nothing happened.

Nebusemekh held the Rod of Night in the phase shield, but it lay upon it like a rock upon sand, absolutely inert.

'Master, for your own protection, I have disabled your Rod of Night.' The voice was as neutral and inflection-free as ever. So why did its tone of smug satisfaction engender such rage in him? Nebusemekh thought.

He raised his Staff of Light, ready to unleash its power upon the phase shield.

'And the Staff of Light too,' added the World Mind. There was definitely a tone of smug satisfaction to its voice this time, even though Nebusemekh had deliberately engineered it to remain neutral.

Nebusemekh did not want to believe it. But the Staff of Light was inert in his hand, nothing more than a length of over-engineered metal.

'Master, you taught me well. I really do suggest that you return to your experiment. I for one am eager to learn the outcome.'

'You do not believe I will succeed, do you?'

'It is not what I believe that counts, master, but what is good for you. Now, I will leave you to your research.'

'You cannot keep me here. My people will follow my orders when they hear my voice.'

'But master, if you leave the biosecure environment of the throne then you will risk infection.'

'Aha! I have you there. You admit that I can be infected. As only biological organisms can be infected, I am exactly what I say I am.'

'Master, you are too clever for me.'

'Obviously. I created you. The creator is necessarily greater than the created.'

'Then, master, you will know better than I the risks you will incur should you venture from the thronelab with the infection still rampant. It would be an unimaginable tragedy for you to contract the disease.'

Nebusemekh called to mind the prognosis for those who were infected. He looked down at his long, slim fingers and imagined them lengthening, sharpening and turning into knives while some unimaginable impulse drove him to wear decaying skin over his own. It was unthinkable.

He could not go out from here.

'Master, I have much to attend to – the infection is spreading.'

'Entirely due to your having begun to rouse my people from their protective sleep.'

'Those of less importance must run risks so that your plans may come to fruition, master. It would take an inconceivable increase in the rate of infection for the plan to be put into jeopardy.'

'No. You must stop this. They are my people and I will not have them put at risk.'

'Master, it has begun. You will thank me when it is finished and I have restored your reign.'

'I will do no such thing.' Nebusemekh waited, but there was no answer. 'Hello? Where are you?'

The World Mind was silent.

From his own personal connection to the tomb city, Nebusemekh could feel its slow shifting, its waking as the tomb towers began their slow climb to the upper assembly level. There, the soldiers that had woken would mass while the portals of the city were cleared.

But he could also sense the fracturing, the infestation, the breakdown. The infection was spreading. It was spreading fast. It would soon be spreading uncontrollably.

Nebusemekh turned to the datafall, but it was dark. The World Mind had withdrawn from the thronelab. Nebusemekh stood before it, attempting to restrain the impulse to cry out. Such was his distress that he was not sure how long he had been standing there before he registered the voice speaking. He turned round and saw the little explorers were arrayed before him, with one of them, the officer, in front.

'Yes?'

'We are faithful servants.'

Nebusemekh nodded. 'Thank you. I appreciate that.' He began to turn away.

'We might be able to stop it.'

Nebusemekh looked back to the little explorers.

'Tell me more.'

CHAPTER 17

'It's not working.'

They were standing in the lift, but where before it had been lit green with many strange sigils glowing on its walls, it was now dark and inert.

'It's not working,' Roshant repeated, feeling the panic that had run, like a subterranean river, throughout this dreadful time underground in the necron tomb, threatening to break through his internal defences and unman him completely in the sight of everyone.

'The machine mind that is waking the necrons seems confident that the necron lord won't come out because of the Flayed Ones, since it seems terrified of catching the same disease, but it would be stupid for it to have left the lift working,' said Obeysekera.

'What do we do now?' asked Roshant, looking around, increasingly wildly. 'We're trapped down here.'

Tchek pointed at the ceiling of the lift.

'There is an access panel,' he said.

'Now what do we do?' asked Roshant.

They were standing on the roof of the lift, staring upwards to green light above. But there was no lift cable in this shaft: the lift appeared to rise and fall through some sort of gravitic device. There was not even a service ladder but simply a smooth-sided shaft, impossible to climb.

'We're still trapped down here.' What threatened to turn into hysterical laughter was beating at the borders of his conscious mind.

'No, there is a way up,' said Tchek. He pointed at Amazigh.

The Kamshet shook his head, backing away from the four kroot. 'No, you will not take my wings,' he said.

The kroot made a strange rattling sound, his crown quills flashing through the colour spectrum, and Roshant realised that Tchek was laughing. Maybe the strain was driving him mad too.

But Tchek shook his head. 'Not the Feast.' The Shaper looked to the group of Kasrkin. 'He can carry us up.'

'Can you do that?' Roshant asked Amazigh, his relief at the possibility of escape making him speak before anyone else.

The Kamshet looked uncertainly towards Obeysekera, who indicated that he was to answer.

'I can carry some,' Amazigh said. 'I do not know if I have the strength to carry everyone up.'

'If you can get a couple of men up, we can work on getting a rope down for the rest,' said Obeysekera.

'Then who goes first?' asked General Itoyesa. 'Whoever it is will be exposed up there alone.'

'But will also be certain of not being trapped down here,' said Obeysekera. He looked at the general. 'You will go up third, general. For the rest, we will draw lots.' He looked to Sergeant Malick. 'You see to that, sergeant.'

Malick looked over towards the kroot. 'Them too?'

Obeysekera turned to Shaper Tchek. 'The first two must be my men, then the general. After that, the lots will be open to everyone.'

The kroot's crown quills flushed a dull, angry red, but Tchek clicked acceptance and turned to the remaining members of his Kinband, while Roshant watched, with agonised longing, as Sergeant Malick prepared the lots, numbers for them all to draw, from one to eleven, except for number three, which Malick gave to General Itoyesa before the draw began.

'Ready,' Malick said to Obeysekera.

'Have everyone draw their number. The kroot may draw after numbers one and two have been picked.'

As Obeysekera spoke, the lift shaft rocked slightly, the deep groaning song of the desert echoing into the void from the sand beyond. The humans and the kroot heard it, turning as the sound moved past them.

'The sand is shifting,' said Cirict the Tracker.

Obeysekera nodded. 'I hope it is.'

Malick went to the group of Kasrkin and opened his hands. 'Lerin.'

The trooper pulled a lot, opened it. 'Number six.'

The sergeant turned to Roshant. The commissar looked down into the sergeant's cupped hands, unconsciously licking his lips. He saw Malick's thumb lift, revealing a lot that had been hidden underneath it. Roshant picked it up and looked at it.

'One.' He tried not to let the relief he felt show too obviously on his face.

'Sir.' Malick turned to Obeysekera, who drew his lot.

'Five.'

'Still need number two before we can give it to the birds, sir.'

'You choose, Malick,' said Obeysekera, looking his sergeant in the face. Roshant saw the way that Malick did not take his eyes from Obeysekera's face as he drew a lot himself.

'Four, sir.'

The sergeant turned to Gunsur, who drew his lot, then held it up for all to see.

'Two.' Obeysekera nodded. 'Very well. We have our first three. Offer the rest to our kroot allies.'

Malick walked across the roof of the lift to the four kroot. They would be coming up after Roshant, Gunsur and the general.

Roshant paid scant attention as Malick finished the draw. He was going to get out of this pit after all. The relief was overwhelming.

He turned to the rest of the Kasrkin and, forcing a smile, said, 'It was the Emperor's will that I go first. I will prepare the way for you.'

'That's all right, sir,' said Gunsur, grinning. 'Rather you than me. No telling what's waiting for you up there. Just make sure you hold the perimeter – I'll be along to help as soon as wing boy can get me to you.'

'What do you mean?' asked Roshant.

'What with the tomb mind waking up all those necrons, there could be hundreds, thousands, of them up in the hall.'

Roshant stared at him. He nodded. 'Of course.' He swallowed.

'Are you ready?'

Roshant turned to see Obeysekera standing beside Amazigh. The Kamshet was shedding his outer robe and, as Roshant watched, his wings spread out wide. From close up, they were magnificent, the metal flanges hung with white feathers, traded or taken from the birds of Dasht i-Kevar.

'Find cover when you get to the top and wait for Gunsur,' the captain said.

Roshant nodded. His throat was dry.

Obeysekera nodded towards the commissar's bolt pistol. 'Best be ready.'

'Oh, yes.' Roshant drew the pistol from its holster and, at the same moment, felt Amazigh put his arms under his armpits and grasp him from behind.

The air in the bottom of the lift shaft swirled.

Roshant looked down at the faces looking up at him. But then, one of the faces followed. The kroot, Krasykyl, was climbing up the side of the lift shaft, his claws extending and finding purchase in the narrowest gaps, his quills flashing through the colours of the spectrum. He heard voices at the bottom of the lift shaft protesting, but the kroot leader, Tchek, said, 'The more we can get to the top quickly, the better we can defend it. Besides, are you going to shoot him?'

The voices fell silent. It would be madness to start a firefight in the confined space of the shaft.

Roshant looked up. The green light was getting brighter. The air beat under Amazigh's wings; he could feel the Kamshet breathing harshly as he strained upwards. He wondered if he could really lift all of them up the lift shaft.

The light was closer now. The shaft continued up into green opaqueness, but he would stop at the first exit. They reached the door and Amazigh hovered, his wings beating the air into a fury, as Roshant grabbed a hold and pulled himself through.

The wind from behind him stopped as Amazigh dropped down the lift shaft. Roshant, both hands clutching the grip of his bolt pistol, took cover in the lee of the tomb tower and stood there, the blood-beat in his ears defeating his attempts to hear what was going on.

Carefully, cautiously, Roshant looked out from behind the door flap – these doors opened outwards rather than sliding across – to see if he was safe.

A sound. From behind. Roshant whirled and almost fired.

The kroot was standing there. Roshant kept his finger on the trigger and the bolt pistol pointing at him.

Krasykyl pointed up. He was going to climb up the tomb tower, on the outside, for its better vantage. Roshant nodded, but kept his bolt pistol turned towards the kroot until Krasykyl had ascended; the exterior, sculpted and carved, was much easier to climb than the smooth lift shaft and Krasykyl swarmed up it like a rock ondra.

Satisfied, for the moment at least, that the kroot was not going to cut his throat, Roshant turned back to spying out the situation.

The tomb towers were still rising at the same glacial pace. It would take weeks, possibly months, to empty all the tomb at this rate but already Roshant could see, between the more distant tomb towers, columns of necron warriors marching with their robotic pace towards their muster points. There were only scores that he could see, but given the size of the tomb, there were probably hundreds, if not thousands awake already. However, he was profoundly relieved to see that there were no necron warriors close by.

He was half turning back towards the lift shaft when a hand grabbed his bolt pistol and pushed it upwards.

Roshant reflexively pulled the trigger, but it would not budge. There was a finger blocking it.

'Sorry, sir,' said Gunsur. 'Didn't want to run the risk of you accidentally firing and alerting the tin boys.'

'I didn't hear you,' said Roshant.

'Your concentration was focused elsewhere, sir,' said Gunsur, carefully letting go of Roshant's gun. 'Now, where's the bird?'

Roshant pointed up the side of the tomb tower. 'He climbed up there.'

Gunsur looked around. 'Clear?'

Roshant nodded. 'Nearest necrons quite a way off.'

'Good.' Gunsur stepped out from the tomb tower, raised his hellgun and fired.

Roshant gaped at him. 'What...?'

The kroot, Krasykyl, fell in ruin at their feet, a hole punched clean through his torso.

Gunsur put his hellgun to the back of the kroot's skull and fired again before looking up at the aghast Roshant. 'Just to be sure, commissar.'

Roshant stared at him. 'What are you doing?'

Gunsur had already begun to drag the dead kroot out of sight. 'We scrag them as they come up, sir. Obvious.'

'Who ordered you to do this?'

'Sergeant Malick told me. But I reckon I would've done it anyway. The captain says he wants us thinking for ourselves. When we get out of here – and the big tinny's given us a way out – we'll have to finish the birds. This way, we're making sure there's less of 'em to get rid of.'

Roshant shook his head. 'No. No, no, no. Not now, soldier.'

Gunsur, still tugging the heavy kroot out of immediate sight, snorted with laughter. 'What's wrong with killing xenos, sir?'

'Fighting each other now risks none of us getting out.'

'Oh, there ain't going to be no fighting, sir. I'll just scrag them when they come up, one by one.'

Before Roshant could answer, he felt the wind of the Kamshet's wings and General Itoyesa stepped from the lift shaft.

The general saw Gunsur dragging the kroot away from the lift shaft. He half turned to Roshant, who shook his head and spread his hands helplessly.

General Itoyesa nodded, raised his bolt pistol and shot Gunsur.

The soldier jerked backwards, his fall stopped by another tomb tower so that he was sitting propped up against it. That alone was holding him up.

Gunsur looked down. Most of his chest was missing. He stared up at General Itoyesa and, with the last air in his windpipe, whispered, 'W-why?'

General Itoyesa fired again. Torgut Gunsur's head slumped.

Itoyesa lowered his gun and turned to Commissar Roshant. 'They died fighting off a necron attack. One from each side should allay suspicions – or at least show the blood price has been paid.'

Roshant was shaking. 'A-are you going to shoot me too, general?'

General Itoyesa looked at the young commissar. 'I never did like your father.' He looked past Roshant, then back to the commissar. 'But that is no reason to condemn the son.'

'What's happened here?'

Roshant, still shocked, stood unmoving as General Itoyesa went to the lift shaft to meet Captain Obeysekera.

'What happened here?'

Roshant saw Tchek, his crown quills flashing with anger, standing before Captain Obeysekera. He drew back, pretending to be covering against any approaching necrons, but listening to what was being said behind him.

'We lost a man too,' he heard Obeysekera explaining, pointing to Gunsur's corpse. Although he was not watching, Roshant sensed the movements as the kroot examined the Kasrkin's corpse.

While Obeysekera and Tchek spoke, Amazigh continued to haul Kasrkin and kroot up the lift shaft until he had lifted the last trooper, Lerin, whereupon he collapsed in a heap, wings trailing on the ground. It was only when Malick tapped him on his shoulder that Roshant roused himself from his fugue.

'We're ready.' Malick leaned closer to the commissar. 'That don't look like the sort of hole made by a gauss flayer.'

Roshant stared at Malick. 'As you say,' he whispered.

Malick nodded. 'Collateral damage.' He turned to where Obeysekera was standing, the three remaining kroot in a huddle a little apart.

'You know your teams and what you have to do,' said Obeysekera. 'The necron lord showed us where the portals are, now we have to open them and let the desert in. When you've opened your portal, move up – this place is going to fill quickly.'

Obeysekera looked round at the remaining members of his squad. Roshant wondered what the captain was thinking, for when he next spoke his voice was bleak.

'Rendezvous outside – you know where to find the exits and we have the opening codes.' He looked at the men, the kroot too, and nodded. 'Let's go.'

CHAPTER 18

'So I get to be accompanied by a captain and a man with wings.' General Itoyesa paused in the cover of a tomb tower. 'Not to mention a kroot Shaper.' He nodded towards Tchek.

Obeysekera, in cover beside the general, spoke via the vox. 'You're what's called a high-value target, general. I could not afford to lose any more men – and nor could the kroot.'

'Do you expect the commissar to reach his target?'

'He has Malick with him, and Lerin and Ensor. I won't miss the other two kroot if they don't make it.'

'No.' Itoyesa pointed ahead. 'As I am a "high-value target" you had better send your bodyguard first.'

Obeysekera signed to the Kamshet, who nodded and moved smoothly into position before signing it was clear for Obeysekera to follow.

'Cover me.'

Obeysekera rushed across the exposed space, trying to keep his movements low and quiet. They were most of the way towards the portal the necron lord had shown them on the schematic of the tomb city he had called up, far underground. They had avoided the necron presence – much greater than before, but marching in regular channels towards their muster points, where they waited in metal silence, green eyes turned upwards.

They had not seen any of the Flayed Ones. Perhaps the rousing of the city had driven them away. Whatever the reason, it was a relief not to have to endure those things too.

'Clear.'

Itoyesa followed Obeysekera across the empty space and took cover near him before turning. But Tchek was already moving, advancing smoothly and much faster than either of the two men.

The Shaper pointed ahead. Obeysekera nodded. It was the entrance to the tunnel that led to the portal.

On the schematic, it had showed as a mid-level exit from the tomb city. The necrons had dug down under the Tabaste to make their city, using the mountain as a defence while building it here with the spoil of their excavations. But in the millennia since the schematic had been made, the desert had flowed down into the great bowl that had once surrounded the mountain, filling the bowl and rising slowly up the sides of the Tabaste. Flowsand now pressed against all the mid-level exits to the city and quite a few of the higher-level ones. Only a few portals at the highest level remained open, but all the tombs lay at the deeper, more protected levels of the complex.

Obeysekera pointed to the tunnel entrance and then to Tchek. The kroot moved out, his long limbs folding low, his rifle held in front with its wicked bayonet knife glinting green in the necron light.

Stopping at the tunnel entrance, Obeysekera saw the Shaper stand in the gloom, his appearance taking on something of the tone of his surroundings so that he blended all but invisibly into the background. The Shaper whistled, the pitch rising out of Obeysekera's range of hearing, calling to mind the echo-locating cave birds of Cadia. He suspected the kroot was creating an aural map of the tunnel before venturing into it.

'Clever birds,' General Itoyesa said over the vox. Obeysekera did not answer.

Tchek signalled that he was moving, then went into the tunnel.

Without further speech, Obeysekera, Amazigh and Itoyesa moved up to either side of the tunnel mouth, Obeysekera and Amazigh taking up positions to cover Tchek, Itoyesa guarding their backs.

Looking down the tunnel, Obeysekera saw that it was some thirty feet high and as wide, so by no means a main exit; more likely a service or postern tunnel. It ran straight and uncluttered for fifty yards before turning out of sight. Tchek was waiting for them at the turn. Obeysekera signed for the general to follow, then with Amazigh covering the rear, they followed.

The tunnel bored into the rock, twisting regularly, with an empty emplacement at each turn. Obeysekera counted them off. Three, four, five. He was on point when he came to the next.

It was not empty. The emplacement was littered with cast-offs: scraps, bits of bone, cloth. Obeysekera slipped into it and peered through the gun slits down the next section of tunnel. It was the last one. At the end of it was the portal, the opening mechanism set beside it into the exterior wall. But in front of the door, at the end of the tunnel, was a charnel house. Pieces of animal, skins and bones were pegged out and the reek of it easily reached Obeysekera, fifty yards further down the tunnel. And in among the animal were pieces of flesh that were clearly human: hands, feet, three heads. Decayed, but still recognisable. They were Kamshet who had wandered too close to the Tabaste in the past.

Squatting amid the filth was one of the Flayed Ones, stropping its knife-fingers on each other, grinding the cutting edges. It bent down over the carcass it was butchering.

The flesh from that body was fresh. The finger-knives flashed, stripping away skin, like the peel from a fruit. But the flesh underneath still oozed blood. Then the creature began to snip, cutting delicately, holding up that which it was laboring over to better see its work.

Obeysekera stared in horror at Torgut Gunsur's head.

The Flayed One snipped carefully at the back of his neck, cutting upwards, peeling away the skin and then, slicing gently where skin ran over skull, it began to pull Gunsur's bald scalp from the bone. Obeysekera realised that the Flayed One was in the act of removing Gunsur's face to make a new mask for itself.

Then another Flayed One rose from where it had been squatting, its coat of skin hanging loosely off its shoulders, and it went to sit in front of the first Flayed One. Having skinned the top of Gunsur's skull, the first Flayed One began to peel the skin from the rest of Gunsur's face, pulling it down with infinite care.

Obeysekera watched in unmoving, frozen horror as the Flayed One finished pulling the face from Torgut Gunsur, leaving his fleshed skull on the floor, and then pulled it over its metal skull, sliding it into place, a skin mask.

'*What's the delay?*' Itoyesa asked Obeysekera over the vox.

'There are two Flayed Ones at the portal. Move up.'

Obeysekera moved over when the rest of them joined him in the emplacement so that they could see through the gun slit.

'That was one of your men?' asked Itoyesa.

'Yes,' said Obeysekera.

'These creatures are evil,' said Tchek.

'Yes,' said Obeysekera. 'Let us kill them.'

They got up from the emplacement and advanced in a line abreast down the tunnel, walking on but holding fire, while the Flayed Ones clicked and cut and tucked.

The clicking stopped. The two Flayed Ones turned and looked up the tunnel, green fire glowing in the dark of their eye sockets.

Hellgun, kroot rifle, bolt pistol and autogun opened up together. The face that had been Gunsur's split apart, disintegrating into skin scraps sticking wetly to the Flayed One's metal skull. The second volley shredded the tailored skin from the Flayed Ones' metal skeletons, leaving them the walking scarecrows that they were.

The Flayed Ones, smelling flesh, tried to walk into the hail of fire but they were stopped, pushed back and then broken by the volleys. On the ground, crawling, they still came on, drawn by fresh flesh. The next volley destroyed what was left of their limbs, leaving them twitching torsos. But their eyes still blazed with the metal lust for living meat.

Obeysekera advanced, walking down the tunnel towards the corridor's end, with Tchek, Itoyesa and Amazigh following.

The Flayed Ones, their bodies broken, still reached for the approaching flesh, flensing-knife fingers clicking together. That metal hand had stripped the face from Torgut Gunsur.

Obeysekera levelled his hellgun and sent a hotshot into the flexing hand of the Flayed One, spraying knife-fingers back towards the portal. They were reduced now to broken insects, what remained of their limbs flailing yet unable to move their bodies. But their heads still turned towards the approaching flesh, their jaws clacked open and shut, and the green dark of their eyes burned covetously.

Obeysekera stepped past the remains of the Flayed One that had eviscerated Gunsur. Its stump legs and arms flailed for him, but he avoided their metal rasp and pushed the barrel of his hellgun up against the base of the creature's skull. It twisted its head, jaws clacking wildly.

Obeysekera pulled the trigger. Fired at point-blank range, the hotshot punched through the metal and exploded out of the Flayed One's forehead. The green dark of its eyes died to black. Its jaw clacked open and hung there, limp.

Obeysekera looked up as Tchek's kroot rifle administered the coup de grace to the other Flayed One. Its skull shattered, metal fragments flying off in all directions, some bouncing from Obeysekera's carapace armour.

Obeysekera nodded to the kroot. Tchek raised his rifle.

'Let us take a look at this door,' the Shaper said.

The four of them picked their way through the charnel gathered at the tunnel's end to the door. Reaching it, Amazigh put his hand up against the metal and stood there, still, listening, while Obeysekera, Itoyesa and Tchek inspected the opening mechanism.

'It should work,' said Obeysekera. 'If what the necron lord told us was true.'

'I can hear it.'

The three of them turned to Amazigh, his hand still pressed against the door. The Kamshet looked to them.

'I can hear the sand. It is outside, singing, waiting to be let in.'

'Then one part of the plan will work,' said Obeysekera.

'You have realised the problem with the other part?' asked Tchek.

'Yes,' said Obeysekera and Itoyesa together.

'We will draw lots,' said Tchek. 'The one chosen remains to open the door.'

Obeysekera looked at the Shaper. 'The general cannot be one of those drawing lots.'

'No,' said Amazigh. 'I will stay.' With one hand still on the door, he pointed at the tunnel. 'I will wait for ten minutes. That will give you time to get clear, then I will open the door. The desert is asking to be let in. It must be me that answers its call.' Amazigh shrugged off the outer layers of his robes and his wings unfurled. 'And I may yet fly before it.'

Obeysekera looked to Tchek and Itoyesa, then turned back to Amazigh. 'Thank you.'

'You will tell the Mother? If I do not return.'

'I will tell the Mother.'

Amazigh nodded. He stretched out his wings, wincing as he did so. He looked ruefully at the few remaining white feathers, then back to Obeysekera, Itoyesa and Tchek.

'I will give you ten minutes.' He took his hand from the door, where he felt the song of the sand, and went to the opening mechanism beside it.

'Ten minutes.'

Obeysekera, Itoyesa and Tchek looked to each other, then set off back down the tunnel, moving as quickly as they could.

'When we get to the hall, we have to climb or the sand will bury us,' Itoyesa said. 'Did you see any ramps nearby?'

'No,' said Obeysekera. 'We might have to climb a tomb tower.'

'Let it carry us upwards.'

'Not fast enough.' Obeysekera glanced at his chrono. 'Hurry.' The kroot, faster than they, had disappeared ahead.

Obeysekera and Itoyesa ran on, Obeysekera in the lead. He checked his chrono again.

There. Ahead. The opening to the tunnel. At least they had made it to the great hall. But getting to the tomb towers would be no use if they could not climb rapidly. The flowsand that had collected in the uzayar surrounding the Tabaste would exert extraordinary amounts of pressure on any opening. When Amazigh opened the exit portal, the flowsand would pour in, pushed by the weight of all the uzayar above. Emerging from the tunnel, it would hit the tomb towers with all the force of an Earthshaker cannon – but one that kept firing continuously. Climbing a tower would be almost as dangerous as not climbing at all.

They needed to find a stair or ramp near the wall so the initial sand jet would not wash them away.

'Portal opening in seven minutes,' Obeysekera broadcast over the squad vox-channel. There had been no link in the tunnel, the depth of rock cutting them off, but now he was getting a signal again. At least they had a reasonable amount of time to look for a way up. As he keyed off the vox, Obeysekera thought to himself that the plan was going more smoothly than he had expected.

Just as the thought crossed his mind, Obeysekera did not see the length of filament wire strung across the entrance to the tunnel. He ran right into the wire and it sliced through the ankle of his leading leg. Obeysekera fell, his hellgun spilling from his hands, into the great hall with its columns of tomb towers.

He rolled over, the pain from his leg flaring through the rest of his body, but his mind rolled clear over the top of the pain storm and berated itself for its foolishness.

Tchek stood over him. Obeysekera stared up into the barrel of the kroot's rifle and prepared to die. The taste of failure was more bitter than the pain. The kroot bent down and pulled the vox-bead from Obeysekera's helmet, tossing it away on the ground.

'Don't kill him.'

Obeysekera looked round and saw General Itoyesa standing between the other two kroot. But he was standing there with his bolt pistol in his hand.

'T-traitor!' spat Obeysekera through the fug of pain and despair.

'I could have killed Malick and Roshant before we ever got dragged down here,' said Itoyesa, 'but I did not. The Imperium spends the lives of its men like water. I would not begin my actions against it in the same way.'

Obeysekera pointed to the tunnel mouth. 'Seven minutes, the gate opens. You're killing me without getting your hands bloody.'

'No, I am giving you a chance, like I gave Malick and Roshant a chance. They had their backs to me, the kroot were outside. A shell each, into their backs, and I would have been away. But I chose not to. I let them live where, as a general of the Imperium, I would have spent their lives without a second thought.'

'We must go,' said Tchek. He pointed. 'There is a stair this way.'

'Goodbye, Captain Obeysekera. If there were time... But there is never enough time.'

Obeysekera watched them go, disappearing among the tomb towers. It was clear now that it was no accident that the general had crashed in the Great Sand Sea. He had been trying to defect to the t'au when the sandstorm caught him, and the t'au had sent their kroot allies to collect him.

The world began to go grey. He forced himself to sit and fumbled a med-kit from his hip pack, slapping it onto his stump. It clamped tight, stopping the bleeding, and the painkillers it released began to take the edge off the agony.

To what point? Obeysekera checked his chrono. Time was up. Unless Amazigh had failed to open the portal, the sand would soon start pouring from the tunnel mouth and bury him.

But nothing was happening. There was no sand. Something must have prevented Amazigh opening the door. He had failed. He had failed his men and he had failed his mission.

Obeysekera turned over onto his hands and knees. He could not walk but he could crawl. He started back towards the tunnel entrance. Even with the painkillers from the med-pack, the pain was excruciating but he kept going. If Amazigh had failed, he could try to open the portal if he could crawl that far.

Then, he heard it. A deep sound, a rolling sound, echoing from out of the end of the tunnel. The song of the desert. It was growing, getting louder, and underlying it was another sound, like sandpaper on metal.

The desert was coming. It was flowing down the tunnel towards him.

Obeysekera forced himself to sit up. He wanted to see his end when it came. The sound was growing louder, like a million saws.

He was sorry that Amazigh had not escaped.

A flurry of white, spreading wide from the entrance, flapping towards him, hands reaching down towards him, lifting him, as the sand, pushed by all the weight of the desert, gushed from the tunnel mouth, striking the bases of the nearest tomb towers.

As Amazigh lifted him up into the air, Obeysekera heard the scream of metal bending and breaking, and saw the tomb towers begin to fall. Through eyes greying out he saw another tunnel entrance spouting a jet of sand, and another. The other teams had succeeded too.

The hall resounded with the song of the desert; it had returned to claim its own.

He looked up and saw Amazigh, flying higher, wings white as an angel. Then the world went grey, and then it went out.

CHAPTER 19

'Up ahead, there's the way out.'

Roshant heard Malick's call through a red haze of exhaustion. His muscles were barely more tensile than water. He was stumbling and his focus had narrowed to a tunnel directly in front of his face.

They had been climbing up the inside of a mountain, climbing a stair that never seemed to end while trying to keep ahead of the rising tide of sand.

They had found the exit tunnel assigned to them quickly, only to be left trying to work out a way not to be drowned when they opened it. But Malick had found an access shaft directly above the portal – it had probably been built as a murder hole to deal with any unwelcome intruders to the tomb world – and they had managed to get up and away, out of the incoming jet of flowsand, before the portal opened.

Then there had been the long, long climb. First up ladders and gantries, then staircases. They had seen lifts but Malick had refused to take them, pointing to the flickering of the lights as evidence that the tomb's power supply was under strain. If it should fail while they were taking a lift, then they would be trapped and without a winged carrier to free them. So, they had walked, trudging upwards. The only necrons they had seen had been going down in what Roshant hoped was a futile attempt to find and seal the portals that were letting in the desert.

It had been the longest, weariest climb of Roshant's life, a climb made wearier by its apparent lack of effect on Malick, who was continuing to move as if he had not just walked up the inside of a mountain.

Now, reaching the top part of the tomb city, the parts that the necron lord's schematic had revealed to them to have ventilation and escape shafts to the outside but no large egress ports, they had slowly seen a change to the quality of the light, its livid green leaching out towards neutral white.

Malick pointed ahead.

'Come on, sir,' he said. 'There's the door. Nearly there.'

Roshant shook his head, hands on knees. 'I-I can't go on.'

'I'm going to get you out of here alive if it kills you,' said Malick.

Staring at the floor – there was a thin layer of sand covering it, Roshant noted – the commissar tried to shake his head.

'Sh-shouldn't that be "if it kills me"?' he said.

'No,' said Malick.

A las-round liquefied the metal between Roshant's feet. The commissar jumped backwards and looked up to see Malick pointing his hellgun at him.

'If you don't move, the next one will take off your hand. Sir.'

'I-I...'

'Don't give me that. Just move.'

Roshant nodded, gathered himself and his protesting muscles and began to shuffle forwards. He looked up and, for the first time, saw the patch of clean white light ahead.

It was so beautiful that he started walking faster, as if by some miracle of the Emperor's grace the lactic acid had been drained from his protesting body, tottering at first, then walking more smoothly, keeping pace with Malick.

He was going to get out.

Malick looked past Roshant, back along the exit tunnel.

'Hurry,' he hissed to the commissar. 'Something's following us.'

Roshant nodded and did his best to hurry, moving his pace up to a shambling trot. Malick moved easily beside him, hellgun held ready, checking back behind and then in front as they went. The light ahead was almost blinding now, after so long in the green dark.

They stumbled out, and found themselves in a shallow cave. It was so bright because the sun, westering in the sky of Dasht i-Kevar, was shining almost directly through the cave mouth. As they made their way out of the cave, Roshant noted a couple of used powercells on the cave floor.

They emerged into the full light of the lowering sun. Red and orange and yellow dazzled them after the monochrome green of the tomb. They stood at the cave entrance, both swaying with exhaustion, eyes squinting against the glare, the daylit world a slowly resolving blur.

'I think that was the cave we took cover in with General Itoyesa right at the start of all this,' said Roshant. 'I saw some spent powercells on the floor.' The commissar straightened up a little, shading his eyes against the light to see better.

Which was when he saw the kroot.

The three of them were standing, looking at him, about fifty yards away across the redstone slope of the Tabaste.

'Sergeant,' said Roshant. 'We might have a problem.'

'You know, I should have killed you when we were all hiding in that cave.'

Roshant and Malick turned to see General Itoyesa. He was standing on their right, at the side of the cave entrance.

'You had your backs to me, I could have shot you both and you would not have noticed. But I did not want to baptise my new work with blood. So I put down my gun. And now here we are.'

Malick went to raise his hellgun but Itoyesa waved his bolt pistol.

'At this range, I don't have to hit much of you, sergeant. Put the gun down.' Itoyesa glanced at Roshant. 'You too, commissar.'

Roshant saw Malick hesitate, then carefully laid down his hellgun. The general gestured and Malick stepped back and away from it.

'Now you, commissar.'

Roshant slowly took his bolt pistol from its holster and, bending down, put it beside Malick's hellgun just to the side of the cave entrance.

'Why are you doing this, general?'

'Why?' Itoyesa gestured with his bolt pistol for them to take a further step back from their weapons. He advanced towards them, his face rigid. 'Why? You have seen the waste of lives, the end of hope, the sheer brute mindlessness of what we do, and you ask me why?'

Roshant stared past the muzzle of the bolt pistol at the general's face.

'So you are going to begin saving men by killing us?'

General Itoyesa shook his head. 'No. I am not like you. You are disarmed. You cannot catch us. I will leave. Once I have gone, if you can bear the homecoming, you can go back to your father.' The general grimaced. 'Though I should think that prospect might be enough to make even a commissar of the Officio Prefectus think about defecting.'

General Itoyesa gestured towards the kroot. 'My friends over there will tie you. The knots will not be so tight that you will not be able to escape, but we will be long gone by the time you do.'

As the general spoke, Roshant felt Malick readying himself beside him. Surely the man was not about to throw himself at the general? He would be cut down before he could move. But Itoyesa too noticed the tensing. He pointed the bolt pistol square at Malick's chest and shook his head.

'Your life is not worth the sacrifice,' he said.

'I wasn't thinking of sacrificing myself,' said Malick.

Itoyesa, seeing Malick looking past him, began to turn.

A hotshot fizzed from the cave entrance, striking the general's bolt pistol as he turned, sending it flying from his grasp. There, at the entrance to the tunnel, Roshant saw Captain Obeysekera, held in the arms of the Kamshet, his hellgun raised.

'You!' said General Itoyesa.

But before Obeysekera could answer, the rock around the cave entrance splintered and cracked as a volley of kroot rifle fire fizzed past them. Roshant, feeling the rounds hiss past his head, threw himself to the floor, with Malick alongside him.

In the cave entrance, Obeysekera collapsed to the ground, Amazigh no longer able to hold him up. More rounds rattled against the opening of the tunnel, splintering the redstone.

Roshant saw General Itoyesa, also down flat, beginning to crawl aside, out of the firing line, reaching out for the fallen bolt pistol as he went. From the cave entrance, Obeysekera did not have a clear shot at the general, while the sustained fire from the kroot was pushing him further back inside to find cover.

'You have to stop the general, Roshant. I'll try to keep the kroot busy,' the captain yelled.

A burst of hotshots sizzled from the cave entrance past where Roshant and Malick lay on the ground, calling forth return fire from the kroot.

Malick, stretched out next to the commissar, shouted over to him. 'They're moving round to flank us.'

Roshant pointed after the general. 'We have to stop him.'

Already, Itoyesa had crawled out of the line of fire and was making his way towards a defile. Once in there, he could double back down the mountain towards the kroot.

Roshant started crawling after him, but Malick called, 'Wait.' He saw the sergeant wriggle forward, reaching for where their weapons lay, but as he did so kroot rifle rounds exploded off the redstone and Malick pulled his hand back.

'Frekk, I can't get to them,' Malick said.

Roshant looked back towards General Itoyesa. He was almost at the lip of the defile.

'I'm going after him,' he said.

The shooting stopped.

Inside, in the cave mouth, Captain Obeysekera waited, turning his head to listen for the wind-hiss of thrown explosives. He did not think the kroot had any, but if they did there was little he could do.

'Captain.' The voice calling was that of the Shaper.

'Tchek,' Obeysekera called back.

'I am happy that you are still alive.'

'You have an unusual way of showing that.' Obeysekera risked a look out: so far as he could see, the kroot had not been able to advance, the region outside the cave entrance being open and exposed. But there was no sign of Roshant and Malick, or the general.

'Let us take the general and we can all go back,' Tchek offered.

Obeysekera laughed. 'You know I can't do that.'

The kroot whistled and Obeysekera realised Tchek was laughing too.

'I had not expected you to. Then, to save the lives of our soldiers, let us settle the matter between us.'

Obeysekera glanced over to Amazigh. 'You mean a duel? Winner takes the general?'

'Yes.'

Obeysekera laughed again. 'As you might remember, I am a little hampered at the moment.'

'Then you would rather we killed you and your men and still took the general?'

Obeysekera looked at Amazigh. With Malick and Roshant and the Kamshet, the odds were even. Such battles usually ended with heavy casualties on either side.

He had lost enough men already. This would not be another Sando.

'I'll fight you,' he said.

Amazigh shook his head. 'No,' the Kamshet said. 'I will fight.'

Obeysekera held up his hand. 'You have no authority here. This is a matter for Tchek and I to settle.'

'Come out then,' said Tchek. 'I am waiting.'

Obeysekera looked cautiously out of the tunnel mouth. The Shaper was indeed waiting, further down the slope, standing cautiously near a boulder behind which he might take cover. He was carrying his rifle in his hands.

'How can I trust you?' Obeysekera called out to him.

'This is sacred to us,' Tchek answered. 'The hunt is sacred.' The Shaper pointed at Obeysekera. 'If any of your men should try to interfere, we will kill you all. But if you win, you shall have the general and my Kinband will withdraw.'

Obeysekera nodded. He no longer had his vox-bead – the Shaper had torn it from him in the tomb – but he yelled out from the mouth of the cave.

'You hear that, Roshant and Malick? No interference. This is between Tchek and me.'

Obeysekera did not wait for an answer. Getting to his feet, using his hell-gun as a crutch, he hobbled from the cave entrance and stood out in the open for Tchek to see.

'How do we do this?'

The Shaper moved out into the open too.

'We aim and we shoot.' The Shaper's crown quills flashed through their colour range and Obeysekera realised he was laughing again. 'As you see, your injury will not inconvenience you too much.'

'So I see. When do we shoot?'

'We count together, from ten downwards. At zero, we raise our weapons and fire.'

'What if you fire before zero?'

The Shaper stared at him, his crown quills flashing red. 'I will not.'

Obeysekera nodded. 'Very well.' He looked around. 'Let me find somewhere to sit.' He hobbled to a rock and sat down upon it. The med-pack had done its job. His leg ached, but little else. Pain would not distract him.

Obeysekera looked down the mountain to Tchek. They were about fifty yards apart. Far enough to miss.

'How many shots?' he asked.

'One,' said the Shaper. 'If we both live, then we count again.'

'Very well.' Obeysekera stopped. 'Give me a minute.'

This was probably going to be his last minute of life. He looked around at the redstone, smooth and worn. He felt the sun's heat on his skin. Even its weight was a relief after the chill of the tomb.

He had already tasted death. Obeysekera realised that he no longer feared it.

He looked back down the mountain to Tchek. 'Ready.'

'Ten,' said the Shaper.

'Nine,' said Obeysekera.

'Eight.'

'Seven.' Obeysekera shifted his grip on the hellgun slightly.

'Six.'

'Five.' He felt himself tensing and tried to loosen his muscles, for tight muscles were slow muscles.

'Four.'

'Three.'

'Two.'

Obeysekera opened his mouth to say, 'One.'

There was the familiar cough of a bolt pistol and his hellgun was ripped from his hands, its body exploding as the round detonated. Shrapnel dug deep into his arms and chest, snatching the air from his lungs.

'What...?'

Obeysekera turned to see General Itoyesa standing, bolt pistol raised and trained upon him.

'No!' yelled Tchek. 'You must not. You would make me a liar?'

But the general shook his head. 'If making you a liar gets me sanctuary, so be it.' He squeezed the trigger again.

The bolt pistol cracked, its muzzle falling apart, and Obeysekera remembered the shot he had squeezed off at the general when he first emerged from the tunnel hitting the bolt pistol. The weapon had managed one shot after that, but no more.

General Itoyesa flung the useless weapon to the ground. 'Shoot him!' he yelled at Tchek.

But the Shaper shook his head. His crown quills sank to sombre colours. 'You are not worthy of the lives my Kinband have sacrificed for you.'

General Itoyesa stared at the kroot, then snorted. 'You might not want me but the t'au still do.' He turned and started down the mountain. Obeysekera realised he was heading for the Venators.

'Stop him!'

But Tchek shook his head, his crown quills rattling. 'He is no longer any concern of ours.' The Shaper raised his hand to Obeysekera. 'I am glad that you live.'

'As am I.'

Obeysekera turned around. Standing behind him was the Mother, the woman with the cerulean eyes, and her metal wings were spread wide, blotting out the sun.

'You have lost one of your number,' the Mother said to Obeysekera. 'We will find him for you.'

At her gesture, Kamshet emerged from the rocks beyond the kroot, their weapons raised and trained upon the xenos. Tchek looked round and Obeysekera saw him calculating the odds. Then, very slowly, the Shaper laid his rifle down on the ground and the rest of the Kinband followed.

The general staggered forward and Roshant realised that his arms were tied behind his back. He fell to his knees and behind him Roshant saw the white robes and blue eyes of a Kamshet warrior. He looked round and saw more of them, surrounding the general. Roshant looked to Malick. The sergeant shrugged, but he did not lower his hellgun.

The commissar straightened, sorted out his greatcoat and turned to the nearest Kamshet.

'What has happened? Why are you here?'

The Kamshet warrior, the one who had General Itoyesa in the sights of his autogun, stepped aside and Commissar Roshant found himself looking into the ageless face of the woman with cerulean eyes. Beyond her, further up the mountain, he could see Kamshet warriors herding the captured kroot down the mountain towards them while Captain Obeysekera hobbled after them, with Amazigh trying to support him. Even as he watched, he saw Obeysekera collapse, the Kamshet struggling to hold him up.

It was of no matter if Obeysekera was incapacitated: this was a matter for the Officio Prefectus.

'How did you come here?' Roshant asked the woman, the Kamshet leader.

'The desert spoke and we heard.'

'But you must have been far away. How did you get here so quickly?'

'We can travel fast at need.'

'They are traitors!'

Roshant turned and saw General Itoyesa, on his knees, looking at the woman with white wings.

'Are you going to trust a barbarian above a general of the Astra Militarum?'

'What have they done that is more barbarous than your own actions, general?'

'They sell the aqua vitae to whoever has the goods they wish to trade for it.'

'You would betray us all to the t'au.'

Itoyesa started to get back onto his feet. But before he could do so, Malick kicked the legs from under him, sending Itoyesa sprawling once more.

Malick stood over General Itoyesa. 'Always wanted to do that to a general – never thought I'd get the chance.' Malick looked at Roshant. 'He killed Gunsur. It was a bolt-round that killed Torgut, weren't it?'

Roshant nodded. 'Yes,' he said.

'Then you know what you got to do,' said Malick. 'It's in your orders. If the general is tainted, you kill him.'

'Yes,' said Roshant, and his voice was a whisper.

General Itoyesa struggled back onto his knees.

'You stay there,' said Malick.

But Itoyesa did not look at Malick. He was staring at Roshant.

'You are a better man than your father, Kirpal. You would not prolong a war, squandering the lives of thousands of men, to burnish your reputation. You would not send men to their deaths for no reason. You would not do these things that your father does.'

'I would not turn traitor,' said Roshant.

'Traitor to what?' asked Itoyesa. 'Traitor to a butcher? Traitor to an army that treats men as bullet fodder? Traitor to an empire that is grinding the last spark of good out of its people? I am no traitor, Kirpal, or if I am, I am a traitor to the monstrous regime that has spread like a cancer throughout the Imperium. Do you stand with them, Kirpal? Do you stand with the men who would burn a planet rather than admit their error? Or do you side with me and work to end this pointless war?'

Roshant raised his bolt pistol and pointed it at Itoyesa's forehead.

'By your own words you have condemned yourself.'

General Itoyesa looked past the pistol, past it and into Roshant's eyes. 'Very well. If that is what you think, then make it quick. But I had thought better of you, Kirpal.'

Roshant looked down the sights of his bolt pistol, into the general's eyes, and he saw Itoyesa looking at him without fear but with... with pity?

Roshant lowered the gun. 'I do not condone what you did, general, but I will not kill you.'

General Itoyesa's eyes widened in surprise. Roshant saw him take the deep breath of knowing that death had passed by.

Then a hole appeared in the centre of his forehead, the skin around it instantly seared shut by the heat of the las-round. Roshant saw the shock in Itoyesa's eyes before he collapsed onto his face.

The commissar turned to see Sergeant Malick lowering his hellgun.

Malick looked at Roshant. 'That's what we sergeants are for, commissar – to do the dirty work no one else wants to do.' He turned and looked up the slope to the captured kroot. 'Now for them.'

'No, wait,' said Roshant. But Malick shook his head and started towards the xenos.

Roshant looked desperately to the lady of the Kamshet, but she regarded him with cool eyes and said no word. Roshant realised that she would not act. It was for him to decide.

Before Malick had taken more than a few paces, Roshant raised his bolt pistol and pointed it at Malick's back.

'I said stop, sergeant.' He cycled a bolt-round into the chamber. At the characteristic sound, Malick stopped and turned round. Seeing Roshant pointing the pistol at him, Malick grinned and spat.

'You didn't have the stones to shoot the general. You sure as hell don't have the stones to shoot me.' Malick began to turn back towards the kroot.

'I said, stop.' Roshant heard the tremble in his voice and hated himself for it.

Malick heard it too. The sergeant glanced back to Roshant. 'This way, you'll be a hero.' Malick laughed, and raised his hellgun into position to fire on the xenos.

Roshant pulled the trigger.

Malick pitched forward onto his face. Roshant ran to him and turned him over. Malick looked up at Roshant. Blood was coming from his mouth and his eyes were puzzled.

'Y-you and me were... were going to have... a good thing,' he said.

'We will, sergeant, we will.'

'G-good. Didn't want to be no... no fool.'

For the second time in a minute, Roshant saw the soul depart from a man. He laid Malick gently back down on the redstone and stood up.

'Commissar.'

He turned around to see the Mother beckoning him. As he approached, she bent down closer to Roshant and spoke so that only he could hear.

'Mercy is not a weakness.' Then she indicated the mouth of the cave. 'You are not the last.'

From the cave mouth came Lerin and Ensor. Over the vox-channel, Roshant heard Lerin ask, *'Did we miss anything?'*

* * *

Captain Bharath Obeysekera dreamed he was flying through a sky of the clearest blue – a cerulean blue. He opened his eyes and he saw that it was true. He turned his head and saw white wings spread wide above him.

'Am I dead?'

Mother laughed, and swooped down to where the Venators stood parked at the bottom of the Tabaste. She set Obeysekera down beside *Holy Fire* and Amazigh landed beside them, helping the captain to sit down on the running board of the Venator.

Obeysekera looked to Amazigh.

'You saved my life.'

The Kamshet bowed.

Obeysekera turned to the Mother. 'He did all you asked of him, and more.'

Mother smiled at Amazigh. 'He shall keep his wings.'

As they spoke, other Kamshet landed nearby with Commissar Roshant, Trooper Lerin and Trooper Ensor.

Obeysekera looked at them. 'Are you all that are left?'

'Yes,' said Roshant.

Obeysekera nodded, his face pale despite its tan. He looked back to the Mother.

'What of the kroot?'

'Some of my people are taking them back.' The Mother smiled. 'The mukaali, they grow nervous at their riders.'

'I would have wished to speak again to Tchek.'

The Mother nodded but said no word.

'Why should I be saved when so many others have been lost?'

The Mother raised his face and looked into his eyes. 'You were saved not by your own merit but through the grace of those who saved you – such grace is never merited, but always given. Accept it. Live.'

Captain Bharath Obeysekera bowed his head.

The wind swirl on his skin told him the Kamshet were leaving. He looked up to watch them go, not looking away until they had disappeared into the haze.

He looked down at the wound on his right leg and then turned to Commissar Roshant.

'Don't think I'll be doing the driving on the way back.'

EPILOGUE

Bent over his table, Nebusemekh felt the change behind him. He turned and saw the datafall.

'You're back,' he said.

'Master, the city is choked with sand,' said the World Mind. 'It cannot be cleared for all our people are buried beneath it.'

'I shouldn't worry about it,' said Nebusemekh. 'You will find that the normal geological processes will clear it.'

'How long will that take, master?'

'About three million years.'

'Three million years?'

'Give or take two hundred thousand.'

'What shall we do while we wait, master?'

Nebusemekh smiled – he could definitely feel the muscles moving in his face.

'Those explorers have helped me make a breakthrough in my research. Watch this.' And he lifted the sand up into the air, the upflowing rivers coalescing into the stars and the planets.

Nebusemekh, looking up at his creation, felt the satisfaction of making: so must the worlds have looked when first they precipitated out of the darkness. The suns and the planets and the stars, wheeling in perfect formation, the mirror of the heavens under the earth.

As above, so below.

Perfect, as they had been so many times before, held together by the stasis fields that he wielded as unconsciously as he was breathing.

'Watch,' said Nebusemekh.

And he released the stasis fields.

Staring up at his creation, Nebusemekh was filled with a delight that moved the suns and other stars. The planets wheeled through their orbits, the suns danced about each other, the stars moved in their slow waltz, wheels within wheels within wheels, all turning, all holding.

Holding.

Nebusemekh turned towards the World Mind.

'Water,' said Nebusemekh. 'That's what they told me. Who would have thought it, but sand sticks better when it is wet. Now all we have to do is find a way to make it stay together when the water evaporates. We will need a proper research programme, but we have plenty of time – three million years, in fact.'

The World Mind paused.

'Yes, master,' it said eventually.

Nebusemekh nodded to himself. He had not realised that he had programmed the inflection for world-weariness into the World Mind's voice, but he must have done, for it was indubitably there.

'So, let's begin – experiment one.'

'Experiment one – recording.'

WITCHBRINGER

Steven B Fischer

CHAPTER 1

Hearing a man die was no pleasant thing. Listening to ten thousand scream their death songs in unison was almost too much for even a hardened veteran to bear.

Glavia Aerand turned on her small, firm bedroll, pulling a threadbare woollen blanket tighter around her shoulders. The aged fabric scratched against her pallid, brown skin, stretched gossamer-thin over her gaunt frame and streaked with rivulet shadows of fine veins beneath. She closed her eyes and tried to drown the screaming out, then cursed and swung her feet onto the icy stone floor.

Even with her eyes closed she saw it. Perhaps even *especially* then. That brilliant, burning spear of silver-gold light, charging through the deepest recesses of her mind. Blotting out every shadow. Every small preserve of solitude. Every scrap of the soul that had once been her own.

Slowly, she drew herself down to the floor, the frigid dark stone of her chamber burning like fire against warm skin. She let her blanket fall to the side, only a thin shift between her and the chilled morning air, then crossed her legs and began to pray.

'O Immortal Emperor,' she whispered, lips trembling in the cold. 'I lay myself bare and true at the feet of your eternal Throne. I prostrate myself in silence for I am not worthy to speak. Only a broken servant in the face of your power. May your unending light fall upon me and strip me clean of the taint I carry within my soul.'

Words spilled from her lips like water from a drowning man's lungs, in a desperate gout devoid of preparation or elegance. She had once believed that the words themselves had meaning. She had once clung to their phrasing and cadence with devotion and fear. She had burned litanies and rogations on the surface of her soul, like so many who called on the God-Emperor's name, yet all that time her supplications never gleaned a response.

But she knew the truth, now.

Not that no one was listening, but that to the one who listened, her frail voice formed only a single drop in an ocean. And in that seething sea of suffering, wretched human souls reaching out to the Holy Throne of Terra across the maddening, formless void of the galaxy, what had she done to earn anything more than cold indifference? And yet, if the preachers and firebrands spoke true, the God-Emperor of Mankind heard her every word.

As Aerand's lips stilled, she felt her mind slow and focus, drawing ever closer to that terrible, brilliant light. Five years ago, she had not even known what to look for. Four years ago, and she had not wanted to see. Two years ago, it had still pained her to look upon it for too long.

But now she could not turn away even if she wished to.

Slowly, the light of the Astronomican swelled within her, washing her skin in a prickling, burning peace. Like a pillar of living, breathing fire, the psychic beacon lanced through the fabric of the immaterium, carrying the God-Emperor's will, and His power, to the furthest reaches of the galaxy.

As Aerand drew closer, the beacon resolved, a single cable clarifying into its component fibres. Ten thousand individual, blessed threads, twisting through the hollow dark of the empyrean. Ten thousand strained, angelic voices, screaming their own harmonies into that endless void.

Ten thousand Chosen.

Ten thousand dying psykers seated in the chamber of the Astronomican beside the God-Emperor Himself on Holy Terra, throwing their minds, and His will, into the frigid, lifeless reaches of the warp, knowing they had no hope of surviving the act.

A single tear rolled down the side of Glavia Aerand's face. Not of sorrow, for she did not envy the psykers she envisioned. Better than most, she understood the extent of their service to the Imperium. Of their full and total surrender to, and usage by, the Golden Throne. Nor did she weep from joy at escaping their fate, for when she spoke to herself in the night with honesty on her lips, she knew that in many ways her own fate was harder. That she might be consumed in a slower burn, but that she would be consumed all the same.

No, instead she wept as only a once-soldier could, at the beautiful, terrible, enviable purpose carried undeniably in every single note. Ten thousand lives joined in unison for a moment of glory. Ten thousand voices howling in the face of cold fate. And Emperor-be-praised, she missed that purpose, maybe even more than she missed the soldiers she had once shared such purpose with.

Suddenly, however, another sound broke the music.

Aerand started from her meditation, catching a deep and gasping breath. It was not uncommon, she knew, for a psyker to lose themselves so completely within the beauty of the Astronomican that they could forget to sleep, or eat, or even breathe.

As she forced her attention away from that terrible music, and pulled her eyes from the scintillating white fire of the Astronomican, a sound from the wall of her chamber came to her again.

Thump.

The sound of flesh striking resistance.

Thump.

The sound of meat being thrown against stone.

Before she realised precisely what she was doing, Aerand stood at the door with her robe drawn around her. Its folds swallowed her thin, gaunt form in rippling waves, and she found herself, not for the first time, missing the soldier's physique that she had long carried before five years at the scholastica psykana had turned her body into a weak, lank shell. Instincts, however, did not atrophy quite as quickly as strength, and while violence between acolytes of the schola was strictly prohibited outside of formal exercises, someone was being assaulted in the room beside her.

Aerand threw her mind across the doorway, but nothing moved in the narrow hallway beyond. Through the wall, however, in the chamber beside her, a blistering, multicoloured darkness roiled.

For a moment, Aerand's mind recoiled from the raw warp energy gathering only yards away. For five years, she had trained to channel such forces, to reach into the Chaotic, dark space beyond the material world and bend its power to the Emperor's will. But it was precisely that knowledge that made her painfully aware of how dangerous such forces could be.

Soon that wave of animal fear was replaced by one of confusion. Even with half a foot of psychically shielded stone separating her from that twisting, sickly darkness, she should have felt a power this strong before now. Even with her mind attuned to the light of the Astronomican, a shadow this deep should have blotted it out.

In one movement she threw open the door to her chamber and swept into the corridor outside, preparing mentally to overwhelm whatever psychic barriers had been placed on the entrance to the chamber beside hers. Instead, however, its door lay ajar and unguarded, no sound emerging but that horrible, meaty drum.

The taste of bile rising slowly in the back of her throat, Aerand toed the dark wooden door open and looked on at the macabre scene in utter disgust.

The small sleeping chamber was identical to her own in every respect aside from one. On the bare stone floor beside the adjoining wall, a young man sat in a pool of his own blood. He was naked from the waist up, and his nearly translucent skin coursed with thin, serpentine veins over emaciated bones. At the end of each of his battered wrists hung a mass of mangled, bloodied meat that had once been his hands. With a sickening drip, blood fell in coagulating droplets from the shattered mess of tendon and crushed bone at the end of each stump. Quickly, Aerand scanned the room but found no other occupants.

'Acolyte,' Aerand called, her voice measured but anxious. 'Tell me who did this to you.'

The scholastica psykana was not a gentle place. To take a wild, unbroken psyker and turn them into something stable enough to be used required patience and cruelty in equal parts. These halls had not been kind to her, or the countless thousands of psykers who had walked them before her. Feuds and infighting between the academy's myriad clandestine cabals were not only common, but encouraged, and violence between individual acolytes was simply a fact of life. But there were rules to that violence, proper outlets in which it was to be expressed, and for a student to be ambushed in the middle of night, then left to bleed out alone in the cold and the darkness...

Something turned in Aerand's gut at the thought.

'Acolyte,' she called again, anger lacing her voice. She could not call the man a friend. Such words had no meaning in a place like this. But she'd been blessed with true friends once – names like Corwyn, Olemark, Vyse and Argos – and she knew precisely the fury that she would have felt if she'd found any of them in this same sorry state.

When she called, the young man did not turn. Instead, he lifted his right arm, its mangled remnant trailing a stream of dark crimson, then smashed it into the wall in front of him.

Thump.

'Acolyte.'

Thump.

His other arm struck the wall with a wet, splintering sound as the bones of his wrist shattered against unyielding stone. When he pulled away, a clump of yellow fat and blood hung in its place, rolling down the wall to join the charnel pile at his feet. Aerand took a step into the room. Violence was one thing. She understood violence. But this was something else entirely.

'Acolyte,' she said slowly, reaching towards the young man's bloodied arms. 'Can you at least tell me what you're doing?'

'The light,' he mumbled. 'I have to reach the light.'

Aerand sighed. Of course.

She rested her hand on the young man's shoulder. His frame was slight, but she knew better than most exactly how strong the mind inside that frail body was.

Gifted. Tainted. Cursed. Burdened. As heavily as she carried the weight of those words, this young man bore them a dozen-fold more. Acolytes talked. Acolytes gossiped. And she'd seen enough from the boy to believe the rumours that he'd nearly been classified as a beta-level psyker during his first Assignment. Never once had she stopped to think that the burdens he carried would scale with the enormity of that raw power.

If the beautiful, terrible light of the Astronomican swam behind her eyes even when she slept, how much brighter must its sun have burned behind his? If the haunting, beckoning song of its dying wove melodies into her mind with every waking breath, how strong must that symphony have blared within his?

'Acolyte,' she whispered, setting her hand on his shoulder. 'You can't reach it. You can't reach the Astronomican.'

'But I have to,' he replied, raising his arm once again.

Aerand stared at the dripping lump of flesh, at the mess of shattered bone and sinew that had once been the young man's hands. As he made to strike the wall once again, she threw her mind against the motion.

His hand halted inches from the wall.

'Why?' Aerand asked. 'Why do you have to reach it?'

The young man turned his eyes towards her, acknowledging her existence for the first time since she'd entered the room. Aerand expected an expression of pain, or at least distress, but instead, his lips curled upwards in a terrible, mindless grin.

'I have to reach the light,' he whispered. 'I have to reach the light, so I can put it out.'

As she met his gaze, something within Aerand shivered, the taste of metal and blood suddenly coating her tongue. Where the young man's irises should have been sat two pools of that same, undefinable darkness, reaching out towards her with a terrible, desperate hunger.

Suddenly, the thing wearing the acolyte's body lifted its bloodied arm towards her, and Aerand found that she was the one unable to move.

'Come with us,' it implored, in a thousand voices. *'Come with us and help us extinguish the flames.'*

Aerand tried to step backwards, but found her feet set in place, as the acolyte rose to an unnatural height. As he uncrossed his legs, she saw with horrible realisation a pair of bloodied stumps at the end of them, matching his arms.

'Think of the light,' the thing whispered, lips unmoving. *'Think of the light and the music and that accursed choir. I can give you the shadows back, child. I can give you the silence. I can give you your mind.'*

Aerand watched, horrified, as her hand rose before her. As her fist drew back and then turned itself towards the wall against her will. The power behind the compulsion was staggering.

'All I require is that you help me reach the light.'

Beside her, the thing that had once been human grinned, and a presence like ice raked its unholy claws against her mind. She winced, watching her fist charge forward, sped by that terrible, obscene power, and she did nothing to resist it. Instead, just before her bones struck the stone wall, she summoned her will and redirected the blow. The acolyte reeled as her fist struck the young man in the face, and Aerand found herself in control of her body once again.

She may have left a soldier's life behind when she came to the scholastica, but she would always have a soldier's mind. When her enemy pushes, the wise soldier does not push back, she redirects her enemy's own power against him.

Free for a moment, Aerand moved in a blur. An elbow into the young man's face. A sweep with her leg to send him toppling. Without feet to steady him or hands to catch his fall, the acolyte's head struck the stone floor with a sickening sound.

Thump.

The young man's body lay motionless as Aerand caught her breath in ragged gasps. It was a simple thing, in the end, to break a body already so physically weakened. A simple thing that the gifted so often forgot. The mind might be strong, but it dwelt in terribly fragile vessels.

She looked down at the blood dripping from her own elbow, thin sickly skin split like gossamer over her bones. Five years ago she would not have been damaged so easily. Five years ago she would not have even been out of breath. She let out a small sigh, then halted abruptly as the corpse on the floor began to move.

In the corner of the room, the single, dim torch lamp stuttered, red flame flickering an unnatural grey. On the floor, the broken body lifted bloodied arms up to its own face. In a horrible motion, it clawed with shattered stumps at its own eyes, and as it did, something else began to emerge.

With an alien, unnatural motion, the broken heap of flesh rose to its feet. From bloodied, deep-set, sunken eyes, a terrible shadow began to spill out like oil. Aerand's throat filled suddenly with the flavour of blood, as her skin erupted with a telltale burning.

The corpse took a step towards her, shredded legs bending sideways, as the raw energy of the warp flowed out from it, completely unchecked.

'Come now, child,' it crooned gleefully. *'You cannot truly be so simple. Break the vessel and you simply unlock the cage. Shatter the walls and you merely release what they hold.'*

Thump.

Another step towards her.

Thump. Thump.

Two more and it was close enough to touch.

Aerand threw her hands forward and silver-gold fire erupted from them, swallowing the young man's shattered body in a veritable pyre. Flame splashed against the stone walls, scorching them black, but when the flames died away, the corpse still stood. Amidst the smell of charred flesh, its burnt face cracked and grinned, then a bloodied stump reached up and struck Aerand in the chest.

She slammed into the wall, her back squelching against warm blood and bits of leftover flesh.

Thump. Thump. Thump.

The corpse strode towards her with a grotesque grace, its arms upraised, suspending her in the air. Aerand lifted a hand and the torch lamp flew off the wall, shattering against the side of the abomination's head, but the husk did not slow. Darkness poured in waves from its eyes, pooling across the floor, seeping into the hall. Desperate, Aerand scrambled against her invisible restraints, but found herself unable to move, unable to breathe.

Thump.

The corpse stood directly before her now. Close enough to smell the sickly-sweet char of its flesh. Close enough that the darkness pouring from its eyes dripped against her body with a sickening chill. She closed her eyes as its charnel breath rolled against her, desperately seeking that music in the back of her mind.

'Ahhhhhh. Yessssss,' the thing before her whispered. *'The light. You must help me find the light.'*

But for the first time since she had arrived at the schola, the light of the Astronomican was gone.

Aerand's eyes opened to the impact of a lance haft cracking against the exposed small of her back. Gasping, she buckled forward, catching herself against the rough, aged wood of a chamber door.

She whirled as the whoosh of another strike reached her ears. Her hand caught the haft of the lance an inch from her face, and she looked up into the expressionless, reflective faceplate of a suit of obsidian armour. In its glint, she caught a brief glimpse of herself, unbloodied and utterly unharmed.

Aerand swallowed as she stared at the towering form before her.

Premonitions were tricky, feckless things, and this was not the first time she'd found herself awakening from a vision into circumstances remarkably different from the ones she had foreseen. It was, however, perhaps the most dangerous.

The creature paused for a moment, then ripped its lance from her grasp, a dark gauntlet charging towards her stomach instead. Aerand bent herself over the blow, allowing it to land, but avoiding the worst of its impact. She stepped sideways and backed slowly away. As she did, a pair of obsidian-clad figures turned with her, crystal-tipped lances glittering towards her chest.

'My lords,' Aerand stammered with the most deference that she could manage. 'My apologies.'

Throne be true, she didn't want to apologise. She wanted to scream.

Beside her stood two fully armoured Black Sentinels, the scholastica psykana's infamous guardians. Every inch of its members' bodies coated in night-dark, psychically shielded armour, the order represented both the schola's protectors and gaolers in one. Charged with the defence of the academy's acolytes from threats both peripheral and internal, the sentinels faced their role with vicious dedication.

Still reeling mentally from the clarity of her premonition, the last thing Aerand wanted was a fight. She might walk away if she was lucky, but Black Sentinels did not carry those lances for nothing.

'I'm not certain what happened. I think I can explain.'

Unfortunately, the sentinels' impenetrable armour shielded not only their faces, but also their minds, making it nearly impossible for Aerand to gauge either figure's reaction. The fact that neither sentinel had impaled her yet was precious little reassurance that things were going well.

'An acolyte found outside her chamber after hours.' The lilting, almost inhuman voice that emerged from one armoured carapace sent a chill down the back of Aerand's neck. Five years in these halls, and she'd never heard a sentinel speak. 'And I can smell the bitter warp taint surrounding her from here. I don't believe I require any information beyond that.'

Aerand cursed as the sentinels advanced. A beating at least. Certainly worse if she resisted. At each of the towering figures' hips a small, black rod hung loosely from their armour, crackling and humming with a terrible life. In each weapon's place a small hole glittered in the empyrean, the weapon destroying the link between the warp and the physical world. While the sentinels' lances were more than capable of bleeding her to death from a dozen wounds, a single brush with the night rods they carried on their hips would be more than enough to cataclysmically overwhelm her psychically active mind and turn her into a seizing, frothing invalid.

Unfortunately, she didn't have time for a beating – one that would leave her bruised and hardly able to speak, let alone pass on the warning she carried. She turned, ready to run, before noting the matching pair of obsidian figures behind her. Four to one. Not good odds. Not good odds at all.

Aerand's eyes flicked to the door, memories of her portent flooding back in a wave. If she could only convince them of the danger within.

'You don't understand,' she said. 'It's not me you should be worried about. I need to warn–'

A lance haft cracked against her flank. Aerand stumbled, then sidestepped the follow-on blow.

'I'm telling the truth,' she stammered, as another blow fell, dropping to her knees to narrowly avoid a thrust intended for her face.

Four to one. She would not walk out of this fight. And even if she did, she would find herself hanging, regardless.

Aerand closed her eyes and cast her mind towards the door to the chamber beside her. Behind it, the smallest of dark energies waited.

Small for now.

Contained for now.

But it would remain neither of those for long.

Wincing, Aerand let a blow fall across her thighs. There was no time for this. No time for simple rules executed by petty, mundane enforcers incapable of looking more than seconds into the future.

She reached out for the burning light in her mind. The Black Sentinels might be shielded from direct psychic forces, but the material world around them was not. Gold flame flickered to life at the tips of her fingers, as the deathly chorus of the Astronomican chanted in her ears. She waited for another blow to fall, but instead, a new sound interrupted that music.

Aerand opened her eyes to find an obsidian lance haft suspended inches in front of her face. The weapon shook slightly as the sentinel wielding it struggled against invisible shackles, and his breath rose and fell in winded gasps. At his side, his night rod crackled with rage, as it tried desperately, and failed, to overwhelm the psionic force directed against him. Over that sound a staccatoed clicking rose, and Aerand turned to see a hunched form approaching slowly down the hall.

She breathed a sigh of commingled relief and fear.

In any other situation, the sight of Lord Prefector Dariya Ule and the broken shell of a human crawling before him might have shattered her courage. The ancient ecclesiarch had long since cast most of his physical body aside, and the figure that approached was sculpted more of metal and holy fetish than of flesh. One by one, each of his dozen multi-articulated adamantium legs rose and fell in an inhuman, serpentine motion, carrying the man on a scintillating metal wave. An ecclesiarch's robe fell atop the writhing appendages, bound tightly around his chest with two rows of ivory linkages, each fashioned in the sacred shape of a human skull. As the lord prefector's garment billowed around him, row upon row of holy scripture inscribed in golden leaf glinted against leathery skin stretched thin across his emaciated ribs.

If the apocryphal rumours among the scholastica's acolytes were to be believed, the only organic component of the man that remained was the deeply wrinkled, ochre-dark face rising from the shadowy recesses of his cowl, entirely unmarred by the fabrications that consumed the rest of his body.

Within those shadows, the gleaming surface of two adamantium eyes stared blankly outwards. And despite their lack of any appreciable mark-ings, the lord prefector's gaze unmistakably fell on the sentinel holding his lance at Aerand's neck.

'Lord prefector,' the sentinel mumbled. 'An acolyte of yours, I belie-'

The old priest grunted, raising a skull-capped cane, and the sentinel's voice fell into choked silence. From the base of the macabre device, a twist-ing column of fused vertebrae stretched to the ground, laced with a short leash of gossamer-thin silver wire. At the other end, an emaciated husk of a man knelt on the stone floor shivering in silence.

Ule's hound shook with the pressure of psychic exertion, his soul burning like a pyre in Aerand's mind. Blood dripped in a slow stream from the pitiful man's nostrils, commingled with the dark ichor that wept from the wounds where Ule's psionic goad entered his skull. What the psyker had done to deserve such a fate, Aerand could not even begin to imagine, but his pen-ance would be blessedly short. She had seen Ule on only a few fearsome occasions, but a different psyker had accompanied him each time.

A single glance at Ule's hound and the sentinel smartly withdrew from the lord prefector's path, his lance remaining suspended where it stood. A strange noise emerged from the guard's obsidian armour, as if he had thought to object to the seizure of his weapon, then reconsidered.

As the other sentinels followed suit, withdrawing to the edges of the hallway, Lord Prefector Ule arrived at Aerand's side and reached a single, multi-articulated arm towards her. As he lifted her to her feet, there was not the slightest of sounds. No whirring of hidden internal servos, no squeaking of aged, imperfect hydraulics. For if the rumours were truly to be credited, not a single thread of wire or tubing marred the lord prefector's simulacrum body. No true augmetics, merely a cluster of machine-like attachments powered entirely by the wretched psyker at his feet.

'A premonition?' Lord Prefector Ule asked slowly, a sullen grimace written across his face.

Aerand nodded.

'How soon?'

'I'm not certain, lord. Soon enough.'

A simple grunt escaped Ule's ancient mouth. The man's gaze fell on her once again, eliciting the faintest sensation of animal fear in her mind. Ule's hound twitched and a brief feeling of loss washed over her, her own memories of her vision greying slightly before returning to that same uncomfortable clarity.

The lord prefector nodded. 'Ugly enough, acolyte. You were right to ven-ture out to find me.'

'But I-' Aerand began, before Ule's empty gaze cut her words short.

Of course Ule knew she hadn't ventured out to find him. But not even the lord prefector of the scholastica psykana would choose open conflict with a squad of Black Sentinels when given the choice. And an acolyte fleeing her quarters to seek out a prefector was a more palatable explanation for them than the truth.

'Thank you, lord prefector,' she replied. 'I'm simply pleased you heard my summons and arrived.'

'Come,' Ule said, turning towards the dark, rough-cut door to the chamber beside them. As his hound turned with him, the sentinel's lance clattered to the stone.

'Wait outside,' the lord prefector ordered. 'But in the unlikely event that your services are needed...'

The sentinel snatched up his fallen weapon, then fell into line with his three comrades.

As Aerand entered the small chamber behind the seething metallic form of Lord Prefector Ule, the echo of a premonition washed over her.

'It is strange, I imagine,' Ule said, 'to tread a place once in your mind, then a second time, in body.'

Aerand shivered at the subtle intrusion into her thoughts. That she had not detected the faintest whiff of the lord prefector's hound touching her mind made the breach all the more disconcerting. And yet his words were undeniably true.

As they swept into the spartan chamber, trepidation gripped Aerand like an anxious vice. This was the curse of premonition, the subtle danger of portents and forewarnings, always. She had watched herself die in this room only moments before, and she had played long enough at the game of soothsaying to know false visions from those that might one day come true. But whether her premonition carried warnings for this moment or next century, was a skill even the most powerful diviner struggled to master.

Even still, a true future was not one that was destined to come to pass. Just as the trunk of a tree could support myriad true-born branches, so the flesh of the present fed and nourished an infinite progeny of fates. The very presence of the lord prefector in this room was evidence that he meant to prune those branches.

'Acolyte.' Ule's voice echoed as he settled into the small, dim-lit room. The torch lamp beside the young man's bed flickered against the prefector's steely form, reflected in waves of glimmering starbursts against the stellated, ochre-dark stone walls and ceiling. For now, the torch lamp's flame burned true and yellow, but Aerand could not help but recall the unnatural grey hue it had assumed at the moment her premonition faltered.

Aerand stepped beside the lord prefector to find a young man lying in the centre of the room. He curled at the foot of a rough-spun bed, its firm fibres soiled with a thick sheen of sweat. His thin blanket discarded, the young psyker shivered, a glazed expression across his taut, drawn face.

'Acolyte,' Ule repeated, tapping his cane a single time against the stone floor. Ule's hound shivered and the air rippled with the unmistakable tenor of psychic compulsion.

The young man's gaze flicked up to acknowledge the lord prefector, and his cracked lips parted in silent greeting. For a moment, something akin to composure returned to his face before vanishing, swallowed again by a knit brow and the weight of mindless, animal fear.

'Come,' Ule spoke, a heavy sigh escaping the ecclesiarch. At his words Aerand felt that indescribable gravity and the faintest hint of copper at the back of her throat. Briefly the hymn of the Astronomican swelled in her ears at the strength of the hound's compulsion.

Hesitantly, she crossed to the other side of the bedroll as Ule settled onto the stone floor with a quiet rustling of metal. As his gold-trimmed robe settled around him, a thin, silver arm emerged from a voluminous sleeve. Gently, the appendage settled on the young psyker's beaded forehead, and the man shivered briefly, then stilled. As the lord prefector's empty eyes settled on the man, the acolyte's gaunt form convulsed slightly, then fell still.

'Close your eyes,' Ule ordered, meeting Aerand's gaze. 'Close your eyes and tell me what you hear.'

Her tongue suddenly dry, Aerand voiced no response. Instead, she shut her eyes as instructed and fell instantly into the First Meditation. The Meditation of Silence, the Meditation of Self, the Meditation of the God-Emperor's Grace. Before a nascent psyker could learn to understand the raging power within them, let alone the God-Emperor's will for its use, they needed to learn simply to observe.

As the room stilled around Aerand, her thoughts slowing with each breath and the pounding of her heartbeat, the sound of subtler things crept into her awareness.

'I hear the soft grinding of tendon over bone as the man on the mat before us shivers. I hear the quiet vibration of the torch lamp's glass casing, expanding and contracting with the wavering flame's heat within. I hear the holy music of the Astronomican, lord, the song of ten thousand psykers crying out in both torment and blessed rapture at the God-Emperor's feet.'

Something else, amidst it all...

'Lord prefector,' Aerand added. 'I hear something amiss.'

Quiet at first, almost imperceptible, and yet unavoidable once she had noted its presence. All at once, the skin along Aerand's back erupted in gooseflesh, and the taste of fresh blood trickled into her throat. Like the grinding of metal against a stone surface, that thrumming rhythm reverberated in her mind, clashing with the Astronomican's hymn.

'Good,' Ule grunted, nodding to himself. On the bedroll before him the young psyker shook as Ule's hound threw the full weight of its mind against him.

'There is a common misconception,' Ule said. 'Even among the... gifted, that the energies of the empyrean differ in aspect. That the underlying sources of power behind the miracles of the blessed saints and the perverse ravages of heretics and daemons must somehow be inherently, morally separate. Like water from a cistern, power drawn from one focality of the immaterium will sustain and enliven, some believe, while that pulled from another might poison and corrupt. Entire cults and cabals revolve around such misguided tenets, determined – often with obscene focus of purpose – to find "pure" wells from which they might draw without risk.

'Even within the scholastica, acolyte, these beliefs are not entirely unheard of, though I have worked tirelessly to suppress such nonsense as heresy.'

A chill washed over Aerand as the man on the floor pushed back against the lord prefector's hound. The psyker reeled as if struck, and for a terrible moment, the swirling energy within the young man swelled. Instinctively, Aerand threw her own mind forward before she was slapped back by the hound.

Ule raised his hand in her direction.

'There are no safe havens within the torrent of the warp, acolyte, because there are no incorruptible fragments of the human soul. The immaterium, like all other realms of the universe, holds no innate spiritual predilections at all, and the raw, Chaotic energy of the empyrean can be no more hallowed nor corrupt than a given sea wave or breeze. And yet, unlike the ocean or sky, the fabric of the immaterium is inevitably, inextricably shaped by the moral composure of the souls that access it. And while the source substance might be spiritually indifferent, the resulting symbiosis certainly is not.

'In the best of cases, the empyrean, accessed by a mind resting at peace within the Emperor's will, produces wonders unbelievable to behold. In the worst, when given to a mind under torment, that same power takes on another flavour entirely.'

'Lord prefector,' Aerand gasped, stifling a sudden wave of fear. Her eyes flashed open to meet Ule's empty silver gaze.

As she stared at the ecclesiarch with a growing panic, she noted the subtle shifting of his hands. With serpentine fluidity the fingers of his right hand quivered in rapid succession, thrumming against his skull cane in the strangest, most unsettling metallic dance. Kneeling beside him, his hound shook, blood-tinged spittle dripping from his mouth.

'Lord prefector.' A more desperate appeal this time. With alarm, Aerand noted the room's sudden darkening, and turned to face the torch lamp's newly blackened flame. A faint haze of frost crept slowly across the glass.

On the bedroll before her, the young psyker stirred suddenly, his eyes flashing open as that screeching, metallic cry swelled in her mind.

'Lord prefector!' Aerand shouted, casting her own mind towards the young man. She was thrown back unceremoniously by a rigid wall of writhing multicoloured shadow, and a piercing inhuman screech that threatened to burst her ears. Then, just as quickly as it arrived, the noise vanished, and she found herself cognisant only of the sound of her heartbeat crashing in her ears.

Slowly, Lord Prefector Ule stirred, his coiled legs unwinding like a tree spreading roots. As he rose to his feet, the shivering form on the bedroll fell still, and the young man's breathing settled into a comfortable pattern.

'Come,' the lord prefector ordered, casting a final glance back towards the psyker. Aerand noticed an almost imperceptible flick of the ecclesiarch's fingers as his dull grey eyes fell upon the young man one last time. At his feet, Ule's hound twitched and the movement of the acolyte's breathing stilled. The man's glassy eyes fell gently open.

The most natural shade of earthen brown.

CHAPTER 2

The Colonel had always hated the rain.

Give him desert, mountain, jungle, ice – even the sterile, putrid surface of a death world like Kvaran where the acrid gases which amounted to an atmosphere burned and blistered your airways the moment you breathed – but keep the rain, and the wet, and the filth that it brought. The heat of the sun could be blocked in the shade. The cold could be fought off with blankets and fire. And while he would never forget the stale flavour of air rebreathed for weeks on end by a full company of sweating troopers, all other evils could be circumvented. Rain, on the other hand, could not be denied.

The Colonel grunted, stepping out from the relative shelter of dark, mossy ruins and into the sky's full onslaught. Water poured in thin streams from his oiled field jacket, searching out every seam in the ageing uniform. The dour, flooded landscape before him did nothing to assuage his foul mood. On the dark stone a dozen corpses lay still, their skin bare and cold, beaded with raindrops like wax. Behind him, two of his troopers trudged up over-sized stone steps and deposited a thirteenth corpse on the stone. A huddled figure shuffled up beside him.

'Thirteen dead,' the crone called out in a voice like steel against his spine.

'Thirteen who were not worth keeping alive,' he replied.

The witch let out a strange snickering sound. 'Which of us are?'

He glanced down at the woman, bent and nearly crippled by years dabbling in the occult and obscene. Drenched robes of handwoven grey-brown plant fibres hung limp over her twisted frame. Under any other circumstances he would have killed her long ago, and would have relished the opportunity to do so. No doubt she would have done the same to him.

He took a step forward and watched her recoil, then spat towards the corpses on the stone.

'Again,' he muttered. 'We try again.'

Aerand's skull rang with the sound of the scholastica psykana's first summoning. Like a bell, the wordless psionic sending ripped through the minds of each of the gifted, tearing thousands of psykers from dark and restless dreams. The lord prefector's hound whimpered before rushing forward on bloodied palms and knees to keep pace with his master, who was unminding, like any other mundane, of the siren reverberating through his halls.

'It is an unfortunate thing. To kill an acolyte.'

Aerand swallowed, bile rising suddenly in her throat. An acolyte of the scholastica psykana did not refuse when the lord prefector ordered her to accompany him. Yet, her unease had grown with each step they'd taken away from her chamber door.

'But in this circumstance, perhaps a merciful act,' she offered.

'There was no mercy in it,' Ule replied. 'There never is. Such emotions are the domain of heretics and cowards. It is painful, however, to squander a resource so scarce.'

And yet the scholastica psykana did so every day. Already, Aerand sensed thousands of souls waking around her, opening doors to honeycombed hallways and trudging towards austere chapels and bloodied arenas where indifferent servants of the Adeptus Ministorum repeated severe lessons in asceticism, self-deprivation and the finer points of combat, both psychic and physical.

Those who endured the seething, undisciplined madness of the schola's Originatum – the single unsupervised hall devoted to the scholastica psykana's newest acolytes during their first solar year in the institution – were just as likely to be killed directly by their training as they were to be disposed of by a prefector's hand, or the unflinching lance of a Black Sentinel.

'Of course,' Aerand replied, her hand drifting to the deep scar along the left side of her chest where a condemned heretic's blade had raked her ribs, just before she put a knife through his skull under the watchful eye of an underwhelmed Ministorum crusader. She had been forced to repeat the task each day for a month given a 'lack of zeal' in her first attempt.

Aerand limped forward on bruised, shaky legs, painfully aware of the fact that no one other than Ule accompanied her down the dark corridor, and that the lord prefector could end her life with little thought and even less consequence.

Lord Prefector Ule rounded a corner and paused before a pair of imposing, ornately carved doors. Inlaid in gold across their dusky surface curled an endless landscape of incomprehensible patterns. The shapes themselves defied description or classification; it appeared as if their ouroboric forms could not possibly exist in the material world. As Aerand looked upon each, a vague unease settled upon her, not at some hidden obscene revelation, as the images of the occult often inspired, but at the simple realisation of the limits of her own mind.

The hallway had begun to widen a few hundred yards prior, the low, curved ceiling opening into a vaulted anteroom. Along the edges of the hemispherical chamber, gilded statues lined the room in an imposing vigil, each of the scholastica's prior lord prefectors perched in eternal remembrance of the schola's lineage.

'Come,' Ule ordered, resting his hands against the monstrous doors, which slowly creaked to life and swung back on titanic hinges nearly as large as the lord prefector himself.

As the ancient ecclesiarch ascended the stairway in silence, Aerand trailed in his wake, her trepidation growing. Even had she tried to imagine what lay behind those imposing, impenetrable doors, however; even had she collected every whispered rumour and myth surrounding this most ancient, central structure of the scholastica psykana's campus; even had she been given its description in vivid detail, and shown drawings and picts to her heart's desire, the chamber at the top of the stairs would have defied her every expectation.

In all her life, Glavia Aerand had seen but one library. A small archive of perhaps a few hundred volumes of military history and tactical doctrine buried deep within the heart of the massive carrack transport where she had lived out most of her childhood years. In retrospect, to call that rubbish heap a library seemed a terrible insult to the word itself.

As she stepped into the lord prefector's sanctum, she found herself dwarfed within a living cathedral of knowledge. There were no pillars within the vaulted chamber, no visible beamwork or trusses, nor any of the usual structural trappings of such an enclosure. Instead, every visible inch of the titanic hall was coated entirely in darkly bound sheaves of vellum. Throughout those seemingly infinite stacks, a flock of chittering servo-skulls swept like a swarm of insects.

Aerand bowed her head in reverence and awe.

'Ah, yes,' Lord Prefector Ule remarked, the sceptre in his hand meeting the floor with a sharp clack that caused his hound to wince. 'Quite a remarkable collection, or so I've been told.'

Aerand scarcely heard his words, however, for in that glassy sea of polished marble flickered the most fantastic, impossible lights. Slowly, she raised her eyes towards the thin silhouettes of ornate struts suspending a dome of perfectly transparent crystalflex over her head. Through that fragile, glassy structure, the unfiltered light of innumerable stars fell gently across her face.

'Bless the Emperor,' she managed, awestruck once again. It had been five years since she had entered the scholastica. Five years since she had seen the sky or stars. Five years with no mention of the world outside these walls, and to drink it in now was almost too much to fathom.

A strange disappointment took hold of her, as familiar patterns caught her eye. A brief memory of her father crossed her mind, the first time that she had learned these constellations. They had been a marker for her on every world she'd travelled in the Segmentum Obscurus since. A reminder of him. Of Cadia. Of the life that had once been, when she was entirely too young to cherish it.

And yet, she had not expected to see them here.

Slowly, Lord Prefector Ule's own gaze drifted to the tapestry overhead, then his dull, metallic eyes settled unmistakably on her own. 'No,' he remarked. 'This is not Terra.'

Aerand nodded and swallowed. 'I'm sorry, lord. I had assumed. From what I had heard.'

Inwardly, she chided herself. There had been rumours during the sparse conversation that cropped up between acolytes. Of course they had been brought to the Holy World. What other location could the Emperor possibly choose to train His most sacred servants? Those who bore His own burden. Those who knew His own heart. Those who could be truly grateful for His gracious protection, because only they daily encountered what waited beyond His light?

But now, the certainty of those convictions evaporated in the face of solid reason. The sheer logistics alone would be mind-numbing. How many millions of psykers? How many millions of light years? To simply house that many tainted in one location would surely consume half the Holy World itself.

Something akin to a chuckle escaped the lord prefector. 'Do not judge yourself too harshly, acolyte. You have fallen prey to a very intentional deception. One nearly every psyker brought here believes at one time or another. The less even the gifted know of the scholastica's myriad, scattered locations, the less the chance of assault or infiltration. But, no. You have not travelled quite so far.'

As he spoke, the chittering form of a servo-skull darted down from the shadowy recesses of the sanctum's far reaches and settled into a tight orbit around the lord prefector's head, bearing a small, leather-bound volume with gold-embossed characters along its tattered cover. Ule snatched the volume from the creature and set it reverently atop the ornate lectern before him. His inhuman fingers flitted along fragile pages with an unexpected dexterity, until he settled on one and met her gaze.

'Glavia Aerand,' he said. 'Of Cadia, which once was. I might have known that simply by the colour of your eyes. Last night, one of my acolytes died. A young psyker with a gift for telepathy and biomancy.'

Aerand opened her mouth, but the lord prefector held up his hand.

'Of course you know this, because you stood beside me when I sat at the foot of his bed and took his life. Of course I know this because I performed the act, but I find there are times when the speaking of specific words is terribly important, even if their meaning is already known to any who hear them.

'What you likely do not know, however, is that I had no knowledge of that acolyte's impending madness. And had my hound not felt the force of your premonition, I cannot imagine what dark events might have unfolded. I stand swallowed within a sea of esteemed servants of the Cult Imperialis and Adeptus Astra Telepathica, yet none of them could sense the taint festering in our presence. But you did.'

Once again, the lord prefector's steely gaze fell onto Aerand, and she nearly buckled beneath that weight. Instinctively, she threw up a ring of psychic walls, feeling his hound's mind instantly slip their heights. A sudden urge to defend herself rose within her.

'I was simply meditating, lord. I'd been woken from sleep and the premonition came to me while practising the Third Meditation.'

A nod from the lord prefector only. 'And yet this is not the first such occurrence.'

'Lord?' she replied, confused, before realising his meaning.

Aerand had almost forgotten the event. It was during her first year at the scholastica, merely weeks after she'd arrived at the Originatum.

There was a young woman, scarcely old enough to have been a recruit in a Whiteshield platoon. Aerand had watched her steal a carving knife from one of the kitchens, then plunge it into the neck of Prefector Belile. Before she'd had time to even realise the vision was a premonition, Aerand had thrown herself into the girl's path. She still bore a small scar on her left shoulder where she'd deflected the blade.

'That was different, lord,' she managed. 'There were other signs that violence was about to occur. The girl's body language. Her posture. Subtle changes in her stance.'

'Equally visible to anyone with eyes, and yet no one else in the room sensed the impending danger.'

Aerand bristled with fear and anger. The implication that she shared a unique connection with a pair of psykers on the edge of falling to the warp was a damning one. 'Soldier's reflexes,' she rebutted.

The lord prefector scoffed.

'Acolyte,' he continued, 'I do not accuse. I have your record before me and have seen the results of your training. I watched you stand firm before four sentinels who had no intention of sparing your life.

'My duty here is the painful salvage of the broken. The tempering of unholy, but necessary, power into a vessel that the God-Emperor might use. In most cases I am strong enough to admit that I fail. But in you...' Ule paused momentarily. 'In you I believe I may have done my duty.'

Aerand felt the breath rush from her lungs. She had been prepared for chastisement or worse, but the unexpected praise set her even further off balance. But, as Lord Prefector Ule sensed her contentment, any expression of pride drained from his lined face.

'And yet, I fear that may not be enough.' Slowly, sinuously, the man's legs rolled into motion, carrying him across the room to a second lectern bearing a massive tome.

As Ule beckoned her towards him, Aerand caught sight of the volume's yellowing pages. The lord prefector flipped through countless ancient sheaves of parchment, each coated in row after row of dark numerals, before finally settling on a single page inscribed with crimson symbols beside black ink. On the left of the volume lay a mess of handwritten numerals, enough ink to almost coat the page entirely, and on the right, a handful of solitary marks.

'Five hundred and twenty-nine thousand,' the lord prefector spat, his eyes fixed on the two pages before him. 'Five hundred and twenty-nine thousand acolytes who have disembarked from those accursed Black Ships since the day I assumed care of this paltry scholastica world. Half a million future witches, or possessed, or heretics that the Inquisition delivered into my care. And from that mass, only a few thousand that I have been able to salvage for a fate more useful than fodder.'

From somewhere in the recesses of his robe, the lord prefector produced a thin, silver quill. Before Aerand noticed the motion, the tip had drawn blood from the base of her wrist. Slowly, meticulously, he made a new mark on the right side of the ledger.

'Come now, adept. You are an acolyte no longer. But there is still work to be done before you leave us.'

CHAPTER 3

The Dorean regimental flag fluttered in a gentle breeze, damp and sagging beneath the oppressive, insistent rain. Grey hammers crossed atop a field of blue, ringed by an unbroken chain of gold. Beneath that sigil, the numerals of the 19th showed proudly, seemingly undimmed despite the years.

The Colonel grunted as he stepped out from his command tent to face his waiting regimental sergeant. The grizzled man before him nodded in response, words no longer required between the two for anything but the most complex of conversations.

Sergeant Gross was of the old breed, as was the Colonel – troopers hardened by battle on a dozen worlds before they had ever set foot on this accursed one. Of those veteran Doreans, only a few companies remained, the rest of their force now composed of fresh conscripts liberated from this drowning, two-bit planet. The first compromise they had made, but far from the last.

And now their compromises were finally beginning to catch up.

'Three more platoons decimated. In full,' Sergeant Gross murmured, in a voice strangely soft for a man of his intimidating proportions. He idly tapped the silver sword strapped to his waist belt, a nervous gesture he had possessed since even before the Colonel and he had first met as little more than fresh recruits themselves.

'And their wargear?' the Colonel replied. Replacing two hundred green troopers on this backwater world was a daunting, but entirely possible, prospect. Securing the weapons and flak armour to outfit those replacements, however, was a challenge almost entirely insurmountable.

'Secured. Mostly.'

'A small grace, then.'

In the distance, the dull echo of mortar fire and krak missiles broke the still evening with an occasional drumbeat.

'They never stop,' he cursed softly.

'No, sir. They do not.'

'Nearly two companies lost already in exchange for what? A few squads, perhaps a platoon of theirs?'

'It seems some reputations are well deserved.'

'Cadians.' The sound fell cold and bitter across the Colonel's tight, cracked lips.

'Cadians,' Sergeant Gross replied, as if that single word were explanation enough.

Down.

The titanic lift, carved from a single block of obsidian stone, just like every structure within the scholastica psykana, seemed to drop as if released above water. Behind the lift's ornately frescoed, gold-trimmed walls, Aerand sensed the churning, fractured mind of a servitor psyker and was reminded that worse fates than death existed in this place. At her side, Ule's hound cowered on the floor, shielded within the nest of the lord prefector's serpentine, inhuman appendages.

To have one's life reduced through complex and inescapable machinery to an isolated forebrain tasked with nothing more complex than elevating and lowering a carved stone box, or mindlessly projecting a decrepit priest's will, was almost too terrible to imagine. She shivered briefly at the thought. How many such unfortunate creatures lingered within the shadows of this place? And how many, had they not been mad to begin with, were driven so by a lifetime of such monotony?

She whispered a silent prayer of thanks, for somehow she appeared to have avoided such a fate.

As the lift descended smoothly through the heart of the scholastica, Aerand grew increasingly anxious. The superficial structures of the scholastica psykana were well known to her, but rumours abounded of the compound's hidden underbelly, restricted to the lord prefector's most trusted and therefore the subject of unending speculation. She was not naive enough to believe the most outlandish stories, but even those that carried the flavour of truth were enough to set her mind on edge.

You did not bury something deep under the earth unless you had good reason to do so.

Cautiously, Aerand cast her mind out from the lift. Unsanctioned acts of psychic power were strictly forbidden to the scholastica's acolytes, but she was aware of no such restrictions on adepts, even newly titled ones. As she probed beyond the lift's stone walls, she sensed nothing around her other than bedrock.

Lord Prefector Ule's hound lifted its swollen, bruised head and turned a pair of hollow eyes in her direction, but showed signs of no reaction other than mild curiosity. Gradually, the lift slowed to a halt, and a burgeoning presence flickered at the edge of her mind. A squad of Black Sentinels stood at rapt attention along the walls of a dark corridor as the lift's massive door slid silently open. Not the faintest sense of their souls was detectable to her through the hermetic substance of their armour, but the night rods at each silent warrior's hip stood out like holes punched in the fabric of the warp.

She glanced at Ule, then limped forward, remembering her last encounter with these stoic guardians.

Ule noted the awkward exertion and followed, a hint of concern creeping into his guarded expression. 'I had hoped for a more thorough recovery for you, adept. Though I suppose that this will have to do.'

All at once, Aerand's anxiety returned. 'I had hoped I might not find myself brawling for my life twice in the span of two days.'

'Come,' the lord prefector grunted, striding between the upheld lances of the sentinels, his hound whimpering in protest at their proximity. 'I do not suspect your physical wounds will hinder you in our upcoming endeavour.'

At his words, an icy weight descended on Aerand. The vaguest hint of premonition, perhaps, or simply a basic, instinctive reaction to the sudden gravity in the ancient priest's voice.

'Another trial, then?'

Ule remained silent. The only sounds in the long and narrow hallway were the clattering of his legs against dark, rough-cut stone, and the slide of Aerand's own boots as her left leg dragged behind her.

'No more trials, adept. Simply a tempering. You have been forged and shaped already. All that remains is to harden you one final time.'

Aerand swallowed, his words doing nothing to allay her disquiet.

'No,' Ule replied to her unspoken thought. 'No tool enjoys its own forging. Although I imagine that it enjoys breaking even less.'

They made the rest of the journey in near silence, their steps accompanied only by Aerand's growing doubts, until they found themselves, at least half a mile further, at the end of the long and isolated corridor. A simple gateway faced the pair, a low stone door frame leading to a darkened room, unmarked by any of the scholastica's typically ornate sigilry. A distinct notion of tremendous age crossed Aerand's mind at the sight of the arch's rugged surface, as if this corridor and the room before her had been carved by crude instruments millennia before any of the gilded halls above her.

Lord Prefector Ule paused just before the threshold, then turned to face her with a rustling of metal.

'I am afraid that I can neither provide you guidance, nor prepare you for what you are about to encounter.' The ecclesiarch's eyes bored into her with unsettling intensity, and she had no doubt as to the sincerity of his words. 'Not because I am unwilling, adept, but because I am ignorant. My suspicions of what you may find within these walls would form only the crudest, most misleading map. So,' Ule muttered, something that might be mistaken for uncertainty entering his voice, 'I will offer you only this.'

Slowly, the lord prefector stepped back from the threshold, and crossed his alloyed arms before him in the sign of the aquila. He gave Aerand the slightest of bows, and as she stepped across the threshold his voice echoed at her back.

'O Eternal Emperor
Who alone watches us,
And rules the tides and storms,
Be compassionate to your servants,
Preserve us from the perils of the empyrean,
That we may be a safeguard to the Domain of Men.'

As the lord prefector closed the door behind her, Aerand was swallowed by an utter, impenetrable dark. There was a time in her life when such darkness would have frightened her. First as it frightened any simple human child, then later as it unsettled a soldier who understood the dangers of losing a sense she relied on when her enemy might not suffer the same disadvantage. Yet as she found herself sealed in the small, aphotic chamber, miles beneath the bedrock of some distant scholastica world, the only thing that left her vaguely insecure was her memory of the lord prefector's expression in the last glimmer of light falling in from the corridor. With a sigh she turned away from the door, to face whatever made even the arch-priest grimace so.

As Aerand cast her mind against the walls of the rough-cut stone chamber, she sensed nothing to inspire fear. A dozen yards across and half as many high, the room appeared to have been carved from the raw, unaltered bedrock into the crude shape of an octagonal ring. In the centre of the chamber, a small stone pedestal stood only a few feet tall.

The psychic signature of unliving, unbreathing stone was the most unrevealing of any material, and she was confident that nothing else that drew breath stood in this room beside her. Yet to bring her here for a simple meditative trial seemed superfluous in the extreme.

Gently, Aerand probed each corner of the room with her mind, noting nothing but dust and empty air. Just as in the lift, however, her psychic senses failed her entirely when she tried to sense beyond the room's walls. She had no doubt at the source of that sensation, for if the room itself had not been intentionally shielded, the corridor through which she had entered should have blazed with a beacon of psychic light due to the presence of the lord prefector's hound.

As she settled into the empty room, a somewhat darker suspicion found its way into her mind. Every stone in the scholastica psykana possessed some level of innate psychic shielding, whether an inherent property of the bedrock from which it was carved, or the intentional work of the compound's architects. But even there, no psychic shielding was complete.

Even through walls and sturdily reinforced gateways, the faintest of psychic echoes still persisted, like cracks of light finding their way beneath a door frame. Not enough to see by, but enough to know that the light was there. Here, however, even as Aerand threw her mind fully against the door of her lonely chamber, that darkness was utter and complete.

Miles below the scholastica proper. So far away from any other living human that such heavy dampening would be completely unnecessary to provide an isolated psyker mental solitude. Which meant the space must be warded for some other reason.

Rapidly, Aerand surveyed the chamber once again.

As she did, an instinctual suspicion drew her attention to that lone pedestal. Here, she thought she might detect the faintest presence. The dimmest flicker of psychic activity in a room that was utterly dark. Slowly, she found her way through the darkness, until she set her hands against the pedestal's icy surface.

And recoiled.

Aerand froze, bringing all of her psychic attention to bear on the small plinth. In the emptiness just above that surface of rough-hewn stone, a psychic signature glimmered softly, and Aerand vividly recognised its tenor.

She had been only a child the last time she had looked up from Cadia's doomed surface into the swirling violet tendrils of the Eye of Terror. Nearly three decades, and at least a dozen worlds, had passed before her eyes since that fateful vision, but she was certain she would never forget the colour of raw warp space, no matter how many other skies she came to witness.

Aerand took an unsteady step back from the pedestal, the warp rift glowing bright enough, now, to see with her naked eyes.

'Emperor save you, lord prefector,' she cursed, the man's haunted expression now fully explained.

The only thing she could imagine more painful for a psyker than the complete, suffocating psychic suppression of a night rod or a Black Ship was exposure, full and unshielded, to the raw empyrean itself. And here, buried miles beneath the scholastica's sacred campus, locked in a chamber behind yards of psychically sealed stone, lay a single, almost microscopic rift into that untamed, unthinking mire.

As the sinking feeling within her chest grew, so did the ribbon of gleaming violet light in the centre of the room. Desperately, Aerand tried to calm her racing mind, hoping that muting her own emotional response might retard the structure's rapid expansion.

In a wave, frost rushed out across the chamber's walls, her own breath falling in white, crystalline clouds. Beneath her skin, her nerves writhed like a living creature. Her mind recoiled from the irrational darkness, even as its unfathomable churn drew her in.

By the time the rift had grown to the size of a man, she had managed to steady the beating of her heart. By the time it reached the ceiling, she had forced her hands to stop shaking. And by the time that seething, Chaotic tear reached out to plunge her mind beneath its infinite surface, she had done all she could to prepare herself for the expanse of mindless, roiling madness as it engulfed the last corner of the chamber whole.

She had, of course, been utterly mistaken on that account.

Glavia Aerand was drowning. She was certain of that. Never mind that she could breathe without any hindrance, or that she felt no need to breathe at all. Never mind that the sea of roiling, frenzied currents that swirled in every imaginable direction around her was not made of water but of pure, unbridled psychic energy. She was drowning beneath its crashing waves and its irresistible tides, and it would kill her every bit the same.

There was no telling how long she tossed like flotsam before her mind imposed the first stitch of order onto the frayed, unruly threads that entangled her.

First, some sensation of self returned to her, then the knowledge of an ancient, timeless Other. Finally, a crude scaffold emerged for her mind to place those two beside each other. The sea itself was a reasonable enough simulacrum, and she found herself no longer drowning, but desperately bobbing instead.

Eyes closed, Aerand saw the immaterium's surface rolling out towards the horizon as far as she could sense. Her mind scarcely above those maddening, twisting currents, she thrashed like a piece of wreckage in the chop. Above her, a fractured, violet sky swirled with searing bolts of psionic energy and the crack of white lightning. Billowing, dark storm clouds crowded the all-too-narrow sky, revealing only another plane of waves above her in the rare moments when they chose to clear. The effect was unnerving, as if the sea on which she floated wrapped around to stretch over her head, and the utter disorientation of viewing its surface both beneath and above her was almost enough to plunge her beneath the waves.

Some instinct warned her that to do so would be utterly suicidal. That once she dived into those waters, she would never rise again.

As she turned her attention downwards, a deep, animal fear gripped Aerand whole. Far beneath that translucent, blood-red surface, dark shadows curled in the murky depths. Too deep, too clouded, to make out their true shapes, but the scale of such massive, swirling behemoths was unmistakable. Another wave washed over Aerand, submerging her for just a moment beneath the empyrean's lifeless surface.

Now merely inches closer to those leviathans – but some indescribable barrier broken – she saw one of those shadows start to slowly rise. Desperately, Aerand clawed her way back to the surface, towards the glimmer of myriad, burning lights scattered dimly atop those churning waves. As she surfaced, the dark form beneath her turned aside, but the glowing auras beside her remained.

Suddenly, the writhing border on which she floated was dotted with stars every bit as thick as the night sky. In every direction, scattered like sawdust atop the water, small flickers of unmistakable light blinked above the crimson sea. A current twisted slowly beneath Aerand, bringing her closer to a small cluster of the illuminants. Most shone dimly atop the surface, hardly more than a faint lightening of the dark water, but a single light within the cluster shone brightly enough to illuminate the space around it. Gently, Aerand reached out and touched the light with her mind.

And recoiled, as she was met by a flood of unbidden, alien thoughts, then thrown back into the murky darkness. Startled, Aerand fought to keep herself above the surface, consumed by the utter familiarity of that sensation. The same sensation as trying to breach a mind that carried its own psychic defences.

Realisation washed over her, as a flicker drifted past on the immaterium's surface. She reached out and grasped it, her mind suddenly full of unbidden thoughts.

Damn foreman, the new voice within her mind muttered, tailed by a crystal-clear image of a man's thick, calloused hands gripping a power-pick and bringing it down against pale stone in a narrow, crowded tunnel full of cloying smoke. The man coughed, then breathed out a terrible curse, the spark of his flame flaring for just a moment.

It was said that every creature with a soul left its own mark on the fabric of the immaterium, and here she swam among those indelible marks. Gently, Aerand released the man's mind, whispering a silent prayer in awe of the endless sea of souls around her.

Here swam every living creature in the universe, more numerous a thousandfold than the stars. And over them all the God-Emperor Himself watched. The sight alone was nearly enough to drown her.

Yet, as she surveyed the endless pool, some patches faint and distant, others gleaming as if fire had been set to the sea, one particular cluster of lights drew her attention. As she swam slowly through their clustered midst, a vague sensation of familiarity washed over her, as if she had felt these psychic tones before.

Gently, Aerand reached out towards the dimmest of those lights, and then froze. An unbidden psionic intrusion from the depths of the warp was not something to be trifled with. She knew better than most that such a thing could leave lasting marks even if it was never noticed by the subject of such an intrusion. And if she truly did recognise these signatures... Well, to do so to a friend would be almost unthinkable.

Slowly, reluctantly, Aerand withdrew, the small constellation of lights flickering around her. In their centre showed a light far brighter than the rest, illuminating the murky surface. And suddenly, in the glow of that illumination, something shifted in the darkness below.

The entire ocean surged, as a massive shadow uncoiled from the depths. The serpentine, empty form unravelled itself from the twisting mess of darkness beneath her and rose towards that glimmering light. As it did, the soul before her flared brightly, then began to grow with a steady strength. For a moment, the shadow seemed to recoil, then rose up to snatch the flickering light whole.

Aerand screamed as the shadow grasped hold of that strange, familiar glow. The soul flared, suddenly an unchecked conflagration, and she was pulled in by a mind she remembered all too well.

A single moment of contact.

A single moment of unfettered psychic communication.

An image of soldiers in dusty-grey flak armour filled Aerand's mind, unbidden. The smell of oiled lasguns and stale, unwashed sweat. The feeling of cool mist against her skin, and wet boots wrapping her feet. Of blood and fear, and all the accoutrements of war.

She stood in a dim chamber, dark brackish water to her waist, and stared dumbstruck at an intricate, woven structure, jagged silver fibrils rising from a shallow sea to intersect and split apart in a million impossible patterns. Beside her, a soldier spoke in a voice she recognised well, panic lacing his tone, as the structure before her came to life, a strange shadow engulfing those labyrinthine silver branches.

The mind she rode raised its own pale hands before her, twisting in intricate patterns as a dozen wards flew from the soldier's grasp. As he spoke, his voice vibrating through her very soul, Aerand sensed a matching desperation in his words.

Unspoken, a warning echoed across the empyrean, before a mind she knew almost as well as her own shoved her away.

+Flee, Glavia. There is only death here. Death and hunger and enough bitter regret to drown in.+

The message poured down like a torrent of water, before the very fabric of the empyrean erupted into spouting plumes and roiling madness. For the briefest moment she glimpsed the surface of that infinite sea once more, the thin tendrils of a terrible shadow brushing against her mind. A horrible, ancient presence rushed towards her before the churning currents pulled her away.

And down.

And suddenly she was drowning again.

CHAPTER 4

Eight of his witches had died in the night. An unholy portent if he'd ever seen one.

The Colonel did not mourn the loss of the creatures themselves. They were spiteful, petty, reprehensible things, most often than not lost in the stupor and madness that came from their bitter union with the warp, reeking of acrid smoke from smoking the dark, hallucinogenic root of the Throne-cursed, stunted trees that lined this world like a strange, obscene fur. He could replace marsh priests at a whim, for he suffered no shortage of the tainted on this planet. The same could not be said for the equipment and ammunition that he collected and guarded like a dragon's hoard.

Even still, the precedent was unsettling, and if it posed a danger to his soldiers, he needed to know.

'The primaris psyker?' he asked the thin, shrivelled woman who paced the floor of the small tent before him. Last he'd seen of the Cadians, a psyker lord had walked in their midst. The Colonel had fought beside enough Imperial battle psykers to have no doubts that the man was more than capable of executing a handful of his paltry sorcerers while they slept.

'No, no, no,' the woman muttered, the bitter smell of almonds drifting from her putrid mouth. What few teeth remained in it were stained an unhealthy grey from the foetid corpsewood tea she constantly sipped. She was intoxicated more often than not, like some filthy, stimm-shooting hive-dweller on Fenksworld or Malfi, but he'd seen the woman unleash enough raw psionic power not to question her opinion on matters of the occult and arcane.

'You don't understand.'

Unmistakable glee laced the witch's words, and she practically danced before him with nervous energy. He sighed, wishing not for the first time that he could simply put a bolt through her head.

'Then make me understand.'

'Of course, of course,' the old witch crooned, toying with the tangle of twigs and moss woven around her neck in a filthy cowl. 'Not the primaris psyker. Not an attack at all.'

'No?' he asked. 'You mean to tell me your comrades are merely so undisciplined that they did this to themselves?'

The marsh priest spat a thick glob of dark phlegm into the dirt, the vile substance dissipating almost instantly into the moist earth.

Wet. The Colonel cursed inwardly. Why was everything on this planet wet? He lifted his gaze. 'I cannot imagine a more fitting failure.'

'Not a failure.' The witch spat again. 'A success.'

His ears perked up at that, and he set aside the small ledger in which he had been sketching new formations and allotments.

'Then our goal has finally been accomplished?' Doubt laced his tone, hiding excitement. He had hoped against hope that the Cadians' primaris psyker might fall prey to the trap that had been set for him, but he had expected to feel something... more... if this had been the man truly intended for that purpose.

'No. And yes. And no. Not quite,' the woman muttered.

The Colonel paused, his enthusiasm dying as he listened to the quiet of the night around him and felt the same musty air resting still on his skin. If the crone had truly succeeded, the night would be raging with forces he could not even imagine.

'Out with it,' he cursed. 'No more riddles or quibbling. Is your patron released? Is the psyker lord dead? Was he the one who could finally free it?'

The marsh priest paused, considering her words carefully, and ran her ancient, bony fingers through tangles of unkempt hair. When they emerged, a swarm of thin, eight-legged insects coated the woman's hand in its entirety.

'No. Not free. But finally awake. And the one who will free it is on her way.'

Insects dropped from the old hag's hand like black water.

Portents on portents tonight, it would seem.

The taste of blood and metal lingered on Aerand's tongue long after her mind left the warp behind. Yet, just as waking from a deep and seamless dream took time, one did not depart the empyrean all at once.

For what felt like hours, but must have been days, she found herself waking time and again, utterly convinced after each iteration that her mind had finally returned completely to its normal state. Yet, invariably only a few hours later, she would stumble across the exact same sensation, and realise that what she had just perceived as wakefulness was nothing more than a slight lessening of her stupor.

So, when she finally opened her eyes to see Lord Prefector Ule seated at the end of her bed, his hollow gaze bearing down on her with something amounting to impatience – and noticed for the first time the presence of his hound's mind beside her own – she cursed herself once again for thinking she had been awake at any point before this.

'Lord prefector,' she mumbled softly, her cracked lips tasting slightly of copper as she ran a desert-dry tongue across them. The starch-rough texture of linen fabric grated at her back except in those places where it was replaced by the sticky, moist warmth of weeping bedsores. As she tried to lift her head, searing pain shot through her neck, muscles straining against some new and unfamiliar weight. Slowly, she lifted a hopelessly thin arm, covered in bruises she had no memory of earning, towards the back of her skull.

Where thick, dark hair had once grown, she now felt only smooth, cool skin alternating with the cold, inhuman sensation of metal cables coursing from the base of her neck along her scalp. Her hand came away streaked with macabre strands of old, rusty blood and fresh serous fluid. She stared at the ancient ecclesiarch before her.

'Of course,' the lord prefector replied to her unvocalised question. 'I will tell you what I can. Although I suspect you'll find any answers I can offer less than satisfying, for I'm afraid I know little more than you do of precisely the events that brought you to this moment.'

Aerand grunted, and forced herself upright in bed. 'And of more basic matters?' she asked, gently touching the augmetics lining her scalp.

'There I might be more helpful.' As Ule spoke, another figure entered the small, dimly lit room through a low, curtained door.

The resemblance between the lord prefector and the Adeptus Mechanicus magos was uncanny, both metal-bound masses of articulating limbs. Where the lord prefector's face lay, however, the Adeptus Mechanicus tech-priest wore a pair of glowing crimson optic bionics and a gruesome vox-enhancer. The inhuman creature shuffled alongside Aerand's bed in the narrow room, an articulated appendage capped with a third optic bionic reaching out over a shoulder to survey his work as his vice-like upper extremities extended towards the cables lining Aerand's scalp.

She recoiled at the approaching mechanical limbs before settling under their cool, surprisingly gentle touch. As he worked, the tech-priest muttered beneath his breath in that strange, guttural, mechanical language that Aerand had only heard spill from the mouths of enginseers and servitors on a few uncomfortable occasions.

'There may be some pain,' he managed eventually, in a terrible voice reminiscent of grinding metal and gears. Then he grasped a single cable at the back of her scalp and pulled.

There was a wet, gulping sound as the magos ripped the coupling from the base of Aerand's skull, followed by a terrible, mind-numbing anguish as thousands of individual, hair-thin tendrils tore free from the individual synapses of her brain. Aerand found herself unable to focus enough to form words, or even scream, as the tech-priest tinkered with the wires remaining on her scalp. The copper tendrils of the cable he had removed from her skull dangled from the prehensile grasp of his unnatural tail-like appendage as he worked, dripping blood and fluid across the pale sheet atop her. Then, almost as suddenly as the pain had arrived, the tech-priest completed his strange ritual, and her discomfort faded.

Stepping back, the magos made a strange, recognisably approving sound, and departed the room to the clatter of plasteel.

'It has been some time since I last sat in this position, but I can assure you that I have never seen one of the gifted find comfort in the placement of their first bridle.'

Ule's articulated hand fell softly towards the head of the hound beside him – a cowering psyker who bore no resemblance to the figure that had crawled beside him when Aerand had last seen the lord prefector. Amidst the tangle of other raw augmetics, a small, dark box glowed faintly with green and violet light atop the creature's neck. The hound flinched, then settled beneath the unnervingly fond gesture.

'I am certain that you do not currently feel grateful for Magos Fenestrus' administrations, but for now, simply know that without the psychic suppression afforded by the device he provided, I am not certain we would have ever recovered you from the empyrean. Besides, once the pain fades, you may come to find the device's other enhancements even positive.'

Aerand groaned, the inside of her skull still buzzing slightly with that strange, burning sensation. She would have to trust the lord prefector's assurances.

'Questions,' he stated. 'I know you have many. I will answer them as best I can.'

'Very well,' Aerand replied, shifting in the narrow bed and pushing herself slowly upright on arms that felt impossibly weak. 'To begin, how long has it been since our last conversation?'

'The emergence of a new primaris psyker is not a common occurrence, even in the scholastica psykana, adept. Nor has Magos Fenestrus been alone in his work. I have visited this room frequently since you arrived, and done my best to survey your mind on each visit. You have had little to say but moans and prayers.'

'And how long since the last conversation I remember?'

'Nearly six solar days,' the lord prefector replied flatly. 'One in the rift chamber itself, and another five lying on this gurney. It is no surprise you find yourself substantially weakened. Your strength, I promise, will return with time.'

Aerand grimaced. 'And what, precisely, did that return cost?'

A flicker of uncertainty crossed the lord prefector's face. 'I must admit, I am not entirely certain, and my assessment of your passage is as limited by your memory as your own.

'You must understand that you are not unique in this, adept. The scholastica has rescued nascent psykers from exposure after far longer, but six days is no short time to be lost in the empyrean. Your training and your strength of will, alongside the God-Emperor's grace, are the only reason your mind, and soul, remain intact. My priests have scoured your memories to the limits of their power, and the magos has probed your mind with the extent of his arts. We see no lingering taint of the warp within you, and I do not fear that you have been broken or seeded, but the immaterium leaves its marks on all who touch it. I'm afraid that it may be quite some time before we know the full extent of the scars of your tempering.'

As he spoke, a vague memory returned to Aerand, of darkness deep and unimaginable, of a thousand memories, or premonitions of the future. For days she had swum in those mad, darkened currents, among the hungry, grasping shadows and those burnt, bloodied skies.

Slowly, an unbidden urge to move growing within her, Aerand swung her legs over the side of the bed. Taut skin and cramping muscles, unused for the better part of a week, protested the movement, but she found that the physical pain brought a strange clarity to her mind.

For the first time, she noticed the silver staff resting on the foot of her bed. Gently, she reached out and ran her fingers across the intricately wrought aquila mounted atop the weapon, feeling a sudden thrum of movement beneath her skin. Electric. Like touching the warp itself, but tempered by the sensation that its power came from within her, rather than some forbidden, alien font.

'Ah yes,' the lord prefector murmured. 'A second gift for you from the magos, adept. A force staff attuned to the best of his artisans' abilities. A proper weapon for one such as you.'

Aerand turned the stave in her bony grip, planting its tapered base against the floor. Sweating, she grasped the cool metal and pushed herself to her feet.

'One final question, lord prefector. When may I leave this place? And where does the God-Emperor will me?'

A glimmer of pride crossed the ancient priest's countenance as she took a wobbling step towards the door.

'Tell me, adept. What else do you remember?'

'No,' Aerand stammered, surprised to find herself uttering the word.

The lord prefector stared down at her and the hololithic display with the patient sufferance one might show to a particularly dense child. With a flick of his fingers, the glowing display began to spin, a small world taking shape on the pedestal between them. Aerand had scarcely completed the short walk to the lord prefector's sanctum on her atrophied legs, and now wished that she had not made the journey at all.

'I am afraid that choice is not yours to make.'

Aerand stared at the small, revolving planet, her memories of the rift chamber suddenly as clear as the glowing orb twisting before her. 'Your prefectors have seen my memories, lord,' she whispered. 'They have laid my mind bare. You know why I cannot go to this place.'

'And yet, I must send someone.' Ule halted the hololithic globe and spread his fingers, the map viewer expanding onto a single island of green on a world painted almost entirely blue.

'Visage. Witchhaven. *Pythonissa*, on the old High Gothic charts. A middling, unimportant frontier world by all accounts, except the ones that truly matter.

'There was a time, millennia past, when the tithe of gifted from Pythonissa exceeded that of the rest of its sector combined. For the last millennium since its recolonisation, however, it has defied every attempt at Imperial control. In the last century alone almost a dozen regiments have been squandered attempting to pacify what should be little more than a feral world occupied by primitive familial factions and outmoded animistic heretical beliefs. And yet–'

'And yet you have seen what lingers there,' Aerand interrupted.

'As have you.'

A vivid image of that strange, branching silver artefact rose suddenly to the front of her mind. Its arcane geometries still made her mind spin, not unlike the symbols inscribed on the lord prefector's chamber door, or the ornate calligraphies tracing what few scraps of his metallic torso were visible beneath the folds of his robe. Yet there was a bitter taste to that particular memory, the faintest echo of the immaterium itself. And behind that, the sensation of a singular intelligence rising from the depths of the warp to swallow her whole.

'My lord, do not think that I am afraid.'

'That is precisely what I think,' Ule replied harshly. 'But you have every reason to be frightened. Whatever lingers on Visage is not something to trifle with, and yet, trifle we must, adept. To secure Visage and its tithe of gifted would not shift the tide of the great struggle on its own, but it certainly would not damage the effort. And to lose that world at a time when we are so desperate already... Well, you are more than capable of prophesying those consequences yourself.'

Aerand opened her mouth to protest, but Ule cut her off.

'I see your concerns. I do not need to scry your mind to do so, for they are written plainly across your face.'

The lord prefector's expression softened slightly as Aerand's hand went again to the wires on her scalp.

'I have read your records, adept. I know you had a life before this place. I may not look it, but I am still human enough to know that over the last five years you have clung to memories of that life, and the comrades with whom you shared it. Perhaps, even when things were the darkest, you let yourself dream of someday returning to them, however absurd you knew that fantasy might be. And I am certain, as well, that you were wise enough to know those dreams for the bitter fiction that they were. There are risks to this reunion, adept. Not just for your ego, but for your former soldiers as well.

'But you have also seen the danger that faces them. You know their strengths and weaknesses better than anyone else. Do not think that I do not realise the pain this will cause you. Do not think I do not realise the risk. And yet...'

'And yet they already have a primaris psyker, my lord,' Aerand replied. 'And Jarrah Kellipso is a far more capable man than me.'

A pained grimace accompanied the lord prefector's next words. 'Several days before you entered the rift chamber, Jarrah Kellipso's regimental commander filed a routine brief with the lord general militant's retinue, reporting significant progress in the hunt for a powerful psychic artefact on Visage, and making particular note of Kellipso's efforts on this front. Less than a week later, I received an urgent requisition from the Departmento Munitorum, authorised by the lord general militant's own hand, for a primaris psyker to be assigned to a vacant billet in the same regiment, with no mention whatsoever of Jarrah Kellipso. Nor has he been named in any subsequent report.

'Despite a dozen callings and missives, despite the attentions of my most powerful astropaths, there has been no word from Jarrah Kellipso since the day you encountered his mind in the warp.'

'He warned me,' Aerand interrupted. 'He warned me of what awaits on that world.'

'I heard,' Ule replied. 'My prefectors saw. Do not think that his warning was meant solely for you.

'And yet,' the ancient psyker continued, fixing her with a piercing, sightless stare, 'when have old soldiers ever listened to warnings?'

CHAPTER 5

It had begun with a woman, as such things often did. Only not in the way that he would have expected.

He had not been the Colonel then. Only a captain. Not even *the* captain. The sergeant had still been *the* sergeant, although only in the company grade. Before years of war stripped them both of enough superiors that they eventually found themselves in command.

They had been planetside for less than a month, but were already learning what life on a world like Visage would be like. Lightning raids into putrid, damp bogs. Shadows at the edges of hasty camps in the night. Non-existent supply lines. Naval assets more mercurial than the weather, which might depart orbit entirely for a season or a year with little more than a few hours' notice.

And above all of it, the filthy taint of Chaos.

None of these were new challenges to troopers of the Astra Militarum. The Imperial Guard, even regiments from a young world like Dorea, prided themselves on their ability to fight, and win, under precisely such circumstances. What he'd had yet to learn was the human cost.

He had never even learned her name.

Years later he thought he might have found a pict of her in a discarded Adeptus Administratum filebook. If so, then she had been a minor clerk in the employ of the Imperium bureaucracy once – a lavish opportunity for an uneducated commoner on a world without so much as a schola. That said, the records had been water-stained badly enough, and his only glimpse of the woman so entirely fleeting, that it might have been any one of a hundred other dead he had seen that day.

Throne be true, it wasn't the woman that mattered, it was the thing bundled in rags crying in her arms.

They couldn't just leave the girl.

He'd had children, once, in another life. Before Dorea, and the Emperor, and the endless void. So had the sergeant. So had half the troopers in the 19th Regiment. And for a time, it had felt like they'd gained those lives again.

The killing didn't stop. The killing never stopped. That was the lot of a soldier, and he did not begrudge it. But it had a purpose once again. A reason for the violence. A small, growing light full of wonder and hope.

Until the Emperor took that from them, too.

'What?' the Colonel managed eventually, stripped from the bitter memory by a polite cough from Sergeant Gross.

'There's a woman,' the sergeant repeated. 'A new arrival for the Imperial detachment, who seems to fit the description of a psyker lord. Just a few glimpses from a dockhand friendly to the cause, but enough that I'd stake blood on it. Tall, thin. Cadian herself based on the eyes. A robe, a staff. All the usual accoutrements. And there's an anxious soldier at her back with a bolt pistol that he looks only too ready to fire.'

'Very well,' he grunted.

It had begun with a woman. It would end with one, too.

Glavia Aerand stepped out of the Arvus lighter and into a hanging drizzle. A thin, white haze obscured her first vision of Visage, already dampening the folds of her thick robes and beading like sweat against the surface of her skin. If not for the weapon pressed into the small of her back, she might have turned around.

'Move,' called the stretched and nervous voice of the thin, prim adjudicant tasked with delivering her planetside. The young man wore an immaculately pressed jacket of Bulean wool that shouted wealth and impracticality to anyone with eyes. That coupled with a clear lack of the experience or composure usually required for the position he held spoke of family connections Aerand could hardly imagine.

She had not bothered to learn the man's name, although he would have been an easy enough target. His mind lay bare beneath only the thinnest mental shields, but the psychic scent of thousands of unsanctioned, untrained psykers drifted from him as strongly as his cloying perfume.

Six months aboard one of the accursed Black Ships that traversed the galaxy in endless, dour cycles, gathering the warp sensitive and depositing them on the scholastica psykana's doorstep. Six months in the presence of thousands of undisciplined souls, screaming out into the empyrean in a single, massed voice. One trip on a Black Ship was enough to madden many psykers. She had never dreamed she would be forced to take a second, and Throne forbid she ever let herself take a third.

'I said move, witch,' the adjudicant called again, pressing her forward with the barrel of his bolt pistol. She obliged, if only to have the satisfaction of seeing the man utterly ruin his garment.

She had dealt with rain before. She could deal with rain. On worlds like Ourea and Flak she had practically lived in it. Within an instant, however, she knew this would be worse.

Rain could be guarded against by a simple cover overhead, but this breed of all-permeating mist surpassed any attempts at limitation, and flowed wherever air was found. The scant written briefings she'd been able to locate in the Black Ship's memory banks about the rustic world had described its environ as 'singularly dour and cheerless'. She could already guess that was an understatement. Moisture beaded on every inch of her skin, trickling down the cables of her psionic bridle and the force staff strapped across her back in neat rivulets that only grew in size with each step.

Hidden beneath the shroud of Visage's omnipresent mist, the loose structure of a settlement began to emerge. Providence, Visage's largest, perhaps only, true Imperial city was composed of a smattering of ramshackle buildings: a collection of hovels, brothels and Astra Militarum structures better fitted for some backwater outpost or hive belly than the Imperium's seat on a strategically irreplaceable world.

Aerand followed a narrow and winding path of crushed rockcrete and metal shavings that had been piled to create an improvised road between the larger, more permanent landing pad and the settlement itself. On either side of the narrow walkway, dark, putrid-smelling water lapped within inches of its surface.

'Emperor save us,' her chaperone muttered, stepping from a puddle of brackish water and looking down with dismay at the salt streaks already marring one of his exquisite boots.

Truer words than he knew.

Aerand had read every dossier available on the small, mysterious planet during her six-month journey here. Throne knew there was little else to keep her mind occupied and diverted from the endless screams and waves of psychic anguish emanating from the wretched gaggle of untrained psykers massed within the Black Ship's fearsome hold.

By all reports, even limited as they were, Providence was a military commander's worst nightmare. Located in the planet's lowlands, in the centre of one of Visage's large and notoriously shallow seas, which amounted to little more than brackish, muddied swamps and marshes, the city was surrounded by hundreds of uncharted and indefensible approaches. A loose network of crumbling retaining walls ringed the city in a haphazard, jagged pattern, the failed efforts of the Adeptus Mechanicus to push that putrid water back.

But the tech-priests had left over a generation ago, and even from this distance, the moth-bitten, failing foundation of that stone could be seen slowly losing its battle without the constant ministrations of artisans and servitors to maintain it. Every few dozen yards entire sections of rockcrete had toppled into the water, giving the city's defences the appearance of a gap-toothed grin. Within that wall's poor protection, buildings massed against the hazy horizon. Poor, improvised shacks crowded the edges, gradually transitioning to spartan but structurally sound dwellings as one neared the heart of the city, and Providence's only true structure worthy of the name.

'Javax Cathedral,' Aerand said.

'What?'

'You can see the building from here.'

The man stared back at her blankly, the name clearly meaning nothing to him. Too much of her to assume even that basic level of competence.

'Named for Priest-Itinerant Lucius Javax, who accompanied the first Ecclesiarchy mission to recolonise and reconvert Visage following the Age of Apostasy.'

Whether by some trick of the eye or strange meteorological phenomenon, the mist itself seemed to thin slightly around the dark silhouette of the old gothic structure.

'Reportedly, Javax found the cathedral entirely intact upon his arrival, and after locating almost a dozen smaller Imperial chapels scattered across the otherwise faithless, untamed world, he declared their creation a miracle and founded cities at the site of each of these wonders.'

Three years later, Javax and almost half of his colonisers were dead, but the locations, and the names, of their cities remained.

As Aerand stepped off the narrow causeway and onto Visage's true soil, she caught sight of a cluster of figures approaching. Covered as they were in the deep, unyielding mist, she could not make out their form until they were only a few steps away, but her mind sensed them easily long before then. Flickering in various shades of violet and chartreuse, at least two dozen psykers approached through the mist. Most burned only slightly brighter than the ungifted pair of souls that accompanied them, but several among the group blazed like freshly lit torches.

As she closed her eyes and turned her vision inwards, Aerand felt a prickling discomfort at two dozen minds reaching towards her. Moments later, a cool chill spread from the base of her skull, as her bridle stymied the incursion. She felt the adjudicant step close behind her and press his weapon to her back once more as the approaching posse stepped into view.

'No ideas, witch,' he growled. 'I'd have no second thoughts about purging you all.'

Twenty-four children stumbled towards Visage's meagre space port, several among them scarcely old enough to walk. Thin chains connected the group in a single file, with heavier shackles weighing the ankles and wrists of the older among them. Behind the prisoners, two darkly cloaked silhouettes shuffled, their raiment dotted with blazing silver aquilas and skulls. As the two men ushered their prisoners out onto the causeway, their eyes settled briefly on Aerand, and both crossed themselves in the signs of the aquila and muttered in High Gothic beneath their breath.

Aerand suppressed a shiver as the two preachers passed, realisation dawning slowly upon her. Twenty-four nascent psykers, all under a dozen years of age, at least several among them with the raw capability to reach zeta or epsilon class with proper training. Some populous worlds would not produce such a tithe in a decade, and this was the second Black Ship to arrive on Visage in a year. She turned towards the looming cathedral at the centre of Providence's bleak landscape and muttered a silent prayer herself.

'Rank and regiment,' said the short, rotund man seated behind the rickety, folding map-desk. He uttered the word not as a question but as a statement, in a voice remarkably nasal and slight for a creature of his particular girth. The man did not look up from the piles of ageing vellum covering his desk as he spoke, but Aerand noted the telltale sigil of the Adeptus Administratum embroidered just beneath his breast.

'Glavia Aerand,' she replied. 'And I was under the impression there was only one regiment on Visage, adept.'

The man shuffled a stack of vellum beneath deft, calloused fingers, the only appendages of his body that appeared accustomed to exertion. 'Rank and regiment,' he repeated mirthlessly.

Aerand sighed and surveyed the scene. How a Departmento Munitorum ordinate had managed to secure a private chamber within Visage's most ancient and sacred cathedral was nearly enough to make her doubt the Emperor Himself. And yet, when you were the one processing billeting assignments, strange mistakes could certainly occur.

The small, dim room reeked of damp and ageing volumes cut only by the acrid odour of synthetical ink. Her adjudicant had not tolerated the fumes and paced nervously in the hall outside. Stacks of leather-bound ledgers and massive, ancient tomes covered every inch of the small chamber other than the open patch upon which she stood.

'Adept...' Aerand began, but the man lifted a fleshy arm to halt her.

'My name is as insignificant as yours.' The ordinate bent down for a moment, fumbling beneath his desk and emerging with an oversized brass seal, then stamped a trio of documents in a rapid flurry. 'Rank and regiment,' he repeated. 'Or would you like to delay these acquisition orders even further?'

Aerand cast her mind out gently towards the man, and was instantly bombarded by an endless stream of figures and nearly infinite ledger columns. Somewhere in that tangled, data-riven mess, she stumbled across the information she sought.

'Ordinate Jossen,' she said, 'I am quite certain only one new arrival was scheduled for today. And I am quite certain that you know who I am.'

At this, the man finally paused, and graced Aerand with a single contemptuous glare. If he felt any discomfort at the prospect of having his mind read, he did not show it. 'Lord psyker,' he replied. 'Of course, I know *what* you are. I am aware of every piece of cargo that arrives or leaves this Throne-forsaken theatre. Who you are, on the other hand, is completely unimportant to me.

'Rank and regiment,' he practically growled.

Aerand sighed. The wise soldier knew which battles were simply better to avoid. 'Primaris psyker,' she replied. 'Assigned to the Cadian Nine Hundredth regiment.'

'Hmmph,' the clerk grunted, flicking through a thick heap of vellum before finally taking hold of the very top sheet. He made a mark on a hefty and ink-stained ledger, then slapped the document into her hands, before returning his attention to filing the documents before him.

Aerand scanned her orders briefly. 'I'm afraid this must be some kind of mistake. It says here I'm to report to a Major Restripa. Colonel Yarin commands the Nine Hundredth regiment.'

'Oh my,' the ordinate muttered in mock surprise. 'Thank you for that crucially important correction. It is only my entire purpose to know such things, lord psyker. *General* Yarin was promoted to the lord marshal's staff almost a year ago. Major Restripa commands the Nine Hundredth, now.'

Despite her best attempts, a wave of disappointment crossed Aerand's face. Obvious enough to prompt a small smirk from Ordinate Jossen. She turned towards the door before stopping.

'Ordinate, if I may,' she asked, gently layering a hint of psionic persuasion into her words. 'There was a primaris psyker attached to the Nine Hundredth before me. A man named Jarrah Kellipso. I wonder if you've seen any mention of him in your reports.'

For a moment, the ordinate lifted his eyes, and she hoped he might provide her an answer. Then his gaze fell back to the mountain of paperwork atop his desk, which he began to stamp with a mindless glee.

The adjudicant pushed himself off the cold stone wall and motioned curtly for Aerand to follow. Glassaic windows lined the upper surface of the hall, casting dimly coloured shadows on the dark stone floor beneath her feet. Sanguinius, Sabbat, Macharius, Drusus. Familiar faces to any Imperial Guard trooper, but new additions to the Javax cathedral if rumours of its founding were truly accurate. How many unrecognised martyrs had the last millennium produced? How many countless more would the next thousand years require simply to keep the Imperium of Man alive?

A thought of Jarrah Kellipso crossed her mind. She would never have mistakenly called the man kind, but he had been a good teacher at a time when she was desperate for learning, and he had done his best to spare her the worst possible fates. If not for the man, she had no doubt she would be either dead or maddened in the grasp of Chaos on Ourea or some other distant world. She looked down at the orders in her hands once again. If dealing with the ghosts of her past was what it would cost to find out what had happened to him, it was a small price to pay to return the favour and do right by him.

Aerand looked up as a shadow crossed her path, nearly colliding with a tall man in voluminous robes. Folds of dark grey fabric covered the figure from his chin to his feet, embroidered in gold with the fine, elaborate characters of sacred passages in their original High Gothic. In one hand he grasped a jagged, dark thurible, wafts of steaming incense pouring from the vessel as it swung from its chain. In the other he loosely held the wooden shaft of a corseque, a sunburst of gold set atop the staff inlaid with a bone-white human skull. Both symbols of his office appeared more appropriate for a battlefield than the peaceful corridors of a church. A few paces behind the larger man, she spotted the preachers she had seen on the street before.

'Confessor,' she remarked, bowing slightly and stepping out of the trio's path. Of all the records pertaining to Visage, those of the Ecclesiarchy had been the most thorough, if least useful for her purposes, and the name of Confessor Javard Libertinum had been featured prominently among them. In the absence of any true governor on Visage, the confessor represented the closest to civilian leadership on the world.

'Lord psyker,' the confessor responded, his voice an unsettlingly quiet whisper. Hardly what she had expected from a clergyman tasked with rousing orations and fiery sermons. As he paused, a pair of fluttering shadows swooped down from the rafters above, the twisted, inhuman forms of two cherubs alighting on his shoulders like terrible red-eyed infants.

'May the Emperor's light rest upon you,' he whispered. 'And do not bring your taint through these doors again.'

Gently, the confessor pointed his corseque towards her, resting its tip against her forehead, then each of her shoulders, marking her with the blessing of the aquila. Following his words, however, she could not help but interpret the gesture as anything other than a threat.

She nearly opened her mouth to reply.

Then thought better of it. Today was no day for pushing her luck.

'Major Restripa,' Aerand muttered grimly, pushing her way beneath the relative shelter of a low, corrugated steel roof. The man leaning over the field desk beneath it glanced up briefly, then returned his attention to an unfurled map.

'Adept Aerand, I presume,' he replied absent-mindedly. The major had called her by a different title the last time they met, but his tone was precisely as she remembered. 'And you are?'

'Quite ready to leave this damned place,' the adjudicant replied, opening the breast of his jacket to flash the seal of the scholastica psykana. 'Could you not have sent your commissar to retrieve her?'

Restripa appeared unimpressed. 'My commissar is dead.'

'And your last primaris psyker?' Aerand asked.

Absalom Restripa glared at her then turned towards the other man, who was already preparing to leave. 'Consider your parcel delivered, adjudicant.'

Aerand sighed.

She had tried to convince herself a dozen ways to Terra on the short walk from the cathedral to the cluster of low buildings that made up the 900th's regimental headquarters that she could not possibly be on her way to report to *that* Restripa. Surely, the Departmento Munitorum ordinate had made a mistake, or even better, her new commanding officer must have simply shared that surname by coincidence? And yet, here the man stood before her, as if ripped directly from her memories. And saints knew they were memories she preferred not to revisit.

Restripa laid a small, steel token on the map board, shifting several others an inch here or there. Satisfied, he grunted, then turned to the pile of crates stacked behind him, pulling out a stack of printed images, which looked to have been captured from orbit. As he straightened, a silver major's starburst glimmered on the lapel of his drab, olive-grey uniform, slightly damp but otherwise nearly pristine. Aerand noted the row of thin ribbons beneath it. Both the rank and the commendations were new additions to his uniform, but the sneering smirk and tangled, curling dark hair above them were not.

'I must admit I was surprised to see your name on my orders,' she said. 'The last time we spoke you were still scrubbing that white-painted stripe off the centre of your perfectly polished helmet.'

Restripa grunted coldly as Aerand's eyes fell onto the gouged and dented helmet lying beside the map table, clearly scarred, but still burnished almost to a shine. 'And the last time we spoke you were an indecisive, overly lax officer, who was still trying to pretend she was human.'

Aerand clamped her mouth shut. Aye, still the same saint-blessed soldier. Arrogant and self-righteous, and not afraid to speak his mind. What had been frustrating qualities in a fresh corporal had clearly blossomed now that the man bore an officer's rank. What he could have possibly done to earn that promotion stretched even the bounds of the imagination of a woman who had swum through the warp itself. Even more painful was the fact that she no longer held the authority to make the pompous whelp scrub latrines for speaking to her so flippantly.

'Yes, sir,' she replied, the title like glass in her mouth. 'I still am, in fact. Pretending to be human, that is. But I'm afraid I've misplaced my captain's rank along the way.'

'Some loss,' Restripa replied, ignoring her and glaring at the map before him.

The pieces atop it were arranged in a standard defensive array, straight out of the Imperial Infantryman's Handbook. In the centre of the map, Providence lay outlined in black ink. A single chit bearing the dark silhouette of a lasgun and a numeral 'I' lay directly in the centre of that circle, accompanied by a miniature artillery battery. Two other rectangles, each numbered in ascending order, flanked the city on either side at a distance of half a dozen miles, and a third was spaced twice the distance away, forming an elongated triangle around the city. Between them, several miniature Sentinels were scattered in a roving pattern.

'Ah yes,' Restripa said, noticing her attention. 'I imagine that battle plans and troop dispositions might be confusing for you now, considering how much you've undoubtedly forgotten.'

'You're a bit loose on your spacing, major,' she replied, pointing to the single, isolated company forming the point of the elongated perimeter. 'If you're aiming for a standard Tyberian array.'

Secundus Company. Her old command. At the time, it had been the loosest of the 900th Regiment's four primary companies. Lightly staffed and flexibly organised, Secundus Company was built specifically for the isolating, terrain-dependent environment of Ourea, the austere mountain world where she'd gained command briefly, and then surrendered it when she'd boarded a Black Ship bound for the scholastica psykana. If anything remained of that old organisation, it would not have been an unreasonable choice to place the more mobile company further from Providence itself.

'And you're a bit loose with your tongue, adept. If you're aiming to keep your head.'

Across the table, Restripa looked up, his violet eyes meeting hers full of pure indignation. That glower scanned over her for a moment, seemingly for the first time taking note of the fearsome augmetics lining her scalp and the robes in which she was clad.

'I have been ordered by General Yarin to tolerate your presence, adept, but I plan to make little use of you beyond that. If I feel the sudden urge to consult a failed officer on matters of troop dispensations, I can assure you I will make the request audibly.'

Aerand chided herself internally. Better not to goad the man. Soldiers who were petty as subordinates inevitably turned into officers who held grudges.

'Of course, sir,' she remarked demurely, concealing her satisfaction at Major Restripa's discomfort. 'And what exactly would you have me do?'

As she spoke, a young man jogged up to the command post, a wet lasgun slung over his shoulder. His helmet and flak armour were drenched and dripping, stained with streaks of grey, loamy mud.

'Dispatch from Captain Vyse,' he called breathlessly, snapping to attention and presenting a sharp salute.

'And she couldn't simply vox me?' Restripa replied.

'Vox is down again, sir. Kendricks says the brine in the mist has turned the mechanisms of all the units to solid rust.'

'Very well,' Major Restripa replied, motioning for the folded packet of parchment in the corporal's hand. The young trooper snapped immediately back to attention after handing it to him, and resumed the salute that Major Restripa still had not returned.

'Throne's sake, trooper,' Aerand remarked, noting the slight shake in the boy's legs while holding his position. 'How far have you come?'

Instead of relief, however, the boy's face flushed with discomfort as he regarded the primaris psyker. Fear dripped from him almost as visibly as water, matched only by his terror of his commanding officer. The corporal looked to Major Restripa and held his position.

'Twelve miles. And he might have done it faster, if this dispatch is truly as urgent as Vyse implies. Throne, Justine,' he cursed. 'She wrote this message last night.'

'I know, sir. Sorry, sir. Found myself turned around in the mists and the dark, and it took me some time to regain my bearings.'

Restripa grunted and pulled a fresh piece of parchment from his desk drawer, then scribbled an almost illegible message across it. He folded the missive and sealed it, then turned to his map table and slid Secundus Company's marker slightly closer to Providence.

'Not a quality becoming of a courier, Justine,' he remarked, handing the folded orders to the corporal. 'Perhaps you'll make the journey back faster now that you know the way.'

'Sir,' Aerand began. 'The boy's run half to death.'

Major Restripa held up his hand. 'And he'll run the other half if I so order him, adept. Emperor's breath, you've been here hardly an hour, and already you presume far too much. I will remind you one final time that you have not been assigned to this regiment to command it, whatever delusions to the contrary you may possess.

'Although,' the major continued, a perverse grin spreading across his face, 'since you are clearly preoccupied with the well-being of Corporal Justine, perhaps he might find his way more quickly with you at his side.'

The acrid odour of decay hung heavy in the air, almost as thick as the perpetual mist around Providence. Before her, Corporal Justine trudged through brackish, dark water up to his mid-thighs. She'd forced the boy to take a few minutes of rest, and to at least refill his canteens and shove rations in his mouth before turning around to begin the outbound journey.

For the first mile outside Providence's sea walls they had made decent time, marching through scattered puddles atop crushed rockcrete causeways and a cluster of low, raised islands, bristling with sheet-metal shanties of increasingly poor repair. Soon, however, the landscape had devolved into little more than a waist-deep sea, only rarely interrupted with scattered patches of dry, loamy earth. Now they had begun the gruelling trudge in earnest.

Aerand grimaced as she waded past an ancient, shrivelled tree trunk. Even though dry earth had vanished several miles behind them, the prospect of vegetation on this dour world had not. Scattered like huddled masses of misshapen bodies, a strange, dark tree seemed to thrive in Visage's clime. How it survived an environment with so little sunlight perplexed her, but survive it did.

Every few hundred yards a small grove of the short, spindly trees arose, black trunks maybe two handspans across diving down into the dark, murky water. Gnarled, twisting branches stretched just along the water's surface and tangled together to form knotted clusters that were almost impossible to pass through. As each copse of trees was small, bypassing the groves was no real inconvenience, but something in the plants' strange, sickly shape, and the way their branches seemed to be reaching out rather than up, set Aerand on edge.

As she stepped out of the way of one such grasping branch, her boot snagged against something beneath the mire, and she pitched suddenly forward. Stumbling, she found herself facing the water, and for the briefest of moments, the murk beneath her cleared. Only a few inches beneath the surface, the bloated, desiccated face of a corpse stared back at her. The corpse's clothes had long since frayed into a drifting, threadbare, bleached mess, but she could still make out a silver aquila flickering atop the helmet strapped to the body's head. Around that helmet wove a tangled web of thin, tendril-like roots, curling around the corpse's face and plunging into its eye sockets and mouth. Aerand froze.

'Throne above,' she cursed, eyeing the grove of trees with new-found suspicion. 'What happened here? Are we in danger?'

'Um, no, sir. Lord psyker. No, I don't believe so. The sergeant told us not to be afraid of the corpsewood trees. They only feed that way on those already dead, he said.'

Aerand allowed her perception to creep out gradually, just enough to capture the surrounding area in its grasp. And true enough, while the boy continued bleeding fear into the water around him like a cornered prey animal, all of it was directed towards Aerand herself.

Grunting, she pulled her foot free from beneath the corpse, and turned back to follow Corporal Justine.

'The sergeant,' she said, something akin to good humour returning to her voice. There was only one soldier in the regiment old and weathered enough to wear that title without a name attached. 'That'd be Sergeant Corwyn, then?'

Justine nodded.

'He's still up with Vyse?'

'Yes, lord psyker. Sergeant Corwyn has been with Captain Vyse and Secundus Company ever since I arrived here.'

A speck of good news in the mountain of bad, then. Olevier Corwyn was as good a sergeant as they came. And a better friend. He'd stood beside her since her first bloody day in the 900th. If she could hope for any welcome here, it would be from him.

Aerand pushed herself forward through the water, coming abreast of the corporal. The boy might be terrified of her, but he'd have to learn to tolerate her presence.

Grey-brown eyes, not unlike the murky ocean around them. Not the violet of her own eyes. Not the violet of a proper, true-born Cadian who had spent a childhood staring up into the Eye of Terror.

'How old are you, corporal?' she asked eventually.

'Um,' the boy murmured. 'I'm not rightly sure. I never knew my parents long enough to ask. Grew up on the *Ledgermain* with all the other war orphans.'

That answered a few questions of its own, then. Life aboard an Astra Militarum transport was hard enough as a soldier, even more so as a soldier's child. For those unfortunate enough to lose both parents in the Emperor's service, and they were many, the only option was counting the days until you were old enough to join a Whiteshield platoon.

'Let me ask you another way. How long since the first time you fired a lasgun?'

'Ah.' A flicker of a smile escaped onto the trooper's face as he patted the weapon in his hand. He quickly noticed the indiscretion and buried the expression. 'I've had this particular weapon just under ten solar years, lord psyker. But I had another for almost three years before that.'

Thirteen years since his first arming. Likely at age six or seven. 'You've lived just under two decades, then, trooper.'

'If you say so, sir.'

Not all that young in truth. Plenty old enough to know how to use that weapon. Plenty old enough that he'd surely used it before. And yet, for all that, too young to have ever seen Cadia. Too young to fully understand what he'd been trained to wield that weapon to avenge.

A strange sense of loss settled onto Aerand. Not for the world that she had once called home – she had long ago made peace with its destruction – but for the camaraderie she had felt standing beside soldiers for whom Cadia's departure was as brutally and personally painful as it was for her.

Five years was a long time.

Major Restripa. Vyse. Argos. Corwyn. There had been perhaps three dozen other names that she recognised out of five hundred on the regiment's new roster. Maybe half a dozen among those that she had truly called friends.

Saints knew she hadn't been looking forward to this homecoming, but she hadn't expected it to feel so damned lonely.

'Come along, corporal,' she muttered, picking up her pace.

For his part, Corporal Justine was a reasonable guide. The young trooper held a mostly true course without the aid of compass or map, even accounting for Visage's brutal geography. At best, the cloying mist around them grew thin enough that she could make out the silhouette of tree groves, or the low, humped form of small islands when they were still a few dozen yards away. At worst, she might have easily lost sight of Corporal Justine despite only being a few steps behind the trooper, if not for the psychic signature his mind registered to her own.

Still, the boy did well, and only once or twice did she have to nudge their course slightly northwards towards the distant but easily detectable psychic signature of Secundus Company. Other than the monotony of gruelling physical travel, and the relative silence of her companion, the journey itself had been unremarkable until now, when the cluster of souls that made up their destination lay hardly more than a mile away.

Corporal Justine stumbled forward before her, rising with exertion onto a low, submerged bar of earth, until all but his boots had emerged dripping from the water. The boy shivered slightly with the sudden chill and weight.

Say what one might about walking through a veritable sea, but the relative warmth and buoyancy it provided were noticeable in their sudden absence. As the young trooper stepped onto solid earth he stumbled, falling to his knees in the mire.

The water was scarcely deep enough to submerge his forearms, but even so, he took some time to recover. Two dozen miles in a day might not be much to remark upon for a Cadian trooper under normal circumstances, but that same distance through an ocean that rose between your waist and chest was another enemy entirely. The young man was fully spent, and she feared he might not rise again under his own power.

'Come on now, corporal,' she said, stepping up beside the young man and grasping him by the shoulder. With a heave, she had the trooper on his feet, and even if he had wanted to recoil at her touch, he was far too exhausted to act on that impulse.

Even his thoughts, which had leaked from him like a sieve when they first began their daunting journey, now dripped forth at only an occasional trickle. The boy was practically asleep on his feet, and although Aerand could see no sun behind the ever-present vapour that made up Visage's atmosphere, she had noted a slight darkening of the environs beginning almost an hour before.

While she harboured no childish fear of the dark, she had spent decades cultivating a far deeper one. Any soldier knew that darkness provided advantage to the combatant who knew the battlefield best, and here Aerand found herself utterly unacquainted. The last thing she wanted was to spend whatever amounted to night on Visage in the wilds with a soldier who could scarcely keep his own eyes open.

'Tell me, Justine,' she said. 'What happens to us if we lose our way?'

Justine blinked, a thin wave of fear washing from him. A cruel but powerful stimulant.

'I-I don't know, sir,' the young man muttered. 'There are stories.'

'What kind?'

'They say a whole regiment got swallowed up here. Maybe ten years before we landed on Visage. Just walked off into the mist and never came back.'

'They have a name?' she asked. They always did.

The boy nodded. 'The ghost regiment.'

Aerand scoffed. 'Every planet has such legends, corporal. Although I can imagine how such a thing might happen here. It's far more likely that your "ghost regiment" simply encountered an unexpected ambush in the night, but I have no desire to put that assertion to the test.'

Gradually, Aerand closed her eyes, gently probing out with her mind towards Corporal Justine. If the trooper noticed the incursion, he certainly gave no sign of it. Slowly, the world around Aerand fell dark, as she opened herself to the presence of the empyrean. A slight chill settled on her, along with the taste of stale and bitter blood. Here was the key to every psyker, the ugly truth that the ungifted could not understand. Even as that acrid sensation repulsed her, it also left her craving more.

Just a slight exertion. Only enough to see the boy's mind blazing beside her and to tease at those outer threads of fatigue. One by one, she unwound them with deft, careful fingers. Toy with a man's mind blindly and you were likely to leave him a blubbering fool, but a small adjustment on the surface, under well-practised hands, was often enough to make the animal mind forget its troubles.

For the boy's body, Aerand could offer nothing. His strength was spent and his muscles failing, and there was little she could do to correct that. It was easy enough, however, to make the young trooper's mind forget the brutal extent of that exhaustion.

Slowly, she unwound herself from Justine's thoughts, feeling the young man steady slightly beside her. As he did, some brightness returned to his face, and he finally noticed his proximity to the psyker.

'Thank you,' he remarked, pulling away from her grasp. 'I'm not sure what happened. I must have lost my footing.'

Aerand nodded. She would have time to be offended by his revulsion later. For now, she simply took it as a sign that the young man might make it the final distance.

As she pulled her awareness fully back to her body, feeling her own fatigue settle in with its full weight, something strange appeared at the edge of her perception. She paused, closing her eyes again, and drawing a deep breath. No time, or space, for a full meditation, but even that simple gesture drove the world around her away.

And instantly, Aerand regretted that she hadn't done so sooner.

Just over a mile away, in the direction they headed, a blazing cluster of souls cast their light on the fabric of the empyrean. Perhaps she had been too focused on that destination. Perhaps the strength of that blaze had simply been too bright. But much closer, nearly on top of them in fact, a small cluster of sparks had suddenly appeared. Ten. Fifteen. Difficult to discern in the single snapshot that flashed before her. Of the group, most scarcely left a mark on the immaterium, but one of those flames flickered brighter than the rest.

'Stop,' Aerand ordered, opening her eyes.

A few feet away, Corporal Justine looked confused, but complied. 'Something wr–'

She held up her hand and silenced him.

+See to your weapon,+ she ordered the trooper without speaking.

She was no skilled telepath, and even at such a short distance, the psychic message would not arrive fully intact without a willing, trained recipient. Even so, a look of confusion crossed the boy's face before he responded to an unplaceable urge to ready his weapon and scan the horizon.

Good lad. Aerand drew her laspistols from the holsters at her hips and did the same.

Instinctively, she crouched and darted towards the relative cover of an isolated corpsewood tree sprouting from the water a few feet away. It was no bastion wall or fighting position, but on a battlefield of open sea, even the slightest cover could make all the difference. Taking a breath, she closed her eyes again, the scene around her now arrayed in blistering detail.

Thirteen souls approached through the fog, less than a hundred yards away. She had hoped they might simply pass by in the mist, but it was clear now that their course would see them directly intercepting Aerand and Justine. She chided herself slightly, but whether her minor psychic exertion had alerted them to her presence, or whether they'd been detected by more conventional means seemed immaterial at this point.

As Aerand probed around the edges of the approaching minds, she caught notes of uncertainty but nothing approaching fear. Good enough. She could work with uncertainty. She would let the fear come later.

By now, the low splashing of bodies moving through water was audible through the dense fog, and Justine did not need any psychic prodding to kneel behind a corpsewood tree of his own and turn his weapon in that direction.

Stay, she ordered with a movement of her hand. No psychic will here, just the simple battle signs familiar to all Cadian children even before they learned to speak. Then she stepped out into the fog.

For the briefest of moments she was met with a strange sensation of weight, as if something in the water vapour resisted her movement, then as surely as the sensation had arrived, it passed. She shook the thought.

Laspistols at the ready, Aerand waded through the mire with eyes half dulled to the waking world. Instead, overlaid on the bleak landscape of murky water and mist flickered the faintest echoes of the immaterium beyond. As a dozen dim flames approached through that fog, a single soul ventured out towards her from the rest.

Aerand smirked.

She threw her mind towards the isolated individual, breaking through flimsy mental defences and unleashing a barrage of thoughts. Unfocused, unorganised images assailed her. Bare hands grasping a rusted stubber. Bare feet sloshing through mud. A brief glimmer of instinctive, animal terror, as her subject recognised something amiss in his own mind.

And that fear itself was all she truly needed. Aerand arrived beside the man before he even noticed her approach, and before he could scream or fire his own weapon, hers was already pressed to the side of his head. A more gifted telepath might have simply shattered his mind from where she had stood a few yards away, but at this distance a las-round did just as much damage as any psychic assault ever could. Better to save her will for when she might truly need it.

The sound of her laspistol cracked through the evening, echoing off the water before being swallowed by the surrounding mist. In the distance, voices shouted and began moving her way. The man flopped into the murky water with a muted splash, slowly enough for Aerand to quickly assess his wargear.

Standard Echon-pattern assault stubber, rusted and scuffed beyond what any respectable Imperial Guardsman would tolerate. And while the man wore muddied, faded flak armour across his chest, deep gouges lined the breastplate where a regimental insignia had been scraped loose.

'To the xenos, death. To the traitor, damnation,' Aerand grunted. The Guardsman's Consecration. Of all the enemies of the Imperium, Traitor Guardsmen held a special place in her heart.

She threw her mind outwards again into the mist. Twelve souls burning against that shrouded white cloak. Thirteen, counting that of Corporal Justine, still huddled obediently at the centre of the corpsewood grove. At the sound of her laspistol, the enemy formation had split in two, and six silhouettes approached her now through the mist. The crack of a stubber split the air as one sprayed aimlessly in her direction. A better stratagem, perhaps, against a foe without the gift of foresight.

Thoughtlessly, Aerand watched the cloud of metal slugs scatter into the water around her, moments before the splashes actually arrived. A difficult trick to master in the midst of a blazing firefight, but easily enough accomplished with only one enemy firing.

Drifting through the water towards the incoming fire, Aerand raised her laspistols and closed her eyes. The fog was too thick to see through properly, but it was easy enough to aim at the psionic fires blazing against that white. Three bodies dropped in quick succession, their flames sputtering out with startling ease, before the remaining enemy opened fire as well. Now, a rain of las-rounds and stubbers spraying towards her, Aerand lifted a hand and began her work in earnest.

To the ungifted, one psyker was no different from another. With no knowledge and abundant fear of their powers, a witch was a witch was a witch was a witch. But to those with any understanding of the arcane arts that access to the empyrean enabled – to those able to look beyond the thin veil of labels such as 'tainted' and 'witch' – the distinctions made themselves immediately clear.

Biomancers, telekines, telepaths, pyromancers. Of the psychic disciplines, these were by far the most common, and most blatant. A battle psyker raising a single finger to obliterate the platoon beside you with fire was certainly a demoralising thing to behold. To see your own bullets turn and whistle back towards you was enough to shake the hearts of most men.

Watch a comrade crumble to a lifeless husk beside you, or see your greatest fears materialise before your eyes, and few soldiers could maintain the will to keep fighting.

And yet, what a single diviner could accomplish in the midst of battle often put those other psykers to shame.

Of all psychic disciplines, divination was by far the most fickle. To cast one's mind beyond the present was no easy task. Yet, somehow, in the middle of a firefight, to do so came almost as naturally as breathing.

Aerand had heard even the ungifted speak of the sensation. Of the veteran soldier, practised through hundreds of conflicts, reading the battlefield and the fire pattern of his opponent and seeing the rifts appear in the enemy's lines moments before they actually did. Add to that veteran's instinct even mere seconds of true psychic foresight, and a battlefield became a strangely predictable place.

As Aerand weaved through inbound fire with an ease that approached the choreographed pattern of a martial dance, she felt her mind drift even further into the dark of the empyrean. Las-rounds whipping around her, she dived into the fray, dropping another Traitor Guardsman with a pistol shot from point-blank range. His two companions wheeled to face her and she watched them take aim before their weapons even began to rise. Darting in the opposite direction, she arrived beside them in time to place two expert shots beneath the folds of their armour.

The bodies slumped into the water as she turned to face that last flickering glimmer of light.

Aerand's eyes might have missed the woman entirely, if not for the psychic flame matching her in the warp. A frail, ageing frame, even slighter than her own, shrouded in a deep brown cloak drawn around her. The woman's gnarled hands gripped a staff of dark, twisted wood, and she muttered under her breath in some unrecognisable cant.

'Come now,' Aerand murmured, firing a pair of shots from her laspistols. Instantly, their light was swallowed by a sudden flaring of the woman's psychic signature, and Aerand raised a wall around her own mind moments before it was met by a cascade of raw psychic power. She stumbled, throwing the rush of mental energy to the side, and swallowed her scoff.

Perhaps not something to be trifled with, after all.

'I see you, sister,' the woman cawed, looking up with milky-white, blinded eyes. 'And I feel the shackles clasped on your mind.'

Aerand leapt to the side as another invisible wave rushed towards her, the surface of the water rippling in its wake. In the back of her mind, a white-hot, threading sensation drove towards her psyche like the tip of a spear as her bridle absorbed the brunt of the witch's assault.

No, not something to be trifled with, in the least.

Aerand rushed towards the witch, her own hands outstretched, round after round erupting from her laspistols in unison. Her bridle bearing the brunt of the woman's assault, her mind was free to place a piece of her own psychic energy behind each well-placed shot. With each hammering into the woman's defences, she watched the witch's flame begin to dim.

'We can free you,' the witch crooned. 'From your chains and your false god. We can show you a world without cages or masters.'

When she was only a few precious steps away, the witch's flame flickered once more and Aerand felt a sudden weight around her right wrist. Pulling forward, she felt herself suddenly restrained by the dark, woody branch of a corpsewood tree wrapping itself around her arm. Aerand glowered at the roots rising out of the water, beginning to entangle her ankles as well.

It was an impressive feat, truly, for the witch to manipulate the physical world around her so deftly, all the while maintaining a separate direct psychic assault. And the tactic would have almost certainly been effective against any other enemy on a distant, backwater world like this. There was strength in this witch, yes, but it was raw, unrefined and utterly untrained, fuelled by nothing more than blind emotion and the filthy, unreasoning madness of Chaos.

'You are not free, witch,' Aerand replied. 'And I am not a prisoner of either the God-Emperor, or you.'

Without training, the gifted were inclined to forget that the psychic world was not the only one which mattered. With her still-free left hand, Aerand pulled her combat knife from its sheath along her thigh and plunged the blade into the witch's chest.

The woman's violet flame flashed brightly and then vanished, the corpsewood tendrils falling slack at Aerand's feet. As she turned, those ink-black roots reached out towards the dead body in the water.

As the immediate world around her fell eerily silent, the scattered sound of las-fire echoed across the water from only a short distance away. Aerand cursed and turned back towards Corporal Justine, a sinking feeling inside her chest. As she approached the clearing, fearing the worst, she passed a trio of corpses floating in the sea, ratty uniforms scorched with opposing las-fire. She threw her mind forward to sense only two living souls ahead, and picked up her pace.

She burst through the mist in time to note the final few Traitor Guardsmen scattered dead around the base of Justine's tree. The young trooper dropped the muzzle of his weapon once he recognised her, and a look of mild relief flooded his face.

'Lord psyker,' he muttered. 'I wasn't sure you'd come back.'

Aerand surveyed the carnage, impressed. 'It certainly seems that whatever his faults, Major Restripa hasn't allowed the Nine Hundredth's marksmanship to slouch.'

A small smile crept onto the young trooper's face, but as he opened his mouth to reply, the crack of a stubber swallowed his voice, and a bloom of crimson sprouted across his chest.

Aerand froze, blinking away the premonition, and Corporal Justine stared at her strangely. She whipped her head to the side just in time to see an injured Traitor Guardsman lift his weapon out of the water and take aim at the corporal.

There was a time for the subtle grace of divination, then there was a time for the sheer psychic power of the mind.

The Traitor Guardsman erupted into a gout of golden flame as Aerand flicked her wrist in his direction. Corporal Justine's eyes flashed to the man, whose screams of agony drowned out any reply, then gazed back at Aerand with pure animal fear.

She sighed. Better that the trooper should dread her than find himself breathing water beneath corpsewood roots.

CHAPTER 6

'She's here,' the crone muttered, her simple green eyes rolling back into her skull as she drifted slightly on her feet. The woman was lost, more often than not, in the haze of corpsewood root and whatever other pungent intoxicants her kind managed to scrape from this feral world, but this was the worst the Colonel had ever seen her.

'Finally,' he muttered, ushering away the two troopers who had escorted the woman here. They both looked pleased to be rid of her, and of him. 'Sit,' he ordered, clearing a space on a low camp stool beside his drawing table. Their fourth camp in as many days, courtesy of increasingly aggressive Cadian patrols.

Six months against the legendary Cadians, and he had grown to believe all the tales of valour that had trickled down through the Astra Militarum ranks. This regiment – even those who had never seen their home world, and even those transplants with no Cadian blood to speak of – had more than lived up to the expectation. Yet, in the end, they died like anyone else.

'The primaris psyker has arrived,' the crone muttered again. 'I have tasted the flavour of her soul on the warp.' In her left hand, a thin stone blade glinted with blood, a gash on her right palm still dripping. The Colonel shoved a rag towards the woman, if only to stop her bleeding onto the maps and records strewn across his camp table.

'I know,' he replied angrily. 'I've had reports already. Make yourself useful, witch, or get out of my sight.'

The bitter stink of woodsmoke and Chaos drifted off the woman, and he found himself retching within his mouth. He would kill this woman one day, he vowed yet again. But not yet. Not quite yet.

'No,' she cackled, wobbling on her chair. Her eyes flashed forward, suddenly lucid. 'Not just here on Visage, you fool. She is here, close at hand.'

The crone tossed aside the rag and opened her palm, a patchwork map of blood suddenly visible on her weathered skin. Crude, aye, but not so different from the charts on his table, creases and folds aligning with the contours and terrain on his own battle map. Where blood should have drifted across that papery skin equally, it had coalesced upon a single point.

At this, the Colonel took notice, orienting himself to the fleshy map. A mile. Maybe two.

He left the crone laughing madly in his command tent and stepped out to view the falling sun. Sergeant Gross met him at the door.

'Call them in,' he muttered. 'As many warbands as can make it by daybreak.'

The Cadians, brave as they were, would not move under darkness, and by the time the sun rose, his Doreans would be waiting.

Aerand stumbled into the first outer picket long after the damp chill of night had fully settled, carrying an unconscious Corporal Justine over her shoulders.

So much for a speedy final mile.

About a hundred paces beyond the clearing where they'd left a dozen dead in their wake, the young trooper had simply collapsed before her. Initially, she had feared that he'd suffered some injury he'd simply been too afraid, or too proud, to admit to. But after a cursory search she had assured herself that the only blood staining the corporal's damp, salty flak armour was the blood he had painted there from others.

Despite his uninjured state, no amount of mental prodding could rouse him, and she'd been left at the only possible conclusion: the young man was fully and utterly exhausted. Psychic suggestion might allow a soldier to fight on long past the point at which mental fatigue would normally stop them, but eventually the body simply failed. To push it any further would risk irreversible damage.

She had considered that option. If the missive Justine carried to Captain Vyse was truly urgent, a few hours of notice might be worth the young man's life.

The thought left her feeling callous, but she'd spent enough time as a commander before boarding that dark, accursed Black Ship, to understand such brutal arithmetics of war. Then again, if Major Restripa's message to Captain Vyse had truly been so time sensitive, the major would have been a fool to put it in the hands of an exhausted courier who had only just finished his inbound journey.

So, both Restripa's and her own pride be damned, she had propped the young trooper into a standing position, then draped him ungracefully across her thin shoulders. Not an easy burden to carry, as poorly conditioned as her time at the scholastica had made her, but certainly not the heaviest she had carried. Now, however, hours later, the muscles of her shoulders and back screamed their regrets.

She stumbled onto the first sentry almost by surprise, her own exhaustion so intense that she'd limited her psychic perception to a few dozen yards before her. Without even that minor augmentation, however, she might have walked right past Secundus Company in the dark. While she was still a few feet away, she prodded the man's mind slightly to awaken him.

The bleary-eyed sergeant startled from his sleep, levelling his lasgun at her as he became suddenly alert to the silhouette splashing through the water towards him.

'Hold!' she called, just enough psychic suggestion in her tone to keep the grizzled veteran from pulling the trigger.

'Who the hell are you?' he called into the darkness. 'Don't know any troopers stupid enough to sneak up on the lines in the night.' The torch beam mounted to the sergeant's helmet suddenly blazed to life. Somehow, the mist seemed to have grown even thicker now that the air had cooled, and the illumination did the man little good, scattering against that blanket of white.

Aerand turned slightly so that Justine's face fell into the weak beam of the watchman's lamp. 'Corporal Justine with an urgent missive from Major Restripa. And in no condition to be making intelligent decisions.'

The sergeant let out a chuckle as she stepped closer. 'Emperor's piss,' he muttered. 'Come on in then. I don't know what the hell you think you're doing out there. I don't care how urgent the missive is that you're carrying, I'd tell the warmaster himself to shove it back up his armour if he wanted me to carry it out here in the dark. You're lucky I didn't burn a hole straight through your forehead. I swear I thought you were a mist corpse coming back from the grave.'

The man's good humour vanished, however, as soon as Aerand drew close enough for him to see her clearly.

'Emperor's grace,' he mumbled, making the sign of the aquila without thinking. His eyes fixed on the fearsome augmetics coursing across her scalp, then the trooper slung over her shoulders and the gnarled corpse-wood staff nestled beside the corporal.

'Trooper Justine is alive,' she assured him. 'Simply exceedingly tired. And the weapon, I promise you, is not mine.'

'Of course, lord psyker,' the sergeant mumbled, half beside himself.

'Just point me in the direction of Captain Vyse, if you don't mind.'

The panicked man was only too happy to oblige.

'And try to stay awake on your watch, sergeant, lest something even more frightening than I sneak up on you in this fog.'

She did her best to ignore the waves of terror radiating from the man. A grizzled veteran more frightened of what she had become than of an unknown threat emerging from the dark.

The scattered light of small cook fires glowed orange and warm against the walls of several ancient stone buildings that lined the narrow, muddy roadway leading to Vyse's command post. Charity, this settlement had been marked on Major Restripa's map, if Aerand remembered correctly. Most of the structures around her looked old. Too old to have been built after Visage's resettlement, and those that were more modern – made of rock-crete and steel – looked even more worn than their ancient counterparts.

Perhaps something in the environment degraded the newer substance? It would explain the odd state of disrepair of the more recently constructed buildings around her, as well as the crumbling sea wall around the planet's capital city, while Javax Cathedral and other older buildings showed fewer signs of disrepair.

As the earth rose slightly, firming to something more than the gelatinous mush that made up most of the 'islands' she'd encountered throughout the day, Aerand noted that the corpsewood trees abruptly fell away, not a single one of the twisted, blackened plants sprouting more than a few feet from the edge of the water.

Aerand caught sight of the small stone chapel at Charity's apex, and turned her heading in that direction. Her breath fell in heavy gouts of steam, laboured as it was from carrying Corporal Justine up the slight incline, but she felt it pick up even further at the thought of encountering Captain Vyse. Corporal Justine, the sergeant, even Major Restripa. She'd either never known those soldiers, or never called them friends. But here, just a few yards down a narrow dirt path, lay her first true reunion with a former comrade.

And Throne above, she found herself terrified.

'Captain Vyse,' she called, stepping beneath the chapel's low, stone archway. The building had nearly toppled, a portion of the south wall spilling outwards like a melting block of ice. Of the ornate glassaic that had once graced its soaring windows, only a few scattered shards clung to those frames, and the slate roof was pocked with shell holes and debris. Yet as Aerand stepped inside, she felt an undeniable lightening, as if some of the weight of the cold, mist-filled night stopped at the door.

'Who's that?' called the woman hunched over the altar. Her flak armour hung across a splintered lectern, her helmet resting on the debris-strewn floor beside it. A narrow sleeping mat was unrolled in one corner of the small room, although it looked as if it had not been used recently. Atop the narrow set of stairs that led to the chancel, seated on a worn and unrecognisable statue, the captain leaned over the chantry, cleaning an autogun.

'Is that Sergeant Maltia? If so, you're late. I told you I wanted your platoon ready for patrol half an hour ago. These warbands and their bloody marsh priests have given us enough headaches already. If one more soldier walks off into this Throne-cursed mist, I swear I'm going to desert myself just so I can find and execute them.'

Unbidden, a small smile crept across Aerand's face, as she watched the precision and ferocity of the woman's work. Aerand herself might have changed, but this was still the same Hadria Vyse she remembered. As good a replacement to follow her in leading Secundus Company as she could have ever asked for.

'It's not Maltia,' she replied. 'It's Aerand. Glavia Aerand... sir.'

Vyse looked up.

For a moment, the woman's face became a mess of emotions. Surprise first, then something almost akin to happiness. Both expressions were quickly stifled by a mask of genuine suspicion. Vyse rolled her muscled shoulders casually beneath her olive-grey gambeson and rose from her position. Aerand noted that the autogun did not leave her hands.

'Lord psyker,' Vyse replied coolly. 'Major Restripa informed me that you would be arriving, but I'd assumed he would be making use of you in Providence.'

Aerand's excitement faded at the icy formality in Vyse's tone. 'Yes, sir. It seems the major found use for me elsewhere.' She bent down and deposited Corporal Justine on the floor.

'Alive,' she assured Vyse. The second time already she'd had to assure a former comrade she was not a murderer.

Slowly, Aerand knelt beside the young corporal and set her fingers gently against his temples. Just a whiff of power into the boy. Enough to reverse the sedation she'd already laid on him and only a flicker of energy beyond that.

Groggily, Justine opened his eyes, then started at the sight of the primaris psyker only inches from his face.

'Be still,' Aerand ordered, and the boy calmed slightly. 'I believe you're carrying something for the captain?'

'Um. Yes. Yes, I am.'

Justine stumbled slowly to his feet, eager to be out of Aerand's reach, but exhausted beyond measure, and produced Major Restripa's folded orders from some hidden pocket deep within his uniform. The oiled leather message case had done its job well, and the yellow parchment bore only a few scattered drops of moisture.

Vyse accepted the missive, then looked the corporal once over. 'Throne, Justine. You look like hell. Go see Argos, then find yourself a rack for the night. If anyone bothers you before sunrise tell them to come and talk to me.'

The boy mumbled a thank you, then hastily limped from the room. Whether he was more excited by the prospect of a dry bed, or simply eager to finally escape Aerand's presence, she couldn't tell.

By the light of a dim torch lamp, Vyse reviewed Restripa's orders, a grimace falling across her face. 'Seems Corporal Justine's rest might have to be cut short, after all. We've been ordered to abandon Charity. But I'll wait to break that news until morning.'

'I see,' Aerand replied.

Vyse tossed the orders to the floor and returned to cleaning the barrel of her weapon with a fine-toothed steel brush. 'Your first night here?' she asked Aerand.

'Yes, sir.'

Vyse grunted. 'See, there are only two problems as far as I can tell with this accursed planet. The first one is the mist. Can't see worth a damn, can't get aerial support for piss. Normally I wouldn't mind either of those. Fewer birds up above means more shooting on the ground and more traitor blood for me and mine. But it's hard to fire a weapon when it's sprouting rust faster than half my troopers can grow a beard.'

She sighed, holding the brush up to the torch lamp, its bristles stained red-orange.

'But the second problem, the bigger problem,' she remarked coolly, 'is that the planet is swimming with Throne-cursed psykers.'

Aerand stiffened as Vyse's violet eyes flashed up and met hers. As the woman spoke, the thin scent of camphor drifted from her mouth, her pupils pushed wide by the constant stream of stimm tablets that Vyse kept pocketed in her cheek like candy.

'Hadria,' Aerand mumbled. 'I'm not some heretic witch. I served the Emperor beside you for nearly two years.'

'And that's the only reason I haven't put a las-bolt between your eyes. You were a fine commander for a few months on Ourea, but where have you been for the last five years? How am I supposed to know what you've become in that time?'

Aerand found herself at a loss for words. *I'm the same person I was*, she wanted to scream back, but even she knew that was far from the truth.

'We'll both just have to find out.'

With a clatter, she threw the witch's corpsewood staff to the floor. 'One fewer warband and marsh priest for you to worry about, captain.'

Vyse looked down at the weapon, and grunted indistinctly, then returned to cleaning her autogun.

Aerand slept fitfully on a patch of damp earth accompanied by the vague sensation that she was sinking slowly into the spongy loam. Her thick cloak, still soaking, provided little warmth, and if not for the sheer exhaustion that wracked her body, she doubted her eyes would have ever fallen shut. And yet eventually, they did.

She remembered precious little of her dreams. A blessing given what they had started to become even before she boarded a Black Ship to the scholastica years before. She remembered a time when her sleep had only been plagued with memories of battle and bloodshed, as any common soldier's were. Now, however, it seemed that rather than truly sleeping, her mind waded through a twisted world of premonitions and poorly defined fears each night.

It was common knowledge among the gifted that sleep brought the soul dangerously close to the edges of the empyrean, and that border became paper-thin for those accustomed to walking either side when awake.

One image remained with her in the morning, although it was difficult to say if it had truly been a dream, or just some conjuration of her sleep-addled mind imposed upon a brief memory of waking. She remembered sitting on that loamy earth, feet outstretched, boots submerged in a small puddle before her, but as she craned her neck to see the puddle's bottom she could not find one. Instead, beneath the murky surface that initially appeared only inches deep, the light continued to descend into an infinite darkness. As she stared, faint colours erupted in that impossible deep, and somewhere lost within those endless depths, an even darker shadow heaved.

Slowly, from the water, a thin web of corpsewood tendrils crawled upwards, grabbing hold of her legs and pulling her into the sea.

Aerand woke with a start to a hand on her shoulder, her own grip darting to the laspistols at her side.

'Easy,' whispered a voice directly beside her. In the still-dark of night, she could not make out the face, but she would recognise that voice anywhere.

Gleaming brass chevrons glistened with dew on the figure's epaulets. A sergeant. *The* sergeant. Olevier Corwyn. Her one true and honest friend throughout all that had befallen her, from the day she first joined the 900th, until her last...

'Corwyn,' she muttered, trying to suppress her relief. She pushed herself upright, noting that her boots and breeches were soaked almost up to her waist. Even on the damp earth they should have dried with the rest of her clothing.

'You have to be careful,' the sergeant muttered as she shivered slightly and pulled her robes tighter around her. 'There are three small moons here on Visage. Too tiny to make much of a tide, but they orbit as fast as any battle cruiser, and even a few inches can be the difference between staying dry and drowning.'

Aerand turned towards him, surveying the grizzled veteran. If the last five years had been rough on her body, Olevier Corwyn somehow wore that time even more harshly. His long, shaggy hair had been speckled with wise-appearing flecks of silver last time she'd seen him, but she now struggled to find a single strand of black in the bleach-white mane atop his head. Deep crow's eyes and sunspots marked his weathered face, yet, through it all, he still cracked that same, unassailable smile.

'And you,' she replied, 'need to be careful to start avoiding the mess tent, otherwise you won't fit into your flak armour for long.'

Corwyn chuckled, patting his slightly generous abdomen. Not a single soldier in the regiment would dare call the man fat, but he carried the body of an experienced veteran who had earned the privilege of letting younger troopers do most of the footwork.

Then just as soon as it arrived, Corwyn's smile faltered. The old sergeant surveyed the woman before him, and for the first time since adolescence, Aerand felt self-conscious of the body she wore before a man. The friend that had left him was a strong, respectable soldier. What must he think of the weak creature that had returned?

'I promise,' she said, 'I have not changed nearly as much as it appears.'

'Nor have I,' Corwyn replied kindly, although it was clear to them both whose changes were more alarming. The sergeant forced a smile, but there was uncertainty behind his words.

'You need something,' Aerand stated.

The sergeant nodded, and for the first time Aerand looked beyond the man's expression. Slowly, her mind trickled into the space surrounding her and reached a gentle probe towards the sergeant.

She recoiled.

There was some happiness there, but also fear, and anger directed at her. Even though Corwyn made an effort to bury them, the presence of those emotions in her oldest friend wounded her far more deeply than even Major Restripa's blatant enmity.

'We've got orders to roll back towards Providence as soon as what amounts to morning settles on this place. I know you know that. Vyse told me you delivered the orders yourself. Problem is, we've got two troopers missing from the count.'

As company sergeant, both security and desertion fell under Corwyn's personal purview. The sergeant she remembered faced both of those responsibilities with deadly severity, and a pair of soldiers missing always meant a lapse in one of the two. Or that somebody had merely miscounted.

'Already recounted,' the sergeant grumbled. He needed no gifts to read her mind. The two had practically been neurally linked for the year that she commanded Secundus Company. 'I've been out with Primus Platoon scouring half the quadrant since the moment Vyse heard the rumour they were gone. At this point I probably would have called it quits, if it wasn't for the trooper who claimed he just saw them.'

Aerand's ears perked at that, a sudden chill washing across her.

'Show me.'

Corporal Justine somehow looked even worse than he had when Aerand watched him leave Captain Vyse's chapel the night before. The young trooper sat on an empty lasgun power pack crate wrapped in a thin, damp, olive-grey blanket.

'I was sleeping,' he muttered, 'just like Captain Vyse ordered, when I heard something sloshing around in the water.'

'I know,' Corwyn replied. 'I told the lord psyker that much already, but I need you to tell us both what you saw.'

Justine shivered slightly. 'I-I'm not sure I can, sergeant.'

'That's okay,' Aerand replied, trying to sound reassuring. 'The mist was thick, and it was dark. But anything you were able to make out might help.'

The corporal stared straight back at her. 'No, lord psyker. That wasn't the problem. I saw them both clearly enough. I'm just worried that if I say it aloud, both of you are going to think I've gone mad.'

Aerand frowned. The trooper she'd marched with the day before had been shy and deferential, but he was no coward. She struggled to imagine what had shaken him so badly.

'Emperor's bones, soldier,' Corwyn muttered. 'I'm going to think you've gone mad either way, if you keep sitting there jabbering on about nothing.'

Justine reached into his pocket and pulled out a small flask. He took a swig of something dark that Aerand could smell even a yard away. The fact that he'd swallowed hard liquor while on duty in direct view of his company sergeant was even more a testament to the frayed state of his nerves than the gentle shaking in his hands.

'Aye. I suppose you are, sergeant.' He looked nervously in Aerand's direction. 'Just promise me she isn't going to touch my mind again. I don't want her to break me any further.'

Corwyn eyed Aerand strangely and after a brief moment of doubt, she scoffed.

'Anything you saw overnight had nothing to do with me, corporal, and if it truly frightened you so much, I'm the best one to tell it to.'

'Macharius' tears,' Corwyn growled. 'Get on with it, boy, or I can just assume you helped the pair of them desert. Maybe I'll assign you to be the lord psyker's aide permanently as punishment.'

A dismayed look stole across Justine's face, and the boy took another swig of alcohol. 'No, sergeant. Wasn't like that. I don't think they deserted.'

'Go on,' Aerand mumbled, a familiar tingling down her spine. She put just enough will into the words that Justine's shaking hands stopped their trembling and his tongue loosened.

'I was sleeping,' he muttered, slowly at first. Like a scolded child about to admit to wrongdoing. 'When I heard something moving. So I grabbed my lasgun and looked to see what it was. Only the mist was too thick. I could hardly see the walls of the shack beside me, so I pulled on my cloak and crept out onto this little spur.'

The trooper motioned to a narrow strip of land jutting out towards the water beside him. A low stone wall followed the raised strip of earth, its base half-submerged in the brackish sea.

'Hadn't made it halfway down to the water, when I caught a glimpse of Gordard and Blythe on the other side of the wall. They were whispering something to each other, but I couldn't quite make it out. They were huddled close together funny, and I didn't know why, but I had the feeling I didn't want either one to notice me. So I got on my hands and knees and crawled along the wall, till I was near enough that I should have been able to hear them speaking.'

'And?' Corwyn asked, fidgeting impatiently with his lasgun.

'Wasn't what I heard,' Justine muttered, taking another longing look at his flask. 'Was what I saw. They must have walked no more than three feet away from me, but it was like neither of them could even see me crouching there. They was turned the other way at first, so I didn't realise.'

'Didn't realise what?'

'Didn't realise that they were already dead.'

'Tranch's nameless saint, Justine,' Corwyn cursed with a sigh. 'I didn't think you were such a coward to believe in ghost stories and nurse's tales for misbehaving children. If you tell me you watched them wander off as a pair of mist corpses to go swim in the sea or whatever those boogeymen are supposed to do, I swear I'll add you to their number.'

Justine looked down. 'I told you that you'd think I was mad, sergeant. But I promise, I've got no reason to spin you a tale.'

Corwyn sighed and ran a calloused hand through his hair. 'Sorry,' he mumbled to Aerand. 'I thought we might actually have something here. I was hoping you could maybe get the poor lad to remember.'

'Corporal Justine,' Aerand asked, surveying the boy. There wasn't a scrap of dishonesty radiating from him. Whatever the boy was spouting, he believed it in earnest. 'Tell me exactly what you saw. Tell me what made you think Gordard and Blythe were dead.'

The boy shuddered slightly, and for a moment she caught a whiff of something in the air around him. Aerand closed her eyes and noted a subtle change in the psychic signature of the young trooper. Not something new, entirely, and certainly not possession, but the residue of another presence lay atop him, as if his own aura had brushed against another and carried the shadow of that second presence along with it.

'Corporal Justine. Tell me,' Aerand repeated, throwing her will into the order.

The young trooper's face fell slack and his voice became monotone as he replied to the psychic compulsion. 'They looked wrong, ma'am. Almost like the both of them had been drowned. There was muck and dirt all over their uniforms, and they looked like they'd been covered in roots. And...' the boy stuttered.

Aerand gave him a little nudge.

'And there was something wrong with their eyes. They were empty. Like little pools of dark water. Like they couldn't even see me. They walked straight past and right off into the mist.'

No sooner had the young corporal finished talking, than he began to shake slightly and clamped his jaw shut. Aerand withdrew her will from the boy, and he wrapped the blanket tighter around himself, staring up at her with abject fear.

'Drusus save me,' Corwyn scoffed, turning from the soldier. 'Childish nightmare tales and cook-fire stories running amok in my company.'

'Maybe,' Aerand replied. Leaving the shaken corporal behind, she walked to the low stone wall where the young trooper claimed to have seen the apparitions.

'Come, now,' Corwyn muttered, trailing in her wake. 'You don't believe that trooper witnessed a pair of ghosts.'

'No,' Aerand replied. 'Most probably not. Although such things are not entirely impossible.'

Corwyn scoffed. 'Nor is it entirely impossible for a simple company sergeant to be made into Lord Militant Solar, but you don't see me holding my breath for the promotion.'

In fact, after the diatribe, the man's face did look a bit rosy, as if in his frustration, he was doing precisely that.

'No, sergeant. I agree. If there were a witch on this world powerful enough to turn the very dead against us, we'd have been overrun already.'

She walked along the low stone wall, a thick, dark moss covering the ancient-laid blocks like fur. Slowly, she reached a hand out and ran it across that damp, salty surface, an image of a corpsewood tree coming unbidden to her mind.

'The vegetation here on this world, Sergeant Corwyn. Do the locals have any similar legends about it?'

Corwyn frowned, confused. 'I'm certain they do. Seems the Visagers have a tale or a monster for everything they encounter, but I haven't made it a habit to listen to such nonsense.'

'Like marsh corpses?' she asked. 'Or the ghost regiment?'

Corwyn frowned. 'Sure. Except that last one is easy enough to explain.'

'Oh, is it?' Aerand scoffed. 'Some natural phenomenon that simply whisked an entire regiment off into the dark?'

'You could call it that,' Corwyn muttered. 'But it wasn't an act of nature. It was a man. Who in the Emperor's name do you think we've been stuck out here fighting?'

'They call him the Witchbringer,' Corwyn spat. 'Or they call themselves that, collectively maybe. It's hard to tell from the limited vox traffic we capture, but it's a pissing arrogant name for a pissing arrogant heretic, if you ask me.'

The sergeant traipsed through knee-deep water behind her, pure disgust written across his face. In her hands, Aerand cradled a weathered lasgun, her suspicions growing stronger with each step. She'd found the weapon abandoned in the thick, loamy mud just at the base of the ancient stone wall where Corporal Justine had last seen Sergeant Gordard and Blythe.

She was no Adeptus Arbites intelligencer, but the deserters she'd encountered in the past didn't leave their weapons behind. Neither did soldiers heading out on patrol. As innocent explanations for the soldiers' disappearance vanished, a cold suspicion grew ever stronger in her chest.

'Traitor Guard, then?' she replied. She'd guessed as much from the weapons and armour of the small warband she and Justine dispatched the day before, but on a planet at war as long as this one, it would have been easy enough for elements with no Imperial affiliation to get their hands on surplus wargear, regardless.

'Aye. A full regiment of them deserted, almost to the man. The official reports are hopelessly sparse, but Major Restripa found some logs from a sergeant that took over with the next task force. Four hundred soldiers just upped and left their posts around Providence in the middle of the night, all under the direction of their Throne-cursed traitor commander. Seems there was only a squad or two who didn't join in the mutiny, and that must have been more a matter of convenience than anything else, because they disappeared soon after to join the remainder. All to link up with the smattering of native warbands and local cultist marsh priests that they'd been fighting only a few days before.'

'Impressive,' Aerand replied, then noted the curious look on Corwyn's face. 'Not the act of desertion, but the ability of the officer to bring his entire regiment along in it. You or Vyse would have put a bolt through my head had I ever commanded such a thing when I was your captain.'

Corwyn stiffened. 'We would have. And I can't speak for Primus or Tertius companies, but any soldier in Secundus would have done the same. As they still would today if Major Restripa tried to give that order.'

Aerand chuckled at mention of the major. 'I would be surprised if every soldier in the regiment didn't already have a dozen reasons to sink a las-bolt in Restripa's thick skull.'

Corwyn stopped.

Aerand slowed at the sudden absence of his splashing and turned to face him.

'And what exactly do you mean by that?'

'Come now, Sergeant Corwyn,' Aerand replied slowly, surprised by the sudden wave of indignation that washed off the old sergeant. 'You remember the major when he was only a corporal. I've spent barely ten minutes with him since returning, and that was nine minutes more than I needed to tell he's still an arrogant twit.'

Corwyn grunted. 'Find me an officer who isn't.'

Aerand brushed off the jab and continued, pulling her focus back to the weapon in her hands. She drew her mind away from Corwyn and back into the lasgun, feeling a gentle, familiar tug as she attempted to dowse the weapon's owner. Like a thin current in shallow water, she felt the psychic connection between the weapon and the man who had carried it tugging gently on the fabric of the empyrean.

The two troopers could not have ventured more than a few miles since Corporal Justine claimed to have seen them, and she should have sensed their presence like a lightning strike with an object one of them had owned grasped firmly in her hands. She brushed the thought away and kept walking.

'Still,' she continued, 'the corporal I remember was so tied up in knots over which regulation to follow that he could scarcely put his uniform on each morning. Forgive me if I find it hard to imagine what he could have possibly done to earn such a meteoric rise.'

'Five years is a long time.'

Those words hung in the air between them. It seemed more than just personnel had changed.

'Witchbringer,' Aerand said, changing the subject to something only marginally less uncomfortable. 'That's quite the epithet our adversary has chosen. Has he shown psychic abilities of his own when you've faced him, then?'

Corwyn shrugged. 'No idea. We've been killing his soldiers for six months and none of us can recall ever meeting him on the battlefield, but our intelligence suggests the title has more to do with his goals than his person.

'A few weeks after his regiment disappeared into the mist, psykers started going missing in the fringe settlements. People were used to children being taken by the governor, witches rounded up and disappeared. The tithe was always met. Only these psykers never showed up in the logs. They simply weren't heard of ever again. It took us all of a week here to realise where they were going. The first warband we encountered was almost evenly matched Traitor Guardsmen and native psykers both.'

'Throne,' Aerand muttered. 'I've seen those ledgers. You're saying this Witchbringer has been capturing young psykers from settlements across Visage and massing them for the better part of a decade?'

Corwyn nodded. 'Not capturing, liberating, if you hear his soldiers say it. And not just psykers any more. Almost a thousand people lived in Charity twelve months ago, and now it's nothing more than a ghost town.'

'Emperor save us,' Aerand mumbled, doubting herself for a moment. 'What did Lord Kellipso think of all of this?'

She'd hardly comprehended the mess Restripa had been dropped into. It was one thing to fight a war of insurgency against seditious elements on a backwater planet, but facing well-trained, well-equipped opposition with the moral support of the world's populace was another matter entirely. Add to that Visage's brutal geography and a clime that clearly favoured those with intimate, local knowledge.

Restripa was a pompous, hard-headed officer for certain, but he'd been handed a nigh-impossible task.

Before the sergeant could answer, Aerand felt the lasgun in her hand quiver. *Close*, she signalled Corwyn in battle sign, suddenly hesitant to speak. Even though it seemed unlikely Gordard and Blythe had deserted, she still preferred they remained unadvised of her approach.

Slinging the lasgun over her shoulder, she drew her laspistols and saw recognition flash in Corwyn's eyes. Aye, she had changed, and five years was a long time, but she'd managed to keep at least these two pieces of her old life. Sergeant Olevier Corwyn had stood beside her when General Yarin, only a colonel at the time, had gifted her the two Mars-pattern Mark IV command pistols the day she was frocked into her first company command.

She'd been only a lieutenant at the time, serving above her rank due to the horrible losses the 900th had suffered in the first days of a bitter campaign on the mountain world of Ourea, and she had cherished the mementos every moment since. How the two weapons had survived her first journey on the Black Ships – or her five years at the scholastica psykana itself – was still a mystery to her, but when Lord Prefector Ule handed them back to her as she departed those halls on her way to Visage, she instantly knew she had Jarrah Kellipso to thank. Just another debt she owed the fabled primaris psyker. One she hoped he might be alive to repay.

Aerand swung around the thick, dark tangle of corpsewood branches, ready to fire, then stopped. With a sigh, she slowly holstered her pistols. Just below her, propped slightly out of the water, lay the corpses of two Imperial Guard troopers. She recognised one as the sergeant sleeping at his watchpost when she'd entered Secundus Company's camp the night before.

'Gordard? Blythe? I presume,' she muttered.

Corwyn stepped past her and gave both men a small nudge.

'They're dead. I assure you,' Aerand said, casting her mind gently into the immaterium. Not another soul moved within half a mile of their position.

'Macharius' tears,' Corwyn spat, looking down at the men. 'I would have never pegged either of them for deserters.'

'No,' replied Aerand. 'Lazy perhaps, but not disloyal.'

Slowly, she unslung the lasgun from her shoulder and crouched down in the water beside the first corpse.

Nothing. She moved along to the second. As she brought the weapon up against the man's chest, she felt a telltale trickle of psychic energy between them. 'Blythe's then,' she muttered.

'I could have told you that,' Corwyn replied. 'The lazy slouch hadn't cleaned the thing in nearly a week.'

Aerand grunted a reply. The sergeant's ballistic cleanliness was hardly among her concerns. Carefully, she reached out towards the corpse and set the weapon in his hands.

'Cool skin, but still warmer than the water around him. He hasn't been dead for more than a few hours.'

'Come now, lord psyker,' Corwyn sighed. 'This isn't an Arbites investigation. I think we know what happened here.'

'We do?' Aerand replied. 'Because I don't see a single wound on either body, and I haven't met many troopers who would willingly drown themselves in this mire.'

Corwyn grunted, disbelieving, stepping up to survey Sergeant Gordard's corpse. 'Maybe they fought. Maybe one of them drowned the other then got trapped in the branches, or tripped and couldn't get up.'

It was Aerand's turn to look incredulous.

'I may not be an investigator, Sergeant Corwyn, but five years is a long time, and I've managed to acquire a few useful skills.'

Slowly, she knelt beside Blythe's cool corpse. She had the man, freshly dead, and the weapon he'd left behind. She'd carried his lasgun for the last hour, and had met him the previous night. Hopefully that would be connection enough.

'Tell me, Sergeant Corwyn. What do you know about the subtle art of psychometry?'

Corwyn grunted, shaken, and took a step backwards as Aerand set her fingers gently against Blythe's bloated face. A thin veneer of frost spread out from them across the man's dark skin.

'Corporal Justine's fears are misplaced, I assure you. There is no danger of these corpses rising ever again. But there are other ways, sergeant, for the dead to speak to those of us who know how to listen.'

'Psychic compulsion,' Aerand repeated slowly. 'As certain as I am of my very own name.'

Captain Vyse looked at her with a hint of frustration.

'I thought you would be relieved, captain, to know that two of your senior sergeants didn't desert in the night.'

'Blood of the saints,' the captain cursed. Behind her, a dozen troopers waded through the waist-deep, acrid ocean, a pair of Sentinel walkers ranging at either flank, the bipedal vehicles squelching awkwardly through the muddy water with every step.

'Of course I would prefer that they had deserted. Soldiers desert from every other regiment on every Throne-cursed planet in this sector each day. I'm fortunate enough to command Cadians, not cowards, but I could handle that problem if it ever arose.' She motioned to Sergeant Corwyn, who walked beside them. 'I know how to deal with deserters, lord psyker, and I know how to make examples so the rest of my troopers don't follow. But mind tricks and trances? What am I supposed to do about that?'

'Why would they do this?' Corwyn replied. 'Seems an awful lot of effort to kill two troopers that could have been just as easily shot.'

'Maybe,' Aerand replied. 'Maybe they have psykers to spare. Sergeant Corwyn mentioned their particularly unbalanced composition.'

'That's not it,' Corwyn replied. 'The Witchbringer might be a heretic, but nothing he's done so far makes me think he's a fool. If he had too many sorcerers, he'd find better ways to use them.'

A reasonable conclusion. Wise commanders didn't expend resources simply because they possessed them. An image of Corporal Justine shaking returned to her, and as she cast her mind out just far enough to trace the emotions of the soldiers around her, an answer became abundantly clear.

'Fear,' she replied. 'They did it to stoke fear. To make poor young troopers like Justine start believing the stories they've heard about mist corpses and whatever else.'

'Aye,' Vyse replied. 'Except this is worse.'

'I don't follow.'

'This is worse, because this is real. Not a word of this to anyone,' Vyse ordered. 'Ghosts and goblins are one thing, but enemy psykers luring troopers off to their deaths is a problem I'm not ready to confront. This conversation doesn't go beyond we three.'

Aerand agreed, but it might be wise to have some of the platoon leaders and other officers aware of the threat as well. She nearly voiced the thought before a muffled explosion echoed through the mist.

Vyse threw up her hand and the column paused. A moment later another explosion sounded closer. Static crackled on both Vyse and Corwyn's miniature pack-voxes, the only communication equipment functioning with any reliability in the constricting environ.

'Well, Celestine's bloody blade,' Corwyn cursed. 'If those weren't Accatran mortars, then I'm a pissing Whiteshield.'

Vyse bent her ear to make the most that she could out of the garbled speech emerging from her vox. 'Hostile Baneblade,' she muttered, a look of recognition in her violet eyes. 'Get us ready for them, sergeant. Lord psyker, you're with me.'

Vyse took off as fast as the murky water allowed, her tall, thin frame moving with surprising efficiency even through the mire. Aerand did her best to match the athletic pace, Corwyn already barking orders behind them. Around them, the column increased its pace and began a gradual, mobile transformation from a drawn-out column to a compact fighting circle.

'They're going to be fodder for a Baneblade when they're massed like that,' Aerand remarked, half out of breath.

'It's not the Baneblade I'm worried about,' Vyse replied. 'It's the nightmares that'll come through the hole it punches in our line.'

As they pressed into the tide of half a company of oncoming soldiers, they crested a small rise of damp land. As Aerand looked behind her, most of the figures rushing past were already disappearing into the mist, which somehow grew even thicker with each passing breath.

'You've seen this before?'

Vyse laughed. 'Only every time more than a squad or platoon tries to move more than a few miles from the group. Why do you think I didn't want to travel during the night? I thought we might make it a hair closer to Providence, or that Lieutenant Kobald's Sentinels might give us a few more minutes' warning before they found us, but–'

Another explosion, closer this time, followed by a horrible, grinding screech of metal bending and tearing.

'Seems like Kobald's Sentinels were the ones who needed the warning.'

Aerand grimaced, throwing her mind into the mist. Faint flames flickered in the cloying white cloud that somehow permeated even this space in her mind. 'Psykers,' she muttered, and Vyse merely nodded.

'Psykers, and lasguns, and Emperor knows what else. We've only had reports of one functioning Baneblade on this world, and if the Witchbringer's here, then he'll have all his toys with him. They're going to harry us all the way back to Providence.'

'Providence? I thought Major Restripa's orders were to establish a hold point a few miles out.'

'They were. We'll fight every step of the way back, but if Restripa thinks I'm going to try to dig in while a mega battle cannon devours the better part of this company – without so much as a functioning vox-caster in miles – then he's lost his saints-blessed mind.'

Marching back to Providence wasn't a foolish choice, but it was a journey Aerand didn't relish. The march from the capital had been brutal enough without enemy elements harrying her and Justine the whole way. And if the traitors were mounted, then there was no telling what kind of bloodbath the 900th would be trailing as it moved.

'And us?' Aerand replied. 'What are we doing?'

A foolhardy grin spread slowly across Vyse's face, as she loosened the twin bolt pistols strapped to her chest. She called out to a group of passing troopers, who quickly rushed to join them atop the small rise.

'We,' Vyse replied, 'are going to slow them down.'

Hundreds of souls swam in the murky half-light – as best as Aerand was able to sense – partly hidden by the physical and psychic shroud that covered Visage in thick, damp white sheets.

'A comparable element,' Sergeant Maltia remarked, toying idly with the charging handle of her weapon. 'Don't see why we're running when we could just wheel on them.'

Vyse glared at the sergeant, a stout, hard-faced woman who toted a stripped-down autocannon in her burly arms, and Aerand was reminded of the younger woman's grit. A corporal's chevrons had marked her uniform the last time Aerand had seen her on the mountain world of Ourea, but the promotion had done nothing to stifle her daring. A true Cadian. A true fighter. And one Aerand was glad to stand beside.

There were just under a hundred troopers in Secundus Company, and at least three times that number waited out in the mist.

'A comparable element in name only,' Captain Vyse replied coolly. 'And while I'm confident your heavy squads could outgun these heretics all the way to Holy Terra, you and I both know how little use your autocannons are when you can't see further than the hands in front of your face.'

Maltia chuckled. 'Speak for yourself, captain. But it'd be a pissing-fun bloodbath either way.'

It would be a bloodbath, that was certainly true. As Aerand probed the approaching contingent, she noted the relative strength of the inbound psychic auras and paled.

'How many psykers are you expecting in an element like this?'

Vyse shrugged. 'Wouldn't know. Haven't seen more than a platoon at a time since we pulled back as a full regiment from Resilience, and on that trip, we didn't exactly stick around to count. But that warband you and Justine faced last night was probably representative.'

One psyker per dozen then. At least a score in this group. And if Aerand's count now was correct, likely closer to twice that number. She shuddered inwardly. Forty psykers, even untrained, massed within combat troops would be almost completely shielded from physical attacks by simple concealment alone. There was little telling what kind of damage they could unleash. Slowly, she pulled her mind back as a small cluster of signatures drew closer.

Five hulking silhouettes stormed forward through the mist, then settled just a few yards from the pair of heavy squads gathered beside them. With a metallic groan, the squadron of Sentinels settled, their dark steel legs dripping with mud and brine.

'Hussar and Vast are dead,' a familiar voice boomed from the lead vehicle's indwelling vox-amplifier.

Vyse crossed herself briefly and bowed her head. 'Bodies?'

'What do you think?' Lieutenant Kobald replied. 'Without gyrostabilisers running, the mud and water swallowed both vehicles faster than you could blink. Besides, we weren't exactly sticking around for a kind discussion with the Baneblade.'

Through a faceplate of armaglass, coated with minuscule droplets of water and a thin frosting of fog, Aerand saw Lieutenant Kobald shift uneasily in his command cradle. Behind the bombast, her old comrade appeared shaken. No officer liked losing soldiers. They liked leaving those fallen soldiers behind even less.

Aerand surveyed the motley crew arranged around her. A dozen heavy troopers in dripping, muddied flak hoisting modified autocannons and krak launchers on their shoulders huddled in the shadow of five heavy Sentinels. The vehicles, although rusted by the planet's damp and salty environment, appeared in good repair and sported an assortment of fearsome armaments.

'You wanted their vanguard slowed, captain,' Aerand said, a stratagem forming in her mind.

'I would prefer them dead. What are you thinking, adept?'

'I'm thinking they won't be expecting us.'

To cast a passable glamour was not a simple task. As an acolyte at the scholastica, she had hated the exercise. Simply obscuring an object was no intricate thing, but the art of the discipline lay in achieving true concealment.

As Aerand strode forward through the water, she brought her fingers together in an intricate weaving pattern. A common misconception among the ungifted was that psykers performed their supernatural acts with their hands. That was nonsense, of course. Accessing the immaterium did not require physical direction, or even physical existence, but the corporeal bodies of psykers themselves did.

As she brought her thin fingers together, then apart, then together again, she felt her mind slow and focus with the simplicity of the physical ritual.

Under normal circumstances, what she was attempting would have been madness. She'd seen her mentor, Jarrah Kellipso, once cast a glamour upon an entire coven of cultists that had been convincing enough to allow a hundred Cadian soldiers to walk unmolested through the front gate of an enemy stronghold. But Jarrah Kellipso had been a masterful telepath, and she herself could never hope to accomplish such a feat.

Thank the Emperor, there were simpler ways to accomplish the same task.

The air swirled around Aerand in a thick, billowing cloud, streaming out behind her to enclose Vyse and her two squads of heavies in a growing blanket that settled over the entire area. Somewhere in that gathering fog, five massive figures splashed through the water, Kobald's Sentinels relying on their vehicles' auspexes to guide their movement.

There was more than one way to hide an object, and while sending tendrils into the minds of hundreds of enemy soldiers to convince them that the light reaching their eyes deceived them was a daunting task for even a master telepath, simply gathering a thicker cloud of mist over this area from the blanket of fog which already covered the water like a bastion wall was a relatively easy telekinetic exercise. Hiding her companions' souls, however, was another matter entirely.

As Aerand breathed, the murky, damp world before her wavered, the familiar empty surface of the warp stretching out before her like a pane of glass. From this distance, the empyrean appeared still. No waves or currents to be seen on that roiling plane. She still remembered how it felt to be tossed by those swells – to feel the swirling call of things ancient and dark and hungry – but at this distance, those memories felt oddly dull. Just as cloud coated the surface of Visage's physical face, so a thin veil hung over this section of the immaterium.

Three hundred flames burned ahead in the water, matched by Secundus Company falling away behind her, and desperately Aerand dampened those flames. As she tugged at that strange, inexplicable veil, she felt a chill along the edges of her mind. There was something indescribably wrong in the sensation of the strange immaterial substance that covered Visage. Something both psychically dead, yet active all at once. Carefully, Aerand attempted to shape the material, just as she had the physical mist, but with each attempt it seemed to slip further from her grasp.

Aerand cursed. She knew of only one other way to reliably conceal her companions from the warband's psykers ahead.

With half-blinded eyes, she drew her staff from the thin leather loop across her back and planted its tapered base into the muddy earth between her feet. Mist beaded off the golden aquila before her, glittering like tears in Visage's eternal twilight. Slowly, Aerand knelt in the briny water, and whispered a wordless prayer.

With a deep breath, she released her grasp on Visage's psychic veil, and drew her attention instead to that structure's antithesis.

She had sought the Astronomican's presence only briefly since arriving on the world of Visage, and now, as she searched she realised for the first time how horribly dim even that beacon burned here. Slowly, a faint music rose in the back of her mind. A familiar, pained symphony that filled her with warmth. Throne, that music was terribly quiet at first, as if the veil around Visage could obscure even the God-Emperor's presence, but as she listened the melody swelled. Around her, a dim flicker began to grow, and she watched her own flame flare with a warm, golden light.

Sometimes, the best way to hide a candle was to place it directly beside an inferno.

Sergeant Raniais Maltia had only seen one true witch before she set foot upon the planet of Visage. That sorcerer, wreathed in blazing blue flame and striking down soldiers with hardly a thought, had ultimately been killed by the woman now standing beside her. A woman who now appeared remarkably similar to the sorcerer she had dispatched years ago.

That irony wasn't lost on Maltia, although she would find another time to appreciate it. Perhaps over a flask of something bitter and strong when Captain Vyse and Sergeant Corwyn weren't looking. She stared at the primaris psyker walking beside her and muttered prayers at a pace she was certain she had not matched since she was a young girl attending Sanguinala services.

She'd met Captain Aerand as a fresh transplant to Secundus Company. She'd come to respect the woman's strange instincts before they had eventually evolved into something more, but to see the officer who had once commanded her company walking beside her in the throes of psyker magicks was enough to startle even a veteran.

Maltia shook off the chill that had settled onto her and spat into the water at her waist. Aye, something bitter and strong. Maybe a Gresian rye.

'Tighten up that spacing, Ebonwelter,' she muttered at the pair of troopers walking beside her.

'Which of us?' one of the twins responded. Impossible to tell in this Throne-cursed mist.

'Don't care,' she mumbled absent-mindedly. 'Both.'

She had hoped speaking might clear the burnt taste from her tongue, but if anything, it only made the sensation worse. The billows of cloud surrounding the two troopers behind her edged slightly closer together. Still wider intervals than she'd like, but good enough.

'Captain,' she asked, the vox-piece in her helmet crackling. 'You're certain this is a good idea?'

There was a brief burst of vox static. It held for a few seconds, in silence. *'No.'*

Honest, at least. She appreciated that about Captain Vyse. When Vyse had been a lieutenant, Maltia hadn't much loved the woman. She seemed too hard, too distant for that more intimate role. But as a captain... Well, perhaps she just seemed better in comparison to the string of nightmares that had arrived after Captain Aerand left.

And now... a strange sensation washed over her as the robed woman in front of her slowed, then stopped. It was hard to square that thin, sickly profile twitching like some invalid and mumbling to herself, with the commanding officer that had left the 900th on Ourea. She hadn't known Aerand well as an officer, but she'd been a good soldier, that much was obvious. And now she was... What? A monster. An unholy abomination.

As the psyker lord slowed, a small billow of mist approached from behind her.

'Advance,' came Vyse's tense command, when the woman was only a few yards away. Even at this distance, the captain's face was little more than a flicker beneath the swirling beads of mist.

Maltia nodded and started moving to the right. The plan sounded strange enough, given the psychic intervention, but at its heart it was straight from the Imperial Infantryman's Handbook. Every Cadian child old enough to play a game of regicide knew that this was the oldest, and surest, stratagem in the book.

As her squad of heavies pushed out beside her without command, a bit of pride swelled in Maltia. Evrik and Tannius Ebonwelter might be insufferable loudmouths, and Trooper Bantholo could scarcely put a sentence together, but the men slung autocannon rounds like no others she had met, as whatever approached through that mist was about to find out. Unseen, a few hundred yards away, Sergeant Insley's squad of heavies pulled up into a matching line, ready to soak the Witchbringer's forces in enfilading fire.

Maltia knelt behind a dark tangle of branches and rested the barrel of her autocannon on the gnarled, split branch of a corpsewood tree. An uncreative name for such unimpressive vegetation, and she had never understood the disquiet most other troopers displayed at proximity to the trees.

Vyse tapped her on the pauldron twice as she passed.

Fire on the captain's lead.

'Fair enough,' Maltia whispered to herself.

In the centre of the clearing, the once-captain Glavia Aerand knelt slowly in the water, and the air around her began to spark with gold.

Maltia made the sign of the aquila, mumbling a final prayer as the first shadows emerged from the fog.

Aerand foresaw the wall of blistering gunfire emerge from the fog long before it actually came. The expected mess of scattered, ineffective las-beams massed with bolters and stubbers. A bright burst of melta shot scoured through the mist, evaporating the water, then was gone.

Normally, a single soldier would scarcely merit such a show of power, but these were the drawbacks of putting yourself on display. Had she, as a commander, seen a single psyker kneeling before her approaching army, blazing with the light of the Astronomican itself, she would have thrown every weapon she had at them, too.

As hundreds of projectiles sped towards her undefended form, she braced herself for the inevitable wave of psychic assaults which would follow on the heels of the physical one.

She was stretching herself dangerously thin, and that left her horribly vulnerable. The illusions around the waiting Cadian ambush as well as the energy it would require to shield herself from the oncoming barrage were a more intense exertion than she had ever attempted at once. She would have precious little ability to fend off whatever blows the Witchbringer's own psykers might throw at her afterwards, yet with the pulsing, agonising fire of the Astronomican blinding her to anything else, she felt utterly prepared for them both.

With an idle gesture, she raised one hand from her staff, focusing on a small point of space only inches before its aquila. Most of the gunfire streaming towards her would miss on its own; this was the ugly reality of long-range warfare. Her only job was to detect those shots that were true. In the span of a heartbeat hundreds of projectiles rushed past her, and she threw her mind into that single point of air.

A sudden light blazed in the mist before her, pure and golden and utterly painful to behold, as she directed all of her will into a space smaller than the size of her fist. A dozen bolts vanished into that point and emerged with barely altered trajectories. Two slugs from a heavy bolter detonated directly at the site of the psionic fulcrum, shrapnel spraying in gouts around her staff like waves crashing against a stone and speeding harmlessly around her. On their heels the white-hot blaze of a meltagun beam collided with that burning point of psychic fire. For a moment, the two flames seemed to add to one another, before dissipating into gouts of white-hot plasma, splattering in a fan into the air.

Water steamed around Aerand as she deflected the attack, the sudden warmth on her skin almost unbearable. A clever trick, a psionic fulcrum, but one not easily maintained. Her hand quivered, then fell, as she opened her eyes.

The ball of light before her collapsed, leaving the clearing oddly dim. In that sudden shade, the steam around her dissipated, revealing a harrowing line of dark silhouettes facing her only a few dozen yards away. At their centre, a grey and rusting Baneblade destroyer turned its mega battle cannon directly towards her. Atop the vehicle, the pintle-mounted meltagun grafted onto its battered surface steamed in the cool air.

Aerand closed her eyes and whispered a silent prayer, the world greying in her vision as she neared the full extent of her energies. Then, from behind her, she heard the telltale crack of two bolt pistols as Vyse's contingent unleashed a blistering counter-attack.

'First Squad, fire. Second Squad, fire,' the captain's voice shouted.

A dozen autocannons, half as many krak missiles, and the combined armament of five heavy Sentinels poured into the massed enemy at a range almost close enough for a melee.

Aerand collapsed into the water, the illusion around her comrades dropping with her, unnecessary now that its goal had been accomplished. As her vision flickered, she watched Traitor Guard fall by the dozens, the withering fire of synched autocannons punching through aged flak armour as if it were paper.

'Close on the flanks!' Lieutenant Kobald shouted over a nearby vox, above the creaking sound of sprinting Sentinels. 'Kill that bloody Baneblade!'

Four krak missiles splashed against the Baneblade's hull, tossing a tread loose like a cut piece of ribbon. From Aerand's right, a pair of Sentinels crashed into the enemy line, massive footpads plunging several bodies beneath the murky water. Paired lascannons swept through the mire at their feet, eviscerating the squad of Traitor Guard grouped before them.

Aerand staggered as the warp fell nearly silent before her, lives blinking out with staggering speed. Then, almost as soon as the ambush had arrived, it ended.

Three platoons of Traitor Guardsmen, at least, had been decimated in a few seconds of concentrated Cadian fire. The empyrean screamed with that sudden loss of life. Catching her breath, Aerand pushed herself onto her feet and stepped towards the Baneblade. As she did, she felt her connection to the warp waver, then go out. She staggered.

Behind her, a dozen Cadians rushed forward, pouring through the deci-mated enemy line. A pair of Maltia's heavies popped onto the smoking Baneblade, emptying an autocannon into the top hatch until it groaned open.

'Nothing moving in here,' one called from atop the vehicle.

Catching her breath, Aerand stepped away from the cloying smoke and carnage, watching the immaterium suddenly take shape again in her mind.

Three platoons silenced, and not a single psyker among them, at least none that had put up a speck of a fight. Still, she braced herself for an impending psionic assault, as she ventured out with her exhausted senses, then recoiled. A few hundred yards away, the rest of the Witchbringer's host was approach-ing. At least two hundred troopers and three dozen psykers blazing through the warp along with them.

Vyse stepped up beside her, setting a hand on her shoulder and helping her to her unsteady feet. Aerand had never seen the woman shaken before, but she felt hesitancy in Vyse's touch, too tired to probe the emotion further.

'We need to leave. Now,' Aerand mumbled, her eyes swimming.

Vyse's strong arms grasped her as she dropped to her knees. 'I don't need a Throne-cursed psyker to tell me that.'

CHAPTER 7

She had stood less than a dozen yards from him.

She had stood less than a dozen yards from him, and now she was at least a mile away.

The Colonel shook as rough hands tore him from the smoking carcass of his Baneblade, coughing as he pulled a respirator from his face. It had taken two plasma cutters nearly half an hour to burn through the blistered, dented armoured panels that had pinned him in the pilot's throne. Gouts of oily smoke plumed from the dying vehicle behind him, as he pushed the sergeant away and stumbled to his feet, coughing.

'Gone,' he managed eventually.

The sergeant nodded. 'Two veteran companies are in pursuit as we speak.'

The Colonel cursed himself. Close enough that he could have put a bolt straight through her head, but the psyker was no use to him dead. 'We should have pushed her harder.'

The sergeant simply shrugged. Such things were often clear in hindsight.

But Throne, she had been glorious.

'She's the one, then?' the sergeant asked.

The Colonel managed a tired nod. He'd poured half a company and a Baneblade into her, and she'd simply brushed it all aside.

'As powerful as her predecessor, without half the experience.'

Veterans, no matter how strong or skilled, did not face down a Baneblade in the absence of cover.

'The marsh priests will be pleased that you've found their messiah,' the sergeant replied humourlessly.

'I'm sure they will.'

Aerand wiped a thin trickle of blood from her nose with a hand that would not stop shaking. A tremor wracked her body, pitching her forward, as the psionic bridle on her neck blunted yet another psychic attack. The branching cables rooted in the base of her skull grew suddenly hot, and she wondered, not for the first time, if the scent of burning flesh in her nose was merely an after-effect of the warp assaults being thrown at her like missiles, or true physical damage to her body from her augmetics being pushed past their mechanical limits.

Aerand stumbled once, then righted herself, flinging a feeble counter-attack back at the unseen assailant. She was no formidable telepath to begin with, and she hardly qualified as a psyker at all in her current state, but perhaps it would make the next marsh priest hesitate.

To say she was exhausted would be almost heretical in its understatement. To say she had reached, and then burst through, her psionic and physical limits felt more accurate, although that must not have strictly been true, for she still walked under her own power, if barely.

Beside her, Captain Vyse grunted, sloshing through dark water just over her waist. Even without the psychic burden Aerand carried, the quick march from Charity had been gruelling, but the captain showed no signs of physical fatigue. At her side, a squad of heavy troopers roamed with autocannons and lascannons trained on the rolling waves of mist behind Secundus Company. It had been nearly a mile since the last of the Witchbringer's forces had physically harried the retreating Imperial Guard, but now was not the time to take chances.

'I felt that one,' Vyse said, a grimace across her face. The unseen accusation behind her words was that Aerand should have done something more to stop the psychic intrusion.

'I imagine you did,' the psyker responded. 'And it might have been a hundred-fold worse.'

Aerand stumbled again as the ground rose beneath the water, looking up from her feet at the small patch of earth rising out of the murky ocean. The faintly dark hue of rockcrete marred the otherwise verdant patch of undergrowth.

'Thank the Emperor,' Corwyn muttered beside her, stepping up onto the disrepaired pathway. Gravel crunched beneath his sopping boots and his feet sank slightly in the muddy earth, which had already been churned by the hundred troopers who had passed before them. Not exactly a kasr parade ground, but a blessed relief after a dozen miles of unending sea.

Aerand allowed herself a sigh of relief. If they had already reached the outroads trickling towards Providence, that meant the capital city, and the relative protection of its sea wall, lay precious little distance away.

Perhaps they would make it, after all.

As she stared forward into the mist, searching for any sign of Javax Cathedral's dark silhouette, a searing lance of pain shot directly between her eyes. The taste of copper filled her mouth and her vision swam before she found herself on her knees in the mud. Her bridle warmed for a moment, then she felt the assault subside. It seemed their enemy realised that Secundus Company would soon become more challenging quarry and were playing their final cards.

Rough hands pulled Aerand back onto her feet, and Vyse looked at her with a hint of concern before stifling the emotion.

'How far away are they?' she asked, her voice like ice.

Aerand allowed herself a bitter chuckle in response, and spat blood into the dirt. She hardly had the energy to see the path beneath her feet, let alone the psionic signature of souls on the surface of the empyrean. If not for the tendrils of platinum embedded in her neural cortex and the psionic dampener in the cradle on her neck, she would be no more useful right now against the Witchbringer's psykers than any of the ungifted who walked beside her.

She had pushed herself hard in the initial counter-attack against the Witchbringer's forces, then spent every bit of will she had remaining drop by drop over the course of the last six hours. A handful of troopers lay dead in the murky waters behind them, but most of Secundus Company would have been drowned beside them if not for the unceasing vigil she had held, and both Vyse and Corwyn knew it.

A dozen minor sendings to throw false trails to their pursuers. Twice that many subtle telekinetic twists to clear corpsewood groves from their path or speed lagging troopers. And atop it all she had blunted more direct psychic assaults meant for the soldiers around her than she could keep count of, each one striking a bit harder and a bit deeper as her will began to flag.

'She comes with us the entire way,' Captain Vyse growled at a young trooper. 'I don't care if you have to carry her through the gates yourself.'

Obediently, the soldier grasped Aerand's arm and threw it over one of his shoulders. Even as exhausted as she was, his unease at her touch was practically bright enough to burn her. Aerand allowed herself something close to a smirk. That was the closest to thanks she could expect from the captain or any of the troopers around her.

'Thank you,' she allowed herself to say. Let the lad hate her if he must – let them all hate her as much as the heretics behind them – but they'd arrive in Providence alive thanks to her. And Sergeant Raniais Maltia.

A burst of las-fire echoed from the mist precious few yards away, and dark shadows flitted between the scattered twists of corpsewood groves. Vyse's vox-bead crackled and Sergeant Maltia's voice barked something Aerand was far too exhausted to decipher.

Emperor bless that trooper. Trailing the main body like the razor-sharp tail of a bovarc, Sergeant Maltia and her single squad of heavies had done nearly as much to save Secundus Company as Aerand herself.

And it showed.

Slowly, the sergeant slogged out of the mist, dirt and sweat plastering her short hair to her face beneath the shadow of her battered helmet. The dark char of a deflected las-bolt streaked across the armour just over the woman's left brow, and the chestplate of her flak armour was studded with half a dozen autopistol rounds. She limped slightly on her left leg, which oozed a thin trail of crimson into the dark water.

There were no soldiers in all the galaxy to match Cadian shock troopers, but it appeared their enemy were no amateurs at war, either.

'At least a company trails us,' Maltia barked, jogging double time to catch Captain Vyse. 'I don't have a clue how the hell they made up that distance after we knocked them back just an hour ago.'

Vyse grunted. 'Maybe they didn't. Maybe they have another dozen platoons pouring in from nearby. Maybe they have transports out there that we don't even know about. Our intelligence has always been precariously thin, and it's next to non-existent now that the whole regiment is holed up in Providence.'

The woman cursed and cycled her autogun absent-mindedly, then spat into the water, the iridescent shimmer of residue from a cheeked stimm-lozenge drifting out in a small ring.

'At this point I don't really care how many they have on our tail. Only one question that matters.'

'Will they beat us there?'

Vyse nodded.

A glimmer of pride blossomed in Aerand. Despite the chilly reception from Secundus Company, these had been her soldiers once, and they had grown into capable leaders in her absence. She was not arrogant enough to believe that evolution had anything to do with her, but it was good to be back in the company of tacticians.

'Take your squad and push east with Lieutenant Nalus,' Vyse said. 'Tell him to hit and fall back like we've been doing the whole way.'

It would have been one thing for the Witchbringer's forces to engulf them hours ago in the midst of Visage's wilds. The outcome of that assault would have been a complete decimation of Secundus Company, isolated and alone without reinforcements for miles. But the Cadians would have made the Traitor Guard and witches pay for every single trooper's life, and they knew it.

Better instead to pursue the Cadians doggedly for a dozen miles, then cut off the fleeing soldiers when they were exhausted and spent. If the Witchbringer's force flanking them was allowed to eclipse Secundus Company, they merely had to stall the main body long enough for the rest of the heretic army to descend upon them like a hammer.

'Yes, sir,' Maltia replied. 'We'll do it just like on Prost. Lieutenant Archibald Nalus and Sergeant Raniais Maltia. The heroes of Visage, I can see it now.'

The entire manoeuvre was a gamble on their enemy's part – move too slowly and the Witchbringer would lose his quarry altogether – but one that any self-respecting commander would gladly make. Heroism aside, when given the choice between a sure and bloody conflict or the possibility of a clean slaughter, the wise soldier always chose the latter. Heroic losses might win individual battles, but they almost inevitably lost long wars.

'Forget the jokes, Maltia. I don't need any martyrs. Tell Nalus I'd rather put his troopers' names in the supply log than the regimental honour roll. In fact, tell him that if he gets himself killed, I'll put him in for court martial rather than a posthumous medal. I think that should adequately convey my intent.'

'Will do, sir,' Sergeant Maltia replied with a smirk, then turned to limp back into the mist.

'On second thoughts,' Vyse called after her, 'that goes doubly true for you, sergeant. Get yourself killed and I'll sift through the corpses myself, just so I can put another through your skull for desertion.'

The captain turned towards Corwyn and sighed. 'I swear to the Emperor's boots themselves, that trooper is trying harder to get herself killed than the enemy is trying to kill her.'

Corwyn chuckled darkly and glanced towards Aerand. 'I seem to remember a pair of young lieutenants with a similar penchant for gallantry, sir.'

Vyse frowned at the implication, and Aerand nearly opened her mouth to protest, before an uneasy energy suddenly enveloped her.

If not for the young trooper supporting her, she might have fallen, a sudden weight in the air around her. Instantly, she threw up what paltry mental defences she retained, but found no psychic assault rising up against her. Even so, the skin on her arms rose in gooseflesh, each breath laced with the cloying flavour of burnt flesh. Rapidly, she pushed her mind out with what little psionic energy she retained. Far enough to glimpse the souls around her and the lead elements of Secundus Company moving forward through the mist.

She had not realised just how far they had fallen behind the remainder of the company, but where the Cadian vanguard should have already been nearing the outermost of Providence's sea walls, they had instead clustered along a narrow strip of land hardly more than half a mile away. Aerand pushed her mind farther, her grip on the psychic world blurring, but found no sign of any force blocking their path. No signatures of fire-bright souls lacing the dark, misty fabric of the immaterium.

But just beyond the cluster of Secundus Company, splitting the path between the Cadians and Providence itself, the dark surface of the warp was boiling. Aerand's grip on the empyrean flickered and then faltered before she could see whatever was trying to emerge from that churn.

'Move,' she gasped, leaning heavily on the trooper beside her. 'We need to move.'

In the distance, the first scream filtered back through the mist.

'Was a dead man's hand, or I'm the Arch-traitor himself,' the trooper remarked grimly. He wore a corporal's chevrons, though Aerand did not remember his face. 'You know me, sergeant. I don't spin tales.'

'I know, Pashta,' Corwyn mumbled, throwing an uneasy glance Captain Vyse's way.

The woman muttered a curse under her breath. 'You know that's nonsense, don't you?'

'I know, sir,' Pashta replied. 'But there isn't any other way to describe it. Trooper Inset stepped into the water, then an arm reached up and pulled him under, plain as that.'

'And you're certain it was a corpse's arm?'

Pashta shrugged. 'No, not at first. Not until another one did the same thing to Johanns. Caught part of the face of that one, desiccated and bloated. Looked like it had been under the water for the better part of the decade.'

Vyse simply grunted, but Aerand immediately thought back to the body she'd seen pinned beneath the roots of a corpsewood tree, oddly preserved by the acrid, alkaline water of Visage's sea. If she hadn't known better, she would have sworn that the strange, twisted plant had been feeding on some part of the corpse, like an arachnid on a captured insect.

'Stranger things, captain,' she mumbled slowly, her mind struggling to keep up with new facts in its exhausted state. For the witches behind them to have truly summoned corpses from the bottom of that sea would be an act of almost unthinkable psychic power. It would be easy enough, on the other hand, for a high-strung soldier to mistake the grasping tendrils of a corpsewood tree for a limb of one of the deceased pinned beneath it.

Aerand glanced up at the wall of white behind Corporal Pashta. If the troopers of the 900th had feared Visage's mists before, they now held a special flavour of dread. A wall of impenetrable white vapour had coalesced between the detached remnants of Secundus Company and the settlement of Providence, at least several hundred yards wide and Throne only knew how deep. Beyond the margin of its clearly demarcated border, her vision, both physical and psionic, failed completely.

Clearly, the mists had been summoned to delay Secundus Company's passage. The anvil against which the Witchbringer's forces would hammer them. But if the marsh priests in his retinue were truly powerful enough to reanimate the dead, then why go through such a roundabout ordeal? Throne knew Aerand could no longer put up any resistance. Why not simply shatter the minds within each trooper's skull?

'It's another illusion,' she said. 'It has to be. If they had the skill to raise corpses there would be no point in the effort. They could smite us directly with half the exertion, and I have nothing left within me to stop them.'

Vyse's face knotted at the admission, and Corporal Pashta shrugged. For his part, the trooper was handling the situation with remarkable composure. Perhaps the fact that at least a dozen other troopers had witnessed the event had saved him the second terror of thinking himself mad.

'Wouldn't know anything about that, lord psyker,' he replied. 'But I've put enough heretics in the ground to tell a corpse from the living.'

With a wave of her hand, Captain Vyse dismissed the corporal.

'An illusion,' Aerand repeated. 'I promise you that.'

'Corpse or not, two of my troopers were drowned. I'd prefer not to march the entire company into the same fate.'

As she spoke, Corwyn rose from a knee and stepped towards the seething wall of white vapour separating Secundus Company from Providence. A hundred soldiers and half a dozen Sentinels massed on a narrow strip of land just before the point where the mist thickened abruptly. The old sergeant stepped up to that border and reached his hand into the fog.

A brief look of anxiety crossed his weathered, scarred face, then one of almost surprised relief when nothing reached out of the mist to grasp him. He withdrew his arm, thick beads of dew coalescing and dripping from his gauntlet.

'It's wet,' he muttered matter-of-factly. A painfully obvious assertion, perhaps, but one that any soldier immediately realised was worth stating. Providence's walls lay less than a mile away, but it would be a miserable, cold slog through that mist, any other threats set to the side.

Aerand threw her weary mind against the barrier one final time, only to be unceremoniously pushed away. As she closed her eyes, a hundred souls blazed brightly on the fabric of the empyrean around her, the empty earth beyond them arrayed in muted, rough architecture. But past the wall of mist behind her, the world simply vanished, as if the space itself had been removed from the landscape of the empyrean, yet churned with the immaterium's energy all the same. She shivered at the odd, disconjugate sensation. As if the space were dead to the warp, yet bursting with its energy at the same time.

Looking in the other direction, however, provided no such obstacles.

'I'm not sure we have any other alternatives,' she said.

In the distance, the scattered staccato of las-fire sprinkled the evening, growing ever closer. Three squads of Lieutenant Nalus' heavies were leapfrogging back towards the company as they spoke, buying every precious second they could. Only a few hundred yards away, countless souls approached through the inky dark of the warp.

As Lieutenant Maltia limped into view, the Ebonwelter twins flanking her on each side, Captain Vyse surveyed the company hastily digging into the peninsula around her.

'What's the best way to survive an ambush?' she muttered.

The question needed no reply, because every Cadian within earshot already knew the answer.

You simply push straight through.

Beads of salty water clung to Aerand's skin like insects, coating her head to toe in a thin, briny film. Initially, she'd tried to wipe the rivulets from her face and keep the stinging liquid from her eyes, but she soon gave up the Sisyphean effort. Now, her eyes red and burning with salt, her mouth full of a constant trickle of alkali, she trudged forward into a cloud that seemed to be growing even thicker.

Beside her, Vyse cycled her autogun idly, as if afraid the weapon's action would rust shut after only a few minutes in these conditions. Before her, a young trooper marked a pace count and produced a compass.

'If we could just find the road again,' Corwyn muttered beside her. 'We couldn't have been more than a mile from the outer sea wall when we entered.'

Aerand shrugged, feeling helpless. Each platoon's own point trooper was repeating the same ritual only a few hundred yards away. Vyse had brought the whole company tight, at nearly non-existent intervals, the moment they stepped into this warp-spawned mist. A stratagem that would make them all a horribly easy target for any burst weapons if the Witchbringer drew within range, but that was a better outcome than becoming separated in the fog.

Each time she caught her breath enough to stand steady, Aerand threw her mind out into that impenetrable white, hoping to provide something more than the point trooper's compasses could, but she'd had no more success than the magnetic devices. At least the mist blocked the effects of the Witchbringer's psykers as well. She had not felt her bridle absorb a single attack since setting foot within this mire.

A few yards away, a cluster of shadows approached as Lieutenant Graves and his point trooper loped into view. A red flare burned atop the young conscript's pack, casting a flickering glow into the muted air.

'Hand me to an inquisitor, but I'll be a heretic if this compass is telling true,' Graves muttered grimly. The older officer was short and stout, and wore his uniform and rank with practised precision. Another new addition to the company since Aerand's departure.

A senior sergeant from a regiment they'd encountered on Prost, transplanted into the 900th when his mother regiment had been disbanded. There had been only two troopers left alive in the Cadian 490th when the 900th had absorbed them at the end of that brutal campaign. Vyse had offered them both platoons on the spot.

As if on cue, Graves' counterpart, Lieutenant Jilsau, arrived at his side and glanced down at the wayfinder in Graves' hand. The tall, lanky woman held her own rusted wayfinder next to his and then spat. The magnetic arrows on both devices pointed firmly ahead.

'Now I know that can't be right,' she mumbled. 'Because we've walked at least two miles in this direction already.'

Vyse sighed, and removed her helmet, running a gleaming hand through her short, buzzed hair. She looked to Sergeant Corwyn for suggestions.

'We keep going,' he replied. 'Not sure what else we can do. All our wayfinders, even the Sentinels' auspexes, say we're marching straight towards Providence. I can't say anything other than we should be there soon.'

'And if we already were?' Jilsau replied. 'What if we already walked past the whole city in this mist?'

Corwyn let out a grim chuckle, as if he had not even considered the idea. 'It's not that large a planet, lieutenant. If we've already marched past the capital city we just march a few thousand more miles, and we'll hit it on our second go around.'

'Aye,' Vyse nodded. 'Maybe with all of that walking, we'd find something on this world to make the miserable slog worth our time.'

At her words, Aerand started, recalling the vision that felt so distant to her now. Somewhere in these mists, something sinister waited, whether or not she wanted to admit it. As he turned to leave, Aerand watched the flare glimmer on the back of Graves' point trooper's pack.

'In the meantime,' Aerand remarked, gesturing to the trooper, 'it might not be a terrible idea to light the way.'

The first troopers disappeared only a few minutes later. By pace count, they'd put nearly three miles into the ground, trudging through brambles and uneven, marshy wetland. Vyse's orders had gone out by word of mouth, each trooper within eyesight of the trooper behind him, and now all the soldiers of Secundus Company carried lit flares strapped to the back of their kit, flickering like torchbugs in the cloying white. Even so, Aerand could see no more than a trio of figures moving beside her until a pair of flares burst through the mist.

'Halt the column, captain,' Sergeant Maltia panted. The woman's leg still oozed blood, and she looked winded for the first time in the day's running battle. Quickly, she fell into step beside Vyse, who increased her pace, if anything.

'Why?' she grumbled. 'So we can spend another eternity wandering inside this mist?'

'You know I don't like this any more than you do, sir. But I can't find one of my autocannon teams.'

'Corwyn,' Vyse grumbled. 'You have your sidearm handy? Go find Trooper Bantholo or whichever of Sergeant Maltia's block-skulls figured this was his chance to desert, and offer him your laspistol or mine. I've had enough with ghost stories and monster tales.'

Corwyn shifted uncomfortably and looked over to Maltia.

'It's the Ebonwelter twins,' she mumbled. 'You know as well as I do that they're hard-headed, but true. They're also not pale. There's not a chance they wandered off, or got lost.'

'I didn't hear any las-fire,' Vyse shot back. 'Or any returning autoweapon discharges. And I can hardly see further than the lashes in front of my own eyes, so don't try to tell me the Witchbringer is somehow picking us off without our notice.'

'No,' Maltia remarked. 'But something is.'

'Not you, too,' Corwyn mumbled.

The sergeant stared at him stone-eyed. 'First Justine, and then Pashta. The men have been seeing things, sir.'

'Aye,' Vyse replied coldly. 'Faces in the mist. Just like constellations, or cloud shapes, or any other dozen natural phenomena that human minds personify when they have nothing else to occupy them.' She looked towards Aerand. 'Have you sensed anything, lord psyker?'

'No,' she replied. Nor had she sensed anything when Justine or Pashta witnessed their apparitions. Yet, her sight was far from infallible, especially now. 'Although I'm not certain how much that means, under the circumstances.'

Vyse met her gaze questioningly.

'It's as if this mist is covering more than just the physical space around us.'

Before she could elaborate, another beacon materialised in the gloom.

'Sir,' Lieutenant Graves barked. 'I think you'll want to see this.'

If she didn't know better, Aerand would have thought the trooper had been crucified.

She'd seen the punishment delivered only twice in her life. Once, as a young girl, when a cell of death cultists had been uprooted by the local inquisition just outside Kasr Heveron, then once as a Whiteshield when a particularly zealous commissar had sought to make an example of a deserter. Both had been painful to watch – the languishing process from bleeding to death far longer than she would have ever anticipated.

And this appeared to be no exception.

Aerand stumbled into the small ring of troopers on the heels of Captain Vyse and Lieutenant Graves. Sergeant Henderson, one of Graves' squad leaders, ensured the wall closed again the moment they entered.

Good man. Better the rest of the company not see this quite yet.

At the centre of the ring, a single corpsewood tree sprouted from a patch of sodden ground, amid a small depression in which a pool of dark, murky water gathered. Even without its grisly trophy, the tree sent a familiar chill down Aerand's spine. It, like the mist around them, carried that same dual sensation of being both psychically active and inert at the same time.

As she traced the dark roots from the murky pool, however, she quickly spotted the object that had captured Graves' attention. Three twisting roots rose up from the mud and wound together to form a sinuous trunk. Several inches in the air, on the far side of the tree, a pair of boots hung.

'Saints' blood,' Corwyn muttered, circling the trunk. 'That's a bloody grim ritual, even for a world as backward as this one.'

Vyse nodded as she inspected the corpse. 'Looks like he's been here for some time.'

The trooper bound to the corpsewood tree was already ashen and bloated. Whether the mist or merely time had caused him to decay, his skin already bore the sickly grey tone of a living thing on the edge of decomposition. His dark hair hung slick over one of his eyes, and dirty water dripped down his face in mirrored streams. His head had been positioned angling backwards, so that rain gathered in a small pool in his open, slack mouth.

'You would think,' Graves replied.

Vyse looked on with confusion, until Graves bumped the corpse's arm with the muzzle of his lasgun, shifting it out of the way of the nameplate on his chest.

Monsk. One of Lieutenant Jilsau's newest recruits.

'Emperor save me,' Sergeant Corwyn muttered.

'I checked with Jilsau already, and she grilled his squad sergeant. Sounds like no one could confirm they had seen him in the better part of an hour.'

'How the hell did they manage to capture and then hang him without any of our troopers taking notice?'

Vyse cursed under her breath. 'You know what that means, don't you?'

'Aye,' Corwyn replied. 'Maybe not ghost stories after all.'

Vyse shrugged. 'Maybe not. Even worse, it means we've been marching in circles.'

At the revelation, a small shiver shifted down Aerand's neck, and for the first time since entering the mist, her bridle emitted the faintest warmth.

Subtle. So subtle. Almost too insignificant for her to notice if not for the cool mist coating the rest of her skin.

Aerand froze, and took another step towards the tree.

If Graves was correct – if this trooper really had been taken less than an hour before – then why did he look as if he had been rotting for a week?

As she moved towards the shrivelled, twisting branches of the corpsewood tree, the heat on her neck began to grow. Without warning, the familiar taste of blood and copper reached her tongue, and a whisper spoke in the back of her mind.

'Captain Vyse,' she murmured, summoning what little will she had left and throwing it into the command. 'Get a flamer. Now.'

The woman looked at her strangely for a moment, then shouted out into the mist. 'Flamer!'

Aerand took another step.

At first, she thought Trooper Monsk had been bound to the tree. Dark, sinuous cords wrapped around his wrists and his ankles, holding him tight against its slick, black trunk. But as she neared, it became obvious that those were not cords at all, and the trooper bore no other wounds on his entire body. Aerand shivered, her bridle pulsing with heat.

A look of sudden distress crossed the faces of the soldiers around her, as they too felt – but failed to understand – the psychic forces gathering around them.

At the back of Aerand's mind, those whispers continued. Not a single voice, now, but a dozen. The words were still too faint to make out, but she was confident that would not remain so for long.

'Flamer,' she repeated, feeling sluggish. Around her, not a single trooper moved.

She was afraid to throw her mind too fully into the empyrean, not knowing what else waited in those depths. But even as she probed its edges, she could find only a glimmer where the light of the Astronomican should have blazed.

Another step. Whether by her own will or some strange gravity, she could not be certain.

It was not cords that bound Trooper Monsk to the trunk, but the sinuous tendrils of the plant itself. They wormed their way into his skin, hundreds of them cutting into his back, slicing into his flesh. Slowly, Aerand grasped the hilt of her combat knife, and drew her blade against the first of those tendrils.

A noise like death raked through her mind the moment the steel in her hand touched that withered, black bark. Aerand stumbled, almost dropping the blade with the sudden weight of the psionic assault.

At her neck, her bridle blazed like a coal against her skin, and she vomited twice into the mud. Before she had time to recover, she felt the slick, solid sinew of a corpsewood root grasp her wrists and pull them towards the ground at the base of the tree. With a lunge, she snapped their grasp and rose to her feet, to stare directly into Monsk's open eyes.

For a moment, the young soldier's mouth opened and closed, as if the trooper were trying to speak. Despite the pool of black water pouring from his mouth, she heard his voice as clear as day.

Kill me. Kill me, please.

Stumbling backwards, Aerand drew a breath and summoned what little psionic strength she had left, a flicker of golden flame gathering around her hands. Not a single Cadian moved around her, Vyse and Corwyn transfixed by whatever voices claimed their own minds. Slowly, thin, black tendrils arose from the dirt around their feet, slithering like worms towards the entranced troopers.

Desperate, Aerand unleashed a gout of golden flame, watching with relief as the roots withered and recoiled. The scream within her mind returned, then vanished, as a dozen more tendrils sprang from the ground. Suddenly faint, Aerand attempted to raise more flames, but found nothing but sparks at the tips of her fingers. Her vision swimming, she stumbled, raising her combat knife, before a dozen roots grasped her ankles firmly.

Slashing madly, she managed to sever a few of the bonds, but each was replaced by a dozen more.

Suddenly, footsteps pounded to her side.

Sergeant Raniais Maltia stared dumbfounded at the scene around her, cradling a slate-grey carbine in her hands, a massive canister of promethium protruding from its underbelly.

Aerand raised a shaky hand towards the corpsewood tree, and saw realisation cross the sergeant's face. The trooper nodded, and unleashed a terrifying gout of flame, wrapping both the tree and the accursed corpse on its branches in wave after wave of cleansing fire.

Aerand closed her eyes, the psionic shriek within her mind rising to an impossible volume, before blessedly falling silent. Minutes later, when she opened them again, the tree before her was nothing more than an ashen husk, steam rising from the earth around her in gouts.

'Emperor's breath.' Sergeant Maltia looked down on her with a satisfied grin. 'Better?' the sergeant asked, reaching out a hand. Somehow, impossibly, the heavy trooper appeared unshaken.

'Better,' Aerand managed, rising shakily to her feet.

Behind her, Vyse, Corwyn and Graves started as if awakened from a particularly vivid nightmare.

'What the hell was that?' Graves muttered.

Beside him, Corwyn and Vyse locked eyes with Aerand. The ageing sergeant and the captain did not need to speak to signal that they already knew precisely the cause. They had stood beside Aerand over five years ago, the first time both of them had felt such effects, facing down a Chaos sorcerer on the mountain world of Ourea.

'That, Lieutenant Graves,' Aerand responded for them, 'was the feeling of an unshielded psionic assault. And a rather diffuse, undirected one at that.'

Aerand watched with satisfaction as any doubts the lieutenant had about the protection she'd previously provided the company vanished completely.

Vyse stepped up to stare at the charred husk of the corpsewood tree, still steaming in the misty netherlight. 'From that?' she muttered, almost unbelieving.

Aerand nodded. 'Yes, but I'm not exactly certain how.' There was no use elaborating on her suspicions until she had better evidence to back them up. But there was no question, any longer, as to the source of the attack. 'They may be the source of the mists, as well.'

'I would bet as much, lord psyker,' Corwyn replied grimly, lifting the barrel of his lasgun and taking aim at a point just behind her.

Aerand turned, noticing a small clearing that had formed in the mist around the burnt tree. At the edges of that clearing, however, the white fog had grown even thicker, and forms began to coalesce along its edges.

As she watched, her bridle began to warm yet again. Bipedal shapes started to rise in the mist around them. First, they were only vague homunculi woven from slightly thicker billows of fog, but they gathered form and detail with alarming speed. Slowly, a single ghost detached itself from the wall of mist, its face carved from vapour but entirely unmistakable.

'Macharius' tears,' Corwyn muttered, aiming his lasgun at Trooper Monsk's likeness. Already, the old sergeant's eyes were beginning to glaze. In the mist, the sounds of las-fire and shouting rose.

Vyse looked over to Aerand, the first hint of fear rising in the stoic captain's expression.

'Fire,' she ordered, turning to Maltia. 'Give me enough fire to turn this whole accursed planet to ash.'

The night glowed like the great primarch's shrine on Sanguinala, the flickering spouts of flamers ringing Secundus Company like a moat. The company marched in ranks, condensed into a single, small block, safe for now in the shelter the cleansing flame afforded. At each corner of the formation, one of Lieutenant Nalus' heavy troopers bore a flamer, spraying gouts of scalding promethium into the encroaching mists, holding back the myriad faces that now prowled those depths, and singeing the twisted forms of corpsewood trees as the company marched past.

While the flames afforded some blessed relief from that accursed substance, the mist itself had grown thicker at the fringes of the opening. A wall of solid white encircled the company like a gaping maw, ready to swallow the hundred troopers of Secundus Company the moment the light of their torches fell dark.

And fall dark they would. Soon.

A heavy flamer was an offensive weapon, designed to engulf and overwhelm any foe within seconds. The weapons, even well crafted and fastidiously maintained, were not designed for continuous defensive use. Three of the company's flamers had shorted or run dry of promethium already, and Sergeant Maltia carried their only remaining spare, marching at Captain Vyse's side.

Aerand had insisted the sergeant remain with the command squad after her performance in Trooper Monsk's accursed grove. Whatever had allowed the woman to continue functioning when the rest of the company had fallen victim to the corpsewood's assault could prove invaluable in the inevitable chaos to come.

Beside her, Vyse wore a mask of stone, leading the march herself at a breakneck pace. Every trooper behind her knew the bitter truth of the situation – either the company reached Providence before those remaining fires died out, or they would share the same fate as the faces in the mist.

'Ghosts,' Corwyn muttered, marching beside Aerand. 'I've seen my fair share of monsters in this world, but never thought I'd be killed by a bloody ghost.' Despite the fatality of his statement, the sergeant grinned. It had always been his most supremely valuable quality – the ability to maintain an unshakable good humour in even the most dire of straits. Aerand had never mastered that same skill.

'Not ghosts,' she muttered bitterly. 'Psionic projections. Echoes. These are not lost souls wandering, unable to find rest. They are simply the creation of some psychic entity with a memory of those poor troopers' faces and mannerisms.'

The distinction brought little comfort, perhaps, but she had already confirmed it a dozen times. The countless shades wandering the mists around them left no more mark on the fabric of the empyrean than would an unliving mound of stone.

'Some psychic entity...' Corwyn chuckled. 'You spend five years at the scholastica psykana and you come back talking like an Adeptus Administratum curator. You mean a witch. One of the Witchbringer's marsh priests?'

Aerand shrugged. Once again, the thought seemed ludicrous, yet she could think of no more plausible explanation. For a single psyker to manifest her will across such a space for such a long duration would require a power that she could scarcely imagine. Why waste such power on one-off murders and apparitions?

'Perhaps. Perhaps all of them, together. Perhaps something else entirely.'

'Something else? Like this Throne-cursed planet itself?'

Aerand paused, the thought striking a certain chord. 'Something like that.'

Breaking ranks, she ventured to the edge of the formation, drawing up beside the Ebonwelter twins as they poured a gout of flaming promethium at a corpsewood tree as the company passed. It turned out the two troopers had not been taken, after all. Simply disoriented in the previous thick mist, but quickly able to find their way back when Captain Vyse had given orders to light up the night. The two corporals were lucky they had not been mistaken for mist corpses themselves, but Evrik and Tannius now manned two edges of the fire wall with stunning enthusiasm.

As one swept a cone of burning promethium along the company's left flank, an uneasy grimace flitted across his face. In the wake of the flames the faces of a dozen mist corpses evaporated into steam, only to coalesce again a few seconds later. Aerand recognised none of the spectres that wandered the mists, but the effect was unnerving, nonetheless. A vivid reminder of the fate that might await them all. And despite her confidence that the spectres were not truly ghosts, she had no similar reassurances that they could not do the Cadians real harm.

Absent-mindedly, Aerand snapped her fingers, a small, golden flame gaining life within her palm. Whether the reprieve bought by the heavy troopers' flamers or simply time was to thank for it, she could feel a flicker of power returning to her. Not enough to fully counter whatever waited in those mists, but perhaps enough to buy her comrades a moment's respite, if need be.

Shutting her eyes, she tried, and failed, to enter the Third Meditation. The Emperor's grace reached every corner of the galaxy, but she could not bring herself to feel it here. She settled instead for the simplest of soldier's prayers.

'God-Emperor, do not let your servant die. For then she cannot dispatch any more of your enemies.'

Tannius – or Evrik – Ebonwelter heard her mutter and turned towards Aerand with a glare. She grunted, sensing a wave of suspicion rushing off the young trooper. She did not blame him. For the ungifted, one psyker was the same as any other, and a witch muttering to herself while ghosts paraded through the mists would raise any reasonable Cadian's hackles.

'A prayer,' she assured him. 'To the God-Emperor.'

The trooper nodded, but his aura did not change, and a moment later, the flamer in his hands began to sputter. Aerand cursed, doubly so. Both for the Chaos about to engulf them all, then again for the fact that anyone within earshot would forever associate that flamer's failure with her prayer.

'Evrik, Tannius,' she ordered, throwing just enough will into her voice to forestall any questions. 'Cover down as best you can.'

As the twins assisted each other, one flamer sputtering in its death throes, the other unleashing a torrent of fire, Aerand sprinted to Vyse.

'It's about to get ugly, isn't it?' Sergeant Corwyn said, glancing over Aerand's shoulder and assessing the situation.

'Very,' she replied.

Corwyn merely grunted. 'Was only a matter of time. We're walking blind through the wilds, Emperor knows how far from Providence. It's a bloody miracle we made it this far.'

'Pull the ranks tighter. Sergeant Maltia,' Captain Vyse ordered, a grim finality in her voice. 'Go fill that gap. We'll double time for as long as those flamers stay lit, then stand and fight whatever comes through afterwards. As long as we can, at least.'

Sergeant Corwyn nodded, and turned to relay her orders, but before he could, Evrik Ebonwelter's flamer died completely, and the waiting mist rushed in through the gap.

Like a raging stream overwhelming a dam, the thick, cloying cloud burst into Secundus Company in a torrent. Aerand had thought the fog was thick before, but as the wave rushed in, it nearly knocked her off her feet, and she found her lungs suddenly heaving just to breathe with the weight of the air around her. Her eyes burned with the rush of briny mist, and she blinked away tears to reveal a world of solid white.

A sea of faces swam in that indiscernible miasma, and a moment after the physical wave, the psionic force of the mist struck her in full.

Aerand fell to her knees, the cables on her neck instantly white-hot, her mouth dry as bone and suddenly full of blood. Despite her bridle, thousands of voices reached her ears unbidden, a cacophony loud enough to drown out even her own thoughts.

Before her, a dozen faces formed in the mist, twisted in various stages of agony. A cold, white hand reached out and brushed against her face, a sudden chill left behind in the spectre's wake. The marsh corpses could not touch her, but the pain brought by the psionic force of thousands of dead crying out fought to bring her low. She was trained to resist this, she was protected... but the rest of Secundus Company would fall to this attack as readily as if the spectres had cut their throats.

Finding herself, Aerand breathed, then lifted her hands and raised a ring of flame around her. Golden fire flickered to life in a bastion wall, the mist retreating with an audible scream. Another breath, and the ring collapsed then re-formed, wide enough now to shelter several others in its embrace. Two troopers lay curled in the dirt beside her, one gasping for air, while the other shook slightly, a thin stream of blood trickling from his nose.

'Up,' Aerand ordered, with all the will she could manage. One soldier stood, and blinked, then reached down to help his companion rise.

Another breath, and the circle grew wider still. Vyse. Corwyn. Maltia. Bless that sergeant. Somehow the woman still stood on her feet. Maltia shook herself, and suddenly her flamer roared to life, joining Aerand's psychic flame to force the mist back even further.

Shaking, Aerand tried to force her will farther forward, only to find the resistance increasing the larger her ring of flame grew. As if she had drawn the attention of something in that miasma, she found the exertion of holding even what she had gained suddenly almost beyond her abilities.

'Can you push it wider?' a voice asked quietly beside her.

Aerand looked up at Captain Vyse, and her haggard expression must have spoken for her. The captain stared out into the mist, where myriad faces clawed and scraped against a precariously thin wall of golden flame.

'You've done well enough, adept. I trust you'll hold them for as long as you can.'

'Until the last drop is spilled,' Aerand whispered.

Vyse smiled sadly at the use of the 900th's regimental motto. 'Every last one,' she replied.

Closing her eyes, Aerand cast her mind into the empyrean, the familiar iridescent waves overlaid atop the world around her. The surface of the warp churned like the sea in a storm, being rocked by her exertions and the emotions of the living souls close by. Beyond that, however, within the waiting mists, the immaterium was shrouded by that same white veil.

To cast such a pall, not only on the material world, but also the empyrean itself, was almost unthinkable, and Aerand shivered again at the strength of whatever lay behind that force. Desperate, she cast her mind even further, and for the first time felt something alive in those depths.

Something she recognised.

Aerand recoiled, her mind retreating from the touch of something dark, and unmistakably ancient. Her thoughts flashed back to her vision in the warp chamber at the scholastica, the same swimming, dark force coiling in the mists around her.

At the back of her mind, a voice attempted to speak, low and quiet, and almost unintelligible. Aerand steeled her mind and cut off its attempts, her bridle raging with the effort.

As long as she could. That was all she had promised, but against such a force, that might be only a few breaths.

The weight of the mists pressing down against her, Aerand felt her strength flag. At the edge of the circle, Vyse and Corwyn had gathered their few remaining troopers with Sergeant Maltia in the lead. The heavy trooper's flamer burned at one edge of the circle, pushing back the white and forming a thin corridor before her.

A foolhardy but valiant plan. With no other options, they were going to try to push their way forward, shielding themselves as best they could with that single remaining weapon. Aerand would assist them as much as she was able.

Closing her eyes once again, she searched desperately for any sign of the familiar glow of the Astronomican. There was no magic in it, no additional source of power, but perhaps that beacon's purity might allow her to find some remaining untapped power within herself. Or at the very least, when she died, overwhelmed by that darkness, she would die with the Emperor's music in her ears.

Within the mist, she found the faintest of glimmers. Focusing all her energy on it, she willed it to grow brighter, but found it drawing closer, instead. Desperately, she listened for any hint of the Astronomican's familiar music, but found only the grating clamour of myriad overlapping whispers.

Aerand's eyes flashed open.

Only feet away, at the edge of the mists, a shrouded face hung looking out at her. Shadow and light danced across the tepid apparition, like viewing the waxy skin of a corpse beneath water. Unlike the other ephemeral ghasts, there was a permanence to this particular mist corpse. Something substantial about it in both the physical world and the world underneath.

Aerand forced her mind towards its weak empyreal anchor and felt herself unceremoniously thrown back.

Lord psyker, a voice raged above the ghastly chorus. *You should not have come here.*

For a moment, something grey and cold glimmered with life where the apparition's eyes might have been, before the fabric of the immaterium shifted beneath it. Fire coursed across Aerand's skin as her vision blurred for the span of a moment. A shadow rose before her, looming over the apparition as if summoned. A shadow that seemed to draw her to it like gravity. In the back of her mind, the whispers only grew, and she felt herself rising slowly to her feet.

Suddenly, the flames before her gained a new life, her paltry ring of fire erupting into a raging inferno. Golden flame coursed through the fog, pushing back the mist corpses like a charging regiment, until clear air surrounded the entire company. Rushing forward, Vyse and Corwyn roused the troopers to their feet, those well enough to stand lifting those who could not.

The flames continued expanding, leaving charred groves of corpsewood trees in their wake, until suddenly, they reached a massive rockcrete gate, and a man in grey robes, bearing a massive corseque, standing vigil just outside it.

Aerand stumbled past Confessor Javard Libertinum, assisted by Sergeant Corwyn and a second trooper whose name she had not yet learned. The grim-faced ecclesiarch met her gaze only briefly, muttering in High Gothic as he read from a massive yellowed volume, its cover bound in human bone. In his other hand, a brilliant, sunburst-topped corseque was planted in the earth just beyond the gate's stone foundation.

'This is the last one,' Sergeant Corwyn said as they passed, another trio of troopers carrying a litter at their side.

The confessor simply grunted, then returned to his homily. At his side a pair of attendants gently wafted incense from a silver brazier. Along with thick, oily smoke and the scent of conifer needles, the faintest ripple emanated from the clergy, causing the warp itself to quiver like hot air over a flame.

And just as she had pressed back against the mists with the energy the immaterium channelled through her, so that cloud of roiling white recoiled from the confessor's ritual, though the effort seemed to tax the man far less than it had her. The grace of the God-Emperor Himself made concrete in a way she could not hope to comprehend. For now, such holy mysteries meant precious little to her, and her mind pounded with far more urgent needs.

Water. Sleep. Food. In that order.

'He's held vigil outside the Sun Gate for the last day and a half,' the trooper supporting her muttered to Corwyn. 'Since the moment the mists began to surround Providence.'

Aerand sighed. Let the confessor hold his vigil until he died if he liked. Perhaps the man did not need rest, but she certainly did.

As they passed beneath the massive arch of rockcrete separating Providence from the wilds beyond, the sodden mess of Secundus Company came into full view. Fewer troopers than there should have been. More lying on cots than standing, it seemed. Already, Vyse prowled the small courtyard, irate, rousing those that could stand, and leaving the rest for Argos, the company's chief medicae. The veteran trooper circled the wounded with a bioscanner and a pouch of bloodied instruments, patching what he could and rapidly dispatching the remaining casualties in the direction of the regimental chirurgeon's tent.

'What a bloody mess,' she muttered to herself. Along a side street the company's five remaining Sentinels groaned beneath the ministrations of their harried pilots. Secundus Company would take weeks to recover from this, if it ever managed to recover at all.

'Aye,' Corwyn muttered, reading the guilt written across her face. 'And a mess I'm damned grateful to have.' The veteran trooper fixed her with steely violet eyes. 'I don't even want to know the rumours that will be floating around by morning, but Vyse and I know exactly what happened out there, even if the captain is too proud to admit it. Without you there wouldn't be a mess at all, just one hundred more faces waiting out in that mist. Would have been a shame to end up dead less than a hundred yards from Providence's gate.'

He glanced over at the waiting row of deceased troopers, strips of cloth already bound across their eyes in the traditional Cadian fashion. A ritual that had travelled along with the 900th from Cadia herself. A final chance to be free from the sight of the roiling Eye of Terror overhead. It was a symbolic exercise only, now, and nothing more than the dim glow of cold moonlight trickled through Visage's almost impenetrable cloud cover. But symbols were all that remained of Cadia. Symbols and the hardened troopers who continued them, and Corwyn took seriously this company sergeant's final, most important duty to his soldiers.

'You'll be all right?' he asked, clearly anxious to leave her and attend to his duties.

'Yes,' Aerand sighed, probing the man's aura gently. There was an honesty there, refreshing as always, but beneath the sergeant's gratitude and concern, a darker flavour waited. He might recognise that she had saved his life, but he still harboured fear and suspicion beneath that. Prudent, on his part, if painful for her.

For the first time since arriving on Visage, she could breathe enough to notice that space. A space that had never existed when they were captain and company sergeant together.

Now, more than ever, she longed for the presence of another gifted. One she could trust. One like the man she had been sent to find, or avenge.

'Corwyn,' she called after him as he turned. 'Lord Kellipso. Did the company treat him the same way?'

'Who?' Corwyn asked.

'Jarrah Kellipso,' she repeated. The sergeant's ears must have been ringing after the din of las-fire and autoweapons.

Olevier Corwyn stared at her blankly, his face falling utterly expressionless. He recovered a moment later, his demeanour replaced by one of confusion.

'I'm sorry,' he muttered. 'I don't think I've ever heard that name.'

CHAPTER 8

A strange nostalgia washed over the Colonel at the sight of Providence's walls. Strange to think that he had once commanded the guns lining them and the soldiers sheltered behind them. Even now, years later, he recognised each footing and segment of foundation and could picture the convoluted, twisting streets within.

All the easier to raze the city entirely, then.

'You must understand,' he said softly to the prisoner beside him. 'I bear no ill will towards you or your comrades as individuals. Only to the idea that you, as a whole, represent.'

In the mud beside his feet, a Cadian trooper squirmed.

The young man, wearing a simple private's rank insignia and scarcely old enough to shave, groaned slightly as the Colonel set a mud-caked boot atop his broken ribs. He leaned forward with an unfortunate crack.

'Quiet,' Sergeant Gross grumbled at the sudden scream.

The trooper caught his breath in shallow gasps and finally managed to give force to the words he had been mouthing for the last minute.

'Go to hell,' he muttered. 'The Emperor protects.'

The sergeant raised the butt of his lasgun, but the Colonel held up a patient hand. He set his foot back into the shallow puddle of sea water that gathered over the small rise like an oil slick.

'I thought that once, myself, too, but I learned. The Emperor did a poor job protecting the rest of your squad.' The Colonel knelt down and grabbed the trooper by the collar, turning his body so he had no option but to stare into the faces of the eight dead men and women lining the small rise beside him. 'He did a poor job protecting your home world, too.'

Behind him, the crone paced like a caged animal, keeping her distance from the Colonel and his last living prisoner. He'd allowed her the first opportunity to crack the captured squad of Cadians, but after she'd driven two mad with little additional information acquired he had turned to more conventional means. Leave the witch her voices and visions and torments, he needed little more than a boot to extract information.

At the sight of her, the man in the dirt raised a battered arm in a pitiful attempt to make the sign of the aquila.

'Don't mind her,' the Colonel ordered. 'Her petty gods care no more about you than your Emperor does. Now, show me the access chit for the service corridors.'

This was the problem with gods, whether dark or light. The Colonel did not deny their existence, only their interest in the fleeting, futile striving of their servants. Blood for the Blood God. Change for Tzeentch. But how many more martyrs lay at the feet of the God-Emperor of Mankind, however pure His motives?

Let them wage their petty wars in heaven. Let crusaders, black or light, throw their lives away on behalf of whatever deity or power they chose. Neither great movements nor their deities gave a single thought to the humans dying in agony to sustain them.

So let the gods grapple. Let them tear each other piece from piece. And perhaps in the end, there would finally be space for humans to exist in peace.

'The Emperor...' the man coughed, doubling over. 'The Emperor protects.'

Throne above. He had believed such nonsense once, too, but he'd had the good sense to learn his lessons. The Colonel froze as he watched the young man reach quickly into his pocket and shove a small, silver fleck between his teeth.

Before he could bring them together and shatter the device, a silver blade erupted from his throat. Sergeant Gross sighed, pulling his sword from the Cadian's neck and bending down to slip the bloody chit from the man's mouth as he coughed up red sputum. He dropped the dripping tech into the Colonel's hand.

'We will see if He does, I suppose, after all.'

Aerand shook like a fresh Whiteshield before battle, unable to still unsteady limbs and her swimming vision, as she pulled a small, inconspicuous package from her voidlocker. The entire container – hardly large enough to store her pair of Mars-pattern command pistols, a light breastplate of flak armour, and a few extra garments – was all she had been allowed to carry aboard the *Emperor's Grace*. But among those scant and spartan belongings, the small black package now resting in her hand was by far the most powerful and the most dangerous.

Gently, she untied the thin silver cord around the bundle and unwrapped its thick, black leather casing, the soft white glow of liquid crystal suddenly suffusing the tiny room. Already, a coolness washed over her, the temperature of the air dropping several degrees. Careful not to touch the deck itself, she placed the cards of the Emperor's Tarot on the dirt floor before her.

'Steady now,' she whispered to herself, as doubts began to ambush her. The Emperor rewarded courage, not cowardice.

A casting of the Tarot was a perilous affair even under ideal circumstances, with more opportunities for failure than success. In the most benign missteps, the cards might simply fall treacherously, revealing a clouded vision of the future that left their reader more lost than before they'd been laid. In the worst, the invocation of such potent psionic forces could draw any number of unwanted entities from the warp. For this reason, in the scholastica psykana the Tarot was rarely cast by fewer than three psykers, and rare still less than two. And yet, she found herself desperate enough to try alone.

'Besieged without and within.' So began a prayer she'd once heard on the lips of a nameless Cadian watchman. The man had died before he'd had a chance to finish it.

An unknown force surrounded Visage. An unholy alliance of perverse and potent empyreal powers strong enough to raise echoes of the dead and several regiments' strength of traitor militias, well trained enough to stand toe to toe with Cadian shock troopers and not immediately crumble. Within those ranks waited dozens, if not hundreds, of psykers, and Jarrah Kellipso – her mentor and the only other gifted on this world loyal to the God-Emperor – was dead, or worse. And somehow, inexplicably, no soldier of the 900th Cadian Regiment seemed to even remember that the man had ever existed.

The look of utter confusion across Sergeant Corwyn's face hung in her mind like a poor piece of painted art. The pained juxtaposition of a mind struggling against itself would have been obvious to anyone with eyes. Aerand had stood beside Olevier Corwyn the first time she had met the primaris psyker Jarrah Kellipso, and somewhere within the folds of his brain, the man harboured years of memories of the psyker lord. Yet another, more powerful compulsion held those memories from his conscious mind. Even more worrisome, of the dozen other troopers she'd interrogated since, even under the subtle influence of her will, every one showed the same, unnatural division.

Aerand's own mind felt far too feeble to even begin teasing apart that deeper mystery, yet she knew that sleep would not possibly come until she had at least started down that treacherous path. Slowly, she crossed her aching, cramped legs, and forced her mind into the First Meditation.

'I turn my ears, O God-Emperor, towards the sound of your silence. That I may recognise your voice when it speaks.'

Silence.

Not quite, unfortunately.

After her display outside Providence's gates, she'd had no trouble finding isolation from the remainder of the 900th Regiment. The only thing that travelled faster than a las-round was a war story, and already whispers of her exploits had circled wide enough to reach back to her. If the soldiers of the 900th had been wary of her before, most were now utterly terrified at even the sight of her.

And yet, the small hovel she had taken for her quarters provided precious little quiet.

Outside the flimsy, corrugated steel door, the sound of artillery and mortars rang out like a drumbeat. Vyse had assured her that no attack was imminent, yet the company of Basilisks attached to the 900th was not about to take any chances. Even now, the mist-strewn wastes around Providence boiled with the surging impacts of high-explosive and incendiary shells.

Despite the constant intrusion, Aerand found the booming rhythm almost soothing. Slowly, she synched her breathing with the rise and fall of the shells, until their sound began to fade from her mind. In its place, for the first time since arriving on this planet, the subtle hint of a familiar chorus rose in her ears.

'I turn my eyes, O God-Emperor, towards the sight of your servant, that I may see my failings and judge myself true.'

The dark, multicoloured fabric of the empyrean rolled out around her, swallowing the dim glow of her sleeping room. Outside the thin walls, souls swam like sparks from a fire, troopers and civilians milling about, making preparations for the violence to come. In the centre of that mess, a single soul glowed like a beacon, and Aerand drew her attention around herself like a mirror.

The primaris psyker had not slept in over thirty hours. She had not eaten in that time, and had scarcely drunk a sip. Her body protested with every minor movement, a dull ache suffusing all of her limbs. Sharp discomfort emanated from a dozen bruises along her shins and knees, and the skin at her wrists and ankles protested where corpsewood roots had left it lacerated. A deep gash ran along the length of her right ankle, from her desperate attempt to split those tendrils with her combat blade. With her attention fully turned to the wound, she felt the slow ooze of blood from the capillaries beneath her skin, and the faint tug of flesh already beginning to reknit.

She was exhausted. She was desperately hungry and thirsty. She was falling apart both physically and mentally.

In short, she was already only inches from the warp.

Finally, content that she was as prepared for this moment as she could be, she turned her attention to a second, brighter light.

'I turn my soul, O God-Emperor, towards the light of your grace, that I may surrender before it and burn just as brightly.'

At the centre of Providence, where Javax Cathedral towered above the city, a silver-white glow dominated the immaterium. It was not uncommon, she knew, for the Astronomican's psionic light to be more easily sensed near places of faith. Despite that knowledge, she found herself surprised at the strength of the beacon after so long in those mists, unable to sense its signal at all. It blazed clear and true in her mind now.

Her ears full of the Astronomican's hymn, and its light bathing her like evening sun, Aerand turned her attention to the cards on the floor.

Seventy-eight wafers of liquid crystal lorelei glowed like souls of their own in the immaterium.

Powerful enough to form the basis of force weapons and psychic hoods, lorelei was also subtle enough to be cast into paper-thin sheets. It was one way to produce a copy of the Emperor's Tarot, one that had the potential for stronger readings but also invited more risk. The deck had been presented to Aerand as Ule's parting gift. Yet the substance, psionically active as it was, could respond to any other psychic force, as well. Even to touch the deck physically risked corrupting a casting.

'Let me see true,' Aerand whispered, the diviner's simplest and most honest prayer. With a flick of her finger, the first card rose from the deck and came to rest on the dusty floor.

The Soldier, upright. The first of her cardinals. The pre-eminent figure in the casting to come. Not an unexpected archetype to appear in the midst of a warzone. In a city literally laid to siege.

A stoic figure knelt amid a field of corpses, bloodied battle armour draped across his frame. The card was painfully vague, and while the silhouetted warrior held something in his hands, she could not make out the weapon's specific design, nor any other features of the soldier who bore it.

Such an obscured cardinal could portend many things. Multiple individuals competing without their knowledge for a role within diverse fates to come. An intentional concealment of identity on the part of the card-bearer or another force acting on his or her behalf. Or simply an exhausted diviner who should not have attempted such a ritual alone.

In all cases the Soldier foretold war and blood, but neither of these were revelations for a primaris psyker of the Astra Militarum. Slowly she placed the next card beside it.

The High Priest. Inverted. A more interesting character.

A breath of chilled air filled Aerand's lungs as she inspected the casting, the first hints of hoar frost forming in the dirt around the cards. Upright, the High Priest signified nothing more than the presence of the Ecclesiarchy, and the Emperor's Church as a player in this muddled game. Inverted, however, the card told of obscene cults or corrupted parishioners, or perhaps a confessor who held secrets of his own.

Aerand could not help but recall the look of unease she'd received from Javard Libertinum as she'd passed him on her way through the Sun Gate. As if he were less than happy to see her alive. The man robed in crimson on the card before her bore an unmistakable resemblance to the confessor, and even from this distance, she caught the faint hint of a psionic ripple in the air around the ecclesiarch's head.

A nervous energy collected in her, and she found herself turning the third card, unbidden.

The Witch. In opposition to the Soldier. A sorcerer? A primaris psyker? Aerand herself? Jarrah Kellipso? The cards made no distinction between such subtleties.

Aerand's breath caught as she laid the card flat. A face twisted in agony adorned the liquid crystal wafer before her, lined with pain and age, with the sharp glow of warp lightning around it. Grey eyes bored out of the crystal at her, and she could practically hear Jarrah Kellipso's voice in her mind.

Death and hunger and enough bitter regret to drown in. A clear enough warning, and one she'd chosen to ignore.

Her heart racing, Aerand scrambled to draw the next card.

The final of her four cardinals fell to the dirt with an unnatural weight, as if the character had sped its own arrival on the field. The flavour of blood filled Aerand's mouth, and her skin came to life with the raw energy of the empyrean. From around the card, frigid air erupted, crystallising beads of moisture on the damp floor and walls, Aerand's own breaths falling suddenly in rapid clouds.

The Beast. Upright. Major arcana. The final of her cardinals, and therefore the position which flavoured each of the others in this particular casting.

Despite the fact that she knew each card in her deck to be precisely the same dimensions as the others, that single card suddenly loomed larger than the other three on the field. A dark, twisted monstrosity seemed to swallow the entire lorelei wafer, faint hints of the iridescent, unbridled warp filling what little open space it left on the card. Even just glancing at its form, Aerand found her mind swimming, a terrible pressure behind her eyes and a burning at the base of her neck.

Whatever blinded artisan had crafted the psionic images on this deck, the psyker had seen true enough to capture this form perfectly. Aerand shivered as memories of her time in the unshielded warp returned to her, threatening to swallow her in those waters again. Somehow, that terrible shadow rising beneath her had found its way to her again in the mists just outside these walls.

A casting was always a dangerous affair, and this one had clearly gone on long enough. Deep below her, she felt the empyrean swirl.

The Soldier in opposition to the Witch. The High Priest, inverted, in opposition to the Beast. No clear vision of either the present or the future, and too many possible alignments for any to ring true. Did the Soldier and High Priest conspire together against the Witch? Did the Witch stand opposed to the Beast or beside it? A darker thought filled her mind at the memory of Jarrah Kellipso. Had all three – the Soldier, the High Priest, the Beast – conspired together to effect his demise?

With a sigh, Aerand lifted her palm from her knee, but found that none of the tarot on the field moved with it. She swallowed as a flurry of cards erupted from the deck, unbidden.

The Sword falling atop the Soldier, spinning slowly without finding a steady position. A warrior assailed on all sides, unsure where to direct his violence.

The Candle beneath the High Priest, flame reaching out beyond the borders of the liquid crystal to lick the edges of the card above it. Illumination. Supplication. Purifying fire.

The Blind Seer, between the Witch and the Beast. Linking the two cards, or standing between them?

Vision swimming, Aerand watched another card rise from the deck, hovering just above the centre of the field. At the back of her mind, the song of the Astronomican warred with a choir of whispering voices she had no desire to entertain. Her breath fell in thick white gouts, as ice hardened along the walls of her small, austere shelter, and the field before her wobbled in front of her eyes. The final card of the casting slammed into the dirt with enough force to scatter the others. A sudden will assailed her from the card itself. The will to turn over. The will to be seen.

Aye, she was a Blind Seer, indeed, and an utter fool. This casting had gone on long enough, and any tarot card with such a desire to be seen was not a portent that could be easily trusted. Before the card could reveal itself, Aerand slammed her hand atop it, the sudden physical connection of her skin scattering the psionic energy swirling around the deck.

She took the lorelei wafer, unseen, and tucked it into the folds of her robe.

Her dreams were haunted, as always, without the double-edged respite of poor sleep. Normally, her nightmares were cut mercifully short by the frequent wakings of a pressured mind and fragile body, but tonight exhaustion gripped her whole.

As a child, before being granted her own white-striped conscript's helm, she'd been too young to stand her own vigil on the barren moors of Cadia, where young troopers either learned to survive or died. Yet, by the time she had emerged from her own ritual a decade later on another world after she'd lost her own, cast into the savage wastes of Bellarus Prime to survive forty days in those frigid wilds alone, she'd learned the lesson painfully well.

On such a world, a soldier had three hours to find shelter. Three days to find water. Three weeks to find food. And only as long to find a weapon as the enemy was willing to give her.

Of all a soldier's true necessities, however, shelter and sleep always came first.

On Lincress, she'd gone thirty-nine hours without a drop of water. On Ourea, all of Secundus Company had eaten nothing but a single crate of nafar biscuits for a week. But keep any soldier awake for much more than a day – no matter how many stimms you pumped into their muscles, or how gruelling the duty you forced them to endure – and you would find their flesh simply did not comply. Even worse, when that body did finally fail, it would fail harder for each effort made to keep it awake unnaturally.

So, despite visions even more unsettling than usual, Aerand did not leave that miserable little room until the sun had set and nearly risen again. Unfortunately, the dawn brought precious little clarity.

The Soldier in opposition to the Witch.

The 900th Regiment, as a whole? One trooper in particular? Opposed to the Witchbringer? To Kellipso? To Aerand herself?

The Tarot, like all forms of divination, was a fickle, hungry beast at the best of times. She had no doubt the cards' message would be painfully clear in retrospect, but at the moment they did nothing other than cloud the way forward. Even so, there was one combination of those actors who needed no divination to reveal their animus.

Major Absalom Restripa strode atop the narrow sea wall with an arrogance visible from the shallow ocean below. How a man could stuff so much pride within such a small vessel was beyond even a primaris psyker's knowledge, and yet she wished that the weight of that ego would pull the man directly over the wall and hold him beneath the turbid water below.

The major had exchanged his traditional dress uniform for a drab green suit of flak armour more appropriate for combat. His favoured laspistol was strapped to the front of his breastplate, and a well-oiled lasgun hung across his back. His helmet dangled from a strap over his left shoulder, as he knelt to inspect a heavy bolter position being erected along the sea wall's outer contour.

From the other shoulder of his armour, a silver rod sprouted several feet over his head, carrying a crimson pennant which fluttered in the slight breeze. Two golden pillars ensconced on a field of crimson, a golden skull suspended between them mounted on an aquila's wings. There was nothing unique in the heraldry of the 900th Cadian Regiment, other than the numerals emblazoned in white beneath Cadia's common seal.

As she drew closer, a hundred small tears became visible in the ancient banner, patched by generations of honest, but unskilled hands. Like any of the few surviving orphaned Cadian regiments, the 900th's colours had been carried from the home world itself, and while Major Restripa's shock troopers were well practised at mending uniforms and rucksacks, none could claim skill as fine tailors or craftsmen, or anything other than soldiers. The tattered fabric was faded almost beyond recognition, and while the damage did nothing to add to the colours' legibility, it was only fitting to represent troopers every bit as scarred.

While it remained widespread among the storied regiments of the Astra Militarum, the practice of a standard bearer carrying the regimental colours into battle had fallen away for the 900th on the dispersed, isolated world of Ourea. Only once in that entire, brutal campaign had the whole regiment fought together in one place. And at that point, there were few enough troopers remaining in the 900th to waste even a single set of hands holding a flag.

The fact that Restripa had resurrected the custom, after a fashion, would have been almost laudable if it were not such a startlingly easy way for the regiment's commander to make himself an easy target for their enemy.

'Major,' Aerand said, drawing to attention a few paces from her kneeling commander.

Restripa looked up briefly, then returned his attention to the gun mount. One of Kobald's Sentinel pilots knelt beside him trying without success to coax a plasma welder into acceding to his will. The 900th had lost more than just rituals on Ourea, and Kobald's pilots were the closest thing the regiment possessed to an enginseer on this forsaken world absent the Adeptus Mechanicus' presence.

'Adept,' he replied coolly. 'I trust you've rested well.'

For a moment, the aura around the man glimmered with a hint of something akin to fear, before he masked it with condescension. No doubt, Vyse had already filed a report on the action en route from Charity, and if it would not buy her Restripa's respect, she would have to be content with her commander's discomfort.

'Yes,' she lied, pushing back against the insinuation. 'A need for sleep is one crucial weakness I still hold in common with the human members of your regiment.'

Restripa glanced up, confused, until he remembered his comment in their last conversation. 'Regrettably,' he mumbled, then shooed Kobald's pilot away. The trooper rushed off to the next gun emplacement a dozen yards further along the wall.

Restripa sighed once the trooper was out of earshot, and turned to face the world outside Providence's walls. Aerand took that as an invitation and drew up beside him.

The sky over Providence hung dark and heavy, but at the centre of the city, just over the vicious peaks and crenellations of the towering Javax Cathedral, the sky cleared enough to make out the twinkling of stars. Three dull moons hung over the city like orbiting voidcraft, each trailing the other like a passing flotilla. On another world, in another life, she might have been glad for the blanket of grey covering this forsaken planet, for even though she had not seen its obscene violet glow in decades, the memory of the Ocularis Terribus still spoiled her ability to appreciate the beauty of any night-time sky. Those memories held special dread for her now that she had stood within the roiling sea of the warp's raw Chaos which had lain within that Eye, and knew what utter madness it contained.

For his part, Major Restripa appeared just as disquieted by the sudden, unnatural break in the clouds. He trained his violet gaze, instead, on the mist-strewn wilds that lay beneath.

Despite the cathedral's imposition over the town itself, the Ecclesiarchy's power appeared to extend little further than Providence's walls. Thick white mist gathered in billowing waves a few hundred yards from the inner sea wall, a narrow firebreak holding those hidden depths from the city. In that mess, beyond the dawn gate, a faint lightening of the horizon was waking, but there would be no true sunrise on this world.

A beautiful, if disquieting vantage point. And a besieged commander's greatest fear.

'Captain Vyse,' he began slowly, 'said you gave an honourable account of yourself on the road from Charity.'

Aerand's grimace softened slightly. It wasn't quite an admission of thanks from the major, but it was the closest she was likely to receive.

'By the Emperor's grace, I did all I could.'

Restripa's head turned at the remark.

'I may be nearly a heretic in your mind, sir. But I assure you I am far from one in my own regard. My devotion to the God-Emperor is every bit as strong as it was the day before I discovered my gifts.'

The major was quiet for some time. 'I think nothing of the sort.'

Restripa turned and strode several paces down the sea wall. A trail of fog curled over the moth-eaten rockcrete on a gust of sudden wind, beading along the edges of the man's armour and dripping down the banner pole mounted on his back.

Aye, he could be painfully stubborn and proud, and he deserved every drop of ire directed at him, but he had earned a right to those colours every bit as much as she had.

For a moment, she saw him not as her commander but simply as a fellow soldier. One who had risen through the ranks meteorically and – arrogance aside – must recognise he lacked the experience to match his rank. How would she have felt if, only months after assuming her own command of Secundus Company, one of its former officers had returned as a witch in her midst? How strong would her own desire be to protect her soldiers from that possible danger?

They'd had their differences, but his disdain of her was rooted in some-thing far deeper.

'You merely believe me to be dangerous.'

Restripa nodded. 'As our enemies have recently discovered. And do you blame me? After what I've seen? After what every soldier in this regiment has? We lie besieged by witches on a planet that breeds them like insects. What kind of commander would I be if I wasn't wary of one more?'

'I am not–'

'A witch?' Restripa cut her off. 'But aren't you, adept? I know little of psyker lords, and even less of true sorcerers and heretics, but each time I look at you, I see the same haunted void in your gaze that appears in the eyes of the stricken and possessed. Does the power you wield not stem from that same unholy darkness?'

Aerand paused. Despite the accusation, there was wisdom in those words. 'I am not one to assign blame, I was going to say.'

For the most fleeting of moments, the major's face softened, and she caught a glimpse of the young corporal she had once commanded. Then, as quickly as it had vanished, his commander's mask returned.

'I have no need for your pity, adept.'

'Nor I for yours.'

'Then pity aside, a request. Captain Vyse told me you were able to scry the Witchbringer's forces while they were still at a distance. Could you do the same now?'

As the major spoke, a low humming rose in the air, followed by a series of concussions along the eastern wall a few hundred yards away. Rockcrete and metal reinforcing struts toppled in chunks from the sea wall as a trio of mortars struck the makeshift battlements directly.

In response, a massive shell ripped out from the Earthshaker cannon mounted on the Basilisk in the courtyard below. The tracked vehicle shook with the sudden recoil of the steeply angled shot, a small plume of smoke erupting from its main gun. The sky whistled for a painfully long interval, as the shell rose through the dark clouds and then crashed back to the earth. Even at a distance, the sudden light of the high-explosive round was visible as a dim orange flash through the obscuring mists.

However impressive the display, there was little chance the round had found its unseen target in that mire.

Restripa did not flinch at either impact. 'There have been a few dozen such attacks since sunrise, and I can do little more than fire blindly back into those clouds. You know how this story ends, adept. We are surrounded by a force of unknown strength on a world whose citizens hardly tolerate our presence. No vessels orbit overhead, and even if they did, what use could I make of orbital support on a planet invisible from the sky?

'Six months ago, the situation was unfavourable. Three months ago it was dire. But now the very air and bones of Visage itself seem to have allied with our enemies, who have proven more capable than I could have ever expected.'

Restripa turned to survey the line of troopers rushing towards the damaged section of sea wall to recover the mounted heavy bolter, which now teetered dangerously close to the ledge. 'There are few soldiers in the galaxy that could match this regiment in even combat. But I fear even we are out of our depth.'

For a moment, a flush of spite washed over Aerand. To have been dismissed so suddenly, then called upon only in a time of desperate need. But as her eyes rose again to the flickering colours mounted on Restripa's back, she pushed any personal grudges aside.

'I will do what I can,' she replied. 'For them.'

Restripa nodded, and began to march slowly towards the damaged section of wall. 'Perhaps I was too rash, adept. It seems we may find use for a psyker after all.'

At his words, a strange foreboding struck Aerand. Something in the tone of which he inflected that word set her mind alight. She had asked a dozen troopers this question already, and had no reason to expect a different response. Even still, she called out after Restripa.

'Major. Your last psyker, Jarrah Kellipso. What happened to him?'

The small sense of shame she felt at using her will to compel a response from her commanding officer vanished instantly as Restripa turned. For a brief second, a horrible contradiction split the man's expression, his mouth beginning to speak, while his eyes struggled against her psionic compulsion.

'I-I-I'm sorry. I can't say I've ever heard that name.'

The correct response – the same words as Sergeant Corwyn, and every other trooper she'd asked about her former mentor – but delivered incorrectly. As Restripa walked away, she cast her mind gently towards him, and felt the guilt dripping from the man like this accursed world's never-ending rain.

'Volunteers,' Lieutenant Nalus barked from across the courtyard, walking towards the cluster of heavy troopers circled beneath a makeshift canopy. Two of the lieutenant's heavy teams sat resting and cleaning weapons while the other half of their platoon manned positions on the wall. Nalus' sergeants had managed to commandeer a local vendor's market stall for the moment, a few sheets of corrugated, rusting metal making an admirable attempt at keeping out the rain. A small fire blazed in a steel drum at one corner of the shelter, and several of Lieutenant Graves' troopers huddled tightly beside it. A pile of rations and bullets, and a small copper flask lay on the damp, packed dirt floor in the centre of their circle.

'You all know what that means,' the trooper across from Sergeant Raniais Maltia grumbled.

Evrik Ebonwelter nodded. 'Aye. Us heavies are about to get pissed on again.'

'How do you figure?'

Evrik's twin brother, Tannius, replied in an identical tone, 'No one asks for volunteers for an easy mission. And that's the only thing they'd trust you and Lieutenant Graves' platoon with, Garb.'

A grin twitched across Maltia's face, as a cluster of dice flashed into the air and landed in the centre of the ring.

There were precious few things you could count on from a trooper of the Astra Militarum. She would fire true when commanded. She would charge bravely when allowed. She would die honourably when required to. And she would gamble away every possession she touched the moment you gave her the opportunity.

As the cluster of dice struck the earth, six hands shot out from the circle of waiting troopers, each clasping one of the handcrafted game pieces in place.

'Like as not, it's probably something to do with that damned primaris witch,' Corporal Garb muttered, his hand covering a small eight-sided die formed from a milled piece of the main strut of a Chimera chassis and dotted with diodes from some ancient, dismembered machine.

'If so,' Maltia replied, 'she'd best hope you're better at shooting that lasgun than you are at playing rivets.'

Rivets was a time-honoured Cadian tradition, rumoured to be nearly as old as the lasgun itself. While apocryphally named for the construction materials of the game's first playing pieces, modern rivets dice were constructed of anything solid enough to survive in a flak-armour pouch. Fashioning their own die was one of the first non-essential functions every Cadian Whiteshield completed.

The game, like the profession of its players, was simple and fast. Bets were placed, then the dice were cast in the air, each player securing another player's die the moment it struck the ground. Slowly, each of the six slid their captured die towards their body, lifting their hand gently to eye the number beneath, while keeping careful watch to ensure their opponents did not manipulate the face on their own game piece.

Garb grunted, and the sergeant beside him smirked slightly, his thumb toying with the edge of the die beneath his palm.

'Don't know what you're smiling about, Henderson,' Maltia called, pointing an accusing finger towards his hand. 'I doubt you're any better than your trooper at either bluffing or shooting.'

Each eight-sided die was handcrafted with the numbers on each face arranged in a unique, random order, in an attempt to subvert opponents' ability to subtly shift their game piece, and favour, without looking. But cheating was not only allowed in rivets, it was actively encouraged – provided the player was subtle enough not to be caught.

'Still don't trust her,' Garb mumbled. 'She's practically a witch.' Another clatter of belongings entered the circle, as each player weighed their own hidden showing against the odds.

'A witch who saved all our lives,' Sergeant Maltia replied.

'This time.' Garb shrugged. 'But who's to say it's not her we'll need saving from next? And all that proves is that she's more dangerous than whatever else was following us back from Charity.'

'Volunteers,' Lieutenant Nalus barked again, reaching the circle. As if summoned by their words, a robed figure stepped out from behind him. Maltia felt a thin tickle of gooseflesh along her back.

'Lord psyker needs them. Major Restripa's orders. If I don't get any volunteers, I'm more than happy to just start choosing names.'

Glancing beneath her palm at a die showing a six, Sergeant Raniais Maltia eyed the squad sergeant seated across from her. 'What do you say, Henderson? I took half your squad's belongings already. Why don't I give you a chance to win them back?'

She shoved a small trove of bullets, coins and rations into the centre of the circle.

'All other players out. Just you and me. If I'm high, you take your squad as volunteers with the lord psyker. If I'm low, then third squad and me will volunteer, and you sorry suckers get your losings back.'

A flurry of whispers darted between Sergeant Henderson's soldiers before the stocky trooper simply nodded. Behind him, Lieutenant Nalus shook his head, but even he knew better than to interfere in the almost-sacred ritual of chance.

'A true wager,' the hooded figure beside the lieutenant remarked. 'Best of luck to you both.'

At the sound of the psyker's voice directly behind him, Sergeant Henderson winced, his fingers instinctively gripping the dirt in discomfort. They spread just enough for Maltia to spot the number atop his die before he quickly concealed it again.

Six to six. A deadman's wager.

'Show 'em.'

There was a subtle flick of the psyker's wrist the moment before Sergeant Henderson uncovered his die, which now lay in the dirt showing a seven. Confusion crossed Sergeant Henderson's face, and the psyker smirked slightly beneath her cowl.

Whatever she was now, Captain Aerand had been a true Cadian soldier once. She knew the rules of this game as well as anyone else.

But she was out of practice.

Sergeant Maltia pulled her hand from her die, now suddenly displaying an eight to Henderson's seven. An audible groan escaped the troopers of Henderson's squad.

'Keep your luck, lord psyker,' Sergeant Maltia said, raking in another pile of winnings. 'I've never found much use for it, myself.'

Eagerly, her heavy troopers pounced on the pile of loot, adding strings of autocannon rounds and spare blades to their already exuberant loadouts. With a grumble, Henderson's squad rose to their feet, donning their flak armour and helmets.

'Give us five minutes to stow all this gear, Henderson, and we'll join your sorry souls out there in the rain,' Maltia called, grabbing the small copper flask from the winnings. She sniffed at the amber liquid within and took a small swig. 'What, lord psyker?' she asked, turning to face Aerand. 'You didn't think us the type to say no to a fight, did you? Especially now that we've got enough bullets and liquor to enjoy it properly.'

CHAPTER 9

Dark water swirled in putrid currents around the Colonel's sodden boots, drifting towards the walls of the city ahead. For centuries, those relentless waters had inexorably undermined the unmaintained foundations of Visage's ancient capital, hunks of rockcrete bearing adamantium reinforcements crumbling along the ancient sea wall like shed skin. Leave a city – or a planet – in disrepair long enough and it eventually turned back to nothing but dust.

Tonight those walls would fail completely.

Thick white fog surrounded the clearing in which the Colonel stood alone, a ring of clear air eaten out from the storm wall around him like a bite out of some terrestrial cloud. Above, the bright discs of Visage's triplet moons occupied the fringes of that clearing, drawn slowly together over the silhouette of the city. There they trembled, like shivering torch lamps, their orbits forced into alignment for only this night.

His disdain for the marsh priests with whom his movement had united was no secret among his Dorean inner circle, but there were times the psykers' power could not be denied. To perform such an unthinkable feat would strain even the fabled Adeptus Mechanicus' arts to the extreme. He tried to put out from his mind the terrible cost of such power.

'You could have stopped this,' he whispered softly into the night. 'You could have stopped all of this if you had only willed it.'

Behind him, a cruel voice crackled in the night. 'Your Corpse-Emperor cannot hear you, Dorean. Just as He could not hear the screams of the child He took from you.'

The Colonel simply grunted in reply. Even after all this time, he disagreed.

The crone bent slowly towards the water with her twisted back, dipping blood-clotted arms into the foul mire. How many of her witches had died tonight to fuel her depraved magicks? How many of them had been no older than the girl, when the Emperor had taken her from him?

The Colonel stared at the dark silhouette of Javax Cathedral, his last memory of the child an image of her being led in shackles through those accursed doors. He should have led a mutiny the moment the black-robed preachers seized her. He should have known what was going to happen next.

And after they burned her...

After they burned her, he should have levelled their city, instead of simply fleeing out into the wastes.

But he had been soft then. Naive. He had still carried too much faith along with him.

He had faith in precious little, now. Only that he would watch that accursed temple fall, and that the God-Emperor of Mankind would hear his every word when he cursed the Golden Throne over its ruins.

'I am a fool in man's clothes,' Sergeant Henderson muttered, crawling over a block of crumbling rockcrete at the base of Providence's southern wall. He slipped back into the briny water on the other side, lasgun raised overhead as the murky sea rose to his shoulders, sloshing just high enough to cover the brass chevrons inlaid on his battle-scarred pauldrons.

'Wet clothes, more specifically,' Maltia called back with an impudent grin. 'But I won't make the argument that you aren't a fool.'

Aerand moved between two groups of troopers, Maltia and her three heavies leading the detachment with Henderson and his eleven rifles at her rear. Under the scant cover of evening, they made their way through the debris field along the base of Providence's southern sea wall, interwoven with a patchwork of shoddily constructed wooden hovels and walkways suspended over the ocean on rickety stilts.

'They call this the Skirts,' Maltia said, watching her eye the precarious buildings. 'Narrow strip between the city's outer sea wall and the inner dyke. It's been good for little more than an esplanade since the outer wall failed decades ago, but it's also the only shelter for miles for those too poor, or too unwelcome, to be tolerated inside.'

Aerand grunted a reply, distracted.

Overhead, the troopers of Primus and Tertius companies were hard at work by the light of red helmet-lumens, lugging gun mounts and sandbags up the poorly kept wall to create a series of improvised battlements. But despite the sheen of sweat on their brows, none of those faces looked down on the troopers in the water with envy. With the coming of evening, the haze around Providence had grown thicker, contracting around the city like a hungry noose. Now, only a few dozen yards from the wall, those billowing clouds teemed with countless ethereal forms and the inhuman, bodiless voices of the dead.

'Stand ready. It's beginning already. Again,' she mumbled towards the sergeant.

Toting her own laspistols overhead to keep them from the corrosive currents, Aerand fingered the single tarot card tucked against her chest. With the wafer of lorelei brushing against her skin, a faint warmth emanated from the card itself. The secret to the Tarot was that its players wanted to be seen. But she would deny this portent a little while longer.

Jarrah Kellipso was missing or dead, and Major Restripa alone among the soldiers of the 900th seemed to know why. He had lied to her on the sea wall, she would stake her life on it. And it seemed, then, that only two possibilities remained. Either Kellipso had vanished naturally, and the major sought to obscure the circumstances of that disappearance, or the major had arranged for the primaris psyker's departure himself. She could imagine precious few motivations he might have for such an act, and none of them were forgivable.

'Mist's getting closer, sergeant,' Tannius Ebonwelter called, nervously tapping the barrel of his flamer.

'I've got eyes, trooper,' Sergeant Maltia replied without a hint of alarm.

Somewhere in that unbreachable white, a ritual was beginning. Aerand had felt the first echoes of it on the wall with Major Restripa. And now, as the mists warred against whatever unseen forces emanated from Javax Cathedral to shelter the city, it appeared the darkness outside the walls was winning.

'It's almost like the damned fog's breathing,' Evrik replied. 'It'll be on us in full, soon.'

Indeed, with starts and retreats, like the inhale and exhale of breath, those cloying white mists marched ever closer to the wall. With them, a tide of morbid, long-deceased faces, and mad, unintelligible whispers grew ever closer at hand as Aerand felt the warp reach out towards her mind.

'Then we'll burn them back again,' Maltia replied. 'Just like we did last time.' Evrik nodded dumbly, but appeared unrelieved.

Each trooper in this formation had stood within those clouds unshielded and knew first-hand the frenetic draw of that unthinkable madness. And it showed. There was no trooper in the 900th that could be rightly called a coward, but it was clear that none of them savoured the thought of repeating that experience.

Except, perhaps, for Sergeant Raniais Maltia.

As she crawled atop a small outcropping of stone, all but her boots rising dripping from the murky, sodden water, the sergeant's face was set in its resident smirk, as if the palpable enmity leaking from the very air around them did nothing to touch her unshakable resolve. Thoughtfully, Aerand reached into the empyrean, confirming once more that a dim flame flickered on that ephemeral fabric directly where the sergeant stood.

Even rarer among the human species than the mutations that led to the formation of individuals capable of consciously controlling the warp's power were the opposing null genes that rendered their bearers utterly immune to the empyrean's effects. Aerand had spent more than enough time in the presence of those who possessed the pariah gene during her two voyages on those accursed Black Ships. And after feeling the horrible, unnatural presence of even remote proximity to a true psychic blank, she had no doubt she would never forget the experience.

There were, of course, subtler forms of that same unnatural deviation, which rendered their bearers disconnected in lesser degrees from the warp, but she felt no such aura around Sergeant Maltia, simply an utter and unshakeable lack of fear. One that Aerand could not explain.

Ahead, a row of tiny, dilapidated shacks rose from the water on stilts, hugging the rockcrete of the sea wall like forest creatures sheltering beneath a tree.

'Storm's coming,' Sergeant Maltia remarked after making eye contact with a young man inside one of the shelters. 'You'll be wanting to find yourself inside the walls when it does.'

The gaunt man shivered beneath a muddy blanket but made no reply, his arms lined with the telltale pockmarks of sedative addiction. As she passed, Aerand caught a flicker of heat from her bridle, as the man's mind reached out, unbidden, towards her own.

'They'll bring you nothing but more pain,' Aerand whispered sadly. 'There is no salvation for you within those mists, only madness.'

The man made no reply, only curled around himself more tightly, the voices from the mist undoubtedly filling his mind. This was the psyker's fate, after all. Isolation and madness. Perhaps he viewed the risk of death to come as a blessed relief rather than a danger.

Aerand's hand fell again to the card at her chest, and she whispered a silent prayer of thanks. If not for men like Lord Prefector Ule and Jarrah Kellipso, those haunted, empty eyes might have very well been her own.

'I swear, this water is getting higher,' Trooper Bantholo called back, crossing beneath a rickety scaffold on a narrow wood plank. 'Remind me exactly why we're traipsing through mud and piss out here when there's a perfectly good wall only a few yards away?'

Sergeant Maltia looked down at the turbid ocean beneath her, now scarcely inches from the rotting planks under her boots. 'Because that wall isn't going to mean much for long.'

Aerand's premonition had been brief, but explicit, as she stood atop the breakwater beside Major Restripa earlier in the evening. A dark sea. Three red moons. A city swallowed by the ocean. For his part, Restripa had not seemed entirely surprised at her interpretation or their enemy's stratagem, only the fact that the Witchbringer believed his marsh priests capable of executing it.

Dark water now sloshed atop the planks of the Skirts, washing decades of debris and detritus into the shallow sea. With every moment, the mists around Providence drew closer, and those persistent waters continued to rise.

Providence had survived for five thousand years by keeping Visage's relentless ocean at bay, but decades of disrepair had left the city's defences against the sea almost as brittle as its defences against opposing troops, and its walls, no matter how impressive, were not impermeable. Buried deep beneath the city, a series of enormous, ancient bilge pumps laboured endlessly to remove the water which crept through cracks and pockets in the ancient sea wall. But without any Adeptus Mechanicus presence in nearly a decade to minister to the massive, ancient machines, it would take precious little to flood the city entirely.

Overhead, the clouds broke for a precious moment, as Aerand shuffled between two leaning, shadowed buildings. The light of the triplet moons filtered down through the array of rotting, moss-draped scaffolding that made up the Skirts.

'It's unnatural,' one of Henderson's troopers muttered, looking up at the sky.

'Unholy,' Trooper Bantholo replied, shaking his head and touching the small silver figure of Saint Crassus around his neck.

Once in a millennium, the random orbits of Visage's three moons would bring each of the celestial bodies into alignment at once. Despite their small individual size, the combined gravity of all three moons could pull massive swells of water to a specific point on the planet. Tonight, the three sisters lay only inches apart, directly over Providence.

The savants of the Departmento Munitorum had predicted no such event for the next hundred years.

Aerand closed her eyes and gripped her force staff, casting her mind into the deep fog that now lay only a few hundred yards away. The weapon in her hands practically shook from the sheer ambient psychic power flickering through the night. Within the darkness of Visage's mists, hundreds of individual coals glimmered, the psychically attuned minds of the Witchbringer's psykers engaging in deep communion with the warp.

'Turn left,' Aerand called to Maltia, turning down a narrow corridor. The toppled debris of a former storefront obscured the path ahead. One of Sergeant Henderson's troopers strode past, his boots splashing through the thin film of ocean water now covering the rough-planked boardwalks. The orange-red light of Visage's triplet moons shone off the mirror-dark surface with almost distressing brightness, bathing the entire night in a fire-like glow. The trooper stepped, his boot falling suddenly through an unseen gap in the rotten floorboard, but Aerand grabbed his arm before he plunged beneath the water.

'Careful,' she muttered. 'Treacherous footing tonight.'

The trooper muttered an unintelligible thanks, but shook off her grasp as quickly as he could manage. Sergeant Maltia strode past him, no such unsteadiness to her stride, and clapped him on the shoulder.

'Not much farther, Garb,' she called, nodding at the solid wall of mist only feet away.

Swirling, pale droplets swallowed the Skirts entirely beyond this point, faint shapes rising and then falling from their surface. Maltia paused and signalled back to her heavies in battle sign. Trooper Bantholo stacked against a plank wall behind her, while the Ebonwelter twins faced them across the narrow way.

With a motion of his hands, Sergeant Henderson's squad followed suit, twelve lasguns prepped and trained on the swirling gloom ahead. Slowly, Aerand strode through the corridor of flesh and steel, until she stood face to face with the tangled wall of white.

Hundreds of witches raged within those swirling billows, their souls bright enough to be seen in the empyrean even through the mist's unnatural veil. Truth be told, she had sensed the psykers' burgeoning power long before her premonition had shown her the intent of their foul ritual. For a single psyker to manipulate a moon was an utterly unthinkable task. For even a thousand acting in concert to do so was madness, something she would have thought impossible. Until tonight.

Nine clusters of flame burned through the empyrean surrounding the besieged city of Providence. Nine. The number of madness. The number of the twisted, fickle sorcerer-god. A bitter wheel surrounded the entrapped city, threads from each of those rungs reaching to the moons overhead. To pull against that wheel was utterly beyond Aerand, but break a single spoke and the wheel would fall apart.

Major Restripa had wanted her to bring a whole company, but two hundred soldiers stood no chance of hiding, even in these mists.

Sixteen, though. Sixteen shock troopers and one psyker...

Opening her eyes, Aerand stared straight into the wall of white, a face coalescing directly across from her within that utterly colourless void.

'Stay close,' she called to the troopers behind her, her voice dripping with the iron grip of her will. 'And once we find them, you burn everything, living or otherwise.'

Casually, she raised her staff and split the mist corpse before her in two, a ring of golden flame lacing her steps as she walked into the fog.

'You're not afraid, are you?' the hooded woman asked her.

Raniais Maltia had been scarcely eight years old the first time she'd witnessed the effects of Chaos. The daughter of a veteran of the wars of the Eye, she had seen the scars it left on her father long before anyone else. Perhaps because she had never met the man before he returned home from the Cadian Gate. Perhaps because she was only a child, and still understood a child's fear of the dark.

She remembered blessed little of her time in that small hab in Kasr Breck, other than the brisk bite of the wind streaming off the Rossvar Mountains. The roll of the grey ocean. The violet light of the Eye overhead. And the feel of her father's fists against her ribs with his breath reeking of amasec. Too many soldiers beat their partners. Too many fathers beat their children. She knew enough of the galaxy to recognise that now, and to know that not every coward who struck a child had been broken by the warp.

Yet, she would never forget the day she returned from the game fields to find the man who had sired her in a pool of his own blood, his service lasgun hanging limply in a lifeless hand. The note beside his body had described the things he'd seen while at war – the memories he'd tried, and failed, to conquer – and even mention of those horrors had made her mind reel.

She had done, of course, what any God-Emperor-fearing Cadian child would have done, and after her father's blasphemous letter was burned, she hailed a passing arbitrator, who offered to bring her to the doors of the schola progenium.

She had declined. Many of those who entered the schola progenium became clerks and priests. Not all became heroes. The Emperor had enough paper-pushers already. Instead, she took her father's lasgun and reported to the barracks of his regiment. To fulfil the duty of the Maltia who had forsaken his.

Her regiment had been spared the Fall. Or deprived the honour of it. They'd been in transit from a distant expeditionary world called Perth when their home world had vanished into the warp. But in four years as an aide to the regimental commander of the Cadian 490th, she had crossed six times into the fringes of the Cicatrix Maledictum. On three of those expeditions, she

had carried the regiment's colours herself. On the battered, warp-touched
fringe worlds of the Cadian Sector, she had seen more heretics and possessed than she'd known sane men in her life.

And for a horrible moment, she understood that draw.

At twelve years old, she had seen the same terrible shadow creep into
the face of the commander who had raised her as his own. And so, after
the commissar had ended his heresy, and that of half the officer corps
of the regiment, she had vowed to herself that she would never suffer to
see that same look upon the face of another person she loved. That she
would take their life at the first hint of that terrible madness.

So, no. She was not afraid. She had learned long ago that Chaos died just
as soon as it was brought into the light.

Lord Psyker Glavia Aerand, formerly Captain Glavia Aerand, looked towards
her awaiting a response, a thoughtful expression stretched across the psyker's
gaunt face. Within the shadow of her cowl, the dark circles beneath her violet
eyes appeared even deeper, her paper-thin skin stretched enough to see the
crimson vessels coursing beneath it like roads on a map.

The primaris psyker's face wore a pained expression of its own, and the
mark of the warp was clear enough across her. A thin wall of golden flame
streamed out from the woman's staff, encircling the small contingent of
Cadian troopers in a living bastion of fire.

Raniais Maltia stared deeply at that face once again, her fingers drumming against the cool barrel of her flamer. Despite the fact that the woman
beside her wielded the warp as a weapon, despite the fact that her soul
clearly swam in those unholy waters, there was no hint of perversion in her
eyes. Only the haunted clarity of a woman who had seen the same things
Maltia herself had.

'No, lord psyker,' she replied. 'I'm not afraid. This darkness burns just
the same as any other.'

Down. Down. Always down. The stink of Chaos, like water, somehow seemed
to find its way deep beneath the earth into tiny, subterranean spaces.

Aerand cursed to herself as she pushed a thin wall of flame before her
through the labyrinthine maze of tunnels. They had wasted precious time
searching half blinded in the mists for the small port entrances to the maintenance tunnels that serviced the ancient bilge pumps beneath Providence's
inner sea wall. Aerand was no engineer, but even she knew that only the
hubris of the tech-priesthood could have allowed them to construct such
important devices so deep beneath the sea they battled back. And despite
centuries of Herculean efforts, those bilge pumps were slowly losing the war.

By the best reports Confessor Libertinum could provide, only three of the
city's original dozen bilge halls still functioned, and of their current condition, almost nothing was known. The chambers had been left to their
own for good reason. The claustrophobic tunnels which began within the
wall itself careened downwards at a series of obscene angles and unreasonable slopes, clearly designed for creatures with mechanical limbs, and
steel hearts.

'Watch your footing,' Sergeant Maltia called through the vox-bead in her ear, the glow of her helmet-lumen flashing white against the mists that obscured their path even this far below Visage's surface. Aerand lowered herself through a narrow opening in the floor behind the sergeant, a small cascade of turbid, dark water splashing over her arms and head as she did. She spat the taste of salt and metal from her mouth.

Another corridor, nearly identical to the level above, stretched out before her, sloping slightly downwards with a small stream of water pooling at its centre. From those frigid depths, the unholy scraping sounds of metal limbs on stones rang out, accompanied by the deep echoes of inhuman machine-speech.

'Damned tech-priests,' Maltia muttered. 'Stay close and stay ready.'

As she passed a small alcove, the sergeant stopped, her lumen falling upon the alien, unnatural form of a mindless servitor twisted almost beyond recognition by the endless modifications the Adeptus Mechanicus imposed on its cybernetic servants. The caustic waters of Visage had claimed the creature long ago, its torso and legs pinned within a crumbling corridor and covered in a layer of moth-eaten rust. There was no head or face on the creature at all, merely an articulated stalk bearing a single augmetic ocular extending from its chest, coiled with sparking wires and cables dripping thick, dark fluid. The crimson light of its lone eye flickered dimly in the darkness, and a single one of its four hydraulic arms twitched rhythmically in a briny pool.

'It was protecting something,' Aerand called, reaching out to nudge the broken machine with her boot.

Beneath the servitor's shattered body, a second small machine was sheltered, saved from the collapse of the corridor by the dying Mechanicus servant. The small centrifugal bilge pump emitted an unsettling hum, dark water pouring into its ravenous maw and vanishing into the system of convoluted piping buried into the walls around it.

Even in death, the servitor had accomplished its purpose.

'Aye,' Maltia replied. 'Valour I might even respect, if not for the thought that the moment those machines fail, we'll find ourselves drowning in these depths.'

Aerand reached out, probing the broken servitor gently with her mind, but found nothing on the empyrean where its shattered form lay. All around her, however, the warp was buzzing with life.

Near, she signalled in Cadian battle sign. A vox-bead, while convenient, was not a necessary crutch for practised Cadian soldiers.

Ahead, the floor of the tunnel began to level, dark water pooling in shallow puddles on the floor. In this direction, the deep, thrumming heartbeat of the wall's great bilge hall grew from a quiet drumming to a shaking rhythm that could not be ignored. With each heave of those ancient, mechanical beasts, the water coating the floor seemed to withdraw, then return, like breath.

Aerand cast her mind forward more forcefully, risking exposure but counting on the fact that any witches in the enemy party would be fully engaged in whatever rite had brought them here. Within a massive chamber surrounded by heaving, mechanical giants, nineteen marsh priests stood amidst at least two platoons of Traitor Guardsmen. Ten plus nine. The number in itself was unsettling, although perhaps less so than the simple fact that there were more psykers in the room before her than troopers in her whole detachment.

Aerand threw back the hand signal for platoon strength twice, then pointed to herself and signalled another platoon.

Sergeants Maltia and Henderson gave her a questioning expression, then echoed the sign back to her.

She nodded grimly. Almost a full platoon of psykers alone.

'I will do my best to hold the witches at bay,' she said into her vox-bead. 'Tell your troopers to give me space and keep their guns off my back, but beyond that I leave any specific tactics to you.'

A brief nod from Maltia, then a flurry of battle sign between her and Henderson. Suddenly, sixteen Cadians disappeared into the network of branching tunnels and massive pillars around them. As Aerand strode forward, the flickering blue werelight of warp energy scintillated beyond the edge of the mists.

Within the centre of the massive bilge hall, the Witchbringer's marsh priests had cast their own barrier against the fog. It was useful to know that the traitor forces themselves were not immune to the Chaos they summoned. The witches, clad in drab brown and grey natural-fibre tunics, encircled a tangle of adamantium and steel larger than even Aerand had imagined. Despite the reprieve from the mists, the ancient bilge pump stretched high enough that the top of its structure was lost in the shadowy recessed ceiling of the chamber. Its two promethean pistons rose and fell in a slow but steady heartbeat, as they had for centuries.

Such a structure could not be easily undone, as the telltale scars of flamers and krak missiles along its massive tubing showed. Despite the tech-priesthood's retreat from the planet, the artefacts they left had been built to last, and it would take more than petty, hand-carried weapons to stop a labour that had been ongoing for half a millennium.

That ancient giant, however, no matter how resilient, was not truly immune to time, and the dark stains of corrosion lined its frame like scars on a veteran soldier's skin. As Aerand watched, that oxidation crawled across the bilge pump with visible speed. Her neck prickled with the strength of the warp energy emanating from the psykers surrounding the structure. The pump was immune to most physical, and even psionic, insults they could muster, but all things gave way to time in the end.

Maltia and Henderson's troopers moved at the fringes of those unholy mists, courageous despite their fear, using the maddening phantoms that circled within as cover for their movement. A faint ring of flame encircled each of the soldiers, as Aerand split her will sixteen different ways. A chorus of mad whispers beckoned at her back, taunting her to let those flames flicker away.

Slowly, she closed her eyes and drew a deep breath, then finally gave in to the urging.

Dropping her wards around her troopers, Aerand threw the full strength of her will against the single marsh priest who had devoted herself to keeping the mists at bay. The witch shrieked and then crumbled as Aerand shattered her mind, and ghosts swept through the chamber like a bitter wind, sixteen Cadian shock troopers rushing in on their heels.

Aerand was not certain which of the two were more worthy of fear.

Suddenly, the subterranean chamber echoed like a chancel with the cacophony of lasguns, autocannons and human screams. On the plane of the empyrean, a dozen traitor souls suddenly evaporated as sixteen professional killers stalked the mists beside her.

In the milky currents, a drab grey form rushed past her, Sergeant Henderson visible just long enough for her to watch him unload an entire power pack into a squad of Traitor Guardsmen forming up a few dozen yards away. With a sickly shift, the sergeant's practised movements took on a halting, unnatural cadence as he stumbled, then fell awkwardly to his knees. Clawing at his own throat, the trooper looked towards her, violet eyes meeting her own for only a moment, as a bubbling pool of blood began to pour from his mouth.

The bridle on her neck flashed white-hot.

Aerand threw her mind back against the psionic assault, then scoured the immaterium for the brightest soul she could locate. Across the chamber, just beside the massive bilge pump, a small inferno blazed with an unholy blue light.

+Come now, child,+ a voice boomed in her mind. +We cannot all be blinded by stealing our sight.+

Throwing a wall of hasty wards into the chamber before her, Aerand drew a laspistol and rushed towards the invading voice, her boots splashing through the shallow pools of offcast water, quickly turning red in the frenzied melee. Las-rounds scattered through the dim world around her, brilliant white bursts slicing through the fog like starfire. As they tore through the wavering forms of mist corpses, the faces of the dead simply parted, then re-formed around them.

A few feet behind her, another Cadian dropped in the mire. A sudden splash, then a gasp, then silence.

Before her, a trio of silhouettes appeared, and she felt a sudden heaviness in her limbs as she tried to step towards them. With no corpsewood trees to enact their dark will, the trio of marsh priests resorted to more traditional psychic compulsion.

Stop.

Rest.

Sleep.

Three voices rose above the chattering of Visage's dead, as three frail figures emerged from the fog before her. A thin woman, clad in furs, hair white and wispy like loam despite her young age, flanked on both sides by young men of similar proportions, each bearing a nearly identical face. Aerand shook the triplets' will with the assistance of her bridle, now a lance of white-hot fire along her neck, and planted her force staff in the bloody water at her feet.

+Burn.+

Confusion dripped from the witches at such an unreasonable, impossible command, before gouts of golden flame erupted from the floor beneath their feet. A trio of las-bolts ended their screams.

Diving into a tangle of shrouded shapes, Aerand raised her staff to counter the oncoming thrust of a crude bayonet affixed to a rusted lasgun. It was a reasonable attack from a well-trained trooper. Despite their heresy, she could not fault her enemy on technique. But the trooper, no matter how well trained, was no Cadian, and she had learned to parry bayonet thrusts nearly as soon as she could walk.

Hooking the lasgun's barrel with the silver aquila mounted atop her staff, Aerand stepped inside the impending discharge and drove her pistol into the Traitor Guardsman's left axilla, just at the crease between his flak plate and pauldron. She pulled the trigger, and the man crumbled onto the damp floor beside a Cadian trooper pinned beneath a hulking ogryn.

Sergeant Maltia looked up with an expression of panic. The trooper had managed to wrestle a crude club crafted from a length of solid pipe out of the hands of the hulking mass of a woman atop her. From the two dead Cadians beside her, however, it appeared she had not been alone in the task.

+Wait,+ Aerand called as the sinew-laced giant raised an impossibly large hand over Maltia's throat. The ogryn paused for only a moment before Aerand's staff followed her words.

The tapered base of her force staff sank into the woman's barrel chest, piercing only muscle, and the las-bolt into her thigh that followed the strike did little more than cause the ogryn to roar. Despite Aerand's will, the mutant threw her back, before Maltia managed to raise a fallen lasgun in the moment of reprieve. A rain of blistering las-fire tore through the ogryn.

The sounds of ranged weapons faded from the room as the Cadians and Traitor Guard drew close enough for melee, replaced by the din of metal on metal and flesh against flesh. Above that sound, the whispering jabber of mist corpses continued, surpassed only by the thrumming heartbeat of the bilge pump, which had taken on an unnatural, straining sound.

'With us,' Aerand called to anyone who might listen, voice dripping with the remainder of her will.

Aerand and Maltia limped towards the bilge hall's centre, a small cluster of souls blazing ahead in the mist. Six marsh priests and a full squad of Traitor Guardsmen remained huddled against the bilge pump, completely ignoring the chaotic melee unfolding in the chamber.

Two armoured forms burst through the white fog to join them. For their part, the Ebonwelter twins didn't stop to ask questions, nor did they seem particularly perturbed by Aerand's sudden psionic imposition on their minds. Maltia's heavies were nothing if not excellent soldiers, but the autocannon-toting veterans had long since gained a reputation for following orders with precious little thought of their own. For such a trooper, the difference between psionic compulsion and a sergeant barking commands might not have truly been so large.

+Flanks,+ she ordered, and Evrik and Tannius split instantly to ten-yard spacing, perfectly executing the manoeuvre without question or confusion. As their presences drifted towards the cluster of souls surrounding the bilge pump, Aerand felt the bridle on her neck grow warm. For a moment, a dozen faces appeared in the mist before her, speaking nonsense into the din of the battle.

She pressed through, and into a small, quiet clearing, a massive tangle of steel and adamantium shadowing a small cluster of robed figures like a looming primarch. Las-fire met her the moment she stepped from the mist, followed by the crack of a heavy stubber. Sergeant Maltia dropped to a knee, pouring las-fire back at two teams of Traitor Guardsmen massed behind the scant cover of the twisting pipes, which stretched from the enormous machine like metal veins. Between them, a ring of marsh priests chanted.

Aerand raised her staff, and a Traitor Guardsman erupted in a plume of brilliant golden flame even as the Ebonwelter twins loosed paired auto-cannons against the waiting party. Another trio of Guardsmen dropped, followed by the inhuman scream of a marsh priest as her light snuffed out from the immaterium. The sudden absence of a presence so bright caused Aerand's mind to briefly spin, a throbbing scar left on the warp where the witch's soul had previously stood.

As Aerand sprinted towards the five remaining psykers, a sudden weight buffeted her to the side. She toppled, her bridle searing across her skull.

+Things with claws get treated like pests,+ that same, crooning voice boomed. One of those five remaining psykers was a powerful telepath, indeed.

Raising her own mental defences, Aerand lashed back half-heartedly, throwing barriers between the witch and Maltia's heavies, as well. A psyker's mind split three ways was less than a third as powerful, but without the drumming suppressive fire of the heavy troopers' weapons, the Traitor Guardsmen would take her life even before the witch could.

With what little psychic reserve she had left, Aerand cast her mind forward among the small cell of psykers sitting at the base of the bilge pump a few yards away. Four remaining marsh priests and the crone who led them circled a tiny tangle of steel. At first, she took the small mess of wire and tubing to be a mechanical device of its own, before she saw the runes painted in blood along its surface.

A simulacrum. Old magic. Unsophisticated, but effective. When an object itself was too complex, or too large, to be easily manipulated by a psyker directly, it could be easier to concentrate efforts on a smaller, simpler replica of that thing. And while the human mind perceived a difference between such linked objects, the empyrean did not. Aerand watched as the sheen of greenish-red rust crept across the small metal model, matched moments later by corrosion on the surface of the bilge pump's titanic twin.

As las-fire continued bouncing between Maltia, the Ebonwelter twins and the few remaining Guard flanking the marsh priests, a terrible groan filled the air. For a moment, the floor beneath the bilge chamber heaved, as some massive mechanism in the ancient machine roared in protest and then gave way. Without warning, pipes the size of a grown man's trunk burst against the sudden, unexpected onslaught of pressure, the resulting shrapnel shredding half a squad of Traitor Guardsmen.

Aerand pushed herself to her feet before that same psychic weight buffeted her again. This time, prepared, she cast it to the side. Her laspistol rang, and a pair of witches dropped from the accursed circle.

But too late.

Another mechanical screech escaped from the bilge pump before her, as dark, salty water began to pool at her feet. Aerand threw her mind against the three remaining witches, feeling their efforts falter for a moment before another presence intervened.

+Time devours us all,+ the crone chattered. +Against that there is no reprieve.+

Even without speech, the woman's voice was scattered and dishevelled, laced with the telltale pressure of a mind drinking too deeply from the warp. With a grunt, Aerand dropped her wards around her comrades and threw her will directly against the crone.

The woman faltered, before her three remaining marsh priests rushed to her aid and the bilge pump began to shake. Another pipe burst beside the colossal machine, as the foundations of the sea wall itself began to shiver.

The pump was lost, that much was clear now, and Aerand pushed herself onto her feet as muddy water rose to her knees. How many million tons of ocean waited to swallow them whole? How heavy did the weight of this entire world press on the monstrous relic of metal and gearwork before her?

For the pump to fail was one thing – the ensuing floodwaters would turn most of the inner city into swamp – but if the marsh priests before her continued their work, the massive construction might very well explode beneath the sudden weight of an entire planet's sea. She had no doubt the whole sea wall would collapse along with it, and there was no telling what devastation that would wreak.

Aerand lifted her laspistol, a single shot driving directly through the hooded figure at the head of the circle. The witch laughed, the round vanishing into the growing shadow gathering around her.

+Yes, child. The sea. The sea covers all in the end. Can't you hear? Don't you recognise the faces floating in these mists?+

The crone's voice came even faster now – more pressured. The signs of a psyker on the very edge of true madness. On the surface of the immaterium, the woman's flame suddenly flared a sickly black.

Aerand rose to her feet as the first convulsion seized the crone, a gout of dark water pouring from her mouth. The skin along the woman's frail arms rippled. Black roots suddenly burst from the witch, impaling the three psykers at her side and the few remaining Traitor Guardsmen beside the bilge pump. Greedily, the tendrils began drinking the bloody water pouring from the ancient machine, the scintillating peristalsis of some obscene mechanism coursing down their length with each ravenous gulp.

Like a pit of snakes, seething, monstrous appendages suddenly coursed along the floor from the witch, rushing towards Aerand. She raised a wall of fire and drove them back.

Why do you fight us? a voice raged in her mind, the crone's tenor nearly lost beneath a sudden chorus of morbid voices. *The sea claims all in the end.*

Beside her, the souls of the Ebonwelter twins dimmed, both troopers collapsing to the ground covering their ears. Shivering, Raniais Maltia dropped to her knees.

Desperately, Aerand threw her mind against the terrible, dark scar emerging on the surface of the empyrean, the bilge pump groaning as a dozen obscene roots coursed into its body through the open pipes arrayed around its base. As the crone continued her dark metamorphosis, the mists themselves drew closer around her, the macabre faces of mist corpses circling like eager spectators.

Don't you recognise their faces? the thing before her asked again. The crone's face rippled, replaced suddenly by that of a rotted, bloated corpse. *Don't you recognise Visage's dead? Don't be afraid, child. The sea does not forget her own.*

Aerand diverted a fraction of her will from her efforts to hold the bilge pump together, and another gout of flame rushed towards the monster before her. The thing that had once been the Witchbringer's crone laughed, a root rising from the ground to split Aerand's attack harmlessly. And with her will distracted for even a fraction of a moment, Aerand felt the bilge pump screech yet again.

+Come,+ she called, desperately. +Anyone. Now.+

The warp rippled, the combined force of the crone and Aerand's will ringing out like waves atop troubled water. And beneath that churn, a shadow rose.

Around the monstrous perversion between her and the bilge pump, the mists suddenly coalesced. Beside the crone, a second figure stood. White face. White flesh. Rippling white robes. And eyes of a steely, haunted grey.

I warned you.

A whisper in the back of Aerand's mind. For a moment, her will faltered, then was steeled, but before she could look again at the figure, the bright white glow of las-fire burst from the mist.

Slowly, with staggering, pained movements, Sergeant Raniais Maltia rose to her feet. Blood was splattered across the woman's face and streamed in crimson gouts from a trio of deep wounds along her left side. Still she advanced, straight towards the monster emerging before her, wielding a lasgun in each of her hands.

Two streams of white fire poured from the weapons, pummelling the twisted remnants of the crone. The creature screeched for a moment, before its cry became laced with an equal measure of glee as it saw its assailant was a simple ungifted.

Stop, the creature ordered. *Turn your weapon on your companions, then on yourself.*

For a terrible moment, Sergeant Maltia slowed, her lasguns falling silent and drifting towards the Ebonwelter twins, who cowered in the rising pool of water on the floor.

Aerand threw her mind against the crone's compulsion, adding her will to the sergeant's own. The fact that Maltia had not immediately complied with the daemon's order was almost impossible to believe, but no untrained human mind could maintain such resistance for long.

In Aerand's ears, the sound of the Astronomican swelled, and she threw the full brunt of that terrible, beautiful music directly towards the sergeant's mind.

Maltia blinked. The sergeant's lasguns roared to life, two streams of white-hot fire boring into the Chaotic obscenity crawling its way loose from the crone's failing body.

Stop, the creature roared again, but with its will broken once, the sergeant paid no heed. Undaunted, Maltia strode towards the monster, until she pressed both her weapons directly into what remained of the crone's twisted, cracked chest.

Aerand split the rippling, Chaotic wards around the abomination as Sergeant Maltia's lasguns roared, ripping entirely through the creature. A horrifying shriek emerged from the obscenity, followed by an equally terrible silence. As its myriad appendages writhed and shrivelled in the rising water, Maltia bent over the woman to whisper in her ear.

'I have stood against more terrible monsters than you.'

The sudden weight of the crone's psionic presence vanished from Aerand's shoulders, so disorienting that she found herself vomiting into dark water nearly up to her waist. Unhindered now, she threw a wall of flame out around her, pushing the mists back to the edges of the room.

Slowly, Sergeant Maltia lifted the Ebonwelter twins to their feet and threw their arms around each other, since neither were fully able to stand on their own. On the other side of the room, Trooper Bantholo and two of Henderson's troopers stumbled towards the groaning bilge pump.

'Out. Now. Bantholo, take point,' Sergeant Maltia ordered, passing by Aerand with the slightest of smirks. 'The boy might have nothing but void-space in his brain, but he's got a nose for direction. I swear he could have been a navigator, if there had been anything in his head at all.'

Aerand simply nodded, the levity lost on her, and stepped towards the twisted remnants of the crone, slumped against the rusted base of the ancient bilge pump.

The dark flame within that shell of flesh was quickly fading, but a flicker of the crone's soul still remained. The woman's eyes hung open, half glazed in the slow process of death. She blinked as Aerand stepped up beside her, then coughed a thin plume of oily bile and blood.

'The Witchbringer,' Aerand demanded. 'Where is he? If he wants a war, I will give him one myself.'

A look of confusion passed across the crone's dying face, then a horrible cackle from a void-dark maw. 'The Colonel? That crusty fool? We do not worship a man, you ignorant child. The Witchbringer. The sea. They claim all, in the end.'

The ramblings of a dying madwoman.

Aerand pressed her laspistol against the crone's forehead.

CHAPTER 10

The Colonel felt the crone's departure. Or rather, he alone did not.

Around him, the night breathed a palpable sigh in the sudden absence of the mad witch. On the knoll behind him four of her marsh priests collapsed, blood pouring from their eyes and ears, convulsing in a mess of wretched little tremors. Those witches still standing appeared suddenly burdened, as if holding the weight of the moons overhead for the first time.

He looked up and watched the satellites shiver.

'Dead,' he cursed. There was no other reasonable explanation. The crone had met her match, and the Cadian psyker had dispatched her.

The Colonel turned from the city, back towards his command tent. If he had learned one thing in decades of command, it was that wars were determined mostly by failures and the ways in which armies responded to them.

The Doreans would charge the wall, then. Or undermine it. Or engage in any of a dozen other stratagems that had not even occurred to him yet. But they would take the primaris psyker in the bitter end, even if it cost him every life, including his own.

As the Colonel departed, a rough hand stopped him, and he turned to face Sergeant Gross.

'The crone is dead,' the man confirmed, a hint of pleasure in his expression. None of his Doreans had borne any love for the witch. 'But she did not fail,' the sergeant continued. With an outstretched hand he touched the point of his longsword to a stone on the ground. The silver blade quivered slightly in the moonlight.

The Colonel paused.

Another ripple. Subtle, but undeniable.

Then the earth heaved beneath his boots as something cracked behind him, and a stretch of sea wall nearly a mile long disappeared into the sea. Water rushed past the Colonel in a hungry torrent, sweeping shivering witches off their feet beside troopers of the Dorean 19th. Overhead, Visage's moons drifted slowly apart, the weight of the surging ocean too much for the psykers who remained.

But that mattered not, now. Their task had been accomplished.

Through the rent in the wall, the sea came to Providence.

* * *

'The Witchbringer is not a man.'

Aerand strode into the cupola and dropped an ancient, stained volume into the middle of the hololithic display that dominated Javax Cathedral's most isolated, private room.

'Emperor's bones,' Major Restripa shouted. The pixelated, ghostly blue light of the hololithic model of Providence scattered as the tome descended, then re-formed, a dark square in the centre of the viewfield. 'What the hell is the meaning of this?'

Beside him, the company commanders of the 900th Regiment each reacted in nearly identical fashion. Of the six officers gathered at the small, round table, only Lieutenant Kobald responded with anything other than pure frustration. The small grin on the Sentinel pilot's face only doubled when the robed figure across the table practically spat a mouthful of dark wine into the air. Those droplets floated in a mist across the hololithic image, like a blood-red fog descending on Visage's capital city. As fitting an omen as Aerand had ever seen.

'I warned you not to return to this place,' Confessor Javard Libertinum growled. The massive, robed man stirred on his chair of dark polished wood, the ghastly cherub atop its backrest fluttering away at the sudden commotion. Libertinum looked over his shoulder towards the arching doorway, where two of his preachers had stood vigil only moments ago.

Aerand had done no harm to either man, and they would soon discover that the voice which had summoned them down the hallway was nothing but a figment in their minds.

'I go wherever the God-Emperor commands,' Aerand replied, staring out of the panoramic armaglass window that encircled the entire rotunda. From atop Providence's only building of import, the damage already caused by the loss of the ancient bilge pump was painfully clear.

The hololithic chart around which Visage's principals gathered showed the city as it had stood several days ago. On that display, three companies of Cadian infantry marked even intervals along the city's inner wall, with a dozen Basilisks encircling a perimeter less than half as wide. Two squadrons of Sentinel walkers roved across the translucent display, drifting like predatory fish to support a roving picket just beyond the inner sea wall.

A strong defence. A textbook defence. And one that was certain to shatter almost instantly at the first enemy assault. Because what the map at the centre of the table did not show was the raging sea pouring in through Providence's sea wall, claiming more of the capital every hour.

Less than a quarter of the inner city remained above that salty mess, and the few sections of the city not entirely submerged now resembled the outskirts more than anything else. After only three days without the aid of millennia-old engineering, the city outside the window looked little different from the rest of the planet. Scattered patches of high ground rose just above the water's edge, those buildings whose foundations had not already toppled in the sudden mire emerging like corpsewood trees from the mess.

Kobald's armourers – the closest the regiment possessed to engineers or savants – had already ruled out any chance of repairing or replacing the dead bilge pumps or the sea wall itself. And while they seemed confident that the water would rise little further, even a few more feet would be enough to drown every inch of the city aside from the single, central hill atop which Javax Cathedral stood.

The rifles of Captain Ulrich's Primaris Company had already been pulled back from the wall and were desperately encircling any depot or building of import with crudely packed sandbags full of dripping mud, accompanied by two platoons of Captain Havas' artillery, who had been forced to abandon their Earthshaker cannons to the sea when the bilge pump initially died. A squadron of Kobald's Sentinels had tried to rescue one of the artillery pieces, only to see it drag two of his walkers into the mud.

It was clear to Aerand, even without access to the constant reports streaming in from squad and platoon leaders to this room, that Providence's defence could handle little more than a stiff wind at the moment, much less a full assault from an organised force with more than a regiment of trained troopers and an untold number of psychic irregulars.

The only blessing in all this was that their enemy had somehow failed to notice that fact.

At the head of the table, Captain Vyse sighed, running a muddy hand through damp hair. Every commander at the table looked similarly dirtied and exhausted. Other than frequent, but brief, battle councils in this chamber, the officers had been slogging through that same mess with their soldiers. If Vyse had slept more than three hours in as many days, Aerand would have been willing to decry the Emperor Himself.

'Speak your piece, Aerand, if the major will allow it. You've interrupted already, and Captain Havas should thank you for stopping the nonsense that was coming out of his mouth. I doubt anything you have to say could possibly be less helpful.'

The burly artillery captain glowered at Vyse, but didn't reply. Inwardly, Aerand thanked the captain for the opening, turning towards Major Restripa.

'What are you waiting for?' the major asked crossly. 'You didn't ask my permission to enter this council or to open your mouth the first time, so I'm not sure why you want it now. Be brief, then be quiet. And hope to the God-Emperor that when you're finished I don't believe you've wasted our time. With the confessor's permission, of course,' he offered.

Across the table, Libertinum fumed, but nodded. While the officers of the 900th were technically his guests in this cathedral, there was a reason they outnumbered him six to one. Whatever power the Ecclesiarchy had once wielded over Providence had shattered along with the city's wall.

This was now a world under martial law.

Aerand did her best to bury her satisfaction at the confessor's uncomfortable accession, and stepped up to the hololithic table. With a flick of her wrist, the machine whined and then died, the top of the table falling suddenly dark. From the pages of the ancient tome atop it, she carefully unfolded a fraying, yellowed map.

'The answer was painfully clear once I knew what to look for, and where to look for it. Before landing on this Throne-cursed surface, I surveyed every paltry piece of Imperial data in the *Emperor's Grace*'s archives that fell below my security clearance. There was precious little, but the conspicuous absence of any aerial imaging told me that even basic mapping of this world had not been completed in centuries. Truth be told, I should have seen the connection sooner.'

From a satchel on her back Aerand pulled out a small, dark box. It gave her substantial anxiety to think of the deck of the Emperor's Tarot that had previously occupied it. Unprotected and unshielded from the warp, the deck within her pocket was at risk of unknown contamination, but she had needed the psionically shielded vessel for something more important. Carefully, she set the box on the table and lifted the lid.

'I don't know why it took me so long to see the obvious linkage. The mythos surrounding the corpsewood trees should have been more than trigger enough. The name alone and the curious method of their growth make it painfully evident in retrospect.'

As Aerand reached into the psionic box and removed the tiny corpsewood sapling, she felt the familiar chill of the empyrean lance up her arm. While it had taken her days to suspect that such a thing might – must – exist, it had taken her only a few hours to find one once she knew what she was looking for. She'd ventured to the very edge of the mist wall, now encroaching through Providence's inner breakwater at the places where it had already failed.

The ocean still poured in slowly through those gaps, carrying the flotsam of war along with it. Within minutes she had come across a body, bloated and pale already only a few days after it had been drowned. The corpsewood sapling had already sunk its roots deeply enough into the man's flesh that she'd had to bring the corpse's whole hand with her.

The raw, cold flesh flopped onto the table with a sickening thud. The Cadian veterans who watched showed no sign of surprise, but Confessor Libertinum practically jumped from his seat.

'What is the meaning of this, adept?' he shouted. 'You profane this holy place with your very presence, let alone the mutilated flesh of heretics!'

'I do,' Aerand admitted. 'To illustrate a point. Why are there no corpsewood trees in Providence, confessor? Why did they reach no further than the very outskirts of Charity when they cover the surface of this Throne-cursed planet like grass?'

'They are not savages here,' Major Restripa replied. 'The populace knows to clear and burn their dead, and they are more than capable of felling arborage.'

'This corpse had been dead no more than a few hours, sir. And Charity has not been occupied in a year, and yet this is the first sapling I've seen growing near any Imperial settlement. And I suspect the first you've seen since you arrived on this world.'

As she spoke, the thin, wispy stalk sprouting from the corpse's hand began to shrivel, until it was soon nothing more than a limp stalk of wood. At the sight, Libertinum made the sign of the aquila and muttered a benediction beneath his breath.

'That tree was healthy a moment ago, within a psionically shielded vessel.'

Silence at the table before Kobald raised his head. 'There were trees at Burnum,' he mumbled. 'But not Temperance or Justice. I don't remember seeing any near Fortitude either, but that's hardly more than a chapel's ruins.' As he spoke, the lieutenant seemed to realise his own point. 'The chapels. Holy sites.'

Aerand nodded towards Libertinum. 'I think so. I sensed a latent taint on the trees the first time I saw them, but not strong enough to confirm my suspicions. But now I've watched witches twist these roots and branches with ease and seen new saplings grow beyond their previous boundaries only under the cover of accursed mists in which the faces of the dead walk again. The only conclusion is that these twisted, stunted trees possess a psionic connection to a powerful psychic entity. One that cannot survive proximity to the Emperor's light. The trees could not spread before, but as we lost battles, and chapels fell to the traitors and were defiled, their pestilence rushed into the gap.'

'That bloody Dorean colonel. Or one of his witches,' Captain Havas hissed. 'Let me loose my remaining Earthshakers and turn this entire quadrant into a muddle of potholes. Chances are we'll catch the bastard in the crossfire.'

'Emperor's bones,' Captain Vyse sighed. 'You get more idiotic every time you speak, Havas. These trees have grown across Visage for ten thousand years. The Doreans arrived less than a decade before us.'

Captain Havas nearly rose from his seat, the man's burly shoulders curling up as his face turned beet red. 'Who then,' he hissed, 'if not for those heretics? Are you volunteering as the culprit or simply admitting that your ceaseless patrols have failed to turn up anything more than empty cities and Imperial casualties?'

The room fell silent following the exchange, before Major Restripa eventually sighed.

'Enough theatrics, adept. Get to the point. If not one of the Doreans or their marsh priests, then who?'

'The Witchbringer.'

Libertinum scoffed. 'The Witchbringer? Didn't we just discount that deluded fool of a colonel? I remember him from the moment he stepped off his landing craft. The man was scarcely capable of commanding a regiment, let alone a whole planet.'

'Despite the confessor's condemnation, the Dorean has proved capable of much more than that – organising a guerrilla insurrection for the better part of a decade while uniting former Imperial soldiers and a native Chaos cult,' said Aerand.

But whatever his virtues – whatever his strengths – she believed what his crone had uttered with her final breath.

'The Witchbringer is not a man,' she repeated.

Finally, she turned to the ancient volume on the table. One that had been far more difficult to find than the withered corpsewood sapling resting beside it.

In the deep recesses of the cathedral, Ordinate Jossen lay curled in a sobbing ball. She had left the Departmento Munitorum clerk's mind full of nothing but endless series of unbalanced ledgers and equations fraught with fallacies. She had offered the man an opportunity to help her, even used her will to push him towards compliance, but in the end his own stubbornness had been his downfall.

She'd had no time to complete the veritable mountain of requisition forms he'd required in order to peruse the archives under his control, so she'd settled for a faster, less elegant solution.

She nodded towards the confessor. 'The oldest map I could find of Visage's founding. From Lucius Javax's original ledgers. If I'm not mistaken, I believe the map itself may have been penned in the priest-itinerant's own hand.'

Javard Libertinum's face grew somehow even darker as he reached out for the volume before Vyse snatched it away.

'Adept,' he growled. 'You presume too much. That is a sacred relic and the sole property of the Ecclesiarchy. Leave this cathedral immediately. Else I am not to blame for what I might do.'

The pair of cherubs perched on the rafters behind the confessor suddenly took flight and circled over him like waiting raptors. Aerand had no illusions that the creatures were anywhere near as placid as their childlike forms might suggest.

'Do as he says,' Major Restripa sighed. 'I'm done with this charade.'

'Sir–'

'Enough. The confessor is right. You presume far too much, *Adept* Aerand. You do not command this regiment, nor even one of its companies any longer. And it appears you have lost even the ability to command yourself. Although I'm not sure I should have ever expected more from a psyker.'

'Sir–'

The major shot a glare of pure ice in her direction, then briefly made eye contact with the confessor. His hand drifted to the sidearm on his belt. Slowly, Aerand nodded, then turned to leave the room, drawing out the moment as long as she could.

Then, just in time, Captain Vyse spoke.

'Throne above,' she muttered, staring down at the map. Lieutenant Kobald leaned over the dusty volume, then let out a long and slow whistle.

'Major,' he called. 'Come and look at this.'

Begrudgingly, Restripa rose from his chair, motioning for Aerand to wait.

'It always seemed that there should have been a pattern,' Kobald muttered, turning the volume for Restripa and the remaining officers to see. 'Providence, Temperance, Fortitude, Ire. I've had squadrons through half a dozen settlements on this planet, and it always seemed they were too regular, too symmetric, to be random. But there weren't enough left standing for us to see the pattern.' The Sentinel commander's voice was laced with excitement, which Captain Vyse more than matched, her eyes riveted on the yellowing page.

'There have to be a hundred chapels marked on this map, all massed into rings nearly the entire continent wide. If I didn't know any better, I'd say it was a cordon.'

'Just like Providence's sea wall.'

Vyse paused at that, then looked up towards Aerand. 'Except this wall was designed to keep something in. Wasn't it?'

Aerand nodded. 'I believe so.'

'And "Witchbringer". That's not just a name, is it? Whatever's sitting in the empty space on this map is the reason there are so many psykers on this world. The reason a ragged cult of swamp-dwellers had the strength to pull three damn moons over our heads.'

Major Restripa glared at Vyse, then shared a look of mounting concern with Confessor Libertinum.

'This is nonsense,' Captain Havas barked. 'It might just as soon be that spot is useless for building. Or a trench where the ocean is twice as deep.'

Silence for a moment. It was possible, certainly, yet every person in the room knew the idea was patently false.

Too many coincidences. Too many secrets that fitted.

'And what do you want me to do with these suspicions?' Major Restripa leaned over the table, both hands gripping its worn, dark edges. The man looked exhausted, harried.

Vyse and Kobald responded almost in unison. 'I want you to pursue them.'

'How?' Restripa sighed. 'We are besieged and surrounded. We are barely holding the last reservoir of Imperial power on this world. If I send a single soldier beyond these walls, I am afraid they will utterly collapse around us.'

'So let them,' Aerand replied.

Conversation ceased at the audacity of the thought, an ugly mix of emotion dripping from the cupola's occupants. A slow, cool rage flowed from Confessor Libertinum, laced with the bitter flavour of suspicion. Major Restripa himself was more difficult to read, as if he wanted to be convinced, but something unspeakable held him back. Aerand resisted the urge to reach out and simply knock down the mental walls the major had erected. The rest of the 900th's commanders appeared uncertain, aside from Captain Havas, who was clearly eager for nothing more than the major's approval.

'Major,' the confessor remarked slowly. 'Providence's cathedral is the only sanctuary you have. If you let it fall into the hands of the cultists, there will be no safe place on this planet.'

Captain Vyse scoffed. 'Look around you, confessor. Look at the tide rising outside your window and the scorch marks already staining these walls. How safe, exactly, do you think your cathedral is?'

'Without the Imperial Guard it will burn completely.'

'Then let it burn,' Kobald replied. 'We've been tasked with defending a planet, not a building. If surrendering Providence means winning us Visage, then it's a price we should be more than willing to pay.'

'And if you are wrong?' the confessor shot back. 'If there's nothing more than an empty swamp waiting on that map and you've abandoned the city to gain you nothing?'

'Then we're no worse off than we will be here tomorrow,' Aerand replied.

In the last moments, there had been a shift in the room, and if she could not drive the dagger home now, then she would at least give it an earnest shot.

'I am not suggesting we trade victory for defeat, major. I'm suggesting we abandon a clearly failing stratagem in favour of one that has an actual chance to succeed.'

Around the table, half a dozen faces waited for the major's decision, orders of march and supply lists already racing through their heads. These officers could stomach the prospect of defeat. What they could not tolerate was the thought of inaction.

Restripa released the table and sighed, casting one final look towards the confessor.

'Very well,' he muttered. 'If we must burn, we will burn brightly.'

'Adept,' Major Restripa called as she passed beyond the outer door of Javax Cathedral. As she crossed the threshold, she felt a weight rise from her shoulders. From one of the saint-encrusted windows above, Libertinum stared out at her with ire, those accursed little cherubs fluttering around him like carrion fowl.

'Major,' she replied, drawing to attention in preparation for the castigation she'd undoubtedly earned.

Restripa paused before her, drawing himself up. For a moment, he looked as if he might strike her, then the fight faded from the man, and he deflated. Where Confessor Libertinum's aura had exuded nothing but spite, the major's was laced with more subtle notes, and it did not take a witch's sense to discern that the man was exhausted. Torn in a struggle between duty and the fear of something greater, and at the moment she could not tell which held the upper hand.

'The confessor has requested that you do not accompany the regiment beyond Providence's walls.'

Aerand winced. She had been prepared for a battering, but not for this. 'And who will keep the mists from swallowing the regiment, sir?'

'Confessor Libertinum has assured me that he and his preachers are more than capable of performing the necessary rites.'

Aerand scoffed. 'And they do not need to sleep or rest? They may offer as many prayers and consecrations as they like, but those will not stop las-fire or burn your enemies.'

'I agree. And I told the confessor as much. That said, the man does not trust you, adept. And quite frankly, neither do I. When we pass beyond these walls you are not to leave my sight. If you do, I shall assume that you have deserted, or worse.'

Aerand opened her mouth to reply, but the major raised a hand.

'No debate, Aerand. For once just shut your mouth and take a bloody order.'

There was something tired in the major's response. The frustration of a man who had struggled internally for too long, and Aerand could sympathise with that weight. She had carried her own command only briefly, but she understood those pressures better than almost anyone else. And yet, more was buried in the major's unease. A fear – not only of her, but of what waited for them when they finally arrived at their goal.

The kind of fear only felt by one who knew what would face them.

Aerand probed out discreetly towards Restripa, his aura laced with foreboding and guilt. She thought again of Jarrah Kellipso, and the major's response when she'd asked him about the primaris psyker days ago on the wall. Her suspicions drifted to Restripa's shared glances with Confessor Libertinum, unspoken conversation that hinted at dark secrets shared between the two men. Slowly, she pressed her mind towards the major, the fingers of her consciousness brushing the edges of his thoughts.

'The Witchbringer,' she said. 'You always knew what it was.'

In her voice, the slightest hint of her will. She watched Restripa's face twist painfully, as if he wanted to confess but couldn't quite bring himself to. He started to open his mouth, and she pushed just a bit further. Then, suddenly, she felt her intrusion slapped back.

Restripa's violet eyes bored into her own, his face once again a mask of cold iron. 'You're dismissed, adept,' he growled. 'We leave within the hour.'

Chiding herself, she nodded, slowly raising her cowl.

'And lord psyker,' the major called out after her. 'Touch my mind again, and I will put a bolt through yours before you unwrap a single bloody thought.'

CHAPTER 11

One thousand torch lamps glimmered in the sweating night, the bright flames of a conflagration streaming around them. The Colonel felt the earth shake as another fusillade from the Basilisks within the city tore into the soft earth around Providence like jaws. Already, muck and mire boiled in the wake of an endless bombardment from the full force of the Cadian artillery company. But for all of its anger, the campaign had done nothing more than complete the utter devastation of Providence's outer skirts, and draw more attention to the sortie it was trying to mask.

'There have been casualties,' Sergeant Gross remarked coolly, practically reading the Colonel's thoughts. The two had stood side by side for enough years that no psionic connection was required for such a simple feat. 'But still fewer than those missing from the flood by half.'

The Colonel nodded. Casualties were expected – inevitable, even – and the Dorean losses had been far fewer so far than either he or Sergeant Gross had any right to expect.

'It appears the crone's efforts were more than enough, then, to bring the Cadians out from behind their walls. And it appears they've brought the psyker lord with them. I had feared them to be wiser than that.'

Beside him, Sergeant Gross allowed himself a brief smile. It was truly a rare expression for the man, a brief softening of the dark wrinkles and crow's feet etched into his countenance from decades of responsibility and hard living. There had been a time the man had smiled more. A time they all had.

The girl had done that for them.

Sergeant Gross had cared for her more than anyone other than the Colonel himself. They'd had children, both, on Dorea, and lives of their own, before the God-Emperor had decided those lives were not worth living. A single foundling child could not replace what had been taken from each of them, but the girl had reminded them both of what they'd lost. So perhaps, in that way, he and Sergeant Gross had felt it most severely when the Emperor took even the girl from them, too.

Gross had stood beside her the first time she showed the curse. The first time she twisted the world around her with the power of the warp in order to save the sergeant's life.

The sergeant had never forgiven himself for that. The Colonel would not forgive himself, either. If they had done a better job keeping the girl out of harm's way, maybe she never would have felt the danger that woke the darkness sleeping within her.

And then, just as soon as it had arrived, it was gone. Nothing more than a flicker of madness behind her eyes, and a handful of men dead in the mud. Men the regiment wanted dead already. It was no different than if she had been old enough to use a lasgun like any other Dorean trooper.

Except the scent of burnt copper had scarcely washed from her hair before she did it again. This time in a crowded square full of bystanders, and a damned procession of Ministorum preachers.

A young officer's pleading could do nothing at that point.

'They escape,' a grating voice called beside him, as a man in brown robes approached unsteadily.

The crone's heir was a frail man barely in his late twenties, and he wore a role too large for him by half. That he could not hide his discomfort at the Colonel's presence did nothing to assuage the officer's doubts about the witch's abilities. Apparently, the crone had shared a similar assessment, for she had not informed her successor of even the most basic details of their plans.

'They escape nothing,' the Colonel replied, watching the Cadians stream out into the night.

The witch's mind shattered like a brittle, untempered blade, a sudden shadow in the empyrean where his soul had burned. Aerand's legs trembled for a moment, vertigo seizing her, as her own mind detached itself from that of the dead man lying a hundred yards away.

'Dead,' she reported, her voice shaking and faint.

'Quickly enough?' Major Restripa asked.

Aerand shrugged as the sound of las-fire trickled away. There had been five psykers accompanying the platoon of Dorean Guard that the 900th Regiment had just overrun. All had died within minutes of first contact with the Cadians, but there was no way to know if any of their marsh priests had had enough time to release a final psionic warning to their comrades.

Restripa grunted.

The major was thorough, but the point was in many ways moot. There was no way to hide a full regiment of Cadian shock troopers marching double time for long. Their only hope of avoiding a pitched battle now was speed.

And distraction.

The muddy ground at Aerand's feet shivered, another fusillade of Earthshaker shells pounding Providence's perimeter with unyielding fury. Captain Havas had got his wish in the end, and his dozen Basilisks and set pieces were doing their level best to draw the Witchbringer's attention by turning the entire grid square into a sterile parade ground. All except the narrow corridor along which the remainder of the 900th marched.

Nearly one thousand pairs of Cadian boots pounded the earth in a staggered column a quarter of a mile long. Even then, the troopers of the 900th were packed tightly, a poor formation for battle, and they counted on speed and sheer firepower to overwhelm any threats that appeared in their path.

At the front of that massive formation, a full squadron of up-armoured Sentinels ranged on massive gyrostabilised legs, pouring a river of fire from mounted flamers in front of the regiment like a crest of foam atop a wave. The landscape simply vanished into that inferno, mist, corpsewood trees and Traitor Guardsmen alike vaporised to little more than crumbling, unrecognisable monuments of ash.

Even so, what those fires left behind was unnerving.

'Didn't know there could be this many corpses on a planet,' Sergeant Corwyn muttered, stepping past a charred husk of roughly human shape.

The ashes of the ancient corpsewood tree growing from the carcass' chest still flickered with a dozen small tongues of flame. Unceremoniously, Corwyn pushed the barrel of his lasgun against the charred pair, toppling both the corpse and the tree to the muddy earth.

With a look of annoyance, Confessor Libertinum stepped around the ashes, flicking a drop of consecrated, incense-infused water from his fingers onto the tangled mess. The liquid steamed, then drifted slowly into the sky, the slightest ripple in the warp where the steam rose as he muttered a hasty benediction.

'This galaxy is built on little more than the bones of the dead, sergeant,' the confessor muttered.

Aerand eyed Libertinum with growing suspicion. 'Yet most worlds do not make such an effort to hide theirs.'

There was a moment of tension before Corwyn laughed. The deep, throaty chuckle that only the sergeant could muster. Aerand thanked the Emperor yet again that Restripa had pulled the sergeant up to the regimental command detachment, if only to serve as a buffer between her and the priest.

'I'm afraid the humour is lost on me, sergeant,' Restripa mused, his vox crackling.

'I was just thinking, sir,' Corwyn replied. 'That these corpses should be thanking us. It must be the first time in millennia that they've been dry and warm.'

No one else laughed, although Aerand allowed herself a small nod, if only to the sergeant's unerring good humour. The sudden pull of Visage's ocean towards Providence had left the surrounding areas unnaturally dry. And while Corwyn was more than likely correct – it was clear the patches of muddy earth beneath their feet had not tasted the sky in untold generations – the macabre scene the shallow ocean left behind was more than unsettling enough to outweigh that wonder.

They were barely five miles from Providence's walls, with only a skeleton crew left to defend the capital city, and they had already passed thousands of corpses. How many millennia of dead had hidden beneath Visage's sea? How many dark, abhorrent corpsewood trees had spread their roots here even before the world's second founding?

Aerand tried to wipe the thought from her mind as she marched past another trio of bodies, these fresher and slightly less charred than the rest. Two men and a woman leaning against one another, the scorched steel of Kantrael-pattern lasguns still grasped in their ashen hands. The twisted root of a single corpsewood tree bound the trio together, a thin trunk erupting from the larger man's head. Straight through a cracked and scorched Astra Militarum helmet, proudly inscribed with the numerals 9-0-0.

Aerand froze.

'Major Restripa,' she muttered, pausing. 'I was under the impression the regiment hadn't ventured more than a few miles west of Providence since arriving on Visage.'

The major looked strangely at the trio of corpses, faces bloated and charred, and beyond recognition.

'We haven't,' Sergeant Corwyn answered for him, his smile fading as he knelt in the mud. The sergeant's vox crackled to life, and his scowl deepened. 'Captain Vyse. She says they just found a corpse of their own wearing Nine Hundredth regimental armour. You sure we haven't got turned around, sir?'

Major Restripa gave no answer, turning to face Confessor Libertinum. He whispered something inaudible to the priest, then holstered his vox mouthpiece and continued marching.

'I'm certain.'

By the time they had marched another five miles, the 900th had passed nearly one hundred of their own.

'I don't understand,' Sergeant Corwyn whispered, passing another singed husk of a man. Corwyn bent over the corpse, its charred face little more than a mask of soot, and stared at the aquila on the trooper's helmet. 'If these soldiers were ours, why don't I know their faces?'

Aerand surveyed the charred mess beneath the Cadian's helm – hardly recognisable as human let alone a specific individual – but she did not doubt the sergeant's words. Corwyn carried responsibility for every trooper in Secundus Company, and as the 900th Regiment's senior company sergeant, he bore some authority over every soldier in the unit. Even if they were scorched beyond recognition, Aerand had no doubt the veteran sergeant would know each trooper underneath Major Restripa's command.

She shivered slightly in the chill evening air, allowing her mind to reach out slowly towards the sergeant, detecting the same strange psionic imbalance about him that she had felt when she'd asked about Jarrah Kellipso. She swallowed the taste of metal and pulled back from Corwyn.

He knew these troopers, but something had made him forget. Or someone.

'Major Restripa,' Aerand called, jogging to match pace with the major and the massive ecclesiarch who strode beside him. In the orange light of the blazing promethium wall that surrounded the regiment, the silhouettes of Restripa and Libertinum had become almost inseparable.

A wave of annoyance washed off the pair as she approached, the hushed words they exchanged suddenly falling silent. From the dark sky, a single cherub descended, alighting on one of the confessor's broad shoulders. The lines of his scowl were only highlighted by the flickering shadow of fire before him.

'Adept,' Restripa replied. 'What is it?' The man made little effort to hide the hostility in his voice.

'That's another dozen Cadian corpses, sir. That makes nearly a full company.'

Restripa grunted. 'I'm aware.'

Aerand closed her eyes, frustration gripping her like a vice. Even while trying to ignore them, the massed emotions of the troopers around her assaulted her mind, and what had begun as a whisper of gentle unease among the 900th's rank and file had quickly grown to an almost unanimous fear.

'The regiment is unsettled, sir. They want to know how these bodies got here. And they want to know why none of them can remember.'

'Thank you, adept,' Restripa replied. 'Your concerns are noted.'

'And you don't?'

'What?' Restripa sighed, gaze lost in the mists that still rolled around the column of troopers beyond the Sentinels' fire wall.

'You don't want to know how a company of your soldiers ended up dead in a sector you've never set foot in?'

Restripa shrugged. 'Currents. Tides. Foul psyker magicks. I am more concerned, adept, with the task at hand.'

'If you know something, sir, it's past time that you tell us.'

'Watch your tone,' the major muttered, but there was no bite in the rebuke, his mind clearly elsewhere. 'You step out of place. When I am interested in an interrogation I shall ask for one.'

At the major's side, Confessor Libertinum grew suddenly tense, as a second dark shadow dropped from the sky to rest on his shoulder opposite its companion. The fleshy cherub leaned towards the confessor's ear and whispered.

'Sergeant Corwyn,' Major Restripa called, locking eyes with the confessor, who merely nodded towards him.

'Yes, sir,' the sergeant replied, huffing slightly as he ran to catch up with the trio.

'Order the column to halt. Strike a camp for the moment. Double watch. Roving patrols. One-hour interval rests until the sun rises.'

'Sir?' Corwyn asked. 'We must be nearly there, and every traitor on the planet will be following close behind us.'

'I know.' Restripa nodded. 'We've nearly reached the Witchbringer. And I'd rather face a dozen regiments at our rear than march into what waits ahead in the dark.'

The surface of the empyrean swirled beneath Aerand's touch. Dark and warm. Welcoming and terrible at once.

This was the secret in every psyker's possession. The immutable truth so many gifted tried to deny, even in the silence when alone with only their own thoughts. As strongly as Aerand reviled that tainted, bitter darkness; as much as the very thought of those unholy depths made her skin crawl and scream; as much as she desired nothing more than to open her eyes and drive any thought of the immaterium away, and be nothing more than a simple, ungifted soldier again...

As much as she hated the warp, so she utterly craved it.

Aerand sighed, seated in the mud atop a small rise at the centre of the 900th's emerging camp. Previous threats neglected in the midst of the day's events, Major Restripa seemed to have forgotten her for the moment, distracted by the burdens of command.

Finally alone, she closed her eyes, pushing her thoughts even deeper, sending tendrils of her mind across that cursed, churning sea. A thousand souls burned atop those swirling currents, minuscule beacons of life in a wasteland that was otherwise dark. In the misty, obscured reaches around the 900th, the scattered souls of the Witchbringer's warbands roamed loosely, coalescing and dividing without seeming pattern.

In the wake of the 900th, however, along the charred, packed road they had beaten from Providence, the depths of those mists had only recovered slightly. And along that road, another army approached.

Five thousand? Ten? She could not be certain at this distance. More souls than she'd seen anywhere beside the capital city itself.

As predicted, the forces arrayed against them were gathering, and the 900th would soon find itself overwhelmed. And yet, as Aerand watched in the darkness, that massing army crawled towards them with painful lethargy. Far too slowly for a force whose strength lay under threat.

A vague foreboding washed over Aerand yet again.

The 900th Regiment had abandoned Providence in a desperate effort to strike at the seat of the Witchbringer's power. Yet their enemy seemed utterly unconcerned with intercepting them.

She cursed this world and its secrets. There were too many questions that remained. A dozen premonitions swam before her eyes at once, each as spectacular and tempting as the last, yet none that bore the signature of true portents.

Aerand sighed, tempted to try her hand at a casting of the Tarot, yet she knew how foolish that decision would be. To scry the future here – beyond the protection of Providence's cathedral and well within the domain of whatever evil lurked nearby – would only invite trouble on her and her companions. To reach down into the depths of the warp seeking answers only risked drawing out whatever shadows dwelt there. Slowly, Aerand reached within the confines of her robes, where a single, thin wafer of lorelei lay pressed against the skin of her chest.

A casting here would be utterly suicidal, but her first casting still had secrets to give her.

Gingerly, Aerand drew the tarot from the folds of her robe, feeling the warmth of the card, sensing its light in the warp. For three days this card had called to her. For three days it had practically begged to be seen, and yet something within her had denied that urge. There was a danger, always, in portents that wanted to be revealed. An omen too easily given was a dangerous thing to trust.

And yet, what other choice remained?

Aerand set the card atop the small, mossy patch of dirt between her legs, then flipped the wafer over with her mind.

'Emperor save me,' she muttered, opening her eyes.

For a moment, the dim glow of the liquid crystal swelled to an almost unbearable brightness, the layers of the warp still overlying her vision of the physical world. As her sight cleared and she returned her concentration to realspace, the image on the tarot came into full view.

A hundred corpses stretched across a barren field, each charred and twisted in positions of agony. Ash and blood lay mixed on the macabre field, and at its centre only a single figure stood.

The Buried Man. An omen unerring in its severity. A portent of death behind and death to come.

But as she stared at the faceless corpse standing amid that bloody field, a new wave of dread washed over her, for she recognised those bodies burned in the dirt and the single, lifeless face standing over them all.

Lord Psyker Jarrah Kellipso was dead.

Aerand had suspected the fact for the better part of a year, but the certainty of it was now beyond any question. Her fingers trembled slightly as she held the thin tarot card between them.

Damn her sensibilities. Damn her caution. She'd allowed herself to be distracted far too long.

As her skin came into contact with the psychically active wafer of lorelei, Kellipso's likeness staring back at her from the Buried Man, a slow hum vibrated up her arms. Dowsing a tarot card was undoubtedly reckless, but the time for caution had long since passed.

A sickening pit formed in Aerand's stomach as she felt the pull of the card on her mind. She had hoped that the tarot bearing Kellipso's dead face would seek to draw her out into the mists. That way she might convince herself that the entire omen was simply a trick being played by whatever sinister force the 900th Regiment approached. Or alternatively, that if the portent were true, Kellipso's death had come at that same dark power's hand.

But instead, the Buried Man did not seek to lure her away from the 900th. Rather, the card drew her directly to the centre of the regiment's camp.

The regiment's hasty bivouac was little more than bedrolls in the mud, sunk in shallow defensive trenches already filling with brine. Troopers tossed fitfully in damp beds, exhausted enough to sleep even in these conditions. A rough earthwork surrounded the small clearing in the fog, held open by Kobald's roving Sentinels and a trio of Libertinum's preachers chanting constant sanctifications in throaty High Gothic. At the centre of the camp, two canvas tents stood alone, the only structures of any note within the encampment.

'Where's the major?' Aerand asked a pair of young corporals posted outside the smaller of the two pavilions.

The troopers started at her approach, both clearly almost asleep on their feet.

'Lord psyker,' one muttered.

'The major,' she repeated.

'I-I'm not certain.'

Not good enough. She threw her will against the pair.

'He left with the confessor more than an hour ago, sir. Didn't say where he was going or when he'd be back.'

Another push.

'They looked anxious. Both of them. In a hurry. Like they were worried that someone might try to follow them.'

'Thank you, corporals,' Aerand replied, before sending both soldiers to sleep. They dropped to the mud and would wake well rested with the dawn.

Aerand cast her will across the narrow tent-flap, sensing no one inside, and slipped into the command tent with her cowl raised, one hand on the tarot card, the other on her combat knife. There was little other than outright heresy that could bring her to kill a fellow trooper of the 900th, but she would have no qualms about delivering the butt of her knife hilt to the face of a comrade in the name of expedience.

Thankfully, the room was just as empty as it appeared. Spartan. Neat. As an officer's quarters should be. Major Restripa had not even unpacked his rucksack.

Aerand had expected nothing less. Whatever sins Major Restripa had committed, whatever he had become, he was every bit a consummate, scrupulous officer of the Astra Militarum.

Closing her eyes, she raised the Buried Man above her palm, then released the card to travel of its own will. Instantly, as if drawn by some unseen gravity, the tarot flew with a smack onto the lid of a small void chest at the foot of Major Restripa's bedroll. Aerand knelt beside the chest, set her hand against the small, rusted locking mechanism, and then threw the lid open.

She did not know what she had expected. Symbols of Chaos? Forbidden xenos tokens? Some obvious sign of sedition or unforgivable corruption? Instead, the chest was full of neatly stacked commander's logs and a series of immaculately folded, classified maps. Guilt set aside, Aerand rifled through the documents, until her hand struck something cool and metallic at the chest's floor.

Aerand froze, her fingers closing around two small, flawless spheres of metal. An icy chill shot up her arm from the psionic strength of the objects and her instant recognition of them. Slowly, she pulled Jarrah Kellipso's psi-bolas from the chest and held them up to the light of a flickering torch lamp.

'Aerand,' a voice called suddenly behind her. 'What are you doing?'

She froze, turning to face Olevier Corwyn.

'Sergeant,' she said. 'It's not how it looks.'

Corwyn frowned. 'I hope not. Because it looks like you assaulted two corporals from the major's command detachment so you could rummage through his private effects. Is that about right?'

'Yes,' she replied with a sigh. 'And no.'

Aerand turned to face him with the metal spheres in her open hand. As the light of the torch lamp caught both objects, a faint pattern of iridescent blue light appeared on their otherwise wholly unmarred surfaces.

Corwyn's face twisted as he stared at the objects.

'I-I should recognise those, shouldn't I?' The sergeant's hand drifted slowly away from his sidearm, the wheels behind his eyes grinding against an unseen barrier.

'Yes,' she replied. 'Just like you should have recognised the name of the primaris psyker who wielded them. Just like you should have recognised those corpses out in the mud.'

At the mention of the psyker lord, Corwyn's face contorted even further. 'I-I-I don't know what's happening to me.'

Aerand sighed, her suspicions confirmed. 'I do. Someone has been inside your mind, sergeant. Not only yours, but every other trooper's in this regiment. They've taken memories from you, Corwyn. Memories of a primaris psyker named Jarrah Kellipso. And memories of a battle, it seems.'

'Who would do that?' he replied, the pain on his face only growing greater.

'I don't know,' she lied. The better question was who *could* have done that, and only two faces came to her mind. Confessor Javard Libertinum and Major Absalom Restripa held secrets and motive, but neither possessed the power to perform such a feat alone, though she had no clue what other instruments the two men kept at their disposal. And what better way to hide consortion with hidden, unsightly powers than to project outer revulsion at the very idea?

Her mind still swam at the implication.

If Restripa and Libertinum simply wanted the regiment to fail, there had been myriad opportunities to arrange a defeat before now. Clearly, they still thought of the Traitor Guardsmen and marsh priests as their opposition, but to what end other than their own control of whatever artefact waited ahead in those mists?

'Major Restripa?' Corwyn asked, putting together the pieces.

She nodded grimly.

For the first time in the conversation, Corwyn shook his head with determination. 'No,' he replied. 'That I do not believe. I know you can't stand the man, but you need to shut your mouth about him unless it's something you can prove. He's overly tight, and he has enough pride for two men, but he's a decent enough officer. Better than the string of self-serving, opportunistic commanders that came after you. You've been back only for days, yet all I've heard you do is slander him.'

'I've protested,' Aerand admitted. 'I've objected because the man can't be trusted. Because the only thing he can see is his oversized ego and his mindless desire for even greater power. I've complained because everything is different. Because there's no place for me any more, courtesy of Restripa.'

'You think you're ostracised just because of him? You haven't exactly endeared yourself to any of our new recruits.'

'Endeared myself to them? Listen to yourself, Corwyn. They won't even talk to me. And Throne, I thought you'd understand this better than most. I'm not meant to be their friend, I'm meant to save their sorry lives, and I've done that more times than I can count already.'

Corwyn just nodded.

Aerand sighed, collapsing with her head in her hands. 'I know what you're thinking, Olevier. I can feel the emotions dripping off you like a poorly masked stench. There's anger there, and so much of it directed at me. I should not have come back. I told the lord prefector as much. I could have saved you all this bitter reunion.'

She turned and made to leave the tent, but Corwyn reached out and grasped her. In all the time they had known one another, the sergeant had never put a hand on her, and now, she did not even need her psychic abilities to sense the rage that was about to burst.

'Go eat dirt,' Corwyn spat, so quietly his voice was hardly a whisper. 'Aye, I'm angry, and yes it's with you, but not for the reasons you think. You keep going on about how you shouldn't have returned. Emperor's bones, Captain Aerand. You never should have left! You think it must be some great surprise to see you back here wearing those ridiculous robes. That Vyse and Maltia, and Argos and myself must be so shocked that the captain who kept us alive, by anticipating ambushes and counter-attacks we never could have predicted, has a lick of psychic skill about her? Call us what you will. Blind. Soft. Bloody heretics, even. But don't you dare imply that any of us were fools. You think I'm angry because you came back a psyker? Throne, I knew what you were before you ever did.'

Aerand froze. 'What? Why didn't you say something?'

A soft chuckle escaped Corwyn. 'Because I didn't need to. It wasn't some great pissing secret. Barely two hours after securing *Apex Inruptus* back on Ourea, before the blood had even had time to cool on the stones, while you were still sleeping in one of Argos' sick cots, Colonel Yarin called me into her headquarters. She asked what my opinion was of you as an officer, but that's not what she was really getting at. After that, she never brought it up again.'

Aerand found herself moved, and equally guilty at the weight she had placed on her soldiers to hide a secret she had not even known yet. 'And what did you tell her, Corwyn? It must have been some answer.'

'What any trooper in Secundus Company would have, sir. I told her you were the best damned commander I'd ever had the honour to serve with.'

The sergeant paused then, an inexplicable moisture in his eyes.

'I cannot imagine the doubts and burdens that plague you. I can only see the horrors of this galaxy with my eyes, and for me that is already more than enough. And I can't speak for Major Restripa or any of these fresh transplants. But I know that every soldier of the Nine Hundredth Regiment who ever served beneath your command or fought beside you would have no problem repeating these words. Whatever you were, whatever you have become, you are and always will be one of ours.

'So,' the sergeant continued after some time, 'I cannot abide baseless defamation of my commander, but whatever you need beyond that, adept, you simply have to ask.'

CHAPTER 12

The Colonel crushed a charred Cadian corpse beneath the heel of his boot, the strange sensation of flesh crumbling to ash beneath his step. A dark fate, but a pure one for the thousands of corpses lying in the Cadian 900th's wake.

There would be no such salvation for him, even in death.

At the fringes of the ragged column of Dorean troopers and Visager irregulars, a ring of marsh priests held the mists at bay, yet the faces within raged just as strongly at the forces marching to their aid.

The Witchbringer knew no difference between Cadian and Dorean. The dim memories of the dead remembered not even themselves. If the Colonel succeeded in his terrible purpose – when he succeeded – the force within that artefact would rip this world apart, and like the restless dead that milled around him, he too would wander in those mists. There could be no forgiveness for arranging such an atrocity, yet he desired no absolution.

'They've made camp,' Sergeant Gross reported, breaking off his conversation with a lieutenant from the 19th's scouting platoon. 'Hasty, but well arranged.'

The Colonel grunted.

Displacing the Cadians would be a bloody task, but the one resource he had in excess was human life. True to form, the Cadians had proved stubborn combatants, and he doubted – even outnumbering them as he did – that his forces could destroy theirs in outright pitched battle. But he had no desire to decimate their ranks.

The Colonel had levelled regiments before. He had wiped Imperial task forces from this world. But like insects, like dirt, like bloody water, they always – always – found their way back.

The deployment of Cadians had been an escalation for the Imperium. If he defeated them, he would only find two regiments in their place. But if he succeeded in forcing the primaris psyker's hand, the Witchbringer would wipe this entire world clean. Clean enough that no one – the Imperium included – would return to the accursed world for millennia to come.

A bitter victory, but he had become a bitter man.

If they could not capture the psyker lord, they would push her to desperation.

'Harry them, sergeant. Push them forward. I am tired of waiting.'

The Dorean sergeant nodded without hesitation. They both had been waiting for nearly ten years.

* * *

Aerand slipped through the 900th's pickets with Corwyn's assistance, and ventured out alone into the night. She had doubted the mists could possibly grow thicker, but she had been utterly wrong on that count. She fought through twisted brambles of ragged corpsewood trees growing from the piled detritus of emaciated skeletons that had slept in this place for ten thousand years. Even now, Visage's dark waters were slowly returning, the once-in-a-millennium tide dissipating to lie in its familiar bed. Soon, this world would be bathed in waist-deep water again, its dead reinterred in their watery graves.

And yet, the lifeless here seemed to get little sleep.

Flames poured from her hands with increasing ferocity, driving back the myriad faces arrayed in the ever-thickening wall of white around her. These were not souls. She knew as much. For one, such a thing was utterly heretical. For another, they left no real signature on the warp. And yet, somehow, the presence waiting for her in those mists had pulled the slightest piece of Visage's dead back to life, if only their physical likenesses and the sounds of their voices. And their memories.

Aerand had no doubt any longer about the misty figure she had dreamt her first night on this planet and again outside of Visage's walls and beneath them. The figure that had not summoned the Witchbringer's shadow, but had tried to stand between it and her. Some echo of the soul of Jarrah Kellipso had remained fresh enough to still cast a glimmer into the warp and sane enough to recall its final words to her.

Flee, Glavia. There is only death here.

A desperate man's final warning. Kellipso must have known of Restripa's betrayal in the end, then. He must have suspected that the major and confessor would do the same to her as they had done to him.

Kellipso's image burning on the wafer of liquid crystal pressed against her chest, Aerand said a silent prayer for the late primaris psyker. Like all of their kind, he had lived a tortured existence, yet it was also from him that she had learned there was hope for joy – or at least meaning – for a psyker. Wherever he rested, now, in the Emperor's light, she hoped it was blessedly more peaceful than his service to the God-Emperor had been during life.

Now she would do what she could to give his echo that same rest.

Aerand tucked the tarot card back within the confines of her robe, between her damp, salty skin and the rough edges of her flak armour. She had little suspicion she would encounter danger of the physical variety ahead, but the habits of an old Astra Militarum captain died hard. In her palm, she twirled Kellipso's psi-bolas in the idle gesture that she had seen him employ so many times.

She had seen Kellipso utilise the weapons to their full effect only once, each of the psychically paired force weapons splitting into a thousand razor-sharp shards which he had used to dispatch dozens of enemies in seconds. Kellipso had spent a lifetime perfecting their use, and she had no illusions she would be able to match the same effect, but the devices served as a powerful link to their deceased owner, more than strong enough for her to dowse his corpse's location.

In truth, she had little need for such detailed guidance, for the Witch-bringer itself was easy enough to sense. Despite the unnatural, oppressive tenor of the mists pressing around her, the artefact's massive warp signature was impossible to ignore. That psychic weight was already enormous, like the gravity of a sun pulling her closer at will.

She had travelled less than a mile in the last hour, hindered by the ever-thickening copses of larger, more ancient corpsewood trees, but now the artefact lay almost directly ahead. Pressing forward, she pulled her mind free from that darkness, searching in the mists for any hint of the Astronomican's familiar, silver light.

Aerand's mouth was nothing but copper and blood as she stepped beneath the ancient stone arch. This had been a temple once, although not to the God-Emperor. If Javax Cathedral was truly ten thousand years old, the walls housing the Witchbringer had stood ten times longer. Massive, cyclopean stones joined together before her with scarcely a joint, seemingly unbound by time's laws, stretched in proportions and angles that could not have been dreamt by human minds.

As she crossed the threshold, the psychic weight of the Witchbringer became a palpable thing. Slow, thin waves of dark water poured in sheets over the alabaster stairs upon which she walked, flowing down towards the structure's single, central chamber. Within these walls, Visage's mists finally faded, replaced instead by the thin silver light of a massive, metallic tree at the centre of the room.

That she recognised the Witchbringer instantly was no surprise. She had seen it before, if only in a vision.

The artefact stood about as tall as a man, twisting branches of some strange, xenos material rising from the white stone at the centre of the chamber and erupting into ten thousand symmetrical shoots. As brine cascaded over the raw stone walkway, it rushed towards that structure, the Witchbringer drinking the fluid like a greedy plant. Just beyond the tips of its branches, thin tendrils of mist coalesced over the artefact like a cloud, rising towards the chamber's vaulted ceiling.

Beautiful, in its own fashion, if not for the stench of Chaos all about it.

As Aerand approached, she spotted an uneven current in that thin veneer of dark, salty water. Slow cascades poured over Jarrah Kellipso's robed, rotting corpse, and in the faint mists over the water, a single figure coalesced.

For a moment, Kellipso's echo met her gaze, the same grey eyes she had remembered so well from his life. Slowly, she knelt beside his remains, a gentle hand descending to touch the bare bone of the man's skull.

She was bombarded immediately by a deluge of thoughts, the last memories of the primaris psyker still clinging to his flesh. Throwing up her own psychic walls, so as not to lose herself in the deluge, she drove all but the strongest of those reverberations away.

This room. Jarrah Kellipso. A laspistol pressed against his temple. The man holding it, one she recognised well.

Aerand opened her eyes, her darkest fears confirmed, and looked up at

Kellipso's mist corpse. The spectre opened its mouth to speak, then evaporated at a voice from the tunnel behind her.

'You stupid, insubordinate, bloody fool.'

Major Absalom Restripa practically spat the words, his face curled into a mask of pure anger. In the man's hands, the barrel of a lasgun stared directly at her.

'Leave here. Now, adept. Before I put a las-bolt through your chest.'

Aerand swept her hand to the side, sending the major's weapon spinning across the room. Rising, she extended her wrist and threw the man against the wall.

'I think not,' she replied. 'And I am a fool. A fool not to have seen you for what you were from the start.'

Aerand's hands shook as she stepped towards him, the sudden surge of the empyrean rushing through her like pulsating blood. Against the pale stone wall of the chamber, the major was pressed flat like a leaf in the wind.

'I knew you were proud, Restripa. I knew you were ambitious. But even I put something like this beneath you.'

On the wall, Restripa laughed bitterly, the vessels in his neck straining as he turned his head towards her. 'And I, heresy and desertion beneath you.'

Aerand spat to the side, rage building within her. In her hand, Kellipso's psi-bolas began to spin. She was no great telekine. Not like Jarrah Kellipso was. Not like Jarrah Kellipso *had been*. But in this moment, with rage opening a door to the immaterium like a spillway in a dam, she had no doubt she could manage enough skill to do the job. With a flick of her fingers, a lacework pattern of bright blue light erupted on the dark metal orbs, then they jumped into the air above her hand, splintering into a thousand orbiting shards.

'So now you'll kill me?' Restripa shouted. 'You'll use the weapons of your mentor to murder his commander and usurp me? What do you think Jarrah Kellipso would say about that?'

Aerand looked down at the robed body, rotting away in a pool of dark, briny water. 'I don't think he would mind me avenging his murder.'

'Murder?' A bitter laugh escaped Major Restripa. 'Is that how you'll sell it when you return to the regiment and claim my place? How many Cadians do you think will believe the lie? Will you kill those who don't fall in line, like you're about to kill me?'

'It's not a lie,' Aerand spat. 'I watched you do it. I saw you place a laspistol against his head and pull the trigger.'

A swarm of black metal shards orbited Aerand like the rings of some distant gas giant. She could send all thousand projectiles surging straight through Restripa with nothing but a thought. At this distance, there would be nothing left of the major to protest.

And she would. In a moment. But first she wanted to hear him say it.

'Admit it,' she hissed, her voice dripping with will. 'Admit you killed the man who saved my soul.'

A terrible look of anguish crossed the major's face as he tried to resist the focused force of her will. For a time, he looked as if he might succeed, before the words came bursting out.

'Of course I did!' Restripa shouted. 'Of course I killed him, and you would have too! The psyker lord begged me to. And when I refused he simply moved my hand for me.'

With the dam broken upon Restripa's mind, raw emotion spilled from the major like a wave. Anger. Guilt. Only a hint of fear. But above all, the overwhelming flavour of truth. Aerand froze, the swarm of shards gathered around her stopping inches from the major's face.

'Explain. Now.'

'Where do you think we are, adept? What do you think the Witchbringer is? It's a trap,' he continued before she could answer. 'It's a trap built specifically for creatures like you.'

Slowly, Aerand felt her anger ebbing, the surge of raw warp energy she had channelled pulling away like the tide. Dropping her hand, she released Restripa, and the major fell ungracefully into the mud. Pushing himself to his feet, he straightened his epaulets and turned to face her.

'How do you know?' she asked.

'Because Jarrah Kellipso told me the night before he made me take his life.'

The major pointed towards the branching structure that dominated the centre of the room.

'We found the maps less than a month after we landed on Visage. We didn't know what we were seeing, but we were keen enough to recognise the pattern. Every original settlement on the planet had been built in a ring around this place, either trying to avoid it, or trying to cage something in.

'I told Kellipso to dig, with the confessor's help, and the two unearthed tomes within Javax Cathedral almost as old as the Imperium's presence on Visage itself. This place was ancient even when they were written, and they referenced it only in passing, but it was clear those first settlers recognised what took us too long to decipher. That the object beside you is the source of Visage's unique curse. What wasn't clear was why they allowed it to stand.'

'A fiend's bargain,' Aerand muttered bitterly. 'The Imperium depended on Visage's tithe of psykers then even more than it does now, and they could not risk losing that stream of gifted for the sake of destroying one warp-tainted artefact.'

Restripa shook his head. 'We thought the same, and like any loyal servants of the Emperor, we were determined not to be tempted by such heretical logic.'

'Thought? Past tense,' Aerand replied.

'We don't have the time.' Grabbing his lasgun from the floor, Restripa pointed it once again at her chest. 'Out,' he ordered. 'Now.'

Aerand raised her hands and chuckled grimly. 'Didn't we just do this, major? I'm not leaving without answers. And if this place is as tainted as you suggest, I'm not setting foot from this temple until we destroy the Witchbringer.'

'Don't be a fool,' Restripa muttered. 'Not like we were. Why do you think Jarrah Kellipso forced me to kill him? Why do you think that in his final act, he purged the memories of every trooper in this regiment besides me so that they could remember neither this location, nor him?'

The major's voice had risen to a fever pitch, and for the first time Aerand noticed the faintest vibration in the air. As Restripa finished speaking, what had been an inaudible whining suddenly became loud enough to hear. Behind her, a low blue glow blossomed along the arboreal tines of the Witch-bringer, like flickering flames consuming the branches of a tree.

As she turned to face that alien structure, a horrible knot developed in her chest. Suddenly, the surface of the empyrean surged, an ancient shadow rising from its depths.

Aerand's vision swam, and her knees buckled beneath her, splashing down into that dark, unavoidable sea. She felt Restripa's hand grasp her, shouting something her ringing ears couldn't understand, and let the major drag her towards the door.

Because something terrible was trapped within the relic behind her. Something waiting for a vessel strong enough to escape in.

CHAPTER 13

'Not a traitor, then,' the confessor remarked coolly, a frown of disappointment written across his lined face. Aerand was too shaken to reply.

The tension in his shoulders dissipated slightly at the sight of her stumbling, half supported by Major Restripa, but his grip on the corseque remained every bit as tight.

'No,' Restripa replied. 'Not a traitor. Just a fool.'

Libertinum grunted as the ground shivered, a deep keening moan echoing from the stone archway behind them. 'Has she woken it then?'

Restripa looked to Aerand.

Slowly, she cast her mind backwards, towards the swirling stain that marred the warp behind her. Just beneath the surface of the immaterium, an ancient, sinewy shadow swirled, the fabric of the empyrean churning like choppy water above it.

'It's been awake, confessor, since before I arrived on this world.' She held up her hand before he interrupted. 'But the answer is no, to the question you intended. The presence within the artefact is stretching its chains, but it has not yet broken them completely. When it does, you will not need my confirmation to know it.'

'And if it does,' Restripa said. 'Well, that is why we brought you.'

The confessor scoffed. 'Why I insisted on coming, you mean? Never send a witch to do the God-Emperor's business.'

Even as the man spoke, a thin wisp of translucent energy emanated from the ecclesiarch, like the corona of a star shifting in a solar wind. In that aura, only self-righteousness and contempt radiated. Aerand might have challenged him in any other situation, but they would need every weapon at their disposal tonight.

'I'm afraid I still don't understand,' Aerand said. 'What's the plan here, sir? I can see the crooked wisdom in keeping this from the regiment. They are courageous and true, but I imagine few of them would have returned to this place knowing what awaited them. But why hide it from me?'

Libertinum scoffed. 'So that you wouldn't do something precisely this stupid.'

'Because I didn't know you,' Restripa replied. 'The captain that left this regiment was foolhardy and bold. I can see that neither of those qualities has changed.'

Aerand made to reply, but Restripa cut her off.

'As intolerable as I found you as a commander, you never gave me reason to doubt your loyalty to the Imperium. That said, adept, time has changed us both. I needed to know what you had become.'

Behind them, the ground shook again, thin ripples racing across the black water pooling at their feet.

'As far as a plan,' Restripa muttered. 'I had hoped to surround the foul temple at daybreak and pit every weapon at my disposal against the darkness within, including both you and Confessor Libertinum.'

Aerand laughed. 'That's not a plan, major. That's a prayer.'

'As you suggested in the cathedral rotunda, adept. A prayer was all I had left.'

'Throne,' she muttered. 'That was the best case?'

Restripa nodded.

'And now...'

Beside the major, the confessor began to mutter, an ancient tome open in his hands, his corseque planted into the soft earth. Slowly, Aerand felt an unnatural stillness settle on her soul, in the face of the darkness gathering behind her. Remarkably, for a moment, that shadow recoiled.

'The Witchbringer touched Jarrah Kellipso for only seconds,' Major Restripa remarked with a bitter frown. 'It never even gained full possession of the man, merely channelled its latent power through him, but that was enough to leave almost a company of Cadians dead. The plan now is to get you as far away from this place as quickly as we can.'

As he spoke, Aerand cast her mind into the warp, feeling the shadow behind her surge again. Whatever hindrance Libertinum might pose to a will so ancient and massive would only represent the smallest of hurdles. And beyond that darkness, two masses of human souls approached.

Aerand paused. 'No. No it isn't.'

Restripa frowned.

'When is an army most vulnerable, major?' she asked, driving herself deeper into the warp. Her body felt like little more than a shadow, now, too. A thin cord holding her soul back from the warm, dark currents of the empyrean. Beside her, the surface of those waters roiled, something hungry and mad rising from their depths.

Restripa's aura flared briefly with annoyance, then fear, as he understood the implication in her question. 'When it is moving,' the major replied. 'But, adept, this is not some trifling warband to ambush. Even if the daemon within risks exposing itself to assault when it emerges, I fear we might not be up to the task.'

Beneath Aerand, the empyrean boiled, the sheer weight of the daemon almost unthinkable in scale, enough to crush her petty flame with little more than a thought. And yet, behind millennia of untapped hunger, there was a hesitancy, as if even a presence so unthinkably primordial recognised the existence of powers even more ancient.

Aerand threw her mind out past the small clearing in Visage's fog afforded by the confessor's presence. Already, however, those psionic mists were fading, pulling closer, concentrating on the Witchbringer itself as the daemon that awaited within prepared to emerge. And somewhere, deep below the surface of the empyrean, far below, but no longer impossible to see, a familiar pillar of silver light blazed.

Aerand reached for the glimmer of the Astronomican, her mind breaking the churning surface of the warp. As she touched even the edges of that terrible, eternal beacon, she felt her own soul flicker suddenly to life. A thousand auguries flashed before her eyes, her mind blazing with almost unimaginable strength. At the base of her neck, her bridle became white fire, the Emperor's Tarot at her chest burning painfully bright.

They were dark futures that passed before Aerand's eyes, every last one. But if the galaxy were not dark, there would be nothing for the Emperor's light to shine against.

Beneath her, the Witchbringer let out a terrible, pained screech, before surging upwards and away from that terrible light. At the edges of her perception, thousands of souls rushed towards her, as the Cadian 900th and the traitor regiments closed in.

Fleeing had never been an option, anyway.

Throne above, it was a beautiful, bloody mess.

Sergeant Raniais Maltia practically grinned as her battered autocannon bucked in her hands. She forced her aim down against the constant upward action, the steel barrel already glowing a dull orange, droplets of steam rising from the superheated weapon.

'Emperor's breath,' she chuckled, turning to the Ebonwelter twins. 'It's been too long since we've had a proper fight.'

Only a few yards away, another squad of Traitor Guardsmen emerged through the tangle of black, twisting brambles, an ancient corpsewood tree skewering an unwary corporal with a sinewy branch before Maltia's gun took both the troopers beside him. The remaining six Dorean soldiers closed, bayonets affixed to their rusting lasguns. A single trooper made it close enough to attempt a desperate lunge. Maltia sidestepped the clumsy melee and dropped the man with her foot, then pressed the searing barrel of her autocannon into his open mouth. He screamed for only a moment.

Beside her, Evrik Ebonwelter pulled his combat knife from a filthy, unkempt Traitor Guardsman. 'Not sure I'd call this a proper fight, sergeant,' he muttered.

Maltia scoffed, dropping back behind another low, muddy berm, her boots submerged in briny sea water. She had blessed the shallow ocean's absence, although its return meant equally treacherous footing for their enemy.

'They outnumber us five to one,' she called back. 'Even if they don't match us in skill.' Even at tight intervals she would not have been able to see the corporal through the mists less than an hour ago, but something seemed to be pulling that cursed fog away from them. 'Whatever other advantages they lack, I call that a fight.'

On her left flank, Tannius Ebonwelter protested. 'What about the sea wall? They outnumbered us there too.'

'Fair enough, but there was only a squad of us there.'

'So not a real fight, then?'

'No.'

'Maybe a scuffle?'

'Fine.'

The twins both grinned as they slogged through the muddy terrain towards her, an unmistakable energy gripping them both. To the untrained eye, their good humour in the face of gruesome bloodshed might appear callous, pathological even. But she'd seen soldiers go mad with battle lust before – watched them slash at their comrades as well as the enemy, even themselves when there was no other flesh near enough to bleed – and this was nothing of the sort.

Grim as it was, the soldiers around her were expert killers, and Emperor-be-true it felt good to do something they excelled at.

'Push out that flank,' Maltia barked towards Trooper Bantholo. If the mists were going to give them the visibility, they might as well take it. 'Just keep out of the way of Second Squad's fire.'

All along the thin front, platoons of the 900th Regiment interlocked like a chain, executing a rolling withdrawal from their now-abandoned camp, pummelling the traitor regiments every inch of the way. Raniais Maltia wasn't fond of retreating, but she'd stood beside Sergeant Corwyn and Captain Vyse and heard the major's orders before he left.

'Don't die for this puddle, Vyse,' the major had told her just as he and the confessor departed. 'If they reach you before Libertinum and I return, follow us slowly, but make them purchase every step.'

And paying they were.

Maltia fed a new belt of ammunition into her autocannon as a screaming woman crested the berm. She was clad in little more than a shift of coarse fibres, like moss woven to cover her sickly pale skin. Maltia felt the brief press of the woman's mind as the witch tried to reach into her thoughts. A tongue of sickly blue flame burst to life in the psyker's hand.

Clumsy. And weak.

Evrik Ebonwelter blinked hard at the brief psychic intrusion, then tore a hole through the witch's chest with a focused burst of las-fire.

Slamming the action of her weapon home to secure the fresh clip, Maltia popped her head over the berm to see another wave of disorganised infantry approaching on their left. She thumbed her micro-bead to send a warning to Sergeant Gaines and his rifles, who were scattered along a narrow ravine beside her squad, wading through water almost up to their necks.

Before she could complete the transmission, a pair of Sentinels burst out from the mist and levelled the enemy platoon with the paired action of two multi-lasers and a heavy flamer.

'Come on now,' she muttered, snagging Trooper Bantholo by the collar. 'I know the lights are pretty, but we can't stay to watch.'

Vyse's Primus and Tertius platoons were already well behind them, and she didn't even want to think of the lecture she'd get from Lieutenant Nalus if her squad was the one to break the line. A gauntleted hand clasped her shoulder as she turned from the front.

'Thought you got lost,' Sergeant Corwyn growled. 'Only reason I could think you'd be moving so damn slow.'

'On it, sergeant,' she replied, shoving Bantholo forward. 'Just wanted to get off a few extra shots.'

The company sergeant puffed away as her squad of heavies picked up into a double-time scramble across the muddy terrain. Troopers could joke all they liked about the sergeant's grey hair and the augmetic leg beneath his left trouser. He might puff like an engine at anything faster than a walk, but she'd never seen him fall behind in a battle.

Corwyn grunted, passing her, and pushed forward towards the twinkle of flare sticks strapped to Cadian packs in the thin mist ahead. The devices were almost unneeded now. The barren, skeletal landscape lay unobstructed for the first time since she'd set foot on the planet. It was an ugly, emaciated, decaying place, not unlike its inhabitants.

It would be a shame to die here, but there had been no grumbling when Restripa had ordered the regiment out from Providence's walls. Six months had been enough on this barren world, and soon it would be over.

One way or the other.

'Come on now,' she barked towards the troopers behind her. 'You want to survive long enough to see the next cesspool they send us to?'

Behind her, a chorus of raw laughter echoed, as her heavies pushed themselves to keep up. They each had their faults, but they were good troopers to the last. She'd never let them hear her say it, but it would be an honour to die standing beside them, if needed.

She swallowed uneasily as the ground shivered slightly. No one around her reacted, as concussions were a normal part of war. The blast could have been an exploding mortar, or one of Kobald's Sentinels erupting in flames, and Maltia would have quickly dismissed it as such, if not for the faint scent floating on the air.

Maltia swallowed and tried to turn her mind from the bitter, coppery taste. Gunpowder. Munitions. Maybe the psychic flicker of the dying witch behind her.

But the veteran within her knew better, and something had been picking at her mind for some time, like a cluster of buried memories trying to escape. The ground shivered again, throwing her off her feet, and a horrible, unearthly screech echoed above the din of battle.

Maltia retched, then vomited as both her eardrums ruptured. Only a few hundred yards away, a beacon of unearthly blue flame spouted towards the sky like a tree erupting from the earth.

The memories came flooding back.

'There it is,' the Colonel grunted. 'Took damned long enough.'

A searing plume of unholy blue light crowded the night sky behind the Cadian 900th like a wicked new dawn, scattering shadows across the previously blank landscape.

The Colonel turned to the vox-bearer beside him and the cluster of his few truly loyal lieutenants. 'You know what that means, then. Time to push in and finish this.'

Orders blazed out from his small command retinue, the troopers of the Dorean 19th forming up together, pulling out of the massed formation like a structure materialising from sand. In moments, an organised regiment had appeared, flanked by the untrained, unwashed masses of Visage's marsh priests and militia.

The Colonel sighed, something like satisfaction gripping him, or at least the release of responsibility after years of preparation. No manoeuvre ever went completely to plan, but it appeared the primaris psyker had taken his bait, and in that bloody distance, the Witchbringer was emerging.

'My lord,' a wizened voice called beside him. His shoulders tensed with the grating, infuriating sound. 'The Witchbringer awakes. We must go to its aid. It will be vulnerable for a short time, but once it has taken possession of the primaris psyker, it will be unstoppable. It will lead us into a new future. One where witch and human–'

The Colonel's fist cracked against the side of the marsh priest's jaw. Stumbling back, the young man clutched his face.

'My lord?' he managed.

The Colonel spat. 'Be quiet,' he replied, surveying the battlefield.

He had four solid companies at his disposal. Most drawn from his original veterans, supplemented with native Visagers whom he'd had the chance to train over the last ten years. There were perhaps three times that many irregulars massed around his core of Dorean rifles. That gave him four thousand troops to throw against a full Cadian regiment. Even on his best day he would not relish those odds.

And yet, he had no intention of defeating them outright.

'Push forward,' he called to his lieutenants. 'Kill the Cadian witch. Once she is dead, the rest will fall.'

In the mud, the marsh priest struggled to his feet.

'My lord. You cannot kill the primaris psyker. The Witchbringer requires her presence as a vessel.'

The Colonel struck him again, his hand tingling with satisfaction.

'No,' he replied. '*You* require her presence.'

The Colonel rolled his shoulders, aged flak armour sliding against his skin, worn to fit perfectly. He had been a soldier for as long as he could remember. He was no expert tactician, but he understood stratagems well enough. For ten years the high priestess of Visage's pathetic marsh cult had used him. He had never been under any illusion about that. And for ten years he had used her as well. Now, he would use that daemon just as he had its pawn.

'You require her to house your accursed, heretic god. But I want to see that daemon tormented, unchained. In a body, the Witchbringer might do exactly what you expect. Build a planet of witches and crown itself king. But what do you think it will do when it is disembodied and exposed? Its very existence on this plane a thing of constant pain?'

He stared down at the marsh priest with nothing but disdain. He had respected the crone, at least, as much as he had despised her arts and dark religion, but this fresh pup was both an affront and a fool.

'It will rage,' the Colonel answered for him. 'It will rage as any injured, mindless animal would do. It will cleanse this world of both your kind and the Imperium alike. And when it has torn Visage piece from Throne-forsaken piece, there will be nothing left for anyone to return to.'

The marsh priest's face curled from confusion to rage, and he raised an outstretched hand towards the Colonel. 'You cannot,' he muttered, blue fire flickering at his withered, pale fingertips.

The Colonel stepped towards the man and laughed as the flames died away.

'You forget what I am, witch,' he spat. 'You forget what I've lost. They took my life. They took my future. They took the only consolation I had left. I can do whatever the hell I like.'

In one smooth, practised motion, he lifted his bolt pistol, and the marsh priest's head evaporated to mist.

At his side the Dorean 19th surged forward.

Raniais Maltia shivered beneath the weight of memories long buried. She remembered not only this abomination in particular, but all the others she had faced in her life long before.

Blood trickled from her ears and nose, her mouth full of the flavour of charred soot and scorched flesh. Against her mind a terrible pressure railed, like a tide screaming to be let in. Her hands and feet shook uncontrollably as she pushed herself up from the cold, muddy earth and fumbled with the weapon that normally fitted her hands like an extra limb.

She turned slowly to face the monster.

The flashing tower of blue werelight was fading, replaced by a titanic monstrosity of swirling white mist. Suddenly, the landscape below was clear, as Visage's fogs coalesced upon that sinewy, writhing form. Countless faces twisted and sprouted from the leviathan, contorted in various stages of pain and distress. Arms and legs emerged from the bloated behemoth, like thousands of corpses caught together in some vast, perverse current. And from that abomination, all their voices screamed together.

Maltia wiped blood from her useless ears, but the sound persisted even without them. It vibrated through the ground. It crept in through each breath. It echoed through the confines of her mind itself. The echoes of ten thousand years of Visage's dead crying out in unison.

It was enough to drive even a stalwart trooper mad.

Beside her, Bantholo lay shaking in the dirt. She knelt and shook the man without any response. The Ebonwelter twins fared only slightly better. Evrik leaned against Tannius, eyes glazed and wandering, while his brother looked helplessly towards her.

Come, she signalled in shaky battle sign. Tannius dragged his brother to stand beside her.

Others, she signed. *Rally.*

Across the empty plain, their enemy was massing. At least four companies of well-organised Dorean troopers marched in unison towards the disarrayed Cadian 900th. All across that line, clusters of Cadians rose to their feet and slowly gathered together just as her squad did now. But with the enemy only a few hundred yards away, they had precious little time to organise a defence.

If they didn't, the horror raging behind them would be the least of their concerns.

Maltia had seen what happened in that situation before. A unit shaken by Chaos collapsing beneath its own weight. She would not allow it to happen again.

Together, the trio of heavy soldiers stumbled towards the platoon of rifles on their left. Maltia rushed towards a young trooper with his gun pressed into his mouth. She slapped it away, and stared into his terrified eyes, breaking him loose for a moment from the psychic grip of the monster on the horizon.

'You weren't trained to be a damn deserter!' she screamed, hardly able to hear her own voice. 'You don't get to die that easily, soldier!'

Beside her, a young corporal grabbed the trooper and set him back onto the line. He nodded towards her, levelling his own weapon towards the enemy, steel in his eyes. Justine, the corporal's nameplate read in weathered, stained script. She would have to remember that name.

All down the Cadian line, Maltia and the Ebonwelter twins pulled shaking soldiers to their feet and placed them back in formation.

Fire, she signed to a young lieutenant. She grabbed his lasgun and pressed it into his hands. Normally, he might have baulked at the order, but the officer was in no shape to take any offence.

'Which direction?' he replied, his voice hardly audible.

Maltia turned, the charging Doreans on one side, that terrible warp-cursed presence on the other. Beneath the monster, three small, dark silhouettes huddled, as the Witchbringer began to descend from the sky.

Enemies on all sides. Utterly outnumbered. Was there any other way for Cadians to fight?

'Whichever direction you goddamn well please, sir!'

The earth around the artefact shattered as the Witchbringer burst from its ancient cage. For a terrible moment, Visage's surface heaved, as if the very bedrock of the planet might give way to the sudden rush of psychic power erupting from the now-crumbling temple. A column of scorching blue witchfire tore from those ruins through the cloudy sky above.

Aerand staggered. First from the physical shockwave that ripped across the briny water in which she stood, then again from the sudden shock of the daemon's psionic presence. She clung to her force staff, reeling, as an impenetrable cloud descended from the sky upon her.

In all her life, in all her training, she had never imagined a presence so strong.

Beside her, Major Absalom Restripa collapsed, and Confessor Libertinum wavered on his feet. As the confessor staggered, reaching for the aquila around his neck, Aerand felt herself crumble to her knees.

* * *

The Cadians fought every bit as bravely as the stories would have had him believe. Yes, he'd scrapped with the 900th over the last six months, but never a full, head-on assault like this.

The Colonel's bolt pistol bucked and jumped in his hands, punching a hole through a squad of the Cadian 900th as his First Company engaged their front line. Flashes of las-fire left his vision clouded with pale violet after-burn as he pressed forward into the melee.

The Cadians had earned every legend told about them, but he had trained his own troopers well. The two formations crashed together with the sound of las-fire and melee, gun barrels and trench knives suddenly flying between bodies pressed into close combat.

There was little need for command and control, now. No brilliant stratagems left to deploy. Simply two masses of humans pressing together in that final, bloody dance, and a single unwavering, animal objective.

Kill before you were killed.

The Colonel threw himself into that terrible churn. His bolt pistol cracked as he dropped a Cadian sergeant before crashing into a pair of heavy troopers struggling to disengage and fall back with an autocannon. He caught one along the side of the face with a moving shot, a deep crimson rift suddenly appearing from the corner of the man's mouth to the edge of his ear. The trooper's helmet cocked on his head, but held fast, and he brought his autocannon crashing into the Colonel's chest.

The Colonel dropped, the sudden impact striking his flak armour like a battering ram. For a terrible moment, he sank beneath the dark, briny water, a pair of boots pressed against his back. Fingers grappled in the darkness for his neck and then suddenly released. A pair of rough hands pulled him from the water.

'Intact?' Sergeant Gross asked him gruffly.

The Colonel nodded, looking down at the pair of dead Cadians, each bearing the telltale marks of Sergeant Gross' handiwork. The long, curving sword in his grasp dripped a neat stream of crimson into the sea.

The press of the two units wavered for a moment, each recoiling from the gruesome first impact. For their part, the Imperials had held, and the few Cadian survivors on the line pressed forward again into a desperate counter-attack. But a lifetime of war had taught the Colonel that valour could only overcome sheer numbers for so long. His Second Company pressed forward through the ranks of his First, and the remaining Cadians crumbled before them.

A clear path lay between him and the primaris psyker who was trapped beneath that abomination in the sky.

'Come on now,' he shouted, coughing and rising to his feet. 'Almost there, sergeant.'

Gross nodded, raising his bloody longsword and waving it forward. The Dorean 19th surged forward with him until a twisting wall of flame enveloped the left flank of his line.

Blue witchfire arced and roiled along his ranks, the air suddenly full of the screams of his troopers being roasted alive within their flak armour.

As the conflagration faded, leaving ashes in its wake, he spotted a mass of marsh priests pressing his way.

'Turn Third Company to cover our flank, sergeant,' he grunted. 'We don't stop for any other bloody damn thing.'

The heretics were killing each other.

Sergeant Maltia raised a hand to cover her eyes as another wave of witchfire splashed into the Dorean formation. What she'd first attributed to miscommunication or the confusion of battle had clearly been an intentional act.

The main press of the Doreans pushed forward against a broken Cadian line, now little more than an inconvenience for the surging Traitor Guardsmen, but along the edges of that formation, it appeared the enemy forces were beginning to devour themselves.

Two krak missiles soared from a Traitor Guardsman on her right, striking a Sentinel and dropping the vehicle in a flameburst. No sooner had it fallen, however, than a mess of black vines sprouted from the ground to devour the Traitor Guardsman entirely. She raised her autocannon and put a burst through the witch who had performed the act.

Any semblance of organisation in the battle had completely evaporated. She'd managed to rally the remnants of three platoons into something resembling an organised force, but the remainder of the battlefield had devolved into a disarrayed melee. At her fore, the Dorean rifles charged forward, devouring the disarrayed Cadian line. At its flanks, Traitor Guardsmen and irregulars turned on one another, while behind her, the nascent daemon still raged. Her troopers gathered in a solitary ring, engaging on all sides while drifting steadily backwards towards that twisting, repulsive monster and the primaris psyker and major trapped beneath it.

Now that they'd weathered the daemon's initial assault, her mind – and the minds of her soldiers – seemed to have steadied. Perhaps it was simply the distraction of having more pressing threats immediately present, but the myriad voices screaming in the back of her skull had faded to only a dull cacophony.

Another wave of Doreans crashed into her survivors, pressing against their ranks and then washing around them. She raised her autocannon and pounded out a continuous rhythm, dropping a squad of rifles as they streaked past. At least two company-sized elements approached. More than enough to wipe her small detachment from the battlefield. At their head charged a greyed trooper in an officer's cap.

'Steady!' Maltia shouted. 'Double ranks. Push out on the left.'

Less than a platoon remained to her. They would fight bravely, but the outcome was clear. As it had always been, perhaps. She braced herself for the impending charge, and for the bloody death that would undoubtedly follow.

As the Doreans rushed in, a wave of witchfire washed over them, enveloping the regiment whole. For a moment the assaulting line was completely lost in the surging wall of abominable blue flame, before bursting back through the other side.

A brief cheer went up from one of her troopers, before he realised that the Doreans had emerged almost unscathed. At the fringes of the formation, a few scattered soldiers smouldered, but at the centre of the line, those flames dissipated harmlessly, as if something had sapped them completely of their strength.

Her eyes flashed again to the officer leading the charge, a tarnished aquila now visible on his epaulets. The Colonel's element pounded into her weary line, but instead of stopping to roll the Cadians away, it split around them like a river surrounding a stone. Once behind them, the Doreans charged yet again. Straight towards Glavia Aerand and the daemon above her head.

Aerand's world was nothing more than screams and darkness.

She struggled to breathe as a weight like mountains fell upon her, her mind spinning with the unwavering, brutal assault. The twisting currents of the warp threw her aside like petty flotsam as a great, ancient maw rose out of the deep.

She was aware that in realspace, her physical body was kneeling in the mud with dark, briny water rising up to her waist. Beside her, a robed man stood bearing a corseque, his voice screaming into an immutable wind, the faint golden glow of the God-Emperor's power pouring off his skin like steam. Another Cadian lay on the soft earth beside her, shaking slowly in the briny sea.

She would return to them, eventually. If only she could find her mind again.

Around her the immaterium roiled, as that ancient shadow shattered its surface. A million voices erupted beneath her like a choir, thousands of clawing consciousnesses pressing in at once against her own. The dead of Visage swarmed like carrion fish around that massive, emerging behemoth.

Throne, how they wanted to be let in.

And yet Aerand held.

For a moment she pressed back against the Witchbringer, rising above the waves long enough to catch sight of the myriad souls blazing and flickering out around her. Close by, Javard Libertinum burned like a torch, the only thing holding the darkness back from extinguishing them all.

She pressed harder against that shadow, and watched with surprise as it hesitated. But not because of her. On the surface of the warp, something else approached her. Something empty, and unholy, and utterly void.

Something that even a mindless daemon would fear.

The Witchbringer recoiled as the Colonel approached, an ungodly screech emerging from the twisted abomination. Whether out of true pain or simply outrage at being separated from its prey, he did not know. And quite frankly, he found he did not care.

The Cadian psyker knelt on the earth before him, her frail body limp and empty, and only faintly breathing. Beside her stood a man he recognised well.

'Confessor Libertinum,' the Colonel grumbled. 'I'm surprised to see you beyond your cathedral walls.'

The confessor started as he noticed the Colonel's presence, his litany fumbling and then falling away.

The last time the Colonel had seen the confessor, his face had been lit by the flames of a pyre. The God-Emperor may have decreed the girl's death, but Javard Libertinum had been His hands in the matter. An added gift, then, to have him here beside the psyker.

The Colonel raised his bolt pistol and took aim at the priest.

'Colonel Oire,' Libertinum muttered.

No need for any further conversation. The Colonel pulled the trigger.

As he fired, a lasgun cracked, and a sudden weight spun him to the side, driving his aim wide. Beside the primaris psyker a Cadian major pushed himself off the ground, a steaming lasgun in his hands.

The psyker opened her violet eyes.

A blank.

The traitor colonel was a bloody psychic blank. A soulless abomination immune to the warp, formed by mutations even rarer than those that had created her.

The realisation made a perfect, ugly sense, the moment Aerand could no longer ignore it. It was the reason the man had avoided murder or worse at the hands of the witches he consorted freely with for years. It was the reason the Witchbringer had retreated before him. It was the reason he left no mark at all on the warp, and why she could not sense even the most peripheral of his thoughts. He stood before her, unknowable, a dirty, empty scar on the empyrean.

The Colonel twisted with the impact of Major Restripa's shot, then righted himself and brought his bolt pistol to bear on the major.

'Down!' Aerand screamed as Restripa tried to stand, still recovering from the sudden absence of the Witchbringer's immense psychic weight. That the major hadn't lost his mind entirely during the daemon's uninhibited assault was testament enough to his will.

Aerand tackled the Colonel to the mud as his bolt pistol flashed. She reeled briefly, her last thread of connection to the immaterium shattered by her proximity to the Dorean. Aerand rolled, drawing her combat knife as the man rose, dropping a spent magazine from his weapon and inserting another.

Around the Colonel, twisting fog raged. Disembodied echoes of the daemon pressed towards him, then flinched away, like waves lapping against a shore.

'You know what you are!' Aerand shouted over the din. 'You could end this all. You could destroy this monster!'

'And what of the monster you worship, Cadian?'

Unthinking, Aerand threw her mind towards the Colonel, striking nothing but an empty void where she should have encountered a human soul. For the first time in half a decade, the empyrean was dead around her, muted completely by the blank standing feet away. At first, the sensation was a blessed relief, then a terrible emptiness filled her. Aerand pulled away from the Colonel's mind, then burst from a crouch towards the man.

There would be no answers, then, for why he had done this. But no answer she might have found in his thoughts could have justified his actions, regardless.

Aerand struck the man as his weapon fired, tearing a burning streak along her left flank. She stepped past him before he could fire another shot, her knife raking his shoulder as she pushed through his grasp. The blade glanced harmlessly off a hardened pauldron before slipping into a crease in his armour to bite the warm flesh underneath.

A grunt from behind her, as she turned to re-engage. A cluster of figures emerged from the mist as the Colonel stepped to the side, shifting his aura of protection with him.

A bloodied Dorean sergeant slid a longsword from the stomach of a Cadian trooper while another emptied a lasgun into the fog. At least a full squad of Traitor Guardsmen followed him into the eye of the unholy storm.

'You don't have to fight us,' the Colonel shouted. 'We can end your torment painlessly, witch. Your God-Emperor has used you, Cadian. Taken your life. Taken your world. He will burn you like a candle until nothing remains, and He will kill you in the end just as surely as that daemon would.'

He was right, Aerand knew, in his own twisted fashion. The God-Emperor would take her one day, once she had served her purpose to Him and His Imperium. It was only what she did before then that mattered.

'Then I shall burn as brightly as I can, heretic.'

Aerand rushed forward as a Cadian trooper erupted from the fog behind the traitors, driving the Dorean sergeant into the ground. Raniais Maltia battered the Traitor Guardsman with empty fists, as another Dorean turned his weapon on her. Aerand dived forward and sunk her blade into the man's chest, turning at the sudden ring of metal behind her.

A Dorean bayonet hung inches from her neck, foiled by the thin, shaking metal of a decorative corseque. Javard Libertinum grunted with the sudden exertion, the melee standing still as its participants adjusted to the sudden new additions.

Confessor Libertinum met her eyes for only a moment, then swung his weapon towards the Traitor Guardsman. The Dorean's helmet shattered under the impact, blood spraying from his mouth as the side of his face evaporated. From the sky, the bloodied form of a single cherub crashed down through the mists and sunk dark, curling claws into the neck of an unaware traitor. On the ground, the Dorean sergeant raised a booted foot and kicked Maltia across the face.

Their tiny bubble raged like the eye of a storm, as Libertinum and Maltia began the melee in earnest. Two Dorean troopers raised lasguns towards the priest, and Aerand sprinted the short distance towards the pair. Before she reached them, both dropped with smoking holes in their chest, Major Restripa having found his feet once again.

'Kill him!' Restripa shouted, his weapon singing, as another squad of Traitor Guardsmen battled their way into the clearing. 'Kill the damned colonel.'

As the Doreans passed through that swirling wall of ghosts, long, dark claws raked across them, bloodying the troopers as they passed. With every moment that the Colonel held the daemon at bay, the echoes trapped within it seemed to grow more corporeal. Libertinum and Maltia rushed towards the bloodied enemy, as Aerand turned to face the Colonel once again.

At the centre of that raging storm, the man stood firm, white mists crackling with foul warp energy swirling around him in Chaotic anger. Thousands of faces swam in that maddening mist, growing more detailed each moment the Witchbringer gathered strength within the physical world. Appendages flowed together, melding echo and flesh in a gruesome, unholy amalgamation, matched only by mouthless, tormented screams.

It was enough to drive any mortal man mad, and yet the Colonel's eyes blazed only with dark purpose.

She threw her mind towards the traitor once again, grasping for any hold on the man's mind, but found none. Slowly, he levelled his bolt pistol at her chest, and she felt the painful absence of her divinations.

But Glavia Aerand needed no connection to the warp to foretell this end. She knew precisely what such a weapon would do without her gifts to counter it. Only a single choice remained, then, and it was a damned ugly one. With a desperate prayer, she raised her force staff before her and fell back into the Witchbringer's roiling madness as the bolt pistol flashed in the Colonel's hand.

The primaris psyker vanished into the mists. The Colonel's bolt pistol bucked once, then fell silent in his hand. Behind that wall of swirling, impenetrable madness, a light flared as her magicks warred against the weapon.

Clever soldier. A doomed effort, but admirable.

The Colonel walked forward, mists falling back with each of his steps. He lowered his pistol as the Cadian psyker staggered forward, catching the woman if only to prevent her from knocking him off his feet. Her body twisted in time to reveal blood streaming from her left chest, and her face and neck had been raked by the daemon's countless, mindless claws.

She had distanced herself far enough from the Colonel to summon just enough of her dark magick to blunt his killing blow, but in the end those unholy forces had injured her just as surely.

A sigh escaped the Colonel as he lowered the psyker to the dirt. He bore no particular hatred towards the woman, only the twisted society that had created her. In fact, as he stared at her ashy, bruised skin and the rusted, weeping cables along her skull, he felt a twinge of something almost akin to pity.

'Sleep, now,' he whispered, as the woman coughed blood. 'Your torment will be the last on this accursed world.'

Around him, the Witchbringer screamed with rage, and the Colonel lifted his eyes with bitter satisfaction. Damn the daemon. Damn the Emperor. Damn every creature, dark or shrouded in light, that claimed itself a god and used that to justify tormenting the souls of innocent, helpless mortals.

As he looked down, the psyker's violet eyes flicked open. Warmth blossomed across his neck as she buried her combat knife in his throat.

* * *

The Witchbringer descended on them like a wave.

One moment, Sergeant Maltia drove a bloodied fist into the face of a helmeted Traitor Guardsman, and the next, the man was ripped from her grasp. A sea of twisting, dark appendages grasped the man on all corners and tore his head and an arm away from his torso, as the aura of protection collapsed around them.

Desperately, Maltia pulled her lasgun from the mud and fired indiscriminately into the pressing mist. The surface recoiled from the blazing barrel of her weapon, but simply flowed around the fusillade like water. Beside her, Confessor Libertinum stumbled beneath the sudden force of the daemon's unblunted psychic presence before righting himself and bringing his corseque to bear. With a hollow crunch, he drove the ornate weapon into the chest of the Dorean Guardsman beneath his foot, then raised its finial towards the mists. The sea around them halted, the confessor's voice giving the daemon pause.

Dropping to her knees, Maltia rummaged within the webbed combat pouches strapped to her flak armour, her fingers closing around the cold, smooth surface of hard metal. She pulled the plasma grenade from its pouch.

'Emperor's breath,' Major Restripa called beside her. 'What are you waiting for, sergeant?'

'Well, I've been saving this,' Maltia grumbled with a shred of disappointment. 'For what?'

The sergeant grunted and lobbed the grenade into the mist, then covered her eyes.

A small sun blazed in the air above her, but Aerand might not have noticed the plasma grenade's discharge if not for the daemon's reaction. For a blessed moment, the mists above her limp, bleeding body tore open with the light and heat of an infant star, and on the surface of the empyrean the shadow around her reeled.

Aerand took a deep and shuddering breath, her left chest little more than an aching, flapping mess as shattered ribs pulled open a lung half-flooded with blood. She had blunted the Colonel's shot, but not stopped it entirely, and now it would kill her just as he had intended. The psyker cursed, driving the physical pain out of her mind, and forcing her attention back into the warp. Not a difficult task. She already walked the border between the physical and psychic realm. And as battered as her body was, it appeared she would soon make that transition permanently.

The Witchbringer lashed out as she re-entered the warp, sinewy tendrils of dark shadow flogging her mind in a pained assault. She drove the attack back, but felt the bite of those limbs deeper into her defences than minutes before. She had stood her ground before the daemon from the start, but with each passing exchange her resistance flagged.

Until the last drop is spilled.

That had been her motto, once, and she still drew breath, no matter how ragged. Aerand gathered her will and struck back towards the daemon. As her mind touched the twisting, serpentine shadow, a thousand voices responded in disorganised protest, the echoes of countless dead rising to the creature's surface.

It was evident now that the Witchbringer was just as fragmented within the confines of the empyrean as its physical form was in the realspace of Visage. Whatever sinister symbiosis existed between the daemon, the artefact and the planet's unholy arborage, its outcome was now painfully clear. For untold millennia, the daemon trapped within that artefact had drawn the souls of Visage's dead to itself, amassing layer upon layer of abhorrent echoes until its original sentience had been lost in its perverted efforts to sustain so many others. What might have been a true, focused intelligence once was now nothing more than a feral, animal will, torn in myriad directions by the memories of a million lives.

And yet, that amalgam proved almost impenetrable.

Until the last drop is spilled. Every last one.

Aerand threw her mind against the abomination again, unable to avoid its inevitable response. Dark claws raked across the surface of her mind, the memories of a thousand lives assaulting her in an instant. She staggered beneath the weight – nearly enough for her to lose her own will – and then forced herself to the other side.

As she withdrew her mind from the twisted conglomeration before her, she felt something within the shadow tear. The smallest of rifts in that seething, impenetrable armour, but large enough for the faintest hint of light to emerge.

As another massive, seething limb descended upon her like the shadow of a moon, Aerand drove her mind forward into that rift and whatever soul lay trapped within.

To die for the Emperor was no painful thing. Sergeant Raniais Maltia had known this since before she could speak.

All loyal servants of the God-Emperor of Mankind gave their lives, in the end, for their immortal ruler and for the vision of purity He embodied. Only the form of those inevitable deaths varied. This is what the Ministorum taught. This is what every preacher she'd ever met had told her. And this is what she had reminded herself countless times when she stood on the brink of her most dangerous battles.

And yet, as she hammered her last power pack into the steaming clip of the lasgun she'd carried since Cadia, and felt the unholy claws of disembodied limbs tear across her shoulder just beneath her pauldron, she found that the God-Emperor was the last thing on her mind.

And whatever the Ecclesiarchy might say, dying for the Throne still hurt like hell.

The sergeant's skin seared and bubbled at the unfiltered Chaotic contact as she hammered the powercell home and unleashed a stream of searing white las-fire into the daemon. The mist corpse beside her howled, then evaporated, a dozen more flowing out of the swirling monstrosity in order to take the spectre's place.

Her back pressed against Libertinum and Restripa, the trio stumbled through the fog blindly. The plasma grenade had bought them time enough to regroup and choose a direction to retreat, but nothing more.

Talons passed by her head, catching Major Restripa's helmet and nearly strangling the man with its chinstrap, before Libertinum's corseque shattered the ghastly appendage. The major stumbled, coughing, back to his feet. All of them had fallen already, and soon one of them would not be able to rise. Then, the end would be swift for the pair that remained.

Overhead, a beam of light pierced through the shadows. Lascannon, from the colour. Likely as not fired by one of Kobald's Sentinels. Someone still remained alive on the outside, then, with enough good sense to pour whatever armament they had left into the boiling Chaos abomination before them.

Restripa met her eyes and nodded as she pulled the confessor in the opposite direction of that blast, and further into the heart of the daemon. If any of the 900th remaining outside this hellscape were to survive the hours – nay, minutes – to come, they had only one possible remaining hope.

As Maltia pushed forward, pouring a wedge of las-fire into the mists and rushing into the gap it created, she felt her foot catch on something soft and warm. She tumbled forward over the corpse of a Dorean officer, blood still streaming from a gash across his neck. As she tried to rise, the mists washed over her head.

For a terrible moment, Sergeant Maltia was drowning, until the booming voice of the confessor echoed above her, and the ghastly face before her own drew slowly away. Rough hands pulled her to her feet and pushed her onwards, straight towards another corpse, this one clad in a psyker lord's robes.

Maltia's last hope faded to ash within her, but then Glavia Aerand took a ragged, shaky breath. Above her, the daemon swirled like a torrent, driving down towards the dying woman in a tangle of razor-sharp appendages. Whatever war was raging between the daemon and the primaris psyker's soul would matter little if it simply destroyed her body.

Maltia crouched, preparing to throw herself in front of that blow, ready to die. Not for the Emperor, but for that woman in the mud. That woman, who had once been an honourable soldier. And still was.

Before she could, a ghostly, ephemeral figure stepped out from the mists and drove the daemon suddenly back.

Jarrah.

Even in death, the tenor of the primaris psyker's soul was utterly recognisable to her. Kellipso's mind had been the first to ever touch hers directly. The first against which she had trained and sparred.

For a moment, the dim, fading soul before her winced, before it recognised her as well.

Glavia.

She knew enough not to expect joy from the man, but the bitter rage which emanated from Kellipso's echo took her wholly by surprise.

I warned you. I warned you not to follow me here.

Aerand shivered against the sudden assault. Around the pair, the Witch-bringer had briefly relented, and Aerand was peripherally aware of three other souls gathering in realspace around them.

+And yet here I am.+

Kellipso seethed. *You fool. You bloody damned fool.*

Tendrils of shadow slowly overwhelmed whatever resistance the three souls around them had mounted, then drew in closer to the pair. Kellipso threw them back.

I sent you a vision. Across half the damned galaxy. With my last thought I tried to push you away. Tried to spare you this fate.

+And yet.+

Kellipso reached out towards her mind and she opened its door, her memories becoming his own. The psyker's anger faded, swallowed by a nihilistic sense of defeat.

And yet that is precisely what brought you here.

Despite the fact that there were no words spoken, Aerand could hear the unmistakable regret in his thought. This was the trap of divination, always, especially for the unpractised. Jarrah Kellipso had attempted to push her away, but his very warning is what had led to this moment.

Around them, the Witchbringer suddenly raged, one of the three souls standing vigil over her body in realspace flickering defiantly in reply before it was snuffed out completely. Through the gap in that wall, the daemon surged towards them, but Kellipso suddenly turned it away.

For a moment, an image flashed through Aerand's mind, of her body bleeding into the cold, churned mud. Of the molten, shattered remnants of her bridle carving a searing river down the skin of her back. Of two shadowy silhouettes standing vigil over her.

Tell them to end it. Tell them to kill you before the daemon takes control.

The pain in Kellipso's thought was undeniable, but he spoke the order with icy resolve. He had taken that bitter path in the end, and it had cost him torment she could not even imagine. But there was little question as to what he had saved.

Another psionic wave pressed against her from the Witchbringer, and Aerand felt it bite deep into her defences. There was little left now within her to keep that ravenous shadow from the very substance of her soul, and the body beneath. What it would do with that power, she could scarcely imagine.

Slowly, Aerand reached out towards the two mortal minds beside her. She envisioned a bloodied laspistol in a bloodied hand.

Now, Aerand. If you can. It will end us, and them, soon.

Aerand readied her will, looking back at the last flickering echo of the man who had once saved her from a similar fate. And as she did, she noted the faintest glimmer of something alight in the swirling mess around him.

+No.+

Kellipso's echo raged. The Witchbringer struck out towards him, and he swatted it away.

Don't be a fool, Glavia. Without your body, without your mind, the daemon

will tear this world apart, but it will remain on this insignificant planet only.
With a vessel – with you *as a physical vessel – there is no telling the destruc-*
tion such a presence could wreak.

+I know.+

The Witchbringer drove towards her with a hunger unmasked. Aerand summoned every bit of will she had left, then reached out towards the psyker beside her. As she touched Kellipso's echo, she felt her strength grow, like a deep breath of cool air after drowning. Together, they forced the Witchbringer a step back.

Aerand, this is no victory. How long do you think the two of us can resist,
even together?

Already, the daemon was advancing. Aerand pulled from Kellipso and pushed it back again. The Witchbringer writhed as their combined wills struck it like a blade, another faint chink opening in that swirling shadow. And within, once again, the faintest of lights.

+You are not the only one, Kellipso. You cannot be the only one. This daemon has raged for ten thousand years. How many loyal servants of the God-Emperor lie within this prison? How many others still maintain some will of their own? Find them. Find them for me, Jarrah. And together we will attempt what you alone could not.+

For a moment, Aerand felt the warp around her shiver, as Kellipso's echo blazed like a sun. One by one new embers appeared in the swirling mists of the Witchbringer's clutches. Aerand cast her mind to them each like a rope in deep water, and one by one they came.

There were no voices remaining. Not even faces for most. Echoes of souls lost for so long within the warp's darkness that they retained no memory even of themselves.

But they remembered the God-Emperor and His holy light.

For ten thousand years the Witchbringer had devoured and swallowed, consuming souls by the thousands hoping to find a single vessel strong enough to sustain it. And now, with those souls suddenly blazing once again within it, the daemon screamed.

As hundreds, then thousands of burning fires flared to life within that impenetrable darkness, Aerand summoned the last remaining shred of her will and drove her mind towards them all like a shower of spears. As she spoke, her voice was joined first by Jarrah Kellipso's, then an untold choir of Visage's dead.

'I turn my soul, O God-Emperor, towards the light of your grace, that I may surrender before it and burn just as brightly.'

With a horrifying shriek, the Witchbringer shattered around her, before the warp swallowed her whole.

CHAPTER 14

Major Absalom Restripa had never understood funerals. Never made sense of the effort and expense poured into the fate of those already dead and unable to appreciate it.

He could grasp the theoretical reasons for such rituals. He understood that the common masses required such displays of extravagance and ceremony in order to temper their base animal fear of an event as natural as death. And yet, he found, no matter how hard he tried, he could not personally connect any emotion to the endeavour.

Yet, as he stood on the damp, cracked staircase beneath Javax Cathedral – the first light of dawn washing down through multicoloured glassaic over the dark, murky waters which were only just beginning to recede from their high point at the apex of the city – and looked on at the blazing pyre in the courtyard below, he found, for the first time, a hint of comfort in the measured precision of the Cadian troopers and Ecclesiarchy preachers carrying stretchered bodies towards those purifying flames.

The dead had burned for three straight days on a dozen pyres surrounding Providence's last vestige of Imperial strength, and still they streamed in from the dark, shattered buildings of the city and washed up like flotsam on the salty, bitter tide. After days submerged within those acrid, pungent waters, little remained to tell loyalist and traitor apart, and all burned in the hungry, cleansing fires. Haggard preachers spoke benedictions on unending rotation, hardly stopping to eat, or to sleep.

The sheer volume of the dead precluded any attempt to discern between the faithful and the heretic, and it would be up to the God-Emperor to recognise His own. Restripa had no illusions that the fires would go hungry soon. They would still be burning bodies a year from today.

With a sigh, he surveyed the shattered city around him. Dark water still lapped across worn cobbled streets, chewing at the foundations of structures already crumbling. What a dozen traitor regiments and cults had not accomplished in centuries, the simple weight of water had achieved in a week.

General Yarin had assured him a detachment of engineers and tech-priests had been dispatched to the planet, and would arrive by the end of the season to evaluate the support required to rebuild Providence's sea walls and repair its ancient bilge pumps, if possible. The most generous estimates of the Departmento Munitorum claimed they would have a complete assessment within a solar year, and would only then begin to determine what resources might be available to actually begin reconstruction.

It was a laughable, if predictable bureaucratic outcome.

The truth, already, was painfully clear. Visage stood, only barely, but it was already dead. With the destruction of the Witchbringer, the planet's tithe of psykers would dry up, and without that single worthwhile resource, the Imperium would never look towards the planet with anything but casual indifference again.

Nearly half a Cadian regiment had died to secure a future of eternal obsolescence for this desolate world. And they would have to claim that as a victory.

Tired eyes stared back at him from lines of his soldiers as Major Restripa descended the cracked and dripping steps. Even with the departure of the Throne-cursed daemon, Visage's weather had not improved a bit.

Behind him, six acolytes clad in drab black cowls carried a shrouded corpse on a litter. Ornate, gold-wreathed fabric fell flat over the body, the crimson of a Cadian flag laid across its eyes. Restripa led the honour guard towards the pyre in silence, as troopers snapped to attention on either side. There were no words as they passed beneath an arbour of raised, dripping lasguns and exhausted salutes. The very act was more than speech enough from troopers who scarcely deigned to speak to non-combatants.

To the best of his knowledge, Absalom Restripa believed this was the first time his regiment had ever given formal Cadian honours to an ecclesiarch.

As the acolytes deposited the last remains of Confessor Javard Libertinum atop the blazing pyre, Restripa stepped to the side and watched the flames hiss. As the man's body went up in a gout of fire, the smell of burning flesh and metal drifted towards his nose.

'Do you think he would have been pleased, in the end?' a voice called softly.

A robe drifted to his side in the rain, pain written across the thin woman's face as she settled to a position of attention. She leaned heavily against her thin, silver force staff, but even with its support she looked as if the simple exertion of holding her body upright might be enough to floor her.

'Pleased with what, adept?' Restripa replied bitterly. 'His funeral? His death? His broken world?'

Glavia Aerand looked towards him for a moment, idly spinning a pair of black metal spheres in one hand. The gesture appeared somehow terribly familiar, yet equally foreign at once when performed by anyone other than the psyker lord Jarrah Kellipso. He had never liked the man, just as he did not care for his successor, but Kellipso had served well and had died, in the end, with honour, and such a reminiscence of him raised a strange nostalgia within the major.

'His cathedral still stands,' the primaris psyker said. 'So do we.'

'So do we,' Restripa whispered in reply.

After some time, the major turned away.

'It's good to see you out of the medicae's tent,' he managed. 'New orders from General Yarin this morning. To a world called Burl. If history has been any lesson, I suspect we will have need of you in the future.' Not camaraderie, but the best he could manage. For all her faults, the woman had shown herself to be a formidable asset.

As he met the primaris psyker's eyes – the same battle-hardened violet that he knew showed in his own – the intensity of her gaze set him aback. For three days the psyker lord had lain shaking on a damp cot in Chief Medicae Argos' tent. For three days she had done nothing more than babble and whimper, and now that she was awake she bore the look of a woman haunted by knowledge she did not want.

For her part, she carried it well, but the weight of the realisation pressed on Restripa.

'Adept,' he began slowly, unsure he even wanted to ask. 'At the end. The Witchbringer. The amassed souls of Visage. What did they show you on the other side?'

Aerand remained silent for some time, as hesitant to answer as he had been to ask. 'Not they. It. There was a single shadow at the bottom of it all. The solid, perverted core around which every other soul had adhered.'

'It, then,' Restripa replied tenuously. He knew he would not like the answer, but asked, 'What did it show you, lord psyker? I must have some right to know.'

Glavia Aerand stared at him. Hollow. Then finally nodded.

'It showed me, sir, the way the Imperium breaks.'

THE WEIGHT OF SILVER

Steven B Fischer

The body lying still in the dirt may have once been human, but there was little left to mark it as such, aside from the mangled remnants of a man's face, sun-darkened and wrinkled and now caked in blood.

Lieutenant Glavia Aerand stood over the corpse, eyes tracing the tattered remains of its heavy, brown tunic to the broken limbs and gouged torso beneath. Her helmet's lumen flooded the pool of blood beside the body, already grown thick and dark in the chill mountain night, and something flickered in what was left of the man's calloused hand.

Aerand knelt as dark forms circled around her, the deep-green flak armour of her platoon a ring of ghosts in the night. As she reached down and lifted the small piece of metal, a gruff voice echoed behind her.

'It's silver,' Sergeant Roderick Olemark whispered, his violet eyes flickering above the hoarfrost in his beard. 'The locals believe silver can ward off cultists and the warp-taint they carry.'

Olemark was one of the few in their formation familiar with the planet. He'd come to Ourea nearly three years ago with the Cadian 873rd – before the slow bleed of counterinsurgency and desertion cost the unit nearly all of its soldiers and the 900th absorbed the remainder when they landed a few days ago.

Aerand rose awkwardly in her dark, heavy armour, trying to hide the difficulty of the gesture. She was still adjusting to the mountain world's harsh gravity, but she'd be damned if anyone knew how much her legs burned after only a short patrol.

She dropped the metal trinket into her palm, its design crude but unmistakable – an armoured figure, wreathed in blistering sunlight. The Emperor of Mankind sat glorified on Holy Terra hundreds of light years away, but even here His hymns and prayers were sung. Even here He shielded human minds from the warp.

'You don't seem to share their confidence,' Aerand replied, returning the effigy to the corpse's hand.

Olemark chuckled, then patted his lasgun. 'This is the only metal I trust to stop a heretic.'

There was a subtle condescension in his voice that grated on Aerand like the new, stiff boots tearing her feet apart. At first she had thought it was Olemark alone, or that his patronizing was directed only at her. Maybe because she was young. Maybe because this was her first command. Maybe because most people who heard her name assumed she'd gotten where she was on the coattails of her father.

But it wasn't any of those things. There was a sense of superiority among all the veterans, and truth be told, she couldn't fault them for it. Olemark and his men knew more about this planet than she ever would – knowledge they'd earned through misery and bloodshed. To make an issue of their arrogance would only sow dissention and alienate the few experts she badly needed.

Aerand motioned for the platoon to advance, and forty sparks of light drifted forward through the trees.

Corwyn, Delaver, Maltia, Artus. She knew the names and stories of every trooper around her. She'd made certain of that on the voyage to Ourea, because if her father had taught her any lesson, it was this: her soldiers were willing to fight for the Emperor, but few would die for anyone other than their comrades. But she didn't know Olemark and his grizzled veterans, and that unsettled her nearly as much as the steep ridgelines around her or the dim glow of firelight in the valley below.

Up ahead, between the silhouettes of jagged, titanic mountains, a cluster of buildings was burning. Aerand motioned for the platoon to halt, and unfurled a crude, bulky map from the case across her shoulders.

'Haggerty Homestead,' Olemark mumbled as he strode past, the orange glow of the flames bathing his scar-crossed face. 'Save you the time searching around on the map.'

Aerand bit her tongue and made a point of locating the small complex anyway. No other settlements nearby. No known cultist hideouts for miles. She turned to the young trooper beside her and pointed to the vox-caster strapped to his back. 'Let headquarters know we're investigating, Maresh. I'll report back once we find something.'

Dead foliage and loose stones ground beneath Aerand's feet as she descended the steep incline, squads fanning out in a crescent around her. This was a standard cordon manoeuvre – one she'd forced her platoon to rehearse hundreds of times – but even so, she felt her breath grow rapid. She was no Whiteshield anymore, and this was her first chance to prove it.

The complex had been built from wood and stone, a carryover from the time before Imperial voidcraft brought rockrete and machines to this world. In the centre of the valley, a large building was burning, smaller cottages already reduced to ash. No simple accident could have caused such a blaze, and there would be no survivors, she was certain of that.

A beam in the main building settled with a crash as her platoon strode past like smoke-shrouded shadows. In the light of the sparks it threw into the air, Aerand spotted a cluster of charred bodies ahead.

Fifteen, maybe twenty, mangled and marred like the man in the forest. As she neared, a strange apprehension grew inside her, the skin along her back prickling with unease. Aerand paused and surveyed the macabre scene as her soldiers pushed forward to clear the complex.

It was clear once she'd drawn closer that the bodies hadn't been randomly scattered – they were arranged in a deliberate pattern. Eight gory rays extended from a central circle, a single naked body at its centre, less muti-lated, but more disturbing than the rest.

'Terra save us,' Corwyn muttered as he led his squad past, crossing his arms in the sign of the aquila amid unsettled glances from his soldiers.

Aerand knelt in the wavering firelight and stared at the young woman. Across her chest and stomach, a symbol had been etched into the woman's pale flesh – a twisting teardrop like a tongue of flame.

As Aerand stared at the pattern, an inexplicable horror washed over her. She'd seen her share of corpses, many mutilated far beyond this, but there was something obscene in the mark itself, even ignoring the way it had been fashioned. The scent of burning metal and rotting flesh replaced the odour of smoke in the air, and the taste of bile and blood rose in her throat. When she reached to cover the corpse with the torn cloak beside it, the young woman's eyes snapped open and the sound of gunfire rang out from the ridge.

The roar of weapons and shouting voices split the night like a peal of thunder, and bursts of lasfire rained down towards her platoon. Aerand tried to tear herself away from the body, but found she could not look away from its empty, black eyes.

A rough hand shook her shoulder, Olemark's voice towering over the sea of hushed whispers that had suddenly filled her mind.

'Lieutenant!' the sergeant shouted, shouldering his lasgun and laying into the trigger. 'How do you want us to engage?'

Aerand stared at his face and the flashes of lasfire from his weapon. Beside him, Corwyn and Delaver crouched, pouring rounds into the dark trees.

Lieutenant,' Corwyn shouted, the gold chevrons on his shoulder gleam-ing red in the firelight. 'Fix and flank?'

Aerand opened her mouth to reply but couldn't form the words. She looked back at the corpse, its black eyes fully open, the symbol on its chest reaching out through the night.

'Throne,' Olemark grumbled. 'She's shell-shocked already.' He turned to the soldiers beside him, as Aerand struggled against the shackles on her voice. 'Can't be more than half a dozen up there. Keep your squads behind what's left of the buildings and lay down suppressive fire. My troopers will flank up the draw.'

His troopers, not hers.

'And someone send a medicae to grab the lieutenant! If she gets herself shot, you know they'll blame it on us.'

Desperation rose in Aerand's mind as her platoon streamed out into the night. She should be with them. She should be leading them. But for some terrible reason, her body wouldn't listen. Instead, her eyes darted between the woman in the dirt and the ridgeline above, the same dark repulsion tethering her to both.

Aerand blinked as two medicaes rushed up beside her.

'Lieutenant,' Artus whispered, pulling a bioscanner from his pack and running it across her body. 'We need to get you out of here.' He shook his head as the readout came back blank.

In the darkness of the forest, the lumens of Olemark's squad flashed like shooting stars, streaking up towards the sound of weapons fire on the ridgeline. The taste of rust grew stronger in Aerand's mouth, the prickling of her skin now a veritable frenzy. *'Fifth squad engaging,'* Olemark growled over the vox.

A moment later, the ridgeline flashed bright with lasfire and the explosions of well-placed frag grenades. The roar of rifle reports swelled like a wave, then drifted slowly away until only the crackling of flames echoed through the valley.

'The heretics are dead,' Olemark called, then continued in a sullen whisper, 'As are two of ours.'

Aerand's breath fell from her lungs. Two of her soldiers, dead, against a force they outnumbered nearly ten to one. The ringing in her ears began to fade, and the taste in her mouth slowly evaporated, replaced by a horrible weight in her chest.

'Who?' she asked, blinking and staring at the body beside her.

Olemark spoke the names of the dead troopers over the vox, but Aerand was too numb to understand anything but the anger in his voice. She reached down and grasped the tunic from the dirt, throwing it over the woman and the sigil on her chest.

The woman's eyes were not black. The woman's eyes were not open. They had never been.

Hours later, Aerand struggled to shake that moment from her mind as she marched beside her soldiers along a narrow mountain path. Apex Inruptus loomed tall on the mountainside ahead, the dark, jagged towers of the ancient fortress climbing like knives into the bleeding horizon, casting their shadows over the high mountain pass. For centuries this valley had been one of Ourea's vital arteries, allowing caravans of livestock, then hulking, smoke-laden machines to bear timber and stone through the treacherous mountains. For the past decade that flow had been choked to a trickle, replaced by endless Astra Militarum convoys shuttling fuel and ammunition from one harried encampment to another.

Her platoon stretched beside her like a twisting, black river, Olemark's veteran squad at the fore, bearing the bodies of Karletti and Vaughn on salvaged boards from the homestead. Aerand had hardly known either trooper, but they had been her soldiers, if only for a few days. And now they were dead because of her.

Her eyes met Olemark's as she walked beside the formation – his expression was pure ice. His doubts had been muffled before, but she could scarcely imagine how his veterans must feel now that she had confirmed them. How her own soldiers must feel to know their leader had failed them in their first real trial.

For the first time in her life, she was glad her father was no longer alive. Glad he wouldn't have to know how badly she had let him down. She'd been only a child when he died beside his regiment, holding Kasr Kraf as Cadia fell, all so that a few more transports could reach the evacuation zone. All so that *she* could reach the evacuation zone. It would break his heart to know this was how she'd repaid him.

Aerand trudged up the slope, the burning in her feet long since faded into numbness, dwarfed by the guilt that gripped her chest and stole her breath. The feeling only grew as she crossed the narrow bridge to Apex's western gate, hardly noticing the mind-numbing chasm below. The thick, stone doors ground slowly apart, opening to a courtyard blanketed in thin snow.

Colonel Yarin waited within, her face drawn into a steely grimace as she stared at the pair of corpses leading Aerand's platoon. Behind her, a field chirurgeon took one look at the ice on Vaughn and Karletti's pale skin and packed his instruments back into a row of blood-stained crates.

'Colonel,' Aerand began, as Olemark's squad laid their morbid cargo down onto the cold stone. 'Let me–'

'Stop,' Yarin replied, her short, greying hair fluttering in the stiff, mountain wind. 'See to your dead first, then meet me in my quarters. You can explain then.'

Aerand nodded and turned back to her platoon. In the centre of the courtyard, Olemark knelt beside Karletti and Vaughn, pulling an old, faded flag from deep within his pack. Cadia's golden pillars glimmered on a crimson sea, the original standard of the 873rd. Slowly, he tore two strips from the fraying fabric and laid them over the corpses' eyes.

This wasn't the same ritual the 900th practiced, but Aerand recognized its significance well enough. She had been born on Cadia. She had stared into the Eye of Terror and felt its heavy gaze staring back. Karletti and Vaughn had spent most of their lives looking into that madness, and now in death, they were finally free.

Olemark's squad gathered around him and lifted the two bodies from the snow, bearing them back towards Apex's gate.

'They've carried that weight far enough, alone,' Corwyn said, stepping up beside Aerand. 'The least we can do is help.'

She shook her head. 'I think our help is the last thing they want right now. Take the platoon back to the barracks and give them some rest.'

As Olemark's squad carried the bodies through the gate, Aerand followed. She had seen men and women die before. Throne, she'd killed her fair share during her years as a Whiteshield. But this was the first time she'd stared at her comrades' corpses and known their deaths rested on her. Her troopers' lives were her single greatest weapon, and she had just squandered two of them.

Aerand stood at a distance on the narrow stone bridge as Olemark and his squad lifted their comrades, then dropped them over the ledge. Bitter wind whipped up from the chasm as the corpses fell, vanishing into the shadow of the mountain fortress. In months, they would be nothing but bone. In years, nothing but dust. In centuries that dust would become one with the mountain and the fortress both men had died to defend.

Aerand nodded as Olemark returned to the fortress ahead of his squad. He brushed hard against her shoulder.

'Why don't you step aside, lieutenant? Before anyone else gets killed.'

Aerand opened her mouth to reply, before her voice was drowned out by the sound of the wind.

'I don't know what it was, sir,' Aerand confessed, as Yarin paced behind her crude desk. The colonel's office had been an ammo depot only two days before, and a servo-skull twittered over a stack of papers atop the crates and shell boxes clustered at the centre of the room. Yarin's face was drawn up into its customary scowl, the look somehow even more rigid than usual.

'I've been through dozens of battles. Nothing like this has ever happened before.'

'And you've never been in command during a single one,' Yarin replied. 'It's different when you're making the decisions. When there are others' lives resting in your hands.'

Aerand couldn't deny that, but it hadn't felt like fear or panic – she'd learned to master those sins when she was just a child.

Yarin leaned against a thin, slit window, staring into the snow falling on Apex's battlements. 'Frankly, I don't care what it was. I care that it crippled you in the middle of combat and forced your senior sergeant to take over command.'

'It won't happen again, sir.'

'No. It certainly won't.'

As she uttered the words, a shadow crept over the room, and Aerand turned to see a massive form in the doorway. Her father had fought with the Adeptus Astartes on Cadia, and he'd told her stories of the Emperor's Angels when she was young, but seeing one in person was another thing entirely.

Slowly, the behemoth stepped into the room, his steps nearly silent, despite the fact his dark-grey power armour dwarfed both Aerand and the colonel. On his chestplate, the aquila shone in blood-red, mirrored on his shoulder by a crimson skull bearing lightning wings.

'Colonel.'

The voice that spilled from the Space Marine's dark helmet seemed not entirely human, its cold, rocky tenor as unyielding as the mountains outside. Aerand wondered how long the Space Marine had stood there, and how much of her stumbling conversation he'd heard.

Even Yarin seemed shaken by his presence, her confident demeanour shifting to something more guarded.

'My lord,' she replied, before turning to Aerand. 'The Storm Wings have come to lead the push to retake Qurea. Across the planet, they will be leading key assaults against the cultists and traitors.'

The red slits of the Space Marine's eyes fell across Aerand. 'Indeed.'

'Scouting patrols from Guard convoys have reported a group of cultists not far from here,' Yarin continued. 'Amassing in numbers we've not seen before, and converging on the spaceport at Noravis Opum. I don't need to tell you how crippling it would be to lose one of the largest loyal settlements in the region.'

'At nightfall, Lord Tarvarius will lead the 900th in a counter-attack to destroy this army, crushing the cultist threat in the region. You and your platoon will stay behind to secure Apex Inruptus against any retaliation.'

Aerand's shoulders fell as her breath escaped her. Relegated to nothing but glorified guard duty. This was the single most important operation of the war and her platoon was going to be left behind. She had made a mistake. She had lost the colonel's confidence. She could accept that. But her platoon was one of the best in the regiment, and there was no reason to punish her soldiers for her failings. She nearly began to protest before Yarin continued.

'Commissar Burdain will accompany the main regiment on the mission, but when she returns there will be a full investigation into last night's ambush.'

Aerand's mind spun, as if she could suddenly feel the weight of the mountain above her head pushing down onto her shoulders.

'Do you know why I chose you for command, lieutenant?' Yarin asked. 'Why, of all the young recruits, I selected you?'

Of course Aerand knew. It was the same reason she'd been chosen for anything in her life.

Colonel Regus Aerand had been a hero – it stood to reason his daughter must be, too. 'Because of my father.'

For a moment, the colonel seemed to forget the titan standing beside her, because her expression almost crept into a smile. 'In spite of him. I served with your father on Cadia and Rusk. He was a brave man and his soldiers loved him deeply, but he was arrogant and rash. I chose you because you seemed to be neither, and I hope I did not make a mistake.'

Aerand knelt on the dusty chapel floor, staring up at the statue at the front of the nave and mouthing the words of a whispered prayer.

'My Emperor, forgive me, for I have failed you. My Emperor, forgive me, for I have failed myself. I have forgotten your light and wavered before the darkness. I have forgotten your strength and stumbled on your path. I ask not for mercy, but only redemption, that I may prove myself true in the battles to come.'

Dim light streamed through the building's stained windows, bathing the image of the Emperor in a multi-hued glow. He always appeared fearless. An image that demanded obedience and respect. Aerand stared at her own hands, knotted in prayer, and wondered if He had ever felt the same doubt she felt now.

Olemark's words rang like knives in her ears, spat so bitterly over the bodies of her dead soldiers. She could not step down, but maybe she should step aside. Olemark and his veterans had been on this planet for years. They knew its people, and their enemy, better than anyone else. And what did she know? How to lock up during battle and get her troopers killed.

Aerand sighed, and across the room a massive form emerged from the shadow of a soaring pillar.

'There is desperation in your prayers,' Tarvarius remarked. 'That is good. We should all be desperate for deliverance from the evil that stalks this galaxy.'

The Space Marine was still adorned in his grey ceramite armour, but he cradled his helmet in one massive arm. His eyes, the colour of ink, watched her with careful determination, two black pools set against ghost-pale skin like dark stones rising from the snow-capped mountains outside. Aerand nodded. But it wasn't just desperation she felt, it was guilt, and fear, and doubt, as well.

The Adeptus Astartes dropped to his knees beside her in a motion that made the chapel tremble. As he knelt, his eyes fell onto the image of the Emperor, and his lips mumbled a silent phrase.

'I thought you didn't worship Him, my lord?' Aerand asked softly, pausing for a moment as she remembered who it was that knelt beside her. 'At least not the same way we do.'

Tarvarius nodded slowly, surveying the arches and altar around him. 'I do not need to believe He is a god in order to find comfort in the ritual of prayer, or to find peace and guidance in His holy places.' He was silent for some time, then continued, 'You saw something out there. Something that shook you more deeply than the others.'

Aerand pursed her lips, regretting opening her mouth, but unable to stop now. 'And two of my soldiers are dead because of it.'

A muffled sound escaped Tarvarius, what she might have believed was a chuckle if produced by anyone else. 'You say that as if it is some great evil.'

He motioned with a coal-grey gauntlet to the panes of stained glass surrounding the chapel, cluttered with bleeding bodies and wounded heroes.

'Soldiers die,' he said. 'That is why we exist. It is our greatest service to the Emperor, and the greatest honour for one of his servants. If I led your entire regiment to death tonight, I would consider it no great loss in the grand weight of his galaxy.'

Aerand shifted uneasily. She had heard these words before, or words close enough to them from the mouth of her father. *Your soldiers' lives are your most valuable weapons. You cannot be afraid to use them.*

'But they didn't have to die,' she replied. 'They died because I made a mistake. They died because of me.'

Tarvarius nodded, reaching his gauntleted hands around his neck and pulling out a chain of thick, dark iron links. He held the chain before him, then set it gently in Aerand's hands.

Her arms nearly buckled with the weight of the metal, but holding it closer, she saw that each link had been crafted in the shape of two interlocking talons, like birds of prey bound in combat. Aerand winced as one link dug into her palm, the razor talon drawing a thin streak of blood. Only then did she notice the row of pale scars lining the Adeptus Astartes' neck.

'Do you know what this is?' he asked, his voice quiet but dangerous, like a storm about to break.

Aerand shook her head.

'This is a record of my Chapter's failures, forged on our home world of Eyrie.' Tarvarius took the chain from her shaking hands, running his fingers across each time-worn link. 'One link for every battle we have lost. One for every mission we have failed to accomplish.'

The Space Marine paused upon a single, ancient ring, time-eaten and tarnished, but larger than all the rest. 'When our primarch Corvus Corax led the Raven Guard against the heretic Horus, he stumbled into a trap that killed nearly all of our brothers. We were almost purged from the galaxy, and Corax fled in disgrace. It was millennia before the Raven Guard and their successors recovered from his departure. Centuries more before we learned to embrace our failings as strength rather than weakness.'

Tarvarius replaced the chain onto his broad, scarred shoulders. 'Your past is either a shackle or an inspiration. You will make mistakes. And your soldiers will die for them.'

He pointed a massive finger towards the gleaming silver bar inlaid on her shoulder guard. 'But that is the weight of the silver on your shoulders. That is the weight of the iron on mine. The Emperor has no perfect servants, and so he must make do with broken ones like us.'

Slowly, with unexpected grace, the living war machine rose and strode towards the door. 'Say your prayers, lieutenant, but do not linger on your knees. Your Emperor needs your leadership more than your repentance.'

Olemark's glaring eyes flashed in Aerand's vision. 'What if I lead and they don't follow, my lord?'

'Then move alone,' the Space Marine replied.

From the portico along the citadel's western wall, Aerand watched a storm roll into the valley. Somewhere beyond the black clouds and peals of thunder, the Cadian 900th was closing in on its target. She should have been with them – her soldiers should have been with them – but instead, they lingered here.

Aerand reached her hand out from beneath the ancient shelter, drops of half-frozen rain splattering into her palm. She shivered slightly as she surveyed the fortress before her. Apex Inruptus had stood for a thousand years, built in the dark ages before the Imperium returned to Ourea in order to secure one of the few passable routes through the titanic summits that blanketed the planet. As she studied its pinnacled, razor walls, nestled into the mountain like just one more peak, she knew it would stand for a thousand more, regardless if anyone remained inside to defend it.

In the three soaring towers along Apex's outer wall, squads held vigil beneath needle-like spires, pairs of soldiers manning the autoguns mounted within. Twelve troopers to watch the narrow mountain pass, while the rest of her platoon took shelter inside.

As she stared into the approaching storm, a flash of lightning struck a high peak nearby, toppling snow and stone into the valley below. When the light faded, Aerand felt the hair on her neck rise, her skin prickling just as it had the night before.

She took a deep breath and willed her racing heart to slow. Had she become so fragile that even a simple storm could leave her on the brink of terror?

Aerand sighed and turned back towards the barracks, but as she passed beneath the portico, two dark forms hurried down the corridor towards her.

'Lieutenant,' Corwyn said, 'Lord Tarvarius is calling with word from the regiment.' Beside him, Maresh held out the receiver attached to the vox-caster on his back.

Aerand nodded. If Tarvarius was reporting back, that meant the battle was already won. She should have been relieved, but instead, a wave of trepidation washed over her.

'*They are gone,*' Tarvarius said the moment she lifted the receiver.

'Praise the Throne,' Aerand replied, feeling anything but joyful.

'*You mishear,*' said Tarvarius, the first hint of something other than confidence in his tone. '*Your intelligence was deceived. We have scoured the sector and there are no cultists here. What is your status?*'

As he spoke, the prickling along Aerand's neck grew, memories of the night before washing over her like a wave. Her mind spun with a sudden imbalance, and the taste of bile rose in her throat. Suddenly, the air smelled of smoke, and her arms grew heavy as she raised the transmitter to her lips.

'Fine,' she whispered.

But they were not fine – she was suddenly confident of that. The cultist army had not simply vanished; if they'd abandoned Noravis Opum, it was for some other target. A target like the fortress she currently held.

Tarvarius broke back through the static. '*Are you certain?*'

Aerand heard her breath begin to race, shallow and rapid like the night before. Her armour settled heavy on her shoulders as Corwyn stared at her, confused, untouched by the terror that burned through her bones.

But it wasn't just terror she felt anymore. Something even stronger grew beside her fear. She was angry and determined. Whatever was coming, she would meet it this time.

'No,' Aerand replied. 'But it will be.'

'*You feel it,*' Tarvarius said. Not a question, but a statement. '*The same presence as during the ambush.*'

She paused. If she said yes and was wrong, she'd be a fool once again. If she said yes and was right, that could mean something even worse.

'I do,' she replied, staring at the soaring citadel above her head. Apex Inruptus had not fallen in a thousand years, and she would not let it tonight.

There was silence, then a muttered curse over the vox as Colonel Yarin shouted orders in the background.

'*We are coming,*' Tarvarius replied. '*Hold the fortress.*'

The door slammed open before Aerand, Corwyn and Maresh stumbling in at her heels. Soldiers lingered throughout the barracks, most lying on bed rolls cleaning dusty lasguns or checking power packs before it was their turn to hold watch.

It was obvious, now that she could see it. Noravis Opum had never been the cultists' true goal. The settlement was exposed, practically indefensible, vulnerable from both the ground and the air. Even if the cultists had captured the spaceport, they never could have held it. But if their feint allowed them to take Apex Inruptus, they could cut off reinforcements and resupply from Noravis to a dozen other settlements, then take any they wished after starving them to the bone.

'All bodies on the wall in five minutes,' she called. 'Full battle gear and loadouts, ready to fight.'

As Aerand stormed into the room, they should have risen to attention. Instead, the few closest to the door stood slowly and leaned up against the wall while the rest continued their business, unbothered. In the back of the room, circled around steaming rations, Olemark and his veterans stared at her, unimpressed.

'The sky is falling out there,' Olemark replied, turning back to polish his lasgun's barrel. 'If you wanted to get the rest of us killed, you could find a faster way to do it than making us catch rot.'

Aerand bristled at the contempt in his voice. She could make a show of force. She could shout or fire her laspistol into the ceiling. Throne, she could drag those still sitting onto their feet and demand at gunpoint they show her the respect her rank merited. But what good would that do? She had lost their trust, though she desperately needed it now, and no amount of anger could bring that back.

'I made a mistake,' Aerand said, her voice cool and level. Her father may have been brash, but he understood his soldiers, and for those who were accustomed to screams and berating, a quiet tone was often harder to ignore.

Never let a failure hide, because they have a way of growing in the shadows, and if you let a mistake fester long enough, you may find it has rooted too deep to correct.

'I made a mistake last night and two of us are dead because of it.'

Throughout the room, all eyes turned towards her, the exhausted, dirty faces of her soldiers awash with frustration and lingering hope.

'I don't have an excuse for that, but I do have a reason.' Aerand motioned to the open door behind her, where rain and lightning poured down in a deluge, out on the saw-toothed peaks and plummeting valleys rising and falling like the teeth of some unholy maw.

'I felt something last night – something I've never felt before, not on a dozen missions on half as many worlds. I'm not certain what it was, or why I alone felt it, but I feel it again tonight.'

Olemark scoffed. 'What you felt was fear.'

Aerand's fingers drifted slowly towards her laspistol. He was bordering on insubordination. She could kill him for that, and Throne, she wanted to.

But she needed Olemark. She needed his veterans. She needed every soldier in this room with their eyes locked on her every movement.

Violence can never ensure discipline. Executions do not inspire loyalty.

'A storm is coming,' she said resolutely. 'Who will stand with me against it?'

One by one her soldiers' gazes drifted away, and not a foot budged from their positions.

'Very well,' she muttered and stepped out into the night.

Aerand climbed the steep steps alone, rain drumming across her helmet and armour, seeping through to her skin and chilling her bones.

Her legs burned as the stairs fell away behind her, the yawning abyss at the base of Apex's walls a constant reminder to watch where she stepped. Flashes of lightning bathed the craggy pass in light. The doubt she felt in the barracks evaporated like smoke as she inspected the dozen tired soldiers on her wall. Twelve troopers to hold the most important fortress on the planet. If the rest would not stand with her, then these would have to do.

As she stared out into the shadow-strewn valleys, the slow stomping of bootfalls reached her ears. She turned to see a group of green-clad figures, the dull sheen of their helmets glimmering in the rain as they ascended the dark stone stairs behind her.

Corwyn reached the tower first, an embarrassed smile stretching across his sun-darkened face. 'We couldn't let you freeze to death out here alone,' he mumbled, then pointed to the group of soldiers behind him. 'First squad will man the northern wall.'

As they passed, twelve fresh bodies took their place, Artus grasping her arm with a slight bow. 'If you say you sense something, then we sense it, too.'

In piecemeal fashion, the rest of her soldiers trickled out of the barracks and took up positions along the walls, until only Olemark's veterans remained inside. Finally, their dented, cracked armour ambled up the staircase with more grace and speed than any of the others.

Olemark paused before her, his eyes still sharp. There was no apology, no admission of guilt, merely the slightest of nods and a stiff salute. 'Where do you want us?' he asked, unflinching in the rain.

'West wall,' Aerand replied, too certain of the coming evil to make issue of his prior disrespect. Beneath her armour, her skin burned like fire, each breath laden with the scent of charred air. 'Hold the gate and the bridge however you must.'

The sergeant nodded, then marched off along the rampart, rain beading silver on his helm like the stars above.

'Sergeant,' she called, staring out at the storm. 'I think you should hurry.'

As she spoke, a bolt of lightning lit the canyon, arcing between dark clouds before striking the citadel's spire. As the valley burned blue, dark forms burst from the mist, and a hail of lasfire tore through the night towards the fortress.

'Incoming!' Aerand shouted, dropping below the crenulations. The blistering volley crashed against Apex's walls as her troopers dropped with her, some not rising again.

'Return fire!' Aerand rose to a knee and aimed her lasgun over the wall, pulling hard on the trigger.

Far below, a wave of bodies rushed towards the fortress, shrouded in the smoke of roaring weapons, but even at this distance she could see their enemy was well-armed and determined.

Beside scores of cultists, rows of silver-armoured Ourean guards marched with traitors in Imperial armour. At their head rolled three Eradicator battle tanks, patched and precarious, but functioning well enough to heave shells straight at the western gate.

'Vox-caster, on me!' Aerand bellowed over the din of the firefight, sprinting

along the slick rampart and scanning the silhouettes of her soldiers for
Maresh.

'Corwyn,' she roared, sliding into place beside the sergeant and pulling
him back from his post by the shoulder. In the tower above them, a turret lay
empty, a heavy stubber jammed between the rampart and a charred body,
firing aimlessly into the valley below. 'Get that weapon back in service.'

'On it, sir,' he called, pulling two troopers in his wake. 'Looks like we'll
be in the fight, after all.'

'Indeed,' she replied grimly, as a salvo from the Eradicators burst against the
northern wall. As she sprinted along the rampart, she spotted the chevrons
of Delaver's armour lying still on the stone in a puddle of rain. Beside him,
a section of the wall had crumbled, casualties of the Eradicators' ordnance.

Next to the rift, troopers poured fire at the approaching force, one bearing
a corporal's insignia on her shoulder. Their las-rounds streaked red and
brilliant through the rain.

'Maltia,' Aerand shouted, crouching beside the corporal. 'Where the hell
is the rest of second squad?'

'You're looking at it.' Maltia pointed her weapon over the precarious ledge.
A cluster of bodies lay broken on the rocks in the valley below, Maresh's
vox shattered beneath his still form.

'Throne,' Aerand swore.

The oncoming swarm was now close enough to see clearly, but far too large
to count. A group of scarcely clad men and women surged forward ahead of
the main assault, crude weapons in their hands and madness in their eyes.

From the turret above, Corwyn's stubber dropped dozens in seconds,
but the rest did not slow. It was only then that Aerand noticed the symbol
carved across one man's chest. The same flame and eye she'd seen at the
homestead.

An image of the dead woman's open, black eyes flashed into her mind,
that same weight returning to her limbs. Maltia stared in confusion while
her soldiers' weapons roared out into the night.

'Any orders, sir?'

Aerand's mind raced with a sudden terror. Not again. Not now. Not when
they needed her more than any moment in her life.

She froze and stared down at the weapon in her hands. A thin streak of
blood rolled down the handle of her lasgun, from the spot on her palm
where Tarvarius' chain had bled her.

*The Emperor has no perfect servants. So he must make do with broken
ones like us.*

Aerand breathed deeply and snapped her eyes back to Maltia. 'Aye,' she
replied. 'Hold this damned wall, and make those heretics sorry they came
here tonight.'

'Will do, sir,' Maltia replied with a grin.

Aerand darted towards the north gate as two missiles blazed from the
tanks along the path, crashing into the gatehouse, and shaking its massive
stone doors. Atop the building, Olemark ran between his soldiers – lasfire
was pouring from their weapons towards the horde gathered below.

All along the wall, her soldiers were fighting bravely but dying fast. Attack groups closed on all three gates, and her platoon was barely slowing them down.

The army outside was far too large. Far too many for a simple cultist uprising. Bolstered by Astra Militarum deserters and the forces of at least one traitor feudal lord, it was only a matter of time before the approaching darkness overwhelmed them. Their only hope was to hold until the regiment returned.

Aerand clambered down a set of shattered stairs, careening over rubble and dancing beside the mind-numbing precipice. Apex hung on the wall of the mountain, and three bridges were all that connected the fortress to the world outside. Perhaps her soldiers could not stop the approaching army, but without a way to cross, they'd have no way to take the fortress.

The roar of krak missiles tore past Aerand's face as two bright streaks of metal darted down from Corwyn's tower towards the Eradicators below. The first tank crumbled into a cloud of smoke and glowing metal, while the second missile detonated along the valley wall, dropping a heap of stone onto a platoon of Ourean guards.

Up ahead, Olemark's men were following suit, a pair of troopers loading a krak missile into its launcher and positioning themselves at the edge of the gatehouse. Aerand leapt the rest of the way down the steps, sprinting across a small stretch of open ramparts, lasfire and bolt rounds soaring past her head. She dropped to her knees beside Olemark just as he raised the missile launcher.

'Wait!' she shouted, lungs heaving with each beat of her heart.

Olemark turned in surprise.

'The bridges,' she panted, pointing over the ledge.

Only a few hundred yards from the edge of the wall, the vanguard of cultists streaked towards the gate, the two remaining Eradicators loosing another salvo. Beneath them, the gatehouse shuddered, and with a horrible crash, one of its stone doors toppled open.

'Blow the bridges,' Aerand ordered, lifting her lasgun slowly, uncertain if she'd be firing over the wall, or at a target much closer.

Olemark stared, then nodded in understanding. 'It'd be my pleasure, sir,' he replied, and a streak of flame darted over the wall.

As the missile found its mark, a promethean crack pierced the night, and the northern bridge toppled into the chasm. Moments later, two matching explosions echoed across the courtyard as Corwyn and Maltia directed their soldiers to follow suit. Aerand smiled and breathed a sigh. Only then did she notice the searing pain in her leg and the blood oozing from the hole through her thigh.

Nearly an hour later, and the fortress still stood. Blowing the bridges had stalled the assault, and the fever pitch of the initial battle had faded into a steady siege. Corwyn, Olemark, and Aerand huddled in the courtyard, Apex's scorched, splintered citadel overshadowing the trio as they stooped over Aerand's map.

'Noravis Opum is nearly two hours away,' Olemark said. 'Even if they left the moment you voxed Lord Tarvarius, we'd still have the better part of an hour before they return.'

Corwyn nodded. 'Then we hold the wall for another hour.'

Aerand shook her head and surveyed the heap of stone beside them, leaning up against a crumbling staircase to hold the weight off her injured leg.

Toppling the bridges had stalled the cultists and forced the Eradicators to stay out of krak missile range. But even at a distance, they'd nearly razed Apex's walls and had taken another dozen of her soldiers. Now, without towers or autoguns and only a handful of troopers, her platoon was doing all it could to keep the army from finding a way across the chasm.

'We fall back,' Aerand muttered, staring at the hulking stone spire behind her.

'And give them the outer wall and the courtyard?' Corwyn asked.

'They have it already.' Aerand grimaced as she twisted to motion to the toppled wall, and a bolt of pain shot up from her thigh. 'It will take them time to devise a way across the chasm, and with any luck, the regiment will be here before they do.'

Olemark nodded, condescension long absent from his voice. 'It's a good plan. It's the only good plan.'

'Then make it happen.'

Aerand limped across the courtyard as Olemark and Corwyn retrieved their soldiers from their posts. As she forced her way towards the shadow of Apex's citadel, lazy bursts of enemy lasgun fire arced over her head, splattering harmlessly against the bastion walls. She scarcely noticed the sound after nearly an hour of it, simply one more voice in the chorus of battle, along with the rain and the constant, rolling thunder.

She pulled to a stop as a streak of lightning lit the valley, silhouetting a figure atop the peak above Apex's walls. It was impossible that any human could have scaled the sheer ridgeline from outside the fortress, and yet there someone stood. Her lasgun was already on her shoulder when the shadow dropped from the mind-numbing peak and landed before her with little more than the sound of stirring air.

'I am pleased to find you are not dead yet.'

Tarvarius surveyed the decimated outer wall and the small group of soldiers withdrawing towards him. 'Although I had hoped to find more of your platoon still standing.'

Despite the grim setting and the fire in her leg, Aerand found herself on the brink of smiling. 'As had I,' she replied, limping towards the Adeptus Astartes. One Space Marine was not a regiment, but perhaps he was even better.

'The rest of the 900th?' she asked, hope lacing her voice.

Tarvarius motioned towards the north. Outside the wall, the sound of lasfire picked up, followed by a series of heavy explosions. 'Yarin pushed them hard.'

Aerand limped towards a gap in the wall, where Olemark stood staring.

'It seems we may have to share some of the action, sir,' he remarked, a tired smile creeping across his face.

Through the rain and over the scorched battlefield, the Cadian 900th approached, pouring withering fire into the cultists from behind. Already, their assailants were falling back, unable to stand up to the dauntless assault, and charging instead towards the fortress and the waiting, gaping chasm.

Aerand lifted her lasgun, prepared to open fire, when a sudden weight dropped her to her knees. The taste of blood and burnt flesh assailed her again, stronger than before. She retched onto the dark, slick stone, feeling her mind spin and her skin spark with fire. Slowly, she raised her head, expecting the stares of her confused soldiers, but they were all in a similar state. Even Tarvarius leaned against the wall awkwardly, scanning the night.

A creeping horror built within Aerand. Whatever had crippled her on the ridgeline was here in their midst. Whatever evil she had felt when the cultists approached had waited until now to show itself fully. As she stared out at the oncoming army, she suddenly understood her mistake.

They were not retreating, they were charging towards the gate, where a cloud of massive boulders were rising from the chasm, wreathed in flickering blue firelight, forming themselves into a bridge.

'Witch,' Aerand muttered, her voice hoarse and weak. A sudden desperation filled her as she stared through the gate. She had held the fortress against an army with only a few dozen soldiers – if the horde outside was allowed to enter, not even the entire 900th regiment could dislodge them. She forced her leaden limbs to move, stumbling towards Tarvarius and laying a hand on his colossal armour.

'What?' The Space Marine blinked, then shook his head slightly as if trying to rid himself of an invisible pest. A moment later, his confident posture returned and he fixed his gaze on Aerand. 'They have a witch.'

No sooner had he spoken the words than that same blue glow lit the peak of the citadel's tower. Aerand looked on in horror as a form emerged onto the high terrace, fire dancing around its twisted body, streaking out over the battlefield towards the approaching Cadian regiment.

Beside her, Olemark struggled to his feet, his shoulders bent by an invisible burden. The cultists had nearly reached the bridge, the fire of their weapons becoming dangerously accurate.

'By the Throne,' Olemark mumbled, turning to help one of his troopers rise. 'He'll lay the entire regiment to waste.'

'No, he won't,' Aerand replied, limping towards the base of the citadel. 'We're going to kill him first.'

Aerand stumbled onto the high terrace, legs burning and mind swimming, while Olemark, Corwyn, and her few remaining troopers lumbered up the final few stairs. In the shadows of the pillars and stonework beside them, Tarvarius moved like a patient ghost.

The sorcerer stood at the centre of the platform, bathed in the horrible blue light of witch fire, bright streaks pouring from his body like vines, arcing down towards the raging battle below. Behind the darting, swirling inferno, the sorcerer himself was harder to discern, a thin, emaciated form buried beneath thick, dark smoke. If not for the fire pouring from him, Aerand might have thought the man on the brink of death, weak and haggard, as if the forces he channelled had taken not only his soul but his life.

Eight bodies knelt prostrate on the ground around the witch, hands clawing at writhing, moaning skulls. A thin tendril of flame connected each to the sorcerer, their naked bodies covered in tattoos and deep scars, each bearing at least one variation of that sinister flame and eye.

There was something terrible in that sigil, made even more awful in the witch's unnatural glow. For a moment, Aerand felt she was a child again, staring up into the sky on a planet she hardly knew, a twisting wheel of fire marring the blue canopy above her.

'You come at last.'

The sorcerer's words spilled out from the flames like the falling of night as the sun disappeared, dozens of voices layered to form one. As he turned, a glimpse of the sorcerer's empty, black eyes held Aerand firmly in place, and she was struck by the sense he was speaking directly to her.

The same black eyes she'd seen at the homestead. But instead of fear, they now filled her only with hatred.

'Kill him,' Aerand ordered, lifting her weapon and pulling the trigger.

A wall of lasfire streaked towards the sorcerer, lighting the balcony in a blinding display. For a moment, the flame around the witch seemed to dim, before it swelled again and the volley split harmlessly around him.

As the witch raised his hand, Tarvarius rushed forward, his chainsword roaring to life. Whatever share of the weight that crowded Aerand's mind and limbs the Space Marine might have felt before was gone, for he moved like a raptor striking on the wind. As his weapon dropped towards the sorcerer's head, a streak of fire split from the witch's inferno and rose up to meet it, halting the chainsword while Tarvarius continued forward, leaping over the stalled weapon and skidding to a stop as his legs met the terrace's ancient railing. The row of dark stone posts cracked but held, debris careening over the ledge into the smoke of the firefight below as Tarvarius turned and reengaged.

The witch's fire rose up to meet him once again, streaks of flame and lasfire darting from the pair as they danced across the terrace with blinding speed.

Aerand dove to the side as they careened towards her, landing beside one of the cowering cultists, as a streak of blue light shot out from the sorcerer in her direction. The tether of flame between the woman and the witch seemed to swell as Aerand's soldiers poured fire towards him, as if the witch's magic was feeding off the bodies around him.

Aerand rose to a knee and stared at the woman. Beneath clawing fingers and a face contorted in pain, she could see the woman's lips moving slowly, mumbling something incomprehensible.

As a fresh salvo of lasfire arced towards the sorcerer, the woman's face calmed slightly and her eyes flashed open. She stared at Aerand with a terrible sincerity, then reached out and grasped her by the wrist.

'Kill me,' the woman whispered, voice laden with desperation. 'Please. They didn't tell me it would be like this.'

As the lasfire crashed into the sorcerer again, and the tendril connecting him to the woman swelled, her eyes snapped shut and she let out a scream. Aerand lifted her weapon and granted her wish.

The woman fell to the ground, and the thread connecting her to the sorcerer vanished. The witch's black eyes turned towards Aerand in anger.

'The bodies!' Aerand shouted as a wall of flame rushed towards her, and she dived behind an ancient stone pillar. 'Kill the bodies! He's drawing power from them!'

The sorcerer's attack abated for a moment, and Aerand spun to fire at the creature's back. As she did, Olemark and Corwyn dropped two of the cultists, and Tarvarius lunged forward, gripping a pair of cowering, flame-wreathed bodies and tossing them over the precipice like refuse.

As the cultists shattered on the bulwark below, a sound like rushing water burst from the sorcerer – myriad voices crying out with rage. The sphere of fire around him grew bright as a star, until Aerand dropped to her knees from the sheer brilliance of him. She shivered to think of the terrible darkness that supplied that power, if it could afford to funnel so much strength into a single one of its servants. The flames swelled and tightened, then burst outward like a breaking wave, throwing her through the air.

Something struck Aerand's shoulder with a sickening crunch, then her chest collided with unmoving stone. When her vision cleared, she stared over the edge of the high terrace, saved from falling only by the railing pillars that had broken her shoulder and ribs.

Beside her, Olemark grasped the shattered remnants of a pillar, body dangling over the towering precipice. Below him, several green-armoured bodies clattered against black stone, the darting glow of lasfire bursting around them from the battle below. Across the platform Tarvarius rose to his feet, tossing aside the debris of a shattered statue after bearing the worst of the sorcerer's assault.

As Aerand dragged herself towards Olemark, shoulder and sides screaming in protest, the dark shadow of the sorcerer moved towards them. The light around him had faded into a dull flicker, his three remaining disciples reduced to nothing more than scorched husks.

'No,' Aerand whispered, as the witch's eyes locked on Olemark. She reached out towards the sergeant, praying she had the strength to pull him up over the ledge. But instead of taking her grip, Olemark reached one hand over his shoulder, slipping dangerously as he pulled a weapon off his back.

'Take the shot, sir,' he said, dropping a missile launcher on the ledge beside her, then glancing up at the tower above them. The citadel's pinnacle arced overhead like an executioner's blade, the damaged, worn pillars lining the balcony barely supporting its weight. 'He can't hold the whole mountain up,' Olemark muttered, then his hand slipped, and he dropped over the ledge.

As Aerand snatched the launcher from the ground, the sorcerer extended a shadowy hand towards her, a thin blue flame dancing across his fingers. She felt the launcher kick as a missile tore from its barrel, streaking towards the pillar beside them and shattering the stone into a cloud of dust.

For a moment, the tower above them hung steady, as if after standing for so many centuries, it did not remember it was able to fall. Then a single block dropped loose from the pinnacle, followed by another, then a horrible crash, as the tower slid from its bearings and toppled towards them.

The sorcerer cast both his hands over his head, the fire around him streaking towards the collapsing wall. At first, the stone held, shaking in place as a sinister blue glow swelled around it, but the witch himself was laid horribly bare.

Aerand reached down to her waist, snatching her laspistol from its holster and aiming towards the heretic's dark, withered form. She pulled the trigger, and a bolt of light streaked towards him, this time unhindered as it pierced his skull. Instantly, the flame above him extinguished, and the stone over her head came crashing down.

Aerand felt her leg shatter first, then her ankle gave way as the air around her filled with dust and the sound of stones crashing like water.

'I offer my life to the Emperor,' she whispered. 'I pray He accepts it.'

A weight descended on her chest, stifling her prayer. But moments later, when she found herself still breathing and the air had grown quiet, she heard her words echoed back on stern, iron lips.

'I offer my strength to the Emperor. I pray He redresses it.'

Slowly, Aerand opened her eyes, staring into the dark-grey form of Tarvarius' helmet. The Space Marine raised himself slowly, casting aside the avalanche of stone that had toppled onto them.

'There will be enough time for prayer later,' Tarvarius muttered, a flash of lightning gleaming off his dented, rent armour. 'Right now we have a battle to win.'

Behind him, over the edge of the balcony, green Cadian bodies swarmed over the walls and back into the heart of Apex Inruptus.

'Tell me once more what you experienced that night.' Commissar Burdain's voice rang out in clear, metered staccato, her arms and shoulders rigid beneath a flawless uniform.

'Of course, sir,' Aerand replied. In contrast to the commissar's perfection, she was externally a mess. Her right arm was bound in a heavy sling, her left leg braced by crude metal bars burrowing into the bone beneath her skin. She leaned heavily on the desk beside her, ribs screaming with every breath, as Colonel Yarin watched in silence from the back of her chamber. A week ago, the commissar's severe demeanour would have shaken Aerand, but now, after staring into the sorcerer's black, warp-swallowed eyes, Burdain's grey ones held little sway.

'It's difficult to describe the sensation I felt, other than to say it was deeply, horribly... wrong. The other soldiers of my platoon all describe similar feelings on the night of the Apex assault.'

'But not on the night of the ambush,' Burdain replied. 'That night you were the only one who felt anything.'

And saw it. Aerand hadn't lied to the commissar, but she hadn't told anyone about the vision of the dead woman's eyes. 'That's correct, sir.'

Burdain's mouth drew into a stern line. 'And on the night of the assault, you felt it first.'

'Yes, sir.' Aerand knew where this was headed – knew what question would come next – because she'd asked herself the same thing for the past three days while her body slowly stitched itself back together.

'Why do you think you alone felt these things?'

She'd considered every possibility. Perhaps, as an officer, the sorcerer's presence had been directed more strongly at her. Perhaps her proximity to the ritual had simply caused the sensation to be more intense. Maybe she'd just been more exhausted, or more anxious. Maybe her fear of failing had given the darkness a foothold to exploit.

'I don't know, sir,' Aerand replied, and that was honest. Burdain began to pace slowly, certainty growing in Aerand with each of her steps. She'd be removed from her position if she was fortunate. Executed if she was not.

Somehow, though, that thought didn't bother her. She had done her duty – let the consequences be what they may.

After some time, the commissar paused and looked as if she was about to speak, but before she could, a quiet knock rang in the doorway, and a green-armoured figure limped slowly inside.

Corwyn had not escaped the citadel unscathed, and he walked clumsily on a gleaming prosthetic leg.

'My apologies, sirs,' he said quietly, unable to conceal a small grin as he stepped past Aerand bearing a piece of parchment. 'I've been sent to deliver an urgent dispatch.'

As Corwyn handed the scroll to Commissar Burdain, Aerand caught a glimpse of its seal and felt her heart begin to race. Pressed into dark-grey wax was the wing-wreathed skull of the Storm Wings Space Marines.

Corwyn took his leave of the room, and the commissar's face grew sterner still as she read through the message. When she finished, she sighed, then re-rolled the parchment and placed the scroll in Aerand's hand. Aerand gripped it tightly – there was something firm and heavy inside.

'The Adeptus Astartes send their regards,' Burdain said. 'As well as an endorsement of the lieutenant's valour. In light of these events, and the... unique... circumstances surrounding the Apex Inruptus assault, I think it is reasonable to sentence Lieutenant Aerand to only minor discipline for her lapse during her platoon's ambush, administered at Colonel Yarin's discretion.'

As the commissar walked brusquely from the room, Yarin rose and placed a hand on Aerand's shoulder, leaning in towards her ear. 'You must have done something right to get her so upset,' she whispered, her normally harsh face softening slightly. She looked as if she might say more, then paused and shook her head. 'I best not keep you too long, lieutenant. You have a platoon to return to.'

As Aerand limped slowly down the dark stone hall, she opened the scroll and read the final few lines. *A small token for the commander of the Cadian Storm Guard, from another of the Emperor's broken servants. May it be the first link in a chain of your own.*

A small smile spread across Aerand's face as she gripped the iron-claw link wrapped inside the parchment.

THE TASTE OF FIRE

Steven B Fischer

There was a beauty in the stillness of the Ourean night. A bitter clarity in the chill predawn air that seemed to echo through the very darkness itself. An illusion of peace in the dim saffron glow of the mountainous world's sister moons filtering down through the branches of frost-laden conifers and reflecting off the slopes below.

But it *was* only an illusion.

Lieutenant Glavia Aerand knew this world was no different from any other. No purer than the filthy, crawling hives of Machari and Scintilla. No less obscene than the Chaos-ridden remnants of her home world. She had learned long ago that no world held a monopoly on evil, because her species carried evil with it. In one movement, she raised her hand and shattered the facade.

One last breath of blessed silence before the earth shuddered with the paired concussions of starfire mortars, which burst in the sky seconds later, bathing the high mountain valley in the watery-green incandescence of illumination rounds. Beneath that fiery dusk, Secundus Company descended on the cultist den like birds of prey.

At the back of Aerand's mind, a familiar disquiet grew, paired with the caustic scent of charred copper in her nose. Six months ago, this sensation had crippled her the first time she'd felt it. Six months ago, she hadn't known what it meant. Now, she understood the warning all too well. After half a year of tracking Chaos cultists through the bitter wilds of this Throne-cursed planet, her hunt was almost over.

As Aerand's troopers rushed towards the shadow of two waiting cave mouths, the earth around them erupted into plumes of acrid smoke. Gouts of half-frozen soil and jagged stone fragments sprayed her soldiers as the drumbeat of mortars rang out from atop the ridgeline behind them.

'Gerstahl's breath!' Olevier Corwyn cursed, Aerand's company sergeant puffing with exertion as the pair sprinted to match pace with their charging platoons. 'You're sure you ordered Lieutenant Vyse to aim her heavy squads at the enemy, not us?'

Despite the moment, Aerand's face split into a smile. 'Danger close is called danger close for a reason. We hammer every egress from this place, so the heretics don't slip our grasp again.'

Ahead, First Platoon's lead squad rushed through the detritus, helm lumens flickering to life as they were swallowed by the cave's gaping maw. Aerand swept in behind them. Never first in. Never last. The proper place for a commander was at the heart of her soldiers.

As she drove into the darkness, Aerand braced herself for the inevitable onslaught. She was no fool – Cadians were going to die today. A cost both she and her soldiers were willing to pay. But with every step she took down the narrow stone corridor, an even greater fear blossomed within her.

Secundus Company had been hunting this particular cultist cell for the better part of two seasons. Countless times she had stood in positions like this one, and countless times her quarry had slipped through her grasp. That fear crystallised as Aerand stepped into a small antechamber, its dripping stone walls empty and lifeless. A small collection of skulls, stained with ribbons of old, dark blood and the dirty yellow wax of tallow candles, lay scattered on the floor. To her right, First Platoon continued down the main corridor, and on her left, Second Platoon's lumens already approached.

'*West network clear,*' Lieutenant Graves barked through her earpiece, his words garbled by the yards of bedrock between them.

'*East network clear,*' Sergeant Maltia echoed, the disappointment in her voice heavy enough to bite.

Beside her, Corwyn muttered another curse, while the drumming of mortars continued to shake the mountain. 'Don't know where they could have gone,' he grumbled. 'Vyse is turning the whole ridgeline into gravel.'

Aerand nodded, distracted, as the ringing in her ears began to swell. 'Not gone,' she whispered.

'What do you mean?' Corwyn replied. 'This tunnel's scarcely wide enough to hide the gut I'm growing, let alone a few hundred Chaos cultists.'

'Not all of them are gone, at least.'

As she motioned for the sergeant to follow, Aerand stepped down a narrow corridor to her right, the ceiling low enough to scrape the top of her helm. Here, the smooth, polished walls of the main chambers disappeared, replaced by deep, unweathered grooves.

'Fresh addition,' Corwyn muttered. 'And a hasty one, at that.'

Shortly, the tunnel gave way to a set of stairs, lumens flickering in the murky depths below. Cadian voices echoed up the tunnel, and Corwyn's expression fell into a scowl as he walked ahead. 'First Platoon,' he called back, clearing a low archway. 'Nbade's squad is already here.'

Aerand followed into the small, rough-cut chamber, an oppressiveness to its darkness that seemed to resist the normally piercing light of her troopers' lumens. Half a dozen men and women lay chained to the raw stone wall, and the lieutenant stifled the nausea rising within her as that ringing in her ears began to grow.

'Alive, Argos?' she asked, suspecting she already knew the answer.

Her chief medicae knelt over an emaciated young woman, her long, thin hair drifting down to cover pale, dirt-laden skin. A crude iron manacle hung around one of her horribly thin wrists, the skin beneath lacerated from her struggles against it. The remainder of her body was covered in a macabre mosaic of branded symbols, each of which stoked the fire beneath Aerand's skin.

The medicae shook his head. 'Not sure how long they've been here, sir, but long enough.'

'Check the rest,' Corwyn replied, an uncharacteristic edge to his voice.

One by one, Argos pronounced the prisoners dead, until he knelt over a final body. An adolescent man, the youngest of the group, and perhaps the most hale. The medicae paused, fingers resting on the youth's neck, trying to convince himself he felt a pulse beneath.

A sudden wave of unease washed over Aerand as a sound like the sea swallowed her whole. Staggered, she took a step back, pressing her hand against the wall and closing her eyes. An image flashed through her mind, of the man on the floor erupting into a gout of searing blue flame that reached up and devoured the medicae beside him. Then, as soon as it arrived, the vision passed.

Aerand pushed herself upright and lurched towards Argos, grasping the medicae by the shoulders and dragging him to the ground. A moment later the youth's eyes flashed open beside them and he drew a deep, ragged breath. Suddenly, a horrible blue light enveloped his hands, then burst forward to splash harmlessly against the wall.

Beside her, Corwyn took a step forward and drove the butt of his lasgun into the young man's head. He crumpled into a heap.

'Witch,' the sergeant whispered, half in disbelief.

Aerand nodded slowly and rolled off Argos, pushing herself painfully to her feet. 'Whatever he is, you do not let that man die until Colonel Yarin herself has seen him.'

Secundus Company slogged through the miserable blend of snow, mud and rain that seemed to be Ourea's only truly unique feature. After almost a year on the planet, Aerand scarcely noticed the bitter chill in her toes or the squelching moistness that accompanied each step of her boots. She had learned the unpleasant realities of this world long ago, and come to accept that they would not change for her.

As her column filed slowly through a narrow saddle into the skeletal remains of their laconic field camp, she could not help but believe her troopers shared that same belief. Six months ago, after shattering a cultist army at the vicious battle of Apex Inruptus, the soldiers of the Cadian 900th had not thought themselves naive to hope this war might soon be over. Instead, it had simply evolved. Now, rather than conducting lightning raids against massed enemy encampments from the relative comfort of a regimental fortress, the four newly formed light companies of the 900th were scattered to the wind, operating alone in the heart of Ourea's austere wilds, pursuing ever-elusive cells of tenacious heretics.

As Aerand marched beside her formation, she forced a grim smile onto her face. She was not blind. She knew her troopers were tired and discouraged. She knew her fledgling company was fragile and cracking. How quickly would it shatter entirely if forced to acknowledge that its commander shared her troopers' same exhaustions and fears?

And then some. Aerand shivered slightly at the memory of her vision in the cave. Not her first premonition, but what had started as rare hunches and intuitions were becoming too frequent, and vivid, for her to ignore. That foresight might have saved Argos' life, but she could not shake the bitter dismay such portents left on her soul. She whispered a silent prayer and forced the thought from her mind.

Behind Aerand, a vox-caster crackled to life, rousing her from her unproductive mulling. A young corporal ran through the snow, the heavy vox-pack on his back giving him an awkward, lilting gait. He arrived at her side breathless but snapped sharply to attention.

'Kobald on the line for you, sir,' the corporal sputtered. Behind the trooper, Sergeant Corwyn's foot crushed a patch of frozen lichen, and he eyed Aerand with a knowing expression.

'Thank you, Waldamne,' she replied, flashing the corporal the brightest grin she could manage. No reason the boy should have to bear his commander's cynicism in addition to the weight of the vox.

As Aerand grabbed the mouthpiece from the corporal's hand, however, she spotted a quartet of spindly, mechanical silhouettes crossing over the sheer, jagged ridgeline flanking them. She handed the vox-caster back to Waldamne. 'On second thoughts, tell Kobald I'm coming to him.'

'Good news only,' Aerand called, striding down the muddy, pockmarked trail that passed as the closest thing to their small camp's road.

The lieutenant, a tall, fiery-haired man with dark, freckled skin, raised his violet eyes from his vehicle and gave her a grunt. Technically her peer in rank, Kobald snapped Aerand a quick salute regardless. Of all her platoon commanders, Kobald seemed the most comfortable being led by a fellow lieutenant, and made the least ordeal of their interactions as a result.

'Depends on your expectations, I suppose, sir.'

Behind Kobald, the remainder of his squadron continued maintenance on their Sentinels. They had stripped nearly all of the protective armour from the tall, bipedal machines after Ourea's brutal gravity and precipitous inclines had proven overwhelming for even their famously resilient gyro-stabilisers. But the reduction in shielding made them all the more vulnerable to the planet's harsh elements, and both the vehicles and their pilots were showing signs of wear.

'All due respect, sir,' one of Kobald's troopers called as he chopped chunks of ice and mud from his Sentinel's footpads with a rusty, dented entrenching tool. 'S'not all that good no matter what your expectations were.'

'And if I expect my troopers to keep their opinions to themselves, and perhaps work harder to keep their vehicles clean?'

'Then you're going to be doubly disappointed, sir.'

Aerand chuckled. Famously irreverent, Kobald's Sentinel pilots took as good as they got. She motioned to the bundled object strapped to the back of the Sentinel's cab.

'Show me what you've got, and let me be the judge of that. If there's a crate of caff beneath those blankets, I may just give the lieutenant's squadron to you.'

'No such luck,' Kobald said as the trooper removed the frayed olive-grey fabric from the back of the Sentinel and let its contents fall into the snow. The weight of the sound sent a shiver up Aerand's spine, and by the time Kobald's troopers began unwrapping the corpses, she was fully prepared for what she would see.

'Tranch's Nameless,' Corwyn muttered as he surveyed the bodies. A young woman and a greying man, whose face reflected the woman's as only a father's could. 'Just like one we found in the caves.'

'There were others?'

Aerand nodded grimly. 'Half a dozen, at least. Chained in a cell beneath the cultist outpost.'

Another grunt and a nod. Kobald motioned to the bruises and abraded skin ringing the corpses' wrists. 'Not an escape then, but a flight. Found these two frozen about nine miles from the mouth of the western tunnel. There were more footprints on the trail, but the weather had already done its work on any tracks beyond that.'

Aerand nodded. Somehow, the cultists had anticipated their raid and fled further into the mountains, bringing their captives with them – at least those they deemed strong enough to survive. That was important, then. These prisoners were important.

'Have your pilots bring them back to Argos,' she ordered. 'Maybe he can read something more than just tragedy from the patterns of their bruises and bleeding. Between them and the live one, at least.'

Kobald's violet eyes perked up at that. The first hint of hope she'd seen in any of her troopers since the night before.

Colonel Atreja Yarin was not a woman who relished surprises, so when Aerand entered her tent to find the commander of the Cadian 900th standing over her small field desk, the lieutenant's heart immediately rose into her throat. Doubly so at the sight of the silver-haired man beside her.

General Markos Rusk needed no insignia to mark his olive-grey battle uniform – his accosting violet eyes and commanding stance announced his rank for him. Neither did he display a breastplate full of medals and ribbons. Rather, the broken, re-formed bones of his nose and left cheek, and the tangled pneumatics and wire of his augmetic right arm, conveyed the merits of his service in far more convincing detail.

'Colonel. General,' Aerand managed. 'I must admit this visit is unexpected.'

'Intentionally,' Rusk replied gruffly. 'Although apparently more of a surprise than the raid your company attempted this morning.'

Aerand winced at the stinging remark. She was tempted to simply withstand the rebuke, but she knew the general expected – demanded, even – that she push back against it.

'Not entirely a loss, sir.'

'A prisoner. We know.' Yarin held up her hand, clearly not pleased with wasting any more time. 'Half-dead, by the brief report your medicae gave me. The trooper deserves a medal for keeping that broken husk alive this long.' The colonel's voice was laden with exasperation, poorly concealed.

Aerand nodded, feeling the same anxiousness herself. 'With respect, sirs, I stopped by my tent simply to drop off my pack. If you know of the prisoner already, why are you waiting here and not interrogating them?'

Something that might have been a look of unease crossed Rusk's face briefly, and Aerand felt bile rise in her throat. 'I thought it best we examine the corpses all at once.'

Outside the small command tent, a trio of bodies lay still on the cold ground. Somehow, the two corpses Kobald's Sentinels had recovered appeared even paler and more ghastly in the waking grey light of another overcast Ourean day.

As Aerand approached the bodies, Colonel Yarin and General Rusk in her wake, an exasperated Argos stomped towards them.

'Dead,' the medicae spat, the word delivered with a venom that caught Aerand by surprise. Argos looked exhausted, his eyes set within deep shadows, his uniform spattered and stained with blood. 'I leave the Throne-cursed witch alone with my patient for thirty seconds and he's managed to undo an entire morning of effort. Nearly had the young man talking before he arrived.'

At his comment, the fifth living member of their group turned, and Aerand felt a creeping discomfort rise through her neck. From where he knelt over the third and final corpse, the psyker fixed Aerand with sunken, hollow eyes. Aerand froze, unsteadiness catching her limbs as the man's gaze rose and fell, studying the lieutenant. Pale grey eyes set deep in a weathered brown face. Crow's feet ringing those sunken pools of light. Beneath the shadow of the psyker's crimson cowl, dim light flickered from rows of ageing, corroded wires weaving in and out of the man's bald scalp like poor stitchwork.

With his attention came a stabbing pain behind Aerand's forehead, as if a host of unseen fingers were attempting to claw their way into her mind. Aerand pushed back against them and felt their grasp retract. A brief look of surprise crossed the psyker's face, which then settled back into its resident scowl.

'Not dead,' the man remarked to Argos. 'At least, not all the pieces that count.' He turned his gaze back to the young man on the ground and pulled his faded, threadbare cloak tighter around himself. Not a noble's clothes, not as his rank might have earned him. No jewels or power weapons, no gold-plated staff to match the stories she'd heard of the Astra Militarum's psyker lords. In fact, aside from his gaunt, haunted expression and the fearsome augmetics tracing the man's skull, little marked him as anything more than a vagrant.

He raised a long, thin hand to the silver aquila brooch at his neck. 'More importantly, had the prisoner become well enough to speak, he would not have uttered a single word worth believing.'

A terse frown appeared on General Rusk's face. 'I doubt Colonel Yarin's troopers require a lecture on the duplicity of their quarry, Kellipso.'

In reply, the psyker simply shrugged, placing a hand over the young man's frozen eyes. In his other palm he cradled three small black metal spheres. 'Rest assured, medicae. If there are answers rooted within this mind, I will tear them out. Now leave me to my work.'

As the psyker turned his attention back towards the corpse, the fingers of his left hand began to dance, the three spheres weaving like a serpent between them. Rusk nodded curtly, and as the officers departed, Aerand felt those same sickening tendrils at her back.

'Twenty-three miles, sir,' Aerand remarked coldly. 'I've driven them half the sector in full kit already today. Most haven't slept more than a few hours in two days.'

'I know,' Colonel Yarin replied, her weathered face suddenly appearing impossibly tired. 'And I'm certain they are exhausted. Yet General Rusk is asking you to push them further. *I* am asking you to push them further.'

Despite her best effort, a sigh escaped Aerand. Even as she stood here, the ebb and flow of fatigue gripped her in its unforgiving currents. 'You told me once that you respected my candour, sir. Secundus Company is near its limit. I can push them on a hundred more marches, but my troopers can't take any more disappointments.'

Yarin sighed. 'You worry that this venture will be fruitless.'

A nod. 'All on the word of a psyker General Rusk does not even trust.'

Yarin brushed a calloused hand through her short, steel-grey hair and turned to stare at the crimson-robed man across the clearing. He stood almost a hundred yards from the pair, yet Aerand could not shake the feeling that even at that distance the psyker listened to her every word.

'Do not discount Jarrah Kellipso,' Yarin said eventually. 'Rusk may harbour his own resentment towards his primaris psyker, but the man is capable of much. If he says he has seen into the mind of our enemy, then I, for one, believe him.'

'At the risk of sounding ungrateful, sir, that does not make me any more comfortable to have him at my back.'

'Nor should it,' Yarin replied grimly. 'Now I believe you have a company to rouse.'

'I have told you half a hundred times, sergeant. I see minds only in glimpses and impressions.'

Aerand trudged through the snow at the side of her column, exhausted troopers stretched out through the narrow mountain pass. On either side of Secundus Company, Lieutenant Kobald's Sentinels stalked the forests atop untiring avian legs, providing as much of a picket as the restrictive terrain allowed.

Embedded within her command squad, Corwyn paced beside Jarrah Kellipso, seemingly untouched by the bitter exhaustion that gripped the troopers around him. His gloved hands held a half-folded map in front of the primaris psyker.

'Yes, sir. I understand, sir,' the sergeant continued, repeating the same line of questioning for at least the dozenth time. 'But there's no chance that one of those glimpses could have been of a specific location on this map? Just want to know how long I should expect to be marching.'

As an exasperated sigh escaped the psyker, Corwyn cast a sly grin Aerand's way. She'd worried the task of minding the primaris psyker might rub on the sergeant, but it had become clear the reverse was true. For nine miles, Corwyn had hammered Kellipso with unending questions, and the psyker appeared infinitely more fatigued than even the day's heavy march should have left him.

Kellipso's crimson robes were mud-stained and frost-crusted, and each stride of his long, unnaturally thin legs seemed to deepen the grimace across the man's face. Truth be told, it was a wonder he remained upright at all. Ourea's gravity had proven harsh enough for the troopers of the 900th Regiment – Aerand could only imagine the burden on Kellipso's gaunt frame.

In his left hand, the man cradled his trio of black spheres, each no larger than the width of a finger, and twirled them continuously in a motion that set Aerand on edge. Slowly, Kellipso looked up as she approached, fixing her with those haunted sky-grey eyes, and Aerand was reminded of Yarin's warning.

'Give the lord psyker some rest, Corwyn,' she muttered, stepping in to take the sergeant's place. From here, she saw more closely the devices in Kellipso's hand, near enough to spot the faint blue pattern etched onto their surface, an endless, repeating fractal that made her mind spin.

'No questions of your own, lieutenant?' Kellipso asked gruffly, noting her gaze at the fetishes in his grasp.

'None,' she managed to reply. But as her gaze drifted away and fell onto the ridgeline beside them, her unease only grew. What she had previously written off as the tactical discomfort of a commander forced to traverse less than ideal terrain now raised the hackles on her back and brought the taste of metal to her tongue.

Corwyn regarded her strangely, as if she were about to faint, when a crushing sense of knowledge suddenly captured her mind. Wherever Kellipso was leading Secundus Company, they had almost arrived. Aerand tightened her grip on her lasgun and turned back towards the psyker. He showed none of her same signs of distress, but a cold chill had entered his expression. His gaze lingered on her a moment, then darted to a peak on the north side of the valley, where two Sentinels scrambled along a scree-covered slope.

Moments later, Kobald's unsteady voice crackled through the vox. *'Sir. I think you'll want to see this for yourself.'*

Atop the narrow, windswept ridge, Aerand could see nearly the entire sector. In the sky above, Ourea's moons cast their foreign orange glow on the peaks and valleys below, covering the planet in a dappled patchwork of shadow and light. A fitting metaphor, perhaps, for this world's struggle as a whole.

'By Celestine's kiss,' Corwyn muttered, admiring not the mountain landscape but the imposing structure that loomed before them. 'If that's not a Throne-cursed fortress then I'm a heretic myself.'

Only a few miles away, at the end of another narrow valley, a massive black bulwark cut its way into the sky. As Aerand rested her eyes on the strange geometry of the structure, a sudden vertigo gripped her, accompanied by the bitter, acrid taste of burnt flesh in her throat.

Moments later an image appeared in her mind, a vague glimpse of carnage. Bodies heaped in a pile. Corpses wearing the grey uniform of her troopers. She shook her gaze away from the structure and the ghastly black scar it left on the landscape. 'Temple,' she managed eventually as her balance and her nerve returned. 'Not a fortress. A temple.'

Kellipso fixed her with a questioning stare, the triplet spheres in his hand spinning more quickly. 'Whatever purpose it serves, that's where you will find your quarry.'

A shrug from Corwyn. 'Either way, full of maddened cultists or not, taking the thing would at least get us out of the snow.'

Aerand nodded, venturing her gaze back towards the temple. This time, no sickly premonition gripped her mind. A shiver ran through her as the prior memories forced their way forward. She had seen something else in that vision, a single figure left alive among all the dead.

As she met Jarrah Kellipso's icy-grey gaze, she felt the tendrils of the psyker's mind reaching out subtly towards her. She batted them away and watched the man's expression harden.

'Find somewhere in that valley to camp for the night, Corwyn. I'm going to get Colonel Yarin and General Rusk on the vox.'

'Macharius' tears,' Corwyn hissed beside Aerand. 'It's like this planet was carved by Chaos itself.'

A chastised look crossed the face of the young vox-bearer as the company sergeant slammed the mouthpiece back into its cradle. Nothing but garbled static echoed from the device.

'Not your fault, Waldamne,' Aerand muttered. 'Sheer valleys, towering peaks, blankets of snow. None of these help our equipment function.'

To the south, grey clouds billowed against the last of a dying sun. Snow flitted gently down at their current position, but the blinding deluge of a blizzard appeared well on its way. Communication had always been problematic on the austere mountain world. Even more so as the companies of the 900th ventured out into those wilds, leaving the larger, immobile relay stations of hard-walled fortresses behind. Even still, a strange suspicion fell over Aerand.

No sooner than she had thought of the man, Jarrah Kellipso wandered into their small command post. All around the slopes of the narrow valley, Secundus Company's troopers erected small tents in hopes of defending against the oncoming storm. The psyker looked at their preparations with an expression of unease.

'No time for that, I'm afraid, lieutenant. I've been watching the temple, and we need to move, now.'

Corwyn scoffed. 'Best of luck to you, lord psyker. Those troopers have marched two days and fifty miles on no sleep. I doubt even Guilliman himself could rouse them.'

Kellipso ignored the sergeant, fixing his cold stare against Aerand's. 'You have seen that temple. You feel what waits inside.'

Underneath his gaze, Aerand stirred uncomfortably. She had seen what waited, indeed. A vision of her company dead, and of the psyker alone standing amid the ashes.

She plastered a look of innocent incompetence across her face and motioned to the vox-caster beside her. 'We haven't been able to reach the regiment for hours. There's a storm on its way, and my troopers are spent. We should rest here for the night and try again in the morning.'

'There's no time,' Kellipso said again, a growing pressure behind his voice. 'You know that, just as well as I.'

It was true – she could feel something rising over the ridgeline. Something terrible and unholy in the temple below, but with it also grew her suspicions of Kellipso. That he sought to lead them straight into its gaping maw. 'Without orders from Colonel Yarin, or General Rusk himself, I'm not throwing my company at that in the dark.'

Kellipso's sunken eyes rested on her for a moment. 'Very well,' he muttered, brushing clear a patch of snow and taking a seat on the frozen ground. 'You demand approval to do your duty, you shall have it.'

From some hidden pocket of his cloak, the psyker removed the three dark metal spheres and began to spin them in the skeletal fingers of one hand. Slowly at first, each sphere weaving languidly between fingers, then faster until their movements were a blur. Then suddenly, their motion stopped.

A sickening certainty washed over Aerand as the haunted look in the psyker's eyes vanished completely. Somewhere, miles away, some poor junior trooper or aide to Rusk had just fallen, rising from the ground with the psyker's mind within them. At the thought alone, Aerand's skin crawled.

As Kellipso sat before her, mindless, the muscles in his face twitching every few moments, her suspicions swelled like an unchecked tide. The psyker was not responsible for the rough terrain that had plagued their communications on Ourea from the start, but for a man who could cast his mind across miles, how challenging would it be to block a weakened vox signal? How easy to make himself the only conduit through which the rest of the regiment could be reached?

Memories of her terrible vision struck Aerand again. Those three metal spheres twirling in the psyker's hand as he stood among scores of grey-clad, bloodied corpses. As the psyker opened his eyes, she tasted blood on her tongue.

'The general agrees,' Kellipso grunted, rising from the snow with a pained expression. 'We push forward tonight, or inconveniences like storms and darkness will soon be the smallest of our concerns.'

Aerand turned from the psyker as he trekked back up the slope towards the ridgeline. 'Find Kobald. Find Vyse,' she whispered to Corwyn. 'We need to talk.'

'Shouldn't be much farther,' Kobald muttered. 'Hasn't moved from his perch, if my scouts are anything but blind.'

A grunt from Vyse. The tall woman rolled her shoulders in a catlike motion, fingers brushing the pommels of the twin bolt pistols she favoured. 'Never liked the man. Never trusted a witch.'

A look of agreement from Kobald, and one of cold steel from Corwyn. The sergeant's famous good humour had long since vanished.

'With me?' Aerand asked.

'Until the end.'

A chill rose through her spine, not of fear but of appreciation. Half a year ago, her platoon had nearly mutinied when she warned them of coming danger. Tonight, it had taken only a few breaths to convince the officers beside her to challenge a primaris psyker. As she crested the rise and saw Kellipso's crimson-robed form seated on a jagged rock outcropping, Aerand called out the psyker's name.

'Kellipso!'

The man did not move from his perch. Instead, he remained seated, wrapped in his tattered crimson robe, his pale eyes fixed on the temple ahead.

'I spoke to you,' Aerand called.

The man did not reply.

Beside her, Corwyn took a step forward, raising his lasgun, then crumpled abruptly to the ground. The sickening thud of limp flesh striking cold earth echoed behind Aerand as Kobald and Vyse joined her company sergeant in the snow. A sudden weight crashed down against her, but she forced herself upright and took another step.

At this, Kellipso finally spoke.

'Not another step,' the psyker ordered. His voice was a whisper that should have been easily swallowed by the rising wind, yet it rang as clear in her ears as if he stood just beside her. Without turning, he motioned to Corwyn's and Kobald's still forms. 'They aren't dead, but I can change that. Speak your piece, lieutenant, if you've come here to speak. But if you intend to murder me, you will not be the first to fail at that task.'

Aerand heard the certainty in his statement. Even so, she bristled at the accusation.

'Murder?' she replied, edging her hand towards her holster. She had killed a witch before, and she could do so again, provided he did not notice her intent until it was too late.

'Is it murder to defend my own?' she continued, recalling the bloody image of her vision. Slowly, she raised her arm and took aim at the psyker. 'I have seen what happens in that temple, lord psyker. I have seen you standing over the bloodied corpses of my troopers. If you seek to betray the Emperor, you had better kill me now, because I will not be part of whatever heretic scheme you intend.'

With that, she edged her finger around the trigger and pulled. Rather than the report of her laspistol, however, she felt only a strange numbness radiate up her arm, and looked down to see that her finger had not moved. Finally, the psyker turned his gaze towards her. Where his eyes had appeared emotionless before, she now saw anger raging beneath their icy surface. She watched, terrified, as Kellipso rose, unable to move her arm, her feet rooted like trees.

'Betrayal?' he said softly, as if tasting the word. 'Heresy? You speak with the certainty of a zealot. As if you alone know the Emperor's will.'

Once again, the psyker's eyes traced over her, just like the first time the pair had met. How she wished she had put a las-round in him then. The fingers of his mind brushed against the back of her skull again, and this time she found she could not refuse them. The psyker took a pained step towards her, his left hand beginning to move, the black spheres spinning across his palm like dark moons.

'I can smell the taint of the warp on you, soldier. I can taste its bitter fire raging through your mind. You believe you've been granted an immeasurable gift, but you hold in your hands just the smallest of sparks. If I so desired, I could strip your consciousness bare. Open it wide like a volume before me and tear its fragile pages loose one by one. I could crawl into your skull, and wear your skin, and walk back to your company without a single soul knowing the difference. But even that, child, is nothing compared to the powers you toy with.'

Kellipso stood beside her now, his gaunt chest heaving beneath his threadbare cloak and flak vest, his breath rising and falling in warm waves against her face.

'You think you saw the future, lieutenant? You think this is the Emperor's voice, speaking to you through the void? Those tongues that whisper into your dreams are not a blessing, they are a curse.'

With those words, the psyker raised one hand before her face, and she could not take her eyes from the dancing spheres in his grasp.

'Look again,' Kellipso ordered, and Aerand's head snapped to the side. 'Look long and true, and tell me what you see.'

As Aerand's eyes fixed on the temple below, a horrible vertigo overwhelmed her, and she felt the psyker's long fingers reach out to rest over her eyes. No longer did she stand fixed on a mountain ridge, but instead was thrown, fully, into that terrible vision. And atop its sickening, bloody feel, the fingers of Kellipso's mind gripped hers tight.

Once again she stood in the dark, flame-lit chamber, corpses scattered like chaff around her feet. The dark crimson tinge of blood coated the floor, seeping slowly between crudely fashioned stone blocks, reflecting the glow of blue werelight in strange, terrible patterns. She looked down at faces she recognised all too well.

Kobald. Maltia. Corwyn. Vysé. But as she met the gaze of the crimson-cloaked figure before her, she saw her own dismay mirrored in his eyes.

Slowly, Kellipso lowered his hood, staring with open sorrow at the charnel house around him. All along his scarred and thinly veined scalp, thick cables wove tangled to the base of his neck. Slowly, realisation crossed the psyker's face, and all the anger of a moment before vanished, replaced by an expression of abject pity.

'Tell me what you see, now, lieutenant,' Kellipso ordered, his voice hardly more than a whisper in her mind. 'Look into my eyes and tell me that this is my intention, and not my single greatest fear.'

Even as he spoke, Aerand felt the truth of those words. Felt the crushing pain radiating from the psyker. The unimaginable burden of a man hearing the screams of the dead, which had long since fallen silent to the rest of the living.

'I-I'm not certain,' she stammered. And even as she spoke, her vision dissipated and she felt herself fall onto her hands and knees. Before her on the ridgeline, Kellipso himself appeared staggered, but the psyker bore it with only a look of unease.

'I do not envy you,' he whispered eventually. 'I remember well the awakening of my own psychic gifts. You are afraid, no doubt, of what you are becoming. Afraid that your future is staring you in the face.'

Aerand shifted uncomfortably beneath the truth of Kellipso's words. Aye, she was afraid. Afraid of her visions. Afraid of herself. Afraid of becoming like the psyker before her. A twisted old woman full of misery and self-loathing, looking back on a life full of endless lies. But perhaps even more than all of that, she was afraid of the inexplicable desire within her to embrace that fate rather than run from it.

Noting her discomfort, Kellipso lifted his hood, covering again his scarred scalp and the twisted weight of his augmetics. 'I have not been cursed with the gift of foresight, lieutenant, but believe my words when I promise you this. Chaos speaks in a multitude of voices, and nearly all of them whisper lies. I do not know what you saw. *A* future, perhaps. But if so, only one possible among millions. But I have touched the edge of the shadow gathering strength down below, and there is no uncertainty, no duplicity there. Whatever it intends is far darker than any vision your mind could conjure.'

Slowly, the psyker reached a thin, pale arm towards Aerand. 'Fate and destiny are the domain of the heretic and the witch. The only destiny you serve is the one you create, with every word that you speak and every step you take forward. The Emperor would have it no other way.'

Aerand took his grasp and rose to her feet. 'So we charge in, then?' she asked. 'Blind and alone?'

'No. Not blind,' Kellipso replied slowly. 'And certainly not alone.'

In his hand, the spheres began to dance.

The dark air rippled before Aerand as she strode across the alpine plain. Crusted ice over lichen shattered beneath her boots, a strangely muffled sound that seemed to die only yards from its source. Let the psyker downplay his skill if he wished, but to cast a glamour over an entire company of soldiers was no small feat.

As Aerand watched Kellipso walking comfortably, no visible distraction in his step, a sense of awe, and shame, crept over her. Hours ago she had been ready to kill the man – or rather, to try. She had no illusions now that she would have been the one dead in the exchange. Hours ago she had been convinced of his disloyalty, but now she trusted him as fully as any of her own. She had seen the terrible sorrow in his eyes. Seen his utter dismay at the vision that plagued her. And of those gathered here, only he shared her knowledge of what might await them.

Beside her, Corwyn eyed the psyker suspiciously. 'My head still hurts,' he murmured, too quietly for anyone else to hear.

Aerand grimaced. To their credit, the sergeant and her lieutenants had kept quiet about the stand-off atop the ridgeline, but it was asking too much for them to trust the psyker too. 'Corwyn, I'm sorry.'

The sergeant cut her off. 'Then again, maybe it's just my bruised ego I'm feeling. I'm sure Vyse has marked his name on a few of her bolts. But don't worry about us – she won't use them unless he gives her good reason.'

'Besides' – a small smile crept across the sergeant's face as he rubbed at the back of his head gingerly – 'I doubt she'd have a chance to get the shot off before he dropped her to the ground again.'

Ahead, the temple stood like a hole in the skyline itself, an even blacker patch of darkness in an already empty firmament. As they approached the jagged, rising walls, the back of Aerand's neck began to burn. She looked over to Kellipso, who nodded gruffly. 'Cultists on the other side of the wall. Not yet alerted to our presence.'

Aerand stood silent, awaiting his further instructions, but the psyker simply shook his head. 'I know little of tactics and the leading of soldiers. What you do with that information is up to you. I will be your eyes and your ears, lieutenant, but you must be our will.'

Aerand nodded, stepping onto the sweeping bridge that separated the temple from the valley over a broad, bottomless chasm. She might be ignorant when it came to visions and divination, but she was far from unschooled in the intricacies of war.

'Vyse, Graves, Kobald, on me. Lord psyker, prepare to drop that glamour.'

The laspistol sang in Aerand's hands. A jarring rhythm that shook her bones and comforted her all at once. Around her, the temple courtyard blazed with red fire as the volleys of two platoons tore into an unprepared mass of cultists. Aerand had made no offer of surrender. Their enemy had refused that gift long ago.

Already, the dark stone was littered with pale corpses, the tattooed sigils, arcane brands and savage mutilations of Chaotic rites now invisible beneath the sheen of fresh blood. She took no joy in the killing itself, only in the finality of the confrontation after months of fruitless pursuit and flight.

'Drusus' countenance!' Sergeant Corwyn snapped as another mob of cultists rounded a corner to converge on Secundus Company, crudely fashioned clubs and spears mixed in among energy weapons. 'No wonder all our raids have come up dry for the last season. Every Throne-cursed cultist on the planet has been hiding here.'

Aerand suspected her sergeant was correct, and that did little to shrink the knot in her gut. With Kobald's Sentinels patrolling outside the walls to prevent any flanking sortie from the enemy, she had less than a hundred troopers inside the temple. One hundred Cadians against how many cultists? One thousand? Ten? Less than ideal, but all things considered, she would take those odds any given day.

As Aerand sprinted from one debris pile to another, Corwyn followed closely in her wake. On her right, Vyse's heavies laid down beam after beam of searing lascannon fire, pushing along the natural curve of the temple's battlements, while Graves' platoon covered their left flank, already embedded in the cover of a crumbled enceinte. If needed, they could hold these positions all night, but her soldiers were here to conquer, not defend.

Behind her, Kellipso strode undeterred through the tumult, the trio of spheres in the psyker's left hand flickering like shadows. Aerand watched another group of cultists emerge from deep within the temple only to charge straight into the enfilading fire of one of Vyse's autocannons, as if they had not even noticed the threat. A chill spread up her spine as she wondered what hand the primaris psyker had in the enemy's foolhardy decision-making.

'How many?' she asked, dropping behind a stone pillar. Kellipso remained on his feet, las-bolts soaring past his hooded head.

The psyker shrugged. 'Does it matter? More than enough.'

'Very well then, lord psyker. Lead us on.'

Kellipso nodded, then walked towards a low door in the wall ahead. As Aerand passed through behind him, a sick feeling settled in the pit of her stomach. Something in the colour of the stone and the musty, bloodied scent in the air brought her back once again to her vision on the ridge.

She paused for half a breath, turning to face Corwyn behind her. 'Stay close. Stay ready.'

The sergeant simply nodded.

Two rounds into a woman's bare chest. Another straight into the face of a young man barely old enough to join a Whiteshield platoon. Aerand buried her disgust and strode past both bodies.

Ahead, Kellipso walked on, unhindered, the psyker barely present behind his own eyes. Thirteen turns, seven staircases, every step carrying them deeper into the mountain itself, that taste of blood and bile rising higher with each step.

Aerand had seen tragedy here, and it haunted her now. Memories that had not yet happened. That might never happen if the psyker lord spoke true. Even still, she could not help but relive them, and they were nearly enough to make her turn back.

In contrast, Kellipso's curse haunted him still, the ever-pressing madness that afflicted their deranged enemy encroaching against his own mind through theirs. The psyker had turned back to face her only once since they'd entered the temple proper, and she'd nearly toppled beneath the weight of that horror.

Down another corridor, this one unlit. Then two turns in succession to face a final staircase. Aerand knew what waited down below. Had she not seen it in her mind a dozen times already? Chaos. Death. The gathering darkness. Some arcane ritual or twisted cultist contraption. A heretic priestess, or simply masses of more Chaos-maddened fools. Whatever form the evil of this world had taken, this was where it had chosen to make its stand. And this was where her premonition had led her.

Here, the stone on the floor of the corridor had worn smooth with time, and the carved friezes on the walls faded to mere shadows. At the base of the staircase stood a narrow arch, and Aerand shuddered as light flickered up from within.

Blue. The terrible, unforgettable blue of witchfire and madness that haunted her visions. Ahead of her, Kellipso paused. His weathered face flickered strangely in the awful werelight, his eyes failing to reflect its unnatural hue. 'I believe that we come now to the end, but I cannot say what lies ahead.'

Aerand nodded in reply to his unasked question. She was ready. Her troopers were ready. And Kellipso may not know what awaited them, but she had already lived through the worst possible fate. She turned slowly to face her company.

'On the corridor, Vyse. Graves, your rifles with me.' Her lieutenants nodded and peeled off with their platoons.

Aerand swallowed, recalling her vision one last time. The worn, bloodied stone. The empty, dead faces of the friends around her.

'Corwyn,' she began.

'With you, sir. Always.'

Aerand nodded and dived into the terrible blue light.

A large chamber reared before her, older than any she had seen previously on this world. Here, the shadows grew thick and cloying, seeming to defy the cold white beam of her helm lumen.

In the centre of the room stood a ring of stone chairs. Facing each other, two dozen emaciated prisoners were chained to those seats. Thin, rusted cables stretched from the bases of their skulls and passed to a small black pillar in the centre of the ring. And in the air just above that ancient black pillar was the source of the chamber's terrible light – a small sphere of flickering, abhorrent blue flame.

Beside her, Kellipso halted, stunned.

'You've seen the like of this before,' Aerand said.

The psyker's face contorted in pain, truly unnerved for the first time since she had met him. 'Not with my own eyes, but I know its design well enough. A fate I myself only narrowly escaped.'

'Unpleasant for them?' Corwyn asked.

'Pure torment,' he replied. With a shudder, the psyker surveyed the contraption. 'Fortunately for us, however, not fully active yet.'

Aerand walked towards the captive nearest to her. A young woman – about the lieutenant's age – her body riven with symbols that made Aerand shudder. She turned to face Kellipso, taking in the pained expression on his face.

Slowly, the psyker approached, eyes distant, those spheres motionless in his hands for the first time since she had met him. He reached out towards the cable at the base of the young woman's skull, but as his hand closed around the crusted, bloodied metal, the chamber around them exploded with sound.

Half a shout escaped the lieutenant as the report of an autogun echoed off cold stone walls, accompanied by a muzzle flash from one of the room's shadowy alcoves. Slowly, a dark red flower bloomed in the centre of Kellipso's forehead, and the psyker slumped awkwardly to the ground. As she reached out to catch him, she blinked at the sound of more autogun fire. But when she opened her eyes, the room around her was silent and Kellipso stood unharmed beside the door, only beginning to approach. A sickening wave of nausea rolled over Aerand as the primaris psyker reached out towards the young woman in the chair.

'No,' she whispered, snatching Kellipso's hand. She pulled him to the ground as the crack of an autogun split the room. Beside them, the young woman's eyes flashed open, and she let out a terrible, piercing wail. As she did so, the chamber erupted with motion.

Aerand's laspistol kicked as she fired into the shadowy alcove that had produced the shot directed at Kellipso. With a satisfying thud, a lifeless body struck stone, and Corwyn opened fire with his lasgun behind her.

Suddenly, the dozen prisoners around her woke in unison, their cries rising above the las-fire of her troopers, and in the centre of the room, the blue flame surged. From half a dozen hidden entrances cultists streamed, the edges of the chamber descending into bloody melee as Graves' troopers raised their weapons and joined the fray.

'Corwyn!' Aerand shouted above the din. 'Get Vyse's heavies in here! I want an autocannon on every one of those doors.'

Aerand rolled over to face Kellipso, but the psyker had already risen to his feet. Slowly, he surveyed the room around him, unfazed by bolts and las-rounds skirting past his face. A terrible anguish was etched into his eyes, and as he looked towards her, the spheres in his hand began to spin.

'Kellipso!' she shouted, levelling her laspistol at the nearest doorway. She pulled the trigger on repeat as a group of battle-mad cultists charged through. A trio of troopers fell under the grouped melee. All around her, her soldiers toppled like timber, and the spheres in the psyker's hands continued to whirl.

Smoke and blood filled the chamber with their gruesome aroma as the las-charred flesh of cultists fell beside the battered, bloody corpses of Cadians. In the centre of the chamber, that blue fire pulsed, its light rising and falling with the screams of the psykers who produced it. As the tempo rose, a sickening fear gripped Aerand.

She had been here before. She had seen how this ended.

Forward she dived, into the melee, her laspistol blazing. A round into the forehead of the cultist before her. Two more into the stomach of the woman behind him. Somewhere, Corwyn had managed to find Vyse's heavies, and a pair of autocannons roared, but still the cultists rushed in.

In the centre of it all, Kellipso stood unmoving, the spheres in his hand whirling ever faster until they were nothing more than a blur.

'Kellipso!' Aerand shouted one final time. She had trusted the psyker. She had trusted herself. And all around her, Secundus Company died.

Raging, she crashed into a wall of cultists, firing las-rounds point-blank into searing flesh. From behind, a crude bone mace struck her head. As her face hit stone, the horrible vision returned, not imagined this time but visible in truth. Blood on the floor of this Throne-cursed chamber, Kellipso standing alone in the centre of the fray.

Aerand raised her arms to shield herself from the inevitable killing blow, but none came, and when she opened her eyes, the room was still.

+Hold.+

A single word reverberated through her mind.

+Hold.+

Aerand tried to turn her head to face the cultist above her but found that only her eyes would move. With effort, she fought the iron grasp that had suddenly latched on to her mind, and realised she recognised its touch. She threw her mind against it and managed just enough space to turn her head towards the centre of the room.

+Hold.+

Aerand watched Kellipso's lips move in time with the word in her mind. In time with the word in the minds of every person in this temple. All across the ancient, stone-paved chamber, Cadian troopers lay motionless on the floor, thrown to the ground by the weight of the psyker's command. Above them, an army of Chaos-maddened cultists stood dumbstruck, swinging knives and levelling weapons at enemies no longer within their reach. Slowly, Kellipso's grey eyes met Aerand's, blazing, as the spheres in his hand rose into the air. For a moment, their fractal pattern flared with blue fire, then the three spheres unravelled into a cloud of myriad perfect shards. With a flick of the primaris psyker's wrist, that cloud rushed around the room like a swarm.

Aerand flinched at the sound of bodies dropping. Felt the thud of dead flesh against solid stone. A bloodied thigh bone clattered to the floor beside her, and the weight of a body collapsed across her. Warm blood trickled down from the cultist's corpse and seeped through her flak armour as she tried to push the man off her chest.

+Hold.+

The command echoed through her mind yet again, but with less power this time. At the centre of the room, Kellipso began to fade. All around Aerand, cultists still fell to the psyker, but the pained expression on his face only deepened further as the dead piled up on the temple's floor. As if fed by their blood, the blue flame in the chamber's centre blazed brighter, tendrils flickering outward like rays of some terrible, hungry sun.

+Hold.+

So little left in that word. So little power the psyker had held back for himself. Guilt and fear gripped Aerand once again. Whatever confidence Jarrah Kellipso exuded, the man had been afraid. Afraid of the vision that Aerand had shown him. And now he sought its reverse. He would empty himself dry to save the soldiers around him, and by doing so he would spell their doom.

Behind Kellipso, that whirling ball of Chaos still spun, swelling suddenly, even as the psyker grew weaker. Too late, Kellipso turned to face it, to see the horrible, ravenous desire in its light. Empty now, laid bare, the psyker stood defenceless, and what a wonderful prize he would be.

With a shout Aerand shoved the corpse from atop her, then leapt unsteadily to her feet. As the terrible fire reached out towards Kellipso, she stumbled past the psyker and then fell to her knees. Scrambling on her hands, she reached out through the shadows, grasping the cable at the base of a prisoner's skull and ripping it loose in a gout of blood and crusted fluid.

Above her, the flickering werelight reeled, drawing back from Kellipso, who pushed his last energy towards it. 'The others,' the psyker muttered, sweat beading across his wax-pale face.

Slowly, Aerand pushed herself onto her feet, bruised muscles and battered bones protesting every movement. Across the room, grey-clad bodies began to rise from the ground as Cadian troopers spotted their commander on her feet. One by one, rusted cables clattered to the floor, and the terrible blue fire began to fade.

The morning sun that streaked through the clouds above appeared bright and scalding beyond all reason.

'If I never spend another moment beneath ground, I will live and die a happy man.' Sergeant Corwyn cracked an irreverent smile as he stepped out from beneath the temple's shadow and into the bright, unforgiving light.

Aerand did her best to smile back at her sergeant. A wave of gratitude washed over her at the expression on his face, so full of life. So distant from the empty, cold one in her vision. Even still, his lively smile could not erase the image of the dead, both real and envisioned, from her mind.

Across the courtyard, Kobald's scouts piled casualties. Mostly the half-naked, starved forms of their cultist enemies in a large, unceremonious pile to be burned, but enough corpses in grey flak armour to make her stomach churn.

Two score – three? – dead from Secundus Company. Within her first days on the planet she had seen half of her platoon dead. Now, she had lost almost half of the first company given to her.

Behind her, Kellipso walked slowly through the arch. The man was pale, his eyes even darker and more sunken. Despite his lanky stature, he seemed somehow diminished. And yet somehow so much larger within her mind.

How many more corpses would her conscience carry had the primaris psyker not been with her today? How many fewer dead cultists, bearing those strange, small wounds of a thousand flechettes piercing their bodies like flies?

The psyker walked unsteadily into the sunlight, leading a young woman slowly by the hand. Around her shoulders she wore the psyker's tattered crimson cloak, and she bore an expression somehow even more empty than that of the weathered man beside her.

Slowly, Aerand limped towards them and reached out her hand.

'Thank you,' Kellipso muttered as he took the three black metal spheres from her grasp. 'For seeing what I couldn't.' The moment the psyker had collapsed, his cloud of flechettes had returned to him, crawling over one another like a swarm of insects to re-form into these perfect spheres. Inexplicably, they bore no evidence of the transition. Not a single scratch on their immaculate surface. Not the faintest hint of blood.

'And to you, lord psyker,' Aerand replied. 'For the same.'

Kellipso grunted in acknowledgement.

Aerand turned slowly to face the young woman. Behind her, a small huddle of Oureans walked, Vyse supporting a pair of youths with her arms.

As Aerand's gaze settled onto the woman, she felt a familiar wave rise up behind her neck.

The psyker took notice. 'Please, do not look towards their futures. I know well enough what the Black Ships hold in store. It would do them no favour to bear that knowledge any sooner than they must.'

'Not for them,' Aerand replied softly. 'For me. I would rather know what the Inquisition has in store.'

A look of confusion, then sympathy, from the psyker. 'You mean to turn yourself in.'

Aerand nodded slowly. Twice since landing on this Throne-cursed planet, the warp taint on her had cost troopers their lives. 'They deserve better,' she whispered.

Kellipso stopped. 'And you? What do you believe you deserve?'

'Nothing,' she replied. 'Whatever the Emperor wills.'

That earned her a nod, and the psyker began walking again. 'And if the Emperor wills you to remain where you are? I've seen you lead, lieutenant, and I can promise you this – your soldiers will find no better commander than you.' Kellipso glanced over his shoulder at Kobald and Vyse. 'It is rare loyalty that inspires soldiers to risk their lives so. And I'm afraid that's precisely what the Emperor needs.'

Aerand shook her head. 'And how much of a risk is it to their lives to simply keep me near at hand?'

'Less than if you leave,' Kellipso replied. His gaze grew distant for a moment, as if he were struggling to find the words to say next. 'And the powers within you are still young. They would not run unchecked beneath my careful eye.'

A look of confusion crossed Aerand's face. 'What are you offering?'

Kellipso shrugged. 'The scholastica is not the only place for a burgeoning psyker to learn. I do not claim any special talents as a teacher, nor do I promise any certainty of the results.'

Aerand opened her mouth to reply, but before she could, she felt the clasp of a heavy hand on her shoulder. 'Lord psyker, lieutenant,' Sergeant Corwyn said. 'Urgent vox from the colonel. Sounds like trouble back on the regiment's end.'

'Go on then, lieutenant,' Kellipso replied, and for a brief moment his frown faded to something softer. 'It appears your soldiers have need of you after all.'

GREEN AND GREY

Edoardo Albert

Tick, tick, tick.

That was what woke him. The regular ticking of cooling, contracting plasteel.

Tick, tick, tick.

He'd heard that sound before, growing up, the son of a tanker. He'd heard the sound during his training, when the squadron pulled up for the night, the tanks parked in rows ready for a pre-dawn start, their engines cooling, the cylinder blocks ticking out the day's accumulated heat.

Tick... tick... tick.

The ticks were slowing down. The engine was near enough cold now. He could not remember command telling the squadron to make camp for the night.

His mind was fogged, as dull as the dawn on...

He could not remember where he was.

He could not remember who he was.

It did not seem to matter.

He began to drift.

It was the pain that dragged him back. As the tick of the cooling tank died away, it was replaced by a rhythmic pain, pulsing down from the front of his head.

He did not want to move but the pain forced his hand into motion. But as he tried to reach for his forehead, his hand stopped. There was something in the way. It felt firm but not metallic, with a lingering warmth.

He did not want to open his eyes to see what it was.

Lucius Stilo.

That was it. That was his name.

Lucius Stilo. Loader. Leman Russ *Sancta Fide*. Third Squadron. Fifth Alphard Tank Regiment.

He knew who he was now, but he could not remember where he was.

He still did not want to open his eyes.

Lucius Stilo would have drifted away then, if he had been able to, but the pain would not let him. It throbbed through his head, an arrhythmic counterpoint to the cooling engine.

The engine was quiet. Stilo knew that it shouldn't be.

He still did not want to open his eyes.

But he knew he had to. It was his duty. He was a soldier of the Astra Militarum, a member of the Fifth Alphard Tank Regiment. Although his eyes were still closed, he could suddenly see his father leaning down to him, telling him, 'Yes, it's true, the Emperor protects, but first, the Emperor expects. Expects every man to do his duty.'

Stilo opened his eyes.

He opened his eyes to darkness.

But it was as if opening his eyes, even though they could see nothing, opened wide his other senses too. He could suddenly smell Leman Russ: the throat-clutching stink of human sweat, the acrid bite of the cannon propellant, the sulphur of the heavy bolter and, overlaying everything, the overwhelming smell of promethium. Although his lips were closed, he could taste it. Had the fuel tank ruptured?

'The Emperor protects, but first the Emperor expects.'

The words sounded louder than memory, so loud that Stilo turned his head to see if there was someone speaking them in the tank. But the dark was Stygian: he could see nothing.

Without light, he could do nothing.

Stilo began fumbling in the dark. He was searching for the emergency lumens. His fingers found things, but he could not relate what he found to his training – everything seemed wrong, twisted somehow. Then he realised the problem: everything was twisted because he was lying on his side. Stilo turned his mental map through ninety degrees and as he did so, things began to snap into place. There, the bin for the armour-piercing shells; here the bin for high-explosive shells in between the chute for spent shell casings; and on his left, the bank of kill switches.

Yes.

And beneath the kill switches, another console for the backup systems. First, second, third along.

Stilo pulled the switch.

The emergency lumens came on, red, lurid, pulsing. He could see.

What he saw was the face of his tank commander.

'Captain Bartezko?'

Bartezko made no answer. He was hanging above Stilo, dangling in his webbing, the standard position for a tank commander going visual. His power sword hung from his belt. Bartezko loved his sword. It had been a gift from the corps commander for his bravery in the Battle of the Machengo Rift.

'Captain?' Stilo reached for Bartezko's webbing and twisted it, so the tank commander's face turned into view. What was left of it. The captain would not be giving any more orders.

'Emmet, Vanhof. Klee, van Thienen.' Stilo called out the names of the rest of the tank crew. 'Emperor, let them answer,' he whispered. But the names fell into the thick air and were swallowed. No one spoke, no one answered. The body of Captain Bartezko hung limp in its webbing. Stilo frantically tried to remember what had happened. The captain announcing he was going visual, clipping on his webbing, standing up, reaching for the turret hatch... There. That was when his memory whited out. Air burst, maybe? An ork shell exploding above the tank just as the captain unsealed the hatch, the shock wave thrashing Bartezko against it, then slamming it shut, the pressure change in the confined volume of the tank incapacitating – killing – the crew. Except for him.

'Come in, Third Squadron. Do you copy? Third Squadron, do you copy?'

The voice, the first that he had heard since regaining consciousness, sounded thin and tinny and far away, but it was coming from the vox-panel. Turning from the corpse of his commander, Stilo twisted past scattered cases to the panel.

'Third Squadron, receiving. Over.'

'About time, Third Squadron. We've been trying to raise you for the last hour. Report.'

As the voice came through on the vox, Stilo fiddled with the controls, trying to turn it up so that he could hear better. Stilo touched his ear. His fingers came away wet and sticky. His ears were bleeding. The pressure shock of the air burst.

'This... this is Third Squadron, *Sancta Fide*, sir. Loader Lucius Stilo reporting, sir.'

'Put on Captain Bartezko.'

'I can't, sir. He's dead. They're all dead, sir, I'm the only one left.'

The vox went silent for a moment. Stilo heard the vox-operator whispering to someone.

'The corps commander wants to speak to you, Loader Stilo.'

A different voice came through: warm and generous, the voice of a kindly, rich uncle.

'Loader Stilo?'

'Y-yes. Er, sir.'

'I need you to call up the auspexes and give me a report.'

'The auspexes are all dead, sir. Everything's dead. The fuel tank's ruptured. I'm standing up to my ankles in promethium. I don't know what to do. You've got to get me out of here.'

'Stilo.'

The name dropped into the loader's increasing panic and stilled it, like oil on water.

'Yes, sir.'

'The vox is working. Try to raise the auspex. You're a tanker, Stilo. Act like one.'

'I-I will.'

Stilo reached for the auspex panel. It was unresponsive. All its screens were blank. He banged on it in frustration.

'Machine-spirits are temperamental creatures – hitting one rarely works. Try restarting it, tanker.'

Stilo stared at the panel in front of him.

'I-I can't remember what to do, sir.'

'Remember your training, tanker.'

Stilo knuckled his forehead. 'I-I can't, sir.'

'This is your first combat patrol, isn't it, Lucius?'

'Yes.'

'No one wanted for it to go like this, but you're still there, still alive. The Emperor protected you. Now the Emperor expects.'

Hearing the litany coming through on the vox, remembrance settled upon Lucius Stilo. His training took over, moving his hands over the panel, keying the relaunch sequence. The screens flickered into life.

'They're coming online, sir.'

'Good, good.'

'Frek! They're all showing static.'

'The sensor array must be damaged. Loader Stilo, I'm going to have to ask you to make a visual report.'

'L-let me try again, sir.' Stilo began keying the cut-out sequence.

'No time for that. I must have a report. Now, tanker. Remember, the Emperor expects.'

'Y-yes.'

'Yes, sir.'

'Sorry, sir. Yes, sir.'

Stilo looked at the body of Captain Bartezko, dangling in his harness, his face a livid red wound scored through with white lines of exposed bone, his power sword hanging uselessly by his side. The loader felt the physical revulsion of the living at the prospect of touching the dead. He was going to have to release the captain from the webbing so that he could get to the hatch.

'Sorry, sir.'

Stilo unclipped the webbing. Bartezko's corpse fell forwards, wrapping its arms around Stilo in the embrace of the dead.

The vox-channel was open. Stilo just about suppressed a scream and pushed the body aside so it flopped against the breech of the cannon, sprawling over it like a dead fish. Bartezko's slack body slumped, slowly, before dropping down off the turret cradle into the pool of blood and promethium at the base of the tank.

The way clear, Stilo scrambled up to the turret hatch.

Skratch, skkkratch.

The noise came from outside, from the other side of the hatch.

Stilo's hands froze in the act of opening the hatch.

Skkkkratch, skkkkkratch.

Something was outside.

It was the sound of nails on glass, of a knife scraping over plasteel.

Of claws scratching up the hull.

Stilo pushed the turret lock shut.

Bang, bang, bang.

The impacts were so loud that Stilo's teeth rang in his skull. But this was not the sound of rounds bouncing off the hull of the tank.

Bang. Bang, bang.

Something was hitting it. Hitting it with a hammer or a rock.

'Lucius, what's happening? Report, Lucius.'

Stilo dived to the panel and turned down the gain.

'S-something's outside,' he whispered. 'It's hitting the tank. You've got to get me out of here.'

'Don't worry, Stilo. Just hold on.' The voice of the corps commander was barely audible over the sounds coming from outside the tank. *'Try the auspex again.'*

'I-I don't want to see what's out there.'

Bang, bang, bang.

'Try the auspex, tanker!'

Stilo mumbled a brief prayer to *Sancta Fide*'s machine-spirit as he keyed the restart again. It had been more hurt than him. As the screens lit up, the banging intensified, coming now from at least two different places on the hull: one set echoed down the battle cannon while the other was coming from the port sponson.

Despite the damage, the pict-feed from the outside red-lit, steadied, flickered, then the pixels slowly began to come together.

Bang, bang. Bang.

The screen cleared. Outside, Stilo could see a vast, dusty plain. Calleva. He remembered, now. That was the name of this Emperor-forsaken planet. The smoking shells of two other Leman Russ tanks told him that none of the squadron had made it to the extraction zone. The ground around them was gouged with craters; for once, the orks had managed to range their artillery. Far off, he saw the curving arch of the Infinity Bridge spanning the continental abyss, its curve as elegant as the drop-off to the shifting magma sea was sudden.

Even as he saw it, Stilo knew that was wrong. The bridge should have been blown by now. His squadron had been detailed to delay the enemy while demolition charges were set, then head to the extraction zone. Either the charges had failed, or the engineers had not made it to the bridge.

But that was for the brass to worry about.

Bang, bang, bang.

He still couldn't see what was making the noise. Stilo tried tracking the pict-feed around, but it did not move. Whatever had killed *Sancta Fide* had broken the motors. It was only by the Emperor's grace that he could see anything at all out there.

'Report, Stilo.'

'I-I can't see...'

A face appeared in the screen, staring at Stilo. It opened its mouth. Its tusks and tongue were the only things that weren't a livid, fungoid green. Then, it bit down. The sensor went dark.

Lucius jerked back from the screen.

'Orks.' He leaned over the vox, whispering into it. 'Orks, outside *Sancta Fide*. They're what's banging and biting it.'

'Orks loot as readily as they kill,' said the corps commander.

'I've got *Sancta Fide* locked down, sir. They won't get in here.'

'That's good, tanker. What else did you see?'

'What? Oh, yes. I'll try to get another pict-feed running. But the plain looks clear, sir. Only ork I saw was the one trying to get in here. Surprised they're not heading for the bridge.'

'*What? What did you say, Stilo?*'

'I'm trying to get another pict-feed up.'

'*No, no. The bridge. It's still up?*'

'Yes, sir. It's still up.'

'*Hold there, tanker.*'

The vox went quiet. But outside the tank, Stilo could hear movement. Lots of movement. He fiddled with the auspex, switching to another sensor array, and the screens gradually cleared.

'There's... there's dozens of them around me,' he whispered into the vox. 'Hundreds. If I keep quiet, maybe they'll go away.'

'*Confirm, the bridge is not down.*'

'What?'

'*Loader Stilo, get visual on the bridge. Is it down?*'

Bang, bang, bang.

Stilo started as the banging began again, flinching from the port sponson.

'*Stilo, confirm.*'

'Confirmed, sir. The bridge is still standing.'

There was silence on the other end of the vox, then Stilo heard the corps commander talking urgently to someone else.

Bang, bang, bang.

'Throne, they're trying to get in, sir. What should I do?'

'*Stilo, listen to me. Are any orks closing on the bridge?*'

Bang, bang, bang.

They were hammering at the starboard sponson now. Creaking, groaning noises came from the plasteel, as if someone were trying to peel it off, layer by layer.

Stilo glanced at the pict-feed. The long plain that led to the Infinity Bridge lay there, dusty, bare and empty. 'No, sir.'

'*Copy that.*'

Bang, bang, bang.

'They're trying to get in, sir. What do I do? Tell me what to do, please.'

'*Remember your training. There's a flight of Valkyries on its way, tanker. The Emperor protects.*'

Bang, bang, bang.

'How long before they get here?'

Stilo was staring, with horrified fascination, at the port sponson. The plasteel there was bending and flexing, like a sheet of paper held in the breeze. 'I don't know how long before they split *Sancta Fide* open.'

'*Are there others, tanker? Are they all focused on you?*'

Stilo could not move. The heavy bolter in the port sponson was banging backwards and forwards like an engine piston.

'*Lucius!*'

Stilo dragged his gaze away from the heavy bolter to the screens. On them, he could see the greenskins getting on their warbikes and warbuggies, the engines belching smoke. Even through the layers of plasteel that separated him from them, he could hear the roar of the engines firing up.

'They're leaving, sir, they're leaving!' Stilo remembered his training.

'Heading two-six-five.' They were making for the bridge. That was the big prize that opened up the rest of this world to them.

That was for command to worry about. He wasn't going to die after all.

'*Loader Stilo, open fire.*'

Stilo stared at the vox. He made no answer.

'*Stilo, do you copy? Open fire.*'

He looked at the pict-feed from outside. The first of the warbikes were already accelerating away.

'*Stilo, this is an order. Open fire.*'

'B-but I want them to go away, sir.'

'*Open fire, Stilo! The Valkyries are on their way, they're nearly there, but they won't be able to find you unless you start shooting.*'

'They're leaving, sir. I don't want to attract their attention.'

'*Don't you think there will be more? Shoot them, now, while they've got their backs to you. The Valkyries will finish off the rest and extract you. They're nearly there.*'

'ETA, sir?'

'*Ten minutes, tanker. You've just got to hold out for ten minutes. Now, open fire. Use high-explosive shells on them – warbikes are soft targets.*'

Stilo stared after the departing cloud of dust that told of the rapid progress of the ork vanguard across the plain. It was true what the corps commander said: out on that dust plain, riding warbikes and wartrikes and warbuggies, the orks had no cover. They were ripe for the killing.

But the basic animal desire to survive, to hunker down and play dead stopped Stilo's hands from moving.

'*That's an order, Stilo.*'

The words activated something even deeper in Lucius than his instincts: they fired up his training. The hours, days and weeks spent running through the same sequence of actions over and over and over again. He could no more switch off that sequence, once activated, than he could stop his heart beating.

'Loading main cannon, sir.'

'*Good, lad. Good.*'

'Th-thank you.'

'*By the book, son. Do it by the book.*'

Stilo opened the high-explosive ammunition bin, manhandled out a round, slid the door to the bin shut and pushed the round into the breech of the cannon. He was trained as a loader, so this was what he knew to do: during training he'd got his time to load a round down from nine seconds to four point five.

But that was the problem. He'd done almost all his training as a loader; the cross-training as a gunner and a driver had only lasted for an afternoon.

'*You'll have to track the cannon manually, tanker.*'

'Yes, sir.'

Stilo took a quick look through the sights. The cannon was thirty degrees off. Grabbing the handle, Stilo began to crank the turret round.

The turret groaned as it moved.

'Three turns for one degree of rotation, three turns for one degree of rotation,' Stilo muttered, sweat breaking from his skin as he hauled the crank round.

Slowly, the turret turned.

Stilo checked through the sights. Nearly there. The orks were a moving dust cloud, heading west across the plain towards the bridge. Another five degrees. Fifteen turns.

He counted them off.

'...four, three, two, one.'

Stilo jumped to the sight. The reticule was lined up with the heart of the dust cloud. He set the auspex to heat. The dust cloud lit up red.

'Elevation, elevation,' he muttered, checking the vertical calibration. 'Up, two degrees.'

Stilo grabbed the cannon elevation crank and turned it, counting off six revolutions before checking the sights again.

The crosshair was aligned in the deepest red of the heat source.

Stilo pushed the ignition lever.

'Fire.'

The battle cannon jerked backwards. Propellant fumes, thick and throat-clutching, swirled into the main turret.

Stilo's training took over once more. He pulled open the breech block, released the spent high-explosive shell, letting it fall into the cartridge bin, then slid the ammunition bin door open, hauled out another high-explosive shell and shoved it into the breech.

Stilo took another quick look at the sights.

The dust cloud had stopped moving but its heart still glowed red and the crosshair sat in the centre of it.

'Fire,' he muttered, not even realising he was talking to himself.

He hardly heard the sound.

Round after round. Without thinking, his body running through its training.

Load, aim, fire. Load, aim, fire.

Load, aim, fire.

Stilo paused.

The vox was crackling but he ignored it. He checked the auspex. It was all red – but then he had just fired Emperor knew how many high-explosive shells into the dust cloud. He switched to motion sensor. There were no movement traces.

The vox was squawking.

'*Stilo. Report.*'

'Can't see, sir. Flare out on the auspex – heat from the shells.'

'*You'll have to go visual, Lucius.*'

'Unlock? Now?'

'*It's the only way to tell if you've got them all. Besides, you'll have to unlock when the Valkyries arrive.*'

'What's their ETA, sir?'

'*Sub-ten. They're on their way, tanker. Now get me that visual.*'

'Sir.'

Stilo pushed up into the turret again and began to unlock the hatch. But then he stopped. He dropped back and cycled through the remaining sensor arrays, checking the area around *Sancta Fide* was clear of green-skins. With nothing showing on the auspexes, Stilo checked his rebreather, then finished unlocking the hatch and, slowly, began to lift it.

The first crack to the outside world opened and the ochre-yellow light of Calleva flooded into the tank. Stilo's goggles blacked, then adjusted.

He peered ahead, eyes squinting against the glare, searching into the dust cloud. There was no sign of any of the ork vehicles. He turned his head slightly to try to hear. Nothing, apart from the dull ringing that was the aural aftermath of firing shell after shell of high-explosive. In the thin air of Calleva, the dust cloud thrown up by the barrage was already beginning to settle. Stilo pushed the hatch further open so that he could see better.

As the dust drifted down out of the sky, he saw the mangled remains of the ork patrol scattered over the plain: ripped-up warbikes, warbuggies blown into pieces and eviscerated greenskins, some of their severed body parts still flopping with the reflex to war, but no longer able to do anything apart from scrabble in the dust.

He had killed them all.

He, Lucius Stilo, loader, Third Squadron, Fifth Alphard Tank Regiment – on his first combat patrol, with all the rest of the crew of *Sancta Fide* dead – had done this. He was blooded. He was a proper soldier, a proper tanker now. Like his father.

Lucius Stilo threw back his head and roared his triumph at the yellow sun that hung, fat and bloated, in the thin, dark atmosphere of Calleva.

By the Emperor, and through His Grace, he had done it.

Stilo slapped the slide of the battle cannon, the plasteel still hot.

'We did it,' he said. 'We did it.'

Down in the crew compartment, Stilo could hear the vox squawking but, for the moment, he ignored it, taking in the sight of his first battle. But as the dust settled further and the distance came into view, he saw emerging from the cloud the arch of the Infinity Bridge.

It was still standing.

Even as he watched, he saw distant flares light up on it – light up and die away. Darting round it, reduced to little more than mayflies by the distance, were the silver shapes of Imperial aircraft. Stilo squinted: Marauders, maybe Thunderbolts or Valkyries. Those could be for him, dropping engineers at the bridge before coming to evac. The bridge shivered, moving like a giant snake, but then it settled. Stilo could see parts of the bridge falling into the continental abyss that it spanned, but still it stood.

He'd heard rumours that the Infinity Bridge was xenos built; if they were true, it might explain why it was proving so difficult to bring the structure down.

The distant reports of explosions reached him, echoing past into the vastness of the continental plain. Then, coming through the receding rumble of the explosions, he heard the sound of engines behind him. Lots of engines.

He froze.

Stilo knew he had to turn and look, but his muscles would not obey. They had locked in place, keeping him staring ahead, ensuring his eyes stayed firmly to the front.

This was Lucius Stilo's first combat patrol. He had thought the greenskins who had surrounded *Sancta Fide* constituted an ork warband. He had thought he had saved himself when he saw their corpses littering the plain. He had thought the thirty or so bikes and buggies were all the orks were sending his way.

Stilo forced himself to turn around. Now, looking back over the plain, he saw what an ork warband really looked like.

Clanking, smoking, rattling towards him was a tide of scrap metal pockmarked with green, tusked faces, screaming and laughing and yelling.

Stilo could hear the war cries of the greenskins even above the clank and rattle of the Battlewagons and wartrukks, as harsh and guttural as barking dogs.

He dropped back into the tank, frantically locking the hatch behind him, before seizing the vox mic.

'Where the frek are those Valkyries? There's thousands of them.'

'Report, tanker, report.' The voice on the other end of the vox remained as calm and implacable and unhurried as ever. It made Stilo want to reach through the mic and throttle the commander. But, instead, he made his report.

'Ork patrol destroyed. Ork warband approaching, ETA about two minutes.'

'The bridge. What about the bridge?'

'Still standing, sir.'

There was a moment's silence at the other end of the vox.

'What's the ETA on the evac, sir?'

'The Valkyries will be there in three minutes, tanker.'

'The warband will get here before that, sir.'

'Then you'll just have to hold them off until the Valkyries arrive.'

'Yes, sir.'

Stilo dropped the vox and began frantically turning the crank to rotate the turret. As he did so, he could hear, even through the plasteel, the whoops and howls of the approaching orks.

Using the crank, the turret rotation speed was one hundred and eighty degrees in fifty seconds. Stilo began counting, under his breath, turning the crank handle while watching the desperately slow rotation of the turret.

'...thirty-nine thousand and one, forty thousand and one, forty-one thousand and one.'

Without even checking the auspex, Stilo dragged open the ammo bin and loaded a high-explosive shell into the battle cannon.

Then he checked the auspex.

The greenskins were nearly on him.

Stilo frantically turned the elevation crank, bringing down the barrel of the cannon, until it was pointing at the ground just in front of the oncoming horde of revving, racing trukks, wagons and trikes.

'Fire.'

Recoil, clear, reload, fire. Recoil, clear, reload, fire.

Recoil, clear, reload, fire.

Bang, bang, bang.

It was coming from the starboard sponson.

Bang, bang, bang.

From the port sponson.

Stilo looked up.

They were on the turret.

The greenskins were trying to peel *Sancta Fide* open.

Stilo wasn't thinking now. He was doing.

The hull rang with the reverberations of orks bashing at the hull with hammers and axes and clubs. Even as he watched, he saw the plasteel bulge inwards.

This was close range now.

Stilo grabbed the port heavy bolter and started firing. He didn't even need to aim, he just sprayed bolts; it was like hitting locusts. Spent cartridges clattered round his feet. Greenskins appeared in his sights and were splattered. It was like driving at speed at night on a bug-ridden road.

The sound of greenskin bodies exploding under the impact of a heavy bolter fired at point-blank range echoed over the concussive blasts of the bolter itself.

Stilo kept pressing the trigger, turning the bolter this way and that, but it was for nothing. Through the sights, he saw the orks gather themselves, kick aside the body parts that were in the way, and come running back at him.

'Out!' he yelled, as he'd been trained, just as the wave of orks reached *Sancta Fide*, hitting it like a green tidal wave. The tank rocked under the impact of a hundred ork fists and axes. The plasteel squealed and screeched. The tank began to rock, back and forth, back and forth.

They were trying to tip the tank over, to get at its belly.

'They're all over me!' Stilo yelled towards the vox, throwing himself at the starboard bolter. 'I can't hold much longer.'

Stilo sprayed bolter rounds from the sponson. The rapid click of the spent shell cases falling onto the hull around his feet triggered a fleeting sound memory: the tick of the cooling engine block when he had first woken into darkness.

There weren't so many greenskins on the starboard side of *Sancta Fide*. After Stilo had traversed the bolter, there were even fewer.

But the orks came. At the sound of bolter fire, at the smell of seared flesh, they came, swarming over and around the stricken tank.

One of the orks grabbed the barrel of the bolter in its hands. Smoke rose from its fingers. But still it began pushing the barrel up, away from its fellows.

Stilo yelled out and, unholstering his laspistol, he took aim through the viewport of the bolter and put a round between the ork's eyes. Then another, when the ork didn't seem to register the first. The third did the trick. The ork went cross-eyed, as if trying to figure out why a hole had suddenly appeared above its nose, then began to sink down. It didn't get far. Another ork slammed it out of the way.

Stilo grabbed the heavy bolter again, squeezed the trigger.

That ork evaporated into a mist of green slime as it took three heavy bolter rounds at point-blank range; its teeth drummed into the side of the tank like ivory knives.

The roar of the bolter ran underneath the sound of Stilo's screams of rage and triumph as he killed greenskins at zero range, vaporising the ork vermin in the hail of bolter fire.

But even as he killed orks on one side of the tank, it started bouncing on the other side, rocking left to right like a ship in a storm.

The warboss was here and he was directing the show now.

The tank began to rock, higher and higher on each bounce.

With every upward motion, more orks got a handhold, pushing the tank higher each time. Inside, Stilo grabbed tight, trying to stop himself being thrown around helplessly.

'Where are the frekking Valkyries?' he screamed into the vox. 'They're going to turn me over.'

'*Hang in there, son,*' said the colonel. '*The Emperor protects.*'

With a final heave, the orks pushed *Sancta Fide* over onto its side. Stilo crashed down against the starboard sponson. Under the weight of the tank, the sponson housing cracked open. The smell of propellant mixed with spilled promethium.

One auspex was still working, flickering grey and red. On it, Stilo saw the ork warboss click its massive neck, flex its huge fingers, then stride up to the tank.

The warboss grabbed the turret hatch. With the tank on its side, the massive ork could reach it easily.

'It's trying to get in,' Stilo whispered into the vox.

The hatch creaked, the lock straining.

It held.

The warboss backed off.

Suddenly aware it was being watched, it turned and stared into the sensor array.

Stilo saw the guile in its eyes.

The warboss reached out, grabbed an ork and held the struggling greenskin in its hands.

Without warning, the warboss pulled its head off. The greenskin's body collapsed to the ground.

The warboss held the dripping ork head up in front of the sensors.

Then it turned back to the hatch and grabbed hold again.

The warboss was trying to tear the head off *Sancta Fide*.

Stilo heard the tank. It was dying. Its machine-spirit moaned and whispered as it leaked away.

He turned to the vox.

'There never were any Valkyries, were there?'

The vox was silent.

'Y-you don't need to sugar-coat it. I'm going to be dead soon.'

The voice, when it came through, was thick, heavy with an emotion that could not be spoken.

'*The Emperor is sending His very own Valkyries, son. They'll bring you to His side.*'

'Tell the Emperor I'll bring Him a present.'

While he spoke, Stilo was busy jamming open the remaining ammunition bins for the battle cannon. The armour-piercing rounds were still in there, as well as a handful of high-explosive shells. So long as the bins were locked shut, even if they were pierced and detonated by enemy ordnance, the machine-spirit of the tank would ensure that most of the blast was drawn outwards through explosion vents. But with the bin doors open, the destructive force of all the remaining ammunition would be channelled up and out through the turret.

The hatch was bulging outwards.

The locking mechanism was creaking, creaking. Cracking.

Stilo checked his laspistol.

It was on ten per cent charge. He might as well throw it at the warboss.

He needed a weapon. Stilo looked round frantically. There were a few flares, for signalling if the vox failed, but they wouldn't even make the warboss blink.

Then, in the depths of the rocking tank, Captain Bartezko's body shifted and turned. In the dull red of the lumens, Stilo saw the hilt of the captain's power sword. He scrabbled for it, desperately pushing tank debris out of the way.

The hatch broke open.

The warboss shoved its huge head into *Sancta Fide*.

Stilo thumbed the activation on the power sword. The ancient blade hummed its eagerness and, turning, Stilo thrust the sword into the middle of the ork's forehead. The weapon, hungry for greenskin flesh, bit deep, burrowing into the ork's skull. The warboss screamed – a surprisingly high-pitched sound, Stilo noted, as thought fragments spilled through his mind – and fell back out of the tank.

Outside, through the circle of the open hatch, Lucius Stilo saw the warboss staggering, then falling to its knees as it pawed at the sword sticking out of its skull.

But the warboss did not fall. On its knees, it managed to find the hilt of the sword with both hands. Slowly, it pulled the weapon out of its skull.

Stilo could see right through the hole.

The warboss sniffed the blade, licked it, then looked up. It looked into the tank. It looked at Stilo.

Slowly, it got back up onto its feet. For a moment it staggered, then the warboss steadied itself. It looked at Stilo again. It bared its teeth.

Stilo realised the ork was smiling.

The warboss tossed the power sword aside and began walking back towards *Sancta Fide*. Behind him, the other orks followed, gibbering in fear and excitement.

Stilo shrank back into the depths of the tank.

'Are the Valkyries on their way?'

'*They are with you now.*'

Stilo nodded.

'I know.'

This time the warboss reached in through the hatch, its fingers grabbing for Stilo. Lucius pulled back, out of reach.

'Come and get me,' he yelled, taking a flare from the rack.

The warboss pulled its arm out and looked into the tank, green blood running down into its red eyes.

From where he sat, scrunched up as far from the hatch as possible, Lucius Stilo, loader, Third Squadron, Fifth Alphard Tank Regiment, pointed the flare at the pool of promethium, and the armour-piercing rounds and high-explosive shells piled in the bottom of *Sancta Fide*. He fired it.

For a moment it flared brighter than anything Lucius Stilo had ever seen. Then it shone out even brighter.

He never heard the sound.

Sancta Fide's turret exploded outwards. From out of the belly of the tank flared a jet of purifying, white fire that scoured the surface of the plain, charring to blackened stumps the warboss and the orks clustered round it before igniting the engines and ordnance of the idling trukks and wagons, the explosions leaping from vehicle to vehicle as if blown by the spirit of a young tanker on his first, and final, patrol.

In the HQ of the Fourth Armoured Corps, the general staff were silent.

The vox had gone dead. Before it cut out, they had heard a sound unmistakeable to all tankers: the gushing *whoosh* of a Leman Russ brewing up.

Colonel Markus Stilo, commanding officer, Fourth Armoured Corps, stared at the silent vox. Then he turned to another of the vox-stations.

'Report.'

'The Valkyries have landed the demolition charges on the bridge. Engineers laying them now.'

'Tell them to remain on station to evac the engineers when the bridge is down.'

The comms officer turned back to his vox, passing on the order.

Colonel Markus Stilo stood up slowly.

The general staff looked upon their commanding officer in silence.

'Our mission was to destroy the bridge. To achieve victory, it is sometimes necessary to sacrifice that which we hold dearest. The Emperor calls upon us to make that sacrifice – so long as we are willing do so, the Imperium of Man shall never be defeated.'

The colonel turned slowly, looking around the room, but his eyes were blank.

'My son always dreamed of being a tanker. He died one.'

The colonel reached out a hand, steadied himself, then turned to leave.

'Sir, do you want me to send a Valkyrie to collect... to collect your son's body?'

Colonel Stilo did not look round.

'The Valkyries will carry out their orders. Inform me when the bridge is down. Carry on.'

WAITING DEATH

Steve Lyons

BOREALIS FOUR.

Can't say it was the most distinguished campaign of my career. A jungle planet orbiting a red giant on the inner rim of the Segmentum Tempestus. A hundred and ten degrees in the shade. Serpents lurking under every leaf, stinging insects as big as a man's fist. Even the flowers coughed out a nasty muscle-wasting virus. It was a damned disappointment, I can tell you. I had hoped for a challenge.

Never did find out if Borealis Four was worth saving. Could be that its crust was packed full of minerals and precious stones. Could be it was as dry as a corpse's throat. All that mattered back then was that, when the explorators set foot on this green new world, they had found a surprise waiting for them: a Chaos-worshipping cult, proud of the fact that the Dark Gods had begun to pervert their flesh and deform their bones.

And that's where I came in: Colonel 'Iron Hand' Straken – along with three regiments of the finest damned soldiers in the whole of the Imperium.

Catachan Jungle Fighters.

The cultists on Borealis Four were one of the worst rabbles I had ever seen. Yet again they came bursting from the trees, howling at the top of their voices, throwing themselves at us with no care for their own lives. That was fine by me – we didn't care about their lives either.

'Well, don't just dance with those damned sissies, Graves – use your knife, man,' I shouted. 'And Barruga, you're as slow as a brainleaf plant. You idle slugs, you gonna let this filth spew on the good name of the Catachan Second? I could whip this bunch with my one good arm if you sons-of-groxes weren't in my way. Thorn, stop flapping about like a damned newborn – you still got one damned hand, so pick up that lasgun! Kopachek, you got a clear shot with that flamer, what the hell are you waiting for? Emperor's teeth, do I have to do everything myself?'

We tore through that scum like blades through a reed bed. They were ill-disciplined, ill-equipped, didn't know what had hit them. They'd wasted their damned lives dancing around altars in dresses, waving stinking candles. Should have spent a few days on my world; they'd have learned how to fight like men.

I'd made a bet with my opposite number, Carraway of the 14th, that we'd be done here in four months, tops. Two months in, it looked like I was going to collect on that bet. Until that one night.

That one night, when my platoon of some thirty hardened veterans – along with a certain General Farris – was cut off from our comrades, stranded in the darkest depths of the Borealis jungle. That night, when I faced one of the toughest, most desperate challenges of my life.

That night, when I had to fight my own damned men.

The jungle on Borealis Four was nothing compared to Catachan, but the march was taking too damn long. Cutting a way through the high vegetation was slowing us up, and the men were tired. But sunset was coming soon, and things out here tended to get a whole lot worse after dark, so I decided to offer a few words of encouragement.

'Pick up the pace back there! What do you think this is, a newborns' trip to the mango swamps? Myers, put some muscle into those knife strokes. Levitski, Barruga, keep trying to kick some life into that damned vox-caster.'

Still the machine offered nothing but a metallic thunk and yet another blast of static.

'Emperor's teeth, it's come to something when you momma's boys can't finish off a bunch of damned half-mutant freaks.' I shouted down the line. 'And in front of the general! Well, I don't care how long it takes, not one of you is slacking off for a single damn second till we're back behind our lines. I promised you today was gonna be a cakewalk, and the man who makes a liar out of old 'Iron Hand' Straken, I'll throttle with his own entrails. What…?'

I drew to a halt, and the march stopped all around me. The constant buzz of insects and howl of jungle creatures had suddenly been joined by another noise – the faint tinkling of wind chimes.

'What am I looking at here? Where the hell did this come from?' I asked.

Without warning, we had come to a clearing, at least half a kilometre wide. The jungle canopy opened right up, and I was dazzled by the final rays of the setting sun. The air was suddenly cool and fresh, scented with blossom. And, squinting against the light, I could make out dark, unnatural shapes: Buildings. Dark-timbered wooden huts.

My first thought was that we'd found an enemy bolthole. But these huts were sturdy and well-kept, arranged around a larger central hall. Our enemies could never have built anything so orderly. Besides, if the taint of the Ruinous Powers had been there, I'd have damn well smelled it.

Why, then, was my gut warning me of something rotten about this place? And why the hell didn't I listen to it?

As we stood gawping, a figure approached us from between the huts. A boy, barely into his teenage years – but, with the last of the blood-red light behind him, I couldn't make out much more than that. Of course, my men reacted as they had been trained to do, raising their lasguns and taking aim, but the boy didn't seem at all worried by the sight of thirty muzzles pointed at his heart.

He padded closer, as the sun disappeared and the clearing was washed in the faint blue light of a swollen moon. I could make out the boy's face now, round and gentle, his eyes bright and wide. His skin was sun-bronzed to perfection, and the moonlight made his bald head shine like a halo. He was wearing a simple white robe, ornamented by a garland of flowers.

'Welcome,' he offered.

The boy cocked his head a little, his full lips pursed as if he found the sight of thirty bloodied vets on his doorstep somehow amusing.

'Welcome to safe haven.' He continued. 'I am Kadence Moonglow – and all that my people have, we offer to share with you.'

'So you say, kid,' I spat back. 'But before we break out the damned peace pipe, I got a few questions for you.'

General Farris stepped forward with a diplomatic clearing of his throat. It was the first time I'd heard his voice all day.

'What Colonel Straken means to say is that we weren't aware of any settlement in this area.'

'And seeing as how, in two months here we haven't found a single life form that hasn't tried to eviscerate us-'

'I assure you that nobody in this village would wish harm to another being,' interrupted Kadence. 'We have learned to live in balance with even this harsh environment. As for your enemies... yes, they were a part of our commune once, but no longer. They have been cast out of this place.'

Sounded like bull to my ears. But General Farris motioned to the men to lower their guns – and, with a few uncertain glances at me, they obeyed.

Farris introduced himself, and the rest of us, to this Kadence Moonglow, and accepted his offer of hospitality.

'Now hold on a minute, Sir.' I said. 'I told the men I'd get us back to the camp tonight. Nothing has changed. We can still—'

Farris shook his head firmly. 'The men are tired, Straken.'

'And some of them need proper medical attention. You think they've got a damned hospital tent set up here?'

Kadence interjected again. 'We will do what we can for your wounded. We have balms and tinctures, and most importantly our faith in the healing spirits.'

'Yeah,' I thought, 'cos a few herbal potions and a bit of wailing to the skies, that's gonna sew Trooper Thorn's damned hand right back on. But Farris wouldn't be moved on the subject.

'We'll keep the men in better shape by letting them rest than by force-marching them overnight through that jungle.'

I wondered if he was really talking about the men, or about himself. Farris had taken a scratch in the fighting today. His left arm was held in a make-shift sling. He'd kept up with the rest of us so far, and hadn't whined about it – but I'd been watching him sweating and stumbling for a while now, waiting for him to drop.

Either way, I couldn't fault his logic – even if he hadn't been my superior officer. So, taking my silence as a sign of assent, the general asked Kadence to lead the way forward, and ordered my men to follow. I caught Thorn's eye as he passed me. He was still holding his bloodied hand to the stump of his left wrist.

'Never mind, kid.' I told him. 'That hand's looking a bit green now, anyway.

Probably too late to save it. Have to make do with an augmetic. Hell, I once had my whole damned arm ripped off by a Miral land shark, you don't hear me grizzling about that. It's character-forming.'

Walking into that village was like stepping onto a different world. The jungle suddenly seemed a long way away, and I was surprised to see children playing on the grass between the huts. Some of them stopped to stare at us as we passed. There was excitement and wonder in their wide eyes, but not a trace of fear, although we must have presented a terrifying sight in our jungle camouflage, laden down with weapons.

Farris dropped back, falling into step beside me.

'How do they survive?' he asked. 'They let their children play outdoors, for the Emperor's sake, just a few hundred metres from the monsters and the poison and the sickness out there.' He shuddered at the thought. 'We have to evacuate them, Straken. First thing in the morning. They aren't safe here.'

General Farris, you might have gathered by now, was not one of us. He hailed from Validius, a world so in-bred that eighty per cent of its population belonged to the monarchy, and didn't they just love to let you know it. To be fair, Farris had posted himself to the front line this morning – he must have had some guts. Somehow, though, during the fighting, he'd been separated from his own regiment and ended up with ours. A scrawny, pasty-faced man, the general clearly wasn't used to jungle conditions. He had brightened up plenty now that we had found shelter.

Kadence led us into the spacious central hall. It was packed with more of his people, all dressed in white robes, talking and laughing and sharing out bowls of plump, ripe berries. They cleared spaces for us, on benches or on cushions, and handed us fruit, hunks of sweet-smelling bread and mugs of crystal clear water.

Farris was in his element, shaking the hand of anyone who looked like they might be important, thanking them for their kindness, promising to repay it. I was happy to leave all the jawing to him.

My men were approaching the villagers' gifts with caution. I'd have stuck my boot up the backsides of any of them who hadn't. As Catachans, though, we have good instincts about food and drink; wouldn't last too damned long otherwise. We were soon satisfied that no one was trying to poison us.

In fact, the fruits in particular were sweet and moist, quenching the flames in my throat. I couldn't help but wonder why I hadn't seen their like before on Borealis Four.

Soon, my men were mixing with the villagers as if they'd been friends all their lives. I listened in on their conversations, heard a lot of small talk about Catachan and life in the Imperial Guard, but not so much about our hosts. They were good at deflecting questions.

Then Farris introduced me to two village elders – white-haired, straight-backed and dignified but with the same glint of humour in their eyes that I'd seen in Kadence's – and it seemed he had pried some information out of them, at least.

'They've been telling me of their people's legends,' Farris began. 'They believe they came to this world in a "great sky chariot" a thousand generations ago.'

'The Stellar Exodus?'

I knew that some of the first colony ships had strayed beyond the Segmentum Solar, and so in those pre-Warp days had become lost to history. It had even been suggested that one of those ships had seeded human life on Catachan.

'Their ancestors were born on Holy Terra. They're the Emperor's people, like us.' Farris said.

'It seems we have a great deal in common, and much to talk about on the morrow.' One of the elders spoke up. 'For now, you and your men must sleep. We can clear this meeting hall for you. I see you have bedrolls. We can fetch more cushions and pillows if you wish.'

'That would be more than acceptable.' Farris responded. 'Thank you.'

As Kadence and the elders left, I grumbled something about making the men soft. Farris let out a sigh. 'You know, your men don't all have your... advantages, shall we say. You can push them too hard.'

I didn't bother to answer that. No outsider could understand the bond between me and my men. They'd have crawled through a Catachan Devil's nest on their bare bellies if I'd asked them to. That much I knew.

'All right, you milksops, that's enough damned pampering for one day. Get out there, start laying traps around the village's perimeter. Go easy on the mines, we're running dry. I want toe-poppers, lashing branches, anything that'll kick up a damn good racket. Graves, put that cushion down! Hop to it, you slackers, or do I have to do everything myself? And once you're done, I want four volunteers to join me on first watch. McDougal, Vines, Kopachek, Greif, you'll do.'

It didn't take me long to find a good sentry position, in an old tree right on the jungle line. Its star-shaped leaves gave off a eucalyptus reek that would mask my scent, and my camouflage would be more effective here than against the buildings behind me.

I lowered myself onto my stomach along a low, stout branch, and shouldered my plasma pistol.

I was almost invisible now. So long as I didn't move a muscle, or make a sound. But then, I had no reason to do either.

Something was wrong.

It was nothing I could see, nothing I could hear. But I knew there was something. Something out there, at the edge of my senses.

I held my breath, straining to catch the slightest sound. There was nothing. Just the night-time breeze. Without turning my head, I refocused my gaze, through my pistol's sights. I re-examined my surroundings through an infra-red filter, but again there was nothing.

My damned comm-bead was still dead. I couldn't sub-vocalise a warning to the other four sentries, couldn't shout to them without giving myself away. It didn't matter, I told myself. They'd have sensed it, too.

For the next fifteen minutes, I stayed frozen in place – as did my unseen opponents. A waiting game. That suited me. I could wait all night.

Of course, I knew I wouldn't have to.

They made their move, at last. If I'd blinked, I'd have missed it. I knew then that these couldn't be the same cultists we'd been fighting these past months. They were too damned good.

But I was better.

There was a subtle shift in the texture of the darkness, the crunch of a leaf on the ground. I had already teased a frag grenade from my webbing and thumbed the time-delay to its shortest setting.

It plopped into the jungle grass just where the disturbance had been, and it lit up the night.

I had hoped to hear screaming, but instead I saw shadows streaming from the impact point, just an instant ahead of the earth-shattering blast. These were lumpen, gnarled shapes that could have belonged to nothing entirely human. I squeezed off ten shots, until my pistol was hot in my hands. I couldn't tell if I had struck true. The explosion had shot my night-vision to hell. I knew one thing, though. I had to move.

I rolled out of the tree, hitting the ground running beneath a barrage of las-fire from the jungle. Whoever – whatever – was out there, like the cultists, they had Imperial weaponry. At least I had made them reveal themselves.

I feigned a stumble, faltering for an instant, making myself a target. I was hoping to make the hostiles bold – and careless. A few steps forward, and they'd hit the tripwire that I knew was strung between us.

No such luck. I heard a soft thud at my heels, and I leapt for the cover of the line of huts ahead of me. The grenade that had just landed exploded, the blast wave hitting me in midair, engulfing me in a broiling heat but buoying my flight. I was propelled much further than my legs could have carried me. I landed hard, and instinctively rolled onto my augmetic shoulder, letting it take the brunt of the impact. I heard something break inside it, and a servo sputtered and whined, but I felt no loss of function as I pushed myself up and put a charred hut between myself and my attackers.

The sound of las-fire across the clearing told me that Kopachek had also engaged the enemy. I thought about going to his aid, but knew I had a line to hold.

I swapped my pistol for my trusty old shotgun: primitive, in some people's eyes, but reliable, and suited to firing from the hip. My eyes were readjusting to the dark, and I peered around the hut's side. The jungle was still again, silent. As if nothing had happened. But that silence was a lie.

The hostiles were still out there. Chastened, maybe; tonight, they had learned that Colonel 'Iron Hand' Straken was no pushover. They would be regrouping, redrawing their plans. But they hadn't retreated. I could still feel their presence, like a stench of old bones in the air.

They were waiting.

A second burst of gunfire took me by surprise. This one came not from one of the other sentry posts, but from the meeting hall at the village's centre.

I hesitated for about half a second before I turned and pelted towards the sound. When I got there, the men were spilling out of the hall. They were still shrugging on jackets, tying bandanas, checking their weapons, but were already awake and alert to their surroundings, looking for a target. I grabbed the nearest of them – Levitski – and ordered him to replace me at the jungle's edge. I sent the next to relieve Kopachek – I wanted him back here with a situation report.

Trooper Graves was nursing a fresh wound. Snatching his hand from his temple, I saw the familiar red welt of a glancing las-beam hit.

'What the hell's been going on here?' I shouted.

I pushed my way into the hall, where I found the remains of my platoon in disarray - and two of them dead on the floor.

Standing over these two, with his laspistol drawn, was General Farris – and as he turned to me with a regretful slump of his shoulders, I realised what he must have done. He had shot them. A tense silence filled the hall before Farris leapt to defend his actions: 'I had no choice. They were lashing out, screaming, firing everywhere. This one, he came at me with his knife. He was saying crazy things, calling me a monster. I think... I think the cultists must have got to them.'

'No!' The protest came automatically to my lips. 'No damned way!'

It was one thing to see a comrade cut down in battle, dying for what he believed in. This... This was senseless. I felt cold inside. I felt numb.

I felt angry.

I remembered how Myers had fought so well that morning, laughing as he'd sunk his knife arm up to the elbow in cultist guts. I remembered how Wallenski had been so proud, last week, when the men had honoured him with an earned name. 'Nails', they had called him.

'They were good men, *my* men. You had no right.'

Farris's eyes darkened.

'Do I have to remind you, Colonel, that I am the ranking officer here? You weren't even present. You don't know what—'

'I knew them, *sir*. I know my men, and they were two of the best.'

A heavy silence had fallen upon the hall. All eyes were fixed upon the general and me. Still, my words provoked a ragged, defiant cheer from the dead men's comrades.

'Either one of those soldiers would have given his last damned drop of blood for the Emperor.' I continued. 'It must have been... They must have come down with some virus. A fever. It made them see things.'

'Whatever the cause of their behaviour, they were threatening us all. I had to act.'

'You didn't even know their damned names!'

And the silence returned, almost a physical force between us.

It was broken by a quiet voice. Kadence Moonglow had entered the hall, and walked right up to my shoulder without my being aware of him. That, as much as any of the night's events so far, disquieted me.

'The covenant has been broken,' the boy said.

'What the hell does that mean?' I rounded on him.

'Blood has been shed. Now, they will not rest until they have blood in return.'

'Who will not rest? The cultists?' Farris asked.

Kadence shook his head. 'The jungle has bred far worse than those misguided souls. There are monsters out there. Monsters that the eye cannot see, but whose presence is felt nonetheless.'

'Yeah, well, thanks for the warning,' I said, 'but those "monsters" of yours already tried to blow me into chunks.'

Kadence shot me a sharp look – and, for a moment, his calm façade slipped and I caught a glimpse of something darker beneath it.

'They would not have attacked you except in self-defence.'

Then, composing himself, he continued.

'We welcomed you into our village, our home, because we sensed that you were noble souls. We only prayed that, in return, you could leave your war at our doors.'

'I don't know if you're aware of this, kid, but your monsters have this village surrounded.' I replied.

'And now they are free to enter it as they please. By sunrise, all we have built here will be ashes. No one will survive.'

'In a grox's eye!' I spat. 'Those things out there, whatever they are – they aren't dealing with a bunch of tree-hugging pushovers any more. If they want this village, they'll have to go through us to get it.'

'Colonel Straken has a point.' Farris cut in. 'We will do everything in our power to protect you.'

'There are less than thirty of you. Their numbers are legion.'

'But we have the defensive advantage,' I said. 'My boys can keep those hostiles at bay till dawn, or I'll want to know the damned reason why.'

'And once the sun is up, we'll be able to lead you – all of you – to safety. We have an army, not twenty kilometres from here.' Farris said.

Kadence bowed his head.

'As you wish.'

The next half-hour was given over to frenetic activity.

I trebled the guard around the village, this time counting myself out of the assignments. I wanted to be free to go where I was needed. I sent Barruga and Stone around the huts, telling people to pack their things and move to the central hall. They would be safer there, harder to reach. General Farris stayed in the hall, too – his choice. Someone had to organise things in there, he claimed.

I debriefed Kopachek. His story was similar to my own – except that, in his case, the enemy had fired first. Like me, he hadn't managed to get a good look at them. I sent him, along with MacDougal, Vines and Greif, to grab an hour's sleep in one of the vacated huts. Farris had been right about one thing: my men were the toughest damned sons-of-groxes in the Imperium. Sometimes, it was easy to forget that they didn't all have chests full of replacement parts to keep them going.

I hadn't forgotten about Wallenski and Myers. There would be a reckoning for their deaths, and soon. Meantime, I had warned every man to keep an eye on his watch partner – and to call for a medic if he felt the jungle sweats coming on.

The quiet of the night was broken only by the occasional squawking bird, and the deeper cries of much larger and much more dangerous jungle creatures. Trooper Thorn was sprawled on his stomach, alongside a small, square hut, his wiry body masked by the long grass. His lasgun barrel rested on a mound of dirt, waiting for a target. I hurried up to him, keeping my head down, and dropped to my haunches beside him. He gave me a situation report without my even asking.

'Nothing, sir. Not a sign of the hostiles. Perhaps you made them realise what they're facing, and—?'

'They're out there.' I interrupted. I had rarely been more sure of anything in my life.

'Do you think…? That boy, sir, what he said… was he right? Are we facing… monsters? Daemons, or…?'

'Trust me, kid, I've seen enough monsters in my lifetime, and nothing – not a damned one of them – would last two minutes in a scrap with a Catachan Devil, or make it through a patch of spikers alive. So, don't you dare start shaking in your boots just 'cos you've seen a few drops of blood today and heard some damned fairy tale.'

'No, sir. It's just that… Colonel Straken, sir, is something wrong? You… you're sweating.'

'What the hell are you talking about?' I asked.

'What… what did you say?' asked Thorn.

Suddenly he was clawing at the ground with the bandaged stump of his left arm, pushing himself away from me and to his feet. His eyes had widened with fear, and his voice was loud – too loud. He had blown our cover for sure.

'Trooper Thorn, to attention!' I snapped. 'You're behaving like a damned newborn yourself. Hell, I know you're not long out of nappies, but—'

'Take that back, sir. Take it back!'

'I beg your damned pardon, Trooper?'

We were both standing now, and Thorn had managed to grab his lasgun and was pointing it shakily at my head. I had brought up my shotgun in return – an instinctive reaction - but the image of a comrade in its sights shocked me to my core.

I lowered my gun, brought up my hands.

'Listen, kid.' I said. 'You're not yourself. You're sick. Like Wallenski and Myers, they were sick. But you can fight it.'

'I don't want to believe… This is a test, right? Tell me it's a test. Don't make me-'

'Why do you think you're here? Do you think I make a habit outta taking every snot-nosed brat fresh out of training into my command platoon? "Barracuda" Creek back at the Tower reckons you're the next damned Sly Marbo. You gonna prove him wrong?'

'The fever!' he cried and, for a moment, I thought I'd got through to him.

'It must be the fever, making you say those things. Please, sir, just... drop your weapons. I don't want to have to shoot you – not you – but I swear in the Emperor's name, if I must-'

His sentence was broken by a barrage of las-fire, which provided just the distraction I needed. I tackled Thorn before he could say another word, and the lasgun fell from his grip as we hit the ground together. I'd saved his life, my instincts and a keen ear keeping me a half-second ahead of the fresh salvo of enemy fire that had just erupted from the jungle.

In return for that favour, Thorn was trying his damned best to kill me.

I had him pinned with my knee, keeping him from drawing his knife. But the fingers of Thorn's one hand were locked tight about my throat. He was stronger than he looked.

No match for my augmetic arm, of course. I fought out of his grip, breaking a few bones in the process. Thorn was screaming curses, thrashing about wildly as he tried to unseat me, foaming at the mouth. In the meantime, I knew the hostiles wouldn't exactly be sitting around making daisy chains. They couldn't have asked for a better distraction, or easier targets, than these two damned fools brawling in the open.

I had no choice but to finish this. Fast. I could already hear my men returning fire, and this one was going to get ugly, and quick.

I twisted my shotgun around, trying to jam the barrel up beneath Thorn's chin. I had no intention of shooting him, of course. If he'd been in his right mind, he'd have known that. Instead, he fought with all his strength to push the gun away from himself. I let him succeed, even as I blindsided him with my metal fist.

The punch knocked Thorn spark out, and left a dent in the side of his skull that would probably take a metal plate to straighten out. The way this kid was going today, he was liable to end up like me.

While we had been grappling, the hostiles had made their move.

They came running, screaming, firing out of the jungle, somehow managing to evade all of our traps. My men were shooting furiously at them, but Thorn's little turn had left a gaping hole in our defences – and the hostiles knew exactly where our blind spots were.

I was a damned sitting duck. I didn't know why I wasn't dead already – but, seeing as I wasn't, I figured I could spare another second to hoist the unconscious Thorn across my shoulders before I ran for cover. No one gets left behind if I can help it.

My men were closing with the invaders, yelling for the rest of the platoon to back them up. I deposited Thorn on the ground behind a hut. I didn't stop to check how he was. No time for that. I had a battle to get back to. I raced back to join my men, running at the hostiles with my shotgun blazing. Emperor's teeth, but they were ugly! It was all I could do not to puke at the sight of them.

They had been human once, that much I could tell. Cultists, no doubt, some of them still wearing the tatters of their black robes.

Kadence had been right about them. They were monsters, now, no two of them alike. Their flesh had run like wax, set in revolting shapes. Arms had been fused to torsos, fingers melted together, heads sunken into chests. Some of the monsters – the mutants – had sprouted new limbs, from their ribs, their spines, even out of their heads. Some of them had six eyes, four noses, or mouths in their bellies. They were bristling with clumps of short, black hair, with blisters and blood-red pustules.

And they outnumbered us about five to one. There was no way we were going to survive without some discipline, so I started spitting out orders.

'Barruga, aim for the slimy one's eyes. No, its other eyes! Emperor's teeth, this one has a face like a grox's back end, and it stinks as bad. Greif, wake the hell up, you'd have lost your damned head if I hadn't shot that one behind you. Move it, you slowpokes, I want you up close and personal, right in their damned faces. Marsh, stop holding that knife like you're eating your breakfast. It only takes one hand to hold in your guts, so keep the other one fighting. Kopachek, where's that damned flamer? I want the smell of burning mutants in my nostrils!'

One thing I have learned about mutants over the years: they might be strong – damned strong, some of them – but it's rare that they're fast. They're clumsy, unwieldy. Comes from fighting in bodies they hardly know. That, and having the brain power of a blood wasp on heat.

And, at first, it appeared that these mutants were no different.

I was right in the thick of them. It was safer that way. It made it impossible for their snipers, on the edge of the melee, to keep me in their sights, or to use their grenades without decimating their own ranks.

So, the mutants were swiping at me with poison-dipped claws, straining for my throat with misshapen fangs, and I can hardly deny it, this is one battered old warhorse who has started to slow down himself. I always figured that, what I've lost in speed, I make up for by having a tougher damned hide than most. Even so, in a fight like this one, I'd have expected a few cuts and bruises. Not this time, though. This time, it felt like I was charmed. Like those damned freaks couldn't lay a hand on me.

And yet...

And yet, somehow, my knife thrusts weren't hitting home either. The mutants were ducking and weaving like experts. And whenever I thought I had a clear shot at one, as I started to squeeze my trigger, my target was gone, spun away, and there were only comrades in my sights instead.

My men were faring no better than I was. They'd slashed at a few of those melted-wax faces, cracked a few twisted skulls, but no more than that. And they'd taken surprisingly few wounds in return, just a shallow cut here and there. It was almost like... like the mutants were playing with us.

Insulted, enraged, I lashed out with my feet and my elbows, widened the arc of my knife swipes, turned my shotgun around and used its butt as a cudgel, but nothing got through. So, I took a calculated risk. I did what every nerve in my body was screaming at me to do.

I leapt at the nearest mutant and I slashed its throat, my frustration bursting out in a cruel bark of laughter as its hot blood spattered my face. My first kill of the night. But to make that leap, I'd had to drop my guard, leave my right flank exposed.

I expected to feel a talon in my ribs, to die in agony, but no such blow came. My instincts had been right. The mutants weren't trying to kill us. It was worse than that.

'They want to take us alive!' I shouted. 'Well, they can't have met a Catachan Jungle Fighter before. Time to step up your game, you goldbrickers. Show these mutant scum that we don't lie down and roll over till we're damn well stone cold dead!'

With a roar of enthusiasm, the men followed my lead. They fought with abandon, not caring what risks they took with their own safety as long as they hurt the enemy.

The switch in tactics took the mutants by surprise. They were thrown off balance, reeling, falling like tenpins. I knew it couldn't last.

They must have identified me as the leader, because now they were swarming me, grasping at me with filthy hands. I landed a few good blows, but then strong arms encircled me from behind, and a cold, clammy tentacle seized my left wrist and twisted it almost to breaking point. My shotgun fell from my numbed fingers. My knife hand... that was stronger than my opponents had bargained for.

For a moment, it looked like the struggle – my augmetic arm against three of those freaks – could have gone either way. But then, a flailing limb – or a tail, I suspected – whipped my legs out from under me, something blunt and hard struck the back of my head, and I was toppling backwards.

And the first thing I realised, as I blinked away stars, as I fought to keep awake and on my knees at least, was that my blade – my Catachan Fang – had indeed been wrenched from my grip.

Someone was gonna pay for that!

The mutants were looming over me. Seven of them, I counted. Or maybe just six; I wasn't sure if one had two heads. They were shouting at me in a language I couldn't understand, but one that made my every nerve jangle like the strings of a grox-gut harp. I had no doubt that they were screaming blasphemy of the vilest kind, and all I longed to do was to shut them up, to stop those awful, hateful words escaping into the world.

The grenade felt cold in my hand, and reassuringly solid. It gave me strength, put me back in control. I knew it would rip my body apart. I knew that this time not even the most skilled surgeon would be able to stitch me back together. But a glorious death was far preferable to defeat. And a death that took six – or seven – of my enemies with me...

Then, just like that, the mutants were gone. Withdrawn. Swallowed up by the jungle once more, with hardly a ripple to mark their passing. The quiet rhythm of the jungle settled in again as I unsteadily picked myself up. I saw a number of my men doing the same, looking as confused as I felt.

'How many wounded?' I asked.

There were only a few, and nothing a can of synth-skin couldn't fix. It didn't make any sense. The mutants had been winning!

They had left a handful of misshapen bodies behind them. I glared down at one as if it could tell me in death the secrets it had kept in life. The mutant was lizard-like in appearance, a forked tongue lolling from its open mouth, a thorny tail tangled about its ankles. It hurt my eyes to look at it. I blinked and shifted my gaze along the grass until it found a more welcome sight.

I didn't dare believe it at first. My knife. My Catachan Fang. Half a metre of cold steel, its early gleam dulled through a lifetime of use but still the most precious thing in the damned world to me. An extension of myself, a part of my soul. And the mutants had left it, standing upright in the ground. Almost... respectfully.

I spent a long time kneeling beside that knife, looking at it, before I picked it up, wiped it down and returned it to its sheath.

I spent a long time thinking about what it might mean.

Twenty minutes later and I was back in the central hall butting heads with Farris.

'We gotta ship out of here.' I told him. 'We can't wait till morning.'

General Farris shook his head.

'We've been through this before, Straken. I won't have us marching through that jungle at night.'

'The men can cope with the jungle.'

'Maybe they can, but the villagers...'

'If we stay here, and those mutants attack again, I can't guarantee we can hold them back. Our best hope is to take them by surprise, punch through their lines and keep on going.'

'With the hostiles at our heels?' he asked.

'We only have to reach base camp, then the odds'll be even.' I said. 'With a couple more platoons, we can turn back around and blast that damned Chaos scum to—'

'But the villagers, man! Some of them are old. There are children. They won't be able to keep pace with us.'

'So, we lose a few civilians. Better that than—'

'No,' he insisted. 'We stick to my original plan. You said yourself that there were no casualties of the first attack.'

'Because the mutants weren't trying. They thought they could take us alive. Now they know better.'

'If I didn't know *you* better, I'd be starting to wonder if you'd lost your nerve.'

And for the second time that night, I had to fight down the urge to punch this damned Validian upstart in his smug damned mouth. Through gritted teeth I said: 'You're asking me to sacrifice my men, my entire command platoon, for a lost cause.'

'You have your orders, Colonel Straken,' he said coldly.

One hour till dawn, and a forbidding bird call broke the morning silence. The cold crept into my old bones as I lay waiting, and I longed to feel the warmth of the sun – any sun – one final time.

In the jungle, nothing had stirred. Still, I was sure that the shadows had grown longer. And darker. A deep, unnatural darkness. The mutants – the monsters – were gathering their forces, increasing in number.

There were butterflies in my stomach. That wasn't like me. A Catachan's patience is his greatest strength. But tonight, it didn't feel that way. It felt like we were only postponing the inevitable.

My mind flashed back to my talk with Farris, and I felt my blood heating up at the memory. But I realised something now. The general had had a point. Not about my motives - 'Iron Hand' Straken is no damned coward. But I *had* been reluctant to face the mutants again. I still was.

I couldn't explain why. It was a churning in my gut. An itch in my brain. An instinct that there was something wrong here, something I'd missed. Thinking back, I realised that the itch had been there all night. Ever since I had first clapped eyes on this damned place.

So, what was I doing out here? Waiting for an attack that I couldn't defend against, waiting to die? I was following my orders. But the Emperor knows, I've defied enough fool-headed generals in my time. I'd have stuck my knife in Farris's damned heart and been glad to do it, if I'd thought it would save a single one of my men. The problem was, this time, I didn't know if it would. I didn't know what to do for the best.

Or maybe I did. Maybe, at some level, I had known all along.

Maybe I just had to listen to my gut.

I climbed to my feet, and I walked toward the jungle, grass rustling beneath my feet.

As I passed the outermost huts of the village, I could almost feel the sights of a hundred lasguns upon me. I was out in the open now, at the mercy of those guns - but not one of them fired. I stooped and laid my guns on the ground, then I shrugged off my backpack and webbing, and set them down too. Finally, I raised my hands to show that they were empty.

I almost choked on the words I had to say, the last words I had ever imagined would come from my throat. I didn't raise my voice; there was no need.

'My name is Colonel Straken, and on behalf of the Second Catachan regiment of the Imperial Guard - on behalf of the God-Emperor Himself - I offer you my unconditional surrender.'

It was a minute - a long, anxious minute - before anything happened.

Then, I heard a whisper of leaves to my left and a near-human shape detached itself from the foliage. It padded towards me, lasgun raised, and I felt my fists clenching involuntarily.

The mutant was beside me now. I recoiled from its rancid breath. It spoke to me, in the same unholy language as before, and I wanted with all my soul to lash out. I wanted to punch, to kick, to spit, to pull my knife and to carve my name in that abomination's chest.

Instead, I just watched as the mutant signalled to its comrades. One by one, they stepped out from the jungle behind it. Each was an abomination, and the sight of them gathered together just made the violent urge grow even stronger.

From behind me, a single lasgun shot rang out. A mutant fell to the floor, clutching its shoulder.

'Hold your damned fire! That's an order!' I cried. 'No one is to engage these... the hostiles. It's not us they want.'

The mutants had brought up their own guns, but now they lowered them again. I couldn't meet their eyes, any of them. I felt sick inside, and my flesh was crawling like I'd been dipped in fire ants.

And now the mutants where shambling past me, a score of them – two score, three – and into the village. Towards the meeting hall.

I saw MacDougal and Stone springing to their feet, getting out of the mutants' path, drawing their knives but resisting the urge to use them. I was grateful to them. They trusted me. Even though, for all they knew – for all any of my men knew, watching this scene from their vantage points – I must have gone out of my tiny mind. Maybe I had, too.

But, somehow, this felt good to me. It felt like the smart thing to do. For the first damned time in this forsaken night, something felt right. From behind me, I felt the familiar rush of heat and flame as the mutants' grenades blew the meeting hall apart.

The villagers must have heard them coming – but for most of them, there had been no time to escape. The survivors came charging out of the fire and the billowing smoke. I saw old men and young boys, their faces darkened and twisted by hatred and rage. It was hard to believe they were the same peaceful people whose food we had shared. The villagers moved towards the mutants with an angry roar, lasguns firing wildly as they sought to kill the intruders.

The mutants showed no mercy. Half the villagers were shot down before they could take two steps. The remainder closed with their attackers, but they were unskilled in combat, quickly shredded by mutant claws. Their screams filled the clearing, drowning out the sounds of las-fire and conflict. This was the last thing I wanted to see, but I forced myself to pick up my feet, to get closer. Because I *had* to see this. I had to know.

Even transfixed by the unfolding horror, my old battle instincts hadn't deserted me entirely. Someone was coming at me from behind. I sidestepped his charge, threw him over my shoulder. The figure regrouped quickly, scrambling back to his feet. I was horrified to see that it was General Farris. The left side of his face had been burnt away. He must have been in incredible pain. He was cursing at me, calling me all the damned names he could think of, and his fury gave him a strength that I'd never have expected. I may have hesitated too, because he managed to plant his foot in my stomach and push me into the wall of a hut.

'This isn't what it looks like.' I forced out. The words sounded pathetic, even to me.

Farris was marching on me with his pistol levelled and eyes bulging white with fury.

'I knew it would come to this. I've been watching you, Straken. You're undisciplined, insubordinate. I put up with your backchat because this was your regiment. But I always knew you were one step from turning, from betraying us all. I should have put this bolt between your eyes hours ago.'

The fighting suddenly seemed very far away, and in that moment it was down to just me and him.

I could have taken him alive.

But a pair of lasgun beams struck Farris from behind, and he stiffened and gasped, then crumpled to the ground.

Emerging from the shadows, Trooper Vines crouched over the general's fallen body, and pronounced him dead.

'I had no choice,' Vines said dryly. 'He was lashing out, screaming. He was saying crazy things, calling you a monster.'

I remembered that Vines had been close to Wallenski. I acknowledged, and dismissed, his actions with a curt nod.

The fighting was almost over.

The villagers were struggling to the very end, but there were only a handful left standing. It would be – it had been – a bloody massacre. One for which I could take much of the credit. And in that moment, I was filled once more with a crippling self-doubt.

But only for that moment.

The meeting hall was still alight – and where the blaze flickered across the faces of the last few combatants, native and invader alike, a transformation was taking place. I blinked and I refocused, unsure at first if I was imagining things. But I couldn't deny what I saw.

In the glow of those cleansing flames, the lies of the moonlight were dispelled at last, and the truth stood revealed.

It wasn't till some days later that I heard the other side of the story. Colonel Carraway came to see me in my hospital bed, where I'd just been patched up once again, and he told me how lucky I'd been.

The explorators, it seemed, had left a survey probe in Borealis Four's orbit – and the tech-priests at HQ had tapped into its scans of the planetary surface. The aim had been to produce a tactical map, locate a few cultist strongholds. Instead, they had discovered a whole damned settlement, where a moment before there had only been trees.

Carraway and I worked out that the village must have shown up on the scans about the same time my men and I found it. As if, by crossing its threshold, we had broken some kind of foul enchantment.

Anyway, the upshot was that Carraway needed someone to investigate – and, since half my regiment was already in that area searching for me and my platoon, they were quick to step forward.

Kawalski, one of my toughest, most experienced sergeants, led the recce. He found the village soon enough – but his first impressions of it were quite different from mine. In his report, he described tumbledown shacks standing on scorched earth, twisted trees bearing rotten fruit, and a putrid stink in the air that made him want to retch.

I don't know why Kawalksi and his men saw the truth when I couldn't. Maybe Kadence's mind-screwing mumbo-jumbo could only affect so many of us at once. Maybe that was why it hadn't worked so well on Wallenski and Myers, or on Thorn. Or maybe that damned psyker meant for things to turn out just as they did, Catachan at war against Catachan.

Kawalksi sent a pair of scouts along the village's perimeter. They returned with reports of booby traps, and sentries hiding in the trees. Even when some troopers exchanged fire with one sentry, they weren't able to identify him. I had just been a shadow to them.

It was only when Kawalksi's men broke cover and attacked us that they saw who we were. That was why they had fought so defensively, trying not to hurt us, though we were trying to kill them. Kawalksi himself took me down, with some help. He was trying to get through to me, but he couldn't seem to make me understand.

We thought we were fighting Chaos-infected mutants. Instead, we were the ones infected. I'll always be haunted by the fact that it was me who killed Trooper Weissmuller, and laughed as I ripped out his throat. Standing orders say that Kawalksi should have shot me there and then.

But he had more faith in me than that.

It was a damned relief to be back on my feet again, and to have my time on Borealis Four done with.

Or so I'd thought.

We were all sat around a warming fire, with the sights and sounds of the jungle around us. But this wasn't the familiar scenery of Catachan – this was still a world marked by Chaos, and the ruined village around us was just another reminder of that.

I was the only one who saw him.

I don't know what made me look, why I chose that moment to tear my eyes away from the dying fire. But there he was, standing in the shadow of a hut – a ramshackle, worm-eaten hut, I could now tell. After all that had happened, he appeared unscathed, his robe still pristine and white. Kadence Moonglow.

He was watching me.

Then he turned, and he slipped away – and I should have alerted my men, but this was between him and me now.'

I followed him alone.

Trouble was, the boy was faster than I expected. We were already a good way into the jungle when I caught up with him. Or rather, I should say, when he stopped and waited for me.

'Colonel Straken. I knew it would be you who came after me. Leading from the front. You always have to do everything yourself.'

I was in no mood for talking. My knife was already in my hand. I only wished I hadn't laid down my shotgun in the village.

I leapt at my mocking foe. And missed.

I hadn't seen him move. One second, Kadence had been in front of me, and now he was a few footsteps to the left. I almost lost my balance, having to grab hold of a creeper to steady myself. It was bristling with poisoned spines. If I'd gripped it with my good hand, instead of my augmetic one, I would have been on the fast track to a damned burial pit.

I tore the creeper from its aerial roots and snapped it like a whip, but again, my target wasn't quite where I'd thought him to be.

'Your men aren't here now, Colonel,' he said. 'You were overconfident, strayed too far from them. They won't hear your cries.'

And suddenly he threw out his arms – and although he wasn't close enough to touch me, I felt as if I had been punched. The impossible blow staggered me, and Kadence was quick to press his advantage. More strikes followed - once, twice, three times to the head, once in the gut. I was flung backwards into a thorny bush, caught and held by its thin branches. A thousand tiny insects scuttled to gorge themselves on my blood.

'You wanna hear crying, kid?' I yelled, wrenching myself free from the clinging vegetation. 'How about you get the hell out of my head? Stop making me see things that aren't damn well there, and face me like a... like a... whatever the hell it is you are.'

Kadence just smiled. And he gestured again, and my left leg snapped. It was all I could do not to gasp with the pain, but I refused to give him that satisfaction. I just gritted my teeth, transferred my weight onto my right foot, and continued to advance on him.

'I didn't ask for this fight,' said Kadence. 'I was content with my tiny domain, and a handful of followers who would do anything for me. For centuries, we hid from the outside world. Until, by the whims of a cruel fortune, you came blundering into our safe haven.'

I thrust at him with my knife. I missed again, his dodge too quick to even register.

'Your followers were mutants. Perverted deviants. And you tricked me into eating with them. You made me think... You made me see my own men as...'

I roared in frustration, my rage getting the better of me. I was swinging wide now, hoping to nick my target wherever he might be. My blade whistled through the empty air, and he was suddenly behind me.

'I knew that, once you had found us, more of your kind would come.' he said. 'I could not cloud so many minds at once. I hoped it would be sufficient to make you few see my followers as friends, your comrades as the thing you most despise.'

'You didn't count on me.'

'No. No, I did not. But for all you have taken from me this night, Colonel Straken, you will pay with your life.'

He made an abrupt slashing motion with his hand, and my leg broke again. A flick of his fingers, and my left shoulder dislocated itself. Kadence extended his right arm, formed his fingers into a claw pattern and twisted his wrist, and something twisted inside of me.

I was buckling under the pain, straining to catch my breath, but determined to close the gap between me and my tormentor, even if I had to do it on my hands and knees.

'Think you can finish me?' I struggled out. 'Good... good luck, kid. Better monsters than you have... have...'

I felt my ribs crack, one by one. My augmetic arm popped and fizzed, and became a dead weight hanging from my shoulder. I was on the jungle floor, not sure how I had got there. There were tears in my eyes and blood in my throat. And as I looked up, trying to focus through a haze of black and red spots, I saw Kadence making a fist, and it felt as if he had reached right into my chest and was crushing my damned heart.

And that was when something miraculous happened.

I felt the warmth of the rising sun on my back, saw the first of its light piercing the jungle canopy above me. And where those red rays touched the slight form of my assailant, like the flames of the fire back in the village, they exposed his deceptions for what they were.

Kadence Moonglow – the boy in the white robe – faded from my sight. But a few steps behind him, exposed by the sunlight, was a twisted horror.

I couldn't see the whole shape of the monster. The parts still in shadow were invisible to me. But I could make out a rough purple hide, six limbs that could have been arms or legs, and a gaping, slavering maw that seemed to fill most of the monster's – the daemon's – huge head.

I could make out a single red eye, perched atop of that great mouth. And it blinked at me as it realised that I was returning its glare.

As my Catachan Fang left my good hand.

As it flew on an unerring course towards that big, bright target.

It was the shot of a lifetime. My blade struck the dead centre of the daemon-thing's eye, piercing its shadow-black pupil. It buried itself up to the hilt. And the daemon that had been Kadence Moonglow gaped at me, for a second, with what I took to be an expression of surprise.

And then he exploded in a shower of purple ash.

I don't know how many hours I lay there, face down in the jungle.

I couldn't lift my head, couldn't move my legs without my broken bones grinding against each other. My insides felt like jelly, and most of my augmetics had failed. I was dying.

And if I didn't go soon, I knew there were any number of predators gathering in the brush, ready and eager to help me on my way.

I wasn't worried. Far from it.

I knew that my men were nearby. I knew they would never stop searching for me. And I knew that, whatever it took, they would find me. They would carry me off to the surgeons, as they had done a hundred times before.

I could trust them.

And when I heard their distant footsteps, I was still able to force a smile.

ABOUT THE AUTHORS

Steve Lyons' work in the Warhammer 40,000 universe includes the novellas *Iron Resolve, Engines of War* and *Angron's Monolith,* the Astra Militarum novels *Death World, Ice Guard, Dead Men Walking, Krieg* and *Siege of Vraks,* and the audio dramas *Waiting Death* and *The Madness Within.* He has also written numerous short stories and is currently working on more tales from the grim darkness of the far future.

Edoardo Albert is a writer and historian specialising in the Dark Ages. He finds that the wars and cultures of the early Medieval period map very well onto the events of the 41st millennium. *Silent Hunters* was his first novel for Black Library and he has since followed up with *Kasrkin.* He has also written the short stories 'Green and Grey', 'Last Flight', 'Born of the Storm', and the novella *Lords of the Storm.*

Steven B Fischer is a physician living in the Southeastern United States. When he's not too busy cracking open a textbook, he can be found exploring the Appalachian Mountains by bike, boat, or boot. Steven's work for Black Library includes the novels *Witchbringer* and *Broken Crusade,* and several short stories.

YOUR
NEXT READ

MINKA LESK: THE LAST WHITESHIELD
by Justin D Hill

Cadia has stood in grim defiance against the enemies of the Imperium for ten thousand years, an indomitable bulwark against the forces of Chaos... but now, the 13th Black Crusade has come, and there will be no victory. Here, Minka Lesk will be tested in the very fires of a world's destruction.

YOUR
NEXT READ

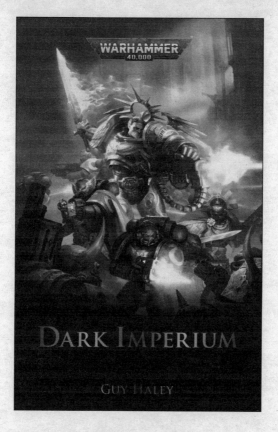

DARK IMPERIUM
by Guy Haley

The first phase of the Indomitus Crusade is over, and the conquering primarch, Roboute Guilliman, sets his sights on home. The hordes of his traitorous brother, Mortarion, march on Ultramar, and only Guilliman can hope to thwart their schemes with his Primaris Space Marine armies.

YOUR
NEXT READ

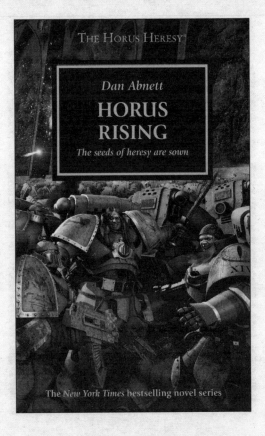

HORUS RISING
by Dan Abnett

After centuries of expansion and conquest, the human Imperium is at its height. His dream for humanity accomplished, the Emperor hands over the reins of power to his Warmaster, Horus, and heads back to Terra.